Gardens in the Dunes

A Novel

Leslie Marmon Silko

SIMON & SCHUSTER

SIMON & SCHUSTER
Rockefeller Center
1230 Avenue of the Americas
New York, NY 10020

Designed by Jeanette Olender
Manufactured in the United States of America

1   3   5   7   9   10   8   6   4   2

Library of Congress Cataloging-in-Publication Data
Silko, Leslie, date.
Gardens in the dunes : a novel / Leslie Marmon Silko
p.   cm.
1. Indians of North America—Fiction.   I. Title.
PS3569.I44G37   1999
813'.54—dc21   98-51987   CIP
ISBN 0-684-81154-5

Special thanks to:

Robert and Caz, for all the love and patience

Larry McMurtry, for all the books and encouragement

Laura Coltelli, for the gardens and all the postcards

For Wendy and Gigi

Gardens in the Dunes

Part One

SISTER SALT called her to come outside. The rain smelled heavenly. All over the sand dunes, datura blossoms round and white as moons breathed their fragrance of magic. Indigo came up from the pit house into the heat; the ground under her bare feet was still warm, but the rain in the breeze felt cool—so cool—and refreshing on her face. She took a deep breath and ran up the dune, where Sister Salt was naked in the rain. She pulled the ragged sack over her head and felt the rain and wind so cool, so fragrant all over her body. Off in the distance there was a faint rumble of thunder, and the wind stirred; the raindrops were larger now. She tilted back her head and opened her mouth wide the way Sister Salt did. The rain she swallowed tasted like the wind. She ran, leaped in the air, and rolled on the warm sand over and over, it was so wonderful. She took handfuls of sand and poured them over her legs and over her stomach and shoulders—the raindrops were cold now and the warmth of the sand felt delicious. Sister Salt laughed wildly as she came rolling down from the highest point of the dune, so Indigo ran after her and leaped and rolled too, her eyes closed tight against the sand. Over and over down-down-down effortlessly, the ease of the motion and the sensation of the warm sand and the cool rain were intoxicating. Indigo squealed with laughter as she rolled into Sister Salt, who was helpless with laughter, and they laughed and laughed and rolled around, one girl on top of the other. They lay side by side with their mouths open and swallowed raindrops until the storm passed. All around them were old garden terraces in the dunes.

Sister Salt remembers everything. The morning the soldiers and the Indian police came to arrest the Messiah, Grandma Fleet told Sister Salt to run. Run! Run get your little sister! You girls go back to the old gardens! Sister Salt was big and strong. She carried Indigo piggyback whenever her little sister got tired. Indigo doesn't remember much about that morning except for the shouts and screams.

Indigo remembers they used to sell baskets at the depot in Needles while their mother washed linens in tubs of boiling water behind the hotel; Grandma Fleet searched the town dump for valuables and discarded seeds. They slept in a lean-to made of old crates and tin, near the river. They learned to talk English while selling baskets to tourists at the train station.

Now, at the old gardens, the girls live alone in Grandma Fleet's house. Grandma had returned a day after they did. Grandma saw Mama escape and run north with the other dancers ahead of the Indian police, who grabbed all the Indians they could, while the soldiers arrested the white people, mostly Mormons, who came to dance for the Messiah. The United States government was afraid of the Messiah's dance.

The deep sand held precious moisture from runoff that nurtured the plants; along the sandstone cliffs above the dunes, dampness seeped out of cracks in the cliff. Amaranth grew profusely at the foot of the dunes. When there was nothing else to eat, there was amaranth; every morning and every night Sister Salt boiled up amaranth greens just like Grandma Fleet taught her.

Later, as the amaranth went to seed, they took turns kneeling at the grinding stone, then Sister Salt made tortillas. They shared part of a honeycomb Indigo spotted in a crevice not far from the spring. Indigo cried when the bees stung her but Sister Salt only rubbed her swollen arms and legs vigorously and laughed, saying it was good medicine—a good cure for anything that might ail you. Grandma Fleet taught Sister Salt and Indigo all about such things.

After the rains, they tended the plants that sprouted out of the deep sand; they each had plants they cared for as if the plants were babies. Grandma Fleet had taught them this too. The plants listen, she told them. Always greet each plant respectfully. Don't argue or fight around the plants—hard feelings cause the plants to wither. The pumpkins and squash sent out bright green runners with huge round leaves to shade the ground, while their wiry green-yellow tendrils attached themselves to nearby weed stalks and tall dune grass. The big orange pumpkin blossoms were delicious right from the vine; bush beans sprang up in the shade of the big pumpkin leaves.

Grandma Fleet told them the old gardens had always been there. The old-time people found the gardens already growing, planted by the Sand Lizard, a relative of Grandfather Snake, who invited his niece to settle there and cultivate her seeds. Sand Lizard warned her children to share: Don't be greedy. The first ripe fruit of each harvest belongs to the spirits of our beloved ancestors, who come to us as rain; the second ripe fruit should go to the birds and wild animals, in gratitude for their restraint in sparing the seeds and sprouts earlier in the season. Give the third ripe fruit to the bees, ants, mantises, and others who cared for the plants. A few choice pumpkins, squash, and bean plants were simply left on the sand beneath the mother plants to shrivel dry and return to the earth. Next season, after the arrival of the rain, beans, squash, and pumpkins sprouted up between the dry stalks and leaves of the previous year. Old Sand Lizard insisted her gardens be reseeded in that way because human beings are undependable; they might forget to plant at the right time or they might not be alive next year.

For years of little rain, Sand Lizard gave them amaranth and sunflowers; for times of drought she gave them succulent little roots and stems growing deep beneath the sand. The people called themselves Sand Lizard's children; they lived there for a long time. As their numbers increased, some Sand Lizard people joined their relations who lived down along the big river, until gradually the old gardens were abandoned. From time to time, Grandma Fleet and others still visited their old houses to feed the ancestor spirits. In a time of emergency, the old gardens could be counted on for sanctuary.

The Sand Lizard people heard rumors about the aliens for years before they finally appeared. The reports were alarming, and the people had difficulty believing the bloodshed and cruelty attributed to the strangers. But the reports were true. At harvest, the aliens demanded and took everything. This happened long, long ago but the people never forgot the hunger and suffering of that first winter the invaders appeared. The invaders were dirty people who carried disease and fever. The Sand Lizard people knew it was time for them to head for the hills beyond the river, to return to the old gardens.

The Sand Lizard people fled just in time; later that year, a fever killed dozens of whites and almost all of the people who remained by the river. The people were starving as they approached the old gardens. From a distance they could see the slopes of the highest sand dunes, and they could hardly believe their eyes; the shoulders of the dunes were crisscrossed with bands of bright colors: bird green, moss green, grass green; blossom orange, blossom yellow, and blossom white. As they got closer, they walked through fields of sunflowers that surrounded the sandhills on all sides.

Only a few Sand Lizard people were left, but they lived undisturbed at the old gardens for years, always ready to flee to the high mountains at the first sign of strangers.

In years when the rains were scarce, the people carried water to the wilted plants in gourd canteens, from the spring in the sandstone cliff. Each person had plants to care for, although the harvest was shared by everyone. Individual plants had pet names—Bushy, Fatty, Skinny, Shorty, Mother, and Baby were common names.

The Sand Lizard people remained at the old gardens peacefully for hundreds of years because the invaders feared the desert beyond the river. Then a few years before Sister Salt was born, in the autumn, as the people returned from harvesting piñons in the high mountains, a gang of gold prospectors surprised them; all those who were not killed were taken prisoner. Grandma Fleet lost her young husband to a bullet; only the women and children remained, captives at Fort Yuma.

This happened before the girls were born; Grandma Fleet was not so old then. She escaped the first night by chewing the ropes off her wrists, untying her legs to crawl away through the burr sage. She headed for the high mountains, where she slept under pine needles and ate acorns, piñons, and pine nuts; the snow sent her back to the old gardens, where the red amaranth was tall and the heads of the sunflowers were heavy with seeds. She hoped to see their mother or others who might have escaped, but there was no one. On the flanks of the big sandhills squash and pumpkins, big and ripe, reflected the light of the sun. How lonely she had been, grieving for her husband, for the others, while all around her the plants they had tended, and their houses, seemed to call out their names. Grandma Fleet was confident their mother and a few of the others would show up in a week or two, but no one came.

Their mother did not escape. Because she was young, she was put to work for an army officer's wife, who taught her how to wash and iron clothes and how to scrub floors. Their mother learned English. She was a prisoner so she was not paid. After the officer's wife left, she remained, washing laundry and cleaning for the post, until a missionary arrived. The reverend took one look at the young Indian woman and requested the post commander allow him to save her soul from temptation. So Mama went to live at the Presbyterian mission, where she learned the preacher himself suffered from temptation. When her belly got big with Sister Salt, the preacher's wife sent her away. One day Grandma Fleet heard the cliff swallows' commotion and looked up to see her daughter. A few weeks later, Sister Salt was born.

The Sand Lizard people were never numerous, but now Grandma, Mama, and baby Sister were the only Sand Lizard people living at the old gardens. A few remaining Sand Lizard people married into other tribes on the reservation at Parker. Grandma Fleet said she would die before she would live on a reservation. There was nothing to eat on the reservation; the best farmland along the river was taken by the white people. Reservation Indians sat in one place and did not move; they ate white food—white bread and white sugar and white lard. Reservation Indians had no mesquite flour for the winter because they could not leave the reservation to gather mesquite beans in August. They were not allowed to go to the sandhills in the spring to gather delicacies—sprouts and roots. Poor people! If they couldn't travel around, here and there, they wouldn't be able to find enough to eat; if people stayed in one place too long, they soon ate up everything. The government bought sheep and cattle to feed the reservation Indians through the winter, but the Indian agent and his associates got more of the meat than the Indians did.

Sister Salt was learning to walk, and Grandma Fleet was holding her by the hand, leading her back and forth on the fine sand outside the dugout house. Mama took the big gourd canteen to fetch water from the spring above the dunes. Grandma played and played with Sister Salt, who was so pleased with herself to be walking; Grandma Fleet heard nothing unusual that morning, but Mama did not return from the spring. Later, when Grandma Fleet searched the area around the spring, she found the empty gourd canteen and the tracks of shod horses and boot prints in the sand churned up by the struggle. Four years passed, and Grandma Fleet believed her daughter must have died at the hands of her kidnappers or she would have escaped by then and found her way back to the old gardens.

One day, at about the same time of year she had disappeared, Mama returned to the old gardens. She had traveled with two women from downriver. The following day more people arrived, and the day after that, others came. The starving people began to harvest the amaranth greens and dig for roots. More people came in the weeks after Mama's return. It was as if a great storm had erupted far in the distance, unseen and unheard by them at the old gardens; then suddenly a trickle, then a stream, and finally a flood of people sought sanctuary at the old gardens. The people were fleeing the Indian police and soldiers sent by the government; the new orders stated all Indians must leave their home places to live on the reservation at Parker.

Mama returned with a sack of mesquite beans on her back and baby Indigo in her belly. Sister Salt was old enough to remember Indigo's birth. How odd it was to see the baby's head peek out from between her mother's legs.

The refugees kept arriving. Grandma Fleet watched their numbers grow each day, weary and frightened women and children. Their men were long gone—to the high mountains or to prison. The spring provided water for everyone, but food became more and more scarce. Before the summer rains ever came, the people were starving. They ate the dried-up seed pumpkins and squash left in the garden the year before as first harvest offerings; they consumed seeds set aside for planting next season. They ate everything they could find. They cleared the wild gourd vines and boiled the roots of weeds and shrubs. They even dug deep into the sand in the old gardens to expose sprouted seeds. Grandma and Mama feared they all would starve to death before the sunflowers and red amaranth went to seed in October.

Grandma Fleet did not like the idea of town, but with a baby and a little girl to feed, they hadn't much choice: to stay at the old gardens meant starvation. The others had already gone. In the railroad town called Needles they managed to find a little to eat each day. Mama washed dirty linens for the hotel next door to the train station. Grandma Fleet carried Indigo on her back while she and Sister Salt scavenged scraps of lumber to build shelter for them on the floodplain of the river. Other women and children lived there, from places even Grandma Fleet had never heard of; they had been driven off their land by white settlers or pursued by the soldiers and Indian police. Their first years there were very difficult, but the Walapai women and the Paiute women shared the little food they had; a kind Mormon woman brought them old clothing. As long as there was no trouble, the authorities left them alone; but they knew they might be removed to the reservation at Parker at any time. Townspeople hired them to work their gardens and to clean house and wash for them.

The older women watched the children and listened for the trains; they took the children to the depot to meet the passengers, who sometimes gave them pennies after they took their pictures. The train passenger especially wanted pictures of the children they called "papooses." Sometimes train passengers, white women, made signs they wanted to hold Indigo; one woman had even shoved paper money into Grandma Fleet's hand, making signs that she wanted to take Indigo away with her. Before Grandma Fleet could throw the money to the ground, the woman snatched up Indigo into her arms. "No" was the only word of English Grandma Fleet bothered to learn, but she knew how to say it, knew how to summon the sounds from deep in her chest and sharpen the edges of the sound in her throat before she flung the word into the white woman's face. "No!" she screamed, and the white woman stumbled backward, still holding the toddler. "No! No!" Each time Grandma Fleet repeated the word, the white woman flinched, her face frozen with fear. Everyone stopped what they were doing on the depot platform and all eyes were on Grandma Fleet and the woman. The door of the depot office flew open and the stationmaster came running with a shotgun in his hand. The woman's husband and the other passengers rushed over to see, and the husband pried Indigo out of her arms and indignantly shoved the toddler back into Grandma Fleet's arms. The stationmaster waved a shotgun after Grandma Fleet and the other Indian women and children as they ran from the depot.

After that, Grandma Fleet did not go with the others to meet the trains. Some days she scavenged in the town dump; other days she sat in the lean-to and watched Indigo play while she soaked and peeled the fibrous strands from yucca leaves she and Sister Salt gathered from the dry hills above the river. She taught Sister Salt how to make little baskets in any shape she wanted simply by cutting the yucca strands in different lengths. Grandma showed Sister Salt how to gather devil's claws and soak them so the jet black fibers would peel away easily. She helped Sister Salt wrap the woven yucca with the fibrous black threads to make eyes for the dog and the frog figures. While Sister Salt made small frog-shaped and dog-shaped baskets to sell to the tourists, Grandma Fleet wove a large storage basket with a lid to keep her treasures from the dump, mostly bits of colored glass and all sorts of seeds, especially the pits of apricots and peaches.

Grandma refused to go to the train depot after the incident, but Sister Salt could not go alone; so as soon as their mother heard the train whistle off in the distance, she left her duties at the washtubs behind the hotel to fetch Sister Salt and the baskets. Sister Salt carried a dog basket in one hand and a frog basket in the other; their mother taught her to smile and say "Hello! Would you like to buy a basket?" Mama stood nearby and watched for trouble, while Sister Salt sold the baskets.

Later on, when Indigo asked Sister Salt to tell her about their mother, Sister Salt recalled how she wanted to go with the other children to get the candy and the pennies the train passengers sometimes tossed to the children from train windows, but Mama made her stay put by the baskets displayed on the depot platform. Mama was strict about that; she was angered by the grinning faces of passengers who delighted at the sight of the children begging, then scrambling for anything tossed out the train windows. Mama learned English from the soldiers' wives at Fort Yuma, but she preferred not to answer the tourists' questions about the baskets or herself. Sister Salt had to do all the talking, but Mama always took the money and quickly stuffed it down the front of her dress between her breasts. The dog and frog baskets nearly always sold; summer was always best; winters were the worst, because the passengers were reluctant to stop on the icy depot platform.

Before deep snow came, Grandma Fleet went with the others to the mountains to gather piñons, pine nuts, and acorns, but they often did not have enough to eat in the winter. The hotel did not have as many winter guests to dirty the linens, so there was not as much work for Mama. The white man who managed the hotel allowed her to take home vegetable crates and other wood scraps to burn on cold nights. As sheets or towels became badly frayed or stained, their mother showed the linens to the hotel manager; if he agreed, she was allowed to take the rags home. When someone smoking in bed burned a blanket, Mama brought home the half of the blanket that remained, and with a quilting needle made from a sharpened wire and string Grandma Fleet retrieved from the dump, Mama sewed them a family quilt with the singed blanket and the ragged towels.

On the coldest days, when the winds whipped the snow and sleet into a blizzard, the four of them huddled together under the family quilt in their lean-to. Grandma Fleet and Mama told the girls old stories about the land of perpetual summer, far to the south, where the ground actually smoldered on the hottest days. Mama recalled her captivity at Fort Yuma, where the army tents filled with white heat at midday and sometimes caught fire. Sister Salt and Indigo imagined the summer heat, and the cold winds were not so oppressive. How delicious the warmth of the fire felt, but fire was also dangerous near the dry willows and scrap lumber of the lean-to. At bedtime, the fire was damped with dry river sand, and Grandma Fleet scraped away the sand floor in the middle of their lean-to and buried hot coals under layers of sand to keep them warm as they slept together under the big quilt. The cold winters made Grandma Fleet homesick for the south, for her dugout house at the old gardens. The refugees might have eaten everything in sight at the old gardens, but her dugout house with its fine roof of layered palm fronds was much more weather-tight, much nicer than the empty packing crates they called home in Needles. The hard years passed slowly.

One day a white man and two Indian policemen walked through the lean-tos. The Indian policemen called out; if someone came to the door, the white man wrote in his black book and they moved to the next shack. Mama was still at work, but Grandma Fleet knew immediately why the men were there. She told Sister Salt and Indigo to hide, quickly, under the big quilt. Whatever happens, she told them, don't make a sound, don't move. Grandma Fleet watched the government men move from shack to shack; when only two other shacks but theirs remained, Grandma Fleet sat down on top of the quilt. She almost sat on Sister Salt's head, but she moved, and Indigo moved her foot that Grandma was sitting on. They got themselves arranged, then Grandma spread her basket-making materials and a half-woven basket around her. She pretended to be crippled when the Indian policemen called her outside. She invited them to step inside, knowing they would refuse; the white man was afraid of disease and the Indian policemen feared witchcraft. They asked to see the two children reported to live there. Grandma Fleet pretended to cry; oohhh, she moaned, she was all alone now, an old woman all alone. The Indian police were not satisfied with her answers; they whispered to each other. They wanted to know about the others. They knew the Paiute women lied, because there were complaints about Paiute children begging for money from passengers at the depot. The Paiute children belonged in school. All Indian children must go to school; that was the law. Grandma Fleet pretended she was afraid of the Paiutes and claimed to know nothing about them. The Indian policemen conferred with their boss.

"Old Sand Lizard woman, dirt digger! You're lying! We'll drag you off to prison with all the rest of them!" one of the Indian police muttered as they left.

Grandma Fleet did not move for a long time after the police left in case it was a trick and they returned. Indigo squirmed because the circulation to her left foot was cut off by Grandma's leg; Sister Salt pinched her to make her be still, so Indigo kicked her in the shin. Grandma Fleet finally stood up and walked to the doorway to look both ways before she pulled back the quilt.

"It's a good thing they were gone when you girls started your commotion!" she said, shaking her head sternly. That evening when their mother came home from work she had news: the government man and Indian police had taken away six Walapai children to school. Grandma Fleet said it was time to go back to the old gardens; Sister Salt was almost a young woman and Indigo was just the age to be sent away to school. Mama agreed but wanted to work at the hotel a little bit longer so they could buy supplies to take back with them; they would have enough money if she worked awhile longer.

Each day while Mama and Sister Salt were at their work in town, Grandma Fleet took Indigo with her. Some days they prowled the arroyos to gather willows for basket making; other days they walked in the sand and sagebrush hills outside town to gather grass seeds to grind into flour. Most days Grandma Fleet and Indigo ended with a walk through the town dump, where they surveyed the refuse and Indigo scrambled down the sides of the garbage pits to retrieve valuables the townspeople carelessly threw away. String, paper, scraps of cloth, glass jars and bottles, tin cans, and bits of wire—they washed their discoveries in the shallows of the river and reused them. Grandma Fleet saved seeds discarded from vegetables and fruits to plant at the old gardens when they returned; she poked her stick through the debris in garbage piles behind the café and hotel. Grandma kept her seeds in the little glass jars with lids they found at the dump; she kept the jars of seeds in her bedding for safekeeping. The apricot pits were her special favorites because she remembered the apricot trees of her childhood at the old gardens. Grandma Fleet held the jar up close to her face and spoke to the seeds;

"Mmmm! You will be my little sweethearts, my little apricot trees!"

◆ ◆ ◆

Grandma Fleet planned to take along Sister Salt and Indigo when she returned to the old gardens after the winter rains arrived; their mother would send food and make visits from time to time. That winter more people came from the north; remnants of many desert tribes, mostly children and women, came to Needles because the winter was so hard and they were so poor.

The Paiute visitors told a strange story; their people were starving but they were not worried because they were waiting for someone, someone named Messiah. A Paiute prophet named Wovoka died and visited Messiah, who gave him instructions to take back to the people. The Paiute women described encampments of hundreds of people all dancing in a circle as Wovoka instructed. The Paiutes were reluctant to talk about Wovoka because many white people feared and hated Wovoka. If white authorities heard the Indians even speak the name, there was trouble. Far to the north there were rumors the soldiers killed dozens of dancers.

On cold mornings, smoke from the campfires drifted across the sky above the river. Now the lean-tos and shacks extended up and down the sandy floodplain on the west side of the river. Their life was different now that there were more people living around them. The smell of roasting meat became more familiar, and so did the sound of voices and laughter at night. A few Paiute boys and old men appeared later on; they stayed in the camp or hunted the river dunes for rabbits. The men were careful not to show themselves in town.

Mama made friends with a Paiute woman who talked about Wovoka. Wovoka lived an ordinary life until one day he died and saw Jesus in heaven. Jesus was sad and angry at what had been done to the Earth and to all the animals and people. Jesus promised Wovoka that if the Paiutes and all the other Indians danced this dance, then the used-up land would be made whole again and the elk and the herds of buffalo killed off would return. The dance was a peaceful dance, and the Paiutes wished no harm to white people; but Jesus was very angry with white people. As the people danced, great storm clouds would gather over the entire world. Finally, when all the Indians were dancing, great winds would roar out of clear skies, winds the likes of which were never seen before; the winds, for weeks without end, would blow away all the topsoil and strip the trees of all leaves. The winds would dry up all the white people and all the Indians who followed the white man's ways, and they would blow away with the dust.

The Paiute woman had seen Jesus surrounded by hundreds of Paiutes and Shoshones and other Indians who heard Jesus was coming. Jesus wore a white coat with bright red stripes; he wore moccasins on his feet. His face was dark and handsome, his eyes black and shining. He had no beard or whiskers, but thick eyebrows. The people built a big fire to throw light on him. Then, as Jesus sang, hundreds and hundreds of people began to dance in a circle around him. They danced until late at night, when Jesus told them to stop. The next morning Jesus talked to them, and talked all day. He told them all Indians must dance, everywhere, and keep on dancing. If they danced the dance, then they would be able to visit their dear ones and beloved ancestors. The ancestor spirits were there to help them. They must keep dancing. They must not quarrel and must treat one another kindly. If they kept dancing, great storms would purify the Earth of her destroyers. The clear running water and the trees and the grassy plains filled with buffalo and elk would return.

The Paiute woman said when the dancers saw their dead friends and family members, they fell to the ground shaking and twitching, then lay silent. When they woke up, they all were happy and excited because they had seen the Earth reborn.

Grandma Fleet said all that was fine and good, but why had these Paiutes run away from the Christ and his dance? Mama shook her head. There were rumors the soldiers were on their way to kill the Messiah and all his dancers. Grandma Fleet shook her head. She wished the Paiutes could have stayed up north, but they had no choice. Now that there were so many Indians living along the river, the white people watched them more closely. Grandma Fleet had watched white people long enough to know they would tolerate a few Indian women and children so long as there was no trouble. But white people got uneasy when they saw numbers of Indians gathered in one place.

One cold morning Sister Salt awoke to the sounds of hundreds of crows. Mama and Indigo were still sleeping but Grandma was up. She had already made a little fire and was squatting next to it. The air smelled moist. The sky was overcast with thick gray snow clouds that dimmed the sun's light. Sister Salt peered in the direction of the cottonwood trees that towered above the riverbank; dozens of crows darkened the bare pale branches of the trees. The birds frolicked, swooping and circling above the trees, playing chase. Grandma gave her a tin can full of warm tea brewed from wildflowers she helped Grandma gather in early fall. Grandma Fleet studied the crows; ordinarily, there were only ten or twelve resident crows, who roosted in the cottonwood trees above the river and roamed the town dump, hopping along the ground with their wings spread as they searched for tidbits. Later that day Grandma Fleet talked with the Paiute woman and learned the flocks of crows were a sign that Wovoka and the Messiah were coming.

One evening after sundown, Sister Salt and Indigo came home from selling baskets at the depot to a strange spectacle: the river sand a short distance from the camp had been cleared of pebbles and debris. Indigo took one look and stopped short. A fire had been built in the midde of the smoothed area and dancers moved slowly in a circle around a fire. The earth under the dancers' feet was the color of old blood. She didn't want to go any closer. The hair and faces of the dancers were painted completely white, and they were all wrapped in white shawls. The girls did not recognize anyone. Sister Salt guided Indigo by the arm away from the dancers and toward home, but nothing looked the same. Someone had gone from shack to shack painting big streaks of ocher red around the entrances; it wasn't dried blood but finely ground red clay. Indigo cautiously touched a finger to the red clay and was about to taste it when Sister Salt batted her finger down; the red clay belonged to the spirits.

The girls hurried to their lean-to. So many people had come; their small bundles and ragged bedrolls were neatly stacked outside their lean-tos of willow branches. They passed a campfire where people were lined up waiting to be painted by a stranger and his two assistants. When they reached home they found red clay dust smeared over the scrap lumber of the doorway, and red dust was even sprinkled on the floor inside, but Mama and Grandma Fleet were not there. The ashes in the fire pit were cold. Sister Salt hid the baskets under the quilt and they went out again to find Mama and Grandma Fleet.

The winter sun was weak and low in the sky, and a cold wind prowled out of the mountains and swirled around the camp. Indigo gripped Sister Salt's hand; gusts of wind flung stinging sand into their faces. Grandma and Mama used to talk about the celebrations in the old days when everyone came to dance and to feast and to give thanks for a good year. The people had not celebrated for years, not since Sister Salt was a baby. They did not see any familiar faces; in one afternoon, hundreds of strangers had arrived. But where were Mama and Grandma?

They slowly approached the line of people waiting to be painted, looking for a familiar face—the neighbor lady, anyone who could tell them the whereabouts of Mama and Grandma. Indigo's dress did not reach her ankles so she huddled down, trying to keep the cold wind off her legs. Sister Salt was wrapped in a piece of an old rug the hotel man gave to Mama. The people stepped back so the girls could warm themselves by the fire, and Sister Salt recognized the Paiute woman who lived next door.

"Have you seen our grandmother or mother?" she asked. The woman nodded and pointed in the direction of the dancers in the circle. The girls started to go, but the woman shook her head and motioned for them to come to her.

"You must not disturb your mother or your grandmother," the woman told them. "They are dancing. They won't recognize you." The woman looked at Indigo, who was shivering, and motioned for one of the men applying the white clay paint. The man reached down to a big bundle near his feet and pulled out a piece of white canvas. The woman helped Indigo adjust the shawl around her shoulders; the white cloth reached past her ankles; its warmth was delicious. The woman helped Indigo wrap it just as the people dancing had wrapped themselves.

"Now," the woman said, "now you won't freeze while we wait for the sacred paint."

The painting and the wrapping in white robes took a long time, but the people were happy and excited. Later, right before the sisters went to join the other dancers, an old Paiute woman gave them each a handful of piñons, the sacred food of the dancers, and she gave them a gourd dipper of warm water to share. The white clay on Indigo's hair and face felt odd when she moved her mouth or eyes; her hair felt stiff. The white canvas robe wrapped Sister Salt's arms close to her body so she reminded Indigo of a big white crow. The twilight was blue-gray giving way to darkness.

Now the dancers were resting on the sand around the fire, drinking water and eating piñons. Indigo looked for Mama and Grandma Fleet among the dancers sitting on the ground by the fire but she recognized no one. Sister Salt pointed across the circle in the shadows where a small group of dancers gathered around a figure moaning and writhing on the ground. Was that Mama? Was that Grandma Fleet? Just then voices began to sing softly and the dancers stood up. They moved together and began to join hands in a circle around the fire. The voices of the dancers rose softly at first from low undertones, but gradually the singing seemed to rise out of the earth to surround them. Indigo held Sister Salt's hand so tightly she expected her sister to pry it loose a little, but Sister Salt didn't seem to notice. Indigo felt shy holding the Paiute woman's hand, but she wasn't afraid. So far the Paiutes had given her a warm shawl and warm water and piñons to eat.

Indigo watched the Paiute woman's feet. She watched Sister Salt's feet. They were careful to drag their feet lightly along the ground to keep themselves in touch with Mother Earth. They were moving from right to left because that was the path followed by the sun. Wovoka wanted them to dance because dancing moves the dead. Only by dancing could they hope to bring the Messiah, the Christ, who would bring with him all their beloved family members and friends who had moved on to the spirit world after the hunger and the sadness got to be too much for them. The invaders made the Earth get old and want to die.

Indigo wondered what the ancestors looked like—Mama's sisters and brothers, Grandma Fleet's teenage husband, and Mama's little baby that died. Around and around they went, singing about the snow: "The snow lies there," they sang, "the snow lies there. The Milky Way lies there, the Milky Way lies there." Indigo looked up at the stars that were the road of the dead to the spirit world. She thought she could detect faint movement on the path of stars.

The dancers stopped to rest after the first song. Indigo and Sister Salt sat down with their backs against the windbreak, where the fire kept off the night's chill. Warm water and handfuls of piñons were passed from dancer to dancer; Sister Salt looked at her but did not speak. When Indigo opened her mouth to ask about Mama and Grandma Fleet, Sister Salt shook her head.

More wood was fed to the fire as the dancers joined for the second song. The Paiute woman told Indigo the words to the second song, but Indigo was not sure if she heard the words correctly. Why sing, "The black rock, the black rock," when they were dancing on white river sand? Why sing, "The rock is broken, the rock is broken"? Indigo was tired now, and the singing voices were so loud she couldn't be sure what the Paiute woman said. Later on she would ask Sister Salt about everything that happened. Indigo kept singing with the others; she was cozy and warm with Sister Salt on one side and the Paiute woman on the other. "The black rock, the black rock, the black rock is broken"; she sang it and saw it with her eyes closed. "The black rock is broken and from it pours clear fresh water that runs in little streams everywhere."

When Indigo opened her eyes again, she was covered with the quilt, alone in the lean-to; dozens of dancers circled the fire; the flames leaped high, crackling and popping loudly. "The wind stirs the willows," they sang, "the wind stirs the grasses." She wanted to see the Christ and his family arrive; they were coming from far away and would arrive just before dawn. She was so comfortable she wanted to sleep a little more. When she woke again, Indigo heard Mama's voice and Grandma Fleet's voice; Sister Salt was talking too, but when she opened her eyes, she saw strange figures wrapped in white. Then she remembered the dancers and the white clay paint.

"Mama! We couldn't find you!" Indigo called out.

"She's awake." Indigo heard Sister Salt's voice. A dancer in a white robe approached. Mama didn't look like herself with the strange white paint on her face and her hands, but Indigo had never seen her look so happy. She knelt down and held Indigo's face between her hands.

"You should see yourself," she said. "Grandma Fleet and I thought we'd never find you girls." They had to get ready because the Christ would arrive soon. Grandma Fleet had to urinate so they all went to the tamarisks to relieve themselves. Indigo pulled the shawl close to herself against the cold. The wind was increasing; clouds moved rapidly across the sky, so the light of the moon was partially obscured. As they returned to the circle the dancers were taking their places; everyone was whispering in excited voices, "He's here! He's here!" Indigo stood on her tiptoes but could see nothing. Here and there, a dancer helped others who had fallen to the ground with joy after their loved ones came down the Milky Way to visit them.

The singers began and the others joined in. "The wind stirs the willows, the wind stirs the willows. How sweet the scent! The wind stirs the sand grass. The wind stirs the sand grass!" the dancers sang. They had to dance; they must dance or the Messiah and the spirits could not come down to them.

The white clay protected her face and hands from the cold wind; the sacred white clay made the wind feel like a warm breeze. Sister Salt did not feel tired or sleepy. She had never felt so happy. Even the sick woman from their camp and the old Havasupai woman who lived with her were dancing and lively tonight. They were about to see everyone who had passed on to the spirit world—beloved family members and old friends. But that wasn't all: the gathering of all the spirits meant the arrival of the storm clouds as well.

The wind calmed and Sister Salt smelled moisture; a warm wet snow began to fall on the dancers. She kept her eyes on the big snowflakes falling into the flames. The voices of the others around her seemed to recede as she entered into the silence of the snow. Each snowflake was luminous and slowly turning as it fell. She saw every crystalline surface, every shimmering corner and bright edge of ice; she was enveloped in the light and then she herself was the light. She felt them all around her, cradling her, loving her; she didn't see them but she knew all of them—the ancestors' spirits alway loved her; there was no end to their love.

Later, Sister Salt and Indigo used to talk about the four nights of the dance. So much happened, so many amazing sights. Sister Salt told Indigo about the snowflakes: "They let me know how beautiful we are, how beautiful we will become." Later she told Indigo she died that night so she wasn't afraid to die anymore. Indigo was disappointed to learn that no ancestors showed their faces to Sister Salt—only the snowflakes. Grandma Fleet said the family spirits didn't bother to put themselves in human forms because Sister Salt would not recognize them anyway—they were all gone or killed off before she was born. Indigo complained that she had seen nothing.

"You are too young to see such things," Grandma Fleet said. "When you get to be a young woman like your Sister Salt, you will understand." The dancers began to rise to their feet. Indigo started to get up to join them but Mama shook her head and smiled while she tucked the quilt around Indigo.

"It's getting too cold. Dawn will be freezing. You stay curled up here where it's warm," Mama said.

All the others were sleeping when Indigo awoke. The sun was already climbing high, and Indigo felt too warm under the quilt with Sister Salt and Mama on either side. The fire the dancers circled had burned down to whitish red coals in circles of ash and mud mixed with the sacred red ocher dust. Indigo checked the position of the sun in the sky once more. It was almost time to take the baskets to sell to passengers on the westbound train. She woke Mama, but Mama said the dance was far more important than selling baskets. Indigo needed her rest so she could dance all night again. They all must dance four nights to move the dead, to help them to return.

While the others slept, Indigo walked around the camp looking at the strangers who had come from all directions for the dance. She heard Grandma Fleet say most of the visitors were Walapai and Havasupai, and of course Paiute; but a few traveled great distances from the north and from the east, because they heard the Messiah was coming. Indigo reached the edge of the encampment and was about to turn back when she heard white people talking. She saw the horses first, hobbled and grazing in a clearing surounded by willow and tamarisk. Then she saw the wagon with bedding spread underneath, with people still asleep; but standing around a small campfire she saw a white woman and a white man. So the Paiute woman's story about the Mormons was true! Small groups of Mormons came because the Mormons had been waiting for the Messiah's return; they became very excited after they heard Wovoka preach. Mormons began to dance hand in hand with the other dancers; these Mormons who believed in Wovoka were generous and donated meat for the dancers. The white canvas for the dancers' shawls was donated by the Mormons.

The second night more dancers circled the fire. Indigo counted eight Mormons—six men and two women; painted with white clay and wrapped in white robes, the Mormons looked like all the others. Indigo watched them that night and wondered if Mormons saw their ancestors when they danced. Watching the Mormons kept Indigo awake; she wanted to see one of them fall to the ground and moan from a visit by the old Mormon spirits. Try as she did, Indigo fell asleep after a few hours, and she had to rely on Sister Salt to tell her all that happened.

Early on the final night, Indigo got to see for herself what happened to a Mormon visited by his ancestors. The young man suddenly fell to his knees with his face in his hands, babbling and weeping before he slowly sank to the earth and lay quietly on his side, no different from any of the other dancers who visited with the spirits. Indigo was wide awake. This final night was the night the Messiah and his Holy Mother would come.

"The whirlwind! The whirlwind! The snowy earth floats before me! The snowy earth floats before me!" Grandma Fleet sang loudly even after dancing hard four nights straight. She squeezed their entwined fingers together firmly—Sister Salt on one side, Indigo on the other. They must sing hard if they wanted the Christ and his eleven children to come down from the mountains at dawn.

Around and around they danced, lightly caressing the Mother Earth with their feet. "Dust of the whirlwind, dust of the mountains in the whirlwind, even the rocks are ringing! Whirlwind in the mountains, rock dust rings. Rock dust rings," they sang. The whirlwind would transform the Earth, the Paiute woman said. When the wind scoured away all impurities, then the Earth's rebirth would follow.

On this final night, more dancers were visited by spirits than on previous nights. Indigo watched Mama stiffen, lean her head back, and sink to the ground shivering, without a word. They carefully stepped around Mama and they kept dancing. "Cottonwood! Cottonwood, so tall! Lush green leaves! Lush green leaves! Cottonwood so tall!" The voices of the dancers rose above the river. Indigo closed her eyes: the sound of the hundreds of voices was not human but mountain, as if out of the depths of the mountains a great humming rose. The Earth announced her labor; the ground must shudder and heave before she could be reborn. Indigo felt the Earth's breathing through the soles of her feet; the sound gently carried her along, so she did not tire dancing. She was determined to stay awake; everyone seemed more alert. Sister Salt said the Messiah and his family were close by, waiting for the right moment to come to them.

As the dancers began the final song, the wind began to stir and the air smelled damp. The waning moon rose but soon disappeared behind the clouds. Big snowflakes began to hiss in the flames of the fire. The clouds and mist reflected the glow of the big campfire and illuminated the hills above the river and cast strange, giant shadows of the dancers. Later Grandma Fleet blamed those odd shadows for the townspeople's fears, which brought the soldiers and Indian police.

Although scattered snow flurries remained, the mass of storm clouds drifted east; the buffalo horn moon was still visible as the morning star appeared on the horizon. While the others danced with eyes focused on the fire, Indigo watched the weird shadows play on the hillsides, so she was one of the first to see the Messiah and his family as they stepped out of the darkness into the glow of the swirling snowflakes. How their white robes shined! Indigo glanced around quickly to see if the others had noticed. She watched the Messiah and the others, who seemed almost to float as they descended the high sandy hill to the riverbank. How beautiful he was, just as the Paiute woman said. No wonder he called himself the morning star!

The others saw him now, but they all kept dancing, as they knew they must, until the Christ reached the middle of their circle. Wovoka the Prophet came too. He walked beside the Messiah's mother; behind them came the Messiah's eleven children. They all wore white robes but their dark faces were not painted. Now the dancers gathered around the Messiah and his family. Indigo held Sister Salt's hand tightly and stood on her tiptoes so she could see between the dancers crowded around.

"You are hungry and tired because this dance has been going on for a long time," the Holy Mother said. Then she opened her shawl, and the Messiah's wife opened her shawl too, and Indigo was amazed to see plump orange squash blossoms tumble to the ground. The Holy Mother motioned for the dancers to step forward to help themselves to the squash flowers.

Now it was so quiet only the fire's crackle could be heard; no one spoke as they waited their turn to take a squash flower. Later, when Indigo and Sister Salt discussed that night, they remembered with amazement that whenever the Messiah or the Holy Mother spoke, all the dancers could understand them, no matter what tribe they were from. The Paiutes swore the Messiah was speaking Paiute, but a Walapai woman laughed and shook her head; how silly, the Messiah spoke her language. When Grandma Fleet and Mama knelt to pick up blossoms, the Holy Mother blessed them in their Sand Lizard language. When the Mormons approached the Messiah, Sister Salt stayed nearby to listen for herself; she was amazed. As the Messiah gave his blessing to the Mormons, Sister Salt distinctly heard the words he spoke as Sand Lizard, not English, yet the Mormons understood his words and murmured their thanks to him.

When Sister Salt excitedly told Mama and Grandma what she had heard, a Paiute man standing nearby smiled and nodded his head. In the presence of the Messiah and the Holy Mother, there was only one language spoken—the language of love—which all people understand, he said, because we are all the children of Mother Earth.

The sky went from dark to pale gray, then from milky to pale yellow as dawn approached. Indigo left the others and went to their lean-to as the dawn lit the sky in flaming reds, yellows, and golds. Away from the people and the campfires, the air was cold and damp though much of the snow had melted. Indigo pulled her white robe closer to her body. She was careful not to crush the squash flower; she wanted to keep it as long as she could.

At home, with the big quilt all around her to keep warm, she sat propped up, facing the east; orange-gold light from the rising sun shined between the lattices of willow and tamarisk branches. Inside the lean-to, everything the sun's light touched turned warm and golden. Indigo took the big orange flower in both hands and held it to her face, with her eyes closed. She inhaled the old gardens after a rain when the edges of the dunes were crisscrossed in all the brightest greens—moss green and grass green and the green of the big pumpkin leaves.

As Indigo drifted off to sleep, she heard one voice and then another voice address the dancers. Wovoka led the dancers in the final rituals of the dance: they all must clap their hands and shake and wave their shawls vigorously to repel diseases and sickness, especially the influenza. They had just completed the final rituals when the alarm was shouted. The dancers remained calm because the Christ was with them and his Mother had already told them the soldiers would come.

The next thing Indigo knew, Sister Salt was shaking her, telling her to get up! Get up! She heard horses' hooves, the sound of wagons clattering, excited voices and shouts. Indigo felt so tired, just sitting up gave her a sick feeling in her stomach; but Sister Salt jerked her to her feet. She was breathing hard as if she had been running.

"Hurry! Hurry! No! You can't take those! We have to run!" Sister Salt pulled her along by the hand while Indigo tried to look back to see what was happening. She saw white men on horses and white men on foot seizing the Mormons, who put up no struggle; she saw dancers running in all directions with Indian policemen chasing them.

The girls ran south into the tamarisks and willows along the riverbank. The deep sand was tiring to run through, and when the sounds of the shouting grew faint, they stopped in the cover of the willows to catch their breath. Indigo knew the rules: when they were on the run, no one must speak even one word; but she wanted to know what had happened to Mama and Grandma Fleet. And the Messiah and his family—were they able to escape?

When Indigo was rested, Sister Salt stood up and pulled her to her feet. Off they went again, not running now but still walking fast; they no longer heard any shouts behind them. Sister Salt followed a game trail down the bank to the river's edge, where the cattails hid them while they drank.

They no longer ran, but they walked steadily until the sun went down; then the cold air from the snow on the mountains drifted down to the river. In the side of a sandy bank above the river, they scooped away the sand with their hands to make a trench; then they wrapped themselves together with both shawls. They laughed at how they must look—two-headed, with four legs; they laughed at how awkwardly they moved wrapped together. They got down into the trench and arranged themselves comfortably before they began pulling sand into the trench over their legs for warmth.

Before dawn, when the air was coldest, Indigo woke Sister Salt with her shivering attempts to snuggle closer. They took turns rubbing each other's hands and arms vigorously; Sister Salt pretended Indigo's hands were a fire drill and stick that would catch fire if only she could rub them fast enough. "Faster-faster-faster," they chanted in unison until they both started laughing out loud. They watched the light seep into the sky—at first a nearly imperceptible glow out of the darkness. Yesterday they all had been together dancing for the dawn that brought the Messiah, then suddenly everything changed.

Grandma Fleet and Mama would meet them back at the old gardens. That was the last thing Grandma Fleet told Sister Salt that morning, moments after someone shouted a warning; the girls knew how to follow the river south to the big wash that led to the canyon of the dunes.

The Messiah and his family escaped; Sister Salt saw them. His wife and children stepped into the river first, then the Holy Mother and he followed them; the fierce river currents of muddy water closed around them but they were not swept away. Their shoulders and heads remained above the muddy water, and they moved across the river effortlessly, as if they were smoke. When they emerged on the far side of the river, the Messiah and his family hurried up the high sandy hill above the river. The sunlight shone on the white robes of the Messiah and his family as they paused at the summit in plain view of the soldiers and Indian police overrunning their camp. But the soldiers and police never saw them; the Messiah and his family escaped.

◆ ◆ ◆

Sister Salt made a digging stick out of a piece of driftwood and dug up cattail roots to eat. Cattail roots didn't really taste like anything but water with a little salt, but Indigo forced herself to chew and swallow them to stop the pain of her empty stomach. For three days they followed the river south; late on the fourth day Indigo noticed the air suddenly felt much warmer. On the morning of the fifth day, they reached the intersection of the big wash and the river.

They dug cattail roots all morning to carry along to the old gardens. They filled their canvas shawls with the roots and wore them bundled on their backs. Before they left the river, they gathered wild gourds to make small canteens, which they filled with water and strung around their waists with cloth torn from their skirts.

All day they walked through the sand and sagebrush; the air was cool but the sun warmed them. Indigo began to notice green shoots and sprouts of new growth pushing through the sand. A few miles west of the river, the big wash meandered southwest, and when they rounded a turn, Indigo shouted, "Look!" Along the sides of the wash silvery green brittlebushes were covered with yellow blossoms.

That night when they huddled together to sleep, the air was cold but it was not freezing. They had crossed into the land of summer. The next day, about noontime, Sister Salt pointed to a big sandstone boulder at an intersection with a smaller wash. Here they left the big wash and walked the small wash for a few hours more before Sister Salt took a game trail that ascended the crumbling clay bank. The trail was steep. When Indigo reached the top, she was short of breath and she had to wipe away the sweat before she could see where they were.

Indigo had been so young the last time they lived at the old gardens she didn't remember how anything looked. She had listened to Mama's and Grandma's stories, and she knew they had been forced to abandon the old gardens after refugees came and ate everything. Despite the descriptions of the ravages of the starving people who left the dunes stripped bare, Indigo imagined the old gardens as they had been before the refugees came: tall corn plants swaying gracefully in the breeze, surrounded with bushes of bean pods and black-eyed peas, their golden-green tendrils tangled around the thick pumpkin vines.

Indigo shaded her eyes with one hand as she surveyed the sandstone canyon; she saw nothing green, nothing growing at all, only sandy ridges covered with dry weeds.

Sister Salt walked faster now, up the path to the head of the canyon. They still had a little river water in their gourd canteens, but for miles Sister Salt imagined how good the springwater would taste. She was grateful to have the river water for their journey, but it was muddy; the water that dripped down the cracks in the cliff was cool and clear.

Grandma Fleet had given Sister Salt instructions: first thing, go to the spring and look for footprints or other signs of people living in the area. Grandma Fleet said they should keep to themselves if they encountered strangers living at the old gardens. Grandma Fleet warned if too many people settled at one location they were bound to attract the attention of the authorities.

Blackened rocks and bits of charcoal from old campfires were partially buried by the sand, but Sister Salt could see that at one time as many as thirty campsites dotted the upper end of the canyon below the spring.

The cool springwater tasted even better than Sister Salt remembered; she and Indigo drank and then scooped water over themselves to wash off the dust. They sat by the spring and ate the last of the cattail roots; the sun felt warm, and the sound of the water trickling down the sandstone was soothing. They spread their canvas wraps on the fine sand next to the pool and stretched out side by side. Sister Salt was on her back looking up at the sandstone walls of the canyon and the sky but she was thinking about Mama and Grandma Fleet. Did the Indian police catch them? She couldn't stop thinking about the soldiers and Indian police galloping toward the dancers to encircle them. In their dark uniforms, on horseback, they did not appear to be humans but giant insects swarming down the hills to the riverbank.

Indigo lay on her stomach and up on her elbows, her chin resting in both hands as she stared into the water. She watched the water bugs scurry around their villages in the yellowish sand at the bottom of the pool. The big bugs moved with dignity, but the smaller bugs darted about as if they were playing chase with one another. Pebbles and stones in the pool were hills and mountains; the green shoots of water plants were the forests. How lovely their pool was! They had all the water and food they needed.

37

From the corner of her eye, Indigo caught the shiver of a blade of grass across the pool, though there was no breeze; she did not move. More blades of grass wiggled, then parted slowly as a big rattlesnake's head poked out cautiously, its tongue moving over the air slowly to read any warnings. The snake's tongue stopped when he caught their human scent. For an instant the snake looked at Sister Salt sleeping, then at Indigo, who held her breath. Grandma Fleet talked about the big snake many times because he was almost as old as she was, and the spring belonged to him. All desert springs have resident snakes. If people killed the snakes, the precious water disappeared. Grandma Fleet said whatever you do, don't offend the old snake who lives at the spring.

"Remember us? We won't harm you, Snake," Indigo whispered softly. "You know our grandmother and our mother." The snake seemed to consider her words before he glided to the edge of the pool. Indigo was amazed at how gracefully the snake dipped its mouth into the water, tilting back his head to swallow a dainty sip. The snake was thirsty and dipped his head to the water many times before he stopped, flicked his tongue at Indigo and then Sister Salt, then backed away and disappeared into the grass around the pool.

Later, when Sister Salt woke up and heard about the snake's visit, she said it was a good sign; if soldiers or others were lurking in the area, the big snake disappeared.

The first night they slept by the spring, but all night birds and small animals brushed past them to reach the water. The next day they went to work on Grandma Fleet's house. The old dugout house was not easy to spot because its roof was low to the ground and partially covered with sand. Sister Salt dropped to her knees, then crawled through the opening. Indigo followed, relieved that her sister was first to go inside Grandma Fleet's abandoned house; the old dugout room looked like a perfect home for centipedes and scorpions. Once they were inside, there was a narrow ledge and then three big stone steps down into the room. Indigo sat on the bottom step until her eyes became accustomed to the dim light. Inside the air was cool and smelled of clean sand; Sister Salt poked around the corners. The room was much bigger than it appeared from outside; there was plenty of space overhead, and the roofbeams were solid, although the wind had disturbed the top layer of desert palm branches on the roof.

They finished the roof repairs and were at the spring for a bath when they heard a strange sound off in the distance; someone was singing. At first the singing was too far away and they could not make out the song;

sometimes the singing grew faint, then loud again, as if the singer had crossed a dry wash. They both listened intently; then Sister Salt recognized the song.

"Grandma!" Sister Salt yelled and took off running in the direction of the singing. Indigo started to follow her but Sister Salt was running much too fast. Indigo watched her sister run through the stands of dry sunflowers below the sandhills toward the mouth of the canyon until she was out of sight. Indigo listened. The singing continued, then stopped. Suddenly she felt a strange fear overtake her, a fearful feeling she was about to be abandoned by Grandma Fleet, and even Sister Salt.

Indigo ran as fast as she could through the deep sand, up and down the sandhills, until her sides ached and her throat burned. She stopped to listen for the singing but the sound of her own breathing was all she heard. She ran, and when she stumbled, she picked herself up and kept running, terrified she might lose them.

At the mouth of the canyon she found them; Sister Salt was kneeling next to Grandma Fleet, who was resting in the shade of a big yucca, leaning herself against a gunnysack full of bundles. Indigo ran to them, her heart pounding wildly. She looked all around, panting; tears filled her eyes as she realized Grandma returned alone.

"Where is she?" Indigo demanded. "Where's Mama? Why didn't she come?"

"Is this the greeting I get?" Grandma Fleet teased as she opened her arms to embrace Indigo, who pressed her face hard against Grandma's bony chest and started to cry.

While Grandma Fleet rested in the shade, Sister Salt and Indigo took turns dragging the gunnysack full of bundles up the sandy path from the mouth of the canyon to the house. Grandma Fleet and one old Mormon woman were released from government custody. Grandma and the Mormon woman became friends on their walk down the river. They did not talk so much as they pointed out things to each other, then smiled and nodded to each other while they walked along.

Later, as she unpacked the bundle, Grandma Fleet talked about Mrs. Van Wagnen's cellar under the floor of the little stone house at Mormon Crossing. So much food put up in glass jars neatly arranged on wooden shelves! From muslin bags kept in big crockery jars, Mrs. Van Wagnen brought out dried apples and dried apricots and even dried venison.

From time to time Grandma passed them a muslin sack to sniff so they could savor the sweet, dry fruit odor. Beans. So many Indian beans! Mrs.

Van Wagnen had great success growing beans because her garden was near the river. Grandma Fleet did not want to take so much food, but Mrs. Van Wagnen had insisted. She could not eat all that food herself, she said, and then she started to cry because her husband and the other wives were arrested, and their children sent away to live with foster families in the new Mormon Church. Mrs. Van Wagnen stopped crying when she talked about the new Mormon Church; she became angry. The old church had been brushed aside by demons, she said. But Grandma Fleet thought maybe the other Mormons got tired of resisting the U.S. government. The government said only one wife, and now the new church said one wife, so the old Mormons moved to remote locations. For years and years, the U.S. soldiers chased Mormons when they weren't chasing Indians.

They thought of Mrs. Van Wagnen each time they ate the sweet dried apricots or boiled a pot of beans, and they hoped she was getting along all right. So many strangers forded the river at Mormon Crossing that a woman alone was not safe there. Poor Mrs. Van Wagnen! She was the first and now the only wife, but she didn't know if she would ever see her husband again.

All the talk about people lost made Indigo cry. Would she ever have her mama again? Grandma Fleet reassured her.

"I would know if something was wrong," Grandma said. "I would feel it in my bones." Even if their mother was arrested, the government usually kept Indian women in jail for only a month or two.

"Before hot weather comes, I'm going to visit my Mormon friend," Grandma Fleet said one day. They had just gathered a great many succulent little plants that grew under the sand at the foot of the cliffs. More than two months had passed and they had heard nothing. Mrs. Van Wagnen might have some news.

"I'll just be gone overnight. You girls won't even miss me," Grandma Fleet said.

"We could come with you," Indigo said hopefully.

"Oh no." Grandma Fleet shook her head vigorously. "It isn't safe for young girls to travel. If the Indian policemen find us, who knows what they might do with you?" Grandma Fleet eased two big gourd canteens of springwater over her shoulder and took up her walking stick. Sister Salt carried Grandma's gunnysack full of roots, seeds, and leaves—spices and medicines Mrs. Van Wagnen might need. After all that wonderful food she gave them, it was the least they could do.

"No one notices an old woman, but everyone sees a young girl,"

Grandma Fleet said as she started off briskly; she allowed the girls to accompany her as far as the big boulder at the intersection of the little wash with the big wash. Indigo tried not to cry but the lump in her throat forced out the tears; she made no sound and kept walking at her sister's side. At the big wash Sister Salt slipped the gunnysack from her back to Grandma Fleet's back.

They watched Grandma Fleet until she disappeared around the first turn in the big wash. Indigo sank to the ground and began to sob loudly. Sister Salt did not like the sound; it echoed off the sandstone on both sides of the canyon. Anyone—the Indian police or a miner or a cowboy—might hear that sound.

"Crybaby!" Sister Salt hissed in her little sister's face as she jerked Indigo to her feet by her arm and pulled her along behind her.

"Shut up before someone hears you! Grandma went to find out about Mama," Sister Salt said, and she was cryng now too.

By the time they reached the house the sun was past midpoint in the sky and it was hot. After a drink and a bath at the spring, they crawled into the coolness of the dugout house and covered themselves with their wet canvas shawls they soaked in the pool. Indigo lay on her bed and stared up at the latticework of willow branches over mesquite poles. Why hadn't Mama escaped by now?

Indigo dreamed she was in Mama's arms, hugged so close and so safe, her face pressed against Mama's chest, breathing in Mama's warm scent of sage and earth. Mama's love surrounded her and rocked her gently. When Indigo woke, she looked around for Mama before she remembered, and some part of her deep inside broke open, and she cried so loud she woke Sister Salt. Indigo expected Sister to scold her for crying, but she put her arms around Indigo and rocked her, saying, "Don't cry, sister, don't cry. Mama will come back, she will." Indigo felt something wet fall on her arm and realized Sister Salt was crying too. As Indigo began to feel more hopeful and stopped crying, Sister Salt cried harder. Indigo hugged her big sister as tightly as she could.

"Don't cry!" Indigo whispered, and patted her sister's back. Sister nodded and wiped the back of her hand across her eyes.

Indigo excused herself to go pee. She was surprised at how much daylight remained as she walked to the latrine below the dunes. The hot days would arrive in no time.

When Indigo returned, Sister Salt was far in the back corner where Grandma Fleet kept the big pottery storage jars. She heard the sounds of

Sister Salt removing the stone lids, and the rustle of dried apples and strips of dried meat in muslin sacks.

At first they were only going to sample the apples and the venison jerky. Indigo rolled the dry apple slice around on her tongue until it was moistened; she sucked on it for a long time until it was too soft and sweet to resist and she swallowed it. They took only the smallest flakes and slivers of jerky to chew and chew, and they had contests to see who could make the jerky last the longer. Indigo looked Sister Salt in the eye and took another piece of dried apple and another piece of jerky; before Sister Salt could stop her, Indigo stuffed both the apple and the jerky in her mouth. Sister Salt grabbed the jerky from her mouth and popped it into her mouth. Indigo laughed and took another piece of jerky. They shared a gourd of springwater and ate as many dried apples as they wanted and more jerky until Indigo began to feel too full and a little queasy, so she gave the half-eaten jerky strip to Sister Salt. Grandma Fleet would be furious when she found out the two of them had eaten enough food in one evening to last three people for a week. Sister Salt finished Indigo's piece of jerky, then she reached into the muslin sack for another and yet another piece of jerky, until the muslin sack was empty. Indigo saw Sister Salt glance in the direction of the back room to the food storage jars; she had never seen Sister Salt eat that way before, not even those times they were without food for days. Sister Salt did not seem like herself; the difference in her behavior made Indigo uneasy. Grandma would be home by this time tomorrow. Maybe she wouldn't notice the lids on the storage jars had been moved, Indigo thought as she drifted off to sleep.

Sister Salt waited until Indigo's breathing was slow and deep before she crept back to the storage jars. Her stomach was so full it felt swollen, but still the hunger raged inside her, demanding that she eat. She reached for the lid on the jar, but stopped herself short; she did not move for a long time. She knew she was full, she knew she didn't need to eat any more. Where did this hunger come from? If Grandma Fleet or Mama had been there they might have explained what the trouble was. She crept back to her bed and reached for the gourd canteen. She drank water until the hunger could barely make itself felt.

The next day they did not talk about the food they took from the storage jars. They gathered succulent green "sand food" from the foot of the cliff all morning, and saved enough for Grandma when she got home that night. The weather was warm; as soon as the first good rain fell, Grandma said, they should start planting.

Around midday time they went to the spring to wash up and rest in the shade. The spring, at the head of the canyon, looked down on the ridges and hills of fine sand that descended gradually to the dry wash that lead to the big wash to the river. Sister Salt wanted to hunt for pack rats' nests, but Indigo wanted to stay by the spring to watch for Grandma. From the vantage point of the spring, Indigo would be able to see her the moment she came around the bend in the wash.

"She won't come until late afternoon. You'll have to wait a long time." Sister Salt wanted Indigo to go with her. "I'll show you the palm grove." Sister Salt knew Indigo wanted to go there.

Indigo followed her sister reluctantly. She wanted to see the wild palms in the box canyon, but she also wanted to be home when Grandma Fleet returned. Indigo kept looking back the direction they had come, and she checked the sun's position in the sky from time to time, determined to be home in time to greet Grandma and hear any news she had about Mama.

The trail followed the spine of the sandstone ridge for a distance before it turned sharply to descend into a narrow crevice. Sister Salt showed Indigo how to brace herself by wedging her legs and shoulders against the sides of the crevice so she could reach the footholds and handholds worn into the sandstone. In a few minutes they were down in the canyon. Indigo was amazed. Pale yellow sandstone cliffs rose all around them; the canyon had no outlet; the crevice they had climbed down was the only way in and the only way out unless you were a bird.

Indigo never imagined the palm trees would be so big. They were clustered together, some trees almost touching others; the larger, older trees were shaggy with dry fronds peeling away below the new green foliage. Dry fallen fronds covered the ground. Here was the place Grandma Fleet got her roof. Indigo rubbed her hands over the odd scales and nubby surfaces of the palms' trunks. She searched the trees' tops for the clusters of little fruit Sister described as sweeter than honey, but saw nothing.

Sister Salt paid little attention to the palm trees; instead she searched among the boulders and big rocks with a short stick in her hand. Indigo watched her; she used the stick to clear away thick barricades of cactus spines meant to protect the burrow. Sister exposed the squirrel's food cache; Indigo recognized the acorns and piñons piled on shredded leaves, but what were all those blackish lumps stuck together?

"Ummmm!" Sister said as she attempted to bite a blackish lump; the dried-up date was as hard as a rock. She took the date out of her mouth and reached for the gourd canteen around her waist. She dropped two dried dates into the canteen to soften. They gathered all the dried dates but left the ground squirrel its acorns and piñons. The afternoon was warm enough to slip off their dresses to use as makeshift sacks to carry home the dried dates.

The sun was setting as they approached the sandstone formations above the spring. Sister Salt stopped and motioned for Indigo to keep still and stay put. Sister Salt listened intently. Soldiers and Indian police were loud-mouths who could be heard for miles away. Sister Salt heard the crickets in the damp sand near the spring; she heard the sundown call of a mourning dove, then the cry of a nighthawk; the darker it became, the more numerous the crickets were. She listened for Grandma Fleet's voice, talking loudly to herself or singing a little song she had just made up a moment before, like the song about the baby tarantula Grandma sang last summer. Sister Salt listened until she thought she could hear the sounds of everything—slithering, rustling, rattling, stirring, chirping, whistling, barking, all the sounds descended around her and deafened her.

When Sister Salt stopped and stood motionless, Indigo did the same; she heard the nighthawks but nothing else. If strangers had been camped near the spring, the nighthawks would be gone. The twilight was bright from the sunset and from the half-moon shining off the pale sandstone and the sand dunes. The air was cooling off, and Indigo felt chilly in only her underslip. At first she thought Sister heard something she could not hear, but after a time, Indigo realized something was wrong with her sister. She touched Sister lightly on the back, and whispered.

"What is it? What do you hear?"

Sister Salt turned to her with the saddest expression Indigo had ever seen. She shook her head slowly, and set off walking again; they were only a short walk from the spring now, but Indigo wasn't fooled. Sister Salt knew something she didn't tell Indigo. Indigo ran ahead of her, past the spring and down the dunes. In the fading twilight, twigs and branches on the sandy trail resembled snakes of all sizes and kinds; Indigo leaped and swerved to avoid them.

Outside the dugout house, Indigo stopped. It was almost dark now; Grandma Fleet should already be home, but Indigo did not hear her stirring inside. Probably Grandma was tired from her journey and asleep already.

"Grandma, it's us, me and Sister. Grandma?" she said as she stepped down into the entryway, but no one was there.

◆ ◆ ◆

Indigo wanted to search for Grandma Fleet at once, but Sister Salt reminded her the moon would set soon and they'd be left out on the trail in the dark.

"She just got a late start and decided to sleep under a bush." Sister Salt's voice sounded tired. She went to her bed. Indigo lay on her bed and listened to her sister's breathing. What would become of them without Grandma Fleet? Indigo started to cry softly for their mother.

The next morning, when the sky was light enough for them to see, they set out down the trail to find Grandma Fleet. They both wore big gourd canteens around their waists in case Grandma lost or spilled her canteen and needed water. Sister Salt dropped a handful of dried dates in both canteens so they'd have something to eat. They were not far past the first turn in the dry wash when they found her. She was sitting up with her back and head resting against the clay bank; her shawl was wrapped around her. At first Indigo thought she was dead, but then her eyelids fluttered open and she smiled, still reclining against the clay bank. Sister Salt ran over and flung herself down beside her.

"Oh Grandma, what's wrong?"

"Now, now, dear, don't be so upset. I'm just tired. I'm getting too old to walk all the way to the river and back in two days. Next time, I'll take a week." Grandma didn't stand up but she hugged both of them close to her. They shared the softened dates and water in silence though they both wanted so much to ask if she had learned the whereabouts of their mother. They could see Grandma wasn't quite her old self yet. Sister Salt expected Grandma to ask where they got the dried dates, but she sat silently stroking both girls on the head with her eyes closed. They sat side by side and watched the sun climb higher until the shade was gone.

The girls knelt down so Grandma could steady herself by leaning on their shoulders and backs as she stood up.

"Ohhhh! I'm so stiff I can hardly stand up!" she said as she steadied one hand on Sister Salt and one on Indigo. "I got a late start, but I didn't want to worry you girls. I must have hurried myself a bit too much."

Grandma Fleet managed to stand up but she was unsteady on her feet, so it took a long time for the three of them to make their way home. Indigo wanted to ask right away what she found out about Mama, but Grandma had to save her energy for the walk.

Grandma slept all afternoon. Sister Salt and Indigo sat on their blankets nearby and watched her sleep when they were not napping themselves. The weather was much warmer than it had been when Grandma set out. No wonder she had been so exhausted when they found her. She only needed a rest and she would be fine, Sister Salt said, but Indigo could tell she was worried by the way she watched intently, each time Grandma exhaled, for her next breath.

Grandma Fleet recovered slowly over the days that followed. She joked that she brought the hot weather with her from the river; she hoped the rain clouds followed her too. The first morning she felt well enough to walk without assistance, she told them to sit down; she had something to tell them.

"Girls, your mama was not among the prisoners taken to prison at Fort Yuma. That's all poor Mrs. Van Wagnen was able to find out." Grandma Fleet took a corner of her skirt to wipe the tears from her eyes.

"Why are you crying?" Indigo demanded. Sister Salt frowned and shook her head at Indigo to be quiet.

"I won't be quiet!" she said and burst into tears. Grandma Fleet held her close to her chest and patted her gently on the back.

"There, there," Grandma said, "don't cry. Our Paiute friends saw your mother slip away from the Indian police."

Indigo stopped crying, and Sister Salt watched Grandma's serious expression and knew there was something more.

"The last time they saw her, she was running up the big sandhill beyond the river. She was following the tracks in the sand made by the Messiah and his family."

The three of them sat quietly. "At least she's not dead and the Indian police don't have her," Sister Salt commented. Indigo imagined Mama running and half crawling up the towering dune beyond the river; just over the crest of the dune the Messiah and his family waited for her and the other dancers who managed to escape.

Indigo wanted to know when Jesus would let their mother come home. Grandma Fleet sighed and shook her head. Jesus and his holy family disappeared into the high mountains to avoid the soldiers and Indian police, who were everywhere. The Mormons were fighting one another too. Poor Mrs. Van Wagnen! She learned her husband was killed by other Mormons, who took him from the soldiers at Fort Yuma. The old Mormon Church and the new Mormon Church could not agree on the number of wives a man might have. The U.S. government had been after the old Mormons for a long time, killing their men and burning their farms wherever they went until they escaped to the west.

The old Mormons believed they were related to the Indians, and the

U.S. government feared the old Mormons and Indians might band together against the government. The old Mormons who answered the call of Wovoka were hated most of all. How dare these Mormons take an Indian to be the Messiah? Federal officials feared the dancers were a secret army in disguise, ready to attack Needles.

From the looks of things, the Messiah and his family might have to stay in hiding a long time, so Mama might be gone a long while too. They would just have to learn to get along without her, Grandma Fleet told them as she began to show them the things they would need to know. They walked through the dry stalks and old debris of the dune gardens, and she told them where to plant the beans, corn, and squash seed and how deep. Plant in late July or early August after the rain came.

The days became longer and the desert heat gathered in the earth, day after day, swelling larger, filling her lungs with heat until there was no space for oxygen. Suddenly Sister Salt felt as if she could not breathe. She was alone at the spring when it happened. She took deep breaths over and over to reassure herself the sensation was only an illusion of the heated air.

Grandma Fleet instructed the girls to do as she did: They got up before dawn and worked until it got too hot; then they rested in the coolness of the dugout house until the sun was low in the sky. As the moon grew full, they worked all night; on the moonless nights they worked until it was too dark to see.

The delicate sand food plants disappeared as the days became warmer and longer. They ate the last of the dried dates. Now Grandma Fleet rationed the dry meat and the dry apples; she had not yet discovered the storage jar with the empty muslin sacks. They knew they had to tell Grandma what they'd done before she discovered the missing food. They waited for the right time to tell her—maybe one hot, drowsy afternoon when Grandma was telling them stories she'd heard when she was a girl. Tonight she was going to show them an old trick: how to get fresh meat.

After dark they filled their gourd canteens at the spring and sat outside with Grandma; they watched the stars and the half-moon as they listened and waited for the coyotes. On three previous nights, the coyotes hunted in the dunes not far from the spring. They listened as the coyotes began their hunt, using yips and barks to signal one another and to drive any small game, rabbits or roosting birds, into their ambush. She taught the girls to distinguish the coyotes' language of barks and howls so they would know when the coyotes got lucky. That was the signal for the girls to take off running as fast as they could, Sister Salt with the old flint knife in one hand

and a gunnysack in the other, and Indigo with a long stick. Grandma said to be careful to leave the coyotes plenty of bones; otherwise next time they might not call out an invitation to share their feast.

Sister Salt ran in the direction of the cries and barks; the cries were high pitched and the barks excited. They had to get there fast before the coyotes ate everything. The light of the moon reflected off the sand so it was easy to see. Indigo fell behind, but she did not dare call out; she ran as fast as she could, but the long stick was almost as tall as she was and it kept getting in the way of her feet. Grandma said the coyotes would drop everything and run at the sight of humans, but they mustn't risk a coyote bite.

As she neared Sister Salt, Indigo saw the last two coyotes disappear behind a sand dune; when Indigo reached Sister Salt she was kneeling on the ground gathering little wiggling pink creatures scattered over the sand by the plundered rabbits' nest. They brought home enough newborn rabbits for a fine stew with the dried roots Grandma tossed in and a little moss gathered from the spring. Grandma Fleet told the girls how proud she was they had come home with such good meat the very first time they ran to the coyotes' prey. They were lucky the baby rabbits were scattered all over; otherwise the coyotes might have eaten all of them before Sister Salt got there.

While they ate the stew, Grandma Fleet told them hunting stories from years ago—about the whitetail deer the coyotes chased down and killed so all Grandma Fleet had to do was take her sharp knife and prepare the meat for the journey home. She told them about the golden eagle that circled high above and watched her hunt the washes and dunes. All day Grandma Fleet crept through the rice grass and weeds between the dunes without result while the eagle dived successfully four times; each time the eagle mother flew away with a rabbit to her nest. It was late and Grandma was ready to give up for the day; she thought the eagle had already gone home for the night. But as Grandma made her way down the canyon toward home, the eagle reappeared, circling high overhead. Grandma was so tired and discouraged she didn't pay much attention to the eagle. She kept walking and for a time she didn't see the eagle and thought it had gone. Then she saw the eagle overhead with a big cottontail rabbit in its claws; the rabbit was still kicking but it was no problem for an eagle. Grandma looked up at the eagle and complimented her on being such a great hunter when suddenly the eagle dropped the rabbit for Grandma Fleet!

As the driest, hottest months approached, Grandma Fleet seemed to slow her pace; she still rose before dawn but now her midday naps lasted longer, sometimes until sundown or the rise of the moon. They had plenty of food stored to take them to the summer rains, but Grandma insisted they go out and gather a few roots and seeds each day.

"You never know," she said; "some years the rains will come late but other years the summer rains will not come at all." The girls gathered moss and watercress from around the pool at the spring. Grandma Fleet showed them how to set bird snares woven from their own hair to trap birds as they landed by the pool. She instructed them to be careful whenever they broke into the pack rat's nest to raid the stores of seeds and mesquite beans.

"Old Ratty does all the work for you, so don't harm her!" Grandma Fleet showed them how to close up the rat's nest after they took what they wanted. Years before, when the refugees flocked to the old gardens, hunger drove the people to eat the pack rats; but the hunger was far worse afterward because there were no pack rats left to gather and store seeds.

Grandma Fleet sorted her collection of seeds while she talked. She wanted to have everything prepared by the time the rains came so they could get the seeds into the damp earth promptly. Every day they watched the sky for the clouds that might signal the arrival of the summer rains. Early one morning coveys of round puffy clouds drifted across the sky out of the southwest, and Grandma became her lively old self as she sang out a welcome to the clouds. Sister Salt was relieved to see she felt well enough to walk up to the old gardens.

Grandma Fleet explained the differences in the moisture of the sand between the dunes as they slowly made their way up the sandy path between the dunes. Grandma steadied herself with a hand on each girl's shoulder; they made their way slowly past the bare terraces where the sweet black corn, muskmelons, and speckled beans used to grow. Grandma explained each of the dunes and the little valleys between them had different flows of runoff; some of the smaller dunes were too dry along their edges and it was difficult to grow anything there; in marginal areas like these it was better to let the wild plants grow.

Grandma Fleet explained which floodplain terraces were well drained enough to grow sweet black corn and speckled beans. The squashes and melons were water lovers, so they had to be planted in the bowl-shaped area below the big dune where the runoff soaked deep into the sand. Wild gourds, sunflowers, and datura seeded themselves wherever they found moisture.

The following afternoon, big rain clouds gathered along the southwest horizon. Grandma Fleet greeted the clouds with tears in her eyes; their beloved ancestors returned to them as precious rain. The morning after the rain, Grandma was up before dawn to unpack her jars of seeds; Indigo and Sister Salt woke to her singing.

"The dampness is sweet on the earth, smell the rain!" Grandma Fleet sang in the old Sand Lizard language, but the girls understood some of the words and got the meaning of the song from Grandma's voice. She was so excited by the arrival of the rain, she told the girls they would eat later; she wanted to be planting the first seeds as the sun appeared. The coolness of the breeze across the damp earth surprised Indigo; she shivered, then broke into a run up the path past the first dune.

Grandma Fleet walked, with only the aid of her cane, at an energetic pace; she seemed to be her old self again. Sister smiled; she had been worried about Grandma's health, but all the old woman needed was a good rain. Grandma Fleet knelt in the damp sand with her digging stick and showed the girls how deep and how closely to plant the seeds. They planted all morning and part of the afternoon with only water from the spring and a few handfuls of dried pumpkin seeds to eat.

Again the swollen blue-violet clouds gathered in the afternoon, and as the rain fell, Grandma told the girls truly they were blessed.

"We are the last remnants of the Sand Lizard clan," Grandma Fleet explained. "So many of us have died it's no wonder clusters of rain clouds gather over the old gardens." The Sand Lizard people of the old gardens were never as numerous as their cousins who lived and farmed along the river before the reservations were made. When Indigo asked why the Sand Lizard people stayed there, if it was easier to grow plants close to the big river, Grandma Fleet laughed. Sand Lizards did things differently than other people. Sand Lizards didn't mind if others found them odd; that's how they distinguished themselves from others. Farming was easy along the river but getting along with the authorities was not.

The Sand Lizards preferred to rely on the rain clouds and avoid confinement on a reservation. Yes, the other people laughed at the Sand Lizards, and it was true their kind was disappearing, but they were proud to be known for their contrary ways. Yes, the Sand Lizards were different! Long ago, when the Apaches used to raid the Sand Lizards' villages, the Sand Lizards fought back fiercely until they were beating the Apache, but then, instead of fighting to the end to crush the Apaches and make them slaves the way the other tribes did, the Sand Lizard people used to stop fighting and let the Apaches get away. Other tribes called them crazy for this, but the Sand Lizards didn't have much use for slaves; they were just more hungry mouths to feed, and slaves had to be watched all the time.

Yes, the Sand Lizards were different. They were stubborn; they refused to allow the churchmen to touch their children. The churchmen were liars; they claimed Jesus Christ died in a faraway country, long ago. They claimed to speak for Jesus Christ; they said Jesus didn't want to see women's bare breasts no matter how hot the summer day was; if the others wanted to pay such a high price to farm along the river, that was their choice.

Grandma Fleet said they did have a few cousins who lived on the reservation at Parker. The girls never met them because the authorities punished the reservation Indians for any contact they had with the renegades.

"If anything happens to me, you girls stay here. You belong here. Your mama knows she will find you here. Otherwise, how will she ever find you? If you need something, go ask our friend Mrs. Van Wagnen. Watch out or the authorities will catch you two and ship you off to school."

The location of the old gardens and the spring was known to the authorities, but they still were safest there, because the journey from the river to the old gardens was difficult for the horses. Miles of deep sand that exhausted the horses were followed by fields of sharp black lava so hard that the horses' shoes wore thin and broke. After they left the river, the horses were without water for two days. Now, as far as anyone knew, the old gardens were abandoned; even if someone did come, the cliff swallows would signal their approach by circling nervously around their nests. All sounds in the canyons were amplified by the sandstone formations. The flash of the sun off metal, the clinking sounds of bits, spurs, carbines, lids of canteens, and the coughs and sneezes of the men and the horses gave plenty of warning.

The sun broke through the clouds in the west and warmed them even as the last raindrops fell. How sweet the air smelled after the rain! Indigo was hungry. She raced Sister Salt down the winding trail, down between the sand dunes to the dugout house. They were at the house only long enough to get dried fruit and a bit of jerky. Grandma Fleet said once farmers finished the planting they might eat a bit of meat. Sister Salt pointed at the empty muslin sack folded neatly at the bottom of the storage jar; Indigo nodded. Next time Grandma sent them for more dried meat they would have to confess the greedy feast they enjoyed while she was gone.

Now that the seeds were planted, they slept in the dunes above the gardens to protect the seeds from rodents. In the heat of the day, when the birds and rodents were less active, they returned to the cool dark dugout house to rest until sundown. Once the seedlings were up, they pulled weeds in the coolness of the moonlight.

On the highest dune, near the spring, Grandma Fleet dug herself a little pit house in the fine sand right below the mound where she planted the apricot seeds. At first Indigo and Sister Salt paid little attention because their grandmother liked to dig down into the sand to find the coolness; but then Grandma Fleet arranged willow branches in a latticework to hold more willow branches to form a roof over the dugout. Now Grandma Fleet no longer bothered to walk all the way back down the trail to sleep at the house; the girls passed the heat of the day alone in the old dugout house. Grandma insisted her burrow below the apricot seedlings was just as cool as the old house, and it saved her energy; the walk up the trail between the dunes was too difficult for her now.

"These baby apricot trees need me close by," Grandma Fleet teased. "Look at them! Aren't they lovely?" The dark green seedlings were knee high by the time the baby squash and baby beans were ready to eat.

Grandma stayed with the gardens, while they went to gather the prickly pear fruit, and later, the mesquite beans. Grandma showed them how to boil the prickly pear fruit into a thick, sweet paste which she dried in the sun. The mesquite beans had to be dried then roasted and stored carefully; otherwise, the little bugs would eat them. After the girls had finished their chores, they played games, made contests to see who could hit the target with a rock or stick from the greatest distance. They made targets out of precarious stacks of flat stones or with piles of kindling wood. They both squealed with delight at a direct hit as the stones or branches fell.

Sister Salt liked to slip away from Indigo when she wasn't watching; then Sister Salt hid and waited until Indigo realized she was gone. Indigo learned to track her in the sand so Sister Salt used sagebrush to wipe away her footprints. She loved to crouch down just around a turn in the trail and jump out at Indigo to hear her scream. When it was too hot to play chase, plunging and rolling down the steepest slopes of the high dunes, they played their favorite guessing game—they called it Which Hand?—with a smooth pebble.

After the first beans and squash were harvested, Grandma Fleet left her shelter by the peach seedlings less and less often. The girls helped her walk through the gardens, where she surveyed the sunflowers, some small and pale yellow, others orange-yellow and much taller than they were; then she examined the brilliant red amaranth. The sunflowers and the amaranth were so robust they would have food all winter. The gardens were green with corn and bush beans; a few pods had already ripened and split, scattering beans on the sand. Sister Salt bent down to pick up the beans but Grandma Fleet shook her head firmly.

"Let them be," she said. That way, the old gardens would reseed themselves and continue as they always had, regardless of what might happen.

"What could happen, Grandma?" Indigo's question brought a groan of impatience from Sister Salt, who made a face at her, but Grandma laughed, then stopped to catch her breath. They had completed their walk past the garden terraces near the spring.

"Anything could happen to us, dear," Grandma Fleet said as she hugged Indigo close to her side. "Don't worry. Some hungry animal will eat what's left of you and off you'll go again, alive as ever, now part of the creature who ate you.

"I've been close to death a few times," Grandma Fleet said as she slowly made her way up the path. "I was so surprised the first time I wasn't even scared; after my first baby, your mother, was born, the bleeding would not stop."

"Did it hurt?" Sister Salt asked.

"Oh no, I felt no pain, that's why I wasn't scared. I thought dying hurt a great deal."

"But you didn't die," Indigo said.

"No, the old medicine woman gave me juniper berry tea and told me, 'You are needed here. We need you. This baby needs you.'" Grandma Fleet paused to catch her breath.

"The old woman scolded me while I drank the tea. 'Don't be lazy, young woman!'"

"Why did she say that, Grandma?" Indigo tried to imagine how one person scolded another for bleeding to death.

"Because dying is easy—it's living that is painful." Grandma Fleet started walking again, slowly, leaning on the girls to steady herself.

"To go on living when your body is pierced by pain, to go on breathing when every breath reminds you of your lost loved ones—to go on living is far more painful than death."

Big tears began to roll down Indigo's cheeks, but she didn't make a sound. Their mother must be dead or she would have come back by now. What had eaten Mama? Was she crawling around as a worm or running as a coyote?

They walked the rest of the way in silence. Sister Salt held her left arm and Indigo the right as Grandma inched her way down, down into her little dugout shelter by the apricot seedlings. Grandma Fleet settled down on her blanket with a loud sigh of pleasure and stretched herself out for a nap. She joked about sleeping so much and becoming lazy in her old age. Relaxed, with her eyes closed, Grandma Fleet talked about their dear ancestors, the rain clouds, until her words came slower and slower and she was snoring softly. Sister Salt felt her heart suddenly so full of love for Grandma, who always loved them, who always was there to care for them no matter what happened. Sister looked at the tiny figure on the old blankets breathing peacefully, and she realized, when the time came, Grandma Fleet intended to be buried there under her little apricot trees.

Indigo was the first one up the path that morning on her way to wash at the spring. As she passed Grandma Fleet's shelter, she called out, "Good morning," but was not alarmed when Grandma did not answer; in recent weeks Grandma slept later and later. Indigo was washing her face at the pool when Sister Salt came running and cried out Grandma was dead.

Indigo refused to help, but Grandma Fleet weighed hardly more than a big jackrabbit as Sister Salt gently shifted her body to wrap the blanket more securely. Indigo refused to scoop sand over the body. She sat flat on the sand, a distance away, with her back to her sister, too angry to cry, too angry to bury Grandma Fleet. All day Indigo sat on the same spot, with her back to the mound of sand, while Sister Salt tended the gardens as Grandma would have, pulling weeds around the squash and beans.

Late in the afternoon Sister Salt came slowly up the trail with gourd bowls in both hands. She placed the bowl full of squash and bean stew on the grave, then filled the other gourd bowl at the spring and arranged it next to the bowl of stew. She did not disturb Indigo but went back to get the remaining stew for her and Indigo to share.

At first Indigo refused to join her sister, who ate stew next to the mound of sand that covered Grandma Fleet. But the delicious odor of the stew finally won her over and Indigo, her eyes swollen and red, sullenly joined her sister. They ate in silence. Sister Salt watched the sun drop behind the sandstone cliffs and felt the breeze become cooler; the days were shorter though they were still quite warm, but the nights were already uncomfortable without a blanket.

Sister Salt continued to follow all of Grandma Fleet's instructions: as the beans and corn ripened, she dried them in the sun, then stored them in the huge pottery storage jars buried in the sand floor of the dugout house.

Indigo refused to sleep anywhere but the shallow hole she scooped out beside Grandma Fleet's grave. All day while Sister Salt toiled in the gardens, Indigo ignored her sister; Indigo had a favorite sandstone boulder next to the pool at the spring; here she spent most days, looking off into the distance, watching the trail to the big wash and the river because this was the trail Grandma Fleet used for her visit with Mrs. Van Wagnen, and when Mama returned, she would probably follow the same trail home.

As the days became shorter and the nights cooler, Indigo spent all day on the boulder, where the sun's heat felt delicious. She carried on imaginary conversations with Mama and with Grandma Fleet to pass the time. She told them how she and Sister Salt worked to put away the harvest, and she imagined how this must please them and the words of praise they would give if they were there. Sometimes she made up stories to amuse herself; she imagined that a golden eagle mother flew down and lifted her by the back of her dress, off the boulder, high into the sky. From so high up Indigo saw the entire world. She saw the river but it looked like a child's belt, thin and green on the edges and muddy red down the middle; the giant dunes glittered like big glass beads. Indigo searched for signs of the Messiah and his followers, but the mother eagle flew too high for Indigo to see human beings.

At night Indigo rolled herself tightly in her blankets and slept next to Grandma Fleet's grave and the apricot seedlings. She was not afraid because Grandma Fleet was right there even if Indigo couldn't see her, and she would protect Indigo from harm. Some nights Indigo heard voices by the spring, people speaking in happy tones with laughter; she knew she must not listen too closely or she might want to join them.

Indigo arranged herself in her sand burrow so the leaves of the little apricot trees shaded her head from the early morning sun. She was amazed at how much the little trees grew each day as the weather became cooler and the saplings did not have to endure the heat to survive. Each day she saw the tender bright green of new growth on the ends of the little branches. Sometimes when she felt lazy, Indigo lay on her back in her burrow to stare up at the rich green apricot leaves against the bright blue sky. She loved the colors of sky blue and leaf green together; only a few desert flowers were as blue as the sky. Her thoughts wandered as she watched the sky; she wondered where Mama and the Messiah and his family were now. Mrs. Van Wagnen might have news of the Messiah's whereabouts. Indigo wanted Sister Salt to take her to find the dancers.

Indigo felt better after she had the idea to visit Grandma's Mormon friend; she immediately joined Sister Salt at the floodplain garden, where the pumpkins and winter squashes waited to be carried to the dugout house. Indigo made a game of the harvest: the pumpkins and their companions, the squashes, were fat babies that hadn't learned to walk yet. Indigo carried them one by one, cradled in her arms, so that she would not damage them. When Sister Salt was out of sight, Indigo dressed the fat babies in skirts and hats she made from the big pumpkin leaves.

Indigo had not been inside the dugout house since Grandma Fleet died and she found that Sister Salt had moved everything around to make room for the shallow yucca baskets in which strips of pumpkin and squash were dried before they were stored in the back of the dugout house, up in the rafters. Every morning they carried the drying baskets outside to the sun, and each evening they brought them inside to protect them from rodents.

The rain was abundant that year and no hungry strangers appeared at the old gardens, and no Indian police watered thirsty mules at the spring. Still, the girls were ready in the event anyone came. Their plan was to run for palm grove canyon, where they'd stay until the danger was gone.

Indigo carried pumpkins and squash all day without stopping to rest; she ate handfuls of baby bean pods, and pumpkin flowers so sweet and tender that they melted in her mouth. From time to time she went to the spring to drink and wash off the sweat. The days were still quite warm, especially if one worked hard in the sun. Sister Salt didn't say much, but Indigo heard her hum a happy tune as she finished. The big pottery storage jars were full, their sandstone lids secure as she covered them with sand for safekeeping in the back of the dugout room.

At sundown, when the air cooled off, Sister Salt built a fire on the hearth outside and boiled a delicious stew of corn, beans, chiles, and pumpkin to celebrate. The harvest was gathered and Sister Salt knew Grandma Fleet was proud of her and Indigo too. After dinner, while the twilight was still bright, they ran laughing up the trail to the highest dune; they raced each other to the dune's steepest side, where they plunged each after the other headfirst, rolling end over end, screaming joyously all the while. So much sand got in their hair that they had to take turns with the yucca brush. Later a big moon, not quite full, flooded the dunes with silver blue light that made the big datura blossoms glow as they perfumed the evening air.

They walked to the springs to fill the big water gourd, and on the way down Indigo rolled up her bedding from the sandy burrow next to Grandma's grave and carried it back to the dugout house. They lay in their beds with the bright moonlight in the doorway, and they talked for a long time before they fell asleep. Indigo wondered what was taking Mama so long to get back to the old gardens; she wondered where the Messiah and his dancers were tonight.

Sister Salt talked about the train depot and the pasengers who used to buy the baskets she sold; a year ago at this time they were all still together with Mama and Grandma Fleet in the lean-to by the river at Needles. Sister Salt wondered if the Paiute women still lived there; they might have heard some news of Mama or at least they might know where the Messiah and his dancers were. The Paiutes said Jesus traveled east across the ocean from time to time, but was careful not to show himself because of the danger from police and soldiers. If the Messiah and his followers crossed the ocean, it might be some time before they returned here. As Indigo drifted off to sleep, Sister Salt said, "We can travel as soon as cooler weather comes."

With the harvest completed the girls were free to do as they pleased. The first few weeks they amused themselves with games of hide and seek and raced each other to the tops of the dunes. With a wad of rags, they even made a ball to kick. When they felt lazy, they played games—Which Hand Holds the Pebble? and Gamblers' Sticks; the loser had to carry water or gather kindling alone. Indigo was ready to try something new every day, but Sister Salt began to feel impatient with the games.

Sister Salt realized if they wanted to find Mama they would have to leave the old gardens; if they went to Needles they would have to find some way to live. Sister Salt began to practice weaving yucca strips until the baskets she wove looked almost as good as Grandma Fleet's baskets. Now when Indigo proposed a race to the springs, or a game of hide-and-seek, Sister Salt shook her head.

While Indigo roamed the dunes and climbed the precarious paths up sandstone formations in the canyon, Sister Salt stayed at the dugout house, peeling thin yucca fibers to weave into baskets the way Grandma Fleet showed her. It wasn't easy: the sharp stiff yucca leaves had to be soaked all night, and even then, while she was working with it, the yucca dried out and cut her fingers until she wet it again.

Indigo did not understand her sister's odd change in mood, but after a few weeks, Indigo no longer had as much fun playing alone. Sister Salt showed her how to take a dried gourd and make a canteen for their long journey. Sometimes they worked in silence, each girl with her own thoughts; other times they talked about what they would do when cooler weather came.

One morning as the weather was beginning to cool, Sister Salt felt a cramp in her abdomen, and later she noticed an odd wetness between her legs. Now she reached to touch the wetness with her fingers and saw her first menstrual blood. Both Grandma and Mama promised last year she didn't have much longer to wait. That day the girls celebrated Sister's womanhood with a picnic at the date palm grove. A light breeze kept them comfortable as they hiked the narrow trail along the precipitous sandstone formations; far below, the giant dunes appeared to be anthills. Ripe orange-yellow date fruit was scattered all around the ground where they sat; scores of big brown ants worked feverishly to carry away bits of the fruit dropped by the birds. The water from the canteen tasted especially good because the dates were so sweet.

When Sister Salt went to relieve herself, Indigo came along too. She wanted to see the menstrual blood on Sister's legs. Indigo tried to peek, but Sister Salt frowned and turned away abruptly. When Indigo tried to look again, Sister whirled around angrily to face Indigo.

"None of your business!" she shouted. Indigo was too shocked to cry until Sister Salt strode away. Indigo meant no offense; how many times had they talked about menstruation with Grandma Fleet and Mama? Today was a day to celebrate. Why had Sister Salt acted so mean toward her? Hot tears ran down Indigo's cheeks. She had been so excited for her sister. Now, if Sister Salt wanted a baby, she could get one; they could raise it together. If it was a boy, they'd call him Raindrop; if the baby was a girl, they'd call her Sweet Black Corn. They wouldn't be alone then. But Sister Salt didn't want her. She wanted a man who could give her a baby. Indigo cried for Mama and Grandma Fleet. Who loved Indigo? Who wanted her? Where was Mama? She must not want her two girls anymore.

Sister Salt walked to the end of the box canyon, where the sandstone formed a natural barrier; she sat on a flattop boulder and closed her eyes. The warmth of the sun felt good on her abdomen. She was tired of being the one who had to teach Indigo everything.

When she returned to the palm grove, Indigo had already left for home without her. Sister Salt felt regret over her short temper with her little sister. She had been fortunate to be brought up by both Mama and Grandma Fleet. Indigo had no one now but her. Sister Salt knew it wasn't good for them to live alone for so long, and as she walked home, she began to think about what to do next.

The wind rustled the dry cornstalks and leaves as the sun went down. At that moment the sound of the wind in the dry stalks seemed like the saddest sound Sister Salt had ever heard; it seemed to say, "All gone, all gone"; her throat constricted with sadness until tears filled her eyes. She watched the evening star rise above the west horizon; somewhere Mama was watching the same star and thinking of her and Indigo.

The terraces in the dunes were still full of melons and squash even after their harvest; what a year for the old gardens! They grew enough to feed a whole family, not just themselves. What they could not store, they left to hungry creatures; ears of sweet black corn dried on the stalks, and big white tepary beans scattered themselves across the sand. Any hungry people who came to the old gardens were welcome to all the food they needed. Sister Salt was so lonely for another human face besides Indigo's; she began to wish someone, anyone—except white men or Indian police—would come.

Later that night, the wind blew in snow and sleet; Indigo fell asleep listening to the hiss of snowflakes in the hot coals. She wrapped up in her canvas shawl and pulled her share of the big quilt right in the doorway, close to the warm coals in the hearth outside. But as the direction of the wind changed during the night, raindrops sprinkled her face and she had to move away from the doorway, closer to Sister Salt. Indigo dragged her bedding across the sand floor, careful not to awaken Sister Salt, who stirred and muttered words in her sleep—something about a basket.

The air smelled wonderfully wet and cold, just as it had the night last year when the Messiah came to their camp at Needles. Indigo imagined Mama and the Messiah and his family and his dancers. The snow was their season; somewhere tonight Mama was dancing so beautifully in the big circle, wrapped warm in her white shawl like the other dancers. As Indigo drifted off to sleep, she imagined how she and Sister Salt would travel north until they located the Messiah and his dancers.

By morning the snow melted and the sky cleared to bright blue; the sun warmed the damp air. Indigo announced that she wanted to go to Mrs. Van Wagnen's house to ask if she knew the whereabouts of the Messiah and the dancers. Sister Salt admitted she wanted to visit Grandma's friend.

They would go to Mrs. Van Wagnen and if she had no news of Mama, they'd return to the old gardens and wait for her. They had plenty of food stored; no need to risk a trip south to the reservation at Parker. If Mrs. Van Wagnen was not at home, they planned to camp near her house, then head north to Needles to see if any of their Paiute or Walapai friends still lived there.

Before they left, Indigo helped Sister Salt heap up rocks and block the entrance to their dugout house to give the appearance of abandonment to anyone who might come poking around the old gardens while they were gone. They filled their gourd canteens at the spring the night before, and in the excitement the next morning Indigo forgot; it wasn't until they reached the big wash and stopped for lunch that Indigo remembered: she forgot to say good-bye to Grandma Fleet and the apricot seedlings, and to the old gardens. Her thoughtlessness brought tears to her eyes and she wanted to turn back; at the same time she wanted to go on to find news of their mother.

Sister Salt noticed the sudden change in Indigo's mood and guessed its source immediately; it was as if the old gardens and Grandma Fleet herself were telling them, "Come home. Don't go." Sister Salt gently patted Indigo's back until she wiped her eyes on the back of her hand and glanced over her shoulder in the direction they had just come. She felt the old gardens' call herself, but the old gardens and Grandma Fleet weren't searching for Mama like they were. Indigo had the saddest feeling they would not be able to return to the old gardens for a long time.

They slept until moonrise, then made their way across the sandy plain of greasewood and cholla cactus between the high sandstone plateau and the sandhills above the river valley. When they reached open terrain, they covered their heads with their bundles and slept until darkness came to protect their travel.

Late the following day they reached the sandhills that overlooked the muddy red water that was edged in lovely willow green and dark cattail green. How exciting to reach the river! They put down their bundles and held hands and danced around to celebrate. Now that they were at the river, they had to be alert and watchful. Indigo wanted Sister Salt to point out Mrs. Van Wagnen's house and gardens, but the groves of cottonwood trees and willows along the river concealed the place.

They followed game trails, sometimes on their hands and knees, through the willow and tamarisk thickets, to conceal themselves from anyone who might also be there to ford the river. Sister Salt moved carefully, and stopped every four steps to listen intently, then motioned for Indigo to come on. The muddy red water slowly threaded between sand bars as its flow waned. In flood season no one crossed the river unless they took the ferry at Yuma, but when the river was low, as it was now, it was possible to wade across here, where the river shallows were bedrock. Sister Salt broke off two stout willow branches and stripped off the leaves for walking sticks to help them keep their footing when they crossed.

They waited for the twilight to darken before they crossed. Indigo gasped at the cold water up to her knees; out in the middle it might be waist deep, so they removed their dresses and tied them to the bedrolls that they balanced on their heads like odd hats. Indigo felt the pull of the river's current, gentle at first but increasing in strength as they reached the middle of the river. The water was scarcely above Indigo's thighs but she had to hold tight to Sister Salt and to the stick to resist the current.

"Use your stick to hold you!" Sister Salt said after she turned and saw Indigo hesitate in midstream. Indigo pushed the willow stick hard into the river bottom ahead of her to keep from being carried along by the red water. Two more steps and the water wasn't as deep; two more steps and the water barely reached Indigo's thighs. It was easy then, and Indigo walked faster; she let go of the willow stick too soon, and as she went to step up on the riverbank she slipped and fell. Sister Salt was only inches away and grabbed hold of Indigo's bedroll to help her out; at the river's edge, the water was only ankle deep. Indigo scrambled up the sandy bank, breathless but smiling because her bedroll and dress were still dry.

There was no moon. At the old gardens the sand dunes reflected the light of the stars, but here the willows and big cottonwood trees seemed to absorb all light. Indigo wanted to go to Mrs. Van Wagnen's house immediately, but Sister Salt said they might frighten the poor woman if they showed up after dark. They would sleep there tonight and go to Mrs. Van Wagnen's early in the morning just before sunup so no one would see them. The coolness of the river bottom settled over them as they ate parched corn and dried pumpkin. They each shared part of the big quilt as they huddled together. Indigo wanted to build a little fire, but Sister Salt was wary. Any strangers nearby would find them, and Mrs. Van Wagnen might see the fire or smell the smoke and be frightened.

Sister Salt listened to Indigo's breathing; a great horned owl hoo-hooed to her mate from the cottonwood trees across the river. What a lovely evening for people and owls, she thought. Sand Lizard people weren't afraid of horned owls the way some people were.

Sister Salt listened intently for a long time for any sounds that might come from the direction of Mrs. Van Wagnen's house—didn't Grandma Fleet mention that her Mormon friend had a dog? Mormons ate cooked food every night—Sister Salt tried to catch a whiff of wood smoke from Mrs. Van Wagnen's stove, but the breeze smelled only of the river mud and the willow leaves.

The cold woke Indigo from her dream just as the sky to the east began to lighten; in the dream, she was at the train depot in Needles. She helped Sister Salt arrange the baskets for sale before the passengers got off the train that approached from the east.

Her breath made steam in the air in front of her so Indigo scooted down under the blanket and cuddled up to Sister Salt. It was too cold to get up without a campfire; she'd wait for the sun. The sky above the cottonwoods was pale yellow; the puffy clouds on the horizon were edged in red, pink, and gold. Although neither she nor Sister Salt had ever been to Mrs. Van Wagnen's house, still Indigo imagined how it looked when Grandma Fleet described her visits there: surrounded by towering cottonwood trees that shaded and protected it from view, Indigo imagined; a big house like the ones she'd seen in Needles with flower gardens and rosebushes in the front yard, and corn, tomatoes, and squash in the backyard.

As they moved through the willow and cottonwood forest, the light of the sunrise was filtered through the flickering cottonwood leaves. Sister Salt listened: long-tail grackles chattered at two crows who scolded them from the next tree, a mourning dove called her mate to the river, and a fly buzzed near her hand. But she didn't hear Mrs. Van Wagnen chop wood or the dog bark, and she signaled Indigo to continue but to move as quietly as possible. From time to time Sister Salt sniffed the air for the odor of wood smoke or the odor of cooked food, but she smelled only the willows' sweet scent and the mossy dampness of the river.

Sister Salt let out a gasp when she saw the burned ruins of the house and the barn; the hairs on the back of her neck stood up. She felt a wave of icy sweat break out on her forehead. Purple daisylike flowers with bright yellow eyes had grown up through the charred debris. The fire must have come in the spring or even last winter. The door to the root cellar had been splintered with an axe, and shards of shattered canning jars littered the ground around the cellar entrance; someone had dumped all that good food in the sand. Who had hated Mrs. Van Wagnen so much? Even the fence wire was torn away from the fence posts around the chicken yard and the backyard garden; here and there among the wild amaranth, wild asters, and mustard weeds were also a few bean and pea plants and a squash vine.

The girls ate the beans and peas right from the pods. Sister Salt found a patch of coriander and they ate it by the handful, though Indigo preferred it with rock salt. Sister showed Indigo the front yard with Mrs. Van Wagnen's "garden ladies" dressed in pink, yellow, white, and red. The hollyhocks stood taller than the fence posts, and the blossoms resembled the sunbonnets Mormon women wore; the round corollas resembled tiny faces.

Indigo pushed her way past the crowd of hollyhock ladies only to discover, wherever their wide skirts of leaves brushed her legs or arms, she itched.

The small garden gate was left untouched, and the climbing red roses grew around the gate so thickly that it no longer closed; long, leafy branches thick with roses reached out in all directions. Sister Salt picked a rose, sniffed it, and handed it to Indigo, who couldn't help herself: the rose smelled so delicious Indigo nibbled the petals and swallowed them.

Beyond the garden gate where the orchard had been, the grass and wild aster grew taller than the girls; but all of the wonderful peach and apricot trees had been chopped down, their dry remains overgrown with weeds. Sister Salt knelt down to examine a dry branch, and among the dead twigs and leaves she found a tiny shriveled apricot. She felt herself give way inside; something broke, and she was overwhelmed by the loss of something that fed so many hungry beings as the orchard had—at the destruction of something as beautiful as the peach and apricot blossoms in the spring. If this was what the white people did to one another, then truly she and the Sand Lizard people and all other Indians were lucky to survive at all. These destroyers were out to kill every living being, even the Messiah and his dancers.

Indigo came running with a skirtful of marigolds and found Sister Salt crying. Indigo patted her on the back and tried to console her but Sister Salt angrily pulled away from her. If that was how her sister wanted to behave, then Indigo would go explore by herself. She avoided the ruins of the house and the barn because she detected a faint but terrible odor still there. She stayed on the ground in the garden, hidden among the hollyhock plants so dark red they were almost black as dried blood.

Later Sister Salt joined Indigo among the hollyhocks and the bees; they sat in silence on their bedrolls, shaded by long snaking branches of fragrant red roses Indigo liked to nibble. Sister still didn't speak; Indigo thought she must be sick because she did not eat when Indigo took out the parched corn and the dried dates. She even refused the gourd canteen when Indigo passed it. All afternoon Indigo watched anxiously as Sister alternately dozed or wept softly.

As the sun made its descent, the great canopy of cottonwood leaves left them in deep shade; the burnt ruins of the house and barn seemed to loom larger in the shadows. The horrible scorched odor from the debris seemed to increase until Indigo could not stop it even with a handful of roses pressed to her mouth and nose. Suddenly Indigo knew they had to get away from this place right away.

"Hurry!" she said, tugging Sister Salt's arm, "get up! I think someone is coming!" Sister Salt jumped up with a wild, confused expression on her face; Indigo grabbed her bedroll and canteen and ran for the river. Once they were deep in the willow thicket on the sandy bank just above the water's surface, Sister motioned for Indigo to stop; the moist air along the river carried sounds a great distance. Now they could hear voices and the creak and low rumble of wagon wheels; they flattened themselves on their bellies in the sand and pulled their blankets over their heads. They held their breaths and listened. The river bottom was slipping into darkness though the sky to the west was still bright gold with the sunset. The wagon sound stopped and more voices could be heard, then the sound of an axe; not long afterward, woodsmoke wafted in the air.

A dog barked. They lay motionless for so long Indigo's legs felt numb. She smelled meat cooking. The voices were no longer as loud and she imagined they were eating. She uncurled her legs from her belly and stretched; she slowly moved each limb one at a time, careful not to rustle even one dry willow leaf.

Sister Salt listened as closely as she could to the voices. They were white people, no question about that; no Indian, not even the Indian police, talked that loud unless they were drunk. If they were only white people, then she and Indigo had a good chance of escaping in the middle of the night; but if this was an army patrol, there would be Indian policemen. Maybe this was how it was meant to be, Sister thought; this is how we will find Mama.

Suddenly Indigo felt something heavy—a pressure on her back that pinned her to the ground; for an instant she thought it might be Sister Salt playing a joke. When she raised up it was too dark to see clearly, but she felt someone grab her by the shoulders and lift her off the ground. She twisted away and fought with all her strength to break free of the hands, but it was no use.

The small white dog the Indian police brought along loved to play with children, so they used the dog to locate them. The dog barked and wagged its tail excitedly whenever children were nearby. Now the white dog anxiously licked the girls' legs and sniffed their hands, tied to the rope knotted above their ankles. The mules, staked out in tall grass near the wagon, were hobbled and tied in the same manner. The policemen knew from experience how fast these wild Indians could escape.

The big policeman lifted them one by one into the back of the wagon with a canvas cover; with their hands and feet tied they landed hard on the rough floorboards of the wagon. The girls wiggled close to each other and managed to sit up; they tried to brace their feet because the wagon was loaded with crates and heavy parcels that shifted dangerously as the wagon bumped along.

The big policeman who drove the wagon was kind enough to lift them out and loosen their ropes so they could step behind a sage bush to urinate. He had younger sisters himself, he said, at White River; he spoke a few words of their language but preferred to talk to them in English to show off. Neither sister would reply to him, but the big Apache did not seem offended or angered; he liked to talk. From time to time one of the other Indian policemen, on horseback, would ride alongside the wagon and converse in Apache; but the six white soldiers rode ahead separately. The soldiers were along only to protect the Indian policemen from angry parents who refused to surrender their children for school.

The first night he untied their hands and fed them the same army rations he and the others ate. He apologized for leaving their ankles tied together and told them about the Mojave and Chemehuevi children who ran away the instant he untied them. He warned them not to throw themselves from the wagon either, because last year a Walapai boy was killed that way.

"He was all tied up so I don't know why he rolled himself out the back," the policeman said, shaking his head slowly as he opened a little can of beans with his knife.

He knows the boy preferred death, but he won't say that to us. What a coward this big Apache is! Sister Salt thought as she moistened the edge of the hard biscuit between her lips. All the way to Parker, the big Apache talked; he talked about his family back at Turkey Creek. He talked about his years at the Indian School in Phoenix, where he played catcher on the school baseball team.

The only time the policeman was quiet was while he ate. He tosssed the empty bean can on the ground and pointed off in the distance toward the south.

"Yuma is right over there," he said. "Don't look so worried, girls. You'll be surprised at how fast the train goes."

Tears began to roll down Indigo's cheeks the longer he talked. If Mama was in prison in Yuma, how could they ever find Mama before the train took them away? Sister Salt whispered her escape plan to Indigo: wait until the policeman lifted them out of the back of the wagon and untied their legs, then dash off as fast as they could for the hills.

"I can't run as fast as you!" Indigo sobbed. "Please don't go without me!"

Sister Salt put her head close to Indigo's and whispered in a soothing tone: "Don't cry, little sister, don't cry. Grandma Fleet got away. We'll get away too.

"We won't get in a hurry. We'll save a little food from each meal, hide it so we can carry a little food with us. Cool weather is the best time to travel."

They whispered strategies and plans to each other all the way to Yuma. They tried to say everything they needed to tell each other because it might be a long time before they were together again.

Part Two

"FIRST CHANCE you get, run!" Sister Salt had whispered to her before they dragged Indigo toward the train, where the other children were cowering or sobbing, crowded four to a seat. Indigo was shocked to learn she and her sister were about to be separated. The authorities judged Sister Salt to be too much older than the others to send away to Indian boarding school. There was hope the little ones might be educated away from their blankets. But this one? Chances were she'd be a troublemaker and might urge the younger students to attempt escape. Orders were for Sister Salt to remain in the custody of the Indian agency at Parker while Indigo was sent to the Sherman Institute in Riverside, California.

Indigo wasn't afraid. Her eyes were dry. She was one of the older children in the group. Cocopa and Chemehuevi girls her own age who had already lived at the boarding school for three years were in charge of new students; only their skin looked Indian. Their eyes, their hair, and, of course, the shoes, stockings, and long dresses were no different from the matron's. The matron gave the older girls orders to seize a little boy who had slipped from the train seat to the floor; she did not want to touch the little wild ones herself. Indigo tried to get one of the older girls to look her in the eyes, but the Cocopa and Chemehuevi girls were obedient; no talking to the new students.

The older girls had learned to be good Christians from the time they first arrived at boarding school. They thought they knew more than she did, but Indigo knew all about the three gods, Father, Son, and Ghost. She knew English words because Grandma Fleet and Mama knew them. The older girls hated her because she already knew English words and she had never been to school. They pulled her hair and pinched her when she recited all the English words she remembered from Needles: Jesus Christ, Mother of God, Father God, Holy Ghost, hallelujah, savior, sinners, sins, crucify, whore, damned to hell, bastard, bitch, fuck. Indigo enjoyed the shock on their faces as she cursed them with English words the teachers never used. The others ran to tell the dormitory matron. The fat matron dragged her to the laundry room with the others trailing along to watch. Indigo did not cry as she was pulled along; she spoke English to the matron, who looked Indian but behaved like a white woman.

"Hey, lady! What's the trouble? I'm talking English—see. God damn! Jesus Christ! Son of a bitch!" The matron was a big Pomo Indian, who gripped Indigo's arm even tighter. At the laundry sink they struggled, and one of the older girls had to help hold her while the matron shoved the bar of brown soap into her mouth. Indigo broke loose from them and spat soap in the matron's eyes. Even with soap in her eyes the matron would not loosen her grip on Indigo. One of the janitors, hearing the commotion in the laundry room, had appeared then; he was one of those mission Indians, and like the matron, he spoke only English. He picked up Indigo by both shoulders and carried her to the mop closet and shut her inside.

She didn't mind the darkness of the closet; darkness was safety. She had to keep spitting to get the soap taste out of her mouth. Light peeked in around the edges of the door, and gradually her eyes adjusted, just as they had when she and Sister Salt traveled at night. The damp mops smelled of mildew and the disinfectant used to clean the bed after a sick student died.

In the months Indigo was at the Sherman Institute, she had watched three girls from Alaska stop eating, lie listlessly in their beds, then die, coughing blood. The others said the California air was too hot and too dry for their Alaskan lungs, accustomed to cool, moist air.

Indigo was locked in the mop closet all night. She relieved herself in a scrub bucket; she did not mind the odor of furniture polish and arranged a pile of dust cloths into a bed. That night in the closet she dreamed about the three dead Alaskan girls; they were happy, laughing together at the edge of the ocean, with great tall spruce trees all around. The ocean mist and the fog swirled around the girls' feet as they ran and chased one another on the beach. The girls did not speak to her, but she knew what their message was: she had to get away or she would die as they had.

The first time the fat dormitory matron turned her back, Indigo took off, running at full speed. She ran past the big boys' dormitory, past the steamy soap and starch smell of the school laundry, past the dairy barn's warm cow smells. She headed for the row of palm trees that marked the eastern boundary of the boarding school property. She did not look back. She stopped by the palm trees to catch her breath; she leaned against the tree and felt the odd curled bark against her back. She could hear voices in the distance.

She crouched low as she moved away from the tree; she glanced once over her shoulder, and seeing no one, she took off running, just as she had the morning she and Sister Salt escaped the soldiers and Indian police who pursued the Messiah's dancers at Needles. Sand Lizard people were not afraid of capture because they were so quick. Grandma Fleet taught the girls to wait and watch for the right moment to run.

Indigo heard the sound of horses' hooves and the rattle of a wagon in the distance; that would be the superintendent with the big boys to track her down. She removed the school shoes so she could run faster; the shoes rubbed sores on her toes and left the soles of her feet too soft. The ground burned her feet, but she found, if she ran quickly, she barely felt the heat. The skin on the soles of her feet would callus in no time. Once before, right after she first arrived, she ran away, but made the mistake of heading directly into the desert, where they easily tracked her and caught her within a few hours. This time she headed for the orange groves down the dusty road from the school. The orange trees would hide her better than the low desert brush.

The ground was cooler in the orchard, and the air perfumed by the orange blossoms; under the canopy of blossoming trees, there was the low steady hum of bees. Here she stopped to rest and to listen for her pursuers, but the only sound was the bees, a soothing sound that reminded her of the bees that hovered at the spring above the old gardens. When Indigo was little, Grandma Fleet used to tease that the bees sang a lullaby for Indigo's nap so she must not disappoint them. The sound usually made her feel sleepy, but not when she was on the run. She did feel a bit tired, so she sat with her back against the tree trunk and closed her eyes. Wherever they were, Sister Salt and Mama must have thought about her at that moment because suddenly she was thinking about them too. She felt their concern for her and their love; tears filled her eyes. Grandma Fleet still loved them and prayed for them from Cliff Town, where the dead went to stay.

The bees' hum, the perfume of the orange blossoms, and the dampness under the trees made the air heavy; Indigo felt drowsy as she sat there. She checked the position of the sun in the sky; it was still early enough that the superintendent and the big boys were probably still driving up and down the dusty farm roads, between the lemon and orange groves, searching for her. The old buggy creaked and rattled so loud she could hear it a mile away, with the jingle of the harnesses and the clip-clop of the horses. She was safe there and would wait for darkness. She smiled because Sister Salt and Mama would be proud of her.

The sound of the buggy and the loud voices of the big boys and the superintendent woke her. There were so many—half the summer staff at the school must be searching for her. She took off running again, deeper and deeper into the rows of orange trees; now and then she caught sight of a grove of tall trees, much taller than the orchard trees, up ahead. She was thirsty, and tall trees meant water nearby.

She left the cover of the orchard and bolted across open ground and a road to reach the tall trees. She stopped and listened. Nearby, the buggy horses moved at a walk while the big boys trotted alongside, talking and laughing as they searched the orchards, row by row. She ran with all her might, all her being. She ran to escape them all—the white teachers with the sour faces, the dormitory matrons with their cruel smiles and quick pinches; she ran from the other children too, because they teased her and pulled her hair. They wanted to make her cry because she was from the Sand Lizard people with their odd ways—they preferred cliffs and sand dunes far from the river, far away from churches and schools.

Get away, get away; the words sang inside her head. She ran until her lungs and legs were burning and the sweat ran into her eyes so she caught only glimpses of the grove of tall trees up ahead. She felt the ground change under her feet. Smooth dirt, a road, then suddenly she stumbled and fell hard; the breath was knocked out of her, but she wasn't on dirt anymore. The surface was absolutely hard and flat, scorching hot; she jumped up breathlessly and she saw the white stone tile that tripped her was part of a walkway into the grove of tall trees. She could hear the wagon and the voices of the searchers. The stone tiles were not quite as hot as the ground. She ran down the stone path until she reached the bushes that enclosed the grove of tall trees. If they were so smart, let them try to find her tracks on the stone walk. She glanced over her shoulder and saw no one; then with both arms in front of her face she dove under the thick green bushes the way Grandma Fleet taught her and Sister.

She lay motionless until she caught her breath. The cool damp of the rotting leaves smelled so good. The palms of her hands and her knees were stinging from skin scraped away by her fall; the damp earth soothed the pain. Her face felt much cooler pressed against the ground. She closed her eyes. Suddenly the sounds of the horses' hooves and the rattle of the buggy were right there on the road across from the bushes. She held her breath and watched; through the leaves she saw the superintendent's angry face as he scolded his posse of Indian boys.

"She can't have got very far," he told them, but the older boys leaned against the buggy or squatted on the ground while they caught their breath. They were tired; they gave up. The superintendent motioned furiously for them to get in the buggy, then took one last look at the lilac bushes as he took the reins in both hands; it seemed as if he was looking straight at her, right into her eyes, but he saw nothing. Then they were gone and silence returned.

Indigo dreamed about the old gardens. Grandma Fleet and she were making little windbreaks for the bean seedlings from dry twigs. Somehow Grandma Fleet made crackling sounds with the twigs, sounds that seemed so odd Indigo had to ask Grandma what she was doing. Her own voice woke her. Only the crickets were awake; desert singers like them knew the night was made for music and love, but the heat of the day was for sleep. Under the bushes it was dark, but beyond she could see outlines emerge from the predawn light that kept shifting—from dark gray, then dark blue, then violet that lifted to lavender that faded to a rosy gray streaked with pale yellow. Faster, faster, faster, the gray sky vanished, and now the eastern horizon was a blaze of red-yellow. Somewhere Sister Salt and Mama looked up at the same sky. She was not so far away from home: some of the same birds lived here—little speckled cactus wrens were calling one another around the lilac bushes, and though she could not see him, a desert curved beak greeted the dawn with trills of praise.

She was thirsty. Grandma Fleet taught them to smell water, to catch the scent of dampness early in the morning before the heat of the day scattered it. She tried to see beyond the bushes, but the foliage was too thick. Her knees and hands were sore as she crawled, head down, pushing aside the twigs and leaves. She saw the trimmed lawn just ahead of her just as she heard a woman's voice call a name over and over. Suddenly a little bearded man no taller than a turkey stood in front of her; he seemed surprised to see her too. He crouched down so he could look her in the eyes. He wore red leather around his little neck. His eyes were golden brown and calm. Timidly he extended his tiny hand toward her face. Just then the woman's voice rang out: "I see you! You little monkey! Come! Come! Linnaeus! Here, sweetie! Come!" As the woman knelt to reach under the lilacs to pick up the monkey, she gave a little shout of surprise when she saw Indigo.

"Oh!" she said as if she had been struck. Their eyes met. She held the monkey close to her.

"Linnaeus," the woman said, "who is this?"

◆ ◆ ◆

Hattie did not try to coax or drag the child out of the bushes; instead she smiled and nodded as if she was accustomed to visitors in the lilacs. Edward had alerted her to the runaways from the Indian school a few miles down the road. No danger. No cause for concern. Only the first-time students tried to run away; after the first year they were not so wild, he said, and she laughed gaily and replied, "Thank goodness we haven't got a penitentiary next door!"

At first she could not determine if this was a boy or a girl, though Edward said the boys were shorn of their long hair; this child's hair seemed long, though it was too tangled with weeds to be certain. Poor little Indian.

She did not want to frighten the child any more than she had already. She carried the monkey to his cage in the old orchid house, damaged some years ago by an earthquake, then abandoned to a white wisteria. Over the years, the wisteria followed the contours of the glass panels of the vaulted roof, snaking along tiny ledges formed by the leaded glass. Long cascades of pendulous white blossoms caught the bright morning light through the glass; the white blossoms gave off a luminous glow as if they were little lanterns. The monkey did not want to go into the cage and clung to her tightly; she tickled him gently and played with him until he loosened his grip, then quickly set him down inside the cage on his bench. She hurried to the house to decide what to do about the Indian child.

The cook was in the laundry helping the new maid iron the linens, but she did not disturb them. Edward's household staff was accustomed to the needs of a bachelor who spent more than ten months of the year away on expeditions. Hattie was in no hurry to make changes; she wanted the cook and maids to feel comfortable with her.

She opened the cupboards and drawers in the pantry in search of something special to lure the child from under the lilac bushes. A peach? Some bread with strawberry jam? Edward said the Indian students were quick to learn civilized ways. In the summer, when he was not away on an expedition, Edward hired two or three Indian boys to help with the weeding and mowing.

She carried the bread and jam and a cup of water on a tray and left them at the edge of the lawn next to the lilac bushes. She wanted the child to see she meant no harm, so she proceeded to measure the grassy arcade created by the lilacs. She had big plans for this area. While she paced off the length of the lawn, she kept watch from the corner of her eye for any sign of the child. She wondered what the school fed the Indian children. Did they feed the children the tribal foods they were accustomed to?

She paced off the width of the grassy area and noted the measurements on one of the note cards she carried in her pocket, a habit left over from her days of scholarly research into early church history. Of course, to Edward, the garden *was* a research laboratory, though she felt he appreciated its beauty. During his mother's last illness the orchid house and gardens were neglected, but the acres of lemon and orange trees were tended by Edward to occupy himself. He did not talk about those difficult years, so Hattie did not press him, but she saw evidence of some sort of breakdown in the neglect of the orchid house.

The rectangle of lawn outlined with lilacs was wasted space she could put to good use. She stood motionless for a good while as she surveyed the area and imagined its transformation. She became so engrossed as she sketched her renovation plans for the arcade, the child under the lilac bushes slipped her mind. She wanted to surprise Edward when he returned from the Bahamas–Key West expedition. She wanted to reassure Edward that she was not at all bothered that the expedition had come so soon after their wedding.

Of course, the expedition had been planned well in advance of their engagement; Edward always kept a busy schedule. Actually, she looked forward to this time by herself to get accustomed to her new home and new life. The day after his departure, she rose at dawn and gathered pink rose petals from the old climbing rosebush that covered the wall of the kitchen garden. While the petals dried she sewed sachets from white satin remnants of her wedding gown; now the musty drawers and closets of the old house were scented with roses. Her mother said no man wanted a professor for a wife, but Edward was no ordinary man; he showed no concern at all over the controversy her thesis topic caused.

The first week Edward was away, she walked from room to room; from the polished oak floors to the oak paneling and high ceilings, she could find nothing out of place. Edward's mother died ten years before they met, but her presence still was there. The rooms had an aura of completion about them that reminded her of her parents' house, with its aura of self-satisfaction rising off its mahogany furniture and emanating from dark oil portraits in gilded frames.

Hattie's mother did not permit the maids to reposition the furniture, and Hattie did not bother to challenge her mother over the furniture or rugs, because housekeeping chores bored her. Hattie laughed at her mother's prediction that she was destined for spinsterhood—she knew she was too pretty to be an old maid. She had a sizeable dowry too. Actually she hoped her mother was right: if she were a spinster she would never have to run a household or take an interest in the shirt starch the laundress used.

From the time she was able to ride her pony alone, she vowed to herself she would not have a husband to interfere with rides along the beach as her parents had when she was thirteen. She discovered books when she was four years old, and Lucille, the cook, held her on her lap, where Hattie loved to listen to Lucille read from the old Bible she kept in the kitchen. Hattie pointed at words and Lucille pronounced them, and before long, Hattie recognized the words when she saw them again. Her father was delighted when Lucille proudly informed him Hattie could read; he went into the city that afternoon to buy children's books of simple rhymes and the alphabet. Hattie rapidly lost interest in the dolls dressed in elegant gowns and the tiny china teacups and plates she was given on her last birthday. With a book in her lap Hattie became a different person, thousands of miles away, in the middle of the action. Her mother worried that books at such an early age would ruin the girl, but Mr. Abbott didn't agree. He admired the theories of John Stuart Mill on the education of women and he was proud of his precocious child.

As Hattie finished noting the measurements, she glanced down and saw the bread and jam were gone from the tray; the cup was empty on the lawn. At that instant she heard the cook call her. Hattie returned her call, and the big woman came down the steps to the lower garden with a telegram in her hand. As the cook approached, Hattie said, "I've found a little Indian hiding in the lilacs."

"I'll send word to the school right away, Mrs. Palmer."

"Oh no—that's not what I meant." Hattie was surprised at the sudden change in the expression on the cook's pink face. With her lips pressed together in disapproval, the cook bent down and squinted to get a better look under the lilacs. But when Hattie pulled back the branches to show her, the child was gone.

"You have to notify the school. It's the law," the cook said.

No one was permitted to employ or otherwise "keep" reservation Indians without government authorization. Edward had explained that out west it was necessary for the government to protect the Indians on reservations; otherwise the settlers would have killed them all.

The cook stared at the lilacs as if she expected a tiger to leap out. In that instant Hattie realized the cook disliked her, and she was embarrassed that her feelings were hurt.

"I'm sure the child returned to school herself," Hattie said stiffly. What did it matter if Edward's cook did not approve of her? The controversy over her thesis topic had shaken her self-confidence; before the thesis committee's decision, she seldom cared what others might think of her, certainly not a servant.

The cook seemed to be waiting for her to open the telegram.

"No need for you to wait," Hattie said. "I'll come inside if there is a reply to be sent." She was annoyed at the cook's attitude. Her mother said leave the cooks in the kitchen, otherwise there would be trouble; if a cook left the kitchen, look out; cooks wanted to run the whole house. Her mother said bachelors like Edward, who were never at home, spoiled good servants because he allowed them the run of the place while he was away. Hattie must be firm with the cook from the start.

She waited until the cook was gone before she opened the telegram. The message was odd; it must have been sent by someone else, a colleague, perhaps, who signed the message "Dr. E. G. Palmer," not "Edward" as he would have. The telegram told her nothing but the arrival time of the train. Had there been an accident? Was Edward ill?

She felt her heart pound as she hurried past the water garden and fountain and up the steps to the house. The expedition was to have lasted three months, time enough, Edward hoped, to allow him to complete the collection of sponges and marine algae of the Caribbean Sea.

She sat down at her writing desk, then realized she might have to break into his desk to locate the name and address of Edward's liaison officer at the Bureau of Plant Industry in Washington. She had not thought to ask for the address, but Edward did not leave instructions for her either. He had been a bachelor too long, her mother said, but he was the only gentleman willing to take a heretic to be his wife.

She paused at the door of Edward's study. They had not discussed what she should do in the event of an emergency. Edward had invited her into his study once, when they first arrived and he showed her their home. The entire third floor of the house was three big rooms, one passing into the other; the walls of every room were lined with oak bookshelves booked solid from floor to ceiling; in the center of the rooms were oak cabinets with dozens of small drawers.

Edward made his study in the first room; the desk in the center, flanked by two vast library tables covered with papers, books, and bits of dry leaves and plant stalks, was Edward's desk, as massive as a throne. She felt uncomfortable as she looked through the papers and letters on top of the desk. No mention of the expedition underwriters, no names or addresses, only Latin names of plants, diagrams of leaf structures, and queries from other plant collectors concerning plants they wished to sell or to buy.

The drawers of the desk were locked. She sat down in the big oak chair and took a deep breath. Her heart was pounding and she could feel the perspiration cling to her clothes and her body. She took deep breaths, as her doctor had instructed, and calmed herself. Easy does it.

She was not about to break open the locks on his desk drawers lest she appear to be overwrought. Her annoyance surprised her. Edward prepared for weeks and methodically reviewed all that he might need for three months in the Caribbean. The floor of his study had been spread with lanterns, candles, tents, tarps, a folding shovel, a trowel, a clock, bottles of chemicals—formaldehyde and alcohol—and a number of handsome cherry wood boxes that contained magnifying glasses, a microscope, a small telescope; and of course, one cherry wood box contained Edward's camera, another the glass plates and bottles of chemicals. Specimen collection envelopes, botanical field guides, a book of maps, blank notebooks, leather boots, rubber boots, rubber hip waders, a wide-brim straw hat, a pith helmet, mosquito netting, a canteen, and a revolver all were carefully packed into huge black steamer trunks. With so much equipment to organize, no wonder he forgot to leave her a name or address to contact in the event of a mishap for himself. The telegram said nothing about illness or injury. She really had made much over nothing. Her nerves were still fragile, though she was much better since she married Edward.

She got up from Edward's desk because walking calmed her. She wandered up and down the aisles of worktables in the laboratory-study. He collected other curiosities as well as plants. On the floor in one corner, a fossilized clamshell as big as an oven cradled a giant yellow tooth. Odd baskets as tall as chairs were filled with artifacts—bows and spears and arrows bristled out of pottery jars painted with serpents and birds. A strange carved mask with a frightful expression gazed at her from another corner stacked high with colorful handwoven textiles. Mineral specimens filled the shelves—fist-size amethysts, flawless crystals, and rows of eye agates watched over glittering pyrites.

As she turned, her ankle brushed a big dark lustrous rock on the floor. A meteorite. Edward had showed it to her because he was quite proud of it.

Too heavy for the shelf with the other meteorites, it was allowed a place on the floor. He was quite keen on "celestial debris," as he called it. Meteorite specimens were nearly indestructible—unlike rare orchids.

In the seventh month of their courtship, Edward told Hattie about the disastrous expedition to collect rare orchids on the Pará River in Brazil. He lowered his voice slightly as he recounted the events. His companions on the expedition were unreliable, and Edward was injured, unable to protect the specimens during the ocean storm. Boxes of rare orchid specimens were lost at sea during a storm, and others were ruined later when they were stored in a damp shed in Miami. Dozens of rare orchids, intended to repay the underwriters of the expedition, mildewed and rotted. Later there were allegations certain plant materials were exported without proper government permits. His companions behaved irresponsibly, and the failure of the expedition nearly ruined him.

Hattie had not expected such frankness from Mr. Palmer, though he was much older than the suitors she was accustomed to. Suddenly she felt too warm, on the verge of a queasy stomach. Was this a test, to see if she would confide her difficulties? How much had his sisters told him about her? Should she tell him how the suitors vanished from her doorstep after the decision of the thesis committee became known? Or how the illness that followed was to blame for her withdrawal? What a relief it had been to stay home with her books. Yes, she would confide in Mr. Palmer.

"By now you must have heard—I am the heretic of Oyster Bay," Hattie said bravely, with a smile. Then Edward Palmer won her heart as he looked at her intently and replied, "Good for you!" He was a man of science himself, he said. He listened quietly to her story of the failed thesis with its scandalous view of early church history. The thesis committee had been unanimous in its determination that her principal reference sources—Dr. Rhinehart's moldy Coptic scrolls—were not authenticated, and in any case the scrolls were unacceptable Gnostic heresy, pure and simple.

"Surely you've heard all about the furor from your sister," Hattie said, feeling bolder. "My heresy was a lively topic of dinner party conversations on Long Island for months!" Edward's laughter at her wit endeared him to Hattie; all the other gentlemen she told looked a bit shocked.

How good Edward's laughter sounded! To hear her mother talk, Hattie's entire life was ruined by her assertions that Jesus had women disciples and Mary Magdalene wrote a Gospel supressed by the church.

Her affection for Edward stirred at that instant, and she could only smile at his neglect to leave her a way to reach him. The hundreds of tiny specimen drawers in the huge oak cabinets stirred her curiosity. She pulled out a drawer: inside was a small manila envelope carefully secured with red string. She unwound the string from the circular clasp and gently squeezed the sides of the envelope to look inside. All she saw was a single shriveled stalk with fragments of dry plant material, remains of leaves, perhaps. She sniffed the envelope but detected only a faint odor. Edward's special interest was in aromatic grasses and plants, which always were highly prized by horticulturists and gardeners. Edward traveled to places so remote and collected plants so rare, so subtle, few white men ever saw them before. He added these rare treasures to his growing collection of roots, stalks, leaves, and, most important, when possible, seeds. His ambition was to discover a new plant species that would bear his name, and he spent twenty years of his life in this pursuit before their marriage.

◆　◆　◆

Hattie did not attend any parties or formal gatherings after she left graduate school, though gradually she accepted invitations to family picnics and outings to the beach—always with a group of her younger cousins, who needed a chaperone. The only reason she agreed to attend a formal event like the Masque of the Blue Garden was because their neighbor Mrs. Colin James served with Hattie's mother on the bishop's fund-raising committee, and Hattie was curious to see the garden so well known for its drama and the spectacle of its mistress.

Hattie's mother wanted the party to mark the end of the seclusion Hattie assumed. Eyebrows were raised when she enrolled in graduate studies in early church history; all the other young women her age were engaged or married. After the scandal over her thesis topic, Mrs. Abbott was relieved to let the dust settle awhile, but she still hoped to find Hattie a husband. In a year or two the incident would be forgotten. By chance, Susan James's distinguished brother, Edward Palmer, arrived from an expedition abroad two days before the blue garden event.

The Masque of the Blue Garden was considered the premier event of the summer season, and Hattie thought it promised to be eccentric enough to be interesting. And so it was. Just as the full moon rose over Oyster Bay, out stepped Susan Palmer James from the arch of blue rhododendrons, dressed all in sapphire blue—blue feathers and blue satin. She strode grandly from the far end of the blue garden along the white marble terrace next to the pool filled with fragrant blue water lilies.

Moments after her triumphant entrance, their hostess introduced Mrs. Abbott and Hattie to Edward Palmer, distinguished botanist and brother.

His face and hands were tanned from his fieldwork just completed in Mexico. Hattie found him quite interesting, and while the others danced, Hattie and Edward talked about Italy. She went to England with her parents when she was a child, but she wanted to see Rome. Edward laughed when Hattie recounted her mother's fears that high church officials might excommunicate her for heresy. But Hattie's father, God bless him, suggested the church's cardinals had more pressing concerns than a Gnostic heretic. Her trip to Italy was scheduled for the following spring.

Mrs. Abbott did not trust Hattie or Hattie's father; after all, they conspired to enroll Hattie in graduate school at Harvard without her knowledge. What respectable man wanted a wife who sat in a musty library all day to pore over heretical texts? Mrs. Abbott's face assumed a stricken expression at any mention of Hattie's thesis, but her expression relaxed whenever she reminded Hattie of the size of her dowry. Mrs. Abbott talked about money almost incessantly—who had money, how they got the money, and who lost their money. Despite her family's impeccable lineage, their wealth was in decline when Mrs. Abbott was a child. She felt quite fortunate to find a husband who did not care about such things.

Despite Mr. Abbott's disapproval of the practice, Hattie had a sizeable dowry that made Mrs. Abbott smile every time she thought of it; she liked to remind Hattie of its size.

"In that case, I hereby renounce my dowry!" Hattie used to reply. "I'd rather spend the money on travel."

"Oh nonsense, Hattie!"

"I'd rather not be married anyway—now that I'm a heretic!" she laughed, but after she got acquainted with Edward, her opinion of marriage began to change. Edward was a remarkable man. He traveled a great deal to the most distant and fascinating destinations, and he had a wonderful gift for recounting his adventures, in which he portrayed himself humorously, as the innocent tourist hell-bent on disaster. The tourist identity was the disguise he adopted to confuse the customs officers. Some foreign governments were quite unpleasant about the export of valuable root stock and seeds.

Edward was quite irreverent about customs authorities in general, which Hattie found appealing. I *am* a heretic, she thought, but Mr. Palmer doesn't seem to mind. Hattie asked her father what he thought of Mr. Palmer.

"He's too old and he travels too much," her father said, "but nothing I say will stop you if your mind is made up."

She linked her arm through her father's. "My mind isn't made up," she said as they walked to the dining room together. "Mother's mind is made up." Mr. Palmer wasn't as young as the others, and like any longtime bachelor he might be set in his ways; still, he didn't seem adverse to children. Indeed, in the months that followed the garden party, Hattie saw Edward again at a picnic on the seashore and at a birthday party on the lawn for Edward's young nieces. On both occasions Edward brought along his view camera and made photographs of the children playing, and later posed everyone for a group photograph that included him too—he tripped the shutter with a long black string as he posed with the group. Edward really could be quite appealing. Hattie had not wanted marriage or children, but Edward changed all that. Children—the child! Suddenly she remembered the Indian child in the lilac bushes. What if the child did not find her way back to the school?

Hattie rushed downstairs and out to the south garden lawn hedged with lilacs. Next to the plate, the cup was lying on its side in the grass. Hattie didn't mind if her skirt got dirty; she crawled and searched carefully under and among the dark green leaves of the lilacs. She found a few late blossoms hidden in the lower branches; their perfume seemed stronger than the earlier blossoms; but she could not locate the child. Hattie blamed the arrival of the telegram for her thoughtlessness; she should not have taken her eyes off the child!

Hattie rushed up the steps to the fountain and pool for a better view. Beyond the lilacs, orchards of lemons and oranges stretched to the horizon. She couldn't quite see the redbrick buildings of the Indian school, but once from the third-floor balcony, Edward had pointed out a cluster of two-story buildings in the distance. The child almost certainly returned to the school; there was nothing but desert beyond the citrus groves.

She checked under the lilacs a last time just to be sure. A late afternoon breeze wafted the perfume of the yellow climbing roses on the kitchen garden wall. She still had to bathe and change clothes before she went to meet Edward's train, but the excitement of the telegram on top of the discovery of the Indian child left Hattie exhausted. On a marble bench that overlooked the gardens and orchards below, she felt herself almost shiver with anticipation, so she closed her eyes and took deep breaths as her doctor instructed. The fresh outdoor air relaxed her. The doctor's orders were to take every opportunity to relax and to avoid fatigue lest she fall ill again. She exhaled slowly, as the doctor instructed. She still had not unpacked her books or papers because the doctor advised against the resumption of her studies until they were certain she was fully recovered. Men were equipped for the rough-and-tumble of the academic world in ways women, unfortunately, were not, the doctor said. Hattie's mother looked sharply at Hattie as the doctor spoke.

Fortunately, Hattie's father entered the room just then. Bless his heart, he reminded them of Hattie's academic honors in her undergraduate studies at Vassar. Women who never opened a book suffered from nervous exhaustion—how ridiculous to blame Hattie's studies! Mr. Abbott encouraged Hattie to continue work on her thesis regardless of the committee's decision, but she could not bring herself to even look at the manuscript or notes, though she did bring them with her to California.

The sun began its descent in the west, and the thick perfume of orange blossoms washed over her in the breeze. Hattie was considering whether to send a note to the superintendent of the Indian school when the cook hurried across the terrace breathlessly.

"Mrs. Palmer! Mrs. Palmer! He's here! Dr. Palmer has just arrived!" Hattie stood up and looked beyond the fountain in time to see him step through the French doors to the terrace. Hattie waved and called out a greeting as she ran. She paused an instant to look him over for signs of injury, then rushed to him. Edward smiled and embraced her.

"I was afraid something was wrong," she said, the words muffled by his chest.

Only the weather was wrong, he explained; one hurricane after another. He kept her close to his side with his arm around her and neither of them spoke as the huge red sun slipped behind the groves of oranges. She found his height and fitness very attractive; men half his age were not as lean and fit as Edward, despite the lingering effects of his injury in Brazil. Before their courtship commenced in earnest, Edward insisted she understand the impediment; he was so tender and ardent in all other ways Hattie was confident he would make a full recovery. She leaned closer to him and kissed his cheek; he smiled and glanced down at her warmly before he looked west again at the sunset as though something was on his mind.

They remained on the terrace in silence even after the sun went down. A gentle wind moved through the white climbing roses heavy with perfume. At last Edward shifted his weight to give his good leg a rest and glanced toward the orchid house.

"How's the monkey getting along?" he asked.

"Oh he's a jolly little thing!" Hattie inhaled sharply as suddenly she remembered the child.

"Oh Edward! How could I forget! Linnaeus found an Indian child hiding under the lilacs this morning."

"A bit late in the season for runway Indians," he said. "Usually by this time they've sent them home for the summer or they've farmed them out."

"I was about to send a note down to the school, but the telegram arrived—in the excitement I forgot."

"Where is the child now?" he asked, looking down past the pool to the lilacs.

"I'm not sure. I went back to find her just now and—"

"Her?"

Hattie felt her face flush. "I think so. I'm not sure. I saw long hair. You said the Indian boys—"

"—have all their hair cut off."

"Yes, but now I can't find her."

"No need to worry. She probably went back."

◆ ◆ ◆

After the sun went down, Indigo crept out of her hiding place under the trellis of cascading white roses. She ran from the lilacs into the white garden because it was enclosed by a low rock wall that concealed her. While the twilight was still bright, she moved cautiously, listening for footsteps or voices. She peeked around the corner of the rock wall and saw the stone walk led to stone steps up to an arch of climbing red roses. What a fragrance they had! Grandma Fleet used to talk about the flowers the Mormon ladies grew, but never had she or anyone ever talked about flowers so fragrant and big as these.

She wanted to run right over to examine these red giants more closely, but she waited until the twilight darkened a bit more. The white blossoms seemed almost to glow and the wonderful perfumes only increased with the darkness. On stalks taller than she was, huge white lilies leaned their faces down to hers. She went from flower to flower, burying her nose in each blossom as deeply as she could, licking the sweet pollen from her lips. The night air was delightfully cool and the sensation of the rich damp soil under her feet made Indigo want to dance. She had to hold the stupid long skirt of the school uniform in one hand to keep from tripping over it; a moment later she pulled off the skirt and danced between the white lilies and white irises, around the white lilacs next to the gate. As she danced, Indigo looked up at the great field of stars like so many little bean blossoms; Grandma Fleet could travel up there now, but where were Sister Salt and Mama tonight?

After she got tired of dancing, she sat on the low wall overgrown with white honeysuckle to watch the moon rise from the same direction she must travel to get home. She made a plan: The school dress with its long sleeves and long skirt would serve as a blanket as well as a pack to carry any food she might find around here. What she really needed, what she really missed most, was her gourd canteen. She didn't have much time. She had to find a place to hide before daybreak. She might need another day to locate the things she would need for the journey home.

The west wind stirred and cooled her face; she inhaled the scent of orange and lemon blossoms, then suddenly caught the scent of roasted meat that wafted down the path from the back of the house. Indigo's stomach grumbled about the scanty food. She crept out from the low wall and made her way to the steps that brought her from the lilacs and past the fountain and pool. From the top step Indigo could see the fan shape of the gardens—in orderly squares and rectangles, outlined by low walls of stone bright with the moon's light. Orange and lemon groves surrounded the house and the gardens and a number of outbuildings and sheds. The place was almost as big as the boarding school.

With the moon high overhead, she could see the white stone steps and paths clearly. She needed to find the best hiding place before morning. She slipped off the school dress and underclothes—how delicious the open air and warm breeze felt against her bare skin. Clothing suffocated her skin; naked in the moon's light, she felt alert and invigorated. Grandma Fleet was right: too much clothing wasn't healthy. She skipped down the steps, two at a hop, past the white garden's snaking branches and thickets of white bougainvillea; she brushed aside the flowering branches and saw three steps down. Below, planted in spirals and whorls, were blood red dianthus, red peonies, red dahlias, and red poppies; bright red cosmos and scarlet hollyhocks made the backdrop along the east wall. Indigo's heart pounded with excitement at all the red flowers—oh Sister Salt would love to hear about this garden of red flowers. By daylight the red garden would be even better.

She picked handfuls of fat rose hips and ate herself to sleep, curled up under the rosebushes with her head at the edge of a stone step. She awoke when the color of the sky was dark red, almost black, the color of the hollyhocks at the burned house. Rapidly the sky became the color of the roses, and finally the sky was blood red. Too bad she had to get going, because Grandma Fleet always advised the girls to collect as many new seeds as they could carry home. The more strange and unknown the plant, the more interested Grandma Fleet was; she loved to collect and trade seeds. Others did not grow a plant unless it was food or medicine, but Sand Lizards planted seeds to see what would come; Sand Lizards ate nearly everything anyway, and Grandma said they never found a plant they couldn't use for some purpose.

There were other gardens she could see only partially because of tall bushes and trees that enclosed them. The sunny gardens, the shady gardens, the damp gardens, the water garden—where was the garden with the beans and corn? Indigo followed the stone path to the point where it forked; one branch turned back toward the house, the other branch led down four steps to a sandy border at the edge of the orange grove.

While she ate oranges in the shade of the trees, she surveyed the house and the gardens. Where did they get all the water? The land here was sandy desert nearly as dry as home—the panic grass and amaranth grew just as they did at home. She heard a buggy and horses, then voices from the road beyond the house; she had to find a better hiding place or the school search parties were certain to find her.

Indigo crept back up the steps, past the garden of red flowers and the white flower garden to the stone path that turned back to the barn and outbuildings behind the house. She listened for footsteps and voices but heard only the cicadas and a cactus wren; she darted around the corner of the barn to the strange glass house she noticed the afternoon before. The whitewash on the glass weathered off to reveal glimpses of green foliage and cascading spikes of white wisteria that grew up and out the roof vent. How wonderful the scent was! She closed her eyes and inhaled again and again; then she heard a sound—tap-tap-tap-tap, silence, then four more taps. She froze in her tracks; the hair on the back of her neck stood up; she turned quickly to locate the source of the sound. Tap! Tap! Tap! Tap! There it was again; someone was tapping on the inside of the glass house. She glanced over her shoulder as she retreated down the stone path to the gardens and caught a glimpse of the shining eyes and face of the little hairy monkey man who found her the previous morning. The monkey motioned for her to come to him.

◆ ◆ ◆

An early hurricane season in the Caribbean Sea had forced them to cut short their expedition. One after the other, the tropical storms lashed the Bahamas and the Keys. They attempted to wait out the first storm in St. Augustine, but a great gust of wind and ocean surge flung the small boat

86

containing all their supplies against the crushed pier. Fortunately, all of Edward's equipment and the precious collections he managed to make were in the hotel room with him. Before the second storm arrived, Edward tried to send a telegram to Mr. Talbot at the Bureau of Plant Industry to ask for authorization to extend the effective dates of their expedition and for funds to replace the lost and damaged supplies, but the high winds from the approaching storm knocked out telegraph communications as far north as Atlanta. Weeks later the downed lines were still not repaired, which was the reason his telegram to Hattie had arrived only hours before Edward. He was dubious when he asked the captain of a freighter bound for Galveston to send the telegram for him.

"The last thing I wanted was to upset you," Edward said as he held Hattie's chair for her at the table. But there was good news as well: when their ship finally reached New Orleans, Edward found a telegram from Mr. Albert at Lowe & Company. Edward's face flushed when he spoke of Lowe & Company. Though he had told her only a few details of the unfortunate expedition to Brazil, she recalled Lowe & Company was involved in a misunderstanding that occurred over certain rare orchids Edward was sent to collect for a group of private investors.

The cook had prepared lamb chops in mint jelly, green beans, and raisin-stuffed potatoes, special favorites of Edward's, and there was mincemeat pie for dessert. Hattie did not care for the heavy flavor of lamb, and the odor of mincemeat pie had repelled her since the one bite of mince pie she took when she was eleven. She was too excited and happy to feel hungry so she daintily picked the raisins out of the potato and pushed the green beans across the plate with her fork while Edward related the new development: Lowe & Company had advanced him $5,000 for an expedition to Corsica. Now Hattie would have an opportunity to visit her aunt in England and they would see Italy as well. In little more than six weeks, they would depart for New York by train to visit their families on Long Island for a few weeks before they departed.

"But I've barely just arrived here," Hattie said, surprised at the news. "I haven't even unpacked our wedding gifts yet." Edward smiled.

"Never mind that!" he said, taking both her hands in his. "You will have years and years to settle yourself here."

He looked so distinguished and stalwart—the military posture from his prep school years in the east. As Hattie listened, she studied the face and the mouth, the intent expression in the eyes, and felt her heart beat faster because this was her beloved, still so new to her; it was still startling to see and realize here was her husband! Did she look as unfamiliar to him as well?

◆ ◆ ◆

The voyage from the Keys across the lower Gulf had taken a week longer than scheduled as the ship was forced to take refuge in protected coves to escape the high seas and winds that scoured the Keys and the coast. When they departed Veracruz the skies were blue and the wind calm, but as they began to cross the Bay of Campeche, the wind speed intensified. The ship's captain steered for Tampico to escape the storm. With the expedition cut short, Edward was pleased for the opportunity to have a look around the public market in Tampico. He had made it his practice to collect samples of local and regional agriculture. The natives might possess unknown medicinal plants with commercial potential or a new variety of citrus or a new source for rubber. He was also eager to purchase archaeological artifacts and curiosities. Weather permitting, he would hire the cabin boy to assist him with his camera so the more interesting subjects could be photographed.

There were only light winds in Tampico; the topaz blue sky was scattered with cirrus clouds in a strong breeze that brought refreshment to the sweltering dockside streets with their stench of dead fish and sewage. Evidence of the civil unrest and the hurricane season were apparent: iron shutters were closed across shops; soldiers loitered in pairs on street corners smoking cigarettes, carbines slung over their backs. The streets were deserted though no one could name the cause. Rumors abounded: an outbreak of yellow fever, or an epidemic of rabid cats. There were always rumors of impending crisis in Tampico.

Earlier the first mate mentioned a recent uprising by half-castes and Indians who claimed to be guided by the Indian Virgin of Guadalupe against the state tax collectors. The early storm season and the dispute left a great many empty spaces and vacant stands; still, Edward was able to find a variety of muskmelon he had not seen before. Its shape reminded him of a human skull; its succulent sweet flesh was bright red. The melons were heaped in great piles on the old flagstones next to clay incense burners shaped like water lilies, filled with lumps of cloudy copal to fuel them. He purchased bunches of mysterious dried flowers beneficial to weak hearts and bald heads; he found strange roots the shape of a baby's fingers, said to aid in digestion. He methodically peered into the stalls and shops that were closed lest he miss some unusual item. He noticed one stall that was actually the front of a tiny house at the entrance of the narrow alley behind the cathedral. He hesitated and nearly turned back because the stall was closed behind an iron gate; but then between the iron bars piled on the ground he saw chunks of lustrous black meteor iron for sale. He was always interested in acquiring meteor irons or other celestial curiosities. He knocked, but no one stirred inside; he would return later.

The massive stone towers of the old cathedral caught his eye; they were built with the stones of the Maya temple that once stood on the site. Edward felt he must photograph the cathedral and the market for his report; he returned to the ship for his camera and tripod and hired the cabin boy to assist him. While the cabin boy steadied the tripod legs, Edward adjusted the camera lens and arranged the black viewing cloth over his head. At this, the market fell strangely silent; Indian and mestizo women of the market hid their faces behind the corners of their shawls as they had when they told the price of a root or seeds.

They moved the camera methodically from stall to stall to photograph the goods for sale. Edward gave the cabin boy centavos to hand out and the odd silence shifted into a low murmur as the Indian women gathered to compare coins, faces still hidden by their shawls.

By midafternoon the local varieties of maize and beans and other market produce had been well documented with photographs, and the specimen bag was full. Edward had just begun to remove the lens board from the camera when he noticed activity outside the stall with the chunks of meteorite ore. A large figure wrapped in a bright red shawl disappeared inside the iron bar gate. Edward hurriedly repacked the camera and sent the cabin boy ahead to the steamer with the equipment while he went to inquire about the purchase of the meteor irons. Recently there had been a great deal of excitement among archaeologists after a meteorite shaped into a frog was found atop the big pyramid at the Maya ruins of Cholula.

He knocked politely but the figure in the red shawl was nowhere to be seen. He became concerned about the lateness and the departure of the steamer, so he knocked a bit harder. The corrugated steel sides of the stall shook. Suddenly a huge blue face appeared in the window and Edward could not help but jump back. The old woman's long tangled hair and her ample chest and arms all had been painted a bright blue that emphasized the woman's Maya features: sharp high cheekbones and aquiline nose. Her glittering black eyes fastened on his, and he felt beads of sweat form above his lip and across his forehead. He pointed at the meteor irons on the ground by her feet.

"How much for these?"

The woman stared at him until he had to look away. He saw the black skin of her legs and realized the woman was African as well as Maya.

"Oh, it's you," she said. "Go away, I'm closed." The tone of contempt in her voice astonished Edward.

"I'll buy all the meteor irons you have," he said as he reached into his specimen satchel for his purse. She leaned her blue face and breasts closer; he felt the heat of her breath and instantly a terrible dread swept over him as if he was in imminent danger.

"Go away! You cannot buy them but you will pay!"

Had she misunderstood him? He held out a handful of silver coins to show her he wanted to buy the irons. She hissed out the words again—go away! The sweat on his forehead felt cold and the hairs on his neck stood up. He got a sudden impression the blue-face woman knew him and she had hated him for a long time.

How silly, he thought later when he was safely in his cabin. He was pleased with the handsome melon specimen and the photographs; the visit to the Tampico market had been a success. He put the unpleasant incident with the Maya Negress out of his thoughts; there would be other opportunities to acquire meteor irons. The encounter only whetted his appetite.

At high tide the steamer departed, but they were under way only a few hours when the wind began to increase and the ship's barometer began to fall. The whitecaps began to slap the sides of the ship and the captain attempted to outrun the storm by heading due north. The ship rolled and plunged as she circled, waiting for the storm to move. In more than thirty years on the Caribbean, the captain had not seen as many storms as there were this season, and all of the winds followed the same path out of the Bay of Campeche.

The wind howled and drove the rain relentlessly against the ship; on the third day the storm gave no sign of abating, and the sailors began to recount old stories about hurricanes that raged for weeks. Edward remained calm. A few years before, he had weathered a far worse storm on the return trip from the Pará expedition.

That time a sudden storm sprung up off the coast of Venezuela; he was convalescing from his injury, immobilized in his cabin alone. Wind-driven waves nearly swamped the ship; the terrified sailors cast overboard much of the ship's cargo to buy the wind's mercy, and all but two crates of the rare orchid specimens were lost.

The sailors believed the storm was the work of the Black Indian of Tampico, who kept two sets of altar saints, one for the day, one for the night. The ship's barometer fell so far that they thought it was broken. Who or what had angered the Black Indian? Edward listened to the men and wondered if she was the same woman who refused to sell him the meteorites. They said she was a daughter of the African spirits and the Maya spirits as well. The sailors heard spirits in the high-pitched whine of the wind.

The Black Indian and her black dogs combed the beaches after big storms to collect the gold and other valuables from shipwrecks. Edward listened to the sailors' comments with amusement. The seamen worked themselves into self-righteous anger: What fool had angered the Black Indian, prompting her to burn black dog hair and rum in a white bowl to call up the winds? No solution but to throw gold coins and valuables overboard. That's what she wanted; gold floated to the shore for her.

Later, when they were alone, Edward asked the ship's captain where in Tampico this Black Indian might be found. The captain had already finished the first bottle of wine and opened another. Her ugly mug was unmistakable—painted bright blue. Edward felt a chill run down his neck. He said nothing about his encounter with her lest they accuse him of bringing down the storm. He excused himself and returned to his cabin. To think that he had inhaled her hot breath reeking of rum!

The rain and wind were relentless, never increasing but never decreasing in velocity; like the other tropical storms this season, it seemed to stall in Campeche Bay. The vessel was in a protected anchorage but they were unable to move. The first mate poured holy water as the ship's captain threw handfuls of gold beads overboard; for good measure, the sailors dumped two palletloads of bananas. The wind seemed to slacken somewhat.

Edward took no chances this time; he kept his trunks and chests full of specimens safely locked in his cabin. The relentless howling of the wind brought on a deafness in his right ear, an affliction Edward first suffered in childhood after swimming in the ocean with his father.

The next morning the sky was blue and the ocean calm as if there had never been a storm. Edward took the opportunity to collect specimens of kelp and seaweeds churned up by the storm before the steamship got under way. As he filled the bottles with salt water and strands of seaweed, he felt a bit more confident the expedition was not entirely wasted; he could not afford to return empty-handed.

Perhaps it was the strain of this worry that triggered the headache that descended on him as he hefted a bucket of kelp and ocean water onto the deck. With the sudden sharp pain over his left eye came a blinding streak of light. He was scarcely able to stopper and label the collection jars before he began to perspire and feel nauseous from the pain over his eye. The headache lasted for two days. The ship's captain sent the steward to administer belladonna, and at one point, the pain was so excruciating Edward begged the steward to put him out of his misery with an overdose. Now as he described the incident to Hattie, he laughed, but Hattie noted the hesitation in his voice. In the fury of the headache he became so disoriented, he believed he was back on the Pará River.

◆ ◆ ◆

"I could smell the burning foliage. I could even feel the broken bone fragments in my leg." Edward took a sip of wine and settled back in his chair across from Hattie.

"At one point, I even imagined my father was in my cabin, smoking a big cigar and laughing at me!"

Hattie smiled. She enjoyed Edward's animated mood. She put a light shawl over her shoulders and they strolled the west terrace arm in arm without speaking. The scent of citrus blossoms suffused the night air and overpowered even the white climbing roses and the lilies. No need to plant scented gardens here, though after a time, one became accustomed to the orange and lemon blossoms. She wanted to plant a garden of scents to contrast the heavy sweetness: wild sage, coriander, basil, rosemary, scented geraniums, and catmint for a start. She saw so many possibilities for the gardens despite the neglect they'd suffered.

Edward's father planted the first citrus groves in Riverside County before the railroad line was completed. But he wasn't a citrus farmer; he called himself a botanist, though he lacked formal training. Edward's father seemed not to care that the family fortune, in decline since statehood and further drained by his obsessive gambling, might easily be renewed with the sale of the sweet oranges by the railroad boxcar to the northeast. Edward's father did not want the bother such business enterprise entailed—orange crates, train schedules, purchase orders bored him.

Instead his father spent all day in the orange groves or in the greenhouses, where he showed Edward the results of his citrus grafts—lemons, grapefruits, and tangerines all grew on the same tree. Every Thursday afternoon found his father at his desk for hours, valise packed and the coachman waiting while he calculated and recalculated his lucky numbers before he left for a weekend of gambling in Long Beach. Edward understood he must never ask to accompany his father.

As a boy, Edward shared his father's enthusiasm for citrus trees; the workshop of the orangery, with its odors of paraffin, sulfur, and damp earth, had been Edward's childhood haunt. The dwarf tangerine trees along the back wall of the red garden were grafts Edward made when he was twelve. Back then, if his mother and sister were in New York, he did not feel as lonely in the greenhouse, surrounded by his mother's orchids.

Edward was seven when she pronounced him old enough to stay with his father. She began her annual summer visit to Long Island with Susan in tow; they took the train the day after Easter because she could not tolerate the dry heat of Riverside in the summer.

For the first few years, Edward dreaded the approach of Ash Wednesday; on Easter Sunday he woke in tears because in a matter of hours his mother and sister would be gone until October. But gradually he learned to overcome the sadness by following his father to the greenhouse or orange groves. His father tolerated him as long as he did not speak unless spoken to. His father's trips to Long Beach or Pasadena occasionally lasted for weeks, and when his father returned, he brought new suitcases full of soiled clothes newly purchased. No one ever spoke about his father's absences, not even after he died during a two-week stint in Pasadena.

A cool wind stirred off the desert, and Hattie pressed herself closer to Edward's side and rested her head lightly against his shoulder. A moment later Edward felt suddenly weary and they went indoors. He was asleep before Hattie came to bed, but after midnight he woke from a dream with a start and sat up in the bed.

In the dream he had been in a narrow bottom bunk in the crew's quarters of a ship. Ocean waves had crushed the sides of the ship and salt water was exploding in all around him. The specimens! He must make sure they were safe. He left Hattie sleeping soundly, to check on the new collections.

One of the containers of seawater had leaked out between Los Angeles and Riverside, and he was concerned about damage to the rare algae. The first thing in the morning, he would send to Los Angeles for fresh seawater. He had not unpacked the dried plant specimens; now he worried they might have been wet by the leaking container of seawater. He dried the sponges before he packed them; if moisture reached them they would rot. He prepared the drying cabinet and took the precaution of opening the specimen envelopes and placed each sponge on top of its envelope for closer inspection. Jacksonville, Lake Okeechobee, St. Johns River, Titusville, Indian River, St. Lucie, Pine Key, Cedar Key, Key West, Cape Florida, Nassau, the Dry Tortugas. He examined each envelope of dried plant material to be certain there was no dampness. Although the hurricane season's early arrival cut short the expedition, he felt confident he had collected an adequate sampling. The Smithsonian Institution and the Bureau of Plant Industry were organizing a joint installation at the World Industrial and Cotton Centennial Exposition in New Orleans the following year. The focus of the exhibit was to be the commerce, industry, and natural history of the Gulf and the Caribbean Sea, with special attention to the commercial and other sponges, the ornamental corals, and the larger species of mollusks and crustaceans fit for human consumption.

Once he was satisfied the specimens were safe, he opened the trunk with his field notebooks and maps marked to pinpoint the locations of each of the specimens collected. After the hurricane season passed, a work party, using his notes and maps, would retrace his steps to collect the large quantities of specimens needed for the displays at the Centennial Exposition. Mr. Talbot showed him the plans. Congress had appropriated $75,000 for elaborate preparations: special curators would bathe the corals and sponges in solutions to preserve and enhance their colors; saltwater display tanks costing hundreds were already being assembled.

The night after his arrival, Hattie woke and saw that Edward was not in bed. Concerned for his health, she went to find him. She noticed light from the third floor study. She did not mean to watch him, but he was so absorbed, she paused in the doorway. What was he doing so intently? He had a wool camp blanket across his lap with the edge of the blanket between the fingers of both hands, examining the blanket inch by inch. Now and then he seemed to find something and pull it free from the wool; then he reached over to a jar on the desk.

She did not disturb him but waited until the next morning to see what he put in the jar. She found delicate grass seed in the shapes of long arrows and others in the shapes of stars. Edward saw her examine the jar.

"Oh those. I wasn't able to finish my collection of grasses but I found some specimens on the blanket."

Something about Edward with his notebooks and specimens in jars awoke Hattie's longing for her books and notes, still packed in the trunks. Despite its rejection by the thesis committee, Hattie still hoped to complete the manuscript. While she was packing for California, one of her notebooks fell open to a page that outlined the teachings of Valentinus, with 365 heavens and 365 different choirs of angels; suddenly she realized how much she missed her work with the old Gnostic texts, so full of exuberant imagination.

The doctor blamed her father's "wild progressivism," as Mother called it, for Hattie's sensitive nervous system. The doctor's orders stipulated that she rest, relax, and avoid intellectual exertion, particularly the overstimulation caused by the reading and writing for her thesis. Her mother blamed the furor over the thesis for another incident so shocking they did not speak about it.

Her father was so proud of Hattie that he accepted any responsibility he might have even for her illness; knowledge did not come without its price. Mr. Abbott planted a white oak tree in the front yard the day Hattie was born. As an ardent student of John Stuart Mill, he believed it was his paternal duty to give Hattie the fullest education possible; so he taught her himself. She was exceptional, he told her, and urged her to look beyond the narrow interests of current feminists—prohibition of alcohol and the vote for women—and look to the greater philosophical questions about free will and God. At Vassar she found the other Catholic women timid or dull, but she disdained the suffragists as well. Hattie preferred her cubicle in the library and the books to the ballroom; she completed her degree with honors in three years.

The peculiarity of Hattie's education separated her entirely from other young women her age. Because Mr. Abbott was a freethinker, Hattie's mother had been adamant about the Saturday afternoon catechism classes at the convent, which were Hattie's only opportunities to socialize with young women her own age. Even after Hattie completed her First Communion and confirmation, her mother continued to send Hattie for religious instruction, in part because Hattie asked to go. Five or six other girls attended the classes, which would have been deadly boring but for old Sister Conrad, who was too deaf to hear them whispering and too eccentric to follow the catechism book.

For years, Sister Conrad had instructed the daughters of prominent families in the creed of the church. The first part of Sister Conrad's classes were too boring to remember; first they stood and prayed in Latin to prove they'd memorized the words, then the old nun talked about goodness and sainthood and heaven. But before long Sister Conrad would drift off the shining virtues to the serious topics, which reddened her big Irish face. Hattie was twelve years old the first time Sister Conrad talked about the devil and the fires in hell, and she was spellbound by the old nun's stories.

Sister Conrad looked each one of them in the eyes as she told stories about the selfish, lying little girls whose behavior was so wicked it caught the attention of the devil himself. Inflamed by their sins, the devil came and hid in their bedrooms—in the closet or under the bed—where he waited to ambush the bad girls. If the sinful girl did not die immediately of fright, then the devil flung her high in the air and let her crash to the floor, where she broke her bones. When Hattie told the devil stories to her father, he appeared concerned and asked if she wanted to stop catechism classes. She quickly said no because she enjoyed her time with girls her own age to gossip and giggle over boys.

Hattie trusted the loving, forgiving God her father described—the God who brought only good to his children and no harm. No devil could harm Hattie—she was confident God loved her too much to allow evil to touch her, and she was curious about the hidden dangers of the world polite people seldom discussed. Her mother's friends whispered about young women who were "ruined," but aware Hattie was nearby, they never disclosed the lurid details.

Sister Conrad dropped hints and made innuendos about "bad girls," who must confess sins of the flesh if they lingered in their warm baths too long. Hattie had no idea what the nun was talking about until she asked the other girls and they told her. Shocked but not surprised, Hattie went home and straight to the library for the set of medical reference books. The chapters on reproduction and childbirth, complete with diagrams and color plates, left Hattie a bit queasy; but she felt sick after her mother described her loss of blood and hours of suffering to bring Hattie into the world! Poor dear! She wasn't able to have more children.

From time to time a Jesuit priest came to lecture them on church history. He was a pale, heavy man who did not look at them but at the wall at the back of the room. Even when a girl raised her hand with a question, the priest stared at a point above her head. The other girls became restless and bored whenever the priest lectured about the dangers of the loss of their immortal souls, but Hattie secretly was thrilled at the drama of the old struggle between God and the devil played out in endless new situations.

The priest began his instruction on the early history of the church with the third day after Christ's crucifixion. Naturally, Jesus' followers were grief-stricken and confused—Hattie felt tears in her eyes as the priest related the event: Mary Magdalene was the first to see the risen Jesus, but Peter refused to believe her. Why would Jesus appear first to a woman like Mary Magdalene? Hattie felt indignant at the injustice; she raised her hand and the Jesuit nodded at her. The other disciples did not like Mary Magdalene, Hattie said; they were jealous of her because of Jesus' regard for her. Boldly Hattie went on: perhaps the reason Jesus appeared to her first was to teach the other disciples a lesson in humility. The Jesuit remained expressionless. A divine mystery, he said; only God knew the answers.

Hattie was fascinated by the early years of the church; heresies sprang up almost as soon as Jesus was crucified. Week after week, the pale Jesuit took them over the great heresies: Gnostic, Arian, Nestorian, Pelagian, Waldensian, Albigensian, Lutheran, Calvinist, and Anglican. The girls made up a singsong chant of the names to memorize them for the quiz. The history of church heresy was far more interesting than the lives of the saints, though the stories of martyrdom by fire and steel were comparable. The other young women in the religion class talked about nothing but young men and marriage; though Hattie was interested, still she preferred books.

At home, Hattie read all the books of mythology she could find. When she finished with Greek, Roman, and Norse mythology, she began to read about the Egyptians. Her interest in archaeology came from her passion for hidden tombs and mummies. She loved to read Shakespeare's plays— weepy Richard II and malevolent Richard III were favorites; suave, brilliant Lucifer of Milton's *Paradise Lost* captivated her.

Her mother insisted she take riding lessons for the benefits of fresh air and sunshine; she wanted Hattie to develop normal interests and hobbies to take her away from her books long enough to find a suitable husband.

She galloped her pony in the dunes above the bay; she loved the rush of the wind in her face and the sensation of flying above the powerful muscles of the horse. Her father sent along a groom at a discreet distance in case of a fall; otherwise Hattie rode alone. A ride along the beach cleared the mind and allowed completely new ideas to spring up. She loved to imagine she was Joan of Arc riding to battle or a knight of the Crusades.

By the time she completed her studies under her father's direction and departed for college, Hattie had exhausted their own library of books about early Christianity. They saw two white swans and a black swan from the train window on their way to Poughkeepsie to settle Hattie at Vassar.

Hattie completed her course work with honors in three years; Mr. Abbott spoke with pride about Hattie's interest in the early church and her desire to continue with graduate studies. A Harvard graduate himself, Mr. Abbott arranged with the Divinity School to allow Hattie to attend lectures as a nondegree student until she proved she was capable of distinguished graduate work.

Mrs. Abbott did not share her husband's enthusiasm for Hattie's continued education; she feared Hattie's reputation might be compromised. How many respectable gentlemen wanted scholars of heresy for wives? Why must she go to Harvard when Columbia was so much closer? But Mrs. Abbott knew when she was outnumbered and graciously accompanied Hattie to the comfortable town house rented near Harvard Square. Mr. Abbott intended to stay home in Oyster Bay with his wind power experiments, but loneliness quickly sent him to them, accompanied by the cook and coachman.

Hattie's father contacted his old friend Dr. Rhinehart in Cambridge and arranged for Hattie to use his private library from time to time. A scholar of ancient Coptic manuscripts, Dr. Rhinehart's library of texts and treatises of early church history was remarkable, an equal of Harvard's collection; Hattie was delighted.

Months later the doctor blamed the overstimulation of the lectures in the presence of young gentlemen for Hattie's illness. The doctor confided to Mrs. Abbott that he treated many more nervous disorders in young women since the advent of Margaret Fuller, Mrs. Eddy, and the like. But Hattie thought her illness seemed quite natural in view of the incidents that preceeded it.

Dr. Rhinehart's library surpassed Hattie's expectations. The sight of so many ancient scrolls in glass cases, and folios of early church history shelved from the ceiling to the floor, took away Hattie's breath. She was silent as she moved around the shelves to savor the scent of leather bindings and glue. The beauty of the bindings caught her attention; the arrangement of the books on the shelves was precise but not by author or title or time period. Here and there volumes bound in red leather and saffron vellum were clustered together amid volumes of fawn, chocolate, and hunter green leather; bindings of black leather formed borders, so the effect was of a lovely strange garden.

From his study, Dr. Rhinehart brought out an armload of leather-bound manuscripts and stacked them on the library table near Hattie. He invited her to read at her leisure his translations of the old Coptic scrolls that were his life's work. She thanked the kind doctor and promised to return as soon as she settled into her classes. The graduate lectures included long reading lists, so the first semester she limited herself to a lecture course on the Crusades and a seminar on heresy. Both classes demanded a great deal of reading and preparation; weeks passed and Hattie was still too busy to return to Dr. Rhinehart's library.

The lectures on the Crusades were exciting, but disturbing as well because of the bloodshed. The seminar on heresy was as fascinating as Hattie hoped it would be. Christ was scarcely in his grave before the first heresies sprang up. As the semester progressed, she found the Gnostic heretics the most interesting and thought she might find a worthy subject for her thesis. Whether she was granted graduate student status depended in large part on the thesis topic she chose; of course, her father thought she should write her book and not bother about a graduate degree.

The Gnostic heretic Basilides was really quite wonderful. He preached Jesus was not crucified, that Simon of Cyrene took on Jesus' appearance and carried the cross and died instead. Basilides believed Jesus came to redeem mankind with the light of divine goodness, but since the material world is full of suffering and evil, Jesus assumed a phantom body that appeared normal but was of heavenly, immaterial origin.

Lecture after lecture Hattie discovered heresies and heretics never mentioned in catechism class, such as Simon Magus, the Samaritan Messiah, who claimed to be the chief emanation of the Deity and was reputed to be the author of a lost gospel, the *Great Revelations*.

The Gnostic Cerinthus taught the world was not made by God but by a power remotely distant from him. He looked forward to a millennium when a Messiah would rule for a thousand years of peace. Carpocrates, a follower of Cerinthus, taught the world was made by six angels, and all believers are equal with Christ; man could be free of vice and sin only after enslavement to vice and sin.

What would the pale Jesuit say if he could see Hattie now? She knew Sister Conrad would have declared her immortal soul in jeopardy! For her first paper, Hattie wrote about the origins of Illuminism, preached by Valentinus, who said he received secret instruction about the secret doctrine of God. "May you be illumined by the Light" was the greeting of his followers to one another. The Illuminists appeared first in Spain with Priscillianus, who preached special enlightenment directly from God, which naturally caused a furor. The Spanish bishops persuaded the emperor Maximus to condemn Pricillianus to death, but Martin, bishop of Tours, who was present at Trier, protested the heretic's punishment by state authorities and insisted excommunication was enough. Martin refused to leave the city until the emperor promised to spare Priscillianus, but as soon as Martin left, the bishops persuaded the emperor to behead Priscillianus and one of his followers. In her concluding remarks, Hattie asserted that A.D. 385 marked the first time the church invited the state to meddle in church business, but not the last.

When the paper was returned to her she found extensive notes from the professor in a tiny cramped script in the margins. Her paper was well written, he said, but her conclusions were impetuous and unsound, and might even be mistaken for an indictment of the Spanish bishops for Priscillianus's execution. Moreover, her paper allowed the possibility that God did give secret knowledge denied to the church hierarchy; that was heresy, pure and simple.

While Hattie was looking over the comments on her paper, she was aware that Mr. Hyslop in the next chair seemed quite interested. Mr. Hyslop was the first of her classmates to introduce himself, polite and even hospitable while the other students continued to ignore her. She glanced up and smiled, but gave him no further notice while she considered the B her paper received.

After class, Mr. Hyslop waited outside on the steps for her and reminded her they had two classes together—heresy and the Crusades, he said with a chuckle. Hattie liked his bright blue eyes but felt her face flush, so she looked down at the steps. The others might feign indifference to her, he said, but they all knew her name because she was the only woman to audit classes that semester. A Presbyterian himself, Mr. Hyslop thought it quite amazing that a Roman Catholic, never mind a woman, was attending Divinity School lectures.

But Hattie didn't even flinch the morning the lecturer asserted that the Crusades were a disaster for Christianity. Afterward, she told Mr. Hyslop she agreed: the Crusades accustomed Christians to killing for the sake of religion. She relaxed as they moved down the sidewalk under the trees away from the lecture hall.

Two women audited classes the year before, he said, and both were quite good students. Hattie replied she certainly hoped the women were good students—why else should they bother to audit classes? Mr. Hyslop's face became bright red. Just then they reached the end of the walk, where the Abbotts' carriage waited each afternoon. The young man stood awkwardly with his hat in his hand as the driver opened the door for her. Hattie called out, "Good afternoon," to him as she stepped into the carriage, and he blushed and waved as they drove away.

For her second paper in the heresy seminar, Hattie wrote about the followers of Valentinus, who prayed to the Mother as the mythic eternal Silence and Grace, who is before all things and is incorruptible Wisdom, Sophia. Valentinus said those who listened to their guardian angels would have knowledge revealed to them because their angels could not enjoy eternal bliss without them. He taught the material world and the physical body are only temporary; thus, there are no sins of the flesh, and no sacrament of marriage is necessary either, since the spirit was everything.

Hattie's attention focused on the equal status accorded the feminine principle in Gnostic Christian tradition. She researched other instances of the equality of the feminine element and discovered the Ophites, who believed the light, or glory, of God is without equal and Christ will reign for 365,000 years. The thrones of the twelve disciples will be near his throne, but the thrones of Mary Magdalene and John the Virgin will be higher than the thrones of the disciples. Amazing! Hattie thought. Fantastic, remarkable. The heresy was plain to see, and yet she was spellbound.

Marcion became another of Hattie's favorites. After he and his followers were expelled from the church, Marcion established his own church, thus adding the sin of schism to heresy. He claimed to preach a purer Christianity than the orthodox Christians, and he and his followers were called the Dissenters. They believed in a supreme God of pure benevolence, not found in the Old Testament; the Just God of the Old Testament was a creating power with anger, jealousy, and the urge to punish, while the God of the New Testament was a Kind God, who sent his Son to rescue mankind. Those loyal to the Just God were inspired by him to crucify Jesus, but this act brought the defeat of their God, who acknowledged his sin in killing Jesus out of ignorance. The Just God was punished by losing all the souls of his followers, who embraced the Kind God. Thus mankind was saved by Jesus' crucifixion, and all that was required for salvation was a belief in God's love. Aha! Hattie thought, and composed her conclusions: Marcion's teachings rendered the orthodox church useless; no need for punishment if there are no laws, only God's love. No need for church hierarchs, or tithes either.

Hattie was curious to read more, but from the pens of the Gnostics themselves; she sent a note around to Dr. Rhinehart, who was about to leave town but was delighted to instruct his household staff to let Hattie into the library and to see to her every need. She opened the first volume of the translations to this passage:

Abandon the search for God and other matters of a similar sort. Look for him by taking yourself as the starting point. Learn who is within you who makes everything his own and says: My God, my mind, my thoughts, my soul, my body. Learn the sources of sorrow, joy, love, hate. If you carefully investigate these matters you will find him in yourself.

Hattie experienced a wonderful sense of pleasure and excitement to find such bold words in the old doctor's translation. As she continued to leaf through the manuscripts, Hattie was astonished to read:

> After a day of rest, Wisdom, Sophia, sent Zoe, Life, her daughter who is called Eve, as an instructor to raise up Adam. . . . When Eve saw Adam cast down and she pitied him and said, "Adam, live! Rise up upon the Earth!" immediately her word became deed. For when Adam rose up, immediately he opened his eyes. When he saw her he said, "You will be called the mother of the living because you are the one who gave me life. . . ." It is she who is the Physician, and the Woman and She who has given birth. . . . the Female Spiritual Principle came in the Snake, the Instructor, and it taught them, saying, "You shall not die; for it was out of jealousy He said that to you. Rather your eyes shall open and you shall become like gods, recognizing evil and good. . . ." And the arrogant Ruler cursed the Woman and the Snake. . . .

At that moment Hattie knew her master's thesis must explore further this female spiritual principle in the early church.

Hattie had difficulty falling asleep because her mind was abuzz with ideas for her thesis. She slept fitfully, and the following morning she woke and realized something felt very different about the world, though both she and the world appeared the same as they had been the previous morning. The names Sophia, Zoe, and Eve came to her again and again like a nursery rhyme, and when she glanced at the small marble *Pietà* on the foyer table, the words "Adam, live! Rise up upon the Earth!" came to mind. On her way to class, as it did every day, the carriage passed the church with the life-size bronze of Christ on the cross; but this morning Hattie found herself scrutinizing the figure. This bronze Jesus was well fed and his posture more relaxed than tortured; the expression on the face was one of peace, even satisfaction. Was this actually Simon of Cyrene, at peace, relieved that he managed to spare Jesus the crucifixion?

The thesis committee declined Hattie's proposed thesis topic, "The Female Principle in the Early Church," and the dean of graduate programs concurred with their decision. Hattie's proposed research materials and corroborating texts were deemed inadequate. Dr. Rhinehart's translations from the Coptic were impeccable, but there was as yet no reliable documentation to authenticate the papyrus scrolls. Little or nothing had been written about the feminine principle, wrote one committee member, "because it was a peripheral detail, too minor to merit much scholarly attention." Still, the committee might have entertained her proposed thesis topic had Miss Abbott *not* rejected all reliable authorities and texts in favor of odd forgeries of old heresies.

Both Dr. Rhinehart and her father warned her from the start it was unlikely the committee could be persuaded of the scrolls' authenticity. Her father cautioned that the scholars of early church history were quite conservative, and she was bound to be disappointed. But the worst of it was the casual suggestion by the Divinity School dean that Miss Abbott should attend the Metaphysical College operated by Mary Baker Eddy in Boston. Hattie was furious to be linked with Mrs. Eddy or her "healer," Phineas P. Quimby. Hattie felt she had been dismissed as a suffragist, but her mother feared far worse—that Hattie was bound to be linked to Margaret Fuller, notorious advocate of free love. More than once, acquaintances of Mrs. Abbott compared Hattie's precocity and ambition to Mrs. Eddy or Miss Fuller, which caused Mrs. Abbott to exclaim she was sure a compliment was intended, however she really must point out Mrs. Eddy was not Catholic and Miss Fuller was not even a Christian and was quite dead.

Though she had been aloof from most of the other Vassar women, still she felt cozy in the classrooms with other women. But at Harvard the atmosphere was far different. The decisions of the thesis committee were to remain confidential, yet news of Hattie's rejected thesis topic leaked out at once to humiliate her. The eyes of the other students no longer were averted from her; there were whispers and smiles because the worst of her proposed thesis had been its conclusion, that Jesus himself made Mary Magdalene and other women apostles in the early church!

As for the behavior of Mr. Hyslop after the committee's decision, Hattie greatly misjudged his character; he was not the gentleman or Christian he appeared to be. From the start, all had proceeded properly enough, and Hattie welcomed his companionship in class and their discussions after class. But Hattie should have been alerted to Mr. Hyslop's intentions when he compared Hattie's ambitious thesis topic to the "lofty and spiritual ambitions" of Margaret Fuller. At the time, Hattie politely assumed Mr. Hyslop's comparison of her to Miss Fuller was strictly limited to intellect and ambition; after all, the Fuller woman shocked polite society with her endorsement of free love and her premarital pregnancy.

Later Hattie realized there was a great deal about Mr. Hyslop that she misunderstood or, worse, that she had imagined for her own comfort. She assumed he was trustworthy because they shared class notes and compared grades and had exhilarating discussions after class. Although he did not seriously challenge the church canons (his thesis topic concerned Irenaeus and the Coptic Christian Church), on numerous occasions he expressed his respect and admiration for her scholarship. But Mr. Hyslop was not honest with her or himself.

In the days that followed the committee's decision, Hyslop began in good form with a gentleman's solicitude after the seminar, consoling her for the rebuff. The glorious spring morning looked so inviting Hattie arranged to walk the short distance home after class. As she and Mr. Hyslop chatted under the big oak tree along the Commons walk, a breeze came off the river and sent yellow blossoms fluttering across the lawn as rain showers drifted in front of the sun. Mr. Hyslop saw she carried no umbrella and kindly offered her a ride home in his coach, which seemed harmless enough, since Mr. Hyslop intended to enter the ministry upon graduation.

But they were no sooner in the shade of the giant oaks along the park drive when Mr. Hyslop oddly complained of the sunlight and closed the coach curtain next to himself, then excused himself and leaned in front of Hattie to reach the curtain next to her. The instant the curtains were closed, Mr. Hyslop suddenly embraced Hattie. He pinned her against the seat with his chest and shoulders, while one hand sought to pull her around to face him and the other hand fumbled, then grabbed her right breast with the cloth of her dress. Too startled to scream, Hattie struggled and twisted away while she gave him a good kick in his ankle. Her dress was askew and her hair pulled loose from the pins. She retreated to the far corner of the carriage seat with her heart pounding and angrily opened the curtain next to her. She stared out at the activity in the park though she scarcely saw anything, she was so shaken. Hattie waited for Mr. Hyslop's litany of apologies to begin momentarily, but she was further shakened after he remained silent and strangely aloof. Hattie felt the blood rush to her cheeks when she realized that Mr. Hyslop was angry with her for disappointing his expectations!

She immediately signaled the driver to stop and left Hyslop without another word. Tears filled her eyes as she hurried home through the park in the rainy mist. She rearranged her hair as best she could and glanced around to see if any of the picnickers or people strolling with their dogs had witnessed her hasty exit from the carriage; but no one seemed to have noticed. While her confidence in her entire life and her very being were changed forever, ordinary life went on without cease.

Lucille opened the front door, took one look at Hattie, and knew immediately what had happened. "Oh honey! He didn't hurt you, did he?"

Hattie shook her head, but tears filled her eyes as Lucille embraced her gently.

"Please don't tell Mother," Hattie whispered. "I'm only shaken up." After she fell ill, Lucille had to tell Mrs. Abbott, and Hattie admitted Mr. Hyslop's crime.

The door latch seemed stuck, or maybe she misunderstood how this one worked. There were so many different sorts of door latches at the school, and now here—press down, lift up, twist left, twist right. Indigo put her face close to the glass door and peered inside. At first the objects she saw made no sense to her; then she noticed identical red clay pots with strange skeletons and dried remains of plants all lined up in rows on the floor. She could not see clearly, but there were vines of green leaves and hanging pods of white flowers that formed a canopy above everything in the glass house.

She wasted no more effort on the door latch because all the slanting windows were open, just wide enough that if Indigo lay on her back and made herself as flat as possible, she could get in. As she rolled in, she noticed the warmth and dampness with the wonderful odor of rich earth; there was an odd animal smell as well. The light inside surprised her with its brightness despite the canopy of vines. The smooth gray branches snaked across and enclosed the ceiling entirely and had begun to push outside through the open vent windows in the ceiling. She saw a flash of motion out of the corner of her eye and turned; it was the little hairy man, jumping from side to side of a big cage. The polished brass cage filled the entire east end of the glass house; near the cage, draped with long wisteria blossoms, Indigo noticed a bench carved out of white stone.

"Hello," she said softly as she approached the cage. "I know you want to get out." She recognized the latch on the cage door was a close relative of the brass latches on the school's closets. Out he came, chattering his gratitude. He wrapped his long curling tail around the bars of the cage to steady himself as they studied each other closely. He had shining golden eyes and he seemed to understand the language of the Sand Lizard people when she spoke to him.

"I'm hungry. Is there anything to eat?"

The monkey blinked its eyes and rubbed its hand on its thigh; it looked down inside the cage and Indigo saw the crockery bowls, one full of water, the other with the remains of chopped vegetables and fruit sprinkled with shelled nuts. The monkey looked over its shoulder at Indigo eating from his bowl, then gleefully bounded up the outside of the cage and disappeared into the wisteria. While she ate, she listened to the rustle of the branches and leaves overhead; then a twig of blossoms dropped on the stone floor next to her. She glanced up but saw nothing. Behind her another twig of pendulous blossoms fell, then another and another; as Indigo reached down to pick up a twig, she felt something thud against her back. This time when she looked up she saw bright eyes in the leaves and she laughed. Her mouth and face felt odd; the sounds she made seemed strange because she had not laughed out loud for a long time. Her laughter delighted the little monkey, who raced through the vine canopy throwing down the fragrant blossoms until the gray stone floor was nearly covered.

They played hide-and-seek among the long rows of benches—most were empty, but a number of them were lined with clay pots of shriveled stalks and leaves. They took turns; the monkey hid first. After she found him, she ran as fast as she could and crawled under one of the wicker chairs by the table, where she lay motionless until she felt his little hands pat her on the back. She got up and sat on the wicker settee to rest; the monkey climbed up and sat beside her. She looked around at the glass house and wished Sister Salt could be here to see it for herself; otherwise she might not believe it when Indigo told her.

Indigo laid her head against the arm of the settee and the monkey laid his head against the other arm of the settee. She knew she had to find a place to hide before she fell asleep. Just then the monkey jumped up and stood on the back of the wicker settee; he looked at the door and rubbed his hands together anxiously. Indigo jumped to her feet and ran to the farthest end of the glass house and looked around desperately for cover. She heard the footsteps and then the sound of the door latch, and she had no choice but to crawl over the dead plants in their clay pots and lie facedown as flat as she could make herself so the rows of clay pots and shade might conceal her.

Hattie was unpacking a box of books in her study when she heard Edward call her name. She hurried to the stairs, where Edward met her with a perplexed expression. Had she fastened the latch on the monkey's cage yesterday? Hattie was irritated that Edward thought she had not properly secured the cage door, but she knew the monkey meant a great deal to him.

He had been out there just now and found the monkey loose in the wisteria, scattering leaves and vines inside the greenhouse. Edward held an empty crockery bowl; the monkey was out of water.

"Oh no!" Hattie put her hand to her cheek. "That can't be! I filled the bowl with water myself!" She hurried down the stairs and out to the conservatory.

Wilting wisteria blossoms and leaves were strewn all over the floor, and over the benches and old clay pots as well. No harm; the wisteria thrived on severe pruning, and the monkey had only done a bit of thinning. The monkey sat on the top of the cage with his head in the wisteria leaves and refused to come down. Hattie stepped inside the cage and was surprised to see no bits of fruit or vegetable peelings on the cage bottom, where the monkey fastidiously tossed all refuse.

Edward brought a handful of peanuts and waved it invitingly at the monkey, but the little creature refused to come to him.

"Linnaeus! Come down! Come! Linnaeus!" Edward stood on a rattan chair to reach the handful of peanuts higher but the monkey scampered away into the thick green canopy.

"This isn't like him at all!" Edward continued. "I don't understand it." Hattie turned to Edward.

"I know what it might be," she said, and she began to walk slowly and look under the benches. "Linnaeus has found a new friend." Edward smiled and nodded his head. Of course, he should have guessed from the start; the little Indian had opened the cage to take the monkey's food and water.

Edward did not want to crawl under the benches among the clay pots to reach the Indian child. He left Hattie to watch that the Indian child did not escape while he sent the cook in the buggy to alert the boarding school superintendent. Although the child had remained motionless since Hattie first spotted her, Hattie could hear the child's fast shallow breathing.

"Please don't be afraid," Hattie said softly. "Nobody will harm you. Please come out. I won't let them hurt you." The monkey climbed down the bars of the cage and crept along under the benches until he was next to the child. Hattie smiled.

"I understand, Linnaeus; she is your friend."

Edward returned after a time with a short length of rope.

"No need for that," Hattie said. "Linnaeus came down of his own accord. He's under there with the child." Edward squatted with the rope in his hands and peered intently under the bench into the mess of pots and debris, and Hattie realized the rope was intended for the child.

"Please, Edward, she hasn't moved. She can't get away. Let's wait until the school authorities come." Hattie took his arm and nodded her head in the direction of a white marble bench strewn with ripped-up wisteria leaves and blossoms. Edward let the rope drop to the floor before he joined her. She appeared upset with him, so he apologized at once. He never meant to imply she neglected the monkey. She wasn't so sensitive as that, Hattie replied; she was concerned about the Indian child. The rope really was beyond the limit!

The rope had been only a precaution—for the child's own good, so that she did not escape and flee into the desert, Edward persisted. Riverside people were familiar with runaways from the Indian school; Hattie had no experience with Indians—certainly not these wild Indians.

Edward took his watch from its pocket. What was taking so long? The boarding school was only two miles down the road. Edward went up to the house to see what had become of the cook and the message to the school authorities.

After Edward shut the door behind him, Hattie sat very still and waited; after a time, she watched the child lift her head to look around. The monkey came out from under the bench first, followed by the child, on her hands and knees, who then stood up. They both ignored Hattie as they marched up the middle aisle of the glass house to the monkey's cage, only a few feet from the marble bench.

She watched the monkey and child sit side by side on the monkey's straw mat, where they took turns rolling the monkey's toy ball to each other. Both the child and the animal seemed to know their holiday together would soon end. A terrible wave of sadness and hopelessness welled up in Hattie, more overwhelming than anything she had felt during the thesis scandal, and her eyes filled with tears. She might not know much about "wild Indians" but she did know they were human beings.

An unaccustomed anger sprang up inside her at that instant, and Hattie became determined the child would not be bound and dragged away like a criminal. She was still angry at the tone of voice Edward had used with her earlier, despite his apology. His tone revealed something disturbing about his impression of her—something she could not yet identify.

Edward returned with an expression of frustration on his face. The school superintendent was away until the following week, and only the janitors and gardeners were on the premises. Any remaining students had been sent home for the summer or placed with local families to work until school started again. The dormitories were closed. The monkey and the child watched Edward's every motion as he explained the Riverside sheriff would take the child until the superintendent returned next week.

Hattie was incredulous that the school personnel so quickly called off their search for the missing child, even if it was the end of the school term. Edward reminded her the school personnel were government employees. Besides, the Indian students ran away constantly. Hattie was not persuaded. The child was too young to simply abandon! It was outrageous! It was criminal. Anything might happen to a child, especially a girl! Hattie noticed Edward's surprise at the vehemence of her words, but she did not feel ashamed, she felt fierce. The Indian child meant nothing but trouble to the school authorities; they didn't care if she was lost or died—that meant one less Indian they had to feed.

"At least she can stay here with us until the school superintendent returns next week," Hattie said in a more controlled voice.

Edward was too surprised by Hattie's display of emotion to argue, although he expressed concern the child might flee before the school authorities returned. Staff personnel at the school had warned him about the girl. She was from one of those renegade bands of desert Indians. She was a wild one.

"Does she speak any English?" Hattie asked. Edward shrugged.

"I wonder how old she is. What would you say?"

This time Edward smiled and shook his head. "You'd be a better judge than I." They both were looking at the child, who sat solemnly on the monkey's mat watching them; the monkey sat quietly beside her.

"We can't leave her here," Hattie said,

The child could stay in one of the spare bedrooms until the authorities came for her. Edward was so relieved that Hattie was no longer upset, he failed to mention the Indian boys he hired from the school always slept on pallets in the tack room.

Edward was annoyed at the sullen expression on the cook's face when he asked her to prepare the spare room for the child. She muttered under her breath about being murdered in her sleep, and Edward recalled the cook used to fear that the Indian boys would leap up from their weeding and shoveling to ravish her.

After Edward left, the monkey came out of the cage and approached Hattie confidently. It hopped up on the end of the marble bench and sat down beside her to examine the lace inset in the arm of her dress. Hattie sat very still while the monkey carefully fingered the delicate threads of the lace.

"Linnaeus, you are a darling creature!" she said as she gently stroked the fur on his back. "I wonder, does your friend over there speak any English?" Hattie watched the girl's facial expression for any shift that might indicate she understood Hattie's remarks, but saw none. The sun was overhead now and the heat inside the greenhouse was quite noticeable; the glass panels badly needed a fresh coat of whitewash. Hattie stood up with the monkey in her arms and walked over to the door of the cage. The child's dark eyes fixed on her every move. Hattie smiled and knelt down; the monkey went over to the child and took her hand as if to lead her to Hattie, but the child stayed put.

Edward returned with a volume of linguistic surveys of various desert Indian tribes. He stood with Hattie at the door of the cage and began to attempt to pronounce words in Shoshone and Paiute to see if the child responded. All this time she had not moved from her place on the monkey's pallet inside the cage. Edward went through the Agua Caliente and Cocopa words and was just beginning to struggle with words in Mojave when a big smile spread across the girl's face and she laughed out loud. The monkey chattered excitedly and climbed to the cage top. The girl stood up and looked down at them confidently.

"I talk English," Indigo said. "I talk it way better than you talk Indian."

All morning Indigo had listened closely whenever the man and woman spoke, and she realized she understood English better than ever; there were only a few big words now she didn't recognize. The monkey made it clear the woman was a friend of his. The appearance of the length of rope had alarmed Indigo, but the woman's words caused the man to drop the rope; the woman's words gave Indigo the confidence to speak.

"Yes, you speak English very well," Hattie said, amused at the child's sudden boldness. Edward looked at the child and then at the photographs of the Indians of various tribes in the book. He tried to determine which tribe the child came from, but the school stripped the children of all evidence of their particular tribes.

Indigo had intended to stay only three or four nights until the people least expected an escape. But the monkey did not want her to begin the journey yet; it was too hot and she would die along the way. The monkey sensed the approach of the desert heat. Hadn't they taught her any better than that? Yes, she told the monkey; Grandma Fleet always said it was best to wait for cool weather to travel.

Every morning she was up and washed and dressed as Hattie taught her; then she hurried down the stairs and out to the glass house to open Linnaeus's cage. They walked in silence through the terraces and gardens in the vivid yellow light after the dawn. The air was warm and would get warmer as the sun rose. They washed in the water lily pool below the fountain and strolled down the steps to the back of the property to pick ripe oranges for breakfast. The monkey had strong fingers and was able to peel his orange and consume it before Indigo had eaten half of her orange. The monkey went into the branches and found ripe oranges heavy with juice. The monkey carried his oranges in the crook of each arm; he and Indigo ate them later in the afternoon. Indigo used the skirts of her dress to carry oranges for herself and for Hattie and Mr. Palmer.

Hattie permitted Indigo to pull the bedcovers off to make a bed on the floor after Indigo told her that she was terrified she would fall. At the school they had tied her in her bed to stop her from sleeping on the floor, and that night Indigo had screamed until she was soaked with sweat. Indigo dreamed the red garden and the white garden were growing in the dunes and Mama and Grandma Fleet and Sister Salt were all there with her. They were all so happy with her because she brought back so many interesting seeds.

Every morning Indigo and the monkey brought the oranges to the breakfast table, where the monkey offered an orange to Hattie, who bowed to the monkey as she accepted it; then the monkey went to Edward, who also bowed formally to the monkey as he accepted an orange. Hattie loved the child's vivid imagination and the make-believe with the monkey; Edward was impressed as well with the rapport the child developed with the creature, and although he was a bit stiff with his formal bow to a monkey, even the monkey joined in the laughter they shared on this occasion.

The lovely morning ritual included breakfast, then more wandering through the gardens, where Edward described the years his mother had spent designing and supervising the plantings that once had thrived there. So many of the more delicate plants and shrubs had died of neglect in the years since his mother's death. Hattie took her notebook along and the child gravely held one end of the measuring tape while Edward held the other. Hattie described her ideas for each of the terraces and gardens and for the lawn and lilac arcades, and made notes of the places she wished to make new plantings. Edward felt a contentment he had seldom experienced, as he spent the morning with Hattie and the child, and the afternoons with his specimens and correspondence.

He understood Hattie's reluctance to travel when they were so comfortable where they were, but the letters from Lowe & Company made it quite clear what must done. The night before the child was to return to the school, Hattie asked Edward how he had arranged for the Indian boys to work for him last summer.

It wasn't difficult, he explained. The school superintendent encouraged the summer placement of students in proper, upright homes because too often promising students went home for the summer and failed to return.

"Please, Edward," she said, placing her hand gently on his arm, "arrange for Indigo to stay with us for the summer."

"But we are leaving for New York in a matter of weeks," he reminded her.

"I feel as if I've barely just arrived. I only began to unpack my books last week."

Edward reminded her how disappointed her parents would be if he arrived alone. What would he tell everyone?

Tell them the truth, Hattie said briskly. The journey by train was exhausting.

Edward did not pursue the matter, because he sensed her opposition strengthen when he pressed further. He wanted very much for Hattie to accompany him. Her presence on the Corsica trip would assure success. He knew only too well from past experience, British or American men who traveled alone aroused suspicion in local authorities and villagers, who refused even to speak to a foreigner, much less permit him to approach their gardens or orchards.

Though reluctant to travel abroad, still Hattie had been agreeable to the trip until the Indian child appeared; now she made it quite clear her intention was to stay in Riverside unless the child came along. Actually, now that he thought about it, he realized the child would be an asset in Corsica; the natives adored children.

The following morning Edward spoke with the school superintendent. He learned the child was an orphan from the remnants of an unknown desert tribe in Arizona. The superintendent was concerned over the child's rebellious behavior, but Edward assured him that they would be able to control the girl. The child would accompany his wife as a personal companion and she would be taught to read and write and, of course, the proper etiquette, while in their custody. The school superintendent supplied the necessary documents to travel abroad. The proposed travel was permissible so long as the child was returned safely to the school by October.

Edward was pleased to see how relaxed and happy Hattie was to have the girl with her. In the short time they'd had her, the child adjusted quickly to her new surroundings, although after Hattie tucked her in bed, Indigo dragged the bedding to the floor. Despite her bold words in the beginning, the girl was quiet, content to listen to their conversation without comment. She followed Hattie in the gardens but disliked the house, perhaps because of the cook's hostility. Indigo repeated the names of the plants and shrubs after Hattie, but otherwise she spoke at length only to Linnaeus when they played in the glass house together.

Edward continued to search through his library for ethnological reports on the desert Indians. He was intrigued with the notion that the child might be the last remnant of a tribe now extinct, perhaps a tribe never before studied by anthropologists. He began to read about the known desert Indian cultures of the Mojave Desert and Colorado River basin. He began to compose a list of simple words gleaned from linguists' work with each of the known desert tribes. When the list was complete, Edward asked Hattie to bring the girl up to his study, where he slowly pronounced the words. The child listened and often laughed at Edward; but asked if any of the words were from her language, she shook her head emphatically.

Neither he nor Hattie were able to pronounce the name the child gave them when they asked her what she wished to be called. The papers from the school had listed her only as "girl child," approximate age eleven years; a name was assigned to her before she was sent on the train, but the child refused to answer to it.

One morning when Hattie was walking with her, the child bolted off toward the desert. Hattie's heart pounded for an instant as she feared the child was running away; but almost as quickly she returned with a plant in her hand. She held out the branch of a tall plant with attractive magenta leaves.

"This is the plant I am named for." Hattie took the plant stalk and examined it carefully. Edward did not have to look at the plant long before he identified a variety of desert indigo.

"Indigo," Hattie said to the child. "Your name in English is Indigo."

Hattie's spirits soared once she knew the child was permitted to stay and to travel with them, and she began to talk to Indigo about the wonderful gardens they would see in England and Italy.

A seamstress was hired to sew clothing for the child. Hattie was pleased with the dressmaker's allowances for the child—nothing must fit too tightly, otherwise the child removed the offending garments and went on playing, quite oblivious to her own nakedness. Attempts to locate shoes wide enough to fit the child had not been a success, so she would have to wear the slippers that did fit until they reached New York. The steamer trunks were brought out by the stable man. The constant activity around the house unsettled the monkey. The little creature chattered constantly and could no longer be trusted indoors after it went leaping from bookcase to bookcase, pausing only to send a vase or bookend crashing to the floor. Edward thought the monkey may have remembered the steamer trunk from the Brazilian voyage; the monkey traveled inside the trunk after its cage was smashed open in the storm. The child was deeply affected by the monkey's odd behavior and refused to stand still for a fitting of her new wardrobe, insisting that the new dresses pinched her. She wanted the monkey to sleep with her, and when Hattie explained it was impossible because of fleas, the child crept outside later that night. Hattie got quite a shock when she looked into the child's room before dawn and she was gone—to the glass house to sleep with the monkey curled up next to her.

Whenever Hattie felt about to lose heart over the travel preparations, she turned her thoughts to the gardens they would see. She talked to Indigo about the English gardens and the Italian gardens and all the new flowers and shrubs they would see. Indigo was not convinced; she took Hattie by the hand and walked with her to the red garden to point out that they already had plenty of flowers and shrubs. Hattie had to agree, but added that in England the climate was much different and so the trees, plants, and shrubs also grew much differently there than here. Indigo was going to see all of this for herself, Hattie reminded her. In the last weeks before departure, the child had become quiet and withdrawn, preferring to play with the monkey in the greenhouse. It was plain that the child did not want to part with the monkey; she had asked Hattie three times if the monkey might go along with them.

Each time Hattie had smiled and shook her head gently; she reassured the child that the monkey would be there when they returned.

"Linnaeus would hate the heat and noise—he will be more comfortable and safer if he stays home."

"He might get sad and die if we all leave him," Indigo persisted. Her voice rose perceptibly.

That night she dreamed she was in her bedroom, where she awoke before dawn to the monkey's terrified screams. In the dream Indigo ran to the glass house, where she found the monkey's cage splashed with blood; she nudged something bloody with her foot and realized it was the freshly skinned hide of her beloved Linnaeus. She ran to the kitchen, where the fire in the cookstove crackled as it burned; she heard muffled monkey cries from inside the oven. Just as she opened the heavy oven door the cook strode in with a big butcher knife and grabbed her by the hair and she screamed for Sister Salt and woke herself up.

She crept outside in the dark to the glass house to be certain Linnaeus was safe. The cook hated her most, that was plain, but now the cook hated Linnaeus too, because he was her friend. Indigo hugged Linnaeus and whispered that she would come back for him. She told him her secret: The train was about to take her home; Hattie had told her they were traveling far to the east, just the direction Indigo needed to go, and a few miles west of Needles, when the train slowed down, she was going to jump off the train when the others were asleep. She would find Sister Salt and they would come get Linnaeus and he would live with them and always be safe.

When Hattie found the child in the morning, she was asleep with Linnaeus curled up beside her on his pallet. Hattie discussed the child's fears with Edward, who admitted that he had been taken aback by the ill temper displayed by the cook toward the child. He was confident, as the child learned more of civilized customs, the cook would mind her manners as well. The downstairs maid betrayed no ill feeling, but she had only just been hired when the child appeared. The household staff would benefit from their absence; they would have time to rest and adjust to the changes in the household. Hattie nodded earnestly.

She was concerned about their itinerary now that Indigo was coming along; perhaps it would be wise to reconsider the length of their visit in New York.

"I hoped we might arrange to depart sooner—while the weather for the crossing is still relatively calm. Later in the season the storms arrive—the child would be terrified."

"Yes, of course. I agree absolutely."

Hattie was quite fond of her father and mother, but she was not eager to return so soon to Oyster Bay and the whirl of teas and dinner parties her mother and Edward's sister would organize to honor their visit. During the dinners and festivities that had celebrated their engagement she had commented that she felt she was on display, and Edward reminded her that he was himself a subject of curiosity because of his expeditions abroad.

Hattie felt tears spring into her eyes when she saw the child and the monkey cling to each other as they watched the luggage and trunks carried outside to the coach. She gently guided Indigo and the monkey away from the activity to the shady garden near the glass house, where the maid brought a tray with bread and milk and fresh grapes. Hattie watched the maid's expression as she spread the cloth and set the plates on the lawn in front of the child and the monkey; she was curious to see if the new maid had been poisoned by the cook's ill will toward the child. Hattie was already thinking about the changes in the household she would make after they returned from abroad.

The bulk of the trunks and luggage had already been sent to the train station the day before; now the last few valises were loaded on the coach. As departure time neared, the child held the monkey, who clutched her shoulder tightly; from time to time she whispered to the little creature, which seemed soothed by her words.

Hattie gently lifted Linnaeus from Indigo's arms and gave him to the maid, who smiled and allowed the little creature to perch on her shoulder. Linnaeus wanted to leap into the carriage but the maid gently restrained him. Indigo watched the white girl closely to see if she liked Linnaeus or if she was only pretending. Indigo watched the cook's fat face for a reaction to the maid with the monkey and saw hatred redden her cheeks. The cook needed someone to hate; with Indigo gone, she would hate the monkey and grow to hate the maid by association. Hattie and Edward had taken the young woman aside to reiterate instructions on the care and feeding of the monkey. The maid had been directed to feed Linnaeus and clean his cage each day, and above all, she was to play with him and take him for walks. Hattie explained all this to Indigo so she would not worry about Linnaeus while they were away, but Indigo was not convinced. Just as Edward knelt down to lift Indigo into the coach, she stepped forward and stood directly in front of the cook.

"Don't hurt the monkey," Indigo told her, "or you'll go to jail!"

Edward and Hattie were too shocked to speak, and the cook blushed beet red. There was no more to say. As Edward lifted Indigo into the coach she burst into tears, and Linnaeus began chattering frantically. Edward followed Hattie inside and the coachman shut the door.

Part Three

THE CHILD covered her ears with both hands as the coach pulled away from the gate and the monkey screamed and fought the maid, who held him. Edward pointed out the Indian school as the coach passed by, but the child only buried her face deep in the cushion of the seat. The drive to the train station in downtown Riverside gave Hattie a last chance to ponder their undertaking; if the child became ill or unhappy and uncooperative, the journey might be delayed or even ended. Hattie had not discussed Indigo's future with Edward, but he seemed to understand how attached Hattie had become to the child.

Indigo gripped Hattie's hand tighter and tighter as she smelled the coal smoke and heard the sounds of the locomotive. The sleeping compartments and the little parlor of the train car looked nothing like the train car with wooden benches that Indigo and the other Indian children had ridden.

Not long after the train left Riverside, the waiter brought a tray of covered dishes to the parlor car, where they ate fried chicken and mashed potatoes and gravy while the groves of lemon and orange trees passed outside the window. After lunch, Hattie unpacked a few of the books she'd brought along for herself and the child, *Chapters on Flowers, Shrubs in the Garden and Their Legends,* and for fun, a book of Chinese stories about a monkey. She had packed a small traveler's atlas of Europe to teach Indigo geography.

Indigo knelt on the train seat with her cheek against the window, watching the trees and fences move past. As the sun sank low in the west, the clouds on the horizon blazed with yellow and red light. The train was headed east just as Hattie had promised. Indigo's heart beat faster as she recognized the tall yucca plants from last year, when she watched at the train window all day and all night and memorized the landmarks to get her back home. Indigo asked if she might walk through the train, but Hattie explained that it was not permitted for children to walk about without an adult. They walked the length of the train and back, Indigo walking ahead of Hattie; the passengers stared at the child, then stared at Hattie before returning to the child, who wore her dress very nicely but went about in her stockings without shoes. "A missionary," someone whispered behind them as they passed from the sleeping car to the observation car.

On their walk through the train, Indigo paid close attention to the passageway between the train car doors, to the steps off the train. She watched for familiar terrain—the sandy dunes below darker basalt hills, the creosote bush and burr sage. Then she would know the train was nearing Needles, where it had to stop to take on water and coal. Indigo was so excited she could hardly wait. She knew what she must do to escape.

All afternoon Indigo knelt on the seat for a better view; mile after mile she watched the land change. The lush green of citrus groves began to fade into pale greens and pale yellows of spring grass and wildflowers; a few miles more and there was only the spidery dark green shrubbery of the greasewood that covered the coarse alluvial gravel. The greasewood forest extended in all directions as far as one could see; far, far in the distance through the blue haze of late afternoon, Indigo could barely make out the blue outlines of desert mountains, which she did not recognize.

Just before sundown, the train stopped at a small train depot named San Bernardino to take on extra water and coal for the gradual ascent through the low mountain pass. Edward joined other passengers who took the opportunity to get off the train to stretch their legs. Indigo watched Hattie hopefully, but she was reading a book and only glanced up when the train stopped and when Edward left the car. Indigo stood up and stepped toward the door. Hattie looked up from her book and asked if she needed to use the lavatory. Indigo shook her head. She wanted to get down from the train and walk. Hattie looked out the windows and shook her head. There wasn't time. Edward was about to reboard. The stop was almost over. A moment after Edward reentered the compartment, Indigo felt the train jerk and move forward and they were off again. She knelt on the seat, her face at the window to watch the blue outlines of the mountains in the distance fade into the lavender-blue twilight.

Later there was a knock and the porter entered the compartment and lit the lamps. Hattie closed the volume of early church history by Eusebius.

"Indigo," she said, "how would you like a nice warm bath before dinner?" Indigo shook her head. She had already bathed that morning and she had never heard of any one bathing more than once in the same day unless they fell into something very smelly or very sticky.

Hattie smiled.

"Well, I think a warm bath would feel heavenly," she said as she approached the door to the sleeping compartment. Edward glanced at Indigo, whose eyes never left the window, then he looked at the telegrams and other correspondence on the small table in front of him. Edward smiled and agreed with Hattie, then went back to his writing.

Without Hattie in the room the scratch-scratch of Edward's pen's steel nib and the occasional tink-tink of steel against the glass neck of the ink bottle sounded much louder to Indigo. Occasionally she heard Edward speak softly to himself or to the piece of paper; she was not certain. He seemed very intent, as if he were arguing with the paper. Indigo watched out the window as the little darkness eased herself over the greasewood forest; far behind her, big darkness came. The lamp's light reflection filled the train window and Indigo could not see outside unless she pressed her face against the glass.

Hattie noticed the child's fixed attention out the train window—entirely normal for a child on a train ride. But as they ate dinner, Hattie was surprised to notice Indigo's gaze out the window had only intensified.

"Indigo, what is it that you see out there?" she finally asked. Indigo glanced at Edward, then looked at Hattie and shook her head. In all the excitement and noise of the journey, the child withdrew into herself, just as Hattie feared she might, though Indigo's appetite did not seem to be affected; she ate the roast beef and vegetables on her plate, and when more food was served, it disappeared from the plate in no time. Edward, who complained of a headache from working on correspondence all afternoon, felt restored by the excellent dinner.

As the waiter served their slices of apple pie, they felt the train slow and the conductor called out, "Barstow," a stop for water and coal. For the first time in hours, Indigo turned away from the train window and repeated the name of the stop. Indigo asked the name of the next stop, and Hattie looked to Edward, who reached into his bag and brought out a leather-bound traveler's atlas that he took on all his expeditions. When he found the page, Edward kindly spread open the atlas on the table in front of Indigo and adjusted the lamp wick so there was enough light.

"See," he said, pointing with his forefinger. "Here is the Barstow stop we've just departed, and over here, quite a distance really, is our next stop: Needles." Indigo's heart was pounding as she repeated the word that meant sharp-pointed objects, a good name, all right, for that town, she thought. Indigo was careful not to betray her excitement; she turned back to the window but over and over she repeated "Needles" to herself in rhythm with the train.

She had prepared as best she could for her escape by taking extra slices of roast beef off her plate to wrap in the napkin with the slices of bread. When no one was looking she maneuvered the bundle under her skirt and into her panties next to her belly. Grandma Fleet said always take food along.

After dinner Edward insisted he felt up to another letter or two and proceeded to refill his fountain pen. Indigo remained pressed to the window. Hattie brought out the garden books with the lovely tinted illustrations, but Indigo shook her head without even glancing at the books.

"You must be exhausted," Hattie said. "I'll go see if the trainman made up the berths."

When Hattie gave her the nightgown, Indigo waited until she turned, then slipped it over her head without removing her clothes. She smelled the roast beef against her skin and wondered if Hattie would notice when she came to tuck her into bed. Now came the wait; she knew she must stay awake so she could creep out of the sleeping compartment at the first sensation the train was slowing for a stop. To keep herself awake, Indigo whispered a message to Sister Salt, the same message she sent to Linnaeus: "I love you so much and I miss you too. I send all my love with these words. I'm on my way. I'll see you soon. I am always your sister Indigo." She repeated the words softly until they were a little song that she sang a bit louder each time until Hattie looked in from the parlor car to ask if everything was all right. Indigo pretended she was asleep and did not answer.

After Edward and Hattie got into their berths, Indigo waited until they both were breathing slowly and deeply, then she slipped out of her berth and crept to the door to the parlor compartment. The door opened silently but the latch closed with a loud click. Indigo froze and held her breath, but heard no one stir in the berths. Indigo took her seat in the dark parlor car and watched the stars; no matter how fast the train moved and the earth moved, the stars remained unhurried on their slow journey.

Indigo was asleep when the train jerked and then jerked again and shuddered as the locomotive began to brake for the stop in Needles. Indigo quickly opened the compartment door, looked both ways for the conductor, then stepped out. She made her way to the end of the car to the exit door between the train cars, where the rush of wind smelling of coal smoke and the grind of steel wheels against steel rails engulfed her. She hid behind the luggage rack of valises and trunks to wait.

Her heart was pounding and she felt as if she might wet her pants, but the urge to urinate passed as the train slowed. In the distance she heard a voice call "Needles"; each call became louder as the conductor approached. Indigo closed her eyes and concentrated on the sand lizards she'd watched, then she flattened herself on the floor behind the luggage just as the conductor entered the car. He called out "Needles" loudly as the train jerked and creaked to a halt. Indigo's heart sank further with each bump and brake's squeal—the stops at San Bernardino and Barstow had been far less noisy and bumpy. She knew Hattie and Edward could not possibly sleep through all the racket.

She scrambled out of her hiding place to reach the outer door and the steps to jump from the train as it came to a stop. Just then she heard Hattie call out her name, and the sound of the compartment door, then footsteps behind her. Sweat ran down her chest and back; she had to get out now! Suddenly the conductor stood in front of her; behind her Hattie called her name. Indigo did not turn; she stood facing the exit door until she felt Hattie's hand gently slip over her hand.

Clackety-clack! Clackety-clack! You left home, now you'll never get back. Clackety-clack! Never get back, never get back, get back, get back, the rails sang; even when Indigo put her fingers in her ears she heard the song. She cried until the tears made a wet spot on the pillow. Hattie sat on the edge of her berth and patted Indigo's back.

Indigo sobbed with disappointment in herself; Grandma Fleet would have been so disappointed too, because *she* always managed to escape the first time she tried. Now that she missed her chance at Needles, the train was speeding her farther and farther away from Mama and Sister Salt. Hattie was a nice person, and her husband was OK; Hattie meant well, but she did not understand.

Indigo cried herself to sleep and dreamed she was back at the old gardens. Linnaeus was up in the top branches of a tree helping Grandma Fleet pick apricots. The apricot seedlings had grown greatly in the dream and their branches were heavy with fat orange apricots. Sister Salt and Mama sat in the shade and split open the apricots for drying in the sun. She stayed with them in the dream for a long time because she felt their love for her so strongly. When she awoke, she could still feel their love, powerful as ever, and she was confident she would return to them before long.

Hattie could not get back to sleep. She was thinking about the child.

The superintendent at the Indian school knew so little about her. When they returned from abroad, Hattie planned to make a thorough investigation of Indigo's background. Edward was agreeable; he was actually quite interested himself in rare or extinct Indian cultures. Edward thought it was a coincidence the child tried to get off the train in Needles, but Hattie had seen the expression in Indigo's eyes, and she knew Needles was Indigo's destination.

The next morning Indigo slept past ten o'clock; she was reluctant to get dressed. When she finally raised her arms so Hattie could slip off the nightgown, Hattie saw the reason: Indigo had not undressed the night before. Indigo looked at Hattie, then reached down the front of her skirt and pulled out the stained napkin with the slices of roast beef.

"What's this? Rations for your journey?" Hattie said softly. "Indigo, dear, you'd be all alone."

"No!" Indigo cried as big tears ran down her face. Hattie felt her throat constrict.

"You must be terribly homesick, Indigo. I'm so sorry for you." She reached out to hug Indigo but the child stiffened and turned away angrily.

"Mama and Sister Salt are waiting for me!" Indigo cried. She did not speak for the rest of the day, and sat listlessly on her berth and refused to eat. She felt better when she thought about the Messiah and the dancers. Hadn't their Paiute friend told them that part of the year the Messiah traveled far to the east to find cooler weather? At that moment Indigo felt reassured; although she missed her opportunity to get off the train in Needles, still there was a chance the Messiah and the others were farther to the east anyway.

"Edward," Hattie said as she returned from looking in on the sleeping child, "did the superintendent at the Indian school mention anything about the child having a sister or mother?" Edward removed his reading glasses and rubbed the bridge of his nose with his fingers and shook his head wearily. He had difficulty getting to sleep the night before, then after the child's near escape, he lay wide awake until dawn.

"Indian school employees are not particularly knowledgeable about their students," he explained.

"Poor child! She must have known she was near her home and she—"

"She nearly got herself lost or killed jumping from the train!" Edward interjected. He mopped his forehead with his handkerchief, then opened the window wider for fresh air.

"Are you feeling ill?"

Edward smiled and shook his head. "Too much reading and writing in a jolting coach for an old man. Shall we play a game of gin rummy?" Edward refolded the pages of a letter and put away the letter and the legal-size documents bound in blue manila. Hattie glanced at the papers as he closed up the leather portfolio.

"Has something come up?"

"There's not a thing to worry about," Edward said as he brought out the deck of cards.

"The Pará expedition?"

Edward nodded.

"Wasn't all that settled at the time?"

Edward removed the jokers and shuffled the deck.

"Shall I keep score?"

"Yes, if you will. Here's the pencil."

Edward continued to reshuffle the cards.

The insurance underwriters had indemnified all the investors. Nonetheless a lawsuit had been filed. His attorney even called it a frivolous lawsuit. Edward smiled reassuringly and passed Hattie the deck of cards.

There was a two-hour stop in Albuquerque for a crew change, and Hattie managed to persuade Indigo to accompany them for a stroll in downtown Albuquerque.

"The fresh air will do wonders for us," Hattie said as she brushed Indigo's hair and fastened it with little silver barrettes.

"These used to be mine when I was a girl. Mother made me wear them whenever I rode my horse so my hair didn't tangle."

"A horse?" Indigo knew of men who had horses, but a little girl?

"Yes, I know, my mother was just as shocked. She begged my father not to allow me to ride. But I had so much fun." Indigo put on the kidskin slippers and Hattie arranged Indigo's new straw hat with the ribbons down her back.

Beyond the depot platform Indigo was surprised to see five or six Indian women in the shade of the overhang from the depot roof, with their blankets spread open to display little black-and-white pottery and small willow baskets, not nearly so fine as Grandma Fleet's baskets. Other train passengers were examining the pottery and baskets as they walked past. Indigo stared at the women's faces and at their woven black dresses with red wool sashes, and the black-and-white pottery they made, and thought they must be related to the Hopi people. Hattie noticed Indigo's interest in the women and thought perhaps the child might be comforted to greet people of her own kind. But when Hattie asked Indigo if she wanted to go over to speak to the Indian women, Indigo shook her head and walked faster to hurry past the Indian women, who were busy with sales to the train passengers.

Indigo was relieved to see that none of the Indian women had noticed her, dressed as she was like a white girl. What did Hattie think? Those women were strangers from tribes Indigo knew nothing about; what was she supposed to say to the Indian women? They would see the clothes and hat she wore and they would laugh and say, "What kind of Indian are you?"

They ate lunch in the dining room of Albuquerque's only hotel, where the white people noticed Indigo and stared at her and Hattie and Edward as they walked through the hotel lobby to return to the train. Indigo smiled to herself; in Needles no Indians were allowed in the café or the hotel lobby. Edward found a two-week-old New York newspaper for sale in the smoke shop of the hotel, and Hattie bought a tin box of taffy.

Back on the train, Edward read the newspaper while Hattie and Indigo opened the candy, only to discover the taffy had hardened like bits of rock. Indigo was not discouraged; she showed Hattie how she and Sister Salt ate the hard dried dates, softening them first in their mouths for a long time; she did the same with the hard taffy.

"If Sister Salt is your big sister," Hattie said, "do you have other sisters and brothers?"

"I don't know," Indigo said as she rolled the piece of taffy with her tongue. "Mama might have a new baby by now."

"Indigo," Hattie began in a soft voice, "I want to talk to you about your mother. The records at the school say you were orphaned."

She was no orphan, Indigo assured Hattie confidently. She knew where her mother was, and her sister too. Her mother had escaped with the Messiah and his family and the other dancers into the mountains.

"The Messiah? Who is the Messiah, Indigo?"

Indigo looked into Hattie's blue eyes to see if she was serious, or just teasing.

"You don't know who the Messiah is?"

Hattie shook her head.

"Sure you do. It's Jesus Christ."

"Yes, but the Jesus I know lived very long ago, far across the ocean."

Hattie hesitated before she said Jesus died in Jerusalem. Indigo shook her head; many were fooled by what happened. The Paiute woman told them after the soldiers tried to kill Jesus, he left that place and returned

126

here to his home up in the mountains. He lives there with his family, but sometimes the Messiah takes his family great distances to visit other believers.

Hattie seemed at a loss for words, so Indigo explained: "When the people dance night after night, the Messiah and his family come down to join the people."

The child's vivid imagination lifted Hattie's spirits. She had begun to feel unsettled, though she could not locate the source of her disquiet. Hattie put the lid on the candy tin and opened one of the garden books she had brought along to amuse herself and the child on the long train ride. She looked forward to the new book about sunflowers the bookseller in Los Angeles sent her just before their departure. She brought an old archaeological guide to the stone shrines of the British Isles because the book contained Celtic legends Hattie thought Indigo might enjoy.

Hattie agreed to accompany Edward abroad only because the travel would be very educational for Indigo; she felt responsible to see the child continued to learn reading and writing while in her care. Indigo was absorbed by the gardening book and studied each illustration for a long time before she turned the page. She asked Hattie the English names of the flowers and seemed especially fascinated with the gladiolus, which reproduced itself with clusters of cormlets.

Edward folded the newspaper as Hattie joined him at the little table.

"Anything interesting in the Albuquerque newspaper?"

"Oh, nothing too interesting, really. Your neighbor from Oyster Bay, Mr. Roosevelt, has been mentioned as a possible running mate for McKinley this time around."

"That's interesting. I expected Mr. Roosevelt to settle for nothing short of the presidential nomination." Hattie thought McKinley the worst of the greedy politicians. Edward smiled. She sounded like her father, Edward teased, "Don't forget: the budgets for acquisitions and independent contractors at the Smithsonian and for the Bureau of Plant Industry were quite generous under the McKinley administration."

Hattie laughed. "So I sound like my father, do I?"

Just then the tray of tea and pastries arrived, and Hattie's expression became serious.

"Indigo says she has a mother and an older sister," Hattie began. "As soon as we return, I want to look into this."

But Edward was doubtful. The government required that strict records of the Indians be kept; Indian mothers did not easily part from their children. Hattie glanced over at Indigo, who had started through the book of gardens a second time. The boarding school was run like prison; it was no place for a child as bright as Indigo. Hattie drew herself up straight in the seat. They didn't care the child was lost—they called off the search after only a day!

"Nothing government employees do surprises me," Edward said. "Remember, I've worked with them in the field. The Indian Bureau employees are some of the worst."

◆　◆　◆

The train stopped in Kansas City to change crews, which was enough time for a stroll through the downtown, though the humidity and heat were considerable. While Edward was at the telegraph office, Hattie and Indigo visited the soda fountain next door. Indigo loved the vanilla ice cream but the fizzing bubbles of the soda went up her nose and brought tears to her eyes. They saw a disabled automobile blocking traffic; the freight wagons and buggies jammed the downtown streets.

Indigo had not seen a Negro woman before, only Negro soldiers. She tugged at Hattie's sleeve and pointed at a tall, majestic dark-skinned woman who passed them in a lovely dress of pale yellow cotton trimmed in green satin ribbon; she wore a wonderful yellow felt hat with a single green feather and amazing button-up shoes of pale yellow leather with pearl buttons. As they walked through downtown Kansas City, Indigo saw a number of dark women dressed in satins and silks of the brightest prints and colors. On the streets crowded with people in clothing as ordinary as the dust, the Negro women were as lovely as hollyhock flowers in all their colors. Indigo decided they were more beautiful than white women in their pale colors of gray and beige.

Back on the train just after dark, Hattie pointed out the window to the great Mississippi River, as they crossed over it; but all Indigo saw was an ominous, surging darkness that went on and on like no river she ever saw. Night was the most difficult time; she missed Mama and Sister, and the thought of Linnaeus, alone in the distance and the darkness, made her cry. Her body was so tired of the motion of the train; her back and knees hurt from all the sitting. She lost count of the days they'd been gone. What if Hattie was not able to persuade the school authorities to let her go live with Sister Salt? What if Hattie gave up and left her at the school? The school authorities never intended to let her go home. Tears filled her eyes when she thought of Sister Salt, dragged away with the others considered too old and unruly for school. Yet she could not think of Sister without remembering her fierce will and her quick wits. Sister Salt would escape the first week. Indigo was so proud of her sister that her spirits lifted and she drifted off to sleep, recalling the fun she had with Linnaeus in the red garden with the pomegranate trees.

They changed trains in Chicago in the middle of the night. Indigo awoke as Edward carried her off the train, wrapped in a blanket in her nightgown. She was embarrassed to be close enough to smell Edward—not just the soap he washed with but his odor. He held her lightly as if he were afraid she would break; women carried her differently. She pretended to be asleep and kept her eyes shut tight as they moved along the crowded platforms until they found the train and their car.

Hattie and Indigo spent much of the remainder of the trip in the observation car with the garden books open in their laps as they gazed out the train windows for glimpses of gardens and parks that resembled those illustrated in the books. The closer they came to their destination, the more Hattie's spirits and the spirits of the child soared.

Edward was relieved to have the parlor compartment to himself the better part of the day as he completed the statement his attorney requested concerning the circumstances of the failed expedition on the Pará River. He consulted his journal for the details from the beginning.

This morning the winds on the great river were high and against us; we were obliged to keep in port a great part of the day, which I employed in little excursions round our encampment. The live oaks are of astonishing magnitude, and one tree contains a prodigious quantity of timber, yet comparatively, they are not tall, even in these forests, where, growing on firm ground, in company with others of great altitude (such as Fagus sylvatica, Liquidambar, Magnolia grandiflora, and the high Palm tree), they strive while young to be on an equality with their neighbors.

The journal entries made no mention of the clandestine itinerary of the expedition; indeed, his attorney advised him to maintain his ignorance of Vicks's mission on the Pará River. All final preparations for the expedition had been made by Lowe & Company when Edward received a telegram from Lowe & Company with news of the last-minute changes that were necessary.

Originally the plan called for Edward to travel alone; Lowe & Company was keen on modest overhead with high returns to their investors. Business was conducted discreetly; buyers or their agents made their requests, and Lowe & Company contracted with independent plant hunters like himself to go into the field to obtain the specimens. This time, however, the consortium of prospective buyers insisted their representative, Mr. Eliot, go along.

During his student years Edward financed his tours to distant and exotic locations by the resale of rare plants and other curiosities he found in public markets. From a trip to Honduras he brought home a lovely *Oncidium sphacelatum* for his mother's collection. How delighted she had been as the plant was unpacked and settled in its hanging basket of bark and moss. It was a robust plant with light green leaves; the flower spike that later emerged was nearly three feet long and well branched; the flowers opened in quick succession and lasted for weeks.

His mother had been so excited the morning the first buds opened, she called him to the glass house to see her "dancing ladies" in their yellow ball gowns, bright red vests, and elaborate tiaras of chocolate brown and butter yellow. The orchid thrived and became a special favorite of his mother.

From that time on, when he collected wild orchids for his mother's collection, he brought back a few extra plants to sell to collectors of her acquaintance. His first sale to other collectors had been specimens of *Brassavola nodosa* he brought back from Guatemala. The orchid was always a favorite because of the heavenly fragrance of its odd white flowers resembling wild swans in flight. His mother lost her specimen to overwatering. Sadly, the loss of this orchid was followed by others as his mother compulsively watered the orchids in the days that followed his father's funeral.

Mr. Albert of Lowe & Company assured him the company had complete confidence in him as a field collector of wild orchids; however, due to the substantial sums at stake, the investors had requested their man come along. Edward assumed the man would be one of the hybridizers who wished to go see for himself the natural habitat of the orchids. Although Edward preferred to travel alone, he had no objection to traveling companions. The list of orchid specimens wanted was quite extensive, and Edward could use the assistance.

When he first traveled the jungle rivers twenty years before, a splendid profusion of wild orchid flowers could be seen along the riverbanks, and specimens were easily gathered. But the orchid mania swept in, and though it ebbed, it did not subside; over the years the demand for wild orchids used by hybridizers made the plants increasingly scarce and difficult to obtain.

Ordinarily, Edward made his own travel arrangements at his own expense; he went alone to enjoy the exotic beauties and curiosities in the solitude of the forests and mountains. He brought along a list of plant material desired by his private clients, wealthy collectors in the east and in Europe. The sales of the specimens he collected ensured that he did not deplete his capital. But during 1893, shocking setbacks had occurred for many investors, and Edward suffered significant losses on the stock market. The remote destination and the magnitude of the specimens sought on the Pará River required far more of a cash outlay than he could afford; so Lowe & Company agreed to advance a large sum to outfit the expedition.

Edward was to receive a generous honorarium, and it was understood he might collect as many specimens for himself as he wished, but he was in no position to object to additional members of the expedition. Mr. Eliot might be helpful with the labeling and packing of the specimens.

The other addition to the Pará River expedition was far more unsettling; Mr. Vicks was an Englishman who came by special request of the Department of Agriculture in cooperation with officials at the Kew Gardens. Mr. Albert swore Edward to secrecy because Mr. Vicks was on a special mission for Her Majesty's government and time was of the essence. A virus, rubber tree leaf blight, was destroying Britain's great Far Eastern rubber plantations. Mr. Vicks's mission was to obtain disease-resistant specimens of rubber tree seedlings from their original source, the lowland drainages of the Pará River. It was imperative Kew Gardens obtain specimens that resisted and survived the leaf blight so stricken plantations in the Far East might be replanted with resistant trees. Otherwise the supplies of cheap natural rubber would be lost to England and the United States; Brazil would enjoy a world monopoly of rubber once more.

The problem was, all British horticulturists were denied entry visas to Brazil because twenty-five years earlier, diplomatic feathers had been ruffled when Henry Wickham smuggled seventy thousand rubber tree seeds past Brazilian customs officers to break Brazil's monopoly of natural rubber. Only three thousand seedlings were obtained from the seeds by the Kew Gardens, but they were enough to open up vast rubber plantations in Malaya and Ceylon.

Before Wickham's daring feat, Brazil and her Portuguese godfathers had jealously guarded their rubber monopoly. Twice before Wickham, agents sent out by Kew Gardens were arrested by the Brazilian authorities in possession of hundreds of *Hevea brasiliensis* seedlings. Clever Wickham chartered a riverboat and smuggled the seeds hidden in Indian baskets; for his daring, Wickham was knighted by the queen.

Since that time, any foreigner found in possession of rubber tree seeds or seedlings was arrested immediately. Thus, as an extra precaution, Vicks traveled under a U.S. passport specially prepared for the mission. The Brazilians and Portuguese would be delighted if the British rubber plantations all were destroyed. The leaf blight virus might well restore Brazil's world monopoly on natural rubber.

Mr. Albert assured Edward Mr. Vicks would be no bother; researchers in Surinam learned deserted rubber plantations were the best sources of disease-resistant specimens. While Edward and Mr. Eliot went out to collect orchid specimens, Vicks would travel by canoe to abandoned rubber stations upriver.

The Pará estuaries teemed with unimaginably diverse animal and plant life; monkeys, colorful parrots, and cascades of rare orchid flowers were not all; the Pará River was the only habitat of the *Hevea brasiliensis,* the most important source of natural rubber in the world.

Hevea brasiliensis, the Caoutchouc Tree, the Pará Rubber Tree, sixty to one hundred thirty feet tall in native sites, floodplains in the watersheds of the Amazon and Orinoco Rivers. Leaflets elliptic, two to twenty-four inches long, thick and leathery. Seeds used as food by natives; the milky juice is the best and most important source of natural rubber.

Edward read over his notes with a growing sense of regret; he felt uneasy about additional companions so near the departure, but he trusted the judgment of Mr. Albert and the company, so Edward did not object.

He had more misgivings after his two companions were introduced: Eliot was a large sullen man who might be mistaken for a prizefighter were it not for the finely tailored white linen suit he wore. Vicks was small and dapper, but his eyes did not meet Edward's when they were introduced. Mr. Albert produced the list of the rare orchids they were to collect, and Edward realized Mr. Eliot knew little or nothing about orchids. Eliot interrupted Edward's descriptions of the orchids' habitats to ask frivolous questions about the wet seasons and the dry seasons. The first time Eliot behaved rudely, Edward looked at Mr. Albert, who returned his gaze; after the second interruption Mr. Albert looked down at the list of orchids, cleared his throat, but said nothing.

Mr. Eliot and Mr. Vicks shut themselves in their cabins before the steamship sailed, and Edward did not see them again until St. Augustine, where Mr. Eliot emerged reeking of rum and accompanied the first mate downtown. Mr. Vicks continued to take his meals alone in his cabin. The weather and currents were favorable and the steamship reached Port-of-Spain in near-record time. Edward's misgivings about his companions gradually waned as he savored the beauty of the lush islands of emerald green in a sea of topaz. He stood at the ship's stern for hours on end, damp with ocean mist, to look down at the subtle shifts of color in the transparent water until he saw an unfamiliar hue. He collected the seawater in a bucket tied to a long rope, then examined the water for rare algae or mosses under the microscope. He was so contented with his algae and mosses he gave little or no thought to Eliot and Vicks. They scarcely acknowledged one another if they happened to meet on the deck. Edward relaxed; it was as if he were traveling alone.

The weather and currents were favorable and the steamship reached Pará on schedule. Their luggage was transferred to a mule-drawn cart that rattled down the planks of the dock to the small river steamer hired for the expedition up the Pará River. The boat captain was a gregarious Frenchman who insisted his distinguished passengers join him in a toast to the success of their journey, which was followed by another toast for favorable weather. The cabin boy refilled their glasses a third time and the captain made a toast to the saints to protect them from savage beasts and Indians. Edward was more worried about the boat's three crewmen, blackened with coal dust, who skulked up from the boiler room to gawk at their passengers before they disappeared below.

Once the riverboat was under way, Edward began to unpack and assemble his traveling laboratory. The boat was to serve as their headquarters while they made excursions on foot and by canoe into the jungle. The rainy season was past and the air was warm and relatively dry—just the conditions that favored the flowering of wild orchids. As the river narrowed Edward spent hours in a deck chair, where he was able to scan the banks with the aid of his binoculars.

Orchids were rare in the dense forests of the lowlands, except in treetops and precipitous rocks above deep ravines and rivers. Few orchids liked deep shade—those few were those with green or white flowers; the colorful orchids came from sunnier, more open terrain. Edward scanned the list of orchids wanted by the consortium of hybridizers and noted which were winter blooming and must be collected now; the others, which bloomed in the spring and summer, could be collected last. These latter genera were the *Laelia* and *Cattleya* much sought by hybridizers, who wanted the rich colors of the *Laelia* flower but with the robust size and graceful shape of the *Cattleya* flower.

The *Laelia crispa* had large fragrant white flowers with yellow-and-purple lips on a rather long stem. The hybridizers were interested in making a fragrant *Cattleya,* so the list included a number of specimens unproven in hybridization but wanted for the fragrance they might contribute to the hybrid that growers dreamed of. Edward was most concerned about this specimen because it did not bloom until summer, uncomfortably near the end of their time on the Pará.

The *Laelia purpurata* circled on the list was sought by the hybridizers for its huge, eight-inch flowers of white suffused with rose, and rich velvety purple on its bell-shaped lip. The *purpurata* bloomed in the spring and Edward was confident he could obtain enough specimens before their departure. Also at the top of the list was *Laelia cinnabarina;* though not large, this orchid was prized by hybridizers for its bright rich red-orange blossoms shaped like stars. Scarce because it was much sought after by collectors and hybridizers, the *cinnabarina* bloomed from spring to late autumn, which made the plant somewhat easier to locate.

Edward was surprised to see *Cattleya labiata* near the top of the list because only a few years before, a great many *C. labiata* had been found and were purchased by two different investment companies, one Belgian, the other British. A dispute arose over which company had the true *C. labiata,* and when word came from scientists that all the specimens were true *Cattleya labiata,* the price of an individual plant fell from $20 to $1 and a number of private investors were ruined.

The Indians and their canoes were waiting on the riverbank when the steamer chugged into the village of Portal. The Indians were familiar with the orchid trade, and two men carried a moss-covered limb with a fine specimen of *Oncidium papilio,* with a long flower spike of bright orange-and-yellow flowers the shape of big butterflies, the so-called butterfly orchid that set off orchid mania years before. The *papilio* did not grow indoors, so there was a steady demand for replacements of those that died of overwatering and the cold.

Now, the Indians knew the value of wild orchids, but frequently white brokers came upriver and demanded their entire stock of a species to corner the market. Indians who did not cooperate were flogged or tortured, much as they were at the Brazilian and Colombian rubber stations. These Indians worked for the French boat captain, who protected them from the violence of the brokers and agents; in return they sold him all of the best plants they found. Edward purchased the *papilio* from the Indians at the price set by the Frenchman—too expensive, really, but it was such a big, mature plant that Edward paid. The Frenchman offered to send his Indians out to gather every specimen on the list, but both Edward and Mr. Eliot declined.

Before dark, Edward followed the muddy track from the river into the old village of Portal, which was a rubber station in the early days of the rubber trade. Years ago the old village was burned during a dispute between rival rubber companies. The new business district of Portal sprang up along the riverbank and consisted of some ramshackle boats and rotting barges tied to big logs. Apparently the Frenchman owned these boats and barges as well and rented space to the merchants and traders for their establishments. Miners and plantation foremen from hundreds of miles around depended on Portal for food and supplies, delivered to distant outposts upriver by the Frenchman's riverboats, the *Louis XIII,* the *Louis XIV,* and the *Louis XV.*

Portal had a violent history from its beginning as a rubber station where an Indian village once stood. All of those Indians were gone; the rubber station at Portal was infamous for the use of torture and killing to increase the output of the indentured Indians who gathered the wild rubber. Rivalry between the rubber buyers erupted into periodic raids and reprisal raids in which dozens of Indians and white and Negro overseers were killed. The Frenchman said the old town and rubber station had been burned to the ground twice before by rivals; the third time Portal burned, the rubber buyer retreated farther upriver. That was when the Frenchman got the idea for a new town, a floating town that could be moved up or down the river in times of danger or floated away to serve the rubber stations in other remote river locations.

The Indians who met the boat did not live here; they lived deep in the forest and were not as friendly as the Indians who once lived at Portal. Edward noticed even the structures not destroyed by fire appeared uninhabited; tree ferns and palms pushed up through roof joists. Inside the abandoned warehouses he passed, he heard noises of jungle creatures that crawled and roosted in the ruins. No wonder the old village site was thought to be haunted; Edward felt uneasy himself, as if someone or something were watching him. The brief twilight of the tropics began to give way to darkness and Edward felt a growing panic that sent him walking faster and faster until he was running for the riverbank.

The motley barges and boats of the floating town were brightly lit with lanterns hung from their decks and rigging to announce the cantina and dance hall, the grocery and dry goods stores were all open for business. The relative coolness of the night brought out mine and plantation foremen from miles away.

The bartender nodded at two young women, a Negro and a mulatto sitting nearby, but Edward quickly shook his head. A crudely lettered sign propped up by rum bottles announced that women were sold by the dance or by the night. The cantina boat and the dance hall barge were connected by a wide plank of wood; Edward bought a gin and sat at a table with a view of the dimly lit dance hall. Three couples moved sluggishly to the music of a large hurdy-gurdy cranked by a monkey chained to the leg of a table. The monkey turned the crank as long as the dancers refilled its tin dish with bits of dry bread, purchased from the bartender. When the tin dish was empty, the monkey let go of the crank and leaned against the hurdy-gurdy box to rest. Edward watched as the little creature's fingers delicately rubbed its neck under the leather collar. One after the other, the dancing couples disappeared across the plank to the hotel barge. The monkey watched the dancers disappear, then looked hopefully in the direction of the cantina and Edward. Before he left, Edward bought a handful of dry bread from the bartender for the monkey's dish; the monkey looked at him anxiously and for an instant their eyes met before Edward turned away.

The next morning they traveled in two canoes as dawn lighted the sky. At a fork in the river Mr. Vicks and the Frenchman took one canoe with two Indians to gather disease-resistant *Hevea* seedlings from an old stand of wild rubber trees the Indians knew. Mr. Eliot and Edward went with the two Indian boys, neither more than twelve years old but already familiar with dozens of wild epiphytic orchids found only at the tops of the highest trees. On each side of the river the great trees towered out of sight in a canopy of foliage. Lianas hung from the branches, interwoven to form webs of coiling vines.

Edward watched closely. Sometimes a tree appeared covered with orchid blossoms that thrived on the lianas. Climbing ferns and vanilla clung to the trunks, and epiphytes graced the branches. Large arums sent down long aerial roots the Indians used for ropes. In the undergrowth different species of palms grew among the tree ferns, whose feathery crowns were twenty feet above the ground. Great broad leaf heliconias, leathery *Melastoma,* and succulent broadleaf begonias grew all around; *Cecropia* trees had a ghostly presence with their white stems and large white palmated leaves that stood straight up like candelabras. Sometimes the riverbank was carpeted with flower petals of yellow, pink, and white fallen from some invisible treetop. The air was filled with a delicious perfume, but in all the overshadowing greenery no source was visible.

The Indians knew exactly where to take the canoes in the branching estuaries; they knew where to find the *Cattleya violacea* by its fragrance. That afternoon Edward and Mr. Eliot returned with the canoes full of lovely rose-purple flowers with a round ruffled front lobe marked with a patch of vibrant yellow streaked with purple. Eliot assisted him with the labeling and packing of the day's collection, and Edward could not help but notice how little Mr. Eliot knew about wild orchids; moreover, Mr. Eliot evidenced no interest in observing the natural habitats of the specimens. While Edward stood at the foot of the great trees to catch the specimens the Indians climbed for, Mr. Eliot napped in the canoe with a bottle of rum between his legs. Mr. Eliot did count the specimens twice and note the number in a small notebook he carried in his breast pocket.

Later Mr. Eliot invited Edward to join him at the cantina, but soon disappeared onto the hotel barge with a giggling mulatto girl. A Negress in a bright red dress joined Edward at the table, but when he offered to buy her a drink, she said she was off duty and only wanted some conversation. She was Jamaican by birth, she said, and if she didn't die of some fever or go crazy from boredom she would be rich when she left the Pará. Already she had saved thousands for the store she would open in her village back on the island.

Edward told her a bit about the expedition, but she shook her head; she didn't care at all for those orchids. They might be costly but the flowers were shaped like giant insects and they were hardly fragrant. She much preferred roses and gardenias. She daintily patted her forehead with a linen handkerchief and he noticed she wore a gardenia blossom on a white satin ribbon at her wrist. He admired the large blossom and she held her wrist to her face and closed her eyes with a big smile as she savored the fragrance. She said she was never without a gardenia because its perfume wards off yellow fever. Some nights the huge jungle moths hovered near her flower; they seemed to recognize her, she said.

The monkey watched them hopefully; the Negress laughed and went and untied the monkey and brought the little creature to sit on the table. People there believed the monkey was good luck, she said; some years ago only the monkey survived the massacre at the rubber station. The monkey was found in the same tree the attackers hung the monkey's dead master, a rubber station foreman. The monkey was specially trained to perform many tasks, so the Frenchman bought the monkey from the police inspector who investigated the crimes. In no time the monkey learned to crank the music box. That happened before the Negress came to work for the Frenchman, but everyone knew the story.

When Edward stood up to go, the Negress carried the monkey back to the music box and retied the leash. Edward paid the bartender and put a piece of bread in the monkey's dish on his way out. The little creature's eyes brightened and it immediately began turning the crank with one hand while it ate the bread.

Sleep was impossible in the small steamy cabin, so Edward joined the others and hung his hammock and mosquito netting on the deck outside his cabin beside the crewmen and the others. The decks were lined with smoldering pots of a fragrant jungle wood to keep away the mosquitoes and bloodsucking insects. The hurdy-gurdy music, the sounds of laughter, and occasional screams and arguments filtered through the constant low hum of the jungle: the rustle of countless serpents, the squeaks and groans of dying prey, with the whir of giant winged beetles and the flutter of great moths at the lanterns. The riverboat deck, draped in netting with hammocks full of sleeping men, reminded Edward of a spider's prey, bound and stored in the web.

One night two weeks after their arrival in Portal, the sound of gunshots woke Edward. Heart pounding, he held his breath and listened for more gunfire and for the sounds he imagined at the massacre and burning of old Portal; but he heard only the hum of the jungle. The next morning the cantina and stores were strangely deserted and the hurdy-gurdy was silent. The little monkey was gone. When Edward reached the riverbank, the canoes were gone and the Indians nowhere to be seen; none of the equipment or day's supply of water and provisions were loaded either. Mr. Eliot paced up and down the riverbank, cursing the Indians and the Frenchman. Just then the Frenchman came, panting and red faced, followed by Mr. Vicks, who appeared calm. The Frenchman carried the little monkey tucked under his arm like a parcel as he gesticulated wildly with his free arm and hand. Nothing to fear, nothing to fear, the Frenchman repeated. The hundreds of rubber tree seedlings already collected were safe in their temporary nursery on the riverbank. A gang of thugs sent by the Frenchman's enemies raided the cantina and stores the night before to disrupt his business. Bullet holes in the hull caused the *Louis XIII* to leak a bit, but no one was wounded. The Indians who worked for him fled into the jungle because they feared a raid like the one that destroyed the old village.

Presently two young mestizo men appeared; they loaded the supplies and the machetes and shovels into the canoes. His sons, the Frenchman said proudly, would come along to help complete the collection of *Hevea* seedlings. The Frenchman lifted the monkey into the canoe with Edward and Mr. Eliot.

"Here is your assistant," he said, grinning broadly as he tied the leash inside the canoe. Point out the plant desired, and the monkey climbed to it and carefully scooped up the orchid bulb, roots and all, in tree moss.

Mr. Eliot laughed but Edward was not amused.

"I can't very well show the monkey the orchid I want when I can't see the tops of trees," Edward said in an indignant tone.

Clearly the Frenchman thought the *Hevea* seedlings of Mr. Vicks and the prestigious Kew Gardens more worthy of his attention than the orchids. His suggestion that a monkey could gather the orchids was quite insulting really. Fortunately he and Vicks had only four orchid species yet to gather, and of the four, only the *Laelia cinnabarina* specimens were required in any number.

"But you have last week's plants, the *Cattleya, non?*" The Frenchman claimed it was only necessary to show the monkey an orchid of the same species and the little creature would bring back all the orchids he could find. That was nonsense, of course, but Edward knew the only way to quiet the Frenchman was to do as he said. While they finished loading the canoes, Edward returned to his cabin to fetch specimens of *Cattleya* and *Laelia;* these, combined with the field handbook with color plates of wild orchids, would be enough to show to the Frenchman's sons, who might be persuaded to climb the immense trees if they were paid handsomely.

Once he showed Vicks and the boys the rubber tree seedlings to dig from a wild grove, the Frenchman, with the monkey on his arm, joined Mr. Eliot and Edward in a clearing.

"Show him what you want!" The Frenchman nodded at the two specimens Edward brought out of the knapsack. The monkey examined each plant closely, carefully fingering the waxy flowers and leathery leaves of the pseudobulbs with the tips of his fingers. Then suddenly the little creature darted off and scampered across a mossy log and up a tree fern, where he disappeared into the jungle canopy.

The monkey was gone for nearly an hour; the Frenchman and Mr. Eliot sat in the canoe sipping rum from a bottle while Edward brought out the orchid field guide with the tinted lithographs to refresh his memory of the rare orchid specimens that remained to be gathered after the *Laelia cinnabarina.* The monkey returned from the opposite direction he departed, with two fine orchid plants in his arms. Edward was dubious, but the little creature extracted the plants without damage except for a flower or two lost from the trailing spikes of blossoms. The Frenchman gave the monkey shelled walnuts each time he brought back orchids.

Once the monkey located the orchids high in the treetops, he moved much faster than any man. A number of the orchids the monkey collected were not needed and as cargo space was limited, those orchid plants were tossed aside. Edward had to admit the monkey did the work of two men. By midafternoon, all that remained to be collected was the small, rare orchids and the *Laelia cinnabarina,* which grew in the same habitat. Vicks collected the last orchid specimens he needed, and the following day, while Vicks and others finished packing the seedlings in burlap, the Frenchman took Mr. Eliot and Edward farther up the river to precipitous granite ridges cut by the river and bathed in the sunshine that gave the *Laelia cinnabarina* her rich colors.

The pale granite cliff with its cascades of wild orchid blossoms above the river mist was so lovely Edward knew he must photograph it. He brought along his tripod and camera despite the bulk for just this sort of location. The dimness of the light under the jungle canopy had precluded photography up until then.

Edward noticed his companions also were preoccupied these last days of the expedition. Mr. Vicks spent much of his time at the temporary nursery where the rubber tree seedlings in their burlap sacks were being carefully concealed inside rolls of woven straw matting for the long voyage. There were reasons for making haste. The Frenchman claimed to receive tips on plots against him by his enemies; he said very soon these criminals might force him to untie his barges and boats and relocate the town downriver. His spies reported growing suspicion among government officials in Belém, who heard rumors of foreigners in possession of *Hevea* seedlings.

On the last morning they went to collect the *Laelia cinnabarina,* Mr. Eliot was late and they were forced to wait for him in the canoe. The

Frenchman brought along the monkey for any orchids they might find on inaccessible rock ledges. Fortunately the weather continued to be dry so the mosquitoes were scarce while they waited for their colleague. How odd that Mr. Eliot should be late on the morning they set out for the *Laelia cinnabarina.* Mr. Eliot showed little knowledge or interest in orchids except for the *Laelia cinnabarina.* He seemed to be aware of the latest developments by orchid hybridizers who sought to create a fragrant bright red orchid to rival the English rose.

What could be the delay? When Eliot came, he was sweating and short of breath from the burden of the bulging knapsack's contents. As Eliot set it on the floor of the canoe, Edward felt the craft list with the weight of the knapsack and he heard the clink of glass bottles against one another inside the knapsack. Bottles of rum, Edward assumed, though he learned later Mr. Eliot brought along something more volatile than rum.

The monkey was not as fleet gathering the *Laelia cinnabarina* from the granite crags and ledges, so the Frenchman helped Mr. Eliot and Edward gather specimens of *cinnabarina* all morning, and by three o'clock they had more than the two hundred robust specimens requested by the consortium of orchid hybridizers. While the monkey watched them carefully wrap the specimens in damp moss and burlap, Edward hiked up the ridge with his camera.

Edward had a clear view of the river and riverbank for a mile in either direction as he climbed. He carried his camera case and tripod up the ledges and over the boulders to make photographs of the amazing granite hillside where hundreds of *Cattleya* and *Laelia* sent out long pendulous flower spikes. Because of the steep incline and the weight of his equipment he stopped periodically to catch his breath and to survey the endless expanses of jungle and the great Pará River as it snaked to the sea.

He stopped and attached the close-up lense so he could photograph a particularly profuse spike of red-orange blossoms of a *Laelia cinnabarina* that appeared to grow out solid granite on the side of the ridge. He was glad the monkey had not found this specimen. As he viewed the orchid flower through the close-up lens, he savored the sublime, luminous glow from the profuse orange-red blossoms that resembled shooting stars. He made exposures of each subject, careful to double-check the lens setting for perfect photographs.

They had agreed they must start back at five; Edward checked his watch and glanced back down at his companions, white specks far below. He had another hour to make photographs and he wanted to make the most of the opportunity because he had not made as many photographs of the wild orchids as he originally hoped. Here the light was lovely, but the steep terrain required numerous adjustments to each leg of the tripod before the camera was level. After the exposure he carefully repacked each glass plate in its padded slot in the camera box. He was so immersed in making photographs he lost sight of the antlike figures of his companions on the riverbank.

He was near the top of the granite ledge with the river hundreds of yards below when he stopped to change lenses for a wide-angle view of the granite cliff face with hundreds of wild orchids in flower. The subtle fragrance of hundreds of orchid blossoms wafted in the cool air rising off the mist from the river. As he attempted to focus the image on the camera's ground glass, he noticed the first gray feather of smoke, followed by another and another. He stepped back from the camera, unable to believe what he saw, when suddenly a greasy black ball of smoke rolled into the sky followed by spidery blossoms of red-orange flame.

This was the dry season, but the forest floor and the lianas and mosses were still moist and green. How could a wildfire break out? He felt the hair on his neck bristle as the plumes of smoke rose higher. Where were Eliot and the Frenchman? Edward quickly removed the lens board and film holder; he shut the camera and replaced it in its box. He slipped the carrying strap over his right shoulder and carried the folded tripod over his left shoulder. He made his way down the slope as quickly as he could. He still did not see his companions, but he saw the canoe safe on the riverbank.

The fire spread quickly and he could hear the birds and parrots screech out alarms. He was beginning to feel winded but he pushed himself on because he feared the flames might cut off his path to the canoe. He regretted the bulk of the camera box and the tripod on the steep slope of rotting granite where the footing was treacherous. The ridge was formed by folds of rock that made terraces and ledges, so the path down to the river, though steep, was not difficult to follow. He stopped again to search, in vain, for a glimpse of his companions.

Edward made his way down the granite ridge cautiously despite his fear of the fire. He was more than two-thirds of the way down the slope when he paused to catch his breath and adjust the camera box and tripod. It was then he saw a strange sight: Mr. Eliot was running madly along the riverbank with his knapsack in one hand, spilling the contents of a bottle over the shrubbery with the other hand. When one bottle was emptied he threw it down and reached into the knapack for another. For an instant, Edward was confused; he thought Eliot was dumping his precious rum; but when he saw the greasy black flames rise into the trees behind his companion, Edward realized the liquid Eliot splashed over the ground and shrubs was lamp oil, not rum.

Edward began to shout at Eliot, who was too far away to hear; the flames were spreading, and Edward realized the fire had cut off his only path to the canoe. He shouted, but the roar of the fire drowned out everything; he gamely held on to the camera box and used the tripod as a walking stick, but suddenly he lost his footing and fell. He did not lose consciousness during the fall, and he never forgot the odd sensation of weightlessness as he fell—quite strange but not unpleasant. He might have escaped this misadventure with only minor cuts and bruises, but the camera box fell against the leg on the rock with a terrible crunching sound. Shattered bone pierced the skin; blood soaked the leg of his trousers, but he felt only the great weight of the numb limb pulling him down as he leaned on the camera box to call out again and again for Eliot and for the Frenchman. Surely they would come to find him when he did not return to the canoe.

Now the fire, fueled by the natural oils of the jungle trees and shrubs, exploded ahead of the flames and sent geysers of fire into the sky. He managed to drag himself into a rock cranny between two boulders just before the wall of flames flashed up the ridge.

The pain woke him from a dream that his leg was burning; in the fading darkness before dawn, bright orange coals still glowed and occasionally flames flared behind the thin veils of white smoke that rose from the legions of blackened tree trunks and the gray skeletons of tree ferns and shrubs. He listened for some sound that might indicate his companions were nearby. He called out their names again and again until the pain in his leg made him feel nauseous and faint.

When he woke again, the sun was just above the horizon. He pulled himself up so he could survey his position; he had come down the ridge and was within a hundred yards of the river below when he fell. The blackened jungle was silent and motionless and Edward felt a chill of horror spread over him: the sunny river's-edge habitat of the lovely *Laelia* and their kinsmen the *Cattleya* and *Brassavola* now lay in ashes.

Nausea swept over him and a cold sweat broke over his body as he recalled his initial misgivings about Eliot and Vicks. Was Vicks with his contraband *Hevea* seedlings a part of this scheme as well? How careless of Mr. Albert and Lowe & Company to allow the investors to interfere, though surely they had no idea of the true nature of Mr. Eliot's mission. Now it was clear: Eliot's only purpose on the expedition was the fire; the fire had been planned months before by the investors, who wished to make certain they possessed the only specimens of *Laelia cinnabarina*. They wanted no unpleasant surprises from rivals to drive down the price of the *Laelia cinnabarina*. Rival hybridizers would be stymied when they sent out their plant collectors now that this Pará River site was destroyed. Habitats for the *Laelia* and *Cattleya* had been disappearing rapidly since the early forties. Now orchid hunters would be forced to go even farther up estuaries too overgrown and narrow even for canoes, where only a few specimens might be found.

As he descended the ridge, he lost sight of the canoe on the riverbank. Surely the Frenchman had seen the smoke and escaped the flames. The fire might have driven them away temporarily, but they would return to search for him as soon as possible. He had suspected Eliot was a scoundrel from the start, but he believed he could rely on Mr. Vicks, who, after all, was affiliated with the Kew Gardens.

Anger suffused his body, and the pain receded. This was an outrage! At the very least, Lowe & Company badly misused him by sending him out with that criminal Eliot; at worst, they had betrayed him, and now the criminals had left him for dead! He was used as a decoy in the service of scoundrels, though he did not see Vicks in quite the same light because he smuggled the disease-resistant seedlings for a noble purpose.

The fire burned the dry sunny exposures preferred by the *Cattleya* and *Laelia* but burned itself out once it reached the deeply shaded damp foliage. The jungle canopy, untouched by fire, came alive as the sun rose above it; the screeching and calling of the parrots and macaws rose to a crescendo, then gradually receded as the morning got hotter. Surely Mr. Vicks would insist search parties be sent out as soon as it was daylight. Edward knew he had to reach the riverbank or his rescuers would never see him on the hillside or hear his voice over the noise of the rushing water.

Carefully he slit the leather and removed the field boot from the injured limb; the leg seemed as if it was a separate object, not his own, with no relation to the pain that left him sweating and nauseous. He removed the bootlace and his belt, pausing from time to time to let the nausea subside. He gingerly maneuvered the leg until it lay parallel to the tripod, then he lashed the leg to the tripod with the bootlace and belt. He knew it was imperative the leg remain immobile, or bone fragments might sever an artery.

Inch by inch he crawled, pushing aside rocks and debris so the injured limb he dragged would have a clear path. He was soothed by this contact with the earth and her gravity that held him close with no danger of a fall. The limb was numb now and the pain seemed to migrate to his other leg, then to his shoulders and arms. After what seemed like hours, he reached the riverbank, though he still was some distance upriver from the site of the temporary camp where the canoes were tied. He was very thirsty by then; the canteen with safe water and the packet of purification tablets were lost somewhere on the hillside, but he knew that to drink untreated river water invited fever and illness more grave than any broken limb. The sun was high overhead now; his rescuers should be along soon.

He dreamed about the white marble pool and fountain in his sister's garden; in the dream he drank and drank the cool pure water to satisfy his thirst. Others at the garden party were sipping champagne, and among them, oddly enough, relaxed as if she belonged, was the Negress from the cantina with the little monkey in her arms. One of the guests, an older man he did not recognize, approached and warned him the water was not safe. He offered Edward a glass of champagne, but suddenly the Negress bared one breast to him and the voices of the other guests called out, "Drink! Drink!"

He woke when he realized the voices in his dream were voices on the river; frantically he called, but from his prone position his cries were muffled by the vegetation and the rush of the river. He must pull himself up now or he was lost. With all his will, with all his remaining strength, he pulled himself up into sitting position and yelled again. Surely the canoes that paddled against the upriver currents could not pass by so quickly; but it was no use; he could see nothing. The rescue party would pass a last time on their return trip downriver. Stand up or die, a voice inside him said. He braced himself against a fallen tree and managed to stand if he leaned back hard against the tree; the trouble was the surrounding foliage would allow rescuers only a glimpse of him as the current of the river sped their canoes past.

Just when he thought he could no longer endure the pain of standing, the canoes came into sight and he began to shout and wave his arms, though each motion caused a blinding pain to shoot up the leg and through his body to his forehead. They were not far away. He could see them clearly; each of the Frenchman's mestizo sons commanded a canoe manned with Indian paddlers. From the banter and laughter between the canoes, they might have been on a holiday; Edward tried to yell with all his might at the top of his voice but managed only a hoarse croak; all the calling he'd done previously and the dryness of his mouth left him mute. Balanced precariously on his one good leg, Edward waved wildly with one arm and then the other, but it was no use; the laughing men in the canoes were passing bunches of bananas back and forth, eating the fruit and tossing the peels into the water.

His associates thought so little of him they had not even bothered to come along with the search parties, he realized bitterly. The first canoe was nearly out of sight and the other was moving away swiftly, and all he could do was wave helplessly.

He slumped to the ground after he lost sight of the canoes. He was sweating and dizzy from the exertion and from the pain in the limb. Fortunately the leg did not seem to be infected, but he knew time was running out. He regretted he had not broken open the camera, for its shutter mirror he might have used to flash signals to the passing canoes. Surely the search parties would not abandon their task so easily.

He felt so much better when he was lying on the ground; he must get a good rest before he stood up again. He pulled off his shirt and wrapped it around his face and head to keep off the mosquitoes and flies while he slept. Thirst tormented him with dreams of clear running streams and deep clear pools of fresh water; he had gone nearly twenty-four hours without water. If he was not rescued by late afternoon he knew he must risk dysentary and fever with a swallow of river water or he would die of thirst. He dreamed of crystalline cascading streams as cold as the snow that fed them from the peaks of the Sierra Nevadas where his father took him to fish for trout. He was kneeling along the trout stream about to take a sip of cool water when he heard his father's voice call him. He wanted a swallow of water so badly he hesitated to stand up and answer his father. Then in his dream he remembered his father died years before, and he thought how odd that a dead man should call him.

He woke from a dream that he had fallen in the river and was choking on the greenish waters, but the water kept flowing into his mouth and splashing over his face. He had to wipe the water from his eyes to squint in the bright sunlight at his rescuers, gathered in a half circle around him. The instant he recognized the faces of the Frenchman's sons he began to babble his gratitude. Over and over he thanked them, but the handsome young mestizos both shook their heads modestly and looked at their feet; no, the señor should not give his thanks to them because really they had given up the search and were on their way home. They said his friends thought he died in the fire; their father sent them to bury his remains and bring back any valuables. Luckily they brought along a helper, the mestizo brother said with a big grin on his face; thank the helper, not them! At that moment his brother lifted something off his shoulder and set it on the ground. The little monkey nervously fingered its red leather collar and looked up from face to face all around until its gaze fell on Edward.

Apparently, the monkey jumped around in the canoe and looked back toward the riverbank to signal it had seen someone or something unusual. They turned back to investigate but at first they could not see him; but again the little monkey chattered and refused to return to the canoes. Finally they came to catch him and found Edward lying unconscious.

The mestizo brothers prepared to administer first aid to prevent infection in the injured limb. They spoke soothingly as they opened knapsacks and removed various implements and a bottle; tribal healing remedies, he thought. The mestizo brothers talked to take his attention from the pain as they cut away the trousers and stocking to expose the injuries. One brother poured kerosene into the wounds on his leg from a glass bottle identical to the bottles Eliot had carried in his knapsack. Edward's shocked expression as he watched the kerosene pour into the wounds caused the brothers to reassure Edward kerosene would kill everything that might try to infect the wounds. Kerosene was used for everything here; even the old-time tribal medicine people swore by kerosene for injuries, infections, and infestations of lice or ticks. The mestizo brothers were smiling broadly by the time the bottle of kerosene had been emptied over the wounds on his leg. Edward nodded grimly at his jolly physicians and drank more water from the canteen the mestizo brothers gave him. It was not until he emptied the canteen and asked for more water that he saw them casually dip the canteen into the river. His rescuers noticed the odd expression on his face when they gave him the full canteen, so again they tried conversation to soothe their patient.

One Indian had to ride in the other canoe to make way for the injured leg. The little monkey rode on the canoe's bow, watching the riverbanks ahead. The water revived Edward, and he was able to raise himself up in the canoe with the injured leg straight out ahead of him. The mestizo brothers praised the little monkey; if it had been them alone, they would not have turned back upriver again. This was summer festival week and they were in a hurry to get back for the revelry that night.

The other brother passed Edward the bottle of rum that went back and forth between the canoes; the burning mouthful brought tears to his eyes when he swallowed it. The mestizo brothers and the Indians let out whoops of celebration. Edward was surprised to feel his spirits lift despite the pain. His rescuers were elated to find him alive and broke out another bottle of rum to celebrate. They composed a triumphant song they sang at the tops of their voices.

"We saved the white man," they sang; "we saved him with the help of the good luck monkey! Otherwise, the white would have died; yes, he would have died."

His friends had departed that very morning at daybreak on the *Louis XV* downriver to Pará, the mestizo brothers told him. Edward was not prepared for such news and his face must have registered the shock, because the mestizo brothers became oddly apologetic about the behavior of his collegues and tried to explain away their abandonment of him: they had to make the departure of a steamer for Havana and they thought he was dead. Yes, they were sorry but they could not wait. They had to go because the authorities were on their way to investigate reports of an English smuggler. With each bit of news, the pain in the leg stabbed harder and he was bathed in sweat. He vomited the river water, then lay back on the bottom of the canoe, shaken by the dry heaves.

When they reached Portal, the Indians carefully lifted him from the canoe and carried him to a hammock hanging on the deck of the Louis *XIV.* The mestizo brothers splinted the leg with parts of a broken chair wrapped with old silk stockings. They poured more kerosene over the leg and pronounced the wound clean, but they warned the leg might need a long time to mend. The brothers attended to all of his needs. They sponge-bathed him while he lay in the hammock, and found his valise with clean clothing and his own kit with tincture of Merthiolate, bandages and plasters, and, of course, tablets of aspirin and belladonna. They took turns feeding him bowls of hot fish soup and tea with odd leaves floating in the cup; for pain, they explained; the tea would help him sleep.

He closed his eyes but was still aware of the sounds and noise from the barges and riverboats nearby; he heard voices in the cantina and he heard the music box begin to play a waltz. He imagined his furry savior intently turning the crank as the Negress, in a red dress, danced with the elder of the mestizo brothers. Later he woke but could not tell if it was evening or early morning due to the lanterns shining along the decks of the boats and barges. He heard the sounds of hammering but they were not close by and he could see no one moving on the barges with the cantina and dance hall. The effort of lifting and turning his head toward the river left him tired and he lay back and closed his eyes again.

He slept heavily for hours and later recalled his physicians came twice to administer their special hot tea. But when he woke he immediately sensed something was different; the little monkey was tied to his valise under the hammock and the *Louis XIII,* which had been tied next to them, suddenly was gone. He pulled himself up for a better look and was shocked to see the barges and other river craft that formed the floating town were gone. Only the *Louis XIV* remained.

Edward saw and heard no one on board except for his rescuer, the monkey, who seemed happy to see him awaken. While he slept the entire town floated off to a new location, free of raids and tax authorities. The long sleep was a healing agent, just as the mestizo brothers said. Edward felt much better and was able to maneuver himself and the injured leg out of the hammock to reach the pair of crutches cleverly carved from branches of mahogany.

He untied the monkey and the little creature danced gaily about, chattering with what Edward imagined was gratitude. Together they sat on the shady side of the boat to share the cache of canned goods and fresh mangoes and guavas left by the mestizo brothers.

At night he allowed himself the luxury of a pot of hot tea, though the little kerosene cookstove was low on fuel. The monkey quickly learned to bring him a mango, then to toss the fruit peelings and pit into the river when he was finished. The floating town of Portal was gone. For six days he and the little monkey were the only occupants of the *Louis XIV;* the leg was much improved so long as he did not move about too much. There was ample water and food, but Edward agonized over the unknown fate of his remaining two boxes of orchid specimens. His "friends," Eliot and Vicks, had taken all of his boxes along with them, the mestizo brothers assured him, except for the two boxes they overlooked. Edward was relieved to see the boxes contained *Laelia cinnabarina* specimens he collected the day before the acccident.

The limb seemed to be healing safely as the mestizo brothers promised, although the healing required he sleep a great deal. He no longer bothered to tie the monkey, who curled up under the hammock while he slept. As each day passed he thought less and less about the past, even the immediate past, and focused only on this place and this time. When a rainstorm and wind threatened to flood the boxes of orchid specimens, he was able to balance himself on the crutches well enough to maneuver the boxes to safety without a thought of the future of the specimens or himself. Although he knew it was only six days, he felt as if he had been alone with the monkey for six months. He felt as if years had passed since his fateful introduction to Vicks and Eliot in the offices of Lowe & Company. Now when he recalled the preceding weeks of fieldwork with Eliot and even Vicks, he felt as if another person, not himself, had lived those weeks.

As he began to feel stronger, Edward passed the time reading; most of the books he brought were botanical texts about orchids and bromeliads—nothing he wanted to read now. He brought a volume of Shakespeare's sonnets, but oddly the sonnets stirred up anxious feelings that left his heart pounding, so he set it aside for a delightful book about ornamental ponds.

On the eighth day, the monkey woke him with excited chattering, and he heard the chug-chug of a boat coming upriver. He expected to see the *Louis XV* round the bend in the river, but it was a Brazilian government boat with uniformed officers at the bow. Edward greeted them warmly and asked which of them was the doctor. They looked blankly at one another and then at the injured limb. They knew nothing about his companions or the accident; they were acting on information received weeks before. The officer was disappointed Edward was not the reported Englishman.

Once Edward identified himself, the senior officer wasted no time; he informed Edward he was under arrest for suspicion of smuggling forbidden plant material. They were quite polite and did not use the handcuffs; they helped him out of the hammock and the three of them assisted him on board their boat. They loaded his boxes and luggage into the police boat. He was so stunned by his arrest and the dizziness and nausea that followed his short trek to their boat, he failed to notice the error made by the police. Just as they reached Pará, Edward noticed the Frenchman's little monkey tied to a handle on his big steamer trunk. The officers permitted Edward to bring the monkey along with him to the jail, and later the monkey accompanied him and the senior officer to the telegraph office across the street from the jail. Lowe & Company responded promptly with a generous advance to cover his medical expenses and all fines and legal fees. Ever discreet, Mr. Albert's cablegram made no mention at all of Vicks or that scoundrel Eliot.

The local magistrate counted the money twice and ordered Edward's immediate deportation; early the following morning, deckhands lifted his stretcher aboard the steamship bound for Miami by way of Havana. Edward tipped the captain and first mate handsomely to keep his two remaining crates of orchids away from the customs inspectors. The little monkey was safely hidden in a compartment of the steamer trunk until they were in open water.

"That was, by no means, the end of my ordeal," Edward wrote in his statement to his attorney. "Within three days the ship encountered a violent storm and we all very nearly were lost; the ship's cargo and luggage were dumped overboard by the terrified crewmen in futile efforts to appease the angry sea.

"All the orchid specimens in the remaining two crates were lost when the crates became soaked with salt water," Edward concluded his account of the expedition requested by his lawyers.

Edward pressed down on his pen so firmly the tip of the nib snapped off and bounced across the floor. Hattie looked up from the book of monkey stories as Edward put away the pen and gathered his papers. They'd arrive at Grand Central station in less than an hour.

Indigo glanced out the window at the lush green countryside with the little settlements and farms; she was glad they were almost there because she was weary of the constant motion and the noise, and her back and legs were sore from sitting in the same place for hours at a time. She wanted to hear what happened next to the monkey born from an egg-shaped stone because nothing could harm the monkey. Even after Hattie closed the book, Indigo felt content to daydream about Monkey, able to change each of the eighty-four thousand hairs on his body into anything he wanted; the little monkey back in Riverside would escape all harm just like the monkey in the stories. Hattie promised when they reached New York they would have news from home and a full report on Linnaeus.

Part Four

HATTIE SAW Father first and waved and called out; she was surprised at how much she had missed him, and pushed her way along the crowded platform to meet him. She embraced him and felt tears in her eyes, then saw him brush away tears of his own. Departure calls and blasts of steam and train whistles rudely punctuated their greeting. Hattie realized Edward and Indigo were caught in the crowd and she turned back anxiously to find them. The smoke and the smells and the noise were worse than she remembered them. Father saw Edward first and called out a booming welcome that caused Indigo to let go of Edward's hand and stop. Almost before Edward could turn around, Indigo was caught in the tide of boarding passengers that whirled her around and swept her back toward the train.

Edward plunged into the crowd and pressed after the child before he lost sight of the top of her head; he called out her name but she seemed intent on reboarding the train. Boarding passengers behind her helped her up the train car steps ahead of them. Edward found her sitting in her place by the window in the compartment they had just vacated. He wished Hattie had come along because the child did not respond to him in the way she responded to Hattie. But as soon as he told Indigo that the train would take her farther away to the north, she stood up.

"I want to go home," Indigo said.

"This is a dreadful noisy place. Perhaps if I carried you, you would feel safer," he said tentatively, aware the child did not trust him as she trusted Hattie. She shook her head.

"I can walk!"

She squeezed his hand fiercely as they pushed through the crowd to the lobby, where Hattie and her father were waiting; their luggage was already loaded on the hired carriage for the ride to Oyster Bay.

Mr. Abbott saw Indigo's big dark eyes scrutinize him. Hattie had written at length about the delightful child she and the pet monkey discovered in the garden one morning. He feared the lingering melancholy that had followed the thesis controversy might have resurfaced while Edward was away. What a difference the child made for Hattie!

Mr. Abbott was not surprised his new son-in-law sailed away almost immediately after a brief honeymoon, to collect algae and mosses in the Caribbean. Hattie applauded Edward's dedication to his collections and said she would rewrite her manuscript while Edward was abroad. She claimed to prefer the solitude of their Riverside home. Still, Mr. Abbott noticed the tone of her letters home changed entirely after the Indian child was found; he felt a great deal of warmth toward the outspoken girl.

Once the coach was under way, Hattie asked if Indigo was afraid, and she shook her head: the giant depot with so many different trains and tracks filled her with hope somewhere nearby she might find a westbound train to Needles. Hattie and Edward both apologized for the noise and crowds on the platform, but this time Indigo did not remain silent; she told them noisy crowded train stations were the best because more tourists bought more baskets.

Indigo asked if they were far in the east, and Hattie said they were, but Edward added that they were going much farther east yet—across the ocean and as far east as Italy. Indigo reconsidered; if she demanded to be sent back to the school, she'd be locked in the mop closet all summer. She had a better chance of finding the Messiah and his followers if she continued to the east. Besides, Hattie promised, as soon as they returned from abroad, she'd take Indigo to Arizona to look for Sister Salt and Mama.

As the coach moved slowly through the crowded streets, Edward pointed out the window at a circus train unloading the elephants and camels. Indigo knelt on the carriage seat and stared out the window at the big steel cages of tigers and lions she had only previously seen on the pages of Hattie's books. Crowds gathered around the circus train and lined the street already crowded with people hurrying along with no interest at all in the circus animals.

Indigo noticed something odd about the faces of the people crowding the street: they did not look at one another or greet one another as they passed. As the coach pulled away from the station, the tall buildings formed deep canyons and Indigo caught glimpses of an expanse of water nearby. The coach traveled a short distance before it stopped at the edge of the dark river.

While the luggage was transferred to the ferry, Hattie took Indigo by the hand to show her the city from the observation deck and to point out Long Island across the East River. Indigo watched the dark water in silence as the ferryboat moved away from shore; how different this river was; she could feel currents of cold air rise off the water although the afternoon air was quite warm.

Behind the ferry, the city rose up like odd stone formations—buttes and mesas surrounded by fields and farmhouses among tall trees; up ahead were lovely meadows of sunflowers and wildflowers lined with big trees. As the ferry drew closer to the shore, the scattered farmhouses gathered into the village where the ferry docked. Indigo held Hattie's hand tightly as they made their way off the ferry through the throngs of people waiting to board.

There were still houses as far as Indigo could see, but now there were farms, planted with corn and beans—Indigo got very excited when she saw this and told Hattie to look out the window. Yes, the farmers in New York grew corn and beans and squash. They left sight of the ocean for a distance as the coach passed through big apple orchards—Indigo became very excited when she saw the small green fruit on the trees. The road curved again and emerged from the trees just above the rocky beach, where dark blue waves splashed the big rocks with foam.

Hattie watched out the window with Indigo so she could show her some of the places she used to ride her pony. Hattie was surprised to see a number of grand new dwellings rising out of the meadowlands above the beach. Years ago after her father concluded that the smoke and dirt of city air caused tuberculosis, he moved them permanently from the house on Fifth Avenue to Oyster Bay, where a great many of their acquaintances kept grand summer houses.

They were among only a handful of prominent families who lived year round at Oyster Bay. Her father relished the ample space on the old farmland, which allowed him to conduct many more of his odd agricultural experiments that aimed to teach the poor to grow food to supplement their diets. Her mother fretted about their isolation on Long Island, though it did not last long.

Hattie rode her first pony up and down the beach to watch as workmen dug foundations and great freight wagons pulled by giant shires delivered cut stone and new bricks to the construction sites. She was not allowed to go near or to speak to strangers, so she kept her pony at a distance from the workmen, but on summer evenings at sundown when the construction sites were empty, she rode her pony through the stacks of lumber and bricks, curious about the construction. She jumped her pony over the trenches dug for the garden maze as the new house was built near theirs, the house of Mr. and Mrs. Colin James, as fate decreed. Like Hattie's father, Susan James sought the old farmland for its fertility, which was crucial in her architect's plan for grand Renaissance gardens.

Indigo never imagined trees could grow as big and tall as the trees towering above the road on either side. She leaned out the window of the coach to marvel at their girth and to try to see the treetops; up ahead, at the end of the tree-lined drive, she saw a tall building of gray stone with a long porch all around, its stone pillars entwined with masses of pale pink flowers. As the coach slowed to a stop, Indigo was amazed to see the climbing rose swallowed up the entire front of the doorway; just as she was about to ask Hattie the name of the rose, the coach stopped and the big front doors of the house swung open, and out came two women followed by a man. Indigo took a step back behind Hattie, where she could not be seen.

They were all talking at once in loud, excited voices. She was relieved the strangers did not notice her as they crowded into the coolness of the entry hall. As she walked behind Edward and Hattie she couldn't help but notice the highly polished wood floor; quickly she reached down to touch the dark wood, hard and smooth as glass.

The air inside the house was not unpleasant or stale, but absorbed a subtle odor Indigo soon learned to identify as old furniture and old books. She was glad her slippers were soft and went lightly across the floor so that no one seemed to notice her. The rooms were not much bigger than those of the California house, but the interior was very different; here the walls were paneled in dark wood. The great tall windows were dressed in pine green velvet draperies that swept down from the carved wood lintels to within an inch of the floor.

They moved through the entryway past the massive oak staircase to the front parlor, where there was much more light from tall stained-glass windows in the pattern of white lilies with green palm trees. Each window was flanked with polished brass pots of dwarf palm trees.

Although this house was larger than the Riverside house, the rooms here contained a good deal more furniture, with a great many little tables with glass or marble tops covered with tiny ceramic figures of animals. Along the walls, cabinets with glass doors displayed larger figurines of clear glass—a fierce glass bear occupied one shelf by itself. The end tables and cabinets were arranged close together with barely a space to walk between them. The matching brown velvet sofas and armchairs were centered at the far end of the parlor near the fireplace, and each sofa or chair was flanked with an end table or little chest of drawers displaying more glass figurines.

Indigo sat at one end of the sofa and looked all around while the others talked. She was most interested in a closer look at the crystal bear in the cabinet because his glittering eyes followed her across the room. She sat up straight and still on the sofa as she saw Hattie sit, but after a time, something on the sofa began to poke her right leg through her petticoats and stocking. Hattie noticed her discomfort and whispered in her ear that she might stretch her legs a bit. For an instant there was a pause; they all glanced at Indigo before resuming their conversation; the attention embarrassed her, and she did not move again until she was sure no one was looking. Inch by inch, she slid herself from the sofa to the floor so slowly Hattie did not notice her absence until the big crash. Indigo froze with both hands covering her face as the others all stood up in alarm at the fragments of broken glass scattered all across the floor.

"Oh my gracious!" Hattie's mother exclaimed, and both Hattie and Edward's sister, Susan, were quite startled. Edward called out sharply to Indigo, but Hattie was by her side with her arms around her, whispering into Indigo's ear. Careful to avoid the maze of glass cabinets and tiny oval tables, she led Indigo by the hand to the door; both she and the child were exhausted from their journey.

As Hattie and Indigo started up the stairs, a voice called out warmly to Hattie; a large Negro woman dressed in white rushed over to hug Hattie.

"Oh I thought we'd lost you to that California for good," Lucille said.

"After a week on the train, I feel as if I'm lost for good."

"Who's this tired girl?"

Indigo stepped behind Hattie so the housekeeper could not see her.

"This is Indigo and she and I both are exhausted." Lucille looked at them both closely and nodded her head.

"I know what you need."

Lucille went up the stairs ahead of them, turning up the gas lamps and calling out for Ceena and Grace, the maids. Indigo looked back down the stairs and saw two young black women come out a door by the stairs.

"Two hot baths!" Lucille called down to the maids as she led Hattie and Indigo down the hall.

Later trays of food were sent up to Hattie and Indigo while Edward dined with the others. All questions concerned the Indian child, so Edward described Hattie's immediate interest in the Indian child lost from the government boarding school nearby. His brother-in-law, Colin James, seemed unconcerned about Indians or children or any worldly care, for that matter, as he downed his fifth glass of wine, but Edward noticed a frown cross his sister's brow for an instant at his mention of the Indian child. She wanted to know why they brought the Indian child. Edward smiled faintly. Hattie was attached to the child, and he found her quite interesting himself. She was generally well behaved and kept Hattie company when Edward was away.

"She's to be trained as a lady's maid," Edward said as he held his plate over the platter. "The Indian schools teach them all sorts of skills and trades." He paused to cut a bite of meat as the others waited to hear more; actually he and Hattie had not discussed plans for the child beyond the summer.

Later, the men strolled outdoors to see Mr. Abbott's latest projects to aid the poor: rammed-earth bricks and fishponds. Susan James and Mrs. Abbott went upstairs to look in on Hattie and the child.

The room was just as it had been the day of Hattie's wedding, some eight months ago, as if perhaps her mother still did not quite believe she had found a husband after all. It was not like Mother to miss an opportunity to redecorate a room, but she gathered from the conversation in the parlor her mother now devoted a great deal of time to the church; she and Susan James organized charity events to raise money for the Catholic bishop's aid society.

Hattie was showing Indigo her scrapbooks of her dried pressed daisies and roses when Mother knocked; before Hattie could reply, the door opened and in came Mother and Susan James. Indigo pulled the bedcovers over her head. They pretended they wanted to visit with Hattie, but she could tell they were curious about Indigo, who remained hidden.

While Susan James talked about her garden renovations, Hattie watched Mother's hand move playfully along the edge of Indigo's bed in an attempt to coax her out; but Indigo refused to budge. Then the attention of the two women turned to Hattie.

"Hattie, you look so thin! We thought by now we might be seeing a 'change,'" Susan said sweetly. Hattie's laughter surprised both women. Children were a subject for the future, she told them. She understood the source of Susan's curiosity: Susan's two daughters would receive smaller sums under the terms of the family trust if Edward and Hattie had children.

At last Susan said good night and Mrs. Abbott leaned over to give Hattie a little hug. It was wonderful to have her home again, Mrs. Abbott said as she followed Susan out the door. Susan's jaw was firmly set and Hattie realized her sister-in-law disliked her. When they were gone, Hattie told Indigo it was safe to come out, but she was asleep with the covers over her head. Hattie pulled back the covers so Indigo could breathe properly, then put out the light.

Edward was sitting up in bed reading a citrus horticulture book when Hattie joined him. She unpacked a nightgown. He laid the open book facedown on the bed and rubbed both eyes.

"Home again, home again—"

"—Jiggety-jig!" Hattie said with a smile.

They agreed Hattie should sleep in the spare bed in the room with Indigo in case she woke in the night and became disoriented or frightened. He put a robe over his nightshirt and walked Hattie down the hall with an arm gently around her shoulders.

◆ ◆ ◆

Just before dawn, Indigo woke to the noisy chirping of dozens of blackbirds in the huge tree outside the window. The big flock reminded her of all the crows that suddenly appeared before the dancers and the Messiah arrived at their camp by the river at Needles. The blackbirds, though only half the size of the crows, were handsome birds with bright yellow beaks and feet. They watched her look out the window at them and she realized they came to greet her and welcome her.

Hattie snored softly in the bed next to hers; Indigo lay on her side in the bed and watched Hattie for a while, but then she had to urinate. The bathroom was a short distance down the hall but she didn't want anyone to see her in bed clothes or a robe, so she got dressed. She tiptoed down the hall and held her breath as she turned the knob on the bathroom door, hoping it would not make a loud noise. She used the toilet but did not pull the chain because of the loud gushing sound the water made; she scooted the little step up to the lavatory and carefully washed her face and hands. She rebraided her hair and retied the ribbons as best she could, then took a final look at herself in the mirror.

"Hello, how do you do, fine thank you, a pleasure to meet you," she said to the image in the mirror. She had to laugh at her dark Sand Lizard face in the gilded oval mirror; now a Sand Lizard girl was loose in the white people's world.

She crept down the stairs to the big front doors with the polished brass latches and studied the mechanism; yesterday the doors opened without a sound. She tried the left latch first but it refused to move; but when she pressed down with all her might, the mechanism of the right latch lifted smoothly and the big door glided open. Once outside, she did not close the door for fear of noise. She inhaled the fragrance of the damp morning air delicious enough to eat: in the distance she could smell tasseled corn plants, squash blossoms, and the flowering beans and peas.

The dawn flooded the porch with golden green light that lifted her as she stepped into its radiance and pulled her toward it. She bounded down the front steps and felt the dampness of the grass through her slippers. She ran into the light pouring between the giant trees near the house along the vast lawns. To run and run over the soft earth while breathing the golden fresh air felt glorious.

She slowed to a walk under the great trees so she could examine them more closely; little mushroom caps dotted the ground under the trees and when she picked one and held it up close, tiny dewdrops glistened in the light. She popped it in her mouth and it tasted as fresh as the earth and the air. She searched for more mushrooms under the trees until her hunger was satisfied. She caught wind of the ocean smell—sharp green and restless; the wind was so cool she started off again.

It was easy walking under the giant trees because there were no rocks or gullies to watch out for; even the bushes of wild roses she had to sniff, and the thickets of fragrant azaleas—yellows, pinks, and whites—were just far enough from the path she need not worry about snagging her dress. At regular intervals the path through the trees opened into little clearings in bloom with blue-and-purple iris scattered with bright gold and bright white narcissus. She could feel the ocean's dampness though she still could not see it. The path went up a slight incline and then suddenly she stepped out of the trees into the brilliant morning light reflected off the bay below. Now she could see the road they'd taken along the edge of the bay, and lesser roads or driveways leading up from the beach and back into the big trees and meadows. As she made her way down from the hill, she came across what appeared to be an old stone wall fallen over in the thick beach grass and sand. Someone had lived there long ago, long before the roads or the driveways; she felt the gentle presence of the spirits of the place in the breeze off the water.

Edward was up before the others for an early breakfast with his sister and brother-in-law before Colin left for his office in the city. He found the front door ajar but assumed Lucille or one of the maids neglected to latch it properly. An old cow trail through the great oaks connected the two properties; he was surprised to see a gray flagstone path replaced the muddy trail. Along the path, clumps of purple foxglove and bright blue delphiniums were edged with lilies of the valley; this was the work of his sister and her new passion for English landscape gardens.

At dinner the evening before, Susan talked of nothing else but the progress of the workmen renovating the Italian-style gardens. Edward thought the word "demolition" seemed more appropriate—he was fond of the Renaissance-style gardens planted when the house was built. It seemed a pity because the trees and hedges had reached full maturity only recently. The sounds of the steel picks and shovels against earth and stone could be heard from beyond the blue garden, which itself was undergoing its annual preparations for the ball. Susan did not want her guests to see the same plants as the year before; she relished the challenge of creating new and startling effects with bedding plants and even shrubs and vines selected for their particular shade of blue; the white-flowering plants and shrubs were chosen for their impact in the moonlight. White blossoms took on the silvery blue of the moon, while the blue blossoms were transformed to a luminous cobalt blue.

The flagstone path emerged from the trees to cross a small stone footbridge over a rill of gushing water; six stone steps led up to the blue garden terrace with its pool and fountain. He paused to admire the tropical water lilies that were his sister's pride. They required special care in the winter, in tubs in the glass house. No matter how clever the plantings of blue flowers or white, the water lily pool was the heart of the blue garden. The huge night-blooming Victoria lily dominated the center of the pool with perfumed white blossoms as big as teapots; it was early enough that the flowers were still open, crowding the smaller blue water lilies that required full sun to blossom.

"Edward!" his sister's voice called out. "What do you think of my Victoria? Isn't she grand?" Susan appeared from the back of the terrace wearing a gray garden smock over her dress; a few paces behind her a tall, unsmiling man in hunter's tweeds despite the warm morning carried an open crate of big bulbs; Asiatic lilies, he thought. Susan introduced Mr. Stewart as her new gardener, from Glasgow. He gave a brisk nod but did not speak. When Susan told him to continue without her, Edward thought the gardener's expression betrayed an impatience bordering on insolence; how much did a Scottish gardener cost per year? he wondered.

Susan paused a moment on the terrace before they went indoors to watch the workmen and teams of horses below as they moved the dark soil, while others with steel bars and picks dislodged the marble tiles and removed the stone blocks of the balustrade. What a ghastly mess, Edward thought, and barely managed a smile when Susan spoke of the improvement the English garden would make to the property.

At breakfast, Edward learned all about the costs of gardeners, workmen, and garden renovations. When Susan was not talking about the price of Asiatic lily bulbs, Colin was talking about the boost to the stock market from the war with Spain. The conversations about costs and expenses began to give Edward an anxious feeling in his stomach; it reminded him of the illness after his rescue on the Pará, and he feared he might have to excuse himself from the table. He took small sips of water and wiped his forehead with his handkerchief, and the ill feeling passed.

To move the subject from finances, Edward asked if his nieces, Josephine and Anna, would be joining them for breakfast. No, the young ladies were away for a weeklong round of parties in Newport. The girls disliked all the dust and noise from the garden renovation. Oh, the expenses that came along with two lovely daughters! Susan gave him a significant look as she said this. Edward felt his heartbeat quicken: had Colin and Susan guessed the reason for his visit? They had loaned him money after the stock market's plunge in 1893 to protect the family estate from Edward's creditors.

Colin managed Susan's financial interests closely, and more than once Colin hinted the sale of the Riverside property might become necessary unless the orange and lemon groves yielded profit. Edward's proposal fit the requirements perfectly. He cleared his throat discreetly, then launched into a spirited description of the profits to be made from the *Citrus medica*. The demand for candied citron by confectioners and bakers increased each year, especially during the holiday season. Candied citron was quite fashionable now, strewn in everything from bride's cakes to oatmeal cookies.

Colin James leaned closer over the table. Edward's mouth felt oddly dry and his tongue felt thick; he knew he had only this chance to win over Colin and Susan to his citron proposal. Currently, Corsica and her French and Italian owners controlled the world's commercial supply of citron. Now, by a special arrangement with the Bureau of Plant Industry, he would own some of the first citron cuttings ever imported to the United States.

Edward relaxed a bit when he saw them smile. He could tell they were interested as he explained the advantages of grafting the newly obtained cuttings of *Citrus medica* onto the limbs of mature lemon and orange trees. They would have a crop of *Citrus medica* in eighteen months or less.

He exhaled slowly and tried to appear calm as he spread strawberry preserves on his toast, but his legs trembled under the table. He smiled hopefully at Susan and then at Colin as he waited for their response. The interval of silence was their answer, he knew that; and the silence was so unbearable he began to babble about the candied citron market. Why, last Christmas holiday, supplies of candied citron were depleted before New Year's Eve!

Edward's forehead felt hot; the napkin was twisted into a knot on his lap; he looked out the window behind Susan, where workmen were tearing out a terrace wall to make way for the English meadow. His thoughts turned without warning to what could happen if he failed on his Corsican mission. Quickly he shifted his thoughts to the present, to the pleasure he would have making photographs of the remaining garden balustrades and the statues before the workmen removed them. As soon as they returned from Indigo's pony ride, he would unpack his camera.

Colin glanced over at Susan from time to time as he spoke, and she nodded almost imperceptibly. They were quite concerned about the pending lawsuit involving him and Lowe & Company; any judgment against his share of the family estate naturally affected Susan's interests.

"A forced sale by the court—" Colin stopped in midsentence, but Susan continued. "Your plan to grow citron sounds quite appealing but we can do nothing until the outcome of the lawsuit is certain." Susan did not want him to worry; she and Colin had a plan: they intended to buy out his share of the estate entirely.

"But it will not come to that!" Edward surprised himself with his own vehemence. As a matter of principle, he did not want to ask Hattie to use her money to finance the citron grove; he wanted to keep matters of his mother's estate out of their marriage.

◆ ◆ ◆

Hattie woke from a dream about England. She had been in an old churchyard sitting on a strange flat stone in front of the church door. She did not recognize the old stone church, nor could she read the gravestones, but Aunt Bronwyn was with her, urging her to slide her seat along on the stone. Hattie tried to scoot herself the length of the stone, but the cloth of her dress snagged on the corner of the stone. In her dream Hattie tugged at the cloth so hard she woke herself with the bedcovers in her hands. She turned to see if Indigo was awake and saw the bed was empty. No wonder! The clock on the nightstand showed ten o'-clock. Still, Hattie was in no hurry as she dressed; Edward was going to breakfast with Susan and Colin, where he hoped to borrow a gentle pony for Indigo to ride. Edward must have taken Indigo along with him to look at the ponies his nieces kept.

Lucille had just served Hattie her toast and coffee with hot milk when her mother came into the dining room to ask Indigo's whereabouts. When she was told the child was with Edward, Mrs. Abbott's eyes widened with alarm; she had just seen Edward, and the child was not with him! Hattie refused to become flustered. She reassured her mother Indigo was nearby, and in any case the girl was quite capable of taking care of herself.

Edward changed into his riding clothes and borrowed his sister's chestnut gelding to search along the shore while the others went up and down the farm roads. Edward lifted the reins gently to signal the gelding he wanted a leisurely pace. He never shared his sister's passion for riding; a horse was a conveyance, not a recreation.

The sky and sea were bright blue. A refreshing breeze blew in his face. Off in the distance he saw sailboats and fishermen in small skiffs follwed by seagulls circling and diving all around them. He crossed the road to follow the path down to the beach because he thought a child might be attracted by the sound of the waves on the rocks. What a mighty sound it was! Edward felt the coolness of the salt mist on his cheeks. Seagulls were feeding on mussels at the edge of the water and scarcely noticed when he rode past. For as far as he could see, the beach was deserted, but he knew he must double-check in case the child was playing among the rocks by the water.

Though he looked up and down the shoreline for the child, he was thinking about the journey ahead—especially Corsica. All he had to do was to complete the task and he would be released from all costs and damages that might result from the pending lawsuit over the orchids. In his letter, Mr. Grabb, the attorney for Lowe & Company, revealed certain silent partners in the Pará expedition wished to settle the lawsuit out of court to avoid embarrassment. These silent partners were willing to settle for cuttings from the *Citrus medica*. Although neither Mr. Grabb nor Mr. Albert of Lowe & Company ever acknowledged it, Edward knew the British and the U.S. government were behind the offer. Clearly the trip to Corsica was going to be one of the most important in his life. He was glad to have the solitude of a ride by the sea to contemplate the course ahead. It would be quite simple really; no need to concern Hattie with the details.

◆ ◆ ◆

"Come on, Hattie, let's take a walk down the road," her father said as he came indoors from his pigs and goats in his dust coat and rubber boots.

"We are likely to find the child on our stroll. She's probably found something more interesting than a house full of elderly Yankees!"

How Hattie loved her father when he made her laugh at her troubles! He was proud of her choice of the female principle in the early church as a thesis topic, despite the furor it caused. Hattie reminded him of Aunt Bronwyn, his mother's sister, who abruptly left the church after her husband died and moved to Bath to live in seclusion and study the prehistoric archaeology of the British Isles and old Europe.

"When you ran away from Lucille, you always ran to the sea," he said, and she laughed and linked her arm in his as they walked the rocky shoreline.

Hattie knew he wanted to know if she and Edward were happy together, but he did not want to pry, bless his heart!

She told him what he wanted to know: she and Edward got along quite well in the marriage. They both had their own interests; although Edward's interests called him to distant places, she rather enjoyed the solitude of the Riverside house and its dilapidated but elegant gardens. Almost as an afterthought she added he and her mother should not expect grandchildren; she felt strangely breathless and regretted her last remark. Her father's expression of disappointment was gone in an instant, replaced by a look of puzzlement and concern. For reasons of health, Hattie said, and offered no explanation. Her remarks left her strangely breathless and light-headed. They were about to walk onto the stone jetty when voices called, "Mr. Abbott! Mr. Abbott! The farmers caught the little Indian!" Here came Ceena and Grace running down from the road.

Indigo had followed the rocky beach for a good distance, examining the bits of shells and kelp and driftwood she found among the gray rocks. The ocean was fascinating and Indigo was sorry when she got too hungry to keep walking along the shore. She left the beach and crossed the road to reach the overgrown meadows on the hillside where she had seen the purple blossoms of wild peas scattered among the sunflowers, goldenrod, and milkweed. She picked green pea pods and when there were no more, she hungrily pushed purple blossoms into her mouth as she continued to walk toward the west, through the old fields not planted for a long time. Where did white people get their food if they didn't plant these fields? She could not see what lay past the sharp curve of the bay, so she kept walking, alert for wild pea pods and berries or anything that might be good to eat. She wished she could locate some drinking water. Where did the stream flowing through Hattie's yard come down the hill? She stopped to empty the sand out of her shoes and to urinate. Up ahead, she was thrilled to see a low stone wall with field of tall corn beyond it.

She easily scaled the wall and went for a nice plump ear of green corn. The white kernels were different—smaller and sweeter—than Sand Lizard corn, but still this was Mother Corn, who feeds her children generously. The baby kernels were tiny, but oh so juicy and sweet! She had eaten her fill and was just about to climb back over the wall to head back home when someone grabbed her from behind and lifted her off her feet.

Instinctively she sank to the ground as deadweight to tear free from the grip. When the hand reached down to lift her she buried her teeth into the sweaty, hairy forearm. For an instant he flinched and lost his hold; she managed to break free. She ran as fast as she could through the rows of corn, back in the direction she had come. She was about to climb over the rock wall when the two farmers cornered her. This time they knew better than to grab hold of her. She watched them and they watched her; they spoke to each other but they didn't speak to her. They thought she was lost. They thought she belonged to someone named Matinnecock.

The bitten man went for the wagon while the other man watched her; she could easily have escaped him, but she was tired. They refused to believe her when she pointed in the direction of the Abbotts' house; its gray slate roof was partially visible through the tall trees on the hilltop.

Lloyd brought the buggy and off they went to the farm down the road. Yes, the farmers had found an Indian girl that morning. She had pointed in the direction of the Abbott house but they thought she must be mistaken. Only minutes earlier his brother left to take her to the Indian settlement on Manhasset Bay near Glen Cove. Hattie barely contained her agitation; she took deep breaths and reminded herself to remain calm; the child was in no danger.

Indigo was skeptical when the white man said he would take her home, but she thought he might know something she didn't know. Not long after they turned west, they passed through a small settlement and then a village similar to Oyster Bay. She was happy to be going west, but she knew there was a great distance south she must travel as well to get back to Arizona.

The farmland gave way to salt marshes that ran to the edge of the ocean. Then the wagon turned off the road onto a narrow sandy trail that led to a cluster of old wooden buildings and beyond them. Two dogs came barking to greet them and Indigo saw heads peek out of doors and windows; the wagon stopped and a small group of women and men gathered around.

Their clothes and shoes and the hats they wore fooled her for an instant, but Indigo saw their faces and realized these were Indians, though their features were very distinct from the people at home. They all looked at her and shook theirs heads slowly when the farmer asked if she was their child.

"No sir, this girl's not from around here."

The farmer looked at Indigo. He had not believed her when she told him that she came from the big house on the hill.

"She looks like one of those desert Indians, don't you think?" one of the women said to the others. "Look how round her head is!"

"Look what nice shoes those were before she ruined them in the sand!"

"She's really dark," said another.

"If she isn't one of yours," the farmer said with a look of concern on his face, "I wonder what I should do." No one spoke. Now that it was clear the lost child did not belong to the small settlement of Matinnecock Indians near Manhasset Bay, the farmer began to reconsider. The big house the child had indicated was the Abbott house; old man Abbott went from one crazy philanthropic scheme to another; maybe this Indian child was part of a new scheme. The farmer paused a moment to decide what to do next.

Indigo looked at the children who gathered around the wagon with the older folks; she saw no one her mother's age. They all looked at her with wide eyes; then from behind the houses a big woman, tall as a man, with big strong legs and arms, approached Indigo's side of the wagon.

"Where did you come from, little one?"

Indigo pointed to the southwest horizon.

"But how did you get here?"

"On the train."

"Where is your mama?"

Indigo again pointed to the southwest. The big Indian woman chuckled and shook her head as she went back to the farmer's side of the wagon.

"She's probably been sent from an Indian school for the summer to work in one of the big houses here," the woman told the farmer. She smiled at Indigo.

"You stay with me. I'll take care of you until someone comes for you." Indigo nodded shyly.

"We'll look after her," the big woman announced. The farmer was hesitant; he was not sure what he would do with the Indian child otherwise, so he agreed. Indigo stepped down from the wagon seat into the big woman's open arms; she squirmed because only babies were carried and the woman set her down. The beach sand was deep and warm through her kid slippers;

she looked past the other children, who were watching her. Tall grass and scrubby little bushes covered the dunes that went on and on until they met the blue-gray sea.

After the farmer was gone, everyone crowded closer to get a good look at her. The younger children touched her dress and her shoes shyly.

"You must be from the Carlisle Indian School," the big woman said. "They put students to work for white people in the summer."

Indigo shook her head.

"No?" The woman looked puzzled, then shook her head slowly and smiled. "You must be hungry."

Indigo nodded her head vigorously.

"Come on, this way," the big woman said and took her by the hand.

Behind the houses and shacks, Indigo saw a number of people who appeared to be digging in the sand not far from the water's edge. An old man and two boys each carried baskets of odd white rocks to the hole. When Indigo got closer she saw the hole was actually a cooking pit lined with smooth flat stones nestled in a thick layer of hot coals. The baskets of flat smooth rocks were emptied into the cooking pit and then the pit was covered with large flat stones. Everyone sat down with their baskets by their feet while they waited for the meal to cook. Indigo was quite interested to learn how the people cooked and ate the odd flat rocks they gathered on the beach; Sand Lizard people knew how to eat nearly everything but they didn't know how to cook and prepare rocks. She expected the rocks might have to cook overnight, but it wasn't long before the flat stones were removed and the people began to use their baskets to scoop up the steaming white rocks.

How amazing! In just that short time, the flat white rocks cooked and cracked open. A little animal lived inside. Indigo watched the other children scoop out its remains, and she copied their example. The meat felt a little odd when she bit into it, but its ocean flavor was wonderful. Indigo ate until there was a small mound of shells on the ground in front of her. The other children no longer stared at her, and as they finished eating, they drifted away in the direction of the ocean's edge. When she noticed the big woman gathering up the shells, Indigo began to help her. They put them in a large old basket by the front door of her little house. Next to the basket was an old bench with a flat stone, the sharpened tip of a deer antler, and a black flint chisel; nearby lay a clamshell with a circle cut out of the shell's thickest edge. The flat stone had long grooves worn into it; bits of shell dust glittered on the stone's surface. While Indigo looked at her workbench, the big woman brought out a small flat basket from inside the shack.

"Look," the woman said as she scooped up a big handful of the shining shell disks and let them cascade back into the basket. Indigo turned the disk over and over in her hand. One side of the disk was pure white shell but the other side was a silvery rainbow of color. The woman held up the antler chisel and the flint awl, then put one of the shell disks on the flat rock; she took a stone hammer and began to gently tap the antler chisel into the center of the shell disk. When she had made an indentation on the shell, she reached for the flint awl and began to roll it rapidly between her hands, to drill a hole in the shell. When one tiny hole was completed, she drilled another.

"A button," she said as she handed the finished work to Indigo. Fifty buttons brought a quarter, and with a quarter they bought lard, flour, and salt to supplement the clams and fish.

"Where are your gardens?" Indigo wanted to know. The woman pointed at the hills above the beach, where Indigo saw only weeds and shrubs. The woman looked at the hills for a long time and Indigo understood her silence as her answer; the land where their gardens used to grow was taken.

Yet they possessed a last, great, bountiful farm, the woman said with a smile as she turned from the hills to the heaving restless blue ocean. Indigo watched as the woman waded into the water and bent over and picked up a long strange ribbonlike plant with a knob on the end. In a tiny freshwater stream that emptied in the ocean, the woman showed Indigo how to rinse off the kelp with freshwater before she cut it into pieces for drying in the shallow basket hanging from the ceiling of the shack. Once the washed seaweed was dried, it tasted much better. She passed Indigo a smaller basket with odd dark pieces of dried seaweed for Indigo to try. The smell of the ocean was strong on the dried kelp as she raised it to her mouth, and at first she only licked the kelp with the tip of her tongue. The faintly salt taste and the strange texture were interesting, so she put the whole piece in her mouth. Dried kelp was surprisingly good. The woman smiled, but then her expression became serious.

"Were the people who brought you here unkind? Is that why you ran away?"

Indigo shook her head. "I didn't run away," she said. "I was just going for a walk when those men grabbed me."

"Then the people who brought you will be very upset, and they'll come searching for you." Indigo nodded. The big woman was nice and the other people and children were friendly, but she was beginning to feel a little tired now. Those men who grabbed her got her lost. Why was it no one ever let her go where she wanted? Sister Salt and Mama would be worried about her by now; they might think she was dead. Indigo sat on the little log stool and did nothing, when big hot tears began to roll down her cheeks.

Edward rode east for nearly two miles along paths in the old-growth trees that crowned the ridge above the sea. From time to time he encountered vast clear-cut sites where excavations for foundations were under way or construction already begun. He rode until he was satisfied no child could have walked such a distance, then turned the horse back.

Hattie was annoyed the farmers had taken Indigo away. She could imagine the child's terror, and it was all so needless because Indigo had pointed to the house, but the farmers refused to believe her. Mr. Abbott asked Lloyd to trot the team a bit faster when he saw the expression on Hattie's face; he had not seen such fierce determination since the debate over her thesis topic.

"Glen Cove? There aren't any Indians in Glen Cove!" Hattie exclaimed. Time was passing and still they had not found her. Mr. Abbott patted Hattie on the back and reassured her; Lloyd knew of some Indian families living on the salt marshes just outside of Glen Cove, on Manhasset Bay.

"I didn't know there are Indians nearby!" Hattie exclaimed. Lloyd nodded his head and glanced over his shoulder at Hattie. He held the reins in one hand to point at the peninsula of land ahead of them. Hattie could see a few small shacks in the sand above the salt marsh and shore.

A large Indian woman was standing outside the shack to greet them as the buggy pulled up. She was smiling but scrutinized her visitors.

"We were told we might find a lost Indian girl here," Mr. Abbott began. The woman nodded.

"A tired little girl," she said. "Please come inside. She's asleep."

Mr. Abbott and Hattie followed the woman inside the shack. On a pallet in the corner, covered with an old quilt, Indigo was sound asleep. The Indian woman knelt down and spoke softly to Indigo.

"Wake up, dear. Your friends are here," she said. Indigo sat up with her eyes open wide. For an instant she did not know where she was, but then she remembered the ride in the farmer's wagon. Hattie knelt next to her.

"Oh Indigo, I'm so sorry this happened!" Indigo rubbed her eyes and got to her feet. As she lifted Indigo into the buggy, Hattie thanked the big woman again and again for her kindness to Indigo. Her father reached down from the buggy seat and extended two silver dollars in his hand, but the Indian woman refused the money.

"If she needs a place to stay, please remember she is welcome here," the woman said as Lloyd lifted the reins.

"I can't thank you enough," Hattie said, then shook hands with the woman before she stepped into the buggy.

"Good-bye," Indigo called out to the woman, who waved at her until the wagon turned onto the road. Her eyes filled with tears.

"I hate that English word!" Indigo said, fiercely wiping her eyes on the sleeve of her dress.

"Don't you have a word in your language that means 'good-bye'?" Mr. Abbott inquired gently.

"No! 'Good-bye' means 'gone, never seen again'! The Sand Lizard people don't have any words that mean that!"

"What do people say to one another when someone leaves on a journey?"

"They say, 'We'll see you soon,' or, 'We'll see you later.' " Indigo replied so vehemently Mr. Abbott was taken aback.

She flung herself down on the buggy backseat and covered her face with both hands.

"She is so unhappy," Hattie said in a low voice as Mr. Abbott glanced back at the sobbing child. "I feel as if I should let Edward go on without us and take the child back to her family."

"But I thought you wrote that the child is an orphan."

Hattie shook her head. "Apparently there is some confusion. She says she has a mother and a sister."

But Edward was depending on her, and Aunt Bronwyn was looking forward to their visit, though it would be brief. The government red tape would take months to untangle; in the meantime Indigo was better off with them than at the school. Hattie reached over and patted Indigo's back soothingly.

"Indigo, I promise. As soon as we return, we'll find your mother." Indigo sat up on the seat and wiped away the tears with the back of her hand.

"And Sister Salt!" Indigo cried out. "Don't forget her!"

They did not get home until nearly three o'clock. Edward and Hattie's mother met them at the door.

"You three look exhausted!" Mrs. Abbott said.

"It was the anxiety that was so exhausting," Hattie said as she removed her hat and duster.

"I'll have the maids heat water for baths." Hattie nodded as she and Indigo climbed the stairs hand in hand.

"That was quite an adventure you had today, wasn't it?" she said. Indigo nodded solemnly.

"We'll bake cookies later this week and bring some to the nice woman who took care of you."

"I would like that," Indigo said. "Maybe we could ride there on ponies." She did not want them to forget. She hoped Edward borrowed a nice pony.

Over breakfast the next morning, Mrs. Abbott announced the arrival of their invitations to the Masque of the Blue Garden, two weeks away.

"How perfect that you'll be here!" Mrs. Abbott exclaimed, her face animated with pleasure. Everyone who had attended the ball the year she and Edward met would be there. Hattie set her cup down in its saucer. During their yearlong engagement, close relatives and acquaintances, both hers and Edward's, invariably mentioned how divine it was they had met at the Masque of the Blue Garden. Hattie was not sure she could endure an entire evening of similar exclamations and remarks from people she barely knew. Hattie looked across the table at Edward to gauge his reaction, but he seemed unconcerned.

Mrs. Abbott knew how to translate silence from Hattie, so she quickly added, if the Masque of the Blue Garden was too much, she and Susan would plan a series of dinner parties in their honor to allow family and friends to visit with Hattie and Edward. Hattie did not relish either prospect and decided the Masque of the Blue Garden was preferable; all the probing glances and questions about them and their new life in California would be relegated to one night, instead of six nights. Hattie was grateful the conversation turned to horseback riding; Indigo was anxious to know when they were going. As soon as they finished breakfast, Edward replied.

Indigo discovered riding horses wasn't as easy as it looked; the pony's fat sides were difficult to grip with her legs. Hattie explained how to press her boot heels down hard in the stirrups to brace herself, though her legs must flex up and down to keep time with the horse's trot. The reins were the tricky part; if Indigo forgot to hold them just right, the pony stopped and refused to move. Indigo tried to pet the pony and talk to it, but the pony's brown eyes were angry.

"He doesn't like to be ridden," Indigo called out to Hattie, who was trotting her horse up and down the paddock.

"Don't worry! He's a spoiled pony but you'll show him who's boss!"

Indigo began to have second thoughts. She didn't want to be the boss of any pony that didn't want to be ridden, but Hattie gestured for her to come on. Indigo cautiously nudged the pony's sides with her heels. The pony pinned back its ears at the irritation but followed the horse Hattie rode. Indigo remembered to post up and down in the stirrups as the pony trotted along. Though Indigo tried to pull the pony's head to the left, the pony refused to take the middle of the path; instead it veered along the path's edge as close as it could get to the branches of trees and shrubs to scrape her boot and riding skirt.

Hattie's horse ran on ahead, but the pony refused to change its course despite Indigo's sharp tugs on the reins. Now the heavy twill fabric of Indigo's riding skirt was pulled and snagged by sharp branches as the fat pony tried to scrape Indigo off its back. She felt the sharp point of a branch poke her right knee through the cloth; closer and closer the pony ran to the bushes and trees next to the path; now the leaves and twigs of the branches were slappping her face and pulling her hair. Suddenly she felt a sharp stab in her ankle and felt the fabric give way with a ripping sound. Her ankle ached from the blow and she felt the stinging sensation of a deep scratch, but she could do nothing but flatten herself against the saddle, head down, and hold on as best she could with a fistful of the pony's mane. The ground flashed by faster and faster as the pony ran out of control.

Hattie glanced over her shoulder and saw Indigo's distress. Hattie pulled back hard on the reins and wheeled the thoroughbred around to block the path of the runaway pony. As soon as the pony saw its stable mate turn back on the trail ahead, the pony began to slow; it stopped next to Hattie's horse.

"Indigo! Are you all right?" Hattie called out as she dismounted and went to Indigo's side. Indigo's heart was pounding as she cautiously released her grip on the pony's mane and sat up straight again in the saddle with both hands on the reins.

"Are you hurt?" Hattie looked anxiously at Indigo's face; she could see the child's discomfort. Indigo shook her head, but two big tears rolled down her cheeks. She leaned down and rubbed her right ankle and felt the torn riding skirt. Hattie pulled back the torn fabric and exposed the long scratch that oozed a bit of blood.

"Oh Indigo! I'm so sorry!" Hattie said as she helped Indigo dismount. The child was shaking and Hattie gathered her into her arms and hugged her.

Edward rode up just then and led their horses behind his horse while they walked home. He was feeling rather discouraged about the success of the visit so far. He didn't blame the child. She was a welcome diversion from the thoughts crossing and recrossing his mind. So much depended on the success of the trip abroad; he could feel the anxiety stir in his chest. He longed to be gone from the Scottish gardener and the Welsh pony, to be under way to Bristol, to be one ocean closer to the citron trees in the dry hills of Corsica.

Hattie assumed Indigo's tears were due to the deep scratch on her ankle, and she tried to soothe the child with promises of medicine for the pain. Indigo did not reply; she felt nothing as sharply as the hurt feelings, the sadness at the fat pony's betrayal of her daydreams about flying along on horseback. She should have known better. Grandma Fleet used to warn her about approaching unfamiliar dogs or mules because sometimes mistreated animals attack without warning. It would have been better to take days or even weeks to make friends with the fat pony before she tried to ride him. Edward might know a great deal about plants and Hattie might know a great deal about books, but they didn't know much about ponies.

Lucille washed and dressed the scratch on Indigo's ankle.

"I won't ride ponies anymore," she told Hattie as Lucille wrapped the bandage, "but a bicycle might be fun."

The afternoon was spent resting; while the child slept, Hattie went to Edward's room, where she found him adding columns of figures. She put her hands on his shoulders and he put down his pencil and took her hands in his. She leaned down and brushed her cheek lightly against his, but felt him tense when she glanced down at the figures.

"Do your figures add up?" she said with a smile. Edward gamely nodded his head as he closed the ledger; he felt hopeful success with the citron cuttings would remedy the financial setbacks he'd suffered in recent years.

"Is the child asleep?" Hattie nodded. Edward removed his reading glasses.

"I could use a nap myself," he said as he rose from the chair to replace the ledger in his valise. Hattie sat on the edge of the bed and removed her shoes; she lay on top of the starched white bedcover. Edward took off his waistcoat and hung it up and turned the key in the lock before he removed his shoes and joined Hattie. The bedsprings creaked as he stretched out his legs, the leg with the old injury first. She was delighted he wanted to join her. Although they had been married for more than eight months, the chronic pain in his leg and the expedition limited their opportunities for intimacy, and they both were still quite shy with each other.

Before their engagement, they both confessed impediments to marriage:

Hattie revealed her terror of childbirth, and Edward revealed the leg injury might impede the performance of certain marital duties. He was no prude; he was a man of science; but the excruciating pain made him nauseous. Their marriage fit their needs perfectly. Hattie wanted the companionship of a man who respected her scholarly interests and her ambition to see her thesis completed. She wanted a man who cared about her happiness. Similarly, Edward wanted a life partner who understood his research interests and the necessity for travel to distant locations unhampered. Hattie hadn't minded a bit even when the Bahamas expedition came so soon after the wedding.

Since the child had joined them, Hattie was aware of a gradual change in her feelings—she no longer feared childbirth as much; she began to see the pain and danger as a sacrifice necessary to bring forth new life. Hattie raised herself on her elbow, her hand under her chin as she looked at Edward.

He closed his eyes; he could feel Hattie's breath on his face, warm and sweet; he opened his eyes to her face, glowing with contentment. Impulsively he embraced her; the sensation was delicious and Hattie pushed closer. Instantly the burning pain shot through the leg and left him motionless with agony. Hattie apologized profusely—she was so sorry to have bumped the old injury—but Edward quickly assured her; it was his own motion, not hers, that set off the pain.

The injured leg had healed quite well, considering his doctors were the mestizo brothers. Even when there was no pain, the healed leg felt strangely unfamiliar, as if it were another man's leg, not his.

They lay quietly side by side, holding hands; Hattie realized she was relieved and yet a bit sad; what a flawed vessel imprisoned the human soul! No wonder the heretic Marcion told his followers not to bother with marriage—the earthly body and what one did with it did not matter; there were no sins of flesh, only sins of the spirit.

Indigo dreamed she was with Mama and Sister Salt. They were driving a wagon pulled by two black army mules, and the entire bed of the wagon was heaped with dirty linens and dirty clothes. She did not recognize the place on the river where they knelt by shallow pools with their scrub boards and big lumps of brown soap; perhaps the place was near Fort Yuma. In the dream Indigo knelt next to them, but the surface of the scrub board she used was uneven. As she scrubbed the white garment, its fine pearl buttons snagged and pulled loose; in dread, she lifted the soapy garment up and saw that it was a white dress of fine cotton, clearly a dress that belonged to a rich woman. Sister Salt yelled at Indigo to be careful and to find the buttons and sew them back on. In the dream Sister Salt looked different; she was as tall as Mama and almost as heavy. Mama said nothing; then Indigo noticed Mama carried a basket full of mother-of-pearl buttons just like the one the nice woman gave her.

Indigo woke with a start. For an instant she did not know where she was, but then she remembered and was filled with sadness as she looked around the unfamiliar room filled with objects she did not know. Indigo felt the pain move around her chest and into her throat until tears filled her eyes, and tears rolled down her cheeks to her chin and ears. Soon the pillow felt damp at the back of her neck. "I'm trying to get back home," she whispered to Mama and Sister Salt, and hoped when they dreamed they'd see her in this room and hear her message She stared at the ceiling's ornate carved moldings that appeared to be leaves and vines with bunches of round fat grapes. Oh, if Linnaeus were there, how much he would love to climb the draperies to finger the carved grapes! He would not be fooled— he would know they weren't real.

Indigo cheered herself with thoughts of Linnaeus and what he might do if he were with her. She was still sleepy and closed her eyes again to imagine Linnaeus and herself romping on the wide lawn edged with lilacs; she sent him a message too, in his dreams of her: she told him how much she loved him and that she would return.

Now she dreamed Grandma Fleet hugged her close and told her to be strong, and she would get back home just fine. When Indigo woke, the scent of crushed coriander leaves in the cloth of Grandma Fleet's dress was still vivid and so was the sensation of Grandma's embrace. Grandma Fleet came to her and she loved Indigo as much as ever; death didn't change love. The dream reminded Indigo she must gather as many new seeds of flowers and trees as she could find on this journey so she did not disappoint Sister Salt and Mama, or Grandma Fleet.

When Hattie woke from her nap, Edward was already awake, but they rested on the bed awhile longer. Hattie asked about his breakfast with Susan and Colin. They seemed quite well, Edward replied. The girls were off for a week of parties with their cousins in Newport.

"They'll be engaged and married before we know it," Hattie said somberly.

"Susan is going all out with her garden renovations," Edward said as he rearranged the pillow under his head.

"I didn't expect to see a Scottish gardener," Hattie said. Edward recalled the odd, almost overbearing presence of the gardener that morning, but thought it rude to speculate about the arrangement. He did not mention the cool reception Susan and Colin gave his plan for the citron orchard, or his fear Susan and Colin wanted to assume control of the estate if the lawsuit turned out badly. Hattie was so earnest in her conduct with him and the child that he felt his resolve waver. For an instant Edward was on the verge of telling Hattie everything, but an ember of hope still glowed on the shores of Corsica, so he patted her gently on the arm and said nothing about the estate.

"I've been mulling over an idea for growing citron commercially—I ran it past Susan and Colin to see if they wanted to invest with us." Edward felt his heart pound in his chest as Hattie asked their reaction.

"Oh, they have no objections," he continued, which was true enough; Colin had perked up at the prospect of the citron; only the finances were in doubt. Edward worried Hattie might feel his pulse race as she fondly stroked his arm. He felt a weakness, a shortness of breath as if he were fleeing the flames on the hillside again. A voice inside his thoughts urged him to confide in Hattie, but he could not bring himself to tell her.

Hattie found Indigo in the front parlor with her mother. They were poring over a book of Renaissance costumes complete with the elaborate hats that reminded Hattie of pillows. The theme of the Masque of the Blue Garden was the Renaissance, and Indigo wanted to see how the costumes might look, though she had to imagine them in all shades of blue because that's what all the ladies wore, to match the garden, of course.

Indigo understood immediately: blue was the color of the rain clouds. She wanted to wear blue from head to toe, she announced, and Mrs. Abbott gave a smile and enthusiastic nod. Hattie reminded her mother children did not attend the ball, but Mrs. Abbott interrupted. Of course Indigo must come! Early, before her bedtime, she must see the blue garden in all its splendor! Her mother looked at Hattie as if to say, "Even this Indian girl can appreciate the ball more than you do."

Hattie realized then it was futile to attempt to resist the Masque of the Blue Garden. All right, Hattie thought, they would make the best of it. Off she went with Indigo to the library to look at more pictures of Renaissance costumes. Indigo was fascinated by the odd ornate collars the Elizabethans wore, so Hattie brought out more books. Indigo lost interest in the costumes when she saw the pictures and diagrams of Renaissance gardens; she spent the rest of the afternoon in the library, kneeling on a chair while Hattie browsed the shelves for other books of gardens and architecture.

Hattie glanced at the shelves of early church history without any curiosity or desire to look at them, and realized her interests were shifting.

Indigo lingered over books with pictures of gardens with water splashing from fountains and statues and even a long stone wall covered with spouts of gushing water. Hattie pointed out what appeared to be extensive stone stairs built for a great cascade of water to a long pool below; in Italy they'd see places like this. They looked at the books together and Hattie pointed out the French gardens and Italian gardens, but Indigo did not see a great deal of difference between them—except the French gardens seemed so empty while the Italian gardens were populated with stone figures of animals and people.

Hattie found the beginner's botany book her father gave her after they moved from the city. Hattie showed her diagrams of a lily bulb and a gladiolus corm. Indigo's expression went from concentration to delight. These bulbs were giants compared to the bulbs of little plants she and Sister Salt used to dig from the sand to eat raw.

They sat on the old leather library couch and began to read about the anatomy of the flower. Indigo was fascinated by the orchids with odd shapes that resembled butterflies and moths to lure insects to pollinate them. When Indigo's interest in stamens and pistils began to flag, they went out into the garden, where Indigo delighted in examining the late tulips and the gladiolus and lilies until her hands, face, and even the front of her dress were streaked with bright yellow-and-orange pollen.

Compared to Susan's garden or even the run-down gardens at the Riverside house, the Abbotts' garden was rather ordinary. Mr. Abbott's interest in gardening was limited to relief of hunger among the poor. Mr. Abbott said if he wanted flowers, he simply went next door for a look at Susan's latest feat.

The Abbott garden was shaded by towering trees that formed a great leafy canopy; simple rectangular plots enclosed by a rock wall were planted informally with scatterings of cosmos and hollyhocks above four o'clocks, snapdragons, and carnations. Along the wall, dwarf plums alternated with cherry trees behind the yuccas in clay pots. Towering foxgloves and fragrant columbines in rainbows of color delighted Indigo. She made her way carefully between the powder blue asters and creamy yellow sunflowers to reach the big yucca plants crowned with spires of waxy white blossoms. Indigo touched the sharp tips of the leaves carefully and watched the bees, fuzzy yellow with pollen, in the throats of the flowers.

Hello, Old Man Yucca, how did you end up here? Indigo thought as she gently touched the sharp tip of the spiny leaves. Hattie said the clay pots kept the yucca roots dry so they didn't rot from all the New York rain.

Indigo liked the water garden best and wiggled her fingers in the water to tempt the goldfish. Mr. Abbott found Hattie on her hands and knees and Indigo on her stomach; both craned their necks as far over the edge of the pool as they could to sniff the big yellow water lily blossoms. He called out with delight to see Hattie so relaxed and happy; he had feared for his daughter's happiness after the thesis controversy, but it was clear the Indian child was just what Hattie needed after her disappointments.

"We got tired of looking at flower pictures in books," Hattie explained. Edward had gone to the city to his lawyer's office to pick up a letter from their Riverside lawyer. Indigo was anxious to have news about the monkey.

"The little monkey is safe, I am sure," Mr. Abbott said; his eyes on Indigo's eyes urged her to share his confidence. He offered his hand to her and to Hattie, who took it; then Indigo shyly took his hand and together they walked down the stone walk past the stables. Mr. Abbott explained how he hoped to banish hunger from the lives of the poor families with dwarf goats and dwarf pigs that could be raised in cities. Her father's enthusiasm was a quality of his generous spirit Hattie loved a great deal; she feared her enthusiasm was ebbing away.

The experimental vegetable gardens formed a large border around the goat pens and pigpens. Lloyd and two young Negro men were shoveling goat manure into wheelbarrows. Mr. Abbott said the dwarf milk goats promised to be a success, but the jury was still out on the dwarf Chinese pigs.

The goats were browsing or lying down, but the instant they heard Mr. Abbott's voice they all jumped to their feet and began bleating loudly. Indigo allowed the goats to nibble the tips of her fingers while others started mock head-butting battles, rearing gracefully on their hind legs.

The small black Chinese pigs were alert and watched Mr. Abbott. They seemed to listen with defiant pride as he recounted their naughty habit of breaking out of the pen. The ingenuity of the pigs amazed Mr. Abbott; they pushed and pressed their bodies against the fencing material—stone, planks, or wire, it didn't matter to them—until they located the point of most weakness. Then day after day they took turns, rubbing and scratching themselves against the same point in the fence until at last the wire or the wood or the stones gave way.

After they escaped the first time, the pigs rooted up the kitchen garden; the following week they escaped again but seemed to remember the kitchen garden was ruined, because they went straight to the barn, where they managed to dump barrels of dry corn before Lloyd herded them back to their pen. Despite extra rations Mr. Abbott thought would calm them, the pigs escaped a third time. He pretended to shudder and shook his head. This time no one realized the pigs' escape until they had uprooted and eaten a dozen imported peonies just transplated by Susan's gardener. It had been a very expensive meal for pigs!

"If the pigs overran Susan's blue garden right now it would ruin her ball," Hattie said; the pigs' eyes followed her as if to memorize the face of one who dared speak against them.

Indigo watched the men rake and shovel the manure while Hattie and her father sat on the garden bench in the shade. She wondered if Lloyd and his sons had pigs and goats of their own; how did they take care of their pigs and goats if they were always here helping with Mr. Abbott's animals?

Her father was pleased Hattie had relented and agreed to attend the Masque of the Blue Garden because the occasion meant a great deal to Edward's sister.

"I know Susan isn't easy to know," he said as they relaxed on the bench and watched the child pet the goats. "But I think a spirit of amity between you and Susan is important, and the ball is the highlight of her year."

The next day, after Lucille cleaned up the breakfast dishes, she mixed the ingredients for gingerbread dough. Hattie rolled out the dough and Indigo used the cookie cutter to make the little dough men. Indigo pressed raisins into the faces for the eyes and nose, and a bit of candied cherry for the mouth.

Later, when the cookies had cooled, Hattie prepared a box of gingerbread men wrapped in wax paper. After Lloyd returned from taking Edward to the ferry, he drove Hattie and Indigo past Glen Cove to the salt marshes and dunes, down the sandy lane to the small, unpainted wood houses with fishing nets hung out to dry. No faces peeked out windows or doors, and Lloyd pointed at the iron padlocks on some front doors.

Indigo recognized the button maker's house by the mounds of broken shells in the front yard. Hattie held the box of gingerbread while Indigo knocked, but no one was home. A strong breeze came off the ocean and the salt marsh grasses rustled as Hattie stood looking in the direction of other houses for some sign of life. Indigo reached into her pocket and touched the shell button the woman gave her; she carried the button with her everywhere she went because the button was her first gift from another Indian and because the shell came out of the same ocean she soon must cross. After Hattie knocked at another door with no response, Indigo suggested they leave the box of cookies on the old chair by the front door. To keep any stray dogs and the gulls away, Indigo took an old wooden bucket and turned it upside down over the box on the chair. Years later Indigo always wondered if her friend the button maker found the box of gingerbread men still under the bucket when she returned.

The sounds of the wind in the grass and the nearby waves gave the deserted village a lonely feeling that did not leave Indigo until the carriage pulled around the driveway to the house and she saw Mr. Abbott walking from the stables with two brown-and-white goats on leashes. He smiled and waved for Indigo to come join him. Lloyd stopped the carriage and Indigo ran across the lawn and took the leash he offered.

As they walked along behind the grazing goats, Mr. Abbott told Indigo all about his plans for poor people to use goat carts for transportation. At the edge of the woods, the goats turned away from the wild blackberry bushes reluctantly, but they came along quite obediently once they realized they were headed home. Indigo helped Mr. Abbott feed two orphaned baby goats with bottles of warm milk. She was happy to see the little goats' gusto as they thrust their mouths against the black rubber nipples, nearly pushing the bottles out of their hands.

Just then Hattie came in the barn with a bright blue garment over one arm; Indigo's dress must be fitted. Indigo left the goats for the upstairs parlor, where the dressmaker and her assistant helped her step up onto the little pedestal so they could pin up the hem of the bright blue silk dress.

"My hands smell like goats," Indigo said, sniffing, then dropping her hands back to her sides. The seamstress and Mrs. Abbott exchanged glances and Mrs. Abbott turned to Hattie.

"You could have taken her to wash up first. When I told you to hurry back I didn't mean bring a dirty child."

"The child is not dirty, Mother; she only petted the goats. Father bathes those goats every day," Hattie said stiffly. "Father is the one who smells of goats." Mrs. Abbott seemed not to hear what Hattie said; she was preoccupied with the fit of the dress around Indigo's waist as the seamstress arranged the fabric. Afterward, Indigo stood barefoot on a piece of paper while Hattie traced the shape of her wide feet for matching slippers.

"Hattie, are you wearing your good slip? You'll be next for a fitting after the child," Mrs. Abbott said.

With the Masque of the Blue Garden only days away, Hattie and her mother joined Susan James and the other women of the bishop's aid society to complete preparations. Place cards were lettered and little blue satin bows were tied for the menus and the individual nosegays that were to grace each place setting. One afternoon the bishop himself stopped by for tea with the women of the aid society to express his appreciation for their generous efforts.

Hattie attended the tea for the bishop out of curiosity, because she overheard the women talk as they curled the crepe paper flower petals with their scissors. The bishop was much younger than his predecessor and quite charming; he was amiable and smiling as he surveyed the centerpieces and other decorations; his face was animated with pleasure as his eyes moved from face to face, as if appraising each woman. Hattie watched the women of the aid society line up to kneel to kiss the bishop's amethyst ring. The bishop's visit was their reward, and she did not begrudge their pleasure with the handsome bishop with only a few flecks of gray in his beard.

The bishop's cassock smelled of church incense and reminded Hattie of the Saturday religious instruction class of long ago. The bishop's booming voice and jolly chuckle rose above the happy hum of the aid society women, who excitedly whispered to one another after they kissed the bishop's ring. Mrs. Abbott made quick little hand motions for Hattie to join her in the line to kiss the ring. Hattie felt her face flush when her mother called out to her as the line grew shorter. She shook her head and fanned herself with a piece of paper. The bishop's presence seemed to saturate the entire ballroom with an odd energy that left Hattie feeling light-headed, as though she might faint. She rose from her chair so suddenly her scissors slipped from her lap, and one blade stuck straight into the hardwood parquet floor. She felt she would faint if she did not reach the door; her mother followed after her into the fresh air and the ill feeling passed.

As the day of the ball drew closer, Susan frequently left Mrs. Abbott in charge of the aid society volunteers while she donned her big sunbonnet to go out to supervise the workmen to hurry the completion of the English landscape garden along the driveway. The newly created hills were bright green with new turf the workers unrolled to fit seamlessly; large azaleas and mature dogwoods were transplanted, but the new hills needed something more to give the appearance of maturity.

The bishop's aid society volunteers were lettering the dozens of place cards when the dour face of the Scottish gardener once again popped around the door of the ballroom where the women worked at the tables. Good news, Susan said as she tied the sunbonnet under her chin. Her gardener had located two great copper beech trees at an old farm on the south shore, and now preparations were completed to move and transplant the beech trees together on the new hills.

The route of the two giant beech trees on their wagons took them through downtown Oyster Bay and necessitated workmen to temporarily take down electrical and telephone lines to allow the huge trees to pass. Hattie was embarrassed by her sister-in-law's excess and stayed behind to letter place cards with the other women. Edward and Mr. Abbott took Indigo along to witness the spectacle of the pair of sixty-foot trees inching through downtown Oyster Bay. People lined the street to stare at the odd procession. Indigo stood on the back of the buggy to get a better view. The slow progress of the wagons loaded with the trees gave Edward time enough to set up his camera to record the event.

Indigo was shocked at the sight: wrapped in canvas and big chains on the flat wagon was a great tree lying helpless, its leaves shocked limp, followed by its companion; the stain of damp earth like dark blood seeped through the canvas. As the procession inched past, Indigo heard low creaks and groans—not sounds of the wagons but from the trees. The Scottish gardener and Susan followed along behind the wagons in a buggy.

The actual unloading and planting of the two beech trees required another two hours after they arrived. Indigo watched with Edward and Mr. Abbott as the workmen attached chains and ropes to pulleys and the horses lifted the giant trees slowly off the wagons and set them in place. Susan joined them to express her concern the trees might not recover their vigor and appearance in time for the ball, but the Scottish gardener gave her a brisk nod that seemed to reassure her.

As soon as the trees were securely planted, Susan turned her attention to the blue garden itself; she invited Edward and Indigo to join her because she needed advice. The spring and early summer had been unusually dry, and the mainstay of blue gardens, the delphiniums, had suffered considerably and replacements must be found. The blue pansies and the violas were stunted, and the salvias, in so many hues of blue, were hardly better; besides, they were so common in blue gardens.

They followed her down the path to the outbuildings behind the house and gardens. Narcissus in July? Wisteria flowers in midsummer? Here was where it was all done; Susan opened the glass door and cold air rushed refreshingly against Indigo's face. The Scottish gardener's cold greenhouse was chilled with blocks of ice delivered three times a week; even the intensity of the light in the glass house was controlled, with muslin shrouds to affect the length of day so the big pots of wisteria, pruned into graceful trees, would bear cascades of sky blue and pure white blossoms for the Masque of the Blue Garden. Pots of blue irises, even big boxes of blue lilacs and blue rhododendrons, would adorn the ballroom, Susan explained.

Whites were as important as blues in the moonlight; on the night of the ball, pots of white wisteria and white bougainvillea would festoon the arches and gateways; cascades of pendulous white and blue wisteria would cover the long marble loggia completely. White lilacs and white azaleas would be scattered among the blue lilacs and blue rhododendrons for drama.

But what to plant in the flower beds around the lily pool? Every year Susan anguished over her choices: blue hydrangeas, blue campanulas, blue cornflowers, blue asters, blue lupines, and pale sky blue columbines were on her list of candidates. Weeks ago, the gardeners had planted every sort of blue-flowering plant imaginable, but now Susan must decide which plants would compose this year's blue garden.

Surely Edward would help her choose; she wanted the blue garden to hold something new and visually exciting, but something resistant to heat as well. Edward and Indigo followed Susan into the adjoining glass house that was much warmer. Here the damp earth smell enclosed them and Indigo felt a thrill when she saw big baskets of orchids hanging from the ceiling structure. This glass house was much larger than the one in Riverside.

The orchids shared the space with the bedding plants for Susan's new English landscape garden and, of course, this year's bedding plants for the blue garden. The glass house delphiniums, the belladonna—both *grandiflorum* and the Chinese—were thriving in here, but outdoors their older siblings, transplanted weeks before, showed the ravages of drought and heat. The *Anchusa azurea,* or blue Asian bugloss, growing next to the delphiniums was far less demanding, though its blossoms not as long lived, but they had to last only one night—the night of the ball. Pale blue spiderworts thrived on the other side of the delphiniums, but they preferred cloudy weather and were planted only in case the summer turned wet and cool.

The blue flowers of the *Gentiana* were wonderful but they would never last in the heat. Edward chose the blue globe thistle and the blue datura for the background, with bluegrass planted with blue *Gladiolus byzantius*. Jacob's ladder and blue balloon flowers went next to the blue Carpathian bellflowers. Of course, a veronica of deep blue must be planted with the myosotis; the forget-me-not and the blue Persian cornflowers should be edged with sapphire lobelia.

In low white marble planters near the coolness of the pool's edge, *Aconitum falconeri,* blue monkshood, and rare blue primulas would be complemented with blue foxglove. For dramatic effect among the blue flowers, there were drifts or scatterings of white lilies and white foxgloves, white hollyhocks, and bushes of white lavender and white tree lupines. In the blue borders bushy white asters and phlox were planted with white artemisia and white Canterbury bells.

Susan took notes as Edward called out the flowers' names, and Indigo examined them carefully. She wanted to remember each detail of the leaf and the stalk for all these plants and flowers so she could tell Sister Salt and Mama. She picked up seeds and saved them in scraps of paper with her nightgown and clothes in the valise so she could grow them when she went home.

The dampness steamed the glass but in the next room Indigo could see the tops of palm and banana trees. Dozens of bark fragments covered with jade green moss were planted with hanging orchids, and big pots of orchids lined the walks between the benches that held dozens of potted orchid plants. Edward stopped when he saw the two big *Laelia cinnabarina,* their fiery orange-red blossoms cascading from their hanging baskets. He felt unexpectedly moved by their magnificent beauty, and the sight of the blossoms overcame him with vivid memories of the fire and his accident. Although he helped collect nearly eight hundred plants, he returned from Brazil without a single specimen of the *cinnabarina* for himself; the storm and the salt water saw to that.

"Expensive specimens," Susan said when she saw him pause to examine the *cinnabarina.*

"Yes, expensive," Edward murmured, and wondered if these two *cinnabarina* were specimens he helped to collect. The humidity of the orchid room suddenly made Edward feel unwell. He looked anxiously at the glass house door.

Once they were outside the glass house, Edward stopped to look back at the workmen digging up old path stones in the ruin of the circular garden of herbs. Edward thought Susan was foolish, so he said nothing; only now had the Italian gardens reached their full maturity to reveal the vision of the architect, yet the gardens were being destroyed. His sister might transplant great trees all she wanted, but she would not see her new English gardens reach their maturity unless she lived to be quite old.

"I'm glad you spared the lemon garden," Edward said, because he was fond of the balustrades of pale limestone with the old lemon trees in their white stone pots along the walk.

"Actually I've not decided," Susan said over her shoulder as she walked up the path to the lemon garden, "but all the statuary must go. The marbles are white Carrara, but they've not weathered well in most instances." Edward noticed no damage; the gardens were well protected. She glanced at the two fat cupids embracing and Edward realized she was concerned about the propriety of the nude figures now that Josephine and Anna were young ladies. The noses and facial features of the marbles naturally softened with time, but there were other prominent features on the marbles not eroded enough.

Edward pointed out the interplay of shade and sunlight and the hues of green were soothing and cool; the Italian gardens here complemented the design of the house and were refreshing havens from the heat. The careful plantings of linden and plane trees, now mature, filtered the light to a lovely, luminous green-yellow, while the darker greens of the hollies and rhododendrons were inside the cool shadows.

Susan gave an impatient wave of her hand. At the time the architect designed the house and gardens she was newly married and had few ideas about gardens. Now she found the arrangement of shurbs and trees according to their hues of green artificial and boring; the geometric topiary forms were ridiculous. She wanted a natural garden filled with color—an English landscape garden with swaths of flowers in all colors from the bright to the shade. Edward asked for a reprieve for the lemon garden.

"I want to make photographs of the statues before the workmen take them away," he said. He could see a number of the statues had already been removed and were lying helter-skelter on the lawn and terrace. He started back to the house to get the camera, but Susan wanted to show the child the birds.

They followed a narrow flagstone path shaded by a canopy of linden trees. Up ahead, Indigo heard excited chirping and the flutter of wings, and then she saw a great many brightly colored birds of different sizes. The aviaries were as large as the glass houses and made of the same steel frame-work; steel mesh took the place of the panes of glass.

The cage of finches fluttered excitedly in the leaves of the big potted fig trees that shaded them. The canaries sat quietly on the perches of their aviary and watched. To hear the lovely songs of the Chinese thrushes one must be there just at dawn, Susan said; their songs were the loveliest.

"What's that bird called?" Indigo pointed at a bright green bird the size of a dove but with a thick hooked beak, alone in an ornate cage behind the aviary of thrushes.

"Oh that's a parrot—I bought two of them because I thought they'd be handsome in that lovely gilded cage in the conservatory among or-chids, but one died and now the whole look is spoiled. One parrot alone won't do."

Indigo tiptoed as close as she could to the cage bars to get a better look at the green parrot. It had a band of bright red feathers across its forehead above its curved beak, and the loveliest feathers of powder blue on the top of its head. The bird was perched on one leg with its head tucked under its wing.

"The bird looks ill," Edward said.

"It hasn't eaten well since it lost its mate," Susan said without looking at the bird.

"What's its name?" Indigo asked.

"Oh I don't bother to name the birds," Susan said. "There are so many."

Indigo watched the parrot open its eye from time to time to gaze at her; it seemed to know it was the subject of discussion, but Indigo thought the bird looked too sad to care what was said.

"What happened to the other parrot?" Indigo asked without taking her eyes off the bird.

"Now, Indigo, it isn't polite to ask questions." Edward turned to go back down the path toward the house, but Indigo didn't move.

"An accident—it was quite unpleasant," Susan said. "I didn't actually see it, thank goodness. Its mate was found dead—accidentally strangled by a toy, a piece of rope in the cage." Indigo saw no toys or ropes in the cage now, only the lone parrot on its perch. As Susan followed Edward up the path, Indigo leaned close to the bars of the cage and whispered, "Don't be sad, green parrot. I'll come visit you every day!"

The following morning Edward left early for a meeting in the city with Lowe & Company's lawyer, Mr. Grabb. Hattie did not sleep well the night before and awoke before dawn from a strange dream that left her oddly tired and a bit low. She asked her mother to give her apologies to Susan and the others making party favors; Hattie felt a great sense of relief after her mother went next door. She found Indigo in the parlor looking for pictures of parrots in a book about birds.

Hattie sat back in the armchair and closed her eyes. The dream itself was almost nothing—at first she saw the bishop at the altar with her mother and Susan and the bishop's aid society gathered around him, but then she realized this was not a church but a dimly lit room, with case after case of empty bookshelves, a library table, and chairs. An overpowering sense of loss and sadness accompanied the dream and she woke in tears. Even to recall the dream stirred a sadness in her, so she turned her attention to Indigo, who was carefully studying a color plate of the parrots. She found herself smiling at the child's serious expression as she searched for a picture of a green parrot like Susan's. Edward was right about the benefits of travel for the child.

Indigo wanted to know more about parrots. She asked Hattie to take her to the aviaries every day, but the green parrot ignored the child. The fruits, nuts, and seeds remained in its dish untouched. Hattie feared the parrot's condition was deteriorating before their eyes. When they were back in the house, Hattie gently reminded Indigo the parrot was ill, and she mustn't become too attached to it. Moments later tears ran down Indigo's face, but when Hattie asked what was wrong, the child accused her of lying about the well-being of the monkey. Hattie promised their lawyer in Riverside would not lie; they would ask him to find Linnaeus a little friend to share his cage.

"Mr. Yetwin will find the nicest little kitten he can and take it over at once for Linnaeus."

Tears welled up in Indigo's eyes; each time she thought of him, she prayed for Linnaeus to be safe until she returned; but she was careful not to think about him too long or she began to feel so lost and alone the knot in her throat wouldn't let her breathe. But now, as she imagined a fat yellow-striped kitten leaping up the wisteria vines behind the mischievous Linnaeus, her tears dried.

"Is there a book with pictures of cats?"

"In the library," Hattie said, and opened the door for Indigo. As she followed the child up the stairs, Hattie thought how odd her parents' house seemed now—even her own bedroom no longer felt her own. Although she knew all the objects by heart, she no longer felt any attachment to them.

Was it all the activity in preparation for the bishop's benefit that made her anxious to be on their way to England?

Hattie recognized the startled sensation in her chest with its urgency that left her perspiring. She first felt the sensation the day her thesis adviser notified her that the committee had grave reservations about her thesis conclusion. The day she thought she might have to kiss the bishop's ring the startled sensation surged up but disappeared as soon she reached fresh air. She worried the anxious sensation might return and incapacitate her as it had two years before.

Hattie was still feeling unwell and went to lie down, so Indigo went downstairs to the kitchen and found Lucille, who gave her a bowl of soup at the kitchen table. While she was eating, she heard Edward's arrival from the city. Indigo could hear Mrs. Abbott's voice clearly; "blue shoes for Indigo" brought her right out of the kitchen into the parlor.

Edward sat in an armchair with his boots off and his stocking feet on the footstool, talking to Mrs. Abbott. He felt overheated and slightly ill from the dry wind that stirred the dust of the city; he was glad to be back at Oyster Bay. Mrs. Abbott smiled when she saw Indigo and pointed at a small package on the table.

Indigo carefully unknotted the string to save for her ball of string before she removed the wrapping paper and folded it neatly. Nestled in white tissue paper Indigo saw sapphire blue satin slippers. Shyly she picked up a slipper to show Mrs. Abbott and Edward, who mopped at his forehead with his handkerchief but smiled. Indigo sat with the slippers on her lap and admired them; from time to time she touched the shiny satin more smooth and wonderful than she remembered.

"Do you want to try them on to see if they fit?" Mrs. Abbott suggested, but Indigo shook her head. Her feet were so wide she feared the beautiful shoes might not fit; but she wanted the shoes anyway because they were so lovely to touch and to see.

After he recovered from his trip to the city, Edward spent the afternoon with his camera as the last of the statues and figures were hauled away to auction. Under his black camera cloth he focused the camera lens on the freight wagon loaded with marble statues and lead figures secured by ropes in wooden crates. In the contrasting light, the pale figures piled on one another in the wagon made a macabre image.

Indigo turned away before Edward spotted her and asked her to pose next to the wagon. She didn't like to have the camera's big glass eye focused on her. The arms of many of the women statues were flung upward in fear, or maybe that was to show off their breasts to men. The statues of men appeared more calm, looking away as if they did not yet realize the destination of the wagon.

She sat at the edge of the big water lily pool to admire the fragrant sky blue flowers on long stems at the edge of the white lilies; the blue flowers stood above the water's surface in row after row like soldiers.

Edward set up the tripod and camera on the lemon garden terrace; terrace and garden both were spared only because of their connection with the blue garden. The Italian gardens were so intimate and refined, so secure from intrusion. Why bother with an English landscape garden when the wooded hills of the island were quite lovely themselves? He wondered if his sister realized how fickle garden fashion was; the so-called English garden was already passé.

He tried a number of different views of the ballustrade and terrace before he realized he needed a human figure in his composition to reveal the Renaissance garden's elegant scale. He almost overlooked her by the pool but he called Indigo to come stand by the life-size lead figures of a stag pursued by hounds.

Indigo came reluctantly, taking small steps and watching her feet move across the ground. She did not like to stand still for so long facing into the bright sun. She didn't care what he said about keeping her eyes open; she didn't like to see the big glassy eye of the camera staring at her. He told her the photograph was ruined if her eyes were closed; when she asked why, he did not answer. After the third plate was exposed, Indigo asked if they might go look at Susan's birds in the aviaries. Hattie was still resting upstairs and Mrs. Abbott was next door.

Edward was annoyed the child would not cooperate when he asked her to pose. He told her he was busy with the camera, to go herself but to find Susan to ask permission first. He was absorbed in making the photographs and gave no further thought to the whereabouts of the child.

Indigo was not comfortable with Susan, but the green parrot was the most beautiful bird she had ever seen and worth the risk of embarrassment. First Indigo went to the two beech trees, where the earth was still damp and bare from the transplanting. Their leaves were beginning to lift themselves and perk up as they settled into their new home. Indigo thought she heard voices farther up the path to the wild cherry grove, but there was no one, only the breeze sweeping fallen petals over the grass. Indigo was relieved not to find Susan, though now she would have to wait until Hattie could take her to see the parrot.

In the center of the grove was a white marble bench; Indigo stretched herself out on the coolness of the polished marble to watch the sky through the leaves and wild cherry blossoms while she listened to the hum of the bees. Maybe it was the bees she heard, and not voices; as she watched the clouds move above the fluttering petals, she drifted off to sleep. When she woke, she heard voices nearby so she did not sit up. She remained flat on the bench with her head turned to one side and watched Susan and the Scottish gardener follow the path into the forest away from the bustle of the workmen.

Indigo watched as Susan picked a lily of the valley and gave it to the gardener, who did a most amazing thing: he kissed Susan on the lips. Indigo took a deep breath as her heart beat faster. She knew Colin was Susan's husband, not the gardener, and she knew the laws of white people: men and women don't touch unless they are husband and wife. That's what the dormitory matrons and boarding school teachers emphasized again and again; girls stay out of one another's beds, and the boys too.

Indigo followed them at a distance, and within the cover of the woods Susan's behavior became more animated—she broke off a white flowering twig of wild cherry and waved it in the gardener's face. He promptly seized hold of her arm and pulled her close to him in a long embrace with his bearded face covering hers. How interesting to watch what it was white women and men did alone with each other. Sister Salt said some white people preferred to keep their clothes on but used special openings in their pants for such purposes. Susan and the gardener took off all their clothes and lay on them. Indigo was fascinated and wanted to see as much as she could. No wonder Susan wanted the English gardens with all the shady shrubs and groves of sheltering trees where two lovers might hide.

Indigo watched through the flowering branches of a wild rosebush as Susan and the gardener lay nearly hidden in the deep shade. She was surprised how bright white their nude bodies appeared; if they had not been wiggling and bouncing around so much, they might be mistaken for marble figures taken down by the workmen. So the marble figures served a purpose after all: who would notice two more reclining among so many other nude figures in the gardens? Indigo watched the gardener bounce and grunt on top of Susan, then roll over on his back with her on top of him. She lost interest after a while because they did more of the same. Just as Indigo was turning away, she saw Susan catch a glimpse of her; for an instant their eyes met before Indigo hurried up the path to the driveway where the workmen were loading the last of the marble statues.

At dinner Mrs. Abbott announced Susan and Colin were joining them after dinner for some of Lucille's fresh peach ice cream. Indigo's heartbeat quickened. She knew Susan had seen her, and now Susan was coming that night. What for?

As the time of Susan and Colin's arrival approached, Indigo chewed the food, but even with sips of water she was barely able to swallow the pork roast and sweet potatoes. Sister Salt once warned her never to peek at white people having sex or they'd go crazy and come after you.

Indigo was relieved to see the expression on Susan's face—a warm smile that did not waver when she greeted Indigo. Indigo held the ice cream on her tongue until it melted, then managed to swallow the cool sweet cream though her throat still felt tight in the presence of Susan and Colin.

After Edward and Colin excused themselves to follow Mr. Abbott to his study for liquor and cigars, the women went to the parlor. Susan sat down beside Indigo on the brocade love seat and leaned close to say she was disappointed to miss Indigo this afternoon; she was told Indigo wanted permission to visit the parrot. Indigo stared down at her hands and swallowed hard before she slowly nodded her head; her heart was pounding so loudly that she had difficulty understanding Susan's words. What was she saying to Mrs. Abbott and Hattie? Did Susan say "bird"? Indigo glanced toward the door, anxious to be excused.

How odd, Hattie thought; the child seemed afraid of Susan. Hattie smiled and patted Indigo's arm to reassure her; she seemed not to understand what Susan had just said.

"Indigo! How wonderful! Susan wants to make a gift of the green parrot to you!" Hattie's voice was full of enthusiasm.

Indigo felt the tips of her fingers and toes tingle as she nodded and shyly thanked Susan. She was too uncomfortable to look into Susan's eyes, but she smiled and thanked her very much. The green parrot! Just like in her dream!

Mrs. Abbott shook her head in disapproval. Where would the child keep the bird? Not in the house! But Susan waved her hand in the air— that was no problem! The bird could remain in her aviary until they departed. Mrs. Abbott shook her head; she disapproved of travel with pets. How would they ever take a parrot to England and Italy?

"I have a lovely brass travel cage with a quilted cover," Susan added.

"But really," Mrs. Abbott continued, "won't that be a great deal of bother?" But Hattie was not listening; she and Indigo were talking excitedly about the bird. Hattie was pleased to see Indigo animated and smiling; the parrot was well worth the extra bother.

Indigo was so excited about the gift of the parrot she woke at dawn. Though Susan pretended she had not seen Indigo watching them, Indigo understood Susan's gift of the green parrot. She did not intend to tell Hattie what she'd seen; to even admit she had watched Susan and the gardener might get her in trouble. Of course she accepted Susan's gift!

What a special day this was! The beautiful green parrot was hers! She slipped on the blue satin slippers for the occasion. She stopped in the kitchen for a cookie, then went to tell the green parrot the good news. As she approached the aviaries, she heard the sunrise songs of the Chinese thrushes; their songs were very beautiful but tragic, maybe because they were born in cages and could not survive if freed.

The green parrot opened one eye at Indigo and seemed about to close it again when she held up the gingerbread cookie. The parrot promptly fluffed his feathers and opened both eyes. Previously Susan ordered the parrot be fed only sunflower seeds, which he largely ignored; but the cookie seemed to interest him a great deal. Indigo broke the cookie in halves and ate one so the parrot could see it was good to eat, then she held the remaining half between the bars of the cage near the bird.

"You can come with me now," Indigo whispered. "You won't be lonely." She pushed her fingers and the cookie into the cage, closer to the bird.

"Ummm! Gingerbread! You'll like this," she urged softly. The green parrot opened its beak as it stretched one wing and then the other and ruffled its feathers as it began to move along the perch to reach the bit of cookie. The parrot took a bit of the piece of cookie and tasted it, watching Indigo intently all the while. How thrilling it was to feel the beak daintily plucking off another bit of cookie! When the last fragment of the cookie was gone, the parrot was within inches of her fingers and Indigo could not resist the urge to touch the ruff of bright red feathers above his beak. For an instant their eyes met before the parrot sank his hooked beak into the tip of Indigo's finger.

For an instant Indigo was shocked by the fiery pain that pulsed in her fingers and hand; tears ran down her cheeks as she clutched the bleeding finger against her body and squeezed it hard to stop the dizzying pain. Her heart was pounding in her ears from the bird's surprise attack.

"But I love you!" Indigo cried as the parrot nonchalantly scratched the top of his head with the claw of one foot. "Then let me out of the cage," the parrot seemed to say with his glittering eyes. When she opened her hand to look at the injured finger there was so much blood she could not see what damage was done. Then to her horror, she saw big splatters of blood across the toes of her lovely blue satin slippers.

Stained slippers in hand, Indigo ran in stocking feet down the path to the fishpond in the Abbotts' garden. She had to wash out the blood before the slippers were ruined.

"Smack! smack! smack!" The big blue-and-red carp sucked the edge of the water lily leaf for the velvet green algae on its edge. Indigo held her breath as the carp raised its blue head out of the water to reach the top of the leaf, and for an instant their eyes met before the carp slapped the water with its tail—splash!—as it dove underwater again.

The injured finger bled a few drops into the water as Indigo thrust it into the soothing coolness. She could see the wound clearly—it was not large but it was deep, the shape of a half-moon, the mark of the parrot beak that parrots gave their human servants so other parrots and creatures would treat the parrot's servant with respect. Oh but why stain the blue slippers? What discouragement she felt when she looked at the shoes. Hattie asked her to save the satin slippers for the blue garden party, but she thought it wouldn't harm them to be worn just once before that night.

She carefully dipped one and then the other satin slipper into the water, and tried to rub away the splotches of blood; maybe the slippers just needed to soak a bit in the shallows on the steps of the pool. While they soaked, Indigo scooped handfuls of algae from the rocks at the edge of the pool and flicked it into the water above the carp's head. She watched the strand of algae float for an instant before the carp opened its big mouth and swallowed it. She was thinking of what she might do to make friends with the parrot when she noticed the blue slippers had floated off the steps and were sinking slowly deeper into the pool. By the time Lloyd fished the slippers out of the water with a leaf rake, the slippers were ruined. Mrs. Abbott was terribly disappointed, but Hattie didn't seem to care. She told Indigo the plain white slippers they brought along would be just fine.

The hot dry weather necessitated the additional expense of workers to pull hoses from the horse-drawn water tank and pump to keep the lawns and flowers of the English gardens in top form. Drought or no, Susan refused to give up the *Delphinium belladonna* because its blue was more pure than any other; dozens of big plants were nurtured in the cool house, and as the ball approached, the gardener directed his assistants who labored to carefully stake each of the stalks of the plants with fine wire before the five-gallon pots were buried discreetly among the white buddleia.

The morning of the ball, the Scottish gardener surprised Susan with two hundred pots of white tulips and white freesias carefully prepared by weeks in the cold room of the greenhouse. The pots of tulips and freesias lined the walks and balustrades of the blue garden and the adjoining terraces. The gardener worked similar wonders in the cold room with the rare blue primulas, which did not leave the greenhouse for transplanting until the late afternoon of the ball.

The blue garden was a lovely sight indeed the night of the ball, despite the dry hot weather. The pots of blue hydrangeas did not leave the glass house until the afternoon of the ball, and the workers were instructed to bury them pot and all in the ground between the powder blue verbena and the sapphire blue lobelia. Along the edge of the walk, a scattering of white mignonettes were transplanted for their night fragrance. Big pots of white and blue wisteria carefully pruned into dwarf trees and forced to bloom for the ball were arranged to create shimmering draperies of the pendulous blossoms. Weeks before, the Scottish gardener had instructed the workers to allow the white rambling roses to overgrow the stone gateways.

Tiny silver lights strung in the shrubs and trees flickered on just as the sun set. On tables draped in white damask, silver platters with real boars' heads, nose to nose, formed centerpieces. Guests began to arrive as the full moon rose over the bay. Even the dry summer provided a lovely clear evening, and the drought only deepened the blue of the sky after sunset. A hush fell over the guests as the pianist began to play the *Moonlight* Sonata and Susan slowly descended the pale limestone steps. The full moon gave off a lovely silver blue glow, which was all that Susan could ask for her dramatic entrance in a white satin Renaissance-style ball gown, trimmed in sapphire blue, which was transformed by the moonlight from mere white to shimmering moonlight blue.

While Edward and Hattie and the Abbotts assisted Susan and Colin receiving the guests on the main terrace, Indigo watched the people from a distance, from the far end of the rectangular pool, where a big silver carp basked motionless at the bottom. She brought crackers and bits of bread from a table of food on the terrace to toss to the carp. The guests began to stroll along the pool's edge to ooooh and ahhh over the fragrant white Victoria lilies big as dinner plates and highlighted by blue lilies of all hues. Indigo was careful to keep herself behind the shrubs and tall flowers where the white women could not see her to call out her name and touch her before she could escape. She was happy alone with the flowers. She loved to inhale the fragrance of the white mignonettes, then hurry down the steps to sniff the gardenias so the scents lightly mixed with each other.

The sound of the voices grew louder, and with her eyes closed and nose pressed into a big white gardenia blossom that appeared blue in the moonlight, Indigo imagined the loud buzz was bees, not human beings. More guests dressed in their Renaissance costumes with ruffled collars and feathered hats came to admire the fragrance of the giant white water lilies. Indigo began to notice then a strange effect of the moonlight: the faces and hands of white people appeared blue, while the skin of her hands appeared almost black.

Hattie, who became concerned when no one had seen the child, found Indigo sitting on a marble bench in the gardenia bower of the blue garden. The child was so serious; what was she thinking? Hattie was relieved their departure day was within a week; when the trip to Europe was behind them, Hattie intended to find the girl's family. She joined her on the bench.

"Did you have something to eat?"

Indigo nodded. She had positioned herself so a branch with a gardenia blossom hung just a few inches away from her head.

"How's the finger?"

Indigo extended it to her and Hattie checked the bruising and swelling, which seemed to be receding. She looked at the child's face and detected fatigue from so much excitement over the parrot. Edward agreed with Mrs. Abbott it was inconsiderate of Susan to present the child with a live parrot without first discussing the matter with them. But Hattie felt the parrot was important to the child's well-being, and the brass travel cage was quite handsome and compact.

"We'll look at the blue garden together and then we'll go home," Hattie said. In the full moon's light the arching bowers of white bougainvillea and white wisteria appeared a luminous silver, and Indigo was reminded of the Messiah and his family and all the dancers in their white blankets all shimmering in the light reflected off the snow.

That night Indigo dreamed she and Sister Salt were running naked in the high dunes; a cool damp wind that smelled of rain swept in low-hanging blue-violet clouds of fog and rain mist. Below them on the sandy floodplain were the Messiah and the dancers, wrapped in sky blue shawls delicate as rain mist, and then the mist swirled around them and they all disappeared.

When Indigo woke the next morning after the ball, the light from the window was dim, and she heard clicks against the window glass and a faint drumming sound overhead. It was raining! She went outside barefooted, delighted at the sensation of the wet lawn between her toes. She could hear the excited cries of the parrot as she neared the aviaries. By the time she reached the parrot's cage the wet cloth of her dress and petticoat were clinging to her body. The parrot was excitedly flapping his wings while dancing up and down the length of his perch with his head turned to the sky, beak wide open to catch the raindrops.

◆ ◆ ◆

The Masque of the Blue Garden was the most successful yet, and the bishop himself offered a mass of thanksgiving in Susan and Colin's private chapel the following Sunday to give thanks to God and to Susan and the other aid society women for the princely sum, which exceeded last year's amount considerably.

Only five days after the ball, they boarded the steamship *Pavonia* for Bristol. The weather was overcast with light rain and the sea was choppy as they steamed out of New York Harbor. Indigo pulled the edge of her coat around the parrot cage as the breeze swept up from the last edge of land disappearing behind them. She watched the dark blue water gracefully encircle the ship; the white mouths of the waves smiled at her. "Don't be afraid, we won't hurt you," they seemed to say. Now she really was far from home. It was too late to jump from the ship. She was crossing the same ocean that the Messiah crossed long ago on his way to Jerusalem. After they tried to kill him, he returned over the dark moving water; Indigo had seen him herself that night as he blessed all the dancers. She took heart because the Messiah and his followers visited the east and returned; she would too.

Part Five

SISTER SALT dreamed Indigo was in a beautiful place full of big shady trees and water and green grass. It was such a lovely dream she didn't cry for her sister when she awoke. She told Maytha and Vedna, two Chemehuevi girls who shared the bunks next to hers.

"Sounds like she died and went to heaven," Vedna said. "No such place exists here." Their faces were nearly identical but Maytha wore braids while Vedna twisted her hair into a knot at the back of her neck. Maytha frowned at Vedna and shook her head to silence her, but Sister Salt didn't care what she said. Indigo was smiling and singing in the dream, so Sister Salt knew she was all right. Maytha and Vedna were Chemehuevis so they didn't have much in common with the other girls, who complained about their strange ways and odd sense of humor. Vedna said that the Sand Lizard people were even more strange than the Chemehuevis, so maybe that's why they were friends. The Cocopa, Yuma, and Mojave girls were not unfriendly but they stayed to themselves, and so did the Apache girls.

Vedna claimed she and Maytha only teased her to cheer her because they loved her. That was their private joke, and it was the signal for the teasing to begin.

"Strange way to show your love," Sister Salt replied, and that set them off. Still laughing, Maytha exclaimed, "We Chemehuevis are strange—it's a relief to know Sand Lizard people are stranger still!" Of course only they and their dear friends, like Sister Salt, were permitted to tease them or make jokes about the Chemehuevi people; the twins were proud and ready to punch any stranger who dared insult their tribe.

Sister Salt laughed. Stories about the peculiar behavior of the Sand Lizard people were known all along the river. In battle, as soon as the Sand Lizards started to win and get the best of their enemies, they'd stop fighting and go home instead of taking prisoners. No wonder the Sand Lizard people were almost gone. Two Sand Lizards on surveillance duty were eavesdropping on enemies when one of the Sand Lizards rustled the leaves of the tree he was hiding in, and the enemies looked up. Desperately, the Sand Lizard imitated the woodpecker's squawk again and again until an Apache threw a rock and knocked him out of the tree. His companion, hidden on the ground, started laughing, and the Apaches got him and killed him, but his companion who imitated the woodpecker got away. Here the Chemehuevi twins laughed out loud, and Sister Salt joined them—these were everyone's favorite Sand Lizard stories. Sister Salt teased them back; she asked where were all the stories about the Sand Lizards' wild sexual practices?

Sand Lizard mothers gave birth to Sand Lizard babies no matter which man they lay with; the Sand Lizard mother's body changed everything to Sand Lizard inside her. Little Sand Lizards had different markings, and some were lighter or darker, but they were all Sand Lizards. Sex with strangers was valued for alliances and friendships that might be made. In Needles the people were too kind to mention Sister Salt's lighter hair and skin to Grandma Fleet or Mama; but down here at Parker, on the Colorado River reservation, Sister Salt found the others looked at her differently. Maytha and Vedna said long time ago some of the other tribes used to smother their half-breed babies because they were afraid of them. This was during the time the white armies came and robbed the people of their fall harvests to starve them, the people killed the half-breed babies. Chemehuevis never did that, the twins assured her. See! Chemehuevis were different too, like the Sand Lizards!

Sister Salt was laughing when suddenly her eyes filled with tears. Yes, her Sand Lizard people were strange, and she felt strange and lost without Mama and Indigo.

For a long time after she and Indigo were parted, Sister Salt dwelled in the numb half world only a step outside the everyday world. She did not remember taking the step outside, only finding herself there after that terrible day she watched the train move away, slowly at first, then faster, until off in the distance it appeared to be the size of a snake, and then it was gone. Her body went numb; her hands and feet felt strange and distant from her; she opened her mouth to yell "Indigo!" but gasped instead. She could not get her breath and sank to the ground, and cried into the hot hard-packed dirt. Though no one could see, a part of herself was torn loose, and the bleeding filled her chest and stomach with a strange weight, so

204

that for days Sister Salt lay motionless on her bunk and managed to swallow only water and a little corn meal soup Maytha and Vedna brought her. All the other girls avoided her; the Mojaves whispered she was suffering from ghost sickness, and the school staff feared typhoid, though she had no fever. The twins brought her the fresh datura root she requested, and she rubbed it against her cheeks and forehead to ask its help.

After the numbness in her body subsided, Sister Salt began to ask about Mama whenever she met Paiute or Mojave people who might know the whereabouts of the poeple arrested at Needles last winter. Yes, they'd heard about that, but no one seemed to know where the arrested people were taken—maybe to Fort Yuma or even Fort Huachuca. She missed Indigo so much, especially in the night, when she dreamed Indigo was lying beside her talking to her, only to awaken alone in the sweltering dormitory. She cried until her tears dried up and the other girls warned she'd go blind.

Next she sought out the Sand Lizard people Grandma Fleet had talked about, the ones who moved years ago to the Parker reservation on the river. But only a few people she spoke with had even heard of her people. Most thought the Sand Lizards were all gone. An elderly Mojave woman who cleaned houses for the white people took her aside and whispered she should be cautious because the Sand Lizard people were still remembered for their odd ways. The woman smiled and patted Sister on the arm as she said this; the old-time Mojaves had a great deal of respect and affection for the Sand Lizard people, who used to hide the Mojaves whenever the Mexican slave catchers pursued them. The help they gave others was one reason the Sand Lizard people got killed off; Grandma Fleet used to say there never were many Sand Lizards in the first place.

The superintendent of the Colorado River Indian agency referred to the old army barracks as "the school," but there were no teachers or books; the school taught them how to boil the dirty laundry of the superintendent and his wife and the other government employees in big steel tubs of soapy water over hot coals. Sister Salt knew all about laundry because Mama did the hotel's laundry in Needles. But the other young women—Cocopa, Yuma, and Mojave—were used to washing their clothes in the muddy water of the river, or not at all.

Each week Sister Salt made an escape plan, then changed her mind; which direction should she go to find Mama? She did not want to return to the old gardens without Indigo. The boarding students were allowed to come home once a year in the summer; so she decided to wait. The soldiers and Indian police brought ragged hungry people out of the canyons to the reservation at Parker every week, and she hoped to find someone with news of Mama.

Years before, the Mojaves and Chemehuevis were given tiny reservations along the river near Needles. The reservation at Parker held all the other Indians who used to live along the Colorado River before the white people came; so it was the most populous reservation on the river, and the largest too. Unfortunately, most of the land was above the fertile river bottom, on old floodplains impossible to irrigate.

Sister Salt had never seen such an ugly place—no wonder Grandma Fleet and the others refused to come in from the hills. White farmers claimed the best river bottom land. Along this stretch of the river not even the cottonwood trees or willows wanted to grow; the ground was hard-packed clay and old floodplain gravel. Only a small portion of the reservation land was fertile river bottom land, already allotted to regular churchgoers; all the others were left to grow what they could, on land that was too far from the river to irrigate and too parched by the sun to grow much.

The Parker Indian school superintendent called it a school, but he ran the place as a moneymaker for himself; he charged the soldiers and survey crews twenty-five cents per bundle for the dirty laundry that Sister Salt and the other young women washed in the school laundry. After the first week, Sister Salt began to mutter under her breath; this was no school, this was a prison. Maytha and Vedna said that all they had to do was get pregnant and the school superintendent would tell them to go as soon as their bellies got big. Sister Salt told them she did not plan to wait that long.

Sister Salt took every opportunity to get away from the school dormitory and laundry tubs to explore. The people were not permitted to farm their traditional fields any longer, and without water nothing grew in the old floodplain gravel. A few old people tried in the beginning by carrying water on their backs uphill to their fields of corn and beans, until they were defeated by the evaporation and the heat. The alluvial plains above the river were good only for sagebrush and rabbits.

The tin shacks built by government contractors were no better than the lean-to they had in Needles. Sister Salt was saddened by the quarreling that went on between the different tribes all crowded together there. The Chemehuevis and Mojaves were lucky to have their own reservations even if they were small, and many of the people at Parker envied the Mojaves and Chemehuevis, although they didn't have enough farmland to go around either.

At Parker, if some poor person had even one parent who was Chemehuevi or Mojave, the others might jeer and tell them to go back to their own reservation. Sister Salt waited for someone to tell her to go home, but no one ever did. The few Sand Lizard people who remained were married to people of other tribes; they went to church every Sunday and spoke English. They did not turn Sister Salt away, but they shook their heads and whispered behind their hands about the fierce young Sand Lizard woman. Poor thing! She lived out in the hills too long!

Sister Salt watched the women who sat outdoors under *ramadas* made of tamarisk and willow branches to escape the oven heat of the tin shacks. Here they threw the old gambling sticks and drank cactus wine to pass the day. Lard, cornmeal, salt, and a little sugar were issued once a week. She saw women quarrel over cards, scream, and pull one another's hair until Mr. Syrup, the Parker reservation policeman, was called to take them to jail.

The men were required to show up every morning to be assigned their work for the day by the superintendent; those who hunted rabbits in the sandhills outside reservation boundaries did so at the risk of jail. The people shuffled along with eyes dulled by the heat, and the tin shacks were to blame; if the people had been allowed to dig old-style houses partially underground they could keep cool until sundown, when traditionally work began in the hot months. But the authorities feared the Indians would take the opportunity to run away, and forbade work at night, when it was coolest.

The superintendent said the Indians must learn to stay put on the new reservation because a great many changes were on the way. Utah won statehood a few years before, so Arizona couldn't be far behind. The surveys were completed for construction of the dam, and the digging for the canal to Los Angeles was under way. No one seemed happier about the construction activity at nearby Parker Canyon than the reservation superintendent. All winter he had important visitors in suits who patted him on the back and shook his hand.

The construction crews began to arrive in big freight wagons. Sister Salt counted the workers, then told Maytha and Vedna she had a plan: they would go into the laundry business for themselves. They hid when the others left for school, and met upriver where the clear side pools stood amid the willows and cattails. They dug soapweed yucca roots and hung them in the willows to dry first before they used them. They had no tin laundry tubs, so one night they borrowed an old oak barrel used to collect garbage from the rear of the dormitory. At first Maytha and Vedna were hesitant, but Sister Salt dumped the contents from the barrel; the stray dogs will take the blame, she told them. They rolled the barrel for what seemed like hours; the hollow noise of the barrel rolling along striking rocks set off the barking dogs, and they feared someone would alert the agency policeman, Mr. Syrup.

"Old Syrup sleeps like a rock," Sister Salt said. "Don't even worry about him. If he comes along right now I know where to touch him so he won't tell anyone." Maytha and Vedna giggled at Sister Salt's remark; she was like the old-time people their mother talked about—before the missionaries came. In those days, the Chemehuevis really knew how to enjoy one another; only Sand Lizards knew how to enjoy sex more, Maytha joked, and Sister Salt nodded proudly. It was true: Sand Lizards practiced sex the way they all used to, before the missionaries came.

Maytha and Vedna complained the site of their laundry camp was too far to walk, but Sister Salt pointed out Mr. Syrup wouldn't walk that far, so they'd be safe. They swore the other girls in the school laundry to secrecy and promised them a share of the money if they didn't tell anyone. The dormitory attendants took roll only in the morning, so afterward they left the other girls in the school laundry while they hurried to the makeshift laundry along the river.

The first Saturday they walked upriver to the edge of the construction camp, only a few of the workers gave them bundles of laundry to wash. But in the following weeks the word got around: clean laundry for half the price the school superintendent charged.

Distinguished visitors from Washington, D.C., and excitement over the beginning of the aqueduct from the river to southern California kept the reservation superintendent occupied for weeks, and he did not immediately notice the decrease in receipts because more workers arrived every day. As their business grew, Sister Salt and the Chemehuevi sisters shared their laundry customers with the others girls, who used the school's laundry facilities to make a little money.

Down along the river Sister Salt sometimes forgot everything but the sound of the water and its coolness over her legs; later when she lay in the shade on the river sand, surrounded with the perfume of the willows, she imagined she was back in the previous year when she and Indigo were still together safely at the old gardens. She knew she must not permit herself to dwell on their separation for fear she might become too sad to move, too sad for her stomach to digest food. Instead, she kept busy; she scrubbed the dungarees and overalls on the flat sandstone. She began to wonder: if Jesus really was such a loving being, why did he disappear with their mother but leave her and Indigo behind?

She saved the coins from her share of the profits each week in a jar buried under a cottonwood tree by the river. The tree was old and so big that Sister Salt could not come close to reaching her arms around its trunk when she closed her eyes to embrace it and lay her cheek on its nubbly bark because she was so lonely for the touch of someone who loved her. With her arms around the tree, she thought of Grandma Fleet and Mama then, and Indigo, and she cried until her eyes felt tiny and hot. She did not know what to do next. Where was Mama? How would she get Indigo home? She saved up money, but what good was it to her? She let go of the tree and let her arms drop down to her sides as she sank down on the river sand.

Suddenly she sensed she was being watched. She jumped up and without taking her eyes off the thicket of willow and tamarisk, Sister Salt reached down and picked up a fallen branch. She carried it raised like a club in both hands as she began to make her way back to the school dormitory. They all knew stories about women and even little girls attacked by whites or black men or Mexicans who worked for them.

She was breathing hard and her heart was pounding so loudly she couldn't tell if the rustle in the bushes was quail or an enemy. The memory of a Cocopa girl beaten and bloodied after an attack filled her with anger. She gripped the stick tighter and felt the anger lift her; her legs felt stronger and lighter; the club seemed light in her hands. Suddenly she wanted very much to find her stalker. She crept along the path next to the river silently as she did rabbit hunting, stopping frequently to listen as she held her breath. She made a circle, crawling under the tamarisks and willows on her hands and knees, dragging the club in one hand. Up ahead she heard the crackle of twigs underfoot—it was a big foot in heavy boots. From around her neck she brought out the rawhide pouch with the flint blade Grandma Fleet gave her.

She crept up behind the large figure squatting in the rice grass and was about to spring on him and stab him in the throat when she recognized the muscular back and huge forearms and hands.

"Hey!" she yelled and the big man startled and never looked back; he tumbled forward on his hands and knees and crawled madly into the tamarisk seedlings in fright. He looked so frightened, despite his size, Sister Salt started laughing. The sound of her laughter made him stop and turn his head with a sheepish grin.

"You almost gave me a heart attack," Big Candy said, pretending to feel his chest over his heart. Sister Salt laughed harder. He was their favorite laundry customer because he was so jolly, always teasing and making jokes about himself and his huge overalls he claimed he ordered from a tent manufacturer in St. Louis. She told him he ought to be more careful or he might get hurt. He'd learned his lesson, he said, with a make-believe shudder and big grin as he looked at the flint knife in her hand. He nodded his head dramatically; all the while Sister Salt watched his eyes—they were even blacker than his face. What beautiful teeth he had; she noticed them the first time he brought his laundry to them. Big Candy was the cook and right-hand man for the construction site superintendent, Mr. Wylie.

"You can see what a good cook I am," he told them the first time they met him, as he showed off his big stomach. After that, even when he was too busy to come himself, he sent his bundle of dirty laundry along with little gifts—leftover cake or pie saved from Mr. Wylie's table. The black and Mexican construction workers were the only ones who acted friendly or tried to talk to the Indian girls. The churchgoing Indian girls ignored them and refused to look them in the eyes because the minister warned them every Sunday about the dangers of Negroes and Mexicans.

In the beginning Sister Salt talked to Big Candy only to practice her English, but he made such funny jokes about himself she found herself laughing as she had with Indigo and Grandma Fleet. Still, Sister was surprised Candy tried to follow her along the river, where his bulk and the tangle of tamarisk and willow made tough going.

"The churchgoers say all you want from us is adultery," Sister Salt said, idly swinging her club by its handle, still gripping the stone blade. Candy brushed the dry leaves off his overalls and pulled twigs from his hair. He smiled and shook his head slowly.

"That's all those churchgoers think about." He looked Sister Salt in the eyes. He seemed relaxed as he sat there on the ground looking up at her. Sister Salt threw down the club and sat on the ground not far from him. She rubbed the stone blade carefully between two fingers to test its edge and waited for him to say something; she and the Chemehuevi girls always laughed at him because he liked to talk so much. She cleaned the dirt from under her fingernails with the tip of the blade, stealing sidelong glances at him. The churchgoers said don't get near the black men or your babies will be born with monkey tails, but Sister didn't believe anything the church-goers said because they were wrong about Jesus Christ. They claimed he died on a cross long ago, but Sister saw him with her own eyes last winter.

Candy stretched out on his back and looked up through the willow and cottonwood leaves at the sky. He was so big he looked like a hill lying there. The man who liked to talk so much didn't have anything to say. Good, she thought, I have nothing to say either. She began to play with strips of willow bark, weaving it into little rings; when she looked over at him, his eyes were closed and his mouth half open; he was asleep, so she left him. The following day when Sister Salt went to the cottonwood tree along the river she found a paper sack with four hard licorice drops. She shared the candy with Maytha and Vedna and they laughed at one another's teeth stained blackish brown with licorice juice.

Even when he could not meet her, Sister Salt found his little gifts to her under the cottonwood tree—gumdrops, a candy cane, or licorice. His given name was Gabriel—but he told everyone to call him Candy because he always had a little sack of penny candies. Sometimes he brought her a piece of red ribbon or an agate marble after a trip to Needles or Yuma, where he went to buy delicacies, fresh eggs, and butter for Mr. Wylie's table. Maytha and Vedna agreed Candy seemed like a nice man, but they didn't think Sister Salt should risk having babies with monkey tails. The first time Candy touched her breast, they were lying on the river sand in the cottonwood's shade; Sister Salt pulled away and sat up. She asked him if it was true what the preacher said, that their babies would have monkey tails. She thought he might laugh at her, but he didn't. His expression became thoughtful, even a little sad, and he shook his head slowly. Sister Salt regretted her question and scooted closer to him on the sand. She didn't really believe it; anyway, people said much worse things about Sand Lizards.

"No, don't waste your time with talk like that," Candy said, stroking her hair away from her face. "The army used to warn us about disease and Indians," he said with a smile, "but my grandma was a Baton Rouge Indian." He laughed. "Don't trust the things the churchgoers say."

Sister Salt was suspicious at first, but for weeks Candy was content just to hug her close and kiss her and touch her breasts without intercourse. What was he waiting for? Later Maytha and Vedna asked what it was like to lie down with such a big, such a black, man.

Ummm! He smelled so good, and his skin was so soft and smooth—more smooth than brown skin and way more smooth than white skin. Doz-ing on the sand under the cottonwood tree he reminded her of a great black mountain she wanted to climb, so she just jumped on his chest and belly while he was dozing; he didn't startle so he must have been watching her from under the brim of his hat. She laughed at the sensation of this mountainous man, wide and soft as a bed mattress, then stretched herself out on top of him so her face reached the center of Candy's chest.

Afterward they dozed side by side on the sand until the mosquitoes came out at sundown. Candy talked about his plans for the future. No more work boots or overalls—he would wear a fine suit, a different color every day with the shoes to match, as he greeted the patrons of his restaurant in downtown Denver. He had lived his whole life in hot climates, first Louisiana, then Texas and southern Arizona. If not Denver, then Oakland or Seattle; the farther north a colored man went, the better off he was.

He was lucky to learn to cook from his mother, in the big house outside Baton Rouge. As an infant, his mother sat the cradle in the corner of the big plantation kitchen. Almost as soon as he could hold a paring knife safely, Candy helped his mother in the kitchen. His mother's cooking made the dinner parties of the plantation famous throughout Louisiana. Now that his mother had passed on, no one knew how to cook fowl and game birds the way Candy cooked them. Even out here, Candy bragged, he could take quails or doves he shot and bake them into delicious pies. Mr. Wylie wanted Candy to return to Los Angeles to cook for him and his family, but Candy wanted a restaurant of his own. He planned to have the money he needed without the job in Los Angeles. Candy did not want to waste time. A man had to work most of his life if he wanted to have anything to call his own; he wanted his restaurant now, while he was still young enough to enjoy the fine food and pretty women that he'd have there.

Would she be one of the pretty women? Sister didn't know what to say—she didn't want to hurt his feelings, so she talked about Mama and the other dancers who followed the Messiah. She dreamed of finding them high in the mountains. Candy shook his head from time to time as she described the four nights of the dancers along the river at Needles.

"I could cook for that many people if I had to," Candy commented, chewing the end of a piece of rice grass.

"I want to go look for her up north."

"See, that's a good sign right there! We both want to go the same direction!"

Before long, the Indian school superintendent received complaints he overcharged for his laundry service and learned of his competitors right under his nose. He was outraged at the cheek of these young "squaws" and ordered a review of purchase orders for soap at the school laundry. Furious at their treachery, the superintendent ordered Sister Salt and her accomplices arrested for petty theft; the federal magistrate in Yuma sentenced them all to three months in jail.

During the months Sister Salt and the Chemehuevi sisters were jailed in Yuma, Candy drove the company wagon down to Yuma for supplies twice each month. He pulled the wagon around back of the old jail's thick adobe walls and parked right next to the narrow barred window of the women's cell, where he could sit on the back end of the wagon and be at eye level with Sister Salt. He pushed licorice drops between the bars and cheered them with reports on the sales and profits from the home brew he sold, and the dice and card games he ran. Mr. Wylie took his cut, of course; that was the cost of doing business.

Candy told Sister Salt to put her ear close to the window bars and he whispered the news: he'd paid off the rest of her fine and now they'd let her out of jail. Tomorrow he was coming to take her to live with him at the dam site. To hell with the reservation and the school! Business was growing faster and faster as more workers arrived to dig the big ditch to Los Angeles; Candy was falling behind with all the work. As Sister Salt was led from the women's cell, Candy called to Maytha and Vedna; he said he would pay their fines too if they wanted to come along, but they were too shy to answer him.

As they rode along in the wagon, Candy told Sister Salt all about his plans for expansion as more workers arrived. Besides the laundry and beer, Candy planned more cards and dice.

Candy stopped the wagon on the sandy ridge high above the construction site. Sister was shocked at the destruction she saw below: the earth was blasted open, the soil moist and red as flesh. The construction workers appeared the size of flies crawling over the hills of clayish dirt. The river had been forced from her bed into deep diversion ditches, where her water ran angry red. Big earth-moving machines pulled by teams of mules uprooted groves of ancient cottonwood trees. Off to the west, the workers were digging a huge ditch to carry river water all the way to Los Angeles.

For the first few weeks, Sister Salt slept with Candy in his tent, big enough for a brass bed and a green velvet love seat, recently shipped from San Diego. When Candy was away on business, Sister Salt woke at first light to bathe in the shallows downriver. In jail she abandoned the stiff tight shoes that hurt her toes; now, free of the agency rules, she used her sharp flint blade to cut away the high buttoned neck on the school blouse, then severed one long sleeve after the other. She left the waistband intact but tore the school skirt into strips to let the cool breeze pass through to cool her belly and bottom. On the hottest days when Candy was away, Sister Salt wore no blouse or skirt at all.

Candy came home unexpectedly a few times on those hot afternoons and found Sister Salt without clothes, resting in the tent by a bucket of water with a gourd dipper to sprinkle herself. The sight of her enflamed Candy's passion, and after the sweet young woman climbed all over and tasted him like gravy, he didn't have the heart to scold her for going naked while he was away. It was so damn hot here! Thermometers lost their accuracy in no time—the mercury simply cooked away in the relentless heat.

Nevertheless, Candy had warnings from the boss about keeping an Indian woman there. Mr. Wylie heard rumors—untrue, of course—Candy planned to start a whorehouse. Sister Salt listened to Candy and agreed it would be better to move to her own place down along the river where she would be free of prying eyes and of clothing if she chose; she could use red clay on her face and body against the mosquitoes, and no white men would become alarmed. So Candy drove her and her possessions a quarter mile downriver from the construction camp to a grove of cottonwood trees and willows spared by the machinery.

She had her own tent, a kerosene lantern, and a little fold-up bed she used for a table or chair because she preferred to sleep on the ground, where it was cooler. All day long explosions sent the rocks and sand of the old floodplain sky high in plumes of smoke and dust. Sister Salt was happy to be close to the river, away from the dust and noise of the camp.

After the river's course was diverted, she was saddened to find silver-green carp belly-up, trapped in water holes in the empty riverbed. She tried to care for the datura plants and wild purple asters on the riverbank suddenly left high and dry. She called them her flower garden, but the asters died and the datura wilted if she did not carry them buckets of water every day. She felt sad but resentful too, at the workers who channeled the river away from its bed. In jail she and the twins heard the Mojave people were terribly upset because their beloved ancestors and dead relatives dwelled down there under the river; witchcraft activity was bound to increase because of the damage done to the river.

She didn't know about witchcraft, but Sister did know about gardens: if the river got moved, there was no way to keep a garden. Angry tears filled her eyes; this place was almost as bad as the reservation at Parker.

She watched the river's angry churning in the bypass channel; torrents suddenly rippled into stiff reddish ridges topped with white foam as the currents surged back and forth seeking a way back to the old riverbed. She sensed the ferocious power of the river and she began to imagine a flash flood that silently enveloped her tent and floated it away so gently the lantern remained secure on its hook. She imagined the river carried her inside the illuminated tent far, far to the ocean lagoon south of Yuma, where she floated out to sea.

Those first weeks alone on the river, in the coolness before dawn she dreamed of Grandma Fleet, Mama, and Indigo at the old gardens; for an instant after she woke, she felt as if they were there with her before she remembered where she was. She walked away from the river up the sandy slopes of the high ridge above the river, where she could see for great distances in all directions. She followed the ridge to its intersection with a big wash and made her way down the steep game trail to the bottom of the wash. As the sun rose, she began to notice a great many colorful pebbles and stones in the old river gravel, reds, yellows, oranges, whites—the pebbles were polished by water—and she was surprised to find rough granular stones of light greens and darker greens just the color of leaves. Sister Salt was delighted. Each visit to the big wash, she carried back as many of the colorful pebbles and stones as she could. The colored rocks and pebbles took a great deal of time to arrange but finally she completed the stone garden on the sand outside her tent—a garden that needed no water.

One morning she returned to find a big load of firewood neatly stacked next to four cast iron tubs; a big slab of brown soap glistened in a tin pail. No one wanted to go all the way to Parker to get his clothes washed when Candy's laundry was right there and far cheaper to boot. Candy brought the bundles of dirty laundry before dawn and drank a cup of coffee with her or asked her to come lie on her bedroll with him before he went back to cook Mr. Wylie's lunch. When she wasn't scrubbing the overalls on the rock, she was folding clean clothes in separate bundles. The first week Sister Salt washed clothes all day and all night in order to finish. When Candy saw she was behind, he tied up the wagon horses and worked side by side with her to rinse the overalls in boiling water, then hang them over bushes to dry.

Sister Salt felt her heart beat faster whenever Candy was nearby. She worked as hard as she could to finish drying and folding the laundry just to see Candy's surprise and pleasure as he realized Sister Salt managed to finish all the laundry by herself. If her hands felt raw or swollen from the hot water and lye soap, Sister Salt only had to remember Candy's warm smile and how good his arms felt around her.

Not long after, Candy told her he had a surprise; first a tent identical to hers went up nearby; then Candy brought four more cast iron tubs. On his third trip he brought back Maytha and Vedna. Sister Salt was delighted to have her friends join her. Candy showed the three of them their accounts in his book; after they repaid him for paying off their jail fines, he would begin to pay them wages each week—four times the wage the school superintendent used to pay them. The laundry work went so much faster with three people to share it and to keep one another laughing with stories and jokes.

Candy was a busy man. Now Sister Salt saw him only when he brought the bundles of dirty laundry or when he loaded the wagon with the clean clothes. Often Candy was so tired when he visited, he fell asleep before he got his boots off, and she didn't get to romp around on his big soft chest and belly as frequently as before. But Candy never failed to take out the rawhide pouch from inside his shirt to show off the $20 gold pieces and stacks of silver dollars, the profits for that week.

While they scrubbed overalls and boiled water, they planned what they'd do with the silver dollars they earned. Buy farmland right on the river! Maytha shouted. With the money they saved, they'd be able to buy some goats and maybe a few sheep, though summers might be too hot for sheep. Chickens? In the winter they might keep them, but when the hottest days of summer came, the hens stopped laying eggs, and they'd have to cook them.

When it was her turn to tell about her plans for her money, Sister Salt hesitated before she spoke. She had so much she wanted to do, she wasn't sure how much money she would need. First she had to get Indigo home, and Big Candy promised to help her. Then she and Indigo had to find Mama before they returned to the old gardens.

"Good luck," the twins said in unison, but they sounded uncertain. The soldiers and the Indian police were under orders to keep the people on the reservations. Besides, good farmland along the river was leased to white people friendly with the superintendent.

On the streets of Needles and Kingman there were so many hungry Indian women and children, Candy brought scraps and leftovers to them when he went to those towns. The women begged him for work, any kind of work, as he handed out bones and skin from the roasted chickens and turkeys; he smiled and nodded and promised them all jobs when he opened his hotel and restaurant in Denver.

Big Candy saw the newspapers every week after Wylie finished with them. The heat that summer exceeded all recorded temperatures in Phoenix and Los Angeles; rainfall the previous spring was far below normal. Wells in Los Angeles and surrounding communities ran dry, and drinking water was brought in by railroad tank cars. A week did not pass without some government official or other paying a visit to the construction site to monitor the progress on the aqueduct and the dam. More workers were hired to keep the project on schedule, and the construction site village of flapping canvas over wood crates and tin expanded toward the river. Big Candy was pleased they were closer to his brewery and gambling tents and the laundry.

The heat made the workers more thirsty than ever—the beer business boomed. Candy's silent partner was his boss, Mr. Wylie; they'd worked together for a number of years from project to project. Wylie came down every evening around sundown to count the empty beer bottles; he liked to have an idea of how much money was taken in each day. After the count, Sister Salt and the Chemehuevi twins washed the bottles and boiled them before they were refilled with fresh brew.

Candy did not allow anyone else to lift the lids on the brewing barrels, and he checked them every day, sniffing at them and tasting them to decide which batches were ready to bottle. The workers joked Candy used river water to make his beer, but he took great care to haul fresh well water from Parker for his beer. He went all the way to Needles to the railroad freight office to pick up the special yeast and hops shipped from Albuquerque. Candy watched the brewing closely because beer was the staple of his business; without beer, the gamblers couldn't hear those voices that urged them to roll the dice again to see how lucky they were. Those voices they heard were the spirits of the alcohol, and Candy tended those spirits very carefully so none were offended. If the brew was bottled too late, it was flat and yeasty; but if it was bottled too soon, too much pressure built up and the glass bottles exploded. Candy left the wine and moonshine to the bootleggers who drove in from Needles or Prescott; wine and distilled spirits took too much time to make.

Candy worried if the heat got any worse, the yeast in the brewing barrels would die; so he instructed Sister Salt and the Chemehuevi sisters to wrap the oak barrels in layers of burlap sacks soaked in the river. Sister Salt loved the excuse to splash around in the warm water, which was still cooler than the air. The moisture evaporated so fast that for a little while her skin felt cool and delightful.

Big Candy kept his word. On one of his weekly trips to Parker he went to the office of the reservation superintendent and made a written inquiry about Indigo. He was told the inquiry must be sent to the Indian Bureau of the War Department, in Washington, D.C.; that would take months. When Candy told Sister, she began to cry from anger and frustration— they'd never find Indigo if they had to ask Washington! But Candy told her to be patient, and he worked on composing a letter, night after night, even when he was so tired he fell asleep at the table. Sister Salt loved him most then, when he tried so hard to help her find Indigo. He was saving money for the train tickets; they'd go to Riverside if necessary. They'd find that girl!

Now the river was unrecognizable—rechanneled and trapped into narrow muddy chambers outside its old bed. The poor cottonwood trees and willows were ripped out and plowed into mounds of debris, where their roots reached out plaintively like giant skeleton hands. Oh poor trees! I'm sad for you. Poor river! What have they done to you? Sister whispered softly.

Two shifts of men worked day and night to complete the dam and canal on schedule. Layers of fine dust settled over everything, even the food and the bedding, and there was always the noise—the scrape and clank of the earth-moving machines, the whinnies of the mules, and the shouts of the workmen. By night the construction site was lit by big coal oil torches that trailed ribbons of flame whenever the wind caught them.

Down at the casino and bar, Big Candy hung dozens of lanterns from the cottonwood trees and from the corners of the tent frames; every afternoon Sister Salt and Maytha and Vedna refilled the lanterns with coal oil; besides providing light, the lantern fumes kept away the mosquitoes. The lamps were their last task before they got off work, and they discussed what they would do that night. After baths they sometimes went to have a beer and see who was winning at dice or blackjack.

A distance away, up on the gravel terrace of the old floodplain, next to the construction camp and the site superintendent's big tent, businessmen from as far away as Prescott and Yuma parked canvas-covered wagons filled with mattresses, and with white and black women who charged construction workers ten cents for fifteen minutes. Mr. Wiley required the wagons with the mattresses to be parked within sight of his tent so that he could keep count of the customers to be sure the businessmen didn't cheat him out of his share. That arrangement was fine with Sister Salt and the twins—they still got more offers than they wanted to have sex for money. Big Candy warned them not to undercut the prices of the wagon women too much, or their managers, the businessmen from Prescott and Yuma, would complain to the authorities and get Mr. Wiley in trouble. Sister Salt and the others took the men into the tamarisks and willows on the smooth clean river sand, so they charged less. Their customers said they much preferred the sand to those smelly mattresses in the wagons. As long as Sister Salt and the twins worked hard at the laundry and brewery, how they earned money in their free time was their business; Candy didn't interfere.

Big Candy loved women, and he said all a man had to do was to let a woman be and she'd love him all the more. Candy's mother had been born into slavery, and after the emancipation she continued to reflect on her position as a slave and then as a free woman. Dahlia was six feet tall and weighed three hundred pounds, so when she talked, people listened, even her employer and his wife. "Wage slave," she called herself and the others; no, they couldn't be bought or sold anymore—now human beings were worthless, and anything worthless was left to starve.

At night in their cabin, Dahlia loved to tell the stories she heard as a girl about the Red Stick people who adopted the escaped African slaves. Even before the Indians ever saw an African, the old Red Stick dreamers described them and said they had powerful medicine that the people here could use. So they welcomed the fugitives when they appeared, and it wasn't long before the Red Sticks were given some of this medicine, which allowed their warriors to move through the swamps as silently and swiftly as smoke. Heavy casualties were inflicted on the French soldiers by only a handful of warriors, and later they routed the British. Of course, the swamps' quicksand and fevers were their powerful allies.

In Dahlia's clan, they knew how to hunt and to cook, especially meat. As Big Candy told Sister Salt more than once, the person who prepares the food has more power than most people think. Candy grew up in the big kitchen where he helped his mother. That was why he preferred to work around women; he explained this to Sister Salt the night he returned from Needles with the Mojave woman. She wasn't young but she wasn't too old; she took one look at Sister Salt and the Mojave woman's eyes clouded with hatred toward Sister. Big Candy only laughed when Sister complained to him later; he reminded her she didn't work near the Mojave woman. He couldn't let the Mojave woman go; she was a good worker. Business was booming and he needed every worker he had.

Money, money! Some nights the sound of coins seemed louder than the sounds of the earthmoving machines and woke Sister Salt two or three times during the night. She felt something or someone was about to come—maybe the letters Candy sent off would bring Indigo home—but she had not dreamed about Indigo or their mother for some time.

Right before dawn it got quiet for a while, and that's when she got up to watch the earth. She walked to the high sandy hill above the river and looked all around: she could see how the vegetation would grow back someday, and no trace of the construction camp would remain. Even their dam would fill up with sand someday; then the river would spill over it, free again.

She gazed off to the southwest in the direction of the old gardens. She was homesick for the dunes, for the peacefulness and quiet; for the good sleep she had in Grandma Fleet's dugout house, which was much cooler than a tent. She missed the cold clear water from the crack in the sandstone of the shallow cave above the dunes.

The only time she wasn't homesick was when she was flirting with handsome strangers or lying with one of them on the sandy riverbank in the shade. The old-time Sand Lizard people believed sex with strangers was advantageous because it created a happy atmosphere to benefit commerce and exchange with strangers. Grandma Fleet said it was simply good manners. Any babies born from these unions were named "friend," "peace," and "unity"; they loved these babies just as fiercely as they loved all their Sand Lizard babies.

Sister Salt took her choice of the men willing to pay a dime for fun in the tall grass along the river. Maytha and Vedna said Chemehuevi-Laguna women like them knew how to enjoy life, but this Sand Lizard woman was lusty! Candy did not mind—he was making good money and busy himself. Her body belonged to her—it was none of his business.

"You can't be everywhere all the time," Dahlia taught him, "so why worry about who or what others do when you aren't there?" Besides, Candy loved women of all ages and colors; every time Candy drove the supply wagon to Needles, Prescott, or Yuma, he took along bundles of clean rags and stale bread to give to the street corner Indian women and to the children alone in the alleys. Sister Salt thought Candy's kindness to women was his best quality. Why should she care if Candy had sex with other women—especially the Chemehuevi twins, because they were best friends? She hoped he avoided that Mojave woman only because the woman was her enemy. It wasn't likely, though, because the poor man seldom had time for sex with any of them; Candy worked all day and half the night seven days a week to earn those silver dollars.

Candy's gambling and brewery tents were packed with miners and cowboys as well as construction workers most of the day and night. He hired another, older Mojave woman to work with the woman who hated Sister; the Mojave women stirred the coals and watched the roasting meat on payday. Sister watched them from a distance and knew they talked about her. Only white men were hired as card dealers or to run the dice games; when he was not cooking Wylie the elaborate meals the man lived for, Big Candy was the overseer, who stood silently behind the customers to observe the dealers to keep them honest while they dealt cards or rolled dice. A young Mexican called Juanito began to drive the wagonloads of laundry because Candy was so busy. More tents for poker and dice players went up under the cottonwood trees along the riverbank.

"I'm this much closer to Denver," he'd say, holding his money pouch close, with a blissful expression on his face to let Sister know he was imagining his hotel's dining room; of course, the main dining table would have to be oversize—he'd have it made in Mexico and shipped to Denver by train. Soon the hard work would pay off. Sister didn't intend to go to a cold climate like Denver's, but she didn't want to discuss it; she hoped maybe he would change his mind and buy a hotel in Prescott or Kingman instead. She didn't want to leave the area where her sister and mother were last seen.

Gamblers flocked to the tents under the cottonwood trees along the river; after sundown a cool breeze came from the river and many men lounged outside to smoke or to count their winnings. Maytha and Vedna confessed they met two handsome young Mexicans, winners at blackjack, and they went off to the willows along the river; they had the silver dollars to prove it!

Next evening when they went, Sister Salt came along with them to see if the Mexicans were as handsome as the twins claimed. The next thing she knew, she was on the smooth sand under the cover of the willows, in the arms of a handsome Mexican with curly black hair. Charlie was different; she loved his smile and his quick, clever remarks that always made her smile or laugh; she never took money from Charlie. She found herself waiting to see him again, unable to concentrate on anything else as she scrubbed overalls with the Chemehuevi sisters.

For a while Charlie visited her almost every evening after his shift ended; Candy was so busy he hardly noticed. But soon Charlie confided to Sister he felt uncomfortable, and feared somehow Candy would cause him to lose his job. In Tucson Charlie was a married man—what if rumors got back to his wife? Nothing Sister Salt said would reassure him; later she suspected a spell cast by that Mojave woman; or maybe some missionary cautioned him. Charlie kissed her good-bye: he'd miss his Sand Lizard girl, but he couldn't afford the risk any longer.

Sister Salt never cared much what other people thought; she never minded the taunts of the churchgoers—Indian or white—who pursed their lips anuslike to spit insults at her. She blamed the loss of Charlie on churchgoers who forgot Jesus loved the prostitute Mary Magdalene and called her sister. Jesus knew there could be no peace without love—why didn't the churchgoers remember that? Wovoka preached the corpse on the cross wasn't Jesus but some poor white man! She herself had seen Jesus winter before last, and he looked like he might be a Paiute, like Wovoka, with handsome dark skin and black hair and eyes.

After Charlie quit her, Sister began to hate the steaming tubs of smelly overalls—now the smell of soap and dirty clothes made her vomit, and so did the odor of the yeast in the brew. Before long she realized she was pregnant; a little Sand Lizard baby was coming to keep her company.

As the flutter of the baby inside her grew stronger, she dreamed a voice she knew was the baby's. "Get a move on," it seemed to say. "We can't go until we get Indigo back," she whispered. It must be Charlie's baby, though she wasn't certain; it might be Candy's—both men were always on the go, no wonder the baby was like them. Probably the baby would resemble both men since both had sex with her regularly. But now that Charlie stayed away, the baby would become more and more like Big Candy until it was his child. That was what sex during pregnancy did.

If she stayed through the winter there was a chance the dancers and the Messiah might come down from the north again and she might find Mama. Anytime a letter might arrive with news of Indigo.

Part Six

JUST AFTER the ship left sight of land, Edward brought out the letter that arrived just before departure. News about Linnaeus! Hattie cleared her throat and began reading; her face lit up as she read this: "I am delighted to report the little monkey is as happy as can be with his new companion. The maid tells me she watched the monkey play with the kitten. The monkey dangles the end of his tail through the bars to lure the kitten to play with it."

Hattie folded the letter and slipped it back into the envelope.

"It was very kind of Mr. Yetwin to write to set our minds at ease. In your next letter, please let him know we greatly appreciated his charming description of Linnaeus and the kitten. We feel much relieved, don't we?"

Indigo nodded her head vigorously as she imagined the monkey playing with the cat. Although the letter told only of the game through the bars, Indigo imagined the door of the cage open wide and the two of them chasing each other among the branches of the wisteria above the cage. She knew the white blossoms were gone by now but she preferred to imagine Linnaeus and his cat playing hide-and-seek among the flowers.

That night as she lay in her berth, a bit unwell from the sway of the ship, she listened to the beautiful rain splash the ship's deck. Rain made her think of the old gardens and Mama and Grandma and Sister, who loved her so much. Tears filled her eyes; she missed them so much! Would she ever find them?

The dark heaving ocean was beginning to lift and drop the ship in a most alarming manner; all water was alive, she knew, but this dark salt water was bigger and more powerful than any freshwater. This ship and everyone on it belonged to the restless dark water until they reached land. Indigo kept the parrot's cage in the berth with her next to the wall so the ship's rocking did not overturn the cage. The parrot seemed unconcerned;

he slept perched on one foot with his head tucked under his wing. She still didn't know the name the parrot wanted to be called.

Indigo pulled the blanket up to her chin and watched the cabin and its contents move up and down. As the rolling of the ship increased, a pencil rolled off the little writing table Hattie used; the hairbrush slid one way and then the other on the shelf below the mirror. She watched as one of Hattie's shoes tipped out of its rack in the cabin closet and began to slide back and forth on the floor. How funny to see these objects suddenly come alive and move themselves around the cabin!

The great rhythmic voice of Ocean resounded through the ship's steel skin; Ocean boasted she made great winds with her waves; the Earth herself was moved by her waves. Ocean was Earth's sister. Indigo felt the sadness overtake her again.

I have a sister too, but this ship and you, Ocean, are taking me farther from her, Indigo whispered. She imagined Sister Salt on the depot platform in Needles, searching for her among the boarding school students returning home for the summer. Now a great ocean lay between them. Her plan for an easy way home had taken her much farther away. Tears filled her eyes and she cried softly into her pillow: Please help me, Ocean! Send your rainy wind to my sister with this message: I took the long way home, but I'm on my way. Please don't worry.

Indigo repeated the message aloud and the parrot opened his eyes and ruffled his feathers as he studied her. Even in the dim light of the cabin she could see the bird's pale gray eyes on her. Soon the parrot would let her know his name and allow her to hold him. How much fun she would have with the three of them—parrot, monkey, and cat! The letter gave no description of the kitten, but as she drifted off to sleep, Indigo imagined she was black with a white face, white belly, and four white feet.

Hours later, after Hattie was asleep, Indigo began to feel an odd pressure in her ears and head; then her stomach began to feel unsettled. The pressure in her head tightened and suddenly she was about to vomit. She woke Hattie, who sent for the ship's doctor and ordered a basin of ice water and wet cloths for Indigo's forehead. Give the child a day or two and she'll get her sea legs, the ship's doctor advised after he administered syrup of paregoric. By morning she only felt worse.

While Hattie cared for the seasick child in one cabin, Edward retired to the other cabin to review his notes on citrus culture, especially the procedures for rooting slips cut from trees. He needed to know the best way to pack the citron slips he obtained for their long journey.

A day later the seas were calm and the sky was bright blue, but Indigo still felt every slow-rolling motion of the ship. Hattie coaxed her to swallow lemon water and plain bread. Throughout her seasickness, Indigo insisted the parrot's brass cage be kept in the corner of her bunk near her feet; even when she was nauseous, Indigo never failed to remove the cage cover in the morning and replace it at night. She found if she talked to the parrot the nausea wasn't as bad. Indigo told the parrot all about Mama and Sister Salt and the old gardens where Grandma Fleet rested next to her little apricot trees to nourish them.

The parrot did not seem interested and sometimes tucked his head under his wing while she talked. She knew the parrot was upset to leave its home to be bounced around in a small travel cage. Worse yet, before the parrot was put into the travel cage, Susan directed the gardener to clip the bird's wing feathers to prevent the bird from flying away. One feather bled and had to be plucked. The parrot blamed Indigo; she could tell by the expression in his eyes.

Fortunately Mrs. Abbott sent along a two-pound tin of ginger cookies, which, with weak tea, were all Indigo could tolerate in her stomach. The parrot did not touch his fruits or seeds, so Indigo fed him bits of ginger cookie, careful to keep her fingertips well clear of the sharp curved beak. Even in the dimness of the ship cabin, the parrot's feathers were brilliant, almost as if they glowed with their own light. Only in a rainbow had Indigo seen such shades of emerald, turquoise, yellow-gold, and blue.

When she felt better, she opened the cage door, but the parrot only gripped the perch tighter.

"Look, I won't hurt you," she said, holding out both hands palms-up to show she meant no harm. The parrot ignored the open cage door, so Indigo left it ajar and opened the book Hattie had been reading to her earlier, stories of the old British Isles, stories about the dun cow and the fairy dog. There was a picture of the dun cow encircled by curious standing stones on the hill where she appeared one day when the people were starving. The dun cow promised each family a bucket of milk every day if the people agreed to take only one bucket each. But a greedy person who thought no one would notice began to fill a second bucket, and when he did, there was flash of lightning and the dun cow disappeared.

As Indigo turned the pages to find the next picture, she glanced over at the parrot cage and saw the bird had climbed out and was sitting on the cage top. Delighted, Indigo put down the book and began to talk to the parrot to try to coax him to come to her, but the bird wanted no part of her.

He fluffed and preened his feathers while he refused to obey, so Indigo turned back to the book and the picture that showed the arrival of the white fairy dog just as the family hurried off to bed. In the picture was evidence the family had been sitting around the fire, enjoying the evening— a man's pipe was still lit on the table; a child's doll and toy ball lay in the middle of the floor. The family had dropped everything to prepare the food, drink, and fire for the visitors about to arrive. In the story, the family could hear the fairies, but the only one they could see was the white dog. Indigo was enjoying the details of the picture, picking out everyday objects she recognized, when she glanced over at the top of the brass cage but saw no parrot.

Immediately she regretted opening the cage door; just because the bird couldn't fly didn't mean he couldn't walk or climb. She wanted to give him his freedom because she was his friend, but now he was gone. She looked carefully in every corner and behind every valise and trunk; just as she began to despair, she thought she saw Hattie's calfskin train case move in the closet alcove. There he was with his beak on the corner of the case. Indigo knelt to pull the case away from the parrot and felt a sharp prick in her left knee. Scattered on the floor near the train case were small brass tacks that used to decorate the leather; the appearance of the case was ruined! Indigo pushed the train case to the back of the closet and began to try to lure the parrot back into the cage. Although only six ginger cookies remained, Indigo broke one in half and put half inside the open cage. The parrot hesitated as if he knew she planned to close the cage door the instant he went inside, but the piece of ginger cookie was irresistible. The parrot ignored Indigo and nibbled the cookie as she shut the cage door.

She sat on the floor beside the cage and watched the parrot.

"How do you like the name Rainbow?" she asked. The parrot looked at her steadily, and daintily trimmed its claws. The parrot book in the Abbotts' library had color picures of wild parrots in jungles surrounded by great trees and lovely flowering plants. The parrot was so far from his beautiful home; no wonder he didn't want to speak!

Sometimes Indigo woke in the middle of the night and could not remember where she was—the smell of burning coal caused her to confuse for a moment the steamship with the train—but then she'd feel the roll of the ship and see the outline of the parrot's cage and she knew immediately where she was. Sometimes in the middle of the night when she woke and reached for the glass of water she saw the parrot watch her. She whispered to the parrot about his family—Edward said the parrots lived in large families in giant dead trees deep in the rain forest. Indigo talked to the parrot about how she imagined the baby parrots played hide-and-go-seek with one another in the big tree. She pulled the blanket up over herself and the parrot cage to form the safe, cozy nest Indigo imagined for the parrots. She pretended she and the rainbow bird were baby parrots in the nest together and all their older sisters and brothers, all their grandfathers and grandmothers—everyone was there with them in one towering tree.

The ship encountered more rough seas, and they discovered that Indigo felt the seasickness less sharply when Hattie talked to her or read her a story. They discussed what Linnaeus and his kitten might be doing right at that moment; scampering up the wisteria in the glass house perhaps. As the ship rolled, sweat broke out on Indigo's forehead; she asked Hattie please to read more of the adventures of the naughty Chinese monkey born from stone.

Already the Chinese monkey was up to mischief, taking bites from the apples of longevity, stealing the golden pills of immortality and gobbling them down with the special wine for the banquet of the immortals; Heavenly King Li sent heavenly soldiers to trap the monkey on Flowers and Fruit Mountain. Indigo leaned back against the pillow with her eyes closed. The seasickness began with a swelling pressure in her ears that ached throughout her head. She wanted Hattie to go on and read the story of the capture of the rebellious monkey by the Buddha. The capture alone took five pages, and Hattie began to tire.

"Monkey refused to believe what he saw and was just about to jump away when Buddha turned the fingers of his hand into five mountains, which buried the rebellious Monkey." Hattie paused and glanced to see if the child was asleep; but just then Indigo's eyes opened wide and she said, "Don't stop now! The monkey is buried under five mountains! Read how he gets away!"

The rolling of the ship had subsided and Indigo's face was not as pale; Hattie glanced at the pages ahead and shook her head.

"Monkey doesn't seem to escape for at least six pages—it's too late to read it now. Tomorrow," Hattie said, firmly closing the book.

"Good night, and sweet dreams."

"Sweet dreams," Indigo replied.

She tucked the covers around Indigo and kissed her forehead. The parrot's head was tucked under its wing but a glittering eye watched as she put out the light. It was after nine so she did not disturb Edward in the adjoining cabin, but she did not feel like going to bed quite yet. During the afternoon she felt an odd lethargy that slowed her motions and demanded her conscious effort to climb the steps to the ship's dining room. She recognized the feeling at once: it was that old companion of melancholy, inertia, which the doctors blamed on her reading and writing and lack of exercise.

When she was first stricken, the doctors mistook her lethargy for a more serious illness; fortunately her introduction to Edward at the ball banished the symptoms. Surely the melancholy had not returned!

How ironic if the malaise were to return during their visit with Aunt Bronwyn. In the months she suffered most from melancholy, the letters from her grandaunt had meant a great deal to Hattie. Aunt Bronwyn followed the latest theories of the mind and emotions, and it was her observation Hattie's illness could be cured if she completed her thesis. After the announcement of their engagement, Hattie's melancholy lifted and she was reluctant to return to the notes and manuscript for fear the anxiety and hopelessness might reoccur. Once or twice during Edward's absence a fatigue tried to take root, but Hattie warded it off with cool baths and green tea. Since Indigo's arrival, Hattie felt so fit and was in such good spirits she assumed herself cured. After travel and a visit with one's family, fatigue was not unusual, but Hattie also felt a vague discouragement that she could not articulate, a feeling similar to the one that preceded her illness before.

She summoned all her energy to break free of the heaviness in her limbs to pick up the portfolio. She did not open it at once; the very sensation of its weight in her hand brought back vivid memories. So much had seemed possible in the beginning; Hattie took pages and pages of notes—copying entire sections of Dr. Rhinehart's translations. She shuffled through the pages of notes until she found the quotations from the Coptic manuscripts she intended to use to illustrate her thesis. Here it was! the passage that had excited her so much, and inspired her thesis—the same passage that caused such consternation on the thesis committee:

> I was sent forth from the power,
> and I have come to those who reflect upon me,
> and I have been found among those who seek after me.
> Look upon me, you who reflect upon me,
> and you hearers, hear me.
> You who are waiting for me, take me to yourselves.
> And do not banish me from your sight.

And do not make your voice hate me, nor your hearing.
Do not be ignorant of me anywhere or any time.
    Be on your guard!
Don't be ignorant of me!
For I am the first and the last.
I am the honored one and the scorned one.
I am the whore and the holy one.
I am the wife and the virgin.
I am the mother and the daughter.
I am the members of my mother.
I am the barren one
and many are her sons.
I am she whose wedding is great
and I have not taken a husband.
I am the midwife and she who does not bear.
I am the solace of my labor pains.
I am the bride and the bridegroom,
and it is my husband who begot me.
I am the mother of my father,
and the sister of my husband
and he is my offspring.

How naive she had been to think her thesis topic would be approved! Hattie could smile now, but at the time of the committee's decision her entire world seemed to have come apart, especially after the dreadful encounter with Mr. Hyslop! Hattie had planned to continue auditing classes until term's end at Christmas, but the morning following the encounter, the symptoms appeared.

The doctor was called, and with one look he pronunced her condition female hysteria, precipitated by overstimulation. He prescribed complete rest and above all no books. Hattie refused to give up all books, but she no longer had the heart to read early church history; it was obviously incomplete, and the orthodox church had no intention to ever acknowledge the other gospels. But now she felt as if she were reunited with an old friend as she shuffled through the pages. She felt the old excitement stir; she wanted to learn more about the Illumined Ones, those to whom Jesus appeared and whom he instructed in secrets not revealed to the bishops or cardinals or the pope himself.

The parrot's damage to the train case was not discovered until Hattie began to pack her toilet articles, and by this time they were only a few hours from docking in Bristol. They were in sight of land, and Hattie was so relieved at their safe Atlantic crossing she only laughed when she saw how carefully the parrot removed the brass tacks.

"Oh it's easily repaired," Hattie said when she noticed Indigo's stricken expression. "Odd how it happened. I don't remember the train case being near the birdcage." They were about to dock in Bristol, where they'd take the train to Bath.

Edward gathered the notes he made from his reading about citrus horticulture. He lingered over his notes on the pome-citron, as the *Citrus medica* was known. The largest groves were in Corsica, but the authorities there were wary of foreigners who might be agents of foreign governments seeking to cash in on the growing popularity of candied citron rind. Agents for Lowe & Company reported the best specimens of *Citrus medica* were to be had in the mountain villages outside Bastia.

Aunt Bronwyn insisted on meeting them in Bristol for the short train ride to Bath. She was the same Aunt Bronwyn Hattie remembered, jolly, bright blue eyes enlarged by the thick lenses of her glasses. She was anxious to get out of Bristol—too much coal smoke and dust, too much noise in the streets.

Hattie watched Indigo's grip on the parrot's cage tighten as she was introduced to Aunt Bronwyn, but the child seemed to relax after Aunt Bronwyn praised Rainbow's beauty. Indigo leaned back on the wide leather seat and clutched the parrot cage tightly as the coach lurched through the port traffic. She had a feeling Aunt Bronwyn was going to be fun to visit.

From time to time she caught glimpses of the waterfront—so many tall ships, so many coaches and freight wagons in the streets. The noise and smoke and the odors of cooking food resembled those in the streets of New York City, except here the overcast sky and high thin clouds reminded Indigo of winter.

Ah, the great port city of Bristol astride the river Avon, Edward thought as he scanned the docks where workmen unloaded bales of cotton and pallets of lumber. The cab passed the wide doors of a large building where people and carts of raw wool darted in and out.

"What is it?" Hattie asked, noticing Edward's attention to the wool market building. Aunt Bronwyn took one look and guessed immediately.

"The site of the old slave market," Aunt Bronwyn said, watching Edward's expression. "No great English port city was without its slave market." The slave market in Bristol had been one point of the golden triangle of world trade. Ships sailed out of Bristol Harbor with English textiles, tin, and glass for the coast of West Africa, where the goods were traded for slaves; in the Americas the slaves were traded for cargoes of tobacco and cotton, which were transported back to Bristol, where the golden cycle repeated itself.

Hattie glanced at Edward, whose face reddened a bit.

"Of course, all the port cities of the Americas had slave markets too," Edward added.

"And we in the Americas kept our slave markets longer," Hattie said as she watched Indigo kneel on the seat to get a better view out the window. Indigo wanted to see the place where slaves used to be sold because Grandma Fleet told them stories about such places, like Yuma and Tucson. In the old days, twice a year, in the fall and the spring, the slave catchers brought their harvest of young Indian children to trade to the cattle ranchers and miners. The Sand Lizards preferred the old gardens because the slave hunters did not usually travel that far; she and Mama always warned the girls to be careful because the slave hunters didn't care what the law was; they tied you to a donkey's back and took you so far away you'd never find your way home.

"My sister and I know how to hide from the slave catchers," Indigo said, turning away from the window. Both Hattie and Edward looked a bit shocked, but Aunt Bronwyn nodded.

"Oh Indigo! There are no slave hunters anymore!" Hattie didn't want the child to make a habit of exaggeration to get attention or approval. Indigo's eyes got round and her face was serious.

"I've *seen* them, Hattie," Indigo said breathlessly. "We were on the hilltop with Grandma Fleet. Off in the distance we saw the children tied together in a line!" Indigo could tell Aunt Bronwyn believed her but Hattie and Edward did not.

As they boarded the train to Bath, Indigo thought her ears were failing her, but then she realized the people here spoke a different language. The people looked a bit different too, with light pink skin, light blue eyes, and light brown, thin hair; the damp cool air and the abundant shade of the tall trees must be the cause, Indigo decided. The people on the train stared at Indigo, but not unkindly.

The motions of the train felt quick and sharp after the days on the ship, and the air smelled of the locomotive's coal smoke. The train left behind the noise and congestion of the waterfront. The dingy tenements at the edge of Bristol gave way to green rolling hills above the river; the sky's color shifted from gray to green-blue. The railroad followed an embankment along the river. How lovely to drive along under the green canopy formed by the old elms and oaks along the meandering river. For a moment, off in the distance on the southern horizon, a shaft of sunlight broke through thin clouds. Indigo excitedly pointed at the sky. The sun had seldom been visible during their ocean crossing. Indigo pressed closer to the window but the sun slipped behind the clouds again.

Hattie was delighted with the beauty of the countryside; here and there between the tall trees and the shrubs—willows, bracken, brambles, and bog myrtle—little clumps of periwinkles, wild pinks, and marshmallows grew above the riverbank. All along the edge of the road foxgloves and primroses stood tall, with wild buttercups and white daisies scattered all around. She was hardly more than a child the last time she and her parents visited Aunt Bronwyn in Bath.

Aunt Bronwyn had been born in the United States, but years ago she married in England, where she remained even after her husband's death, on the estate inherited from her English grandfather. She was regarded a bit odd by the other Abbotts, who disliked the English for their snobbery. "Nonsense!" Aunt Bronwyn liked to exclaim to enliven the discussion. For centuries, the city of Bath had been populated by a great many wealthy foreign princes and other foreigners, who came to gamble and take the waters of the healing spring, so they took no notice of Aunt Bronwyn. The local people thought her foolish because she moved into the old cloister in the orchard, too close to the river, and the structure in disrepair. Aunt Bronwyn was too busy to waste time on teas and dinners, and in Bath they left her in peace. No effort was made to invite her, though they were pleasant enough when she met them on the street or in a shop.

Hattie and her father loved his old aunt, but Hattie's mother found Aunt Bronwyn's eccentricities quite unnerving during their visit years before. They found her beloved Irish terriers asleep in their bed and when Mrs. Abbott tried to force them off with her umbrella, the dogs made ugly growls at her. Mrs. Abbott urged them to stay at a hotel or they would get no sleep as there were cattle lowing and dogs barking all night.

Indigo was amazed at how damp and green the air smelled in England. Water, water everywhere, it seemed—in little ponds and lakes along the river. Through the slit in the cage cover she whispered to the parrot: Aunt Bronwyn seemed very nice, just the kind of person who would not mind a parrot out of his cage. She promised to let him out as soon as they arrived.

"Welcome! Welcome!" Aunt Bronwyn exclaimed again; she was so delighted they were able to stop with her even for a short visit. Indigo shook Aunt Bronwyn's hand but was too shy to speak until she saw the parrot's beak reach between the bars after Aunt Bronwyn's forefinger, then she exclaimed, "Watch out!" just in time to save Aunt Bronwyn's finger. Indigo showed her the half-moon scar on her own finger, the mark of the hooked beak.

They would have a wonderful time together. She had so much she wanted to show them—the new excavations of the Roman temple at the hot springs and a stone circle west of town about to be restored were only two of the outings Aunt Bronwyn had planned. The excavation was yielding a great many interesting artifacts of considerable antiquity.

"I'd like very much to see that," Edward said, turning from the coach window, his expression alert.

Hattie was relieved to see Edward perk up, because he seemed rather preoccupied throughout their ocean crossing. She knew he would have preferred to go directly to Italy, but now the promise of the excavations with old Roman artifacts made their stop in Bath worthwhile.

Edward had visited England before, but he still was amazed at the grand old oaks and elms amidst lush meadows and fields of flowers on the alluvial terraces of the rivers. Susan with her Scottish gardener, troops of workers, and Colin's money might labor for years, but Long Island would never appear as lush, green, and wooded as southwest England.

Here the moist air filtered the sunlight to create a lovely green-blue glow that transformed everything. Edward recalled how lovely Bath was, enclosed on three sides by the meandering Avon. Years before when he visited Bath, he had not bothered with the parks or formal gardens where ladies and their maids strolled under parasols, followed by little dogs. His interest had been in the private clubs where gambling went on as it had since before the reign of Queen Anne. At the time, he believed he had developed a mathematical equation to predict winning hands in twenty-one, but quickly realized his error.

Today the Avon's water appeared almost sluggish, due no doubt to the construction of weirs, built since medieval times to control flooding. Now the Avon at Bath was no longer a free-running river but a series of ponded lengths that overflowed at their downstream ends.

The coach emerged from the trees, and suddenly on the hills above the river grand villas of gray and pale yellow limestone in the Georgian style could be seen. The old walled city of Bath, built on the Avon's old flood-plain, was hidden by great oak and linden trees until they were quite near. Then suddenly the coach clattered across a narrow stone bridge and they entered the narrow twisting streets of buildings crowded together. The foundations and walls of a number of the oldest buildings rested on large hand-hewn limestone blocks Edward recognized as Roman in origin.

Aunt Bronwyn explained they were taking the old road into the town to avoid what she called "ghastly faux colonnades" the city fathers added some years ago when they widened Bath Street.

Edward was a bit startled by Aunt Bronwyn's remark since popular opinion regarded old Bath as among the most lovely cities in England. Down the side streets and alleys, Edward caught glimpses of the renovations ordered by Bath's city fathers to replace old Bath Street, which was too narrow and twisted through a clutter of eighteenth-century structures, mostly tenements, crammed together willy-nilly.

Aunt Bronwyn sat back on the coach seat, her blue eyes shining with enthusiasm as she pointed out the site of the old town. The Romans built over the old Celtic settlement near three thermal springs, sacred to the ancient Celtic god Sulis. On gravel terraces of an ancient floodplain, hot springwater bubbled to the surface with medicinal and magical properties. The Romans, always wary of offending powerful local deities, prudently named their town Aquae Sulis. But the Romans could not permit Sulis to rule supreme any longer, so they built a temple with a great pool over the springs, dedicated to Sulis and to Minerva as well.

The coach slowed as it neared the center of old Bath, outside the Pump House Hotel, so they could see the location of the new excavations in the temple ruins at the spring. Of course they could not actually see the excavations, which were under way in the basement of the hotel, but piles of debris and large screens the archaeologists used to find artifacts in the debris blocked the narrow alley and a portion of Stall Street, so the coachman was obliged to squeeze the horses and coach past a stack of broken stones. A few fragments appeared to have been carved. Edward leaned half out the window to get a better look at a piece of stone carved with the petals of a flower.

Once they passed the baths and hotels, the municipal buildings of handsome pale yellow limestone—the post office and the railway station—came into view, followed by the ornate downtown buildings of new Bath. Aunt Bronwyn found the white and yellow limestone too bright—almost brazen.

Hattie and Edward confessed their "thoroughly American" admiration for the eighteenth-century buildings in downtown. Outside the shops, hanging baskets of geraniums, pinks, and petunias trailed cascades of bright blue lobelia.

Aunt Bronwyn dismissed modern Bath with the wave of her hand and did not look out the coach window again. She talked instead of the surrounding hills, where stands of ancient oaks were preserved since the time of the Celtic kings, only to be cut down now as earthmoving teams carved wide scars in the bellies of the hills overlooking the river. All around Bath, construction was under way for more mansions of gigantic misproportions built for business tycoons from London and Bristol. The threat to the remains of the ancient hill forts and stone circles at the summits of the hills along the river had pressed her into action years ago, even before her husband died. She shook her head. The people nowadays cared nothing about the old stones!

Edward and Hattie exchanged glances; he wanted to follow Mrs. Abbott's advice to stay in a hotel rather than share the old Norman ruins with cattle and dogs. Hattie had loved the old cloister since she was Indigo's age; Aunt Bronwyn's feelings would have been terribly hurt if they went to a hotel. The last Irish terrier died some years ago; besides, it was too late to get a hotel—the summer rush of vacationers was on, and one could scarcely find space to move along the sidewalks outside the shops for all the visitors.

Bath's glory days ended long ago with the laws that restricted gambling. Bath's private clubs permitted gaming, so maharajas and foreign princes still were seen driving through the streets of Bath.

The coach approached an intersection where the left fork appeared to proceed along an old floodplain of the river while the right fork gradually ascended into the fashionable residential parkways up the hills. To Edward's surprise, the coach turned left and then turned left again to double back toward the old town along the lush river bottom thick with elders and willows. Remnants of an old dry rock wall overgrown with mossy sax-ifrages and little ferns could be seen from time to time.

The narrow drive wound through the canopy of lindens and elders that filtered the sunlight to a golden green in a light cool breeze off the river. The old Norman abbey was taken down long ago; now only the old cloister with its walled gardens and the apple orchard remained. Ahead, tucked under great old live oaks and nearly concealed by hollies and hawthorns, was the old stone cloister that once sheltered Norman nuns.

"Oh this is lovely!" Hattie exclaimed. Indigo clutched the parrot cage closer as the coach bumped over a little bridge. Indigo thought no other place could have more trees or be more green than Long Island, but here was a place that had more and bigger trees, and hills far greener. Edward thought the location a bit too close to the river for comfort but he made no comment. Just then the coach slowed to a stop in front of a stone wall and two great iron gates. The coachman climbed down to swing open the great iron gates, then strangely did not proceed but stood there. Edward leaned out the coach window for a look and was surprised to see a white bull blocking the driveway in front of the gate.

Indigo had seen cattle before—thin, wild-eyed, rangy creatures, but never such a fat beauty as this white bull; two white cows emerged from under the apple trees and more cattle followed until a small herd was gath-ered around the coach. Aunt Bronwyn climbed down and took a small pail from the coachman and began to hand-feed rolled oats to the cattle. Ed-ward thought at once of Mrs. Abbott's complaints about the old woman and her animals; it certainly was odd to delay travel-weary guests in order to pet the cattle. Hattie's mother recalled that during their last visit, a door was not firmly latched and they had returned from shopping to find white cattle wandering in the front room. Quite at home, she added, proof that the old woman allowed them to roam at will when no visitors were present.

When Aunt Bronwyn got back into the coach, the cattle seemed to know the treat was over, and they slowly moved back to their grazing un-der the apple trees. But when the coach reached the front of the house, four more cows stood on the driveway near the front step. At the approach of the coach they stared hard at the horses but stood their ground; this meant a difference of only seven or eight feet farther to walk, but Edward felt im-patient with the old woman.

The old stone walls of the cloister were handsome indeed and had been modified very little over the years. The windows were narrow and high;

though it was early afternoon, small oil lamps flickered from their brass sconces in the walls. Indigo was delighted with the odd shadows cast on the bare stone walls.

In the library, Hattie noted the odd placement of the bookshelves, three feet above the floor. Aunt Bronwyn laughed and pointed out the high-water stains faintly visible on the gray stone wall a few inches short of the bottoms of the bookshelves. Edward vowed to himself "a hotel, only a hotel," if they ever stopped there again.

Indigo slipped the cover off the parrot's cage and lifted the cage.

"See," she said, "you're in England now." The parrot looked around the room then began preening its feathers.

"He won't comb his feathers with his beak unless he's happy," she said as she carefully set the cage on the window ledge, then neatly folded the cage cover.

The stone masonry of the old cloister did not tolerate casual renovation. Here and there were indications someone had walled in a doorway or failed an attempt to remove a stone partition wall. Long ago workmen on the old cloister complained that stones loosened and removed by day were found in their former locations the following day. Edward smiled at Aunt Bronwyn's tale.

"So the fairies replaced the stones at night," he said.

Aunt Bronwyn shook her head. The stones themselves had moved without any aid from brownies or fairies. Indigo's eyes widened. Aunt Bronwyn nodded her head decisively.

Oh yes indeed. This is the land of the stones that dance and walk after midnight. Tomorrow she would take them to the giant stones at Stanton Drew.

While Edward and Hattie unpacked, Indigo sat on the stairs with Rainbow in his cage beside her to watch the coachman carry buckets of hot water from the big kitchen stove for their baths. The coachman's wife brought an armful of clean towels and gave Indigo a little round cake of soap that smelled of roses. Rainbow became very excited and flapped his wings with loud squawks at the sound of water splashing as Indigo rinsed the soap from her hair.

The coachman's wife baked a rabbit pie, served with fresh greens, baby carrots, and peas from the kitchen garden. Afterward, Hattie complained of fatigue; she and Edward went upstairs to rest while Aunt Bronwyn showed Indigo the baby calves.

The instant she moved toward the door behind Aunt Bronwyn, the parrot began to screech and frantically flap his wings in the cage. He was afraid she was abandoning him; she could tell.

"Don't worry. You can come along." She opened the cage door, then knelt with her right shoulder next to the open door.

"Come on, little rainbow bird, sweet Rainbow, come on!" The parrot nervously shifted his feet on the perch and looked at Aunt Bronwyn, then at Indigo. Indigo sighed impatiently and started to stand up to go when the parrot climbed out of the cage and clung to the side before he climbed onto her shoulder.

"Good Rainbow! Good bird," Indigo whispered as they followed the old cobbled drive to the dry rock wall of the orchard. All sorts of sparrows and small birds were chirping in the tops of trees above them; Rainbow listened but made no sound; he tightened his grip on her shoulder as Indigo knelt to search for dry pods under a clump of marshmallows.

The sun was low above the trees, and its golden light shifted to leaf green as they climbed the stile's narrow stone steps up and over the old wall that enclosed the apple orchard. No gate was as good as a stile, Aunt Bronwyn explained; gates got left open. The cattle could push gates open, but cattle would not climb over a stile. As it was, the cattle found other clever ways to escape the orchard to browse the willows along the river. More than once the white cattle strayed down Bath Street before dawn, to taste the petunias and geraniums from the hanging planters while they splashed bright green manure outside the shops.

Aunt Bronwyn called the cattle in tones that might have been a song. The calls were lovely and made Indigo think of the old gardens and Grandma Fleet and Mama and Sister Salt. They sat on the steps of the stile in the green-golden light to wait for the cattle to come. Indigo smelled the river nearby and felt the cool air currents move around them. With her eyes closed she imagined for a moment that she was with Grandma Fleet and Sister. The parrot shifted his grip on her shoulder and watched curiously as the tears rolled down her cheeks. Indigo hated the big lump she felt in her throat.

Aunt Bronwyn did not see her face, but she seemed to sense Indigo's sadness. She pointed up at the small green fruit on the branches overhead and began to tell Indigo about the white cattle.

The white cattle belonged to the moon—see the shape of the crescent moon in the cow's horn? Indigo nodded. The sun was only partially visible now through the trees, but in the last shafts of light the cattle appeared to be shimmering white, almost silver, as they emerged from the apple trees. The bull in the lead approached Aunt Bronwyn, who walked slowly to meet him.

At the rear of the herd Indigo saw the cream-colored calves frolicking together; the mother cows stared at Indigo with wide dark eyes, blowing air through their nostrils, wary of any danger she might pose to the calves. Aunt Bronwyn scratched the bull between the horns and spoke softly to him. Gradually the cows came forward to sniff Aunt Bronwyn's shoe or her hat or the hem of her skirt. The calves raced about their mothers, tails held high over their backs, bucking and leaping on one another. They were fond of their mistress, and the bull moved protectively between Indigo and Aunt Bronwyn, who was petting the calves. Slowly Aunt Bronwyn worked her way back through the herd, petting or speaking to each cow. The young bulls watched from under the apple trees at a distance and Aunt Bronwyn went over to greet them as well. As the sun dropped behind the trees at the curve in the river, Aunt Bronwyn pointed at the sky to the southwest, where Indigo saw the thick white horn of the moon.

Hattie watched Aunt Bronwyn and the child with the parrot on her shoulder walk hand in hand up the drive to the house. Hattie's heart felt so full of love for them at that instant tears sprang into her eyes, but she quickly brushed them away. Edward was upstairs with his notebooks. He seemed in much better spirits now that they were on their way. He had an appointment in London later that week at the Kew Gardens.

Hattie felt a bit melancholy. Surely it was travel fatigue and nothing more. At the height of the previous episode, she scarcely had the energy to walk from her bed to the commode. Right now, a walk in the garden might be just what she needed; she called out to them to wait. She strode across the lawn, testing her energy to reassure herself she was fit.

The sun was behind the hills, but the trees along the river were still bright in the twilight's glow. She joined them and followed Aunt Bronwyn and the child with her parrot through a weathered brassbound gate in the high limestone wall off the south wing of the old cloister. Inside they found themselves surrounded on all sides by high stone walls overgrown with old grapevines knotted thick as fists. Stone walks crisscrossed the big enclosure that was divided by high walls into four gardens—Indigo was reminded of a big house without a roof. At the center was a round stone pool fed by water bubbling up from a spring.

Aunt Bronwyn explained at one time the entire area had been devoted to vegetables to feed the Norman nuns, but Aunt Bronwyn didn't need all those vegetables. Now only the sunny southeastern quadrant was planted for the kitchen. The beds were slightly raised above the stone paths that separated them. Flat smooth river stones set side by side upright formed the borders of the beds and gave what Hattie thought was an oddly formal appearance to the vegetable garden. Aunt Bronwyn took pride in old flagstone paths and raised beds and parterres that lay buried under the turf until she hired workmen to unearth them. In old church records she found maps and diagrams of the original cloister garden, its severe plain lines and sparse plantings designed to mortify the soul.

Indigo called out excitedly and ran to the corn plant: she was delighted to see baby pumpkins as well. Aunt Bronwyn took her garden trowel and dug little carrots for the parrot; she picked ripe tomatoes for them to eat while they helped Aunt Bronwyn fill her apron with baby peas and tender spinach for dinner.

The kitchen garden was the modern garden as well, she explained. Plants from all over the world—from the Americas, tomatoes, potatoes, pumpkins, squash, and sweet corn; and garlic, onions, broad beans, asparagus, and chickpeas from Italy—grew with peppers from Asia and Africa.

She led them down the stone path to the northeast quadrant, under a rustic stone pergola that supported a flourishing gourd plant, its pendulous fruits dangling overhead like lanterns. Hattie remarked that this was a good idea to try in Riverside, where shade was always welcome. She explained the Riverside gardens were watered and trimmed but otherwise largely neglected since the death of Edward's father and his mother's percipitous decline. Aunt Bronwyn nodded sympathetically.

So far the trip had been a wonderful opportunity for gardening ideas—Indigo had a small valise full of carefully folded wax paper packets with the seeds she'd gathered. When they returned to Riverside, Hattie planned to show the neglected gardens they were loved again.

Aunt Bronwyn agreed; if a garden wasn't loved it could not properly grow! She was an avid follower of the theories of Gustav Fechner, who believed plants have souls and human beings exist only to be consumed by plants and be transformed into glorious new plant life. Hattie had to smile; so human beings existed only to become fertilizer for plants! Edward and her father would have a good laugh at that!

◆　◆　◆

Years before, when she first moved into the old cloister, Aunt Bronwyn joined the Antiquity Rescue Committee, a local group organized to protect an ancient grove of oaks and yews on a hilltop near a small stone circle.

Old churches and old buildings had defenders but few people cared about clumps of old trees or old stones on hilltops. Not long after the hilltop grove was saved, she joined hands with committee members as they made a ring around the upright stone threatened by dynamite in a farmer's field. Her English neighbors tolerated a good many eccentricities in one another, but the demonstration by the rescue committee to save the boulder earned their group some notoriety in Bath and the surrounding area.

She learned a great deal from the old women and old men who tottered up the stairs of the old Pump House Hotel on the second Saturday afternoon of each month. For many members, the meeting of the Antiquity Rescue Committee was their only social activity other than church or visits from doctors. Aunt Bronwyn smiled and shook her head. They were all gone now, but it had been wonderful to hear the history and tales about Bath and the surrounding countryside from these fervent defenders of old trees and stones.

Aunt Bronwyn paused to apologize for going on so about her committee, but Hattie was eager to hear more, and Indigo nodded enthusiastically. Aunt Bronwyn clapped her hands with a big smile. "All right," she said, "I'll tell you about the toads!" Some of the rescue committee members were also active in the protection of the toads during their odd migrations; Aunt Bronwyn joined them on their hands and knees in the mud to help the toads cross busy roadways safely. But it wasn't until she began to study the artifacts of the old Europeans that she discovered carved and ceramic figures of toads were worshiped as incarnations of the primordial Mother.

She imagined the reactions of her English neighbors to her participation in such activities. How typical of an American! they'd say, although she was the only American in the group; all the other members were English, and many grew up in Bath or nearby towns. Her English neighbors enjoyed hearty laughs over the odd pilgrims and foreigners who trudged through town muttering about solstices and stone rings on their way to Stanton Downs or Avebury, and claimed descent from Celtic kings and druids.

Most rescue committee meetings eventually trailed off into reminiscences and stories—how rotund Queen Anne went bottom-up when her carriage overturned on one of Bath's steepest hills; how Lord Chesterfield preferred to play with card sharps rather than with English gentlemen because the card sharps paid him at once if he won, while the gentlemen sent around a letter and apologies and never paid him. Sometimes after the meetings adjourned they continued lively discussions well into the evening, exchanging stories about the behavior of certain stones that walked to drink water after midnight and stones that turned to follow the sun.

If plants and trees had individual souls, then Aunt Bronwyn decided to acquaint herself with as many different beings as possible. Between the orchard and the cloister odd mounds of broken stone and rubble overgrown with weeds, wild roses, and hawthorn marked the site of the Norman abbey. Here she planted her "wild grove" of silver firs, Scots pines, and yews with black walnut, hazel, and oak. Now, fifty years later, her wild grove reached the back wall of the old cloister garden and shaded the back of the south garden.

A path of pea-size river pebbles curved away from the driveway into the wild grove. Indigo ran ahead on the path with the parrot on her shoulder flapping his wings in excitement; with each breath she could almost taste the damp coolness of the grove.

At the center of the grove was a low circular wall of old stone, overgrown with velvety green mosses and delicate ferns. The water, bubbling and gurgling into itself from an artesian spring, was almost hidden by watercress, moneywort, bog orchids, and yellow iris. After some effort in the local archives, Aunt Bronwyn determined the spring and old wall were the remains of the Norman baptistry.

Indigo offered the parrot a chance to get off her shoulder and walk on the edge of the old wall but the bird nervously scanned the sky and the grove and remained firmly on her shoulder. Indigo told the bird to hold on as she leaned down to taste the water. Nowhere had she found water that tasted as good as the water from the spring at the old gardens. Just then Hattie called out, "Wait," but Aunt Bronwyn said it was safe; the water tasted just like rainwater, so light and sweet it barely quenched her thirst.

Hattie sat on the edge of the old wall to dip her hand into the water, while Aunt Bronwyn pointed to the narrow stone rill that carried the water out of the forest grove through the orchard for the cattle and finally to the river. There were a number of artesian springs in the vicinity of the river but not all of them were hot water like the springs that fed the baths.

"This is a very special place," Hattie said. "I understand why you stay here."

Aunt Bronwyn nodded her head with a merry expression on her face. Yes, the family did not understand her reasons for remaining in England after her husband died; after all, she was an American—"Whatever an American is," Aunt Bronwyn said with a wink at Indigo. She'd fallen under the spell of the old cloister, which was nearly in ruins when she leased it from an English family that wanted fashionable locations in the heights of Bath away from the river and the mosquitoes, not to mention the crowds of tourists downtown or the odors of the baths.

Aunt Bronwyn had more she wanted to show them; a quick look now and they could return for a better look tomorrow. They followed the gravel path to the back of the old cloister along the high outer wall overgrown with ivies and wild clematis. Aunt Bronwyn pushed away the vines to reveal a narrow ironclad door in the wall; she gripped the iron latch firmly and pushed her shoulder hard against the door while she kicked it with her foot. The door seemed stuck for an instant before it slowly opened with the sound of wood dragging against dirt: she had to kick the door to get it open wider. The door was part of a late-eighteeth-century renovation. In the days of the Norman nuns, the cloister garden could be reached only through a door from the kitchen.

The late afternoon light scarcely penetrated the wild grove that shaded the back wall of the west garden. Fortunately the renovators of long ago did not tear out the old raised beds shaped in circles and rectangles—they merely buried them under topsoil. When Aunt Bronwyn began the garden restoration, workmen discovered the intricate river pebble borders and carefully unearthed and repaired them.

The low stone walls that divided the interior garden into four parts were planted with lavender; Indigo buried her face in the blossoms, while the parrot snipped off shoots with its beak. Hattie could see at once each quadrant was quite different from the others.

In the north quadrant, Aunt Bronwyn planted the old raised beds with indigenous English plants—kales, hellebores, dandelions, pinks, periwinkles, daisies. Little white flowering violets cascaded over the edges of the raised beds. The east side of the garden was planted with all the plants the Romans and Normans introduced: grapevines nearly obscured the weathered wooden pergola that slouched down the path between the raised beds planted with cabbages, eggplants, chickpeas, and cucumbers. Hattie was surprised at how few food crops and flowers were indigenous to England; the climate here did not seem unfriendly in the least as compared to the dry heat of Riverside.

The south garden and west garden were planted with plants from the Americas, Africa, and Asia. As soon as Indigo saw the tasseled corn plants along the back wall of the south garden ahead, she broke into a run that caused the parrot to flap his wings excitedly. Indigo stood before the corn

245

plants, which were planted apart from one another—to let the sun reach all of them, she thought. At home they had to shade the plants and help them withstand strong winds, so they planted their corn close to one another, like a big family. Here the corn plants had the protection of the high outer garden walls as well as the old stone walls that formed the garden quadrants. Indigo ran to the hollyhocks along the south edge of the raised beds, and this time the parrot lost his grip. At the last instant Indigo felt him let go, and off he flew, flapping his clipped wings madly for about ten feet before he landed and clung to a pink Persian rose trimmed into a small tree. Indigo ran to the rose tree and returned the parrot to her shoulder.

"Look, here's where all the flowers came from," she called out to Hattie. Aunt Bronwyn broke into a big smile; as she wiped her eyeglasses on the edge of her apron, she explained the roses, the lilies, the hollyhocks, and the pear trees did not originate in England but in the Near East and Asia.

"Your people," she said, "the American Indians, gave the world so many vegetables, fruits, and flowers—corn, tomatoes, potatoes, chilies, peanuts, coffee, chocolate, pineapple, bananas, and of course, tobacco. Indigo felt suddenly embarrassed. Sand Lizard people barely were able to grow corn, and they had no tomatoes, peanuts, or bananas. The Sand Lizard people gathered the little green succulents called sand food; sand food could never grow in England or New York or even Parker. Sand food needed sandstone cliff sand and just the right amount of winter snow, not rain, to grow just under the surface of the sand. Indigo missed sand food with its mild salty green taste better than cucumbers.

Aunt Bronwyn explained a number of the food crops of grains and vegetables and a great many flowers were unknown in England until the arrival of the Romans; thus cattle and pigs, still highly prized for their milk and meat, were once so important they had been gods; even now it was possible to find old churches with the figures of sows and piglets carved in the stone doorways.

In the sunny west garden big dark red dahlias grew at the feet of giant sunflowers with faces like dinner plates. Indigo never imagined so many different sunflowers, some with red petals, some with white flowers—all sizes, with many-flowered branches and single flowers alone. Indigo whispered to the parrot she wished they might have come later in the year, after the plants had gone to seed. Still, she looked carefully on the ground under the plants in case there were any early seed pods. She knew just the place to plant these sunflowers, not far from the spring above the dunes.

She smelled a heavenly perfume and turned to a plant as tall as she was, with handsome dark leaves and little white bell-shape flowers. "Smell this!" Indigo called to Hattie, who did not recognize the plant until Aunt Bronwyn teased her about not knowing this most American of plants, white-flowering nicotiana, tobacco.

The south and west gardens were planted with flowers among the vegetables, with herbs and medicinal plants scattered among them, since they preferred to grow together to protect one another from insects. Indigo caught the scent of the datura before she recognized the plant because it was taller than she was, its blossoms the size of saucers. She pressed her face against the big flower and inhaled so deeply its pollen tickled her nose.

"Hello, old friend. You sure grow tall in England. Are you trying to get closer to the sun?" She showed Rainbow the round spiny seed pods of the datura but told him it was not polite to take it; when she got him back home he could have as many spiny seed pods as he wanted.

She was only a little way into the tomatoes and the bush beans when she looked to the far edge of the west garden and caught a glimpse of the brightest colors, lush flowers on handsome stalks almost as tall as she! The reds, oranges, pinks, and purples of the flowers were so saturated with color they seemed to glow above graceful narrow leaves of deep green. Indigo loved the fancy ones with different colors—white centers and white edges or even spotted petals. These flowers! Sister and Mama would love flowers like these! Aunt Bronwyn was happy to tell her about the gladiolus; originally they were brought from Africa but they'd undergone a great many changes by the hybridizers.

Hattie asked about the medicinal plants. Yes, a great many did require shade and damp—monkshood, belladonna, gentian, valerian—but ways could be found to grow almost any plant, though one might have to take it into one's bed as the old German orchid collectors did every night all winter.

Hattie explained the run-down gardens of the Riverside house as well as Indigo's interest in plants and seeds had renewed her interest in gardening. A medicinal garden would be just the thing for that area of sparse lawn by the lilacs. The location got plenty of sun with just enough afternoon shade for the heat-sensitive plants.

Indigo was captivated by the gladiolus for reasons Hattie could not imagine; hybrid gladiolus seemed to her garish and artificial, though Aunt Bronwyn's clever placement of them did show off their best qualities quite nicely. Hattie tried to interest her in a stand of silvery Casa Blanca lilies, but Indigo wanted to examine a spike of burgundy flowers edged in pink.

While the child roamed among the gladiolus, Aunt Bronwyn pointed out the more modest species of gladiolus and the little white and red gladiolus that grew wild in the hills above the Mediterranean. This was to have been the last year she was going to bother planting the tender hybrid gladiolus, but Indigo's enthusiasm for the long bed of the tall silver and burgundy gladiolus changed her mind. She would plant them every year in honor of their visit and Indigo's enthusiasm for gladiolus.

As Aunt Bronwyn and Indigo paused to watch a big toad catch gnats, Hattie turned to survey the garden and caught a glimpse of another doorway in the west wall, overgrown with a fragrant white climbing rose. She thought she'd like to take a look, but the twilight was fading. Better to wait until tomorrow.

Before she went downstairs for dinner, Indigo put the parrot in his cage; the pupils of his eyes enlarged and he began to shriek; she begged him to please be quiet, she would come right back; but the parrot would have none of that. Indigo knew they expected her at dinner but she didn't want the parrot's screaming to upset Edward and Hattie.

She sat with the parrot until there was a gentle knock at the door and Aunt Bronwyn came in. Was everything all right? Was the bed comfortable? Indigo decided Aunt Bronwyn would understand, so she admitted she didn't care to sleep in beds at all—she moved the bedding to the floor at night but replaced it first thing in the morning. Hattie knew, but Edward didn't. Aunt Bronwyn seemed interested in how she got along with Edward. He was nice, but he didn't like the parrot's screeching; that was why she had't come down to dinner; the parrot didn't want her to go. Aunt Bronwyn took the brass handle of the cage herself and they walked downstairs together.

In the long narrow room that had been the old chapel, they sat around a massive round table Aunt Bronwyn called King Arthur's table because it was so old. Long deep scratches marred its surface, and she laughed and said those were marks from the daggers and swords of the Knights of the Round Table. The coachman's wife served roast chicken, fresh green beans, and potatoes, with carrot cake for dessert. After dinner they did not sit up long because they wanted to get an early start the next morning. Aunt Bronwyn had so much she wanted to show them.

Indigo made a wonderful nest with the sheet and blankets on the floor; Aunt Bronwyn helped her pull the bedding loose and told her she needn't move it from the floor in the morning. Now Indigo felt so much more comfortable. The parrot slept perched on the cage top with his head tucked under his wing; Indigo wondered what he dreamed—probably he dreamed of his old home in the flowery jungle where he used to fly free with his sisters and mother. Indigo felt a heaviness in her chest and tears filled her eyes; she missed Sister and Mama so much, and poor little Linnaeus was left behind. The tears made her face hot and then she felt hot all over and kicked away the sheet and blankets and pushed the pillow to one side so her cheek and ear touched the cool stone floor. She drifted off to sleep listening to the gurgles deep in the belly of the earth; the sounds were more watery here in England.

Hattie dreamed she was walking under the big elms and oaks in the park at the Boston Commons. A cool fall breeze blew across her face. How bright and alive the red maple leaves and golden oak leaves appeared, backlit by the sun; they shimmered so close to her face Hattie reached out to touch them. She woke with a start, shivering, aware she was lying outdoors in the dark. She had not walked in her sleep since she was a child. The sky was clear; how brightly the stars lit the night. She recognized the garden stepping-stones across from her, but she was surprised to find herself lying on a long flat horizontal stone in a raised flower bed. She sat up and saw her feet and the edge of her nightgown were caked with dried mud. As her eyes became accustomed to the light, she realized she was in a part of the garden she had not seen before; only the high stone walls were familiar. It appeared to be an old, abandoned garden of some sort, oddly adorned by stones, many of them broken, carefully sited in the raised parterres with the sweet bay and dandelions.

Hattie stood up, shivering, her arms folded around herself, and realized the stone she'd been lying on was the stone from the dream she'd had in Oyster Bay. In that dream, the stone lay in a churchyard cemetery with old tombstones; of course, Aunt Bronwyn's garden was once a churchyard. What an odd coincidence this was! If her feet had not been so cold, she might have thought she was dreaming. The cool night air was sweet with the scent of river willows and roses. As she followed the stone path out of the abandoned garden she heard a strange noise ahead of her—a loud knock. The loud knock sounded again and to Hattie the sound resembled a club of wood against wood. When she reached the gateway between the two gardens, she saw a strange glow emanating from within. Hattie took deep breaths to calm herself. The light appeared to be on the far side of the grape arbor. At first she mistook the light for a lantern's glow—were they searching for her? But as she observed it longer, Hattie realized the glow was too soft to be a lantern. The loud knock sounded again, and the fine hairs on the back of her neck stood up; she saw something luminous white move through the foliage of the corn plants and the tall sunflowers. Her heart beat faster as she heard the soft rhythmic sound of breathing approach her. She felt a strange stir of excitement and dread at what she would see when she stepped through the gateway. The luminosity of the light was astonishing: was she awake or asleep? How beautiful the light was! Her apprehension and dread receded; now a prismatic aura surrounded the light. It was as if starlight and moonlight converged over her as a warm current of air enveloped her; for an instant Hattie felt such joy she wept.

When she reached the front of the house, Hattie found lanterns lit and the coachman and Aunt Bronwyn up and about. They appeared surprised to see her. Embarrassed, Hattie assumed they were looking for her, but no, the cattle were loose, through an open gate or break in the fence—they were not sure, but the white cattle were everywhere. Three cows and their calves browsed on white climbing roses in front of the house, unconcerned with the commotion. Hattie assured her aunt she was unharmed, but the old woman looked intently at her as if she was not convinced. The eastern sky was already bright pink with the approaching dawn.

Aunt Bronwyn said the sleepwalk might be due to the excitement of their arrival; travel was quite taxing on the nerves, as she learned on a recent trip. She was so exhausted by the train ride from Trieste to Budapest, she hallucinated bad odors in her hotel room. Hattie's heartbeat quickened at the mention of hallucination; the light she saw was no hallucination. Aunt Bronwyn thought perhaps the breakout by the cattle disturbed her sleep and caused the episode.

Hattie shook her head. She feared she might be the culprit who left open both the gates. She pointed at the mud on her feet and the edge of her nightgown, evidence she'd walked as far as the puddle outside the orchard gate, though she remembered nothing of the sleepwalk.

Edward was alarmed about Hattie's sleepwalk. What if she sleepwalked off the deck of the ship? Should they consult a doctor? Edward wanted to postpone his trip to London, but Hattie insisted he take the noon train as planned for his meeting with the Kew Gardens staff. She felt a bit strange after her sleepwalk, but she certainly wasn't ill; there was no reason for Edward to miss his appointment.

Hattie wanted time alone to reflect on her experience in the garden.

She promised to rest for an hour or two, but later, in the darkened bedroom, Hattie tossed and turned but did not sleep soundly; she could not stop thinking about what she had seen. Her thoughts raced—what had she seen, luminous and white, moving through the foliage of Aunt Bronwyn's corn plants and sunflowers? The memory of that instant caused Hattie to weep again with the joy she felt with all her being. Thoughts raced through her mind in swift-moving torrents—glittering and flashing. Words from her thesis notes cascaded before her mind's eye, then suddenly scattered as if suddenly the words were dry leaves blowing away in the wind: poor judgment, bad timing, late marriage, premature marriage, dread of childbirth, sexual dysfunction.

Hattie tried to calm herself with deep breathing but managed to doze for only brief periods. The rooms of the Riverside house would not let her be—that house presided over by her dead mother-in-law intruded into her thoughts, room by room followed by the gardens overgrown and sparse and the glass house of orchid skeletons in pots all around the monkey's cage. Suddenly she realized they must help the Indian child return to her sister and mother! This was all wrong! How foolish she had been!

The rush of thoughts so unnerved Hattie she got up and went downstairs, where she found Aunt Bronwyn and Indigo at lunch on the round table. The child listened to the old woman name King Arthur's knights. They had such strange names; Indigo was confident she could remember them all and tell Sister.

Morfran was so ugly everyone thought he worked for the devil; he had hair on him like a stag. Sandde Angel Face was never attacked in combat because he was so beautiful enemy soldiers mistook him for an angel on the battlefield. Henbeddstr never found a man who could run as fast as he could, and Henwas the Winged never found a four-legged animal as fast as he. Scili the Light-footed could walk above the treetops or above the rushes of the river. Drem could be in Cornwall and see a gnat rise in the morning sun in Scotland. Cynr of the Beautiful Beard endured water and fire better than anyone; when he carried burdens, small or large, the burdens were never seen. If Gwalloig went to a village in need of something, no one in the village could sleep until he got what he needed. Osla of the Big Knife carried a short broadsword he lay across rivers as a bridge so the knights and their horses crossed safely. Gilla Stag Leg could jump three hundred acres in a single leap. Sol could stand all day on one leg.

Stories like these were Indigo's favorites; she could hardly wait to tell Sister. In Needles there had been a Navajo woman, and she used to tell the girls stories about long ago when there were giants, and humans and animals still spoke the same language. Indigo told Aunt Bronwyn about the wounded giant's drops of blood that became the black lava peaks as the giant fled the attack of the Twin Brothers.

Now the rainbow bird refused to go inside his cage, but perched on the cage top at night or whenever Indigo put him down. After lunch, they went to survey the white bull's damage to the corn; by midday light the garden looked very different than she had seen it the night before in the glowing light. They followed Aunt Bronwyn to the back wall; the parrot rode Indigo's shoulder with confidence, squawking and flapping his wings whenever they went outdoors.

Aunt Bronwyn led them to the stone gateway at the back of the garden, the entrance to the stone garden, as she called it; Hattie recognized it at once as the place she woke hours earlier. In the midday light the stone garden looked much different than it had the night before. Hattie examined the vertical stones, which seemed much taller in the darkness. She searched for the long flat stone from the night before, from her dream, which she distinctly remembered being near the tall vertical stones; but she didn't find the long flat stone until she neared the back wall. Hattie asked where the stones came from—she was especially curious about the long horizontal stone.

The grave of Aunt Bronwyn's English grandfather was there, among the standing stones; he wanted no marker for himself. A few of the eldest in Bath still remembered, from their childhood, the old man who carefully searched dumps and trash middens near the old village churches to find fragments of the old stones smashed to pieces by order of the parish priest. He ordered his driver to take the muddy back roads to any new construction sites or newly plowed fields, always with an eye out for any old stones cast aside.

While the child and her parrot walked solemnly from stone to stone, toward the upright boulder alone in the center, Hattie told her aunt about her dream in Oyster Bay: in the dream she sat astride a long, horizontal stone in an old churchyard. Last night she woke on that very stone! Edward was convinced she had seen illustrations of similar old stones in churchyards but had forgotten. Or perhaps as a child Hattie heard the horizontal stone described in family conversations.

The strange glow in the garden the night before was more difficult to explain; she wanted to think it over a bit longer before she told anyone, even Aunt Bronwyn. Hattie certainly didn't mention the light she had seen to Edward because he was already upset by the episode of sleepwalking. Hattie felt on the verge of confiding in her aunt about the light when Aunt Bronwyn asked if she and the child might want to stay on with her while Edward completed his business in Corsica. She had so many things and places to show Hattie, and she wanted time to talk about Hattie's thesis. It was terribly hot and uncomfortable in Corsica in July; worse, there were reports of political unrest. Corsica was always a challenge to the visitor; the mountainous regions were notorious for bandits, who preyed on English and American tourists. It would be lovely to have her and the child stay with her until Edward returned.

Hattie hugged her aunt; what a delight that would be! She wanted very much to learn about the old stones. She promised she would return next summer, but now it wasn't possible to stay; Edward wanted her and the child to accompany him.

Indigo ran back up the path to rejoin Aunt Bronwyn and Hattie. From Indigo's shoulder, the parrot watched sparrows hop along the top of the stone wall where the rock pinks grew from cracks in the old wall and scented the air; mossy saxifrages and catmints grew all along the base of the stone wall and between the old stones with the daisies and dandelions.

Aunt Bronwyn identified the stones. Here was a broken stone with a double spiral carving to help the plants to grow faster. Here were the broken pieces of a stone destroyed by an angry mob of Christian converts. Indigo asked if she had any healing stones in the garden, but Aunt Bronwyn did not know. She'd heard discussions of a standing stone that healed patients who were passed back and forth three times over its top. But over the years, the quack doctors and snake oil salesmen of Bath hacked the old stone to pieces to sell as curative charms. Reportedly there were healing stones that fit in the palm of the hand; they were steeped in water from Bath's sacred springs; they cured any ailment. According to the legend of the healing springwater, the Celtic King Bladud learned from local farmers that pigs with sores were cured by soaking in the mud and warm springwater. The king built a temple and bath at the spring, but later when the king got old he made a pair of wings and jumped from the roof of the temple and was killed.

For centuries, Bath had been overrun by doctors and pharmacists peddling cures for cancer, gout, and heart disease, formulated from such ingredients as live hog lice, burnt coke quenched in aqua vitae, powdered red coral, the black tips of crab claws, and freshly gathered earthworms. Invalids pushed in their chairs by nurses still flocked to Bath the year round to take the waters.

Aunt Bronwyn paused to look over the stones rescued long ago by her grandfather. She pointed out a bluestone no larger than a steamer trunk—in times of drought the bluestone was beaten with hazel sticks to bring rain. Indigo's eyes widened as she went on; Aunt Bronwyn had seen praying stones and cursing stones. There were stones that turned slowly with the sun to warm both sides of themselves, and stones that traveled at night to drink from the river and returned by morning. There were stones that danced at high noon and stones that danced in the light of the moon!

Indigo asked Aunt Bronwyn if she had ever seen the dancing stones. No, when she was a girl about Indigo's age, she observed a black stone the size of a stove move across the road to the south side overnight. Tomorrow they'd take a picnic basket and visit the place. Aunt Bronwyn wanted to drive up on the ridge above the river overlooking Bath; a great deal of construction was going on there. Each week she checked to see if any stones were in need of protection.

Hattie recalled the unkind remarks she'd heard from time to time growing up, remarks her mother made to her father about Aunt Bronwyn's peculiarities. So this is what it was: while other old women fed stray cats and dogs, this old woman took pity on stones. The evening of their arrival, Edward joked Aunt Bronwyn had gone native; what could be more English than an old woman feeding tidbits to her cows?

As they walked back through the garden toward the house, her aunt said something that surprised Hattie. The old people had warned her even would-be rescuers of the old stones must use great caution because it was dangerous to tamper with the standing stones or to cut down the sacred groves. The stones and the groves housed the "good folk," the spirits of the dead. Never interfere with the fairies! When sheep were brought by the English to graze Scotland, the good folk and the people living on the land were displaced, and the fairies waged war against the sheep. An old man heard the sounds of dogs running down the sheep for the angry spirits; the old man was a seventh son of a seventh son and thus was able to hear and sometimes even see the spirits.

The terrible famine in Ireland in 1846 came because the Protestants and the English knocked down the old stones. The wars of Europe were the terrible consequences of centuries of crimes against the old stones and the sacred groves of hazel and oak. Still, the destruction of the stone circles and groves did not stop; now the reckoning day was not far off—twenty years or less.

Hattie found herself taken aback by her aunt's remarks; she was reluctant to link the luminous glow in the garden with the forces of violent retribution. She wished Indigo would not listen so attentively to her aunt's comments; the child might become confused. She felt a faint flicker of ill ease that announced an onset of anxious feelings, so she excused herself and the child. They needed to rest. Aunt Bronwyn invited Indigo to spend the afternoon with her in the garden, but Hattie was firm and took Indigo by the hand back inside the house.

Earlier Edward worried there would be trouble if they did not set some limits for the child. He was concerned about the agreement he signed with the superintendent of the Indian school. It was no use to pretend they were instructing Indigo about the duties of an upstairs maid. Hattie had bristled at the mention of the agreement. She was only a little girl; the boarding school superintendent was a criminal to hire out the Indian children at such a young age. Edward said nothing more, but Hattie wondered if he was concerned over the appearance the child was their adopted daughter, an assumption made by a number of their fellow steamship passengers.

◆　◆　◆

The day of Edward's return from London, Hattie rested upstairs all morning and a good part of the afternoon. Aunt Bronwyn invited Indigo to eat lunch with the parrot on her shoulder and they both laughed with delight at the bird's dainty table manners as he took bits of chicken pot pie from their forks. That evening when Hattie and Edward came to the table for dinner they found the child and the old woman feeding the parrot broth from a spoon. Indigo noticed at once that Edward did not approve and that Hattie was concerned too, but Aunt Bronwyn laughed and told them about the small white dog her grandfather kept with him; the dog sat on a chair with its own china plate beside the old man at every meal, a napkin tied around its neck as it stared straight ahead with great dignity waiting for its master to feed it a tidbit.

Edward smiled and shook his head, as if to acknowledge the old woman made the rules in her house. He had returned from London in good humor, after finding the watercolor supplies he wanted. The visit to the Kew Gardens went very well. The director of Kew Gardens agreed to pay a handsome price for *Citrus medica* cuttings. The French government closely guarded the citron orchards of Corsica to protect their exclusive supply of candied citron to the world market. Edward only smiled when the director commented on the difficulty of the task. The incident on the Pará River left him wary of misplaced trust. He revealed the plan to no one, not even Hattie, though he felt guilty for the omission and planned to tell her everything as soon as they reached Corsica.

The following morning after breakfast, they set out together for a walk downtown to the site of the excavations. Bath had a great many grassy arcades and parks shaded by trees where elegant ladies walked with their maids or drove in smart buggies with their lapdogs. Nowadays the parade of women's fashions was more subdued, but in the last century the ladies went to great lengths to steal the attention from one another during their promenades in the parks. One woman went so far as to have a garden of pinks and violets planted in the framework of the wide hoop skirt of her dress.

Aunt Bronwyn nodded briskly whenever she was greeted by townspeople along the way, oblivious of the gawkers and tourists who stared rudely. Of course they must have made quite a spectacle on Stall Street, Hattie thought; the energetic old woman wearing a brown derby marched ahead, and Indigo with the parrot on her shoulder walked just behind her, followed by Edward and Hattie. As they approached the King's Bath, the streets were crowded with vacationers from London and foreign tourists come to visit the shops and the royal baths.

Aunt Bronwyn pointed out the smaller pavilion, which was the Queen's Bath. Originally there had been only the King's Bath, but the queen became frightened by strange lights in the King's Bath and refused ever to go back. So the Queen's Bath was built. Hattie's heart was pounding; what sort of strange light? she asked.

"Swamp gas caused the light," Edward joked. Hattie was disappointed he felt he had to make a joke out of her question. Aunt Bronwyn was about to reply when they arrived at the hotel entrance, where Aunt Bronwyn was greeted by the doorman.

Rainbow tightened his grip on Indigo's shoulder apprehensively as they entered the lobby of the Pump House Hotel. Hotel guests seated in the lobby stared with open mouths as Aunt Bronwyn marched past, eyes straight ahead, to the back hall and the stairway to the basement. The modern baths were separated from the old baths by a new wall. Kerosene lamps hung from excavation scaffolding to light the stairs; as she descended, Indigo felt the warmth and dampness of the springs below, and despite the odor of the lamp oil, an even stronger odor, of wet clay, old urine, and mildew, wafted around them as they descended.

They approached the edge of the big excavation, where workmen filled wheelbarrows with dirt and stone debris by the light of kerosene torches that projected strange giant shadows of the workmen on the walls. Below them, on the deepest level of the excavation, Edward saw the edge of the old Roman pool that once encompassed an area far greater even than the site of the hotel.

Major Davis left the workmen as soon as he saw them, and he and Aunt Bronwyn exchanged warm greetings. After the introductions were made, the major lit a small lantern and guided them between heaps of old stones and piles of damp earth to point out the periods of occupation: the Tudor and Elizabethan levels were hardly distinguishable from each other and appeared as dark gray streaks; the medieval level was deeper but a lighter gray; the Norman level was the color of ashes. The exposed layers of earth reminded Hattie of the alternating layers of jam and cream in a fancy cake. They descended the wide stone steps the workmen had unearthed only days before; a damp odor of clay and decaying organic material clung to the steps. Indigo was reminded of the odor of the smelly black mud she and Sister Salt tried to avoid at the edge of the river. As Hattie took a step down, the major announced she was now standing on the earliest Roman occupation level, from the time the sacred hot springs were first contained in a pool of cement and limestone; the construction of a Roman temple dedicated to Sulis Minerva followed. Its name was somewhat of a mystery, Major Davis explained, because Sulis was a Celtic diety of the sun and Minerva was the Roman goddess of the moon. He led them past piles of stone and plaster debris.

Edward noticed a number of torches lighting an area that appeared to hold something of great importance. Major Davis led them to it and stepped aside with a flourish to reveal the carved limestone altar of Sulis Minerva. All eyes were on the corner pillars of the altar—each was carved with voluptuous nude figures, two women and two men; fortunately the most prominent features of the statues were weathered enough, so Hattie allowed Indigo to step up to get a better look.

Hattie realized the altar platform stone, though larger and wider, was almost identical in shape to the flat rock in her dream and in her aunt's garden. An odd sensation pulsed through her body when she touched the corner of the altar stone, and left her feeling a bit light-headed, but not unwell.

The parrot became extremely agitated, flapping its wings and screeching on Indigo's shoulder; for a moment the workmen all stopped to stare, but with a stern glance from the major the work resumed. As soon as she moved away from the altar the parrot quieted; Indigo was not surprised to see Edward's frown but she was saddened at the odd expression on Hattie's face, as if she wanted Indigo and the parrot to leave at once.

Aunt Bronwyn took Indigo's hand firmly in hers. The parrot was only trying to warn them the air in the basement was not fresh! The Romans made a mistake when they built structures over the hot springs. Aunt Bronwyn was more interested in the sacred springs before the invasion of the Romans, when the Celts tossed coins and tablets of lead to curse enemies to the spirits of the springs. At the mention of coins, Edward interrupted his examination of the altar platform and turned to the major and Aunt Bronwyn. Was it possible to see the artifacts that were for sale? Of course. Would they like to see the excavation where the Celtic objects were found? It was right on their way to the storage area for artifacts.

They followed the major down the wooden ramp for wheelbarrows, down into the deepest level of the excavations, where workmen removed the layers of sand and peat from the bottom of the pool. Here warm spring-water bubbled up through the sand even as the workmen toiled in rubber boots.

Indigo was fascinated with the bubbling sand and water over the mouth of the spring. The spring at the old gardens dripped cool water down a cleft in the sandstone cliff; here the water bubbled straight up through the sand in a circle that Indigo watched closely for a long time until the circle of bubbling sand reminded her of the dancers bobbing and swaying as they swooned at the sight of the Messiah and his family. Then she felt Aunt Bronwyn gently touch her shoulder to ask if she was all right.

"I was remembering the dancers," Indigo said. "When I think of them and that night, I am happy."

It was a relief to emerge into the fresh air in the back hall of the old hotel. They followed the major to a large storage pantry used to clean and catalogue the artifacts and to label fragments of temple pediments and other carved stone. His assistants excused themselves while the major took the ring of keys to the large oak chests already packed for shipment to Oxford.

The major unwrapped a bundle of canvas and twine to reveal a dozen little wooden artifact boxes with identification labels neatly lettered in india ink. He slid back the tops of the boxes one by one to display the carved gemstones nested in cotton and set them out on the worktable; then he invited them to step closer and have a look. In the later Roman levels, little amulets of ivory and bronze in the shapes of breasts were found; fertility of-ferings, the major supposed. Hattie felt her face flush at the word "fertility" but hoped no one noticed.

Some were superstitious, but not the major; some thought to remove the ancient offerings to the springs invited disaster. Hattie had no desire to touch anything from centuries in black peat mud that reeked of old human waste, but Edward eagerly reached into the boxes. Indigo pressed close to Hattie to get a better look, though she was careful not to touch the carved stones. The little wooden boxes with sliding lids, lined with cotton, inter-ested her more than the stones they contained. What good boxes for stor-ing seeds!

Edward held up a cloudy chalcedony carved with three cattle under an oak tree; the figures of the cattle looked just like Aunt Bronwyn's white cattle. How cruel it was to put the stones into little coffins after their cen-turies out in the world, even if in the bottom of a pool! The major gave a jolly chuckle at her remark and Edward joined in, but quickly cited the ne-cessity to protect ancient artifacts for the sake of science. Aunt Bronwyn did not agree; she shook her head and turned to go just as the major dragged out a trunk with a loud noise that excited the parrot to shrieks. In-digo was relieved the major laughed before anyone could speak; he had been a parrot keeper once himself. Parrots must shriek from time to time for good health.

The major lifted a large canvas-wrapped bundle from the chest and pro-ceeded to unwrap a thin, curved object of blackish gray metal, found by workmen in a drainage culvert. He held it up for them to get a good look; the eyes and mouth were narrow rectangular slits in the tin; the mask was of Celtic origin but was made after the Roman conquest, though its pur-pose was unknown. Did the mask represent the Diety of the spring? Was it worn by a priest, or a patient who came to drink the healing water?

Edward joked the mask belonged to the druids and reached out to touch it; the major handed it to him for closer inspection. Edward examined it, then lifted the tin mask up to his face for a moment and peered out the eyeholes at the others. He supposed it was self-consciousness that caused the odd sensation when he looked through the eyes of the mask; more dis-tance seemed to lie between himself and Hattie and other people, though they did not move. He pulled the mask away and looked at them, then lifted it again and looked before he gave the mask back to the major.

The major talked as he rewrapped the tin mask. The mask showed no relation at all to the fine bronze head of Minerva unearthed in the excavations of 1792. He hoped to locate the rest of Minerva's bronze, though now it appeared unlikely; the funds allocated for the excavations were nearly spent. The cost of running the pumps day and night to keep the excavations clear of the springwater was prohibitive.

Edward examined the carved gemstones again. The bright orange carnelian depicting the goddess Minerva seated with a serpent was even more impressive, and Edward thought he could make a decent profit if he sold it in the United States. He particularly liked the vibrant bloodstone carved with the left profile of Jupiter seated with his mantle draped over his loins, his scepter in his left hand and an eagle on his outstretched right hand. The device of Jupiter holding an eagle was not common on gems, and Edward wanted very much to buy the gemstone.

The major was reluctant to see the pieces leave England, but the circumstances left him little choice; to continue the work additional funds must be obtained. Edward nodded; he understood. He examined a figure of Fortuna, carved into brown agate banded in white; the figure of the goddess held a poppy head in one hand and what appeared to be an ear of corn in the other hand, though it must have been another plant, since corn was a New World plant.

◆ ◆ ◆

Aunt Bronwyn took Indigo to find some refreshment in the hotel dining room while Edward negotiated a price for the carvings and one or two lead curse tablets.

After they returned to the house Edward brought out the lead curse tablets the major sold him. Edward was not sure how marketable the tablets would be—they were dark and discolored, their edges badly broken. Ugly and poisonous, lead was the perfect vehicle for the curses crudely scratched on their surfaces before they were tossed in the sacred spring. The old Celts and the Romans believed sacred wells and sacred springs had the power to expose and punish thieves and cheaters. All that was necessary was to write out the person's name.

Edward was in good humor as he read the inscribed curse: "To the goddess Sulis. Whether slave or free, whoever he shall be, you are not to permit him eyes or health. He shall be blind and childless so long as he shall live unless he returns"—the next word is illegible—"to the temple." Edward speculated on the illegible word while the coachman and his wife brought out the baskets of food for the picnic. Edward was pleased with his purchases from the major; the stop in Bath was more rewarding than he anticipated. He considered pleading a headache to excuse himself from the picnic so he could spend time with his new acquisitions, but the old woman promised circles of ancient stones on hilltops he must see.

Someone must have beaten the old bluestone with a hazel stick while they were at the excavation because by the time they washed up and had a light lunch (Aunt Bronwyn believed no one should go on a picnic hungry), the clear sky and sun gave way to dark blue storm clouds and wind-driven rain. The sky darkened, so hall lamps were lit by two o'clock. As the afternoon wore on, the wind blew harder and the creak and groan of the roof timbers could be heard, along with other noises in the wind—clatters and bangs of loose shutters. The old cloister was in need of repairs.

Edward excused himself and went upstairs; despite the fury of the storm, he was relieved to have the afternoon free to examine the Roman artifacts he purchased and to prepare his watercolor box for Corsica. He sharpened the knife he planned to use to make the twig cuttings and packed it in the watercolor box in a compartment under the brushes. He mixed watercolor washes and practiced pen-and-ink drawings of landscape scenes he copied from a guidebook. The Corsican farmers undoubtedly were accustomed to finding foreign tourists with easels and paint in their fields and orchards; after his undergraduate studies he'd spent the summer doing just that.

The rain drummed against the roof and walls, but the roof and the walls of the old cloister were weather-tight. Oh the wild storms this old building had weathered, he thought; now the rain washed against the walls in waves. Edward held the knife blade up to the light and examined its edge closely; would it cut the citrus twigs fast and clean without crushing the twigs' fragile ends?

Now the wind made a howling sound like the sea monsters in stories Aunt Bronwyn heard as a child. The monsters were not flesh and blood but the great violent storms that lashed these islands. Little wonder there were so many stories of the fairies who were spirits of the dead, often drowned fishermen or others lost at sea.

The stone circle and the standing rock would have to wait; later they'd eat their picnic lunch at the round table. Now the rain poured in a deluge that seemed to rattle every inch of the old slate roof. Aunt Bronwyn listened for a moment, then commented that when the river overflowed its banks the cattle must be brought up from the orchard to higher ground. More than once she found herself in gum boots and slicker in the middle of the night with the rain pouring down, herding the white cattle to safety. She was not concerned now because the ground could take a good rain without a flood.

Hattie brought out her thesis notes at her aunt's request, but she was content to sit all evening and listen to stories and forget the manuscript. The thesis seemed to belong to another lifetime now; she felt oddly detached from her notes.

The rain drummed on the roof harder and the parrot nervously looked up at Indigo. She sat on the little stuffed velvet footstool at Aunt Bronwyn's feet to hear about the magic of King Arthur's knight Cei, who could last nine days and nine nights underwater without air. This was a storm for Cei!

Indigo brought out Aunt Bronwyn's basket of empty thread spools to keep the parrot's beak off the oak molding and the legs of the chairs and sofas. Indigo rolled the empty spools and the parrot examined them with his beak before he broke them to bits. The noise of the storm made conversation difficult, so they sat and listened as the wind accelerated to a high-pitched whine and the rain slapped the window glass until Hattie thought it would break.

Aunt Bronwyn stirred the sugar in her tea and prepared to tell Indigo more about the knights of the Round Table; but she interrupted her introductory remarks about King Arthur with little exclamations at the noises the storm stirred up in the old cloister. After a big bumping noise in the rafters Aunt Bronwyn glanced toward the ceiling and said: "Uchdryd Cross-Beard threw his red beard across fifty rafters in Arthur's hall!" And she continued to name the knights: Clust could hear an ant set out in the morning fifty miles away when he was buried under seven fathoms of earth. Medr from Celli Wig could shoot at a wren in Ireland right between his legs. Gwiwan Cat's Eye could cut off a gnat's eyelash without hurting the gnat's eye. If Gwaddan Osol stood on the biggest mountaintop it would become a level plain. When Gwaddan of the Bonfire walked, sparks flashed from the soles of his feet whenever they touched anything hard, and whatever he touched became molten iron.

Aunt Bronwyn paused to listen to a new sound—an incessant loud knocking that seemed to come from the back of the house.

"Is someone there?" Hattie's heart pounded as she got up from her chair. The sound seemed identical to the strange knocking Hattie heard the night she sleepwalked. Why did the sound set off such a panic in her?

"I think it is only the wind," her aunt said, "though perhaps the wind means to take part of the old cloister with him."

Aunt Bronwyn pointed at the thesis notes on the end table and Hattie picked them up. She explained how intrigued she had been in catechism class by the Gnostic heretics; then later, as she read Dr. Rhinehart's translations, she wanted to write a thesis based on the lost gospels. Hattie flipped through the pages of notes but felt oddly detached from them now. She smiled at her paragraphs that argued Mary Magdalene was an apostle and Jesus treated her as an equal with the others, who resented her. No wonder the gospel of Mary Magdalene had been buried in a cave in the desert for centuries. Mary Magdalene wrote she saw Jesus' resurrected spirit, while Peter claimed they saw Jesus' resurrected body. Why insist on a literal view of the resurrection and reject all others? Here was her answer, which stirred such rancor on the thesis committee: Peter and the others sought to legitimize their authority to exercise exclusive leadership as successors of Jesus.

Aunt Bronwyn laughed and clapped her hands as Hattie finished reading aloud. Good for Hattie! Aunt Bronwyn patted Hattie's arm and told her how proud she was of Hattie's defiance of the thesis committee. That was the old family spirit!

For centuries the clergy made war on the ways of the old ones! King Cormac the Magnificent cruelly supressed the druid religion; in revenge, the druid Maelgin paid a sorcerer who caused a salmon bone to catch crossways in the king's throat at the dinner table.

Indigo let the parrot play by himself with the spools while they listened to Aunt Bronwyn. The Council of Tours decreed excommunication for those who persisted in worshiping trees; the Council of Nantes instructed bishops and their servants to dig up and hide the stones in remote woody places upon which vows were still made. Yet the wisest Christians were respectful of the pagan spirits. St. Columba asked God to spare the sacred oak grove at Derry because while he feared death and hell, he feared the sound of an axe in the grove of Derry even more. Hattie asked if the sacred grove was still there. Her aunt shook her head.

Yet despite the persecution, the old customs persisted—dairy keepers spilled a bit of milk for the fairies, morning and night; on the first night of August, a few people (Aunt Bronwyn was one of them) still gathered around fires on nearby hilltops until dawn, though the church tried to outlaw such practices centuries before. People still bowed to the standing stones at crossroads and threw coins into springs and lakes. At one time the church ordered the slaughter of all herds of white cattle, which were suspected of pagan devotions; fortunately not everyone complied with the order. Aunt Bronwyn's tone of voice grew more intense.

Did Hattie know (did anyone know) how much innocent blood spilled in Derry over the years of the occupation or how much more blood might yet spill? Ireland's suffering began with the betrayal of fairies. Those who cut down the sacred groves doomed themselves and all their descendants!

Hattie was surprised by her aunt's vehemence, and concerned at Indigo's reaction; but Indigo's expression became thoughtful. Jesus was betrayed too, she responded. But after the Pharisees tried to have Jesus killed, he left the Sea of Galilee to return to the mountains beyond Walker Lake, where he was born. As Aunt Bronwyn listened, she glanced at Hattie to see her reaction to the child's comment.

Hattie noded. It was true; six or seven years before, newspapers reported the Indians claimed to have a Messiah, a Christ of their own, for whom they gathered to perform a dance. Hattie followed the reports in the *New York Times*. It all ended rather badly; settlers feared Indian uprisings, and in South Dakota the army killed more than a hundred dancers.

Aunt Bronwyn shook her head slowly; her expression was solemn. Indigo stopped playing with the spools and the parrot, and looked up at them; she told them not to worry: the soldiers would not find the Messiah and his family or the dancers because they fled far away to the east. By winter it would be safe, and the Messiah would return with the first snow.

Hattie was about to caution Indigo about exaggeration and falsehood when Aunt Bronwyn asked Indigo if she had seen the Messiah. Indigo nodded eagerly; they all were so beautiful. Aunt Bronwyn smiled and nodded. Here on the remote islands people sometimes heard the sounds of voices and drums in the night; through the fog or rain mist at night people sometimes saw the silhouettes of dancers around fires on the hilltops. Indigo's eyes were round with delight as she nodded vigorously.

Hattie cleared her throat; she wanted to change the subject before her aunt went any further and confused the child with superstition. But the old woman's face was bright with enthusiasm as she rattled on about sightings along the shore in the fog and mist; the people saw his Mother, sometimes with a child they called the Son of God. Indigo and her aunt exchanged smiles; yes, the Messiah and his dancers were safe.

Hattie was at a loss for words. Her mother had complained of Aunt Bronwyn's growling terriers and the cattle on the front steps, but she never mentioned Aunt Bronwyn's enthusiasm for Celtic mythology. Why, her aunt had left the church altogether! Hattie was critical of developments in the early church, yet she never considered leaving the church entirely. Hattie did not want the child to become confused—certainly not by the notion old stones should be worshiped!

The intensity of the storm seemed on the wane. Hattie returned the thesis notes to the portfolio. Just then Edward appeared in the doorway clutching his left hand in a towel soaked with blood.

Their dinner of picnic food was forgotten as Aunt Bronwyn and Hattie cared for the deep gash in Edward's left hand. Somehow the freshly sharpened knife slipped as he practiced diagonal cuts on green willow twigs. Hattie applied pressure to the wound with a clean napkin while Aunt Bronwyn went to call the coachman to go for the doctor. A dozen stiches were required to close the wound, and Edward was pale and shaken when the doctor finished. By the time they remembered dinner, it was nearly eleven o'clock and they were too tired and overwrought to eat more than a few bites before they all went to bed.

An emptiness in her stomach woke Indigo just before daylight; she could barely make out the silhouette of the parrot asleep with his head tucked under one wing. She took a sip of water to try to quiet the hunger and wished she had more of Mrs. Abbott's ginger cookies. It was much too early to get up, so Indigo lay in bed thinking about Sister Salt and Mama, and her longing for them made her chest ache until tears filled her eyes and rolled down her cheeks into her ears. Her sobs and sniffles woke the parrot, who watched her curiously. She had one hopeful thought that stopped the tears: On their walk to the excavations the day before, she heard Aunt Bronwyn mention a Christ Church to Hattie and Edward, but Indigo didn't see which direction she pointed; she was too shy to ask where it was, but it must be nearby. Today she would ask Aunt Bronwyn to show her the Christ Church. The Messiah and his followers went away when the hot weather came, and though she knew it wasn't likely, still she thought it might be possible that he stopped at his church in England on his way to the Holy Land.

At the first sounds from downstairs, Indigo got up, and with Rainbow on her shoulder, she went to the dining room, where the coachman's wife served her and Aunt Bronwyn tea and hot shortcake. After she ate two shortcakes and drank two cups of tea with sugar and milk, Indigo asked Aunt Bronwyn if Christ Church was nearby. She thought she heard it mentioned and she thought they might find out if the Messiah and his followers had been seen nearby. Aunt Bronwyn's expression was thoughtful—yes, there were a number of churches and even villages with the name Christ Church. Then she smiled. Indigo was right, she said; Christ might be at any of those places. He might be anywhere.

The morning after the storm was clear and sunny and the air rain-fresh and fragrant with the damp plants and new flowers. They left Edward with his citrus books, his injured hand elevated on a small pillow, in a garden chair under the arbor of rambling white roses.

The coach took them up and around to the hilltop park estates of the wealthy, who resided in Bath for a month of gambling and therapeutic baths each year. Hattie asked if these were the old families of Bath, and Aunt Bronwyn laughed merrily. Fled long ago, they had, to escape the milling flocks of tourists and vacationers and the traffic jams like this one forcing their coach to inch past the hotels and shops. The sounds of the street traffic, music from the organ grinders, and shouts of the street vendors made conversation difficult. Indigo leaned out the window to get a better look at the toys—windup dogs and bouncing rubber balls sold on the sidewalk by men and boys dressed in white.

Once out of town, Indigo was excited to see the trees and vegetation of the river valley gradually give way to a rolling plain of grasses that appeared soft and lush in all colors of green, yellow, and copper. Aunt Bronwyn pointed out the window; off in the distance, if one looked very carefully, one could see the largest of the upright stones; next to this stone and still hidden from view was the old church. The lurching of the coach and the shifting sunlight on the plain made the boulder difficult to see until they got closer.

As they neared them, Hattie was quite amazed at the size of the upright stones—they were as tall as the church walls and as broad as the bow of a steamship. She felt a bit foolish because she had expected old stones on the scale of the stones in Aunt Bronwyn's garden.

They parked in the shade of an upright stone that dwarfed the horses and coach, but they no sooner got out than another coach pulled up. Aunt Bronwyn exhaled indignantly when she saw the occupants; the young men appeared to be archaeology students, who eagerly followed their professor with measuring rods and notebooks in hand.

"Curses, curses," Aunt Bronwyn muttered under her breath as the group tramped down the meadow path to the center of the stone ring and began to measure the distances between the giant stones. To avoid the archaeology class, Aunt Bronwyn took them first to see the old Christ Church near the burial cove.

How odd to build a church here, so far from the village, Hattie thought. The church site was down the slope of the hill from the giant boulders, which appeared to dwarf the church structure until one reached the churchyard.

To Indigo, the huge upright boulder appeared to be a giant blackbird's head and the two great overturned boulders on either side were the giant bird's wings outstretched.

A rusted chain and lock secured the church doors, but they were able to peek through the crack between the doors to see the bare stone room. Only the stone steps and massive altar stone, supported by blocks of stone, remained; the altar's stones were cut from the same sandstone as the three giant horizontal stones that formed the entryway to the ancient burial mound.

The location of the church, between the stone circles on the hilltop and the smaller stone ring and burial mound, was intended to discourage the people from their midsummer bonfires and all-night dances. Stories claimed the stones of the circles here were once guests and members of a wedding party who danced all Saturday through the night to the sabbath, when suddenly the sinners dancing in their circles turned to stone. While she was talking, Aunt Bronwyn kept an eye on the hilltop, and when the students and their teacher began to make their way toward the church, Aunt Bronwyn nodded at Hattie and Indigo and they walked briskly up an outlying path to avoid the group.

Indigo touched each of the giant stones along the circular path; the dark stones were rough with melted pebbles and rock fragments. Tiny quartz crystals in the great sandstone boulders glittered in the late morning sun; Indigo ran her finger inside the circles and spirals incised in the limestone—they looked like big eyes to her; and they *were* eyes, Aunt Bronwyn explained, the eyes of the original Mother, the Mother of God, the Mother of Jesus.

Indigo felt a rush of excitement and raced over the fragrant damp turf to the center of the great circle, where she sang out the words of the song from long ago: "The black rock, the black rock—the rock is broken and from it pours clear, fresh water, clear, fresh water!" Yes! The Messiah and his family stopped by this place on their journey to the east; Indigo felt certain of this.

Just then another vehicle—an open buggy full of sightseers—arrived, and Aunt Bronwyn shook her head and Hattie called to Indigo and they walked back to their coach. The best time to visit the stone circles was in the autumn or winter, without the commotion of so many sightseers. She preferred to visit the stones just as the fog and mist of a storm swept over the hilltop, because then it was possible to feel a marvelous energy and life from the stones. Hattie nodded; she took a last look around, embarrassed that she felt nothing from the boulders and curious to know what the measurements of the archaeologists might reveal.

Indigo sat on the edge of the seat all the way back to the house, her face bright with excitement. She did not expect to see Christ at his church, but it was reassuring to see the hilltop and great stones where he and the others stopped from time to time. She hoped Rainbow had not screeched or disturbed Edward while they were away. They'd carefully hung the brass travel cage from a stout rope tied in the main branch of an old yew tree inside the entry yard of the old cloisters, where the coachman's wife, who liked pet birds, promised to reasssure Rainbow he was not abandoned. Loud screeches greeted their coach even before it stopped, but the coachman's wife reported he was quiet until then; a blackbird couple from the orchard kept him company most of the morning.

Although Edward's hand was not quite healed, he booked them on a ship that departed Bristol for Genoa the following week. Hattie no longer slept soundly in the old cloister, and she worried Indigo would be misled by her aunt's eccentric ideas.

The day of their departure for Bristol, Aunt Bronwyn read them an article from the London *Times:* certain Coptic scrolls obtained years before by the British Museum had just been authenticated. Hattie's hands shook as she held the paper. So! Her intuition had not failed her! True words were beautiful words! She must write to her father. Poor Dr. Rhinehart! He died the previous year, before his life's work could be vindicated; but she was more fortunate; now she could petition the thesis committee to reconsider their decision. But almost as soon as she had the thought, she realized she had no desire to return to the committee or to the thesis, though she could not explain this reluctance. She should have felt elated; instead she felt much as she had at the time of the committee's original decision—worn down and sad—though she smiled bravely as she passed the article back to Aunt Bronwyn. Edward did not ask to see the article but he congratulated her, saying science had done its job for the muddled humanists. A bit later she excused herself to finish packing, but once in the room, she felt strangely tired and lay on the bed without removing her shoes.

At the pier, tears filled Aunt Bronwyn's eyes as she smiled and hugged Indigo to her big bosom. "You must bring Indigo again," Aunt Bronwyn said, and promised to visit them next year in Riverside when the weather in Bath was gloomy. Moments before, she gave Indigo a package that held a small silk-bound notebook where Aunt Bronwyn hand-printed the names (in English and Latin) of medicinal plants and the best conditions and methods to grow them. All the other pages in the green silk notebook were blank, ready for Indigo to draw or write anything she wanted. Bundled on top of the notebook with white ribbons were dozens of waxed paper packets of seeds wrapped in white tissue paper. Aunt Bronwyn also packed a large hamper of food and treats for the voyage. Their farewells were cut short by a light rain that gave way to a downpour. Indigo could not fight back the tears after their hug as she and Aunt Bronwyn parted. The parrot made a loud screeching sound that stopped her tears as she petted the bird and whispered reassurances to him.

Part Seven

THE STEAMSHIP departed in the early evening with the tide; despite the rain, the sea was calm. A day away from the Canary Islands they woke to a bright sunlight and blue sky. The warm temperatures reminded Indigo of the desert; the peaks and troughs of the ocean waves made her think of odd barren mountains and hills of salt water. As they neared land the seagulls floated on the ocean's surface and caused Indigo to mistake them for big sea flowers. Rainbow squawked and made no mistake of their identity—they'd kill him and eat him if they could, Hattie explained.

The voyage past Gibraltar was calm and quite lovely. Edward remained in the cabin with his hand in a basin of hot salts the cabin boy changed once an hour on doctor's orders. Hattie and Indigo with her parrot enjoyed the fresh air and sun on walks on the deck. Edward joined them for the evening walk. He continuously squeezed a small latex rubber ball in the injured hand to limber the tendons as Hattie described the schools of flying fish they counted; Indigo had a good head for numbers.

The tedious daily regimen of the hand soaked in steaming water subdued the infection, and the wound was nearly healed. When they were not counting seabirds, Hattie and Indigo practiced spelling the words from the story of the Chinese monkey. Hattie felt relieved to be fulfilling at least a part of the agreement Edward made with the boarding school superintendent—to continue teaching her to read and write.

For geography they accepted the ship captain's invitation to visit the bridge, where he showed them the maps and charts that guided them toward Gibraltar. On the wall chart of the Mediterranean, Hattie pointed out Italy and the town of Lucca, where they'd visit Aunt Bronwyn's friend; here was the island of Corsica they were bound for. The captain expressed surprise Americans would risk a visit to such a lawless place (the mountains were full of bandits and revolutionists!), a place with so little to offer the traveler. Hattie stepped back from the chart at once; she regretted the mention of their final destination, but thanked the captain for his concern about their safety. She signaled Indigo to follow her, though they'd only just got there.

Was it her exhaustion that left her so enervated and shorttempered? She fully intended to discuss dangers in the hills of Corsica with Edward after they reached Lucca and she had time to rest.

Indigo's spelling list for the week included words like "wicked," "hundred," "scriptures," and "scoundrel" because the Chinese monkey was in a lot of trouble. She enjoyed the assignment to use each of the spelling words at lease once in a sentence she made up herself. Hattie was surprised at the sentence in which a policeman was called a "scoundrel" by the Messiah.

Edward locked the cabin doors at night because he feared Hattie might sleepwalk, but she slept soundly every night except the last night before they reached Genoa. That night she dreamed she was awakened in her berth by a soft glow in the corner of the cabin, a glow that seemed to spread even as she watched it. She recognized the glow as the light she saw in Aunt Bronwyn's garden, and when she sat up in her berth she was shocked to see Edward's empty berth.

Where could he be? As she leaned over to get a better look at the little antechamber where Indigo slept, she caught a glimpse of him that set her heart pounding. He was standing by the small writing desk in the dark with a bundle in both hands. She was shaking so badly she had difficulty finding her voice. She did not want to wake the child or disturb the other passengers, so she whispered his name loudly; but the figure in the shadow did not respond. Surely Edward did not sleepwalk! She watched transfixed by the luminous glow that emanated near the figure. Suddenly the radiance increased now as bright as a gas lamp and she saw it was the tin mask from the sacred spring.

She tried to call out to Edward but she could not seem to get the words out. The mask began to advance with the light through the darkness until suddenly it covered the face of the figure in shadow. "Edward!" she called out, and woke herself and Edward. She assured him it was nothing, a nightmare, and he turned in the upper berth to go back to sleep.

Hattie listened to the sounds of Edward's breathing and the beat of her heart, and concentrated on slowing her heartbeat to match the rhythm of his breathing. Certain thoughts sent her heart racing and had to be locked out; all the old feelings swept over her if she permitted herself any thought of her thesis. Somehow the news of the authentication of Dr. Rhinehart's old scrolls only made her feel worse about her rejection by the graduate school.

She concentrated her thoughts instead on the gardens of the Riverside house, aging and neglected, in need of a great deal of attention. She looked forward to the Italian gardens for ideas for plants and shrubs suited to the dry hot climate of Riverside. As she drifted off to sleep, she imagined a pink garden entirely of roses and bougainvillea set off with the rich jade greens of aloes and agaves and large cacti.

Just before dawn, Hattie awoke with a pounding headache and rising nausea; in her haste to the lavatory, she bumped into a chair. The startled parrot flew against the side of the cage and woke Edward and Indigo.

She had never seen Hattie's face so white—poor woman! What was wrong? Indigo dampened a washcloth to wipe her face, then helped her walk back to her berth, while Edward rang for a steward, then rushed off to find a doctor.

Hot pulses of pain expanded behind her eyes until they filled with tears and even her nose dripped. She felt hot, then suddenly she shivered. If she opened her eyes, the room spun so fast she felt she had to grip the sides of the berth to keep from falling. Only the coolnes of the damp cloth Indigo placed on her forehead gave any comfort.

Edward returned alone, anxiously rubbing the bandage on his injured finger. Through the pounding pain in her temples Hattie had difficulty understanding Edward. He said something about the ship's doctor with a woman in childbirth, but not to worry. He'd met a good Austrian doctor the night before in the casino; his new acquaintance would be there at once.

Indigo retreated to her bed in the alcove to play with Rainbow, though she listened closely in case Hattie needed her again. She heard Hattie moan; Indigo wished she had Grandma Fleet's little clay pipe and the crushed blossoms of the healing plants they smoked for nausea or headache. When she or Sister Salt got sick, Grandma Fleet used to recomend someone sit in the darkened room to sing softly or tell stories to the patient, but Hattie behaved as if she wanted to be left alone.

The drumming pain in her head did not permit sleep, but Hattie did not feel entirely awake either; part of her brain whispered the word "delirium." Her thoughts raced out of her control. Over and over she saw the print of the newpaper page, but greatly enlarged—it was the London *Times* article about the authentication of the Coptic scrolls. Giant typeset words were printed in oily black ink on odd paper the texture of the old scrolls themselves. Instead of elation over the news, she felt a lingering sense of futility and loss. She had been right all along, but now it didn't matter.

She did not know how much time passed, but it seemed hours before she heard a knock and Indigo call out, as they taught her, before she opened the cabin door to the doctor. For an instant the pounding in her head made it difficult to understand the doctor's words; she strained to make out the English he spoke until suddenly she realized the doctor was Australian, not Austrian; she could scarcely understand his Australian accent. He introduced himself as Dr. Gates.

While the Australian doctor felt her pulse by gently placing his hands to her temples, he spoke in a soothing tone about the card games he and Edward enjoyed in the evening after she and the child were in bed.

He prescribed belladonna as needed for the pain and nausea; the bitter white syrup turned to heat in her mouth and throat and spread over her entire body like a gust of hot wind. All the while the doctor kept talking in his ridiculous Australian dialect she hardly understood; as she drifted further into the warm, warm sea of her own blood, his odd vocabulary mattered not at all. The pounding pain that enclosed her face and head like a mask receded, and Hattie was able to sleep.

The Australian doctor returned later to massage the veins in the back of her neck; his hands worked their way down and around to the insides of both her arms until suddenly she felt alarmed at his attention. She called Indigo from her game with the parrot in the alcove, and the doctor left off the massage.

Later she told Edward the Australian doctor made her feel uneasy; she feared he might be an imposter or one who touched women with license. But Edward laughed out loud at such a suggestion. He was confident Dr. Gates was no imposter because they had talked a good deal over late night toddies about their professional training. They talked about a great many things, including citrus horticulture, especially the effects of temperature and climate, and Edward was quite satisfied Dr. Gates was reliable. Undoubtedly she was suffering the combined effects of the migraine headache and the belladonna, Edward assured her.

At this Hattie felt a spark of anger at Edward because he had only a modest appetite for female anatomy, and he did not seem to realize other men were not so chaste or honorable. The Australian doctor's fumbling with her bed clothes alarmed her because it recalled Mr. Hyslop's fumbling attack on her breasts.

Dr. Gates came again while Edward was out with the child at breakfast. He entered the cabin without knocking and set off the parrot; for once she was grateful for the bird's loud screeches. The deafening noise unnerved the doctor as he approached Hattie. He might have remained in the cabin alone with her longer but the parrot's incessant noise cut short the doctor's call, and Hattie was spared the ordeal of his groping hands.

After Hattie's recovery, Edward continued to spend a good deal of time in the company of Dr. Gates, who was knowledgeable about a great many fascinating subjects. They discussed Edward's citron scheme and the hot dry Riverside climate so similar to the deserts of Australia; oranges grown in the hot dry climes boasted the highest sugar content. The doctor's face became animated as he contemplated the possibility of irrigated citrus groves in the outback. If he was able to procure suitable cuttings of the citron from Edward, then he was sure of sucess.

The doctor was about to develop a mine to obtain iron ore and cadmium from a meteor crater in northern Arizona. Perhaps they might come to an agreement for an exchange of live citron cuttings for shares of mining stock as well as premium meteorite specimens, which he could sell for a handsome price.

Edward was delighted at the opportunity to obtain meteorite specimens in large quantity because there was a growing interest in the objects by private collectors, and universities as well. The memory of the odd enclosure full of meteor irons near the market at Tampico returned to him again and again, and he regretted he had not persevered with the hideous blue-face woman; he might have had the lot of them—all quite different from one another, apparently from different locations. The increased interest in meteorites by collectors and researchers signaled a rise in the prices paid for specimens. The trade in meteorites had so many advantages over plants, which must be handled with great care or they were lost.

Edward and Dr. Gates made a tentative agreement to become partners once the citron was secured and they returned to the United States. The doctor generously lent Edward a catalogue of the meteorites in North America published a few years before by the American Academy of Science; it was the same reference the doctor used to locate his most exciting acquisition to date: the two-mile-wide meteor crater in northern Arizona. Edward packed the book for safekeeping until he had the leisure to read it on the return voyage. For now he immersed himself in books about methods of pruning and grafting citrus stock.

The ship docked in Genoa at half past eight in the morning and already Edward could feel a dramatic increase in the temperature, although the air was not as dry as he expected.

Genoa was a port and industrial city similar to Bristol in its congested streets and sweltering bad air, although its dust and soot could not conceal the bright sun or deep blue sky beyond the smoke.

Their arrival was overshadowed by the news of the assassination of the Italian king only three days before, in Milan, by anarchists, to avenge the executions of their comrades. Victor Emmanuel III took the throne, but there were rumors of clashes between dissidents and police.

Genoa appeared calm—no soldiers or barricades in the streets, at least not on the waterfront. While they waited on the pier for Edward to fetch a cab, Hattie and Indigo gazed at the piles of cargo, the pallets of polished granite and marble slabs in all colors, carefully crated for export. Indigo pointed them out to the parrot—a rainbow of colors just like you! she told him. On the pier, bundles of hardwood logs sat next to big clusters of bananas. Suddenly, over the noise of the passengers and street traffic, Indigo heard the unmistakable screeches of parrots from behind a pile of cargo on the pier. Instantly Rainbow gave a deafening screech in reply that left Indigo's ears ringing. As a freight wagon pulled away from the pier, Indigo saw a large iron cage filled with parrots of all colors and sizes. The cries of his own kind were more than Rainbow could endure; he called back and flapped his wings frantically. As the wagon with the parrots passed, they saw sick and dying birds on the bottom of the cage. Indigo watched wide eyed, but the sight was too much for Hattie, who was overcome with nausea just as Edward returned with the cab.

Once Hattie was seated in the cab, out of the bright sun, the nausea subsided and she began to recover; the excitement of the new surroundings diminished her discomfort.

As the cab ascended the street into the hills, ruins of the old walls could be seen. As they passed the Piazza de Ferrari and the duke's palace, Indigo pointed out the window and called out, "Look!" at the black-and-white striped facade of the cathedral. The stripes reminded Indigo of those unmistakable black-and-white stripes of the rattlesnake's tail. To cheer up Rainbow after the upsetting encounter with the cage of new captives, Indigo lifted the travel cage closer to the window so he could see the stripes.

Hattie listened to the child play with the bird and realized Indigo believed the parrot understood everything she said. Indigo told the parrot they were much farther east now, near the villages where Christ's Mother had been seen from time to time. Aunt Bronwyn told her about the frequent appearances in Italy, Spain, and France. The Messiah sent his Mother because the soldiers did not try to kill her, Indigo told the parrot.

Hattie and Edward discussed the problem the night before and determined the best course to take with Indigo's exaggerations and fantasies about Jesus was to ignore them. Poor child, such harsh experiences and losses at an early age were bound to leave deep scars! Aunt Bronwyn and Indigo got along so beautifully Hattie didn't interfere, although Edward and she were concerned all that talk about stones dancing and spirits living in stones misled the child. Hattie saw no real harm in the quaintly inaccurate version of Jesus Indigo learned from other Indians.

Hattie took a deep breath and exhaled slowly; then she remarked about the amazing Mediterranean light—the moist atmosphere filtered the light so it was luminous but not burning, as the sun's rays were in Riverside. Hattie felt so much better now that they were on land again. The vibrant colors of the buildings delighted Hattie and Indigo, who made a game of the colors: umber, sienna, ocher, eggshell, sage, tea, mint—they made up names for the amazing new colors they saw. They saw gardens of every sort, even wild gardens of calla lilies and overgrown grapevines in vacant lots along the streets. Hattie was pleased they planned to visit the wonderful gardens of Aunt Bronwyn's friend in Lucca before they boarded the boat for Bastia.

While Hattie and Indigo bathed and rested, Edward took a cab to the U.S. consulate for any messages or mail. Ordinarily the walk to the consulate would have been just the tonic he needed, but the old injury to his leg began to ache, though, oddly enough, the leg was not swollen or discolored.

He found a letter from his lawyer in Riverside, and two cablegrams. He tried to appear calm as he tucked the envelopes into his breast pocket and made small talk with the deputy consul about the hot weather. Edward commented that Riverside got much hotter, but it was dry desert heat. He regretted his idle comment, as the deputy consul seemed to welcome the opportunity to ask questions.

Edward smiled. He and his wife and her maid were on a tour of the Mediterranean area for his wife's health; he thanked the consul again and turned to go before the man asked their destination. The deputy consul clearly relished an opportunity to talk with another American and continued the conversation all the way to the front door. Due to civil unrest since the assassination, U.S. citizens were advised to avoid travel outside of Rome, and certainly not to the south.

Edward felt he must stop and listen politely or his haste might be noticed, and suspicions aroused. The deputy consul remarked the assassinated king was scarcely cold in his grave before political tensions began to rise. Of course, they were quite safe in Genoa; Genoa was an international port of great mercantile importance that all parties to the dispute sought to protect. It almost sounded as if the deputy hoped they'd stay on in Genoa so he'd have Americans to talk to. At the door, Edward shook the deputy consul's hand and assured him they had no intention of visiting the south.

He did not take the cablegrams from his pocket until he was a distance down the street from the U.S. consulate. He had an unsettling suspicion prying eyes at the consulate knew the contents of the cables. The heat on the sidewalk was crushing; the flimsy paper of the envelope stuck to the moisture of his fingers and left dark smudges. He found a bit of shade around a corner and stopped to rest his sore leg; there were no cabs in sight.

He wiped his hands and then his brow on his handkerchief before he opened the first cablegram, sent two days before the other. It was an odd message from Mr. Grabb, at the law firm that represented Lowe & Company: "Agriculture secretary refuses authorization. Do not proceed. Return at once. Company not liable for expenses after August 18."

The second cablegram was also from Mr. Grabb; it urged him to contact Lowe & Company at once concerning a trek to the Himalayas to collect specimens of Asiatic lilies. Edward felt light-headed from the heat and the sore leg, and he feared he might not find a cab back to the hotel before he got sick.

Indigo fanned herself and the parrot with a fan of woven palm fiber she found in the room; the two of them played Keep Away with the fan on the floor of the suite, while Hattie wrote a note to Aunt Bronwyn's friend, the *professoressa* in Lucca. Hattie realized she would prefer to stop in Lucca and let Edward go without her and the child—the English-language newspaper cited instances of suspected unrest. Her skin felt flushed and moist; her underclothing clung in the most annoying way; she was tired of traveling.

On the floor the child and the parrot were becoming more animated; Rainbow picked up the fan by its handle in his beak and flapped his wings before Indigo heard a loud crunch: Rainbow crushed the fan's bamboo handle with his beak, and now he took half-moon bites out of the edge of the fan, leaving broken fibers he plucked out one by one. Indigo laughed so hard she dropped from her knees facedown on the rug. Hattie's annoyance only made Indigo laugh harder because the parrot was able to anger human beings so easily.

Indigo ignored Hattie and invited Rainbow to ride on her shoulder to the maid's alcove, where she already arranged the bedding on the floor the way she and Rainbow liked it at night. She whispered to Rainbow something was bothering Hattie but not to let that upset him because she was there to take care of him. She shut the door so their new game did not disturb Hattie. The fat feather pillows and bedding made a perfect soft landing for Indigo as she practiced flying off the end of the bed with Rainbow on her shoulder flapping his wings, making gusts of air behind them. She told him about all the crows in the bare branches of the trees along the river, the winter the Messiah came. The Messiah especially loved birds, Indigo told Rainbow. Maybe it was because he and his family and followers flew like birds to travel great distances—even across oceans.

Edward's appearance alarmed Hattie; he was pale and complained of soreness in his leg, and the heat had left him queasy. He was about to go lie down when he remembered the letter in his pocket from their Riverside lawyer. Mr. Yetwin reported land values were rising rapidly now that the dam and the aqueduct from the Colorado River were under construction. Edward began to feel better as he read this; a new source of abundant cheap water would assure the success of his new citron groves even in dry years when the wells were undependable. But almost immediately the cablegrams came to mind and again Edward felt too warm and nauseous. He gave Hattie the letter and went to lie down.

Hattie skipped over the paragraphs about real estate prices and other business, to learn how Linnaeus and his cat were faring. Mr. Yetwin reported all was well with the house and gardens, though the cook complained the maid spent too much time playing with the monkey and the kitten. Indigo stopped her game to listen.

While he waited for the pills to take effect, Edward listened to Hattie and the child in the sitting room as they chattered excitedly about Linnaeus and the kitten. He did not wish to spoil their fun, so he did not mention it, but cats were known to harbor diseases dangerous to humans, and probably monkeys too. He was grateful to his new friend, Dr. Gates, for the extra supply of morphine pills he gave them in case Hattie suffered another headache or the pain in the leg flared up. Doctors and pharmacies were few and far between on Corsica.

He swallowed each pill with a generous amount of water, and experienced only a little nausea before a luminous glow rose inside him and all pain in the leg subsided. He lay back on his pillow and basked in the bliss; all anxious sensations in his stomach subsided, and his heartbeat and pulse steadied themselves. He heard footsteps and slipped the bottle of morphine tablets from the nightstand into the pocket of his robe; he did not want to worry Hattie.

But the footsteps passed by and no one came. He tried to keep his thoughts focused on the good news in the letter—abundant cheap water. He visualized the aqueduct snaking through the dry gravel flats and greasewood, and the glitter of the moving water in the sun. He had to keep his thoughts restricted to the water in the aqueduct; otherwise the unsettling message of the cablegram intruded and turned his stomach: Return at once. Do not proceed. Authorization canceled.

Though he could not sleep, still Edward experienced odd dreamlike reveries from the morphine. He followed his father through the groves of oranges and lemons in clouds of heavenly scents as his father plucked handfuls of blossoms into the tin pail he carried. Edward had been only nine years old but he remembered vividly how his father gathered pail after pail of waxy sweet blossoms and carried them upstairs to carefully spread them over the bed in his mother's room.

Edward remembered that summer vividly because his father set up a separate laboratory for perfumery in one end of the library, where he sat for hours, sipping brandy as he pressed whole dried cloves into dainty Persian oranges to make spicy pomanders that might help capitalize his perfume venture after Edward's mother refused to fund it further. She did not mind paying his gambling debts because she herself was quite sucessful at gambling. However, the experiments with citrus perfume were pointless, a waste of money.

Before they parted in Genoa, Dr. Gates prescribed laudanum drops in ginger tea for Hattie. The laudanum permitted her to sleep soundly; after her sleepwalking experience with the odd glowing light and loud knock, she often woke with her heart pounding in the middle of the night. She was reluctant to confide in Edward because it was his nature to demand a rational explanation; he'd call the light she saw in Aunt Bronwyn's garden a hallucination, and the loud knocking noise hysteria. She feared there were no other rational explanations.

She tried to listen to the tiny voice she called conscience, but strangely she could hear nothing; she did not think she was experiencing a nervous collapse like the first one—she remembered that feeling. No, this time she felt quite different: not unpleasant, but she was concerned because she could not think or reason her way to any certainty about that night in the garden. What presence had she sensed? What presence had occupied her nightmare about the tin mask and Edward?

They were up at dawn for breakfast before the cab to the train station. From Genoa the train took them to Lucca, where Aunt Bronwyn's dear friend the *professoressa* met them at the station and graciously invited them to stay with her. Aunt Bronwyn met the *professoressa* at a museum in Trieste, where their mutual interests in Old European artifacts and gardening persuaded them to travel together for the duration of Aunt Bronwyn's time on the continent. Of course, they had only five days before they must leave for Livorno and the voyage to Corsica; but Edward agreed the rest would do them good, and Aunt Bronwyn urged them not to miss the *professoressa*'s gardens.

Hattie was surprised to discover a woman much younger than her aunt when the *professoressa* presented herself at the train station in Lucca. Hattie worried Edward might be reluctant, but he graciously accepted her invitation to visit her home in the hills overlooking the town. Hattie was eager to see the gardens the *professoressa* designed to celebrate her love of Old European artifacts. This would be their only opportunity to stop; once Edward obtained the citrus cuttings from Corsica, they must depart at once for the United States to ensure the survival of as many of the twig cuttings as possible.

Although Edward was anxious to reach Bastia, the stopover in Lucca would give them all a much-needed rest. He was not much interested in the crude stone and pottery figures of the Old European cultures, which he found quite ugly; however, he was interested in the old gardens of the villa. He was curious to see if any of the oldest varieties of Persian roses might be found in an out-of-the-way corner of a terrace or in the family cemetery. Of course he was always on the lookout for old pots of citrus trees on the chance he might see a specimen of the *Citrus medica* in Tuscany, though the mountainous regions of coastal Corsica suited *C. medica* best. Edward smiled. Riverside's climate was ideal for citrus growing, as was the climate of northern Australia where Dr. Gates was from. One day their sweet oranges would outsell all others, and the doctor would produce candied citron for export to Asian markets. Before Dr. Gates parted from them in Genoa, he and Edward arranged to keep in touch to plan a visit in the winter to the site of the meteorite mine in Arizona.

The carriage ride from the station in Lucca to the old villa high in the hills required more than an hour, which passed quite pleasantly for the adults, who discussed archaeological excavations and the citrus known as bergamot, used to make orange water and other perfumes; but Indigo felt ill from the lurching vehicle on the narrow winding road, and she and Rainbow were greatly relieved when the coach stopped outside the golden yellow walls of the old villa.

As the *professoressa* said, the heat made the walled city unbearable in early August, but here in the hills they were cooled by the steady stream of cool air off the mountains. Though the *professoressa* was disappointed to learn their visit must be brief due to Edward's business in Corsica, still there was ample time to show them the restoration of the gardens with her collection of Old European artifacts.

Their rooms had high ceilings richly adorned with frescoes of birds and flowers in lovely delicate colors. Indigo lay on the bed at once to study the painted figures of fluttering gray doves in blue clouds above cascades of white and pale pink roses. The windows were open wide to catch the cool breezes, and the *professoressa*'s housekeeper showed Indigo how to tug, tug, tug on the long cords to lower or raise the window cover to keep out insects or the sunlight.

Indigo opened Rainbow's travel cage and he climbed out to the cage top and flapped his wings. She scratched the top of his head and he ruffled his feathers with pleasure. She looked out the window at the driveway gently ascending the meadow edged with groves of great trees. If this were her place, she would have herds of cattle and sheep graze there.

She opened her valise and took out the green silk notebook with the names of the medicinal plants written in English and in Latin. She took the little pencil that belonged with the notebook and practiced copying the Latin names and the English names on a blank page: monkshood, wolfsbane, aconite, *Aconitum napellus.* Aunt Bronwyn had pointed out how the topmost petal on the dark purplish blue flower spike was shaped just like a helmet or a monk's hood. Indigo drew the long stem of petals, but she had difficulty drawing the top petal so it did not look too large in proportion to the other petals. Below the picture she copied its medicinal uses from Aunt Bronwyn's list: anodyne, febrifuge, and diuretic. Hattie added these words to her spelling list, so Indigo wrote their definitions right beside them. "Anodyne" is Greek for "no pain"; "febrifuge" she remembered as "refuge from fever." Hattie told her the English word "febrile" came from the Latin *febris,* for "fever"; "diuretic" was from the Greek for "urine." Indigo studied the pencil lines of her sketch before she carefully erased the monkshood petal that was too large, and tried again.

Hattie and Edward's room was down the hall. Indigo was amazed to see the big bed with a roof and side curtains on a raised platform. The curtains kept out the cold draughts in the winter, Hattie explained. With a roof like that, one could sleep outdoors in that bed. They laughed together, and Edward joined in. He was seated comfortably in the plump armchair with his shirtsleeve rolled up, soaking his injured hand in a basin of warm water.

The *professoressa*'s house was full of good spirits; Indigo felt them at once. She could tell Laura was kind because her eyes did not shift away when she saw Indigo with the birdcage. Rainbow relaxed his grip and Indigo lifted him off her shoulder and set him gently on her lap, petting his head constantly until he allowed her to cradle him in her arms on his back like a baby. She watched his pale yellow eyes watch her anxiously as his body remained poised to spring away from trouble. She loved how he made her smile even when she was sad. She missed Sister and Mama; were they together now? Hattie was very kind to her but she missed her sister and mother so much.

Hattie opened the French doors to the balcony to show Indigo the Moorish fountain and garden below, enclosing the back of the villa entirely. In the afternoon light, the surfaces of the blue tile on the fountain and pool were instantly transformed. Indigo was amazed and called out her delight with the intense blue. Bright red bougainvillea crisscrossed the blue tiles of the garden wall. Could they go downstairs and walk through it? Oh wonderful!

Indigo leaned into the mist from the fountain and asked Rainbow how it felt; the parrot fluffed his feathers and opened his beak to catch the mist. The long narrow pool of blue tiles was too shallow for fish. Indigo was disappointed and a bit indignant; what were pools for if not goldfish? Hattie explained: In this instance, the pool's purpose was refreshment and beauty for the benefit of people. Fish left the water smelly. Indigo frowned. She enjoyed the fishponds in Oyster Bay a great deal.

The terra-cotta pots of lemon trees around the pool's edge perfumed the air. Indigo was delighted to see green and yellow lemons, and Laura invited her to pick lemons for the custard tomorrow. Great spiked agaves and great python-size cactus were separated from the Joshua trees and big yuccas by the smaller yuccas and aloes of all sorts including a yellow aloe and orange aloe and a red-flowered aloe Hattie had not seen before.

Edward's attention was on dozens of potted lemon trees around the pool.

He hoped he might see the thick scaly rind indicative of *Citrus medica,* though at a glance they all appeared to be lemons. The *professoressa* pointed out the old Persian rose he wanted to see; its root base was thick as a small tree but the branches were carefully pruned and small but fragrant red roses bloomed in profusion. Indigo called in a hushed voice for Hattie to see the hummingbird in the big red hibiscus blossom overhanging the pool. Tomorrow they would see the other old gardens in the woods below.

When Indigo was in her room again she took out the notebook and pencil and tried to draw the hummingbird in the big flower. Rainbow shelled sunflower seeds from his perch atop his cage. Indigo already explained to him what Hattie said: they were guests here, and although Aunt Bronwyn welcomed a parrot and told stories about dogs at the dinner table, it would not be polite to bring Rainbow to Laura's table. When Hattie called her to dinner, Indigo put her face gently against the parrot and whispered for him to wait; she wouldn't be gone for long.

That evening a wonderful display greeted them as they entered the dining room: a flock of white porcelain swans floated and preened amid white calla lilies and fragrant blue water lilies in the center of the dining table. Each place setting was guarded with smaller swan figures in vigilant postures on silvery white linen. Indigo loved the way her napkin was folded and tied with blue satin ribbon; she had not seen so many glasses and forks and spoons on a table before. She slipped the piece of ribbon into her pocket to give to Rainbow, while Hattie expressed her delight with the swans and Edward asked their age.

The dressing of the table must have required as much time as the preparation of the courses of vegetables and pasta. The *professoressa* was happy to hear about their visit to the excavations in Bath. She began her studies with Roman antiquities, but the earlier cultures won her over. Hattie described the tin mask, pre-Roman, crude, but quite powerful, which interested the *professoressa* a great deal because a number of pieces in her collection were figures in masks. Edward preferred to examine the exquisite old glass and porcelain of the place settings, especially the tiny gold cups atop carved marble faces. The *professoressa* and Hattie carried on a lively conversation about masks and terra-cotta figures of goddesses that were half snake or half bird. How clever the Italians were! Edward thought; if one happened to be bored with the topic of conversation, as he was, one had only to turn one's attention to the table settings and the centerpiece and decorations for amusement.

After dinner Indigo brought out her color pencils and drawings; Laura asked Indigo if she might look, and Indigo shyly handed her the notebook. Laura nodded and smiled as she looked at Indigo's drawings and notes on medicinal plants. She got up from her chair, the notebook still in her hand, and opened a drawer in the tall mahogany cabinet. Out came a flat wooden box with a brightly colored label on its top; Laura lifted the lid, and there Indigo saw dozens of pencils in all colors. Would she accept this gift? Indigo looked at Hattie hopefully, and Hattie nodded. Indigo was delighted; now she could draw the flowers with the right colors and make the hummingbird's feathers purple and green. Laura reached deep into her dress pocket and brought out a small brass pencil sharpener. Edward looked at his watch and told Indigo it was time for bed—she could look over the pencils before the light was put out.

One of the pencils was the color of the dune sand at the old gardens—so pale that the first strokes on the white paper of the notebook were difficult to see. She made a low dune, the dune they called the Dog because it reminded Grandma Fleet of a sleeping dog. Runoff from above accumulated there when the big rains came, and the big sunflowers and biggest datura thrived there with the devil's claws they used for decorating baskets. She drew the yellow flowers of the silvery blue brittlebushes after a rainstorm in late autumn, when the datura still bloomed but the sunflower petals dried to seeds.

As she washed her face and brushed her teeth, Indigo studied her dark face in the oval mirror of the washstand and laughed at herself because she realized she was forgetting how dark she was because all around her she saw only lighter faces. Grandma Fleet would really laugh and Sister Salt probably would pinch her and tease her for becoming a white girl, not a Sand Lizard girl. She didn't care. Wait until they saw all the seeds she gathered and the notebook she brought back with the names and instructions and color sketches too.

Later, when they were alone in their room, Hattie remarked at the rapport she felt with the *professoressa*—she asked them please to call her Laura; she was only a bit older than Edward. She was such an interesting woman—not only a scholar and collector of Old European artifacts, she also hybridized gladiolus. Edward looked up from his newspaper; he would like to see the gladiolus hybrids—they were more interesting than crude artifacts from the fifth millennium.

The calls of three fat crows outside the window woke Indigo the next morning. Rainbow cocked his head to one side to get a better look at them in the top of the big linden tree in the garden. The Messiah and the others might have passed this way not too long before, though one could not be certain. She looked down into the garden at the rushing water of the fountain and all the shrubs for shade; probably the crows lived here.

Indigo did not think Laura would mind if she and her parrot walked about the house or went into the garden, but Hattie did not want Indigo to go alone; so she waited by the window with Rainbow in the room until she heard their voices from their room down the hall.

After breakfast Laura excused herself to find the rubber garden shoes for them; the garden restoration left a good deal of clayish mud that stuck to ordinary shoes. What a wonderful story Laura told as they changed to their garden shoes, about the first time she visited the abandoned villa among the great trees. Foreigners, relations of Napoleon's sister, owned the property for more than a century, and the local people stayed away. Rumors told of monsters and strange sounds and lights coming from the old woods. The foreigners and their guests came every summer, then suddenly they came no more.

Later, Laura's family received the property in the settlement of an old debt. The house was abandoned, and the gardens were in ruins by then; the bougainvilleas and red climbing roses had gone wild; the great mounds of yellow day lilies overgrew their parterres and spread into the lawn. The grottoes and formal gardens had been stripped of their marble figures and the terraces stripped of marble balustrades and marble vases.

The first time Laura and her brother came there, they had no idea what lay beyond, in the dense foliage in the dark woods. They ventured down the path to see where the water went. It wasn't until they stopped at the first grotto and looked back that she caught a glimpse of something in the deep undergrowth, where an eroded embankment had collapsed to reveal the head and forelegs of a stone centaur. They found a minotaur spying from the shrubbery in the same area, and when a careful survey was made after the first discoveries, a Medusa head was discovered at the foot of an embankment. Hattie and Edward murmured appreciatively, but Edward was disappointed to learn the statues were only late eighteenth century; still, the pieces were quite fascinating. Only recently, after a fierce storm toppled a great many old trees in the *sacro bosco,* workmen discovered a stone grotto behind a wild thicket, tangled with fallen trees and debris from old landslides.

From the fountain and enclosed garden, four stone steps descended to the lawn of the formal garden, shaded by great trees. The morning light played through the canopy of leaves and Indigo saw more colors of green than she ever imagined—river green, mossy green, willow green, oak leaf green, juniper green, green-golden-green, and shades of grass green all around. She twirled herself around in the delicious green shade as the parrot squawked joyously; around and around she danced, as happy as she had been since she and Sister were parted.

The cries of the parrot attracted the blackbirds they'd seen the evening before. Hattie remarked on the size of the flock; in Bath she remembered only the two or three blackbirds in her aunt's garden. Oh, this area was always known for its population of blackbirds; these hills were thick with hazels and oaks; the local people used to call the run-down old villa the blackbird palace even after she and her husband completed repairs and moved in.

How interesting, Hattie thought; her aunt hadn't mentioned a husband. Was her husband abroad now? Almost as soon as she spoke, Hattie sensed something was wrong. Laura stopped on the path and smiled. She apologized for any confusion: she and her husband were no longer together. Hattie was so surprised at this remark she stammered inanely that she was sorry. Oh, there was nothing to apologize for; all was for the best.

Quickly Hattie turned her attention to the empty stone pedestals and empty niches in the graceful garden walls as Laura explained her reluctance to replace the missing figures with copies; new marble was too bright and would spoil the serenity of the greenery and its subtle shifts of light. When her husband's military command was ordered to Eritrea, she hoped he might obtain interesting stone figures on his visits to Cairo. Hattie glanced about but saw no stone figures; the lichens and tiny ferns and mosses had taken hold on the niches and pedestals where they found just the shade and the sun to thrive. Their eyes met for an instant and Hattie realized the plan to obtain old stone figures from Cairo had gone astray with the husband.

Laura paused to watch Indigo and the parrot on the lawn as they played tag; the parrot waddled after the girl with his wings outstretched and flapping for speed; then the girl chased the parrot as he fled with squawks and ruffled feathers. Shaded by the great lindens and oaks, they played and played; from time to time the parrot flapped his wings fast enough to lift himself so that for a few seconds Indigo scarcely felt him on her shoulder except where he held fast with his feet.

What a sweet child—they were fortunate to have adopted her, Laura commented as they paused in the shade. Hattie felt her cheeks redden and she tried to choose her words carefully. Oh no, they were not so lucky as that. The child was only placed with them for the summer. Hattie could not stop herself—she felt she must explain how the school personnel mistreated the child, that as soon as they returned to the United States they would go to Arizona to search for Indigo's family.

Edward turned back on the path to rejoin them, although the path continued through another stone archway. He wasn't interested in any more old gardens stripped of their ornaments; he preferred to see the hybrid gladiolus; even the crude artifacts of the old Europeans would be more interesting.

Laura glanced up at the sun to judge the time; she had more to show them before lunch. A stream diverted from the hills behind the house fed a stone-paved rill that emptied into a long narrow pool of dwarf papyrus and yellow lotus flowers. The water flowed from the end of the pool into another stone rill that followed the driveway to the edge of the woods; here the waterway abruptly disappeared into heavy foliage.

Two weathered stone pillars dappled with lichens were visible in the lush foliage that marked the entrance to the old woods where the stone figures were found. Laura led the way down the overgrown path. Indigo followed with the parrot on her shoulder, and Hattie and Edward came along behind. As they went deeper into the woods, the parrot settled quietly on Indigo's shoulder, alert for danger.

The path was overgrown with laurel and myrtle but the coolness and the shade were inviting, and Indigo found a variety of lovely ferns and mosses growing between the stones of the path that gradually descended as it went deeper into the dark green pines and cedars with their bowers of box elders, chestnuts, and great oaks. Rainbow clutched her shoulder tighter and leaned forward, flapping his wings, his feathers ruffled with excitement as he looked at the forest all around them. They played a game—Indigo walked slower and slower, which caused Rainbow to lean forward, eager to go faster, and he flapped his wings harder as if to make Indigo speed up. Then Indigo pretended the breeze from his wings was pushing her along with magical power to make her fly. As she walked faster and faster, Rainbow squawked with delight, and as they raced past Laura on the path, Indigo laughed out loud.

Now and then Hattie recognized azaleas and rhododendrons among the overgrown holly and brambles; otherwise Hattie would have believed they were in a primordial forest. The others walked ahead, but Hattie was content to take her time to appreciate what became of even the most elegant gardens over time. She stopped to appreciate the natural effect accomplished with the lindens and elms with the plane trees of a lighter green; as she turned, she was startled to see a creature gazing at her through the twisted branches of a holly tree.

The life-size stone face and bare chest were human, but legs and body were those of a horse. In the foliage so close to the path it appeared almost alive and gave her a terrible start that left her heart pounding. She stopped to catch her breath, face-to-face with the centaur, his hindquarters partially buried in the eroded hillside. Just then Laura came back to rejoin her, while the child and her parrot went ahead with Edward.

They sat on a shady, lichen-covered rock near the centaur as Laura explained the dilemma she had faced: to free the figure of the centaur from his stronghold of earth-slide debris would have required the sacrifice of a young chestnut tree and a bower of azaleas and rhododendrons. The centaur was nicely carved but he was only a copy and was more interesting just as he was, emerging out of the earth. Hattie agreed; this way he was quite dramatic.

They sat in silence awhile; Laura glanced around at the old forest and smiled, then in a soft voice she told Hattie: On the eve of the battle, her husband deserted his army command in Eritrea. The following day, Italian forces suffered terrible losses against the rebels; at first he was feared lost or taken prisoner. It was this confusion that brought such embarrassment later—early newspaper reports called him a "fallen hero," but weeks later army intelligence learned the colonel had fled to Cairo.

They both were silent for a moment; Hattie kept her eyes to the ground, but Laura patted her arm cheerfully and smiled; it was for the best, she said.

Laura pointed at the chestnut and oak trees and the bowers of laurel and bay choked with brambles and holly that grew between the boulders and big rocks of the earth slide. The deadwood and debris were removed, but she did not have the heart to disturb the rest. The old wood remained as it was; fallen trees were left to nurture the earth for seedlings. Repairs were made only to the little canal that brought the stream from the hills to the woods; otherwise, they scarcely trimmed the paths enough to allow one to pass.

The path turned sharply at a stand of silver birches and suddenly there was a marble head of Medusa as big as a cookstove where it came to rest at the edge of the path after it rolled down the hillside. The head was dramatically tilted back to face the sky; she was a giant but no monster. The baby snakes that covered her head were dreamy eyed and gracefully arched above her brow, as unconcerned about the fall as their mistress, whose expression was serene, not furious.

Indigo rejoined them. Well, what did she think? Hattie asked. Indigo's eyes were wide as she slowly shook her head; she wished Sister were there because Indigo knew that when she told her sister later, she'd never believe the head was this big! Wait until she told Mama and Sister! They would be amazed! They'd all heard the old-time people speculate about giants and the offspring of men who had sex with mares or cows.

Now the path began to level out in the dappled shade of the great trees towering above them. Laura described the most recent discovery: A storm with high winds and heavy rain lashed the hills and a number of the largest trees were lost. A lightning-struck oak crushed the rill, and the old woods were flooded; the embankments of the old landslide badly eroded. The morning after, as Laura accompanied the hired man to survey the damage, she noticed odd stonework protruding out of the side of the crumbled embankment a few feet away: it was a hidden grotto!

Edward walked a bit faster and asked what was found; Laura smiled but shook her head. She did not want to spoil the surprise. The stone archway of the grotto was outlined by velvet moss of bright emerald green; inside, splashing water reflected light on the rough stone walls. On a pedestal near the grotto center sat a nearly life-size marble figure of a bald fat man, naked and shamelessly astride a giant land tortoise. Hattie hurried to steer Indigo away from the vulgar marble, while Edward stopped with Laura to examine the figure.

In the stone niche at the back of the grotto Hattie noticed an egg-shaped sandstone that appeared to be far older than the marble fat man, and more proper for a young girl to see. As they approached it, Hattie noticed the stone was engraved with what appeared to be an eye on its end or the outline of a curled snake. She was about to reach out to touch its edge when suddenly she recognized it was a human vulva!

She stepped back so suddenly she bumped into Indigo. The dank odors of the grotto closed around her—she must get to fresh air at once! Outside, the fresh air restored her instantly but Edward and Laura were concerned; Hattie insisted she was all right. Food was all she needed; she only had tea and a biscuit for breakfast. After a short rest and something to eat, she would feel just fine. They could see the other gardens when it was cooler, later in the afternoon.

As they walked back to the house, Edward asked about the "female fertility figure"; Laura smiled at his choice of words. The incised egg was from the fourth millennium in Macedonia; it was the first piece of her collection to be installed in its new home, and the only piece sited in the old woods.

All the other pieces of her collection were in the terraced gardens they'd see after lunch.

Edward asked if she worried about damage to the artifacts from the elements. Oh, Laura laughed, we bring them indoors in the winter. Edward nodded, though he did not approve of such a careless attitude toward rare artifacts. He reached into his pocket for his handkerchief and dabbed his forehead; he was feeling the heat now. He slowed his pace, conscious for the first time of a bit of soreness in the leg.

Now Hattie walked with Laura, who explained the meanings of the symbols found on Old European artifacts: The wavy lines symbolized rain; Vs and zigzags and chevrons symbolized river meanders as well as snakes and flocks of waterbirds; goddesses of the rivers transformed themselves to snakes and then waterbirds. The concentric circles were the all-seeing eyes of the Great Goddess; and the big triangles represented the pubic triangle, another emblem of the Great Goddess.

By the time they reached the house, Hattie felt completely restored. At lunch her appetite returned and she helped herself to the bread while the wine was poured. Before Edward could stop her, the maid filled Indigo's glass with wine; immediately he moved the glass next to his wineglass. The discussion shifted to the question of serving wine to children; Hattie acknowledged the prohibition came directly from their puritan forefathers. The wine wasn't strong! Let Indigo take a sip! But Edward was firm; Indigo must not have wine because she was an Indian; even the least amount might have a shocking effect.

Hattie tried to wash down the embarrassment she felt by drinking the wine. It was such lovely wine—it went down as gently as springwater. A sip would have been harmless, even educational, for the child. Hattie finished her glass of wine and the maid refilled it. She felt the wine begin to calm her, and her irritation at Edward diminished.

Indigo helped herself to the delicious fig bread in the basket on the table in front of her. She loved the feeling of the tiny seeds breaking between her teeth amid all the sweetness. The figs tasted as sweet as the dates she and Sister Salt gathered from the palm grove. The first course was spaghetti with tomato sauce and basil, followed with fried lamb cutlets and peas with ham. Indigo smiled at the cork's squeak when the maid opened another bottle of wine. Then came a warm bowl of stewed sweet red peppers with yellow squash. Indigo's eyes widened at the sight of food she knew, and as she tasted the peppers she thought of them grown so far from their original home; seeds must be among the greatest travelers of all!

They ate lemon ice cream later, while Laura talked about her hobby. The hybridizing procedures were simple enough for the amateur, which is how she began—an experiment that she did not expect to yield results; but she was delivered seed pods the first year. Beginner's luck, she said, and a good deal of effort; for weeks she went into the garden before dawn with her tweezers and paper bags to cover the selected plants to protect them from accidental fertilization.

After lunch, while the sun was too bright and hot to walk comfortably in the gardens, they went to their rooms to rest. Indigo took her notebook and color pencils to her bedding on the floor and began to try to draw Rainbow perched on the cage top. She decided to put all his colors on the page first and then take a black pencil to draw his outline on the colors. The tiles were so cool she stopped from time to time to press her cheek against them, and before long she let go of the pencil in her fingers and stretched out on the bedsheet over the cool floor and fell asleep.

Hattie did not feel the full effects of the wine at lunch until she got up from the table to go upstairs. A sudden rush of well-being was followed by the sensation her body was weightless; each step was effortless but left her giddy. She paused at the top of the stairs for Edward, who seemed a bit unsteady himself. She stifled a smile and took his arm in hers; a nap would be just the cure for their wine-tipsy condition.

As they removed their shoes and loosened their clothes Hattie praised the people and gardens of Tuscany, then Edward gaily interrupted her to praise the wine above all. They laughed together and Hattie felt a sense of camaraderie with her husband that filled her heart with passion. As he sat on the edge of the bed, she leaned over and kissed him ardently on the back of the neck. In the the glow of the wine they forgot themselves and the awkward moments and embarrassments of their previous attempts at sexual intimacy. This session took them quite far indeed, although they stopped short of the act. They lay side by side holding hands in silence, their clothing all askew. Edward listened to Hattie's breathing, slow as she fell asleep, but found himself wide awake, his heart pounding. It was the Indian girl who stirred Hattie's maternal instincts and caused her to change her mind; now she wanted to conceive a child; that was quite clear.

Later, as they dressed to go downstairs, Edward was quite talkative about hybrid gladiolus, as if he wanted to avoid any discussion of the earlier flailing and groping. Hattie planted a kiss on his forehead as he sat on the edge of the bed to put on his shoes. She wanted to put him at ease, to let him know she was not embarrassed by their fling. It must have been the wine, she said with a smile; Edward nodded but did not look up as he tried to decide between a walking shoe and jodhpur boot for their tour of the terraced gardens.

He hoped to photograph the *professoressa's* collection of artifacts, if she agreed; though why would she refuse? A few photographs could not matter when the artifacts were already exposed to the rain and the sun. He told Hattie he still found it difficult to believe. Was the entire collection displayed out of doors? Personally he found the Old European artifacts crude and unappealing; still, he was amazed their hostess, who called herself a scholar, risked rare archaeological artifacts simply to decorate a garden. Perhaps stone artifacts could survive display outdoors, but what about the ancient terra-cottas, exposed to the ravages of the sun and the weather?

Hattie smiled and sat down on the edge of the bed next to him; she put her arm through his. She felt so much affection for Edward at that moment—more strongly than ever before—and she wanted to savor the affection she felt.

But Edward went on: here truly was an affront to science and scholarship! Hattie began to be annoyed by Edward's criticism of their generous hostess. Aunt Bronwyn said the *professoressa* took great care with the installation of each artifact. Shouldn't they see the arrangements made for the artifacts in the gardens first, before they condemned her? No, it was the principle of the matter; artifacts of the early millennia belonged in the hands of scientists and scholars, not in gardens! Edward felt confident in the glow of the wine and continued: a connection must exist between the absent husband and the exposure of the artifacts. Poor Laura must have suffered a breakdown! Hattie frowned; Aunt Bronwyn said nothing of the sort.

Indigo woke from her nap to a snapping, splintering sound of dry wood; for an instant she wondered what it could be; then she jumped up, her heart pounding, just as Rainbow took another colored pencil into his beak from the box. The black pencil that she used to outline and to write words was broken in half, so she could still use it; but splinters and bits of the silver and gold pencils littered the floor around the travel cage, where the parrot was perched on top. She felt lucky to wake up before he destroyed all the color pencils; she did not think she would have much use for those colors anyway. The gold and silver pencils left heavy, greasy marks. Please don't do that again, she told him as he watched her shut the pencil box.

As they came downstairs, Laura greeted them; Indigo and her parrot were already waiting in the green garden. Even the shadows and the shade were green in this lovely garden. Indigo and the parrot raced around to each of the empty niches and pedestals they'd seen earlier.

The afternoon light was a lovely chrome yellow filtered through the great trees. Laura explained as they walked she made her decision carefully, over a year or more, after visits abroad to the most eminent collections of museums in Eastern Europe. The museums, public or private, were dour and depressing, even suffocating; fortunately she met Aunt Bronwyn then, and only Aunt Bronwyn's companionship and good cheer sustained her. The day she stepped out into the sunshine from a museum in Crakow, she made her decision: the figures of stone and terra-cotta must have fresh air and sunshine, not burial in a museum.

Edward set his jaw, determined not to betray his true feelings as their hostess explained how each winter when the first storm clouds gathered, the figures were wrapped in wool and placed in their boxes indoors. Birds of a feather, this woman and Hattie's old aunt; this was what happened when irreplaceable scientific data fell into the wrong hands. What a frivolous woman! She seemed to have thrown over her study of the fourth- and fifth-millennium artifacts to take up gladiolus gardening. Little wonder that her husband was gone!

They stepped down four stone steps through an old stone gateway, and suddenly, everywhere Hattie looked, she saw tall spikes of black gladiolus flowers more densely planted than she ever imagined possible. Hundreds—maybe a thousand—of corms were planted, at heaven knew what cost, to crowd the entire garden with tall spikes of black blossoms—black-rose and black-red was even more amazing. Hattie thought gladiolus came only in pink, white, or yellow.

From the back wall by the gate, terrace after terrace, all the way to the lily tank in the center below, were tall spikes of black gladiolus flowers. Her first glimpse startled her because for an instant she thought something had burned or blackened the garden, before she realized it was a black garden. Here and there the garden of black was accented with scatterings of white, dove gray, and blossoms of mottled lavender and rose. Indigo looked up at Hattie and both their faces lit up with excitement and they exclaimed together: "Look!" Indigo's eyes were wide and she did not gallop about with the parrot but remained next to Hattie. For just an instant when she first saw them, Indigo mistook the tall spikes of black flowers for a big flock of blackbirds sitting among green leaves, swaying ever so slightly in a current of air; in the afternoon light the blossoms seemed almost to glisten like black feathers. Indigo took a deep breath and exclaimed with delight. Smell them! These gladiolus are perfumed!

Edward stopped for an instant at the sight of hundreds, maybe thousands, of the tall black flower spikes, rising out of the terrace flower beds like battalions of black knights. He had never seen such a luxury of Dutch bulbs as this planting of unusual hybrid colors. A display like this cost a great deal, though at least in Lucca's mild climate the bulbs did not have to be lifted in the winter.

The old stone terraces were carefully repaired but otherwise left untouched; the heavy rich Lucca soil had been leavened with the sandy loam favored by gladiolus. Edward had not seen or even read about such a display of gladiolus—tulips and narcissus, of course. He never cared for gladiolus; ordinarily, he found the tall spikes of flowers quite vulgar—tall upstarts and darlings of the florists that intruded here and there among other flowers in borders or in vases; but the grand scale of the old terraced garden displayed these black gladiolus to their best advantage.

Laura's hybrids were quite colorful and of interest for their strong fragrance, though she said they did not reproduce their fragrance in their offspring, a common failing in hybrids.

The old lindens along the walls cast welcome shade; otherwise the terraced garden was open to the sky; the stone path was crowded by spikes of red-black and rose-black flowers as tall as Hattie's shoulder. Hattie had never seen so many gladiolus planted together with not one other plant or flower, and no lawn to border them. Black flowering stems rose out of graceful arched leaves, from terrrace to terrace—black gladiolus descending to the sunken stone lily tank. She could not take her eyes off the hundreds and hundreds of the black blossoms; on closer examination, Hattie noted here and there scatterings of mottled rose-gray and ivory-gray gladiolus accented the black. Pale pink and pale lavender flowers formed a narrow border between the frame of white gladiolus, which were shorter and branched; ah! what a fragrance these white gladiolus had! She closed her eyes for an instant and breathed in the perfume. If she felt tipsy earlier, now she felt drunk, surrounded, even embraced, by the profusion of flowers so tall that they shaded the edges of the garden path. Hattie sat a moment on a narrow ledge of the terrace wall to gaze about and fully realize the effect of the black garden.

Below the terraces of black gladiolus, at the center of the sunken garden, was a stone-paved oval with a shallow lily tank. Hattie saw a stone pedestal with a stone figure of some sort next to the lily tank, but first she wanted to see the artifacts on the other niches and pedestals on the upper terraces.

In a niche of the garden wall, nearly hidden by the tall black gladiolus, sat a white pottery pitcher with black designs. When Hattie got closer she saw the spout of the pitcher was formed by a waterbird's head and beak; but most amazing yet, on the chest of the waterbird were women's breasts! Hattie looked over the tops of the black flowers to see where her companions were; the buzz of the bees in the flowers seemed amplified by the sunken garden, though she could not make out what Indigo was saying to Laura as they examined a figure on the terrace below.

Edward stood in front of a niche in the wall of the terrace nearby and glanced up at the sun from time to time as if calculating film exposures for his camera. Hattie slipped her arm into his as she joined him in front of the stone pedestal. The small terra-cotta was a snake-headed figure with human arms and breasts that held a baby snake, but her legs were two snakes!

"How odd this black garden is!" Edward whispered to Hattie. The sight of the breasts on the waterbird pitcher recalled the designs incised on the egg-shaped rock yesterday. Perhaps it might be better if Indigo took her parrot back up to her room in case other figures were unfit for a young girl.

They joined Laura as Indigo, the parrot gripping her shoulder, began to walk the narrow stone ledge of the raised flower beds; she was careful to push aside the gladiolus as she went.

"I assume black is symbolic of night and death," Edward said; Laura broke into a smile. To the Old Europeans, black was the color of fertility and birth, the color of the Great Mother. Thus the blackbirds belong to her as well as the waterbirds—cranes, herons, storks, and geese. Laura confided she imagined the ancient people as she looked at these figures of clay and stone. After a long brutal winter, how they must have watched the sky of the southern horizon for the return of the nourishment givers!

Edward felt a bit sheepish as he inquired about the modesty of the remaining figures displayed in the gardens, but Laura graciously assured them not to worry. She led the way to the niche, where Indigo stood with her parrot, apparently spellbound by the figure, no more than eight inches tall—another of the crude terra-cottas that Edward did not recognize at once. Whatever it was, it held the child's attention, so he stepped closer to see.

The figure was a seated bear mother tenderly cradling her cub in her arms; Indigo could feel how much the bear mother loved her cub just from the curve of the clay. She stayed by the bear mother even after Hattie and

Edward followed Laura to the next niche; Indigo felt embraced by the bear mother, loved and held by her even as she stood there. The bear mother's affection made her smile for Mama and Grandma Fleet—they'd held Sister Salt and her just like that, even after they were big girls. They all used to laugh when Grandma pulled one of them onto her lap and pretended to cradle a big girl. The girls used to go along with Grandma's joke and pretended to be huge babies that made baby sounds as they laughed even harder.

Rainbow became impatient with her for stopping so long and leaned off her shoulder to reach the black flowers with his claws and beak. She cautioned him to let the flowers be, and walked in the middle of the path, but the long flower spikes leaned toward them and the next thing she knew, the parrot clutched a blackish red blossom in his claws and held it to his beak for inspection. Indigo quickly looked to see if anyone witnessed the parrot's damage.

"Hurry up and eat it if you are going to," she told him; he shredded the petals in his beak but did not swallow them; then casually dropped the remains on the ground. Indigo took a last look at the bear mother with her cub; she wanted to stay with them longer, but she could see Hattie looking back at her and just then Edward gestured for her to come.

Indigo didn't want to miss the figures in the other niches, so she took the long way around to join the others. The clay figure in the next niche was larger than the bear mother; it was also seated and appeared mostly human, but she was painted with black-and-white stripes and over her belly a snake curled in a spiral. She felt a chill of excitement when she realized that the figure had snakes for arms! She'd never seen or heard of anything like this before; she couldn't wait to tell Sister.

Indigo rejoined the others on the terrace below, where they stood before a stone pedestal with a seated figure of carved sandstone that gazed at them with the round eyes of a snake. The snake-headed mother had human arms and in them she cradled her snake baby to human breasts; but instead of legs, she had two snakes for limbs. Indigo took a deep breath and the others looked at her. Well, what did she think? Indigo didn't know what to say. Grandma Fleet used to talk to the big snake that lived at the spring above the old gardens; she always asked after the snake's grandchildren and relatives and sent her best regards.

"It's nothing like the minotaur, is it?" Edward said; he found the grotesque madonnas far more monstrous than the centaur or minotaur.

As they made their way to the niche on the terrace below, Laura described the remnants of snake devotion still found in rural villages of the Black and Adriatic Seas. There, people believed black or green snakes bore guardian spirits who protected their cattle and their homes. In her travels, Laura saw ornamental snakes carved to decorate the roofs and windows for protection. Great good fortune came to anyone who met a big white snake wearing a crown; the crowned snake was the sister of the waterbird goddess, owner and guardian of life water and life milk.

Edward hoped to quicken the pace of their tour as he led the way to the small lily tank; above the lilies was a deep niche that held the bird-snake woman. Fragrant red water lilies as big as dinner plates rocked back and forth when Indigo stirred the green water with her hand.

Previously Hattie agreed with Indigo the bear mother and her cub were the dearest figures they'd seen; but when Hattie saw the carved stone figure of a bird-masked woman holding a bird-masked baby in her arms, she could not take her eyes from them.

Edward called the sculpture primitive, but Hattie disagreed; although the clay figures were simple in form, the expression of the mother's body as she cradled her baby in the arms touched Hattie deeply and she felt a surge of emotion that caught in her throat until tears filled her eyes. The bird goddess loved her baby as fiercely as any mother! Hattie wiped the tears away quickly with the back of her hand. Edward would not understand; he'd think she was ill again. How dare Edward call these Old European sculptures boring or ugly?

Hattie studied the terraces of black gladiolus all around her; the black-reds looked especially striking against the bright blue sky. She would never forget this black garden with its little madonnas, as Laura called them.

Edward knelt on the stone ledge of the pedestal. He examined the terracotta inch by inch to note any erosion of the surface or other damage of the slightest to the rare artifact. He noted one questionable spot on the clay of the right breast, but nothing more.

At first Rainbow was uncertain about so many tall black flowers all around, and he gripped Indigo's shoulder tightly as a breeze caused the black faces of the flowers to bow forward and back, nodding at them. What did the flowers mean by their nods? she asked the parrot. She sat on the bottom step across from the lily tank with the parrot in her lap. She wanted to remember everything she could so she could properly describe the garden to Sister Salt and Mama. She watched Hattie and Edward walk ahead with Laura while she sat with the bird-mask mother holding her baby. I was a baby like that and my mother and my grandmother held me, she told

Rainbow; that's why she wanted to stay there a while longer, though there was another garden yet to see.

As they made their way up the steps from the lily tank to the gateway of the rain garden, Indigo wished she could stay in the black garden longer; she had so many questions about the figures, especially the snakes.

Laura stopped briefly to pull off dried blossoms, while Edward and Hattie walked ahead. Indigo's heart pounded as she worked up her nerve to ask Laura about the snakes. Were there any snakes here in the garden? A few small green snakes and black snakes, but they were very shy. Indigo looked here and there under the foliage and at the base of the stonework, where a snake might rest in the shade. Laura pushed back the tall stems of the flowers to search too, but they found no snakes.

Laura said when she was a girl her grandmother always kept a black snake in the storeroom to protect it from mice and rats. Indigo smiled; yes, Grandma Fleet always thanked the snakes for their protection—not just from rodents but from those who would do you harm. At the spring above the dunes lived the biggest snake, very old—the water was his.

Laura paused and smiled; they'd caught up with Edward and Hattie, who were waiting at the gateway seated on one of the stone benches that flanked the wall.

"We've been exchanging snake stories," Laura said as she sat down. Indigo let Rainbow climb down her arm to investigate the edges of the stone bench with his beak. He examined the stone very carefully, touching the surface with his smooth, dry tongue to get additional information.

One of Laura's favorite stories was about a white princess who returned a lost child from the forest to the village. She helped the sick and gave gold coins to the poor. But she had to return to the forest at night.

A man fell in love with the princess and she loved him, but always she returned to the forest at sundown. She warned him never to follow her; others who did were always found asleep at the forest's edge the following morning.

He promised to honor her wishes, but after some time, her lover became curious. He took food to the blackbirds to ask for help. They told him to tie sprigs of mistletoe berries to his ankles and his wrists first. That night he followed her into the forest; as the twilight slipped into darkness, he feared he would lose sight of her, but the gleam of her fair hair, the white dress, and the pearls gave off a soft glow that seemed to increase with the darkness.

As they approached the middle of the forest, the glow became more luminous and dazzled his eyes—in the center of the brightness she seemed almost to shimmer herself. Then, in a clearing at the edge of lake, she stopped and he heard strange music, a choir of voices, and she began dancing slowly as legions of green snakes and black snakes emerged dancing from the wood. The glow pulsed even brighter and her hair began to glow now with a blinding light. He rubbed his eyes and when he looked again, he realized her hair was a crown of gold, silver, and pearls. On she danced until her very features shimmered, and suddenly he saw the lake's edge as bright as day, where a giant white snake in a lustrous crown swayed gracefully, surrounded by legions of smaller snakes all dancing with her.

Laura paused to see if her guests wanted to hear more; Indigo nodded enthusiastically with Hattie. Edward deferred to them rather than seem rude; it was an interesting folktale, but he was concerned about how little time was left. He lifted his watch from its pocket by the chain; as departure time neared he could feel his blood stir; the palms of his hands were damp; and the scar on his hand itched. They'd never see the other garden if they sat here listening to fairy tales all afternoon!

After her lover confessed his disobedience, the white princess had to go. At the lake's edge they said farewell. She stepped into the water and the swirl of her blond hair on the water's surface became luminous, and then it was a shining crown. At that instant the white snake in her golden crown reared up gracefully out of the water and bowed to him before she disappeared under the water. In her footprints at the water's edge, her lover found coins of pure gold intended for the poor and sick, who became his life's work.

Hattie wanted to ask Laura about the luminous glow in the story—so similar to the glowing light she saw that night in Aunt Bronwyn's garden. She still regretted she had not asked her aunt more about the story of the luminous glow seen in the King's Bath. There must be other, similar stories Laura might know. But Edward was already on his feet and brushing the back of his trousers, clearly anxious to move on to the rain garden.

Along the walls stood treelike aloes on eight-foot stems, some bearded with dead leaves, others towering on scaly stems the diameter of a man's torso, while the tallest plants stood ten feet or more. Dozens of species of aloes—an amazing collection made during the time her husband was in Africa—filled the garden terraces.

African warriors, Hattie thought as she gazed at the spiked leaves and the clusters of tiny red-orange flowers that crowned them. Coarse sand the color of ivory replaced the dark Lucca soil in the terraces, and river-smoothed pebbles and fist-size stones, pale yellow and gray, were scattered beneath them. But what caught Hattie's eyes were the giant clamshells nestled in the sand and pebbles to form shallow basins here and there at the feet of the giant plants. Here and there were conch shells so large Hattie thought they must be from the coast of Africa.

There were no trees even along the wall; the reflected light off the sand and shells was quite intense; here was a garden designed to be seen by the light of the moon or in the cool mist and overcast of an autumn rain. The scent of the first rain on the dry sandstones and aloes must be wonderful. She wanted an aloe garden for Riverside.

Now a breeze stirred; a cluster of fluffy clouds momentarily shaded the sun. Indigo didn't think this sun felt terribly hot—this sun was nothing like the fiery sun above the river back home. Indigo let Rainbow down from her arm to explore the pebbles and sand while she examined a big spiral seashell with long spines down its back at the edge of the path; when she held it up in both hands its inner layers of blue-violet glowed in the sunlight.

The gateway to the rain garden was guarded by two bare-breasted women of terra-cotta holding large basins in their laps to catch the rain. The small statues faced each other on oversize pedestals that flanked the gate. Laura spoke of the link the Old Europeans made between raindrops and drops of breast milk.

Edward felt his cheeks color at the mention of drops of breast milk. A scientist did not blush, but unaccountably his cheeks felt hot, and he quickly bent over to examine a bright red aloe flower—red was a rare color for aloe flowers; most species were yellow or coral.

The figure on the first niche also surprised Edward: it was a sandstone sculpture of what appeared to be a toad, the size of a bread loaf; but on closer examination he realized it was a fat woman on her belly, legs and arms curled close to the body. Big breasts again!

Edward began to feel uneasy about the other figures here, and considered asking Indigo to wait for them in the black garden right then, but he did not want to make a scene. Laura thought her statues posed no moral harm; perhaps not to an Italian child, but for American children, precautions must be taken.

He glanced around and was relieved this garden was smaller than the other gardens, with only four niches and no pedestals other than the two that held the rain catchers and their basins. Best not to take any chances; he went to whisper to Hattie that for modesty's sake the child should be sent to wait in the black garden. But he was too late; just then Indigo hurried from the small stone figures in the shaded recess of the terrace wall and took Hattie's hand.

"Look," she said, pointing at an odd stone figure. "What's this?" Hattie looked up from the leathery speckled leaves of the aloes along the path to the niche.

"What indeed!" Hattie approached for a better look. The strange stone figure had an elongated neck and head, but its large buttocks gave it the appearance of a large phallus. Suddenly Hattie had a stricken expression and quickly stepped back, and Indigo knew at once her guess was correct.

"That's what I thought it was," Indigo said, as Hattie hurriedly guided her away. Edward took one look and insisted Indigo go wait in the black garden. Indigo looked to Hattie and Laura, but Edward was adamant.

Laura's expression was full of concern as the child with her parrot started up the terrace steps; she invited Edward and Hattie to take their time in the rain garden and join her and the child at the garden shed where she made the gladiolus hybrids.

Indigo was still surprised at the sights white people didn't want children to see. Edward's puffed-up concern about the male organ was so silly she had to laugh out loud as she reached the top of the rain garden steps; from the corner of her eye she saw Edward whisper to Hattie. By themselves among the tall spikes of black flowers, Indigo made up a song: "See you can't see what you see. See you can't see what you see. See, see, see!"

After Laura went ahead with Indigo, Hattie walked with Edward, who took a brisk pace to see the remaining niches, which held artifacts for rain invocations—shallow pottery bowls with painted or incised snakes coiled around the inside, and even more impressive were the pottery snakes sculpted on the shoulders of vases. The bowls were incised with holes that represented raindrops.

In the rain garden's center niche was a remarkable fired terra-cotta of a snake coiled into a ram's horn, incised with raindrops and the meandering zigzag representing flowing water. There were no other objectionable objects as Edward had feared but it was just as well Indigo missed the serpent figures. The child was from a culture of snake worshipers and there was no sense in confusing her with the impression the old Europeans were no better than red Indians or black Africans who prayed to snakes. Hattie agreed; they must help the child adjust to the world she was in now.

At the potting shed, they found Indigo at the table with her notebook; carefully she copied the hand-printed words off the envelopes while Laura carefully poured gladiolus seed from the waxed paper envelopes. Laura explained how to prepare the florets of the mother plant for pollination; she let Indigo put the paper bonnet over the plant at the end of the procedure. Only two florets could be fertilized each day. Early morning was better than the heat of the day. Avoid damp or wet weather.

Edward was surprised at the varieties of hybrid colors Laura had developed. The *Gladiolus primulinus* grew on slender, flexible stems with pure yellow flowers. Laura's former husband, the army colonel, acquired the rare plants in Africa for her hybrids. Edward thought perhaps hybrid gladiolus might have a future in the southern California climate, where the corms did not have to be taken up each winter.

He found himself a bit irritated at the *professoressa*'s attention to the child, especially her generous gifts of packets of seeds and corms from her hybrids, although he could see that she made an identical bundle for him and Hattie. It seemed a bit ludicrous for Laura to pretend the Indian child would ever plant the corms or seeds, much less perform the pollination process for hybrids, even if she did take notes on all the necessary steps. Of course Laura could not be expected to know anything about American Indians.

Edward knew all about the process, but Hattie and Indigo were fascinated by the *professoressa*'s descriptions of the hybrid colors she got the first time she crossed the *Gladiolus primulinus* with the species *Gladiolus gladiolus:* she obtained flowers of yellow with a red throat mark, cream yellow, golden yellow with a red-brown splash. She moved on to the dark red and dark rose, at the same time experimenting with blue on light blue and creamy pink with a red spot and a ruffled dark pink with a cream throat. Lavender with purple, tan and brown, brown with a red splash. It was a number of years before she got the black-red and the black-rose flowers and some years of propagating enough corms for the terrace gardens. Currently she was trying to crossbreed the fragrant African species with the European species, but unfortunately the fragrant hybrids did not reproduce themselves.

That evening, newspaper reports of unrest near Rome and points south prompted Laura to insist they remain with her in Lucca at least until the end of the week. But Edward made light of the reports; Corsica could hardly be any more dangerous than southern California, where holdups of coaches and trains still occurred.

Edward fussed with packing long after Hattie was in bed, and it occurred to her he was waiting for her to fall asleep before he came to bed. She hoped they might take up where they'd left off earlier, but when he got in bed beside her he began to talk about the anniversary of his father's death, which was a few days away. He usually marked that day with a visit to the grave under the orange trees. This year would be the first time he would be away.

Hattie shifted and turned a bit so she was closer to Edward, but he remained motionless as though his voice were coming out of the wall behind the bed. Perhaps the dead forgive the lapses of the living, Hattie suggested softly as she stroked the bedcovers lightly over his chest, but Edward seemed not to hear; he was preoccupied with their departure.

Hattie drifted off to sleep recalling the pictures and statues of the Blessed Virgin Mary standing on a snake. Catechism classes taught Mary was killing the snake, but after seeing the figures in the rain garden, she thought perhaps the Virgin with the snake was based on a figure from earlier times.

That night Indigo dreamed she was back home at the old gardens; but where the sunflowers and corn plants and squash once grew, tall gladiolus bloomed in all colors—red, purple, pink, yellow, orange, white, and black. A delightful fragrance and the hum of the bees filled the canyon. Rainbow flew from flower to flower as if he were a hummingbird, and Linnaeus sat beside her on the sand and picked tiny black seeds from a dried pod. She went to find Mama and Sister Salt at the spring but she found the big rattlesnake instead. "Where's my corn pollen?" Snake asked, and Indigo woke up.

The next day Laura put them on the train to Livorno, but only after she got promises from them to come stay with her again. She gave them a card with instructions how she might be reached in case they needed her assistance.

◆ ◆ ◆

By the time the train reached Livorno, Edward's face appeared pale; was he ill? Oh no, he quickly answered, he was only a bit tired. He'd not slept well the night before, he said, but managed a smile for Hattie. Actually he'd barely slept at all; after he managed to fall asleep, he woke shaken and wet with fear from a nightmare about giant African snakes in their bed. Perhaps in her sleep Hattie flung her arm over his shoulder to set off the bad dream.

Of course, all the snake figures he'd seen in the rain garden the previous afternoon were bound to affect his dreams, though yesterday's terra-cotta snakes were small and European. It seemed more likely the nightmare stemmed from an anecdote Laura told the evening of their arrival; as she showed them around the house, she repeated an old rumor—almost a local legend by now. The foreigners who previously owned the villa kept giant African snakes in the wine cellar, then later abandoned the snakes there. According to the story, the great pythons found their way into the foundations of the villa, where they subsisted on rodents and feral cats. Laura reiterated there were no pythons or any other large snakes on the premises; nonetheless Edward dreamed a giant snake embraced him around the shoulders.

The train's arrival in Livorno stirred his blood, and the fatigue dissipated; he felt a tingle of anticipation and excitement; at last he was on the threshold to Corsica and the *Citrus medica* twigs that would free him entirely from debt and secure his share of the family estate. Financial improvements brought other changes as well; actually, the improvement already began on board the ship to Genoa with his aquaintance with Dr. William Gates of Melbourne and a possible investment partnership in meteor ore; the *C. medica* twigs were to be his collateral. It all would work out very nicely; he knew Hattie wanted to go to Arizona to determine if the child had any living relatives, and Dr. Gates's meteor crater was only a few hours by train from Flagstaff.

As soon as they were settled in their hotel, Edward took a walk to reconfirm their reservations on the steamship to Bastia the next morning. He wanted no errors or delays; he double-checked to calm his nerves. He was careful to avoid the U.S. consulate lest he be noticed by the authorities there. He was counting on the inefficiency of the civil servants at the Agriculture Department and Mr. Grabb's busy schedule to give him enough time to carry out his plan. They would assume his reply to their cables had been lost but he would turn back as they had directed; he'd never given them any reason to assume otherwise. Time was of the essence now.

Livorno was a port city, but the downtown area was somewhat low lying and did not always get the breezes off the sea in August. Edward was hot and little out of breath when he reached the steamship office, but an alert young clerk immediately brought him a chair and a glass of water. Edward complimented the clerk on his excellent English, and the young man bowed modestly, replying he had lived two years with an uncle in Chicago.

The reservations for tomorrow were all in order; the clerk carefully printed out receipts good for passage for the three of them. The old injury to the leg was acting up, and the clerk was so hospitable, he sat a while longer. The clerk said he was grateful to have this opportunity to practice his English with an American; British visitors usually declined. Perhaps it was the clerk's friendliness or simply the heat that caused him to ask about the citron industry. He regretted his indiscretion almost as soon as he spoke, then decided he was silly to worry; the Italian clerk was harmless.

The clerk was quite knowledgeable about the citron since the export of pickled citron rind was primarily from Livorno. As it happened the clerk also knew a good bit about the processing of the *Citrus medica* from raw rind to candied spice. Edward was pleased to point out that in the United States, candied citron had become one of the most sought after spices for Christmas plum puddings and those rich wedding cakes guests took home to dream on.

Edward listened with great interest to the clerk's description of the brine tanks used to rot the thick-skinned rinds before it was candied. All this information would be invaluable for Edward's future work with the citron. He promised to send the clerk the recipe for Christmas fruitcake before he excused himself and thanked the clerk for all the information. The man expressed his regret Edward and his family were departing so soon; otherwise, he might have arranged a tour of a citron processing shed.

Edward felt the ticks of the clock drawing him closer and closer to his destiny; he had no appetite at dinner. Afterward, while Hattie wrote and the child and parrot played on the floor, he tried to concentrate on a review of cutting slips from twigs but found it nearly impossible to concentrate.

Hattie wrote Laura a note of thanks for her generous hospitality and for the wonderful opportunity to see the rare artifacts in their lovely garden settings. She regretted the haste that compelled them to depart so soon, but she hoped to return to Lucca soon.

The child and Hattie slept soundly, but he tossed and turned; a nauseous sensation and pounding of his heart continued until he got up and found the paregoric. He was about to possess the first slips of *C. medica* out of Corsica! His future depended on the rough-skinned citrons, those ugly little lemons! He tipped the brown glass bottle and tapped its bottom and managed to get a good dose without opening the last bottle. They must find a pharmacist as soon as they returned from Bastia. He lay back on his pillow and floated away in a glow.

The next morning, while the luggage was taken downstairs and Edward and Hattie completed last-minute details before checkout, Indigo played with Rainbow out on the balcony in the fresh air off the ocean and the bright sunshine. Her head over her shoulder, Indigo loved to watch him spread both wings above her like a mighty eagle; as she ran, she felt the weight of his strong little body lift off as his wings flapped harder, but he did not release his grip on her shoulder. Indigo knew he was too smart to let go because his clipped wing feathers wouldn't carry him. They were having so much fun she did not want to stop although she could see Edward and Hattie were nearly ready to go. She didn't want to put Rainbow in his travel cage until the last moment. She turned to make a last run with Rainbow up the long balcony when she felt the breeze off the ocean suddenly rise against her face, and an instant later, Rainbow lifted off her shoulder in the wind and landed in the top branches of the big chestnut tree in the hotel garden. Indigo could tell by his expression he was surprised, then delighted to find himself free in the top of the tree. Indigo called his name and he looked at her, but she could see he was much more interested in the tree. She watched him climb, rapidly using his feet and beak, and by the time she ran to tell Hattie, the parrot was no longer visible.

Down in the hotel garden, a small crowd of staff and a few curious gathered around the tree to crane their necks and point up. Hattie stood with her hand on Indigo's shoulder and tried to reassure her the parrot could not go far with clipped wings; someone would find him and return him. The head gardener boosted one of his assistants into the lower branches and he disappeared up the center of the great tree. More people gathered to watch the man in the tree. Edward noticed even the cabdriver and the hotel porters stopped loading the luggage to look up at the tree.

For days Edward had not allowed himself to think about his mission to Corsica and the task that awaited him, but now that departure was imminent, anxious thoughts raced through his mind; if they were delayed, they'd miss the only boat to Bastia until the end of the week. The new pink skin of the scar on his fingers itched and tingled though he rubbed it vigorously. They must leave for the pier at once!

Edward held out his pocket watch to show Hattie how little time they had before the gangplank was pulled up, but she was attempting to console the child. Indigo began to cry at the sight of the concierge with the empty travel cage that must stay behind in case the parrot was found. Hattie tried to console her, but Indigo's grief was alarming, far more than she ever expressed before. The hotel kitchen staff brought little trays of candies and sweets but Indigo ignored them. She huddled on the big armchair in the hotel lobby with her face buried in her hands.

"I loved him most of all," she sobbed, and refused to move from the chair; she refused to go anywhere without the parrot.

Hattie was aware of Edward's increasing annoyance at the possibility their departure might be delayed. Hattie assured Indigo someone would find the bird; she sat down on the divan across from the child and wrote a hurried note to Laura about the lost parrot and the generous reward offered for his return; the hotel employees would carry on the search while they were in Corsica, and notify their friend Laura when the parrot was found. Indigo mustn't worry; a seaport like Livorno was bound to be familiar with pet parrots—sailors brought back parrots from their travels; someone would care for the lost bird. The weather there was mild; there were vegetable gardens and vines of ripe grapes when Rainbow got hungry. Now they must not delay any longer. Indigo closed her eyes and slowly shook her head; both her hands tightly gripped the arms of the chair; she refused to leave the hotel lobby. Only when Edward approached as if to carry her bodily did Indigo sullenly get to her feet and follow Hattie to the cab waiting outside the hotel.

Hattie pointed out the cab window at the fountain where pigeons drank and bathed while others scrambled for bread crusts the people threw to them, but Indigo refused to look. Instead she stared at a distant point straight ahead and refused to speak or acknowledge them.

Once on board the boat, Hattie tried to humor the grieving child, first by reading aloud from a guide to Corsica, but the child ignored her. She brought out the book of adventures of the stone monkey and began to read but Indigo covered both ears with her hands. Edward was angered by the child's rejection of Hattie's efforts; they really must come to an agreement about discipline for the girl. Each day she grew taller and the clothing that once hung loose now fit almost too closely. Far more alarming, however, were the child's willfulness and absence of humility; her demeanor was that of a sultan, not a lady's maid.

Indigo refused to touch the soup and bread brought to her. All day and tonight Rainbow had nothing to drink or eat where he was, so Indigo would not drink or eat either. The gust of wind caught him and he landed in the treetop by accident; he only wanted to explore a little. He would not understand why she left him after she promised to always love him and take care of him. Storks and seagulls would try to kill a small bird like him.

Hattie reassured her again someone would find the bird and bring him to the hotel for the reward, but Indigo shook her head angrily and refused to look at her.

The weather for the crossing was perfect—the ocean calm and the atmosphere so clear that off in the distance they saw Elba as they passed.

Hattie explained the island's history, which Indigo ignored except to peer hard into the distance to see some sign of the castle and the tiny kingdom Napoleon made after his first defeat; but the shimmer of the afternoon sunlight off the glassy sea created a glare that made it difficult to see much more than the island's emerald outline against the turquoise sea.

It was dark when they reached their hotel, one of only four hotels in Bastia. Indigo went straight to the maid's alcove, or closet, as she called it, and set down her valise next to the narrow bed. Then she defiantly pulled the bedding loose and rolled up in the sheet and blanket on the floor. The night was quite warm and the floor spotlessly clean, so Hattie did not stop the child. The tile floor felt cool to the touch—the child had the right idea on a night like that.

Hattie was relieved Edward was too engrossed in his book on twig grafts to notice Indigo's display of temper. Otherwise the unpleasant discussion of Indigo's manners and training might continue. Edward was satisfied Hattie was teaching the child geography and reading and writing on their journey, but a docile willingness to serve must also be cultivated. Hattie felt her pulse surge each time she recalled Edward's assertion that she was too soft-hearted to discipline the child. Perhaps the task was more than Hattie wanted to take on, but of course it *was* their duty to educate the child to enable her to survive in the white man's world.

Indigo dreamed she was flying with Rainbow on her back high over the earth. Below she could see the shimmering aquamarine of the Mediterranean; ahead on the curve of the horizon she saw the stormy dark blue edge of the Atlantic as they flew west. Before very long they were flying high above the Colorado River and then over the sand dunes, where Indigo looked down and saw the old gardens were no longer planted with corn or squash but something else. As Rainbow flew them lower to get a better look, she saw the garden terraces between the dunes were streaked with bright colors of the tall flowering spikes of gladiolus three feet tall. Rainbow landed among the gladiolus of all shades of yellow—from the palest white with only a blush of yellow to a yellow so bright it glowed. Rainbow climbed a tall spike of yellow blossoms speckled with red, and Indigo laughed with delight,

She woke just as the darkness was beginning to fade, and looked for the cage before she remembered he was lost. She hoped the dream of all the blossoming gladiolus meant he would come back to her. Indigo memorized the low green hills behind Livorno's harbor; to escape the seagulls and storks, she imagined Rainbow flying to the hills where great trees shaded pale orange and pale yellow houses like Laura's. She recalled too the number of food-bearing trees—olives, acorns, and chestnuts for Rainbow to eat if the grapes, apricots, and peaches were not enough. She felt better as she recalled the train ride from Lucca to Livorno, when she had watched out the train window until dark and saw no end to the fields of wheat, or the vineyards and vegetable gardens.

Italy was the best place to get lost in the summer if you were a parrot, she thought. To be lost in the sweltering dunes above the red muddy river of home might kill a parrot; she must teach him not to fly away before she took him to the old gardens. Great horned owl and redtail hawk and golden eagle all would love to taste a parrot.

◆ ◆ ◆

They checked out of the hotel before dawn to take the train to Cervione; Indigo moved like a sleepwalker and still refused food, though she did take water. Before they left the hotel Edward gave the concierge some coins and the man disappeared into the hotel kitchen; he returned with a burlap sack of potatoes, which Edward tucked into the shipping crate with the camera. Hattie wanted to ask him what he meant to do with the potatoes but decided to wait until he seemed less preoccupied.

The other private compartments on the train were unoccupied, and the conductor who came to take the tickets seemed surprised to see Americans. The only signs of civil unrest they'd seen were a few soldiers at the street corners. The newspapers that Laura consulted before their departure reported no incidents in Corsica. Hattie settled back in her seat and closed her eyes; the motion of the train and its rhythmic creak and clatter enveloped her and were oddly soothing. She was so pleased to have met the *professoressa,* as gracious and generous as she was interesting; Hattie wished they had had more time in Lucca; they barely got to see the artifacts in the gardens, much less discuss the significance of each figure. Hattie wished she had asked about the luminous glow of the white snake goddess. If she got to know Laura a little better, Hattie thought, she might confide about the strange light, the odd luminous glow she saw in Aunt Bronwyn's garden.

Indigo was curled up in a ball on the seat next to the window; her pathetic state brought tears to Hattie's eyes when she remembered how spirited the child had been only the day before; if only they had clipped the parrot's wing feathers as they grew out. Hattie tried to comfort her with a pat on the back, but it was no use; Indigo seemed inconsolable. Hattie recalled the articles she'd read about people who died of broken hearts. She was concerned because the child refused to eat. If the child took the hunger strike too far she was liable to become seriously ill before they could find a doctor. She wanted to take the child and return to Livorno to search for the parrot while Edward completed his business with the citron cuttings.

Edward disagreed. The next boat to Livorno did not depart for three days; by then his business would be completed anyway. The parrot might already have been found; the child was only tired from travel; she'd spring up in no time after some rest. Hattie was reluctant to agree, and gave a deep sigh as she nodded her head. Edward felt his neck and face begin to redden; this was really too much, at such a critical juncture of the Corsica mission!

"When the child is thirsty and hungry enough she will eat!" he said; then the shocked expression on Hattie's face caused him to soften his tone. "By the time we return to Livorno the parrot will be found and Indigo will be just fine."

Indigo watched the world move around her but she was outside the world now; voices sounded distant, but no matter, because there was nothing she needed to hear from these people. She moved when she was told and sat silently until it was time to move again. She forgot her valise on the train when they got off in Cervione, but she could see Edward was in a rush and short tempered so she said nothing. The valise contained all the seeds she'd collected and the notebook and colored pencils Laura gave her, but none of it seemed important now that Rainbow was lost. She remembered Grandma Fleet said if you lost something, you should talk to it, apologize for your carelessness, and ask it to please return to you. She whispered to Rainbow almost constantly to let him know she would find him.

Just then, Hattie looked at Indigo and noticed the valise was missing. Passengers were boarding the train. Where was it? Indigo looked down and shrugged her shoulders. Hattie started to reboard the train but Edward was adamant: There was no time! They must be on their way. It was the child's own fault, Edward pointed out, and she would never learn responsibility if she did not face the consequences.

"Good-bye, seeds. Good-bye, colored pencils," Indigo whispered as their other luggage was loaded on the cab. Then the conductor hurried out of the train car with the little brown valise. The valise came back to her just like that! Rainbow would return too.

Edward tried to soften the tone of his voice because he did regret the child's sadness. "You must learn to take better care of things, Indigo," he said as he gave the conductor a coin. "You would not have lost the parrot if you were more careful."

Dry mountain foothills the color of dust surrounded the small town and blocked the cooling winds off the sea. The town of Cervione was even smaller than Bastia, with few people on the streets in the heat. By the sun's low angle Edward calculated that it was the dinner hour, half past six or thereabouts. Since his accident in Brazil when his pocket watch was smashed, he made it his practice to calculate the time by the position of the sun before he took out his watch to check his calculation. He felt reassured to know the time; one of the worst parts of the Brazilian ordeal had been the sensation time disappeared with the white men, or stopped when his watch was smashed by the same rock that shattered his leg. Without the watch, there was only the same night and the same day that repeated themselves until time itself became the scalding pain of the compound fractures. He had been slowly dragging himself toward the riverbank above the swift currents to let go of himself forever in the rushing water when the monkey and the mestizo brothers came along.

The only hotel open in Cervione during the month of August was named the Napoleon; of course, Hattie thought. The stairs and halls looked and smelled as if they were last scrubbed during Napoleon's era. The hotel's little restaurant was closed for renovations; the hotel clerk indicated that since the heat of the summer months discouraged all but the most hearty travelers, Cervione was a bit too far from the coast to benefit much from ocean breezes; Bastia was far nicer. Most summer visitors stayed there and hired carriages for day trips.

The hotel clerk was the brother of the town's mayor, and before Edward could think of a polite refusal, the clerk sent a boy to bring the mayor to meet their American visitors.

Hattie and the child followed the porter to their rooms upstairs while Edward waited for the mayor to arrive. His brother broke out a dusty bottle of brandy from under the hotel reception desk and wiped three dusty glasses with his clean handkerchief. The mayor, a short heavy-set man in his early sixties, arrived out of breath and sweating. Years before, he lived in the United States, and he never grew tired of greeting visitors from his adopted country. What he missed most from America was baseball; otherwise the wine and the bread of Corsica were far superior. They drank a number of toasts to their countries and to themselves and to tourism before Edward managed to extricate himself with a promise to return as soon as his camera was unpacked, to make the mayor's portrait. He was glad to have the excuse of Hattie and the child upstairs.

By the time the proper lighting was had and the mayor changed his frock coat for the photograph, an hour had passed, and another hour passed while he carefully arranged the mayor's arms and hands on his lap and turned his head for a favorable effect of the flash powder. Then it was time for more brandy all around and big bowls of a savory vegetable soup with little curled pasta and long loaves of freshly baked bread. Finally he left his new companions with promises to send them their portraits once he completed the process of printing them. Both Hattie and Indigo were asleep—the child on the floor of the alcove, which made sense on such a warm night.

Edward closed his eyes but the heat made sleep difficult. His thoughts raced: so many decisons to be made, so many steps to go over to have healthy twig cuttings. The goodwill of the mayor and local officials was essential, especially during this time of civil unrest. One of the mayor's deputies made remarks, in jest, of course, about spies and anarchist agents in disguise, which gave them all a good laugh. The mayor was kind enough to arrange for his younger brother to rent them a buggy with a shade for their tour of the farming villages in the mountains. Edward asked specifically to visit Borgo, the village reputed to have the best candied citron industry. Their appointment was for eight the next morning so they would have a little of the morning coolness for their trip.

His strategy was simple: he would find a grove of healthy-looking trees and pretend to make a landscape photograph that included the citron trees. Then as he set up the tripod and camera in front of the grove of citron trees, he would unpack the two sharpened twig knives from their small wooden box inside the camera case with the potatoes.

All night the bedding felt damp beneath him and no matter how he turned or arranged the pillow, he could not sleep. He listened to Hattie's breathing next to him and the child's soft snoring from the floor in the alcove until he dozed off, only to wake at the creak of the bedsprings when Hattie got up and walked to the window.

The coolness of the tile floor felt wonderful on Hattie's bare feet—no wonder Indigo was able to sleep while she and Edward tossed and turned. For an instant she thought how easy it would be to take a sheet and pillow to the floor to sleep, but of course that was silly.

Hattie was less concerned about Indigo's health after she finished her soup and bread earlier in the evening, but the child still refused to speak or make eye contact. Hattie missed the lively exchanges she and Indigo had, and the child's vibrant reactions and questions about the places and people they saw. Surely someone would find that parrot for the reward! If only their schedule had permitted them another day in Livorno, they might have searched for the bird themselves. Hattie sighed; she was beginning to weary of travel. A day of rest from travel would benefit them all.

Edward got up a little after daybreak while Indigo was still asleep. To Hattie's annoyance, Edward at once began to fuss with the camera case and bumped the floor hard with the tripod. Hattie expected the noise to wake Indigo, but she scarcely stirred in the alcove. The poor child was worn out!

"I think I'll stay here today with Indigo and rest," she said. Edward did not disagree, but as he went on with his repeated repacking of the camera case to ensure against breakage, he pointed out that the hotel dining room was closed for the summer; they'd have only soup and bread again. Moreover, the hotel had no garden for shady walks, only a paved courtyard with some pots of withered dahlias in full sun. The mountains would be much cooler and the mayor's brother promised a home-cooked meal at his house in Borgo; the fresh air and exercise would be good for all of them.

When Hattie woke her, Indigo had just reached the Sea of Galilee, which looked like the river at home, only many times wider and surrounding everything; in her dream, Rainbow was on her shoulder and Linnaeus frolicked along the rocky seashore, whose stones and pebbles were the same colors of pale yellow and pale orange as the stones along the river at home. Up ahead in the distance she saw the white cloaks of the dancers as they lined up to get the sacred red clay dust. When Indigo woke to see that she was back in the hotel room with Hattie and Edward, she burst into tears.

"Why did you have to wake me right then?" she cried in anger. "I was almost to find them!" Hattie felt a surge of compassion in her heart for the child, followed by righteous anger at Edward. They had not argued with each other before, but Hattie was fed up; if he had not insisted on such a haste, the child would behave much better, and so would she!

Edward countered if Indigo were not so spoiled and so stubbornly convinced the parrot would never be found, she might be tolerable. He looked at the child. Pet parrots were lost and returned to their owners every day, all over the world, he said to the child; but Indigo covered her ears and refused to hear of it. An outing in the sunshine and fresh air was just the tonic Indigo needed.

Indigo sat motionless with her eyes closed as Hattie tugged off her nightgown and put on her cotton slip and blue gingham dress. With her eyes closed she could visualize the desert seashore of her dream that took her to Galilee, where Jesus and his family and followers were camped. She didn't care what Edward or Hattie thought; she squeezed her eyes closed and went over the dream again and again until she was confident she could return to the same place in the dream tonight; then she opened her eyes and saw both Hattie and Edward were irritated by her behavior. Good, Indigo thought; maybe they'd find a train and send her back to Arizona.

They got a late start after the mayor's brother had to shoe one of the horses, and the heat rose in waves from the dirt road ahead of the buggy while the dust swirled all around. The ragged buggy cover gave only a small area of shade that left the lower legs and feet in full sun. Hattie found the rolling hills with the terraced fields overlooking the sea strangely appealing in their solitude.

In the heat of the day, they were the only beings that moved along the road. The blazing full sun at midday was entirely too strong for good photographs, but they were passing into the first of the citron groves, so Edward asked the driver to stop. He got down from the buggy and approached the odd pole frame that enclosed the tree—to train it to grow in a vase form, to give the branches the right spread, the mayor's brother explained in an odd mixture of Italian and French. Edward noted how the right spread of the branches enabled them to hold much more fruit without breaking. He restrained the urge he felt to pick one of the small thick-skinned "lemons" and pretended to study the vista of dry rocky hills in shades of umber and sienna streaked with olive and the citrus green of the orchards, framed by the cloudless azure sky. He easily could have taken all the cuttings he needed right here, but he hoped to find a more discreet opportunity.

The buggy passed more roadside orchards of citrons, and Edward saw no one about, not even a dog. Before long the driver stopped the buggy at the front gate of a large old farmhouse and quickly stepped around to help Hattie and Indigo step down. He showed them to the door, which he pushed open with a flourish. Welcome, welcome, came the voices from the next room, and there they found a great table set with many courses and what appeared to be the driver's entire family seated, apparently waiting for their arrival.

Indigo noticed the children her age immediately because they stared at her every move; she saw old grandmas and old grandpas with little children and even a baby on their laps. They were sitting on benches that permitted them to crowd as many as they could around the table; Indigo was reminded of the time all the strangers came to dance for the Christ when they pressed closer together around the fire to make room for everyone. Indigo pretended not to notice their stares; she looked around and saw the farmhouse was one big room with the stove and kitchen in one end and beds of all sizes and shapes here and there along the walls, with boxes and chests of drawers forming little alcoves, some of which had curtains hung from the ceiling for privacy. The delicious odors of hot bread and cooking food made Indigo hungry for the first time since Rainbow's escape.

They all live here in this one room, Hattie realized as she took her place at the end of the bench next to a shy young woman holding an infant. Indigo slid over closer to Hattie to make room on the bench for Edward, and they ate a wonderful meal that began with sweet peppers stewed with onions, followed by a spaghetti dish with tomatoes and little squids, which Indigo liked a great deal.

After wedges of cheese and ripe soft pears, their host announced that they would all walk together to the little schoolhouse at the edge of the village where the image of Jesus' Blessed Mother recently began to appear on the front wall above the door.

Indigo was wide eyed as she whispered to Hattie; this was it! Indigo could hardly sit still while the others finished eating. Had the Mother of God come alone, or were the other family members and the dancers with the Messiah, camped higher in the mountains? Maybe the Blessed Mother could look across the sea and find Rainbow perched in a potted lemon tree on the ledge of a splashing fountain.

Hattie expected their host and perhaps his immediate family might accompany them to the site of the miraculous wall, but the entire family came in a long procession of sorts. The sun was still blazing hot as they set out. Edward refused offers from the young boys to carry the camera case and the tripod, although his leg was beginning to bother him.

Hattie felt an odd energy, a mood of excitement, among their host's family as they walked along, despite the heat, and she assumed it was due to their visit. Their host explained the miraculous wall brought a steady stream of visitors to their village. The mayor's brother tugged at the edge of his neatly trimmed beard as he explained that recently a disagreement between the townspeople and the church officials sprang up. Since the apparition of Our Lady on the schoolhouse wall, the visitors and pilgrims who used to visit the gold and silver portrait of Mary in the abbey shrine seldom went there anymore. Who could blame them? If they knelt or stood long enough in front of the schoolhouse wall, they might get to see the Blessed Mother herself!

Dawn and sunset were the best times to look for Our Lady's image; you must close the eyes, pray, and then slowly open the eyes only a little as you focused on the rough stone wall, their host explained. While the group stood with their eyes closed in front of the schoolhouse, Edward set up the camera behind them. After he made the photograph of the group in front of the miraculous wall, he planned to politely excuse himself to make photographs near the citron groves that surrounded the village. He was relieved to have attention focused on the large group gathered at the schoolhouse wall shrine so he could go among the citron trees unnoticed. Then, he would watch for a moment when no one was watching him, to seize the twig knife and quick-quick-quick cut the best citron twig specimens.

The faithful watched the wall, lips moving in silent prayer as he completed preparations. He put his head under the camera cloth to begin to compose the picture when behind him a distance away he became aware of a low sound growing steadily louder, as if a giant swarm of flying insects were approaching, but soon he heard voices raised in anger. As he turned, he saw a strange sight down the road at the schoolhouse: their host with his family standing behind him was in a face-off with another, smaller group of villagers, led by what appeared to be Catholic monks who brandished large crucifixes.

Now the voices grew louder and arguments broke out between the two groups. Hattie became alarmed and took Indigo firmly by the arm to stay close to Edward in case violence erupted. Bloody Corsican feuds were regularly reported in American newspapers. Indigo did not take her eyes off the wall even as Hattie led her away, although the Blessed Mother probably would not come now that she heard the angry voices. Indigo tried to keep her head turned back at the wall as long as possible, until Hattie became impatient and pulled her along to a safe distance from the dispute.

Edward kept watch through the viewfinder and made one good exposure of their host arguing nose to nose with another man as the monks and the others formed a semicircle around them. Hattie tried to follow the argument as both men gestured at the old schoolhouse and then at the abbey on the hill beyond, but she couldn't make out more than a few words.

Edward seemed unconcerned as he moved the camera and tripod to get another view of the altercation. When the second plate was exposed and safely stored, Edward looked up the road for the best grove of the citron trees, branches arched gracefully over the low rock walls easily within his reach. He carefully balanced the camera and tripod on his shoulder and carried the camera box up the road toward the orchard he'd chosen for its robust trees.

Hattie stayed with Indigo but at a safe distance from the dispute. She felt annoyed that Edward went on with his photographs, but their time there was short. After a time, a friendly woman, their host's sister-in-law, who once traveled in the United States, joined Hattie and Indigo to explain. Recently, church officials contacted the town mayor to order him to put a stop to the devotions at the schoolhouse wall. The mayor replied there was nothing he could do; the image of the Blessed Virgin could not be washed off or painted over—the monks and other church authorities already tried to expose the apparition as a hoax. But the beautiful colored light that formed the image was only enhanced by the whitewash splashed over the wall. Truly this was a miracle, and the people who once went to the abbey for miracles now came here to the street in front of the schoolhouse, where no offerings were required to see the Mother of God.

The abbot alleged the image on the wall was the work of the devil because the miraculous appearance overshadowed the monks' shrine to the portrait of Mary in silver on gold. Still, the people flocked to see the lovely image of Our Lady until the abbot contacted Rome and a monsignor came all the way from Rome and forbade its veneration on pain of excommunication.

By this time other women joined them, curious to hear what their kinswoman told the foreign tourist. Yes, it was true. The abbey was built to house the precious picture of hammered silver on gold. Pilgrims crawled on their knees up the abbey's marble steps to leave offerings. The paralyzed walked; the deaf and blind heard and saw again. When the Greek king lay seriously ill, the abbot himself carried the precious picture to the bedside of the king, who kissed the picture; instantly the illness receded and in a few days the king was well again. Over time, however, the miraculous power of the picture slowly got used up; but now the Blessed Mother herself had come to them.

With Edward barely visible in the distance, bent over his camera, Hattie was grateful for the friendly conversation; at the time she thought his behavior a bit odd, even rude, but he did want to learn all he could about the citron groves while they were there.

Indigo gripped Hattie's hand tightly as she felt the excitement all over her body. The farther east they traveled, the closer they came to the place the Messiah and his family and followers traveled when they left the mountains beyond Paiute country.

After some loud words were exchanged, the monks took up their big crucifixes in both hands and led their followers back to the abbey. Hattie and Indigo followed the other women back to the shrine at the wall, although there was no sign of the apparition with its colorful image of blue, green, yellow, and red. The Blessed Mother was not likely to appear so soon after ugly words were exchanged—Indigo remembered that winter the Paiute women warned the people must be kind to one another or the Messiah and his family would not come down from the mountains.

Indigo studied the surface of the schoolhouse wall intently and from time to time she glanced around at the faces of the others who were looking for the Holy Mother's image in case they saw something she couldn't see, but their expressions were wistful and uncertain. Indigo watched the wall long after Hattie turned to chat with their host's friendly sister-in-law, who brought a pitcher and tin cups for water. As the light changed, Indigo began to see tiny reflections glitter on the surface of the whitewashed plaster that she recognized as the flakes of snow that swirled around the dancers the last night when the Messiah appeared with his family. She could make out the forms of the dancers wrapped in their white shawls and the Messiah and his Mother standing in the center of the circle—all were in a beautiful white light reflecting all the colors of the rainbow, lavender, blue, red, green, and yellow—and in that instant Indigo felt the joy and the love that had filled her that night long ago when she stood with Sister Salt, Mama, and Grandma to welcome the Messiah. In that instant joy swept away all her grief, and she felt their love embrace her.

A murmur rose from those closest to the wall, interrupting their conversation, and when Hattie and the others turned to look, the faithful were on their knees in the dirt. Was it an odd reflection off metal or glass nearby? A faint glow suffused the whitewashed wall and Hattie felt her heart beat faster as the glow grew brighter with a subtle iridescence that steadily intensified into a radiance of pure color that left her breathless, almost dizzy.

The strange light in Aunt Bronwyn's garden might have been a dream, but here she was with dozens of witnesses! Where was Edward? He must see this! Hattie turned and saw him, a dark speck in the distance, too far to call; but when she looked back at the wall again the light was already growing faint. She was surprised to feel tears on her cheeks and saw that the others—men as well as women—wept though their faces were full of joy. Yes, yes, they all spoke excitedly with one another, they had seen her. Yes, Hattie nodded her head, yes! So this was what was called a miracle—she felt wonder and excitement, though she saw the glow of colored light on the wall for only an instant.

The rocky dry hills and their people were poor; their lives were a struggle here; that was why the Blessed Mother showed herself here; the people here needed her. Although she didn't see the Messiah or the rest of the family or her mother with the dancers, Indigo was much heartened; all who are lost will be found, a voice inside her said; the voice came from the Messiah, Indigo was certain.

Edward rejoined them as the crowd began to disperse. He saw the women and even some of the men had been crying. He thought Hattie and the child were rather subdued but he chalked that up to fatigue. He was still a bit out of breath himself from the exertion of carrying the tripod and the camera case, heavy now with dozens of twig cuttings carefully rolled in oil cloth to sustain them until they returned to the hotel. There he would hollow out little receptacles in the potatoes to provide the moisture and nutrients that would sustain the cuttings on their long journey to California.

The buggy ride back to the hotel in Cervione was long, but the night air coolness was invigorating. Edward was in rare high spirits and talked excitedly about the joint venture with Dr. Gates—shares in the citron stock in exchange for shares in the meteor iron mine. Hattie let Edward talk while she considered how to describe what she had seen on the schoolhouse wall; she barely held her temper the first time Edward wisecracked about "religious hysteria." Briefly she thought he might understand if only she explained it in the right words, but as he went on about drilling machines to mine the meteor crater in Arizona, she realized it was no use, not right now.

Fatigue overtook her, limb by limb, until she could not keep her eyes open; Indigo was already asleep, curled up on the buggy seat. As she drifted off to sleep, she recalled the light in Aunt Bronwyn's garden that night—now she was certain it wasn't a dream; it was true; she must write to her at once and tell her about that night and what they'd seen today. Indigo had seen it too, and now the child was so happy and excited before she fell asleep, she asked Hattie how far they were from Jerusalem. Far away, Hattie told her, but much closer than before. Tomorrow Hattie would bring out the atlas for the train ride back to Bastia, and they'd have a geography lesson on the Holy Land.

The ship departed Bastia for Livorno on the evening tide; the light breeze on deck was cool and invigorating as Hattie and Indigo watched the silhouette of the shore recede. A lovely half-moon floated above them in an ocean of stars, and when Hattie pointed to it Indigo smiled and nodded her head. Yes, the eye of the big snake was watching out for them—that's what Grandma said. The wide band of bright stars was her belly and chest, though of course she was much too big to be seen from earth.

When they returned to the cabin Edward was busily wrapping the twig cuttings, their tips stuck in cubes of potato. Later she would be embarrassed she never questioned Edward's authority to cut the twigs from the venerable orchards; it was for science, she thought.

No, she did not suspect anything was amiss until the customs officer on the pier in Livorno motioned for his two assistants to unload the hand trolley stacked with their luggage.

Hattie had walked ahead with Indigo, who was terribly anxious to get to the hotel, where she was sure they would find Rainbow safely in his brass cage waiting for her. She reassured the child the customs inspection would not take long, but when she glanced back to see if Edward was coming along yet, she was shocked to see Edward surrounded by customs officers. Hattie took Indigo's hand firmly in hers and hurried back to find clothing and personal items deliberately scattered over the inspection table. The citron cuttings were in neat rows. They had also set aside the little sacks of gladiolus corms and seeds Laura gave them as well as the seeds Aunt Bronwyn gave Indigo.

Hattie tried to go to Edward's side, but the customs officers politely blocked her path. It was not possible, they said, and motioned for her and the child to step back. Hattie assumed they would be reunited momentarily, so she did not insist. Seconds later she was shocked to see the customs officers lead Edward away; Hattie called out his name, and for an instant he turned his head, and their eyes met for an instant before the officers moved him along. She could not forget the expression in his eyes because its meaning eluded her, yet it remained just near enough to bother her. What expression had she expected to see?

Indigo took Edward's arrest in stride; Mama and Grandma used to get arrested—it didn't mean anything, she tried to reassure Hattie. She was more concerned about the delay; she wanted to get to the hotel to see if Rainbow was found. She sketched and colored a drawing of a green, blue, and yellow parrot while Hattie answered the officers' questions.

Her husband had received a cablegram of authorization in Genoa only last week, Hattie told them. She had seen the two envelopes in his breast pocket when he returned from the consulate. It would be a simple matter, would it not, to ask the cable office to check their records. The customs officers asked no further questions but requested she remain at the American consulate until further notice; they brought around a cab that took her and the child to the consulate.

The deputy consul was on vacation and his assistant away in Rome; the clerk in charge, a dour American with dirty cuffs, announced, in any event, they could do nothing for Americans caught smuggling. Hattie protested; her husband had special authorization from the U.S. Agriculture secretary himself! The clerk stared at her for a moment, his eyes grotesquely magnified by his spectacles; then he rudely turned away and showed her and the child to the door of a sitting room set aside for American citizens in distress.

Hattie had not cried earlier when she saw all their belongings scattered; nor had she cried when the authorities marched Edward away, because then she still believed it was all a misunderstanding. But as she guided Indigo ahead of her into the small dingy room, furnished only with a dark leather sofa and a table and chair, Hattie began to cry.

She sat on the edge of sofa and stared straight ahead at the glass doors to the balcony. Indigo squeezed her hand and whispered, "Don't worry, Hattie. Please don't cry." Indigo wasn't afraid, because the police here did not shove or kick them the way the Indian police and soldiers did in Arizona, and they brought Hattie and Indigo to the consulate as soon as Hattie answered their questions.

To cheer her up, Indigo talked about the way the Indian police tied their ankles and wrists so she and Sister Salt couldn't get away; she told Hattie the stories about the times Grandma Fleet was caught by soldiers or by the Indian police, only to escape later; Mama even escaped Fort Yuma, though it took her more than a year. Hattie mustn't be sad—at home people got arrested for no reason all the time. There was nothing to be ashamed of; this wasn't bad at all.

Hattie was quite touched by Indigo's efforts to cheer her and she had to smile at Indigo's confidence that the police here were not so bad; as she listened, she was shocked at the routine brutality the child described. Indigo was happy to be telling Hattie stories because the telling took her mind off Rainbow; she was certain he was waiting for her at the hotel. If they hadn't arrested Edward, she and Rainbow would already be together again, playing with the quartz pebbles Indigo picked up near the schoolhouse with the miraculous wall.

Indigo sketched and colored gladiolus in her notebook. She recopied the pages of text that she'd copied from Laura's gladiolus books because it helped her to remember the Latin names. One hour passed and then two; Hattie had no idea how long they would be detained there; both she and the child were hungry and exhausted. When she went downstairs with a ten-lire note to ask if they might get something to eat, the American clerk glared at her but snatched the ten lire from the counter and called a young Italian boy from the back to bring them the bread and milk Hattie requested.

Hattie began to fear they would be detained there until the deputy consul returned, and that might be days. The authorities seized all their bags but did return Hattie's purse and Indigo's valise. With a sheet of paper torn from Indigo's notebook Hattie wrote a note to Laura. She apologized for the bother after all the hospitality Laura had extended to them, but there had been a misunderstanding with the customs officials and the American consul and staff were away. Could Laura recommend an attorney in Livorno who might help them?

Hattie consulted her little book of useful Italian phrases and when the boy brought the milk and bread upstairs, she told him to keep the change as a tip. The boy, who had avoided looking at her directly until then, broke into a big smile. His eyes widened when she gave him another ten lire and asked him to send the letter to Lucca the fastest way possible. The boy looked at the ten lire in his hand and at the address on the letter; if he hurried, he said, the letter might still go on the evening train to Lucca.

Hattie stood at the French doors of the balcony and watched the street as she waited, certain Edward would come or at least the clerk would bring her some news. But at closing time the American clerk informed her, for safety purposes, the building must be locked overnight, though they could move about inside until he returned the next morning at eight. Hattie was too shocked by his statement to think to ask him what they should do in case of fire.

The toilet facilities were downstairs, and there was a sink and running water, but no towels. The long leather sofa was large enough for both of them to curl up at each end; the night was quite warm, and while Indigo slept soundly, Hattie lay awake much of the night and wondered how Edward was faring. Was he in jail in Livorno, or did customs have their own detention facilities? Toward morning she did manage to fall asleep but woke with a start, her clothes damp and twisted under her; she dreamed she was in the old woods of Laura's garden on the overgrown path to the hidden grotto but she could not find her way back to the house. In the gray light before dawn, the dream left her with a lingering sadness she had not felt since the incident with Mr. Hyslop; careful not to wake the child, she went to the table and wept.

The boy came again the next morning; this time Hattie asked for oranges and cheese to go with the milk and bread. She unfastened the latches and Indigo helped her open the doors to the balcony for fresh air; they might as well make themselves at home if they were going to be there long. Indigo went out on the balcony and searched the streets and skyline for the hotel with its big tree where Rainbow escaped. She stood very still and listened for a long time until Hattie asked her what was wrong; while the morning air was still cool, she hoped she might hear Rainbow's call.

Indigo got discouraged after a while and came in to lie down on the couch. Hattie reminded her if the parrot was in its cage inside the hotel she would not be able to hear him call—she mustn't give up hope. Hattie was confident, with the help of their friend Laura and perhaps an attorney, the misunderstanding would be cleared up. Hattie reached into her bag and brought out the book of adventures of the monkey king; his wild exploits were just the thing to cheer them up.

Indigo look up at Hattie. How much longer did they have to stay here? Hattie looked down at the book and shook her head. Indigo had been lying down on the couch, her stocking feet curled under her, but now she sat up and restlessly looked out the open doors to the balcony. Hattie went on reading.

Indigo gave a loud sigh; Hattie looked up from the page to see what was the matter. Indigo got up from the couch wiping her eyes on the back of her hand and went out on the balcony to listen again. While she listened for parrot sounds amid the street noise, Indigo watched the donkey carts and buggies in the street and the people come and go on the sidewalks below. Her hair itched because it was dirty; they had not been able to wash or change their clothes. This was beginning to remind Indigo of their captivity by the Indian police before Sister Salt was taken away and Indigo put on a train. If only they could get to the hotel, she was certain Rainbow was waiting there. She was so discouraged.

Edward never wanted Rainbow to come along. The tears came faster as she thought of the little parrot who loved her and trusted she'd come back for him. She set her chin on the balcony railing and didn't even try to blink away the tears. Tears made everything blurry and she saw two or three of the same object when she looked without wiping her eyes; she didn't care. Then she noticed a figure at the end of the street rapidly approaching, and recognized something familiar in the purposeful stride. She wiped her eyes and looked again, and sure enough it was their friend Laura, but what was it that she carried? "Rainbow! Rainbow!" Indigo shouted, and from the street below she heard the parrot screech and squawk in reply.

Laura brought more good news: they were free to go. Hattie wasted no time asking questions; she simply wanted to get to the hotel for a bath and a hot meal and bed. But what news did she have about Edward? Laura put her arm around Hattie's shoulders and told her not to worry; she had posted the bond for Edward's release and he would be along in an hour or two. Still, Hattie could not shake off the vague dread rising inside herself.

While Hattie poured Laura more tea, Indigo sat on the floor rolling pebbles to the parrot, who caught them in his beak, then let them bounce across the tile floor. Laura amused them with the story of Rainbow's return and capture at the fountain in the hotel garden. Laura hoped they didn't mind, but the gardener clipped the parrot's wing feathers to prevent another escape. Indigo's face was bright with happiness and again she thanked Laura, who smiled and told her to thank the gardener, not her.

"But it was so thoughtful of you to bring him along when you came to the consulate," Hattie added. "You've been so kind—I don't know if we could've endured another night on that couch!" They had been at the hotel for almost two hours, and still no Edward; Hattie began to have misgivings. A simple misunderstanding would not take so long to resolve; a sick feeling began to overtake her, from her stomach to her head; her toes and fingers tingled as if the supply of blood was cut off; she stood up abruptly but sank down again in the chair.

Laura helped Hattie to the bed and Indigo, the parrot on her shoulder, gently removed Hattie's shoes as she lay back silently on the pillow with her eyes fixed on the ceiling as tears slid down her cheeks. Laura pulled a chair next to the bed while Indigo refilled the parrot's pottery cups with fresh water and sunflower seeds.

"I am so sorry," Laura said in a soft voice; she looked down at her hands in her lap, and Indigo saw she was almost in tears too.

"Goddamn police!" Indigo said to the parrot, and immediately felt better; both women heard her but neither corrected her. All police were the same, she told Rainbow; they worked for the devil, and the soldiers did too. She lined up the pebbles in a row and pretended they were policemen as she took aim and flicked them one by one across the floor with her fingers. Rainbow watched with great interest as the pebbles clattered across the floor tiles.

Hattie gave a loud sigh and dabbed at her eyes and nose with a handkerchief before she turned to Laura, who reached out to pat her hand and began to speak in a low even voice. Ordinarily, the customs officers did not bother to search the luggage of American tourists returning from Corsica, but the authorities were on the lookout for anarchist secret agents since the assassination of King Umberto. Hattie blinked her eyes but otherwise gave no sign she was listening, but Indigo's ears perked up at the mention of secret agents. She was becoming accustomed to Laura's voice and accent, which reminded her of the English the Mexican people spoke along the river.

Even so, it was the French customs officials—not the Italians—who guarded the citron industry of Corsica so closely. Laura paused, then in a soft voice asked if Hattie wanted to sleep.

"No," she said quickly, "please, the sound of your voice is soothing." Hattie glanced over at the child, who tried to draw in her notebook as the parrot waddled around her and persisted in reaching for the colored pencil between her fingers. Actually it was a game, and Indigo only pretended to draw as she listened to Laura and Hattie.

The killing of the king only four years after Italy's shocking defeat in Abyssinia left the nation stunned. Indigo watched Laura's hands—so graceful when she spoke—with the beautiful rings with their lovely glittering stones of purple, green, and blue.

Many felt there was a connection between the army's humiliation in East Africa and the king's assassination. The prime minister and his cabinet were forced to resign after the defeat at Aduwa. Nothing was the same after that. Laura's voice was softer, and she slowly turned the rings on her fingers as she spoke. Many hundreds dead, and thousands held prisoner, forced Italy to acknowledge Abyssinia's independence. A ransom of millions was paid to the Abyssinian emperor for the return of Italian prisoners.

Hattie sat up and adjusted the pillows to make sure she could hear her friend; Laura's voice became softer as she described her disbelief and confusion when she learned her husband had been absent from his troops days before the battle. Intelligence reports out of Cairo detailed his comings and goings at the estate of a certain Egyptian munitions dealer a few miles outside of Cairo. Not only had he deserted his command; he had divorced her to start a new life, married to the munitions dealer's daughter, with a dowry worth millions. Even now Laura's tone of voice was of one still stunned.

Once the shock had passed, she realized the Egyptians had done her an immeasurable favor; she might have wasted years more of her life with that man in ignorance of his cowardice. This way it was mercifully ended.

They sat in silence for a moment; even the parrot remained motionless on Indigo's arm. Then Laura excused herself; she knew they needed time to rest; Edward would be coming anytime, and she had to catch the train to Lucca.

After Laura left, all Hattie could think about was what to say to Edward; as his wife and life partner, surely she had a right to know the truth about their Corsican excursion! She distinctly remembered the two cablegrams he picked up at the consulate the day they arrived from Lucca—one was authorization from Washington, he said; but the customs officers found the cables and their messages were quite the opposite!

Tears filled Hattie's eyes but she was determined to be strong. When Indigo finished with her bath, Hattie was next; she soaked in the delicious warm water with her eyes closed until the water began to cool. She tried to reconcile her hopes and affection for Edward with the facts before her, but it was impossible—she didn't know where to begin. Instead she sank until only her nose was above the bathwater; in the warm strange silence underwater she recalled the glowing light in Aunt Bronwyn's garden, and a feeling of peace filled her. As she rinsed the soap from her hair Hattie pushed all the doubt from her mind; she would make the best of it, whatever happened; what was most important was to reunite the child with her family.

Indigo had been sitting on the floor so long she lost the feeling in both legs; they tingled as she wiggled her feet to make the blood circulate again. She was tired of being indoors and asked Hattie if she and Rainbow could go downstairs to the hotel garden. The hotel staff all smiled and pointed at the parrot on her shoulder and seemed quite pleased to see them together again; the concierge smiled and said something to her in Italian—maybe a friendly reminder not to let the bird get away again.

The big tree in the hotel garden was full of blackbirds chirping and trilling; Indigo asked Rainbow what they were saying. The parrot tipped his head from side to side, then looked at Indigo and stretched both wings out over his back. It was time to go. The afternoon wasn't as warm as previous days, and Indigo could already see a difference in the position of the sun as it began to move toward the south for winter. The Messiah and the others were probably already on their way home.

Edward did not appear until sundown, long after Laura left. Hattie threw her arms around him in spite of herself. They embraced only briefly; he explained he was exhausted after his ordeal. Fortunately they had allowed him to bathe and change his clothes while in custody. Hattie smiled and shook her head; she and the child had not been so lucky: at the American consulate they shared a couch and had no baths. Edward glanced over at Indigo and the parrot. So the bird was found just as he said it would be! Indigo nodded.

Hattie didn't know what she expected Edward to say to her but he should have said something—given some expression of regret or sorrow over their detention, since his twig cuttings were the cause. Hattie was about to confront him, but just then there was a knock on the door. Customs authorities had released their luggage and the hotel staff brought it to their suite.

Hattie was shocked when she saw the damage done during the search by customs authorities. The interior linings and the panels behind them were ripped open to expose the wood frame, tin, and leather. Evidently the contents of the luggage were searched, then hastily repacked, because Hattie's nightgowns, Indigo's dress shoes, and Edward's books on citrus horticulture were dumped together helter-skelter in the trunk that had been packed with Edward's shirts and trousers. The drawers of the big steamer trunks were jammed into the wrong slots; lace edges of handkerchiefs and parts of stockings dangled out. Hattie's underwear apparently got particular attention because it was wadded up and stuffed into the small leather valise Edward packed with his shoes and slippers. Hattie dropped the valise; she couldn't touch those undergarments again until they'd been washed.

All of their clothing was wrinkled and soiled from the search. Hattie rescued Indigo's underwear and dresses from the camera case, where they were stuffed on top of the photographic equipment. Indigo was more concerned with recovering the gladiolus corms and the seeds spilled from their packets into the bottom of the trunk that previously contained Hattie's books and notes. They both cautioned her to be careful; although Hattie's books and notes were no longer in the trunk, two square wooden boxes of Edward's glass negatives were packed with a bathrobe and pair of Edward's walking shoes. Indigo was worried about the envelopes and tiny boxes of flower and vegetable seeds she had been saving for the gardens in the dunes.

Rainbow was in his cage with the door shut to prevent any damage to the clothes and belongings, but he could see all of the objects, which intrigued him; he protested with a loud series of screeches that caused both Edward and Hattie to look sharply at her and the bird. Indigo could feel the trouble in the air despite the cool breeze from the balcony and windows. Off in the distance, over the evening sounds of the streets, Indigo heard loud laughter.

Hattie was relieved Laura missed the spectacle of the rifled luggage, by far the most humiliating part of their detention. Edward continued to pick through the mess of clothing and papers and books for a clean shirt to send downstairs to be pressed. Did Hattie have anything she wanted to send down for herself or Indigo? Hattie shook her head and sat down on the edge of the bed, suddenly too exhausted to look at another trunk, although Edward warned that if any items were missing, they must make a list to present to the American consulate.

Throughout the evening, during dinner and afterward, Edward talked about the beastly customs men—common thieves who pillaged private property—and about travel arrangements, but still Edward made no mention of her and Indigo's detention. He expressed no regret, nor did he express any gratitude for the sizable bond which Laura pledged on his behalf.

He must be suffering shock from the ordeal, Hattie thought; he really wasn't himself. Even his appearance seemed changed, though she could not say exactly how. He did not look directly at her but at a point beside her as if he were watching for something. His tone of voice had an uncharacteristic edge of bitterness as he blamed the Plant Industry Bureau and the Department of Agriculture. He had already sent cablegrams to Lowe & Company and to the company attorney, Mr. Grabb.

As Hattie listened a sinking feeling began to overtake her; he had been following a clandestine plan all along. She and the child were his dupes— his decoys! She watched him babble on without bothering to listen. Poor Edward, what a desperate creature you are, she thought. At last she shook her head; tears filled her eyes.

"Please," she said, "don't say any more."

Later, after the lights were out, they lay awake side by side in the bed, careful not to touch each other, and talked in low voices so the child did not awaken. The marriage was over, she said. He gave a loud sigh, but did not reply. That was a sigh of relief, she thought angrily, but had to admit she felt a great deal of relief herself. Still, she cried when she recalled their engagement and the high hopes they'd both had; he patted her hand gently to comfort her. The marriage was doomed from the start, and they both shared the blame.

As the ship was towed away from the pier in Livorno, Indigo held up the cage so Rainbow could say good-bye to Italy. The color of the sea before sundown was so lovely—as clear and blue as the topaz of Laura's ring. She would miss this color of blue—there was none like it anywhere in California or Arizona.

Part Eight

AT FIRST she had difficulty understanding the language her baby spoke to her from the womb, but then she recognized the Sand Lizard words pronounced in baby talk. She had not heard the Sand Lizard language spoken for a long time, except in dreams. To hear the baby, Sister Salt had to wait until early morning before dawn, after the night shift quit but before the day crews started. She lay as still as she could, holding her breath, and if the baby was awake and turning restlessly, then she could hear it talk—how its voice reached her ears was a mystery. She did not tell Maytha or Vedna because they were likely to blame the voice on witches.

Sister Salt talked to the baby whenever it kicked and moved inside her; she told the little Sand Lizard about their home and the gardens in the dunes where she and Indigo used to play games. There it was peaceful at night with no drunks or fights to send men falling against the tents. She could feel her baby's impatience grow more urgent.

The baby did not like the noise and the dust. The place was not safe. No place is safe, she told the baby. The baby wanted her to leave at once for the old gardens. How could she leave without Indigo? Indigo was still a child.

"But she is not your baby like I am. You don't breathe for her. You breathe for me!"

Most days he was so busy, Candy did not come to her tent until after midnight, and even then he was only taking a break—the gambling tents were full of players, and sales of beer and barbecued meat were nonstop. She did not see as much of Maytha and Vedna after she quit the laundry. The pregnancy caused her to sleep more, and the twins got busier as more workers arrived to finish the dam. Maytha and Vedna knew Sister Salt wanted company, but usually by the time they bathed in the laundry tent after work (to take advantage of the clean warm water), their "dates" arrived before they had a chance to visit her.

Sundays were days of rest—not because Maytha or Vedna were Christians but because preachers and missionaries descended on the construction camp for Sunday services and scared off their dates. So the three of them decided Sundays would be their day together; after they ate, they talked and laughed as they took turns combing and braiding new satin ribbons into their hair. They were best friends now, and the twins teased each other saying they wished Sister Salt were their twin, not the other.

The camp was a dump, Maytha said, and Vedna and Sister Salt had to agree with her; all the noise and dust drifted to their tents. They were getting tired of sex along the river week after week with the same sweaty workers who never changed what they did; sex with these men was boring and tedious. Luckily the twins had saved almost enough money to retire forever before they died of boredom here.

"It's so bad Vedna's started to read the Bible! All the sexy parts in the Old Testament!" The three of them laughed together. Vedna reminded them about the weird stories too—those were even better than the sex. Chariots of fire! Beasts with seven heads!

The Bible was the only book Vedna could find to practice her reading. They had gone to school and learned to read when they lived in Winslow with their father. Their Chemehuevi clanspeople were troubled because their father wasn't Chemehuevi; he had been from Laguna Pueblo, working on the railroad, and was already married with children when he met their mother. Still, he took them in after their mother died, but kept them away from Laguna in Winslow. Their father was killed in a railroad accident when they were thirteen, old enough to go back to their mother's people on their own. Only one old auntie, their grandmother's sister, welcomed them inside, and poor thing, she didn't have much—a tiny stone house on the dry floodplain of tumbleweeds and river gravel south of Needles. The government took away her farmland on the river to lease out to white men. Maytha and Vedna liked to say they had only two living relatives in Arizona—their old auntie and Sister Salt!

Later Sister had to lie down because her back ached from the baby's constant turning. Candy looked in on her and was concerned about her discomfort; he didn't want anything to harm his first child! His huge hands gently closed around both of her hands, and he kissed the top of her head. He was sorry he was so busy; he could see something was wrong. Nothing was wrong; she was only listening to the baby. Candy exhaled and glanced down at her belly; he had to take Wylie the evening receipts. He wanted to know how the baby could talk, how she could hear it when it was so tiny, but questions would have to wait until he got back.

Wylie was waiting at his counting table in his tent; when he saw Candy at the door, he mopped the sweat from his face and adjusted the lantern to give off more light. Wylie had finished off the pumpkin pie Candy baked the day before; the pie pan and a fork and a few crumbs were pushed to one side. The night was hot without a breeze, and Wylie wore only a night-shirt, which barely covered his private parts; Candy glanced into the ad-joining tent where Wylie slept but didn't see any women in his bed.

Wylie kept two sawed-off shotguns on the tent floor by his feet at all times; he rode his big walking horse with the shotguns in scabbards within easy reach. Candy watched him practice firing both guns from the hip at once; the stack of two-by-fours were blown into sawdust and sticks. The job of the site superintendent was to keep the contractors in line and keep the locals out of the way. Friction was bound to develop; the locals and their politicians sorely resented outsiders and federal projects, though they wanted the dams and levees.

Wylie first hired Big Candy to cook for him on a river dredging project in Mississippi. There the locals pulled out survey stakes and the mules had to be guarded around the clock or they'd be blinded or crippled.

After he counted and recounted Candy's receipts and counted out his share, Wylie liked to open a fresh bottle of brandy and talk. Candy's job was to listen and to keep a fresh pot of coffee brewed for the brandy. Wylie was generous with his brandy, and some nights, even with the black coffee, Candy caught himself falling asleep. If he noticed, Wylie never com-plained; he was a strange one all right. But he took to Candy's cooking at once, and claimed he could detect whether someone was trustworthy after the person had cooked him one meal. Before he hired Candy, he said, he had four good cooks in his life: the cook who was with his parents for sixty years, and three others who cooked for him one after the other. It was an-noying that each cook lasted only five years, but not surprising because of the amount of liquor they drank. Why were the best cooks such drunks?

Candy shook his head; he wasn't a drinker—he preferred to keep busy, making money. Not by stealing the boss's money—Candy laughed at his own joke.

"Let me cook you a meal so you can decide."

Wylie gave him the run of his tent kitchen and supplies, but they were miles up the Mississippi River in the middle of nowhere. It had been quite a test of his cooking skills, all right. What did Candy do? He went walking with a shotgun and a knapsack and two hours later returned with all he needed except for brown sugar, cream, and butter, which Wylie, at great expense, kept on hand. Wylie ate the baked pheasant basted in raspberry preserves, the baby peas in butter cream sauce, and told Candy he was hired even before he tasted the thick cream custard sprinkled with caramelized sugar.

How that white man could eat so much and never get fat! Must have been something wrong inside Wylie for him to eat all the time and stay skinny. Candy began to try to fatten him up—it was a challenge; but over the years Wylie never gained a pound. Candy wanted to keep the boss healthy because he paid Candy so well, but more important, he understood fine cooking and showed great appreciation for Candy's cooking no matter what new concoctions Candy devised.

Until the wee hours of the morning and sometimes until dawn, Wylie did the talking. Generally he talked about food and cooking, and his recollection of the hundred best meals he ever ate. Candy was proud that high on Wylie's best hundred list were meals cooked by him: deep-fried clam croquettes, venison filets marinated in wild cranberry sauce, baked catfish in wild plums.

Candy thought maybe all the food Wylie ate was the reason Wylie didn't need more than four hours' sleep a night. Candy liked to sleep more than that and returned to his own tent for a few hours before he had to cook breakfast for Wylie. Over the years, they had developed an arrangement that gave Candy the business opportunities that someday would finance his own hotel and restaurant in Denver. At the rate they were clearing profits here, they'd both be able to retire after this job, although the big profits brought troubles of their own. Prescott and Needles businessmen who wanted to make money off the construction workers too were angered at the fees charged by Wylie to permit the wagonloads of whiskey and women onto the project site.

Tonight something was up; in addition to the two sawed-off shotguns, Candy saw twelve-gauge shotguns propped in each corner of the tent. Tonight the boss didn't talk about recipes; there was trouble between the state of California and the Arizona Territory over the diversion of the river to Los Angeles. Arizona farmers below the dam site were outraged to see water diverted to farms in California, and gathered in Yuma to burn down the federal courthouse. Rumors had the California state militia on alert, and the Arizona territorial militia preparing for a possible engagement with the California troops on their borderline, which was the Colorado River. Of course, Wylie knew it was all politics and money; lately he didn't trust his two white bodyguards; to be rid of them, he sent them to guard the construction equipment day and night.

Candy never thought those bodyguards were worth a damn anyway. What Wylie needed were some good dogs. Bodyguards could be bribed and bought off; good dogs would lay down their lives. Dogs could sniff out assassins and these Arizona bushwhackers a mile away. He didn't want anything to happen to Wylie. Candy wrote "dogs" on the top of his list of items to get the next time he went to Yuma.

Big Candy had never been friends with a white man before—only Indians and Mexicans and a few Asians. But he liked Wylie at once as he watched him eat the first meal Candy cooked for him. He liked the way Wylie's eyes widened when he saw a special dish or dessert on the table; out here in the middle of nowhere, Candy was hard pressed to find even the most basic ingredients, but on other job sites in populated areas Candy took pride in finding local delicacies—fresh berries, mushrooms, or fresh oysters or clams. In hot weather Candy packed blocks of ice in sawdust under layers of damp burlap to surprise Wylie with thick sweet cream for butter and ice cream. For fifteen years now, they'd worked together, and their happiest times were the special meals—succulent rich delicacies Candy served him at the remote locations, construction sites miles from civilization, as they were here. So far here, Candy surprised Wylie with ice cream in June—he later joked it took a one-ton wagon of ice blocks from Prescott to make one big bowl of lemon ice cream. The lemons were off trees in Yuma, and the heavy sweet cream was from a Mormon farmer in Needles.

To show his continued appreciation for Candy's cooking, Wylie didn't hesitate to let Candy make beer and run dice games and cards on the side; now they both were ready to retire after this project. Wylie was going to Long Beach to live a gentleman's life and he wanted Candy to come along—he only had to cook one fancy meal a week, and he could bring the Indian girl; Wylie didn't care as long as Candy was there to cook.

Candy only smiled and shook his head; before he went to Denver, he'd come to Los Angeles to help Wylie find a cook far better than he was. Candy's dream was to own a hotel and restaurant in Denver near the Rocky Mountains, which he'd only seen in paintings and photographs.

As soon as it was daylight, Wylie wanted Candy to find a hiding place—somewhere down along the riverbank—and rebury the floor safe. If there was trouble, the first place looters would look was under the floor of the tent. Wylie wouldn't put any deed past the Prescott businessmen or the army, and Candy had to agree; during Candy's hitch with the army he had seen drunken troops turn to looters while their officers looked on.

Wylie was philosophical about the changes: they'd done very well here and already had the money they needed to retire. If the state militias clashed at the dam site and the army got involved, Wylie would continue to oversee the actual construction, but his control over the premises and his licenses to conduct business would be taken over by the military. After that, the outlook for Candy's casino and brewery was not good; the military men were bound to favor the Arizona businessman with political connections in Washington.

Candy told Sister Salt one evening after he cooked eggs and bacon for her they might not be here on the river for as long he first thought. He told her what Wylie said about the water feud and the troops taking over. He wanted to make their baby strong and happy, and though they did not discuss it, he knew their baby complained about the place and the food. Once the troops took over, he and she would go straight to California to the Indian school in Riverside and track down her little sister that way. Otherwise, they might wait in Parker forever before any letters ever came back from Washington.

Sister Salt was lying down that evening when Maytha and Vedna surprised her; they had big grins on their faces because they'd just counted it all up and realized they'd made all the money they needed to buy land. Very soon they'd leave this noisy dump for good! They invited her to come with them—they weren't going right away—in a month or two. Think about it. After they went back to their tent, her eyes filled with tears.

I am the only one who will wait for you, dear little Indigo, she whispered that night before she went to sleep. Now both the baby and its father wanted to leave, and the twins were going too!

In mid-July the rains came and the weather began to cool off. Rumors flew around the construction site, but there were no signs of the state militia or the federal troops. Cooler weather made Sister Salt restless; she began to dream about the old gardens, where Mama and Indigo were planting red amaranth and speckled yellow beans.

The baby was big enough to be seen in her belly, so she only had sex with Big Candy now; otherwise the baby's features might resemble other men's. The cloth of her smock shifted just a bit as the baby kicked and turned; the baby wanted her to eat Sand Lizard food, not all this animal grease and cooked food. Big Candy wanted a big strong son and insisted she eat plenty of meat, and each night he brought back big platters of leftovers—beef rib roasts and stuffed pork loins and bowls piled high with orange yams and stewed okra. But now the odor of meat and its grease made her nauseous; she ate the okra and yams but pushed the meat aside.

Why should I talk to you when you don't feed me the food I need? The baby turned and turned but didn't speak again; the baby worried her and she decided to confide in Maytha and Vedna. But when she went by the laundry, the washtubs were turned upside down and the fires were out, and the twins were nowhere to be found. They must have found a ride going north and went to visit their old auntie, who was ailing.

She wished she'd gone with them; now they joked all the time about escaping that place; the earth of the dam towered above them in a sinister hump, they all agreed. The trampled earth of the dam site looked all the same, just as each day's work around Big Candy's casino tent and brewery took on a sameness. The construction workers who preferred to drink beer and gamble at Big Candy's down along the river became regular customers. The men made the same remarks each time they saw Sister Salt— why had she stopped taking them to the willows to roll around on the sand? Why didn't she come inside the casino tent to bring them luck with the dice? She learned to avoid the casino tent and so did Maytha and Vedna because the drunk gamblers who lost often turned nasty and blamed the women for spoiling their luck.

It wasn't too hot yet; a walk would do her good. She left behind the river for the sandy hills above to gather wild greens. The construction noises receded as she walked, so she kept going until she no longer heard anything but the wind and the meadowlarks in the rice grass. She had not planned to walk so far without her gourd canteen, but her legs kept going, and the farther she went the better she felt; even the baby stopped turning so much.

A distance up a dry wash she found a coyote melon vine snaking through the rice grass and thistles. At the first sweet taste of melon, she was overwhelmed by memories of the sweet yellow melons they shared the last autumn they were all together. The salt of her tears made her cheeks itch. They had been so happy together that sunny afternoon a few months before the crows and then the dancers came. That last afternoon, the melon's sugar juice stuck their fingers together and they squealed with delight as they pulled them apart.

She ate one melon and then another like a starving person until her hands and even strands of her hair were sticky; her stomach felt too full and unsettled. She sat with her arms across her belly protectively and waited for the cramp to pass. Grandma always warned them not to eat too much too fast! The baby must like this Sand Lizard food because it didn't complain. She lay back on the fine sand to take a rest. The sky here was pure endless turquoise, and the air here smelled so clean, unmarred by the dust and smoke of the construction. The sun was moving lower in the sky but she didn't want to turn back yet.

What else was there growing wild in this sandy wash, ready to eat? She walked a distance farther up the wash and sure enough she found a stand of sunflowers, many still in bloom but others gone to seed. Her stomach felt uncomfortably full but at the same time she felt so hungry she crammed handfuls of dry seeds into her mouth, hulls and all. Ummmm! The flavor in her mouth was so rich and delightful she swallowed despite how full her stomach felt. She couldn't spit them out and waste them!

A short distance beyond the sunflowers she spotted the bright red fruit of a chile pepper plant; once someone must have had a garden here, and a few seeds replanted themselves just as they did at the old gardens. Oh how she wished she were there!

She ate the sweet hot peppers one after the other, as if they might take her home if she ate enough of them. The heat of the peppers in her stomach eased the odd heaviness she felt; she knew she really should start back to the river before it got any hotter than it was. But all the food in her stomach made her feel heavy and sleepy; the heat was already strong, so she decided to take a nap in the shade of a big boulder and start back when the sun went down and it cooled off.

She slept longer than she intended; the shadows were already long and the sun about to set. If she wasn't back by dark, Big Candy and the twins might worry. She walked only the distance back down the wash, past the melon plant, when another cramp tightened around her belly and back until she knelt in the sand, doubled over from the pain.

She thought it was only diarrhea until she saw the gouts of dark blood glisten on the sand between her feet. How strange that the blood's color was identical to the dark red edge of the sky at sundown. All this blood! How much more blood did she have before she died, and the baby died too? She crawled to clean sand and lay on her side with her knees drawn to her belly; the blood felt warm and thick between her thighs and then it happened: she could not stop her body from contracting and pushed to relieve herself, then realized something else had happened, some part of herself had been expelled. She could feel it pulsate but it beat faster than her heartbeat and she knew it was the baby Sand Lizard, born too soon.

Twilight was fading into darkness as she gathered up the wet bundle still connected to her own body. She smelled blood as she cradled the dark sticky mass in her arms before she bit through the cord that connected them. He was a tiny shrunken old man who refused to stop sucking his own hand long enough to open his eyes. She tore her skirt and gently wrapped him, not too tightly, around and around until she'd made a cocoon with only a small opening above his face to keep him warm. She was still bleeding, and the cramping did not stop, and she thought, My Sand Lizard grandfather has come to take me home.

The sand remained warm after darkness came, and she curled around the little black grandfather, who preferred his own fist to the nipples of her breasts. She did not lose consciousness, but she was so weak she felt the pull of the earth bring her to the ground, and she thought, So this is how we return to Mother Earth. She was happy to return because she missed Grandma Fleet so much.

Toward morning the desert cooled off and she woke shivering in the darkness; the stars were bigger and brighter late at night when they thought no one was watching them. She looked overhead; the stars were closer and bigger now; how they flashed in arcs traveling from place to place. Though she shivered, still she took care not to move her arms or shift the bundle in her arms; she did not look down because she did not want to know if he was alive or dead. Was the bundle warm, or cold? It was so small she couldn't be sure; carefully she pushed herself deeper into layers of sand that were still warm. Oh how soothing the warm sand was on her belly and the base of her spine! How sweet sleep was—let me sleep forever.

At dawn she woke to a black dog gently licking her face. If the dog's motion had not been so gentle and slow, she might have feared an attack. The bundle was secure in any case because she slept curled around it to keep it warm. During the night she woke but could not be sure if he moved or if she had only dreamed he moved. She was still bleeding, though much less than the night before; the afterbirth was in the sand nearby, untouched by the dog. A good sign. The dog had a fat stomach, but seemed crippled; it hobbled backward wagging its tail as she raised up. Did something move in the bundle? She still couldn't bring herself to look. Too bad she hadn't brought a canteen, because she was really thirsty. She wondered if Big Candy came to her tent last night and was looking for her. Maytha and Vedna probably wouldn't get back from Needles until tomorrow.

The dog stood a short distance away watching her face and the bundle in her arms curiously. When they lived in Needles, she and Indigo used to beg for a puppy, but Grandma Fleet said dogs eat too much meat.

Now the sun rose above the horizon but with a partial mask of thin clouds. Her left arm was stiff from holding the bundle and she tried to shift it a bit without disturbing it—if she bumped it and it didn't move, then she'd know he was dead. Just then she was aware of a strange sensation—an odd tingling—and when she touched herself with her right hand, her breasts were swollen and leaked warm milk through the cloth of her blouse. The dog's ears pricked up at the bundle, and when she first looked down, she thought she saw a spider, then she realized it was a tiny black hand reaching out of the bundle.

He was still alive! Now she had to look, but she dreaded to see the poor little thing breathe his last. Yes, she whispered to him, it was her fault he was born too soon, for eating too much greasy white-colored food. She whispered to him as she gently pulled open the bundle to look. Now both little black hands were waving at her angrily and she laughed with relief at how briskly they punched the air. He smelled breast milk and wanted some right now. As she fumbled with her blouse to bring out a breast, he began a high-pitched cry sounding like a river heron; the longer it took for her to push back the cloth wrapped around him, the louder the heron's cries became. His little wrinkled face was contorted in anger—his eyes squeezed shut and mouth gulping like a fish; in her haste to get the breast and nipple to his mouth, milk squirted on his forehead and for an instant he stopped wiggling and opened his eyes in surprise and she saw he was a tough customer who wouldn't die anytime soon.

His mouth was so tiny her nipple filled it entirely but he did not choke or cough as he sucked ravenously. He gave out angry cries as she shifted him to the other breast, which was soaking them both in milk. She was so relieved he was alive she began to cry softly. His vigorous sucking stopped briefly, and she saw a black shining eye open for an instant to see what was wrong. "I'm just so happy," she said in Sand Lizard language. "I was afraid you were dead."

The black dog was lying close by, and watched patiently. Each time she felt his nursing diminish, she started to get up, but instantly he woke and began to suck so strongly she sank back down on the sand again. She man-

aged to scrape away enough sand with one foot to properly bury the afterbirth without disturbing him. Encouraged by that success with him in her
arms, she was able to urinate, then crawled a distance away to clean sand.
She was so thirsty. She'd never go for a walk without a canteen again—not
even in cool weather! Good thing she was only a few miles from the river.
For a moment she wondered why Big Candy didn't come looking for her—
maybe Wylie sent him to Prescott; the twins probably wouldn't get back
from Needles until the next day.

Finally she managed to stand up without disturbing him—he slept
with her nipple in his mouth—and she began to walk back down the sandy
wash the way she'd come. The black dog led the way, stopping from time
to time to look back to see if she was still coming. She had not gone far
when the dog suddenly stopped as it approached a bend in the arroyo. The
hair on the dog's back stood straight up and Sister Salt froze in her tracks;
but then the dog's tail began to wag wildly and it gave a bark and ran fast
on its crooked legs around the bend in the wash.

"There you are!" a woman's voice shouted in Spanish, and before Sister
Salt could decide whether to hide or not, a strange sight met her; around
the corner came a small dark woman surrounded by a pack of black dogs.
The woman seemed as shocked to see her as she was; for an instant Sister
Salt thought the dog woman was about to turn and run.

All the dogs began to bark but the woman shushed them; they obeyed
at once and sank to their bellies; it was then Sister Salt noticed each of the
other dogs wore a burlap pack over its shoulders and back. "They won't
harm you," the woman said in Spanish, but when Sister Salt didn't reply,
the woman repeated the words in English. Sister Salt nodded but didn't
move; she felt him let go of her nipple and begin to squirm in his bundle;
he wanted the other breast.

The woman watched as she shifted him to the other side. She wasn't
much older than herself. The woman looked at the torn bloody skirt, then
at the bundle in Sister Salt's arms, and she looked around to see if there was
anyone else.

"Do you need help?" the woman asked in English. Sister Salt got a good
look at her then and saw a dark purple scar from the middle of her forehead
down the bridge of her nose to her chin.

"Please, some water," Sister Salt answered. The woman turned to the
dogs, who wagged their tails but obediently remained on their bellies.
From the nearest dog's pack she took out a plump canvas water bag that
felt deliciously damp and cool in Sister Salt's hands; water never tasted so

good! She could have made it back to the river without water, but that might have also caused her milk to dry up, and she didn't want to take that risk.

While Sister Salt drank, the woman gazed around them with vigilance, but more than once the woman looked back toward the south, the direction she'd come from. The woman offered to hold the bundle while she washed up, but Sister Salt declined. The little black grandfather would be furious if she disturbed his nest between her breasts to hand him over to a stranger.

In Yuma, the dog woman heard about a wagon town booming upriver at the new dam, so she brought her dog circus to make some money. Sister Salt nodded. Yes, money was waiting up there for entertainment. The workers would flock to see something new for a change.

She introduced herself as Delena, but just the way she said the name told Sister Salt it was not her real name. Delena asked if she lived there, and Sister nodded. For the first time since the baby was born, she began to take stock of her situation. She could see the dust cloud in the distance above the construction site. Her feelings were hurt because Big Candy didn't come looking for her. Even if he was really busy, he should have at least sent Juanito out to search for her this morning. If Big Candy didn't care enough to start a search, she wasn't sure if she should bother to go back.

Maybe she should ask the dog woman for a water bag and start back to the old gardens now. Even before he was born, the little black grandfather hated the construction noise. He might never tolerate the noise now, and all night the drunks and gamblers laughed and cursed around the tents. She'd have to move her tent downriver away from the noise. She had a difficult time deciding what to do; he watched her from inside his cocoon. His eyes said, "You don't want to go back there," but she pretended not to understand.

Rain clouds from the northwest pushed into the sky, and the air felt cooler. The dogs fanned out and trotted ahead of them as they walked along; now and then one of them caught a scent, and they all bolted off yipping and barking, but the lame dog never left the woman's side.

Sister Salt had walked farther than she realized the day before. They had walked for a long time, and only now could the ugly hump of the dam be seen off in the distance, rising toward the sky. Whenever Sister Salt needed to rest, they stopped; invariably the woman looked back toward the south as if someone was following her. As long as they spoke in soft tones, the little grandfather slept; otherwise he screeched like a heron if they talked.

Sister Salt was curious about the contents of the packs the dogs wore. Delena explained each dog had to carry its own water and food, and its circus costume. She was curious to know what happened to the dog's legs; a dog might hurt one or two legs, or in a dog fight, injure three; but this dog's legs all had been badly broken. Sister was curious to know about the long dark scar down her face, but she was too polite to ask.

Sister Salt took her time walking, partly because it was hot and she felt a little weak, but also to see how long she had to be missing before Big Candy noticed and sent searchers. They stopped a number of times to drink water, then to eat the last of the mutton jerky Delena bought in Yuma. How did she keep the dogs from going after the jerky in their packs? Good training, Delena said. Discipline is everything in an army—or a dog circus, she quickly added. The dogs hunted ahead of them and filled themselves with mice swallowed in one gulp; the occasional rabbits they caught caused all the dogs to fight until Delena stepped in to command them to stop. They weren't upset with one another afterward; they seemed to enjoy fighting as a game. Although they were not big dogs, their strength and savagery with one another impressed Sister Salt; one dog must have nearly the strength of a man.

They had almost reached the river when the dogs stopped, their ears and tails up in alert: immediately both women dropped to their knees. The jolt caused the little grandfather to stiffen with anger but he didn't cry out. Someone was up ahead on the wagon road; they could hear the hum of voices and the jingle and clink of bits and steel-shod hooves. A number of horsemen were riding north; the cottonwood trees and river brush blocked them from sight. Whoever they were, they were headed for the dam too.

Sister sat down while Delena and the dogs went to look at the tracks in the wagon road. She looked worried when she returned; soldiers—she could tell by the tracks and manure the horses were in military formation. Soldiers. The little grandfather twisted and kicked in his bundle; he didn't like to be wet, but if she tore up any more of her skirt or blouse, she'd be naked. Her promise of a nice warm bath as soon as they got home seemed to quiet him.

They avoided the wagon road by following the old path that wove through the tamarisk and willows on the riverbank. From time to time the dogs splashed and played in the shallow water; Sister felt her excitement grow as she anticipated Big Candy's reaction to the baby. She didn't show the baby to the dog woman so Big Candy could be the first to see his son. The closer they came to the construction site, the more the little grandfather twisted and turned in his bundle. Off in the distance to the southwest, Sister heard the rumble of thunder and smelled the approach of rain. At the sight of the tents, Delena called her dogs to her; she wanted to stay with them down the river a bit, where they wouldn't be in the way. Despite the gathering storm, Sister didn't press her to come stay at the tent because that many dogs might go after the meat in Candy's barbecue pit or stampede the mule teams that pulled the earthmoving machines. As they parted, Sister thanked the dog woman again for the water, and promised to come visit soon.

Business was booming as she reached the camp; horses she'd not seen before were tied to the willows and tamarisks all around the casino tent; there were workers, their faces streaked with grime, arms full of dirty clothes, lined up outside the laundry tent for warm baths. No more bottles of beer—Juanito dipped it straight from the barrel into the workers' lunch pails. Soldiers in uniforms lined up with workers just off the day shift; overnight the number of customers for gambling and beer seemed to have doubled.

Big Candy smiled and nodded when he saw her but he was striding in his very-busy-in-a-hurry walk, both hands full with decks of cards and the casino strongbox. He didn't seem to notice the bundle in her arms, so she called out for him to come see, but he disappeared under the flap of the casino tent. In the line that formed outside the casino, the men who rolled dice on the sand while they waited stared at her curiously as she began to cry. The little black grandfather peered up at her intently from his cloth cocoon as she wiped at the tears with the back of her hand. She could tell he did not approve of his father's bad manners.

The old Mojave woman gave her a pail of clean warm water out of the back of the laundry tent without any questions. Carefully she unwrapped him on her blankets in the tent and gently wiped him down and dried him with part of a clean sheet she tore up for diapers. The thunder cracked and shook the ground, and raindrops clattered against the tent while the wind pulled at the canvas and rattled the cottonwood branches and leaves above them. "Good for you," she told him. "Your rain cloud ancestors came to greet you." If not properly welcomed, a baby that tiny might give up on this world and leave.

The rain came in gusts that slapped and sagged the tent roof; she pulled the blankets snuggly around them and listened to the creak and groan of the old cottonwood in the wind. Lightning flashed the inside of the tent and shook the ground, but as long as the little grandfather nursed contently, she was not afraid.

She left a lantern burning for Big Candy, but it was out of oil by the time he came to her tent. The wind and lightning had passed but it was still raining steadily. Big Candy shook off his hat and rain slicker—she felt some of the cold droplets on her face but said nothing. He fumbled to light the other lantern on the table, and put down the money sacks; they made heavy sounds on the table.

"Business was booming," he'd say if she were up now. Why didn't she get up then and show him her surprise? No, if he hadn't noticed something different by now, then she wanted to see just how long it took him to notice something was different.

He went out again to get the beer and roast meat he liked to eat while he counted the money. The rich odors of the meat and beer made her stomach growl with hunger, but she did not get up. She listened to him chew and swallow to the jingle and clink of the coins he counted. He taught her gold pieces jingle but silver only clinks. Tears came to her eyes as she remembered his delight in teaching her these things before he got so busy.

"There's plenty of meat here," he said, but she pretended to sleep. Finally he got up and stood over her.

"What's wrong? I thought you went to Needles with the twins."

The sound of his father's voice right above woke the little black grandfather with a start; he pulled his head away from her breast and twisted inside his cocoon as he gave out a loud cry.

"What have you got there?" Big Candy demanded as he knelt down next to her. He thought it sounded like a cat or bird, and at first couldn't see what it was because the baby was so tiny.

"Ohhh," he said in amazement before his expression shifted into concern.

"It's so small."

"He—he's a boy."

"He looks too tiny to live," Big Candy said in a sad voice.

"Don't talk like that to him!" Sister Salt said in low, fierce tones. She wanted to say talk like that could kill tiny babies, but Candy looked so sad she kept quiet. He didn't know the first thing about Sand Lizard babies. His ignorance was more apparent when he asked her to unwrap him so he could get a better look. She pulled the bundle closer and arched her body over it as she shook her head. Later on when she gave him clean dry wrappings, Candy could see him; right now it was important to keep him warm so he could sleep.

Big Candy sat down at the table again; the beat of the rain against the tent was not as heavy now. He sat in silence and he didn't touch the money. He hadn't realized how much he wanted the child until he saw the baby was too tiny to live. He'd seen babies born too soon when he was a child—born to the housemaids, who brought them to the big kitchen to keep warm. He watched his mother help the women try to save babies born too soon—pitiful little things with legs and arms like sticks; they gasped like fish out of water for a day or two, then lay still. He had not thought about them for years, but now the tears sprang into his eyes and he choked up as he had each time the babies died. Poor girl! She doesn't know any better—she thinks this baby will live. He rubbed at his eyes hard with his fist and cleared his throat. He didn't want to add to her hurt so he didn't tell her what he knew.

He'd be back soon; he just had to take the receipts to Wylie. What a mess in this rain! He pulled down the wide brim of his felt hat to better shed the rain, and turned up the collar of his denim work coat. If the rain kept up, the clayish mud would be knee deep and impossible for the machines and mules. Bad for the contractors, but good for beer sales and the casino, especially now the soldiers were in the area.

Wylie was still wary of the presence of the soldiers. For now they might be there to discourage sabotage by disgruntled farmers downriver and slowdowns by workers demanding shorter hours; but the boss had information from his contacts in Prescott his enemies meant to put an end to his strict control of the gambling and beer at the construction camp. Wiley was already through a fifth of whiskey when Candy got there. He grinned when he saw the money sacks Candy put on the table were too full to tie shut.

"They might close us down next week," Wylie said with a grin. "By God we'll make money hand over fist until they do!" He wasn't worried. It was his job to control access to the job site to keep the work going smoothly—to keep the peace between the general contractor and all the subcontractors and their workers. He had to watch the federal inspectors who came from time to time, to make sure they didn't become too cozy with the contractors.

The Prescott businessmen had the hard liquor and the prostitutes in their wagon town within walking distance. Wylie didn't stop them from running dice and card games outside the construction zone; if the men didn't want to walk that far after work and preferred Big Candy's barbecue, beer, and the casino tents along the river, well, that wasn't Wylie's fault. The construction zone and workers' camp had to be kept in an orderly manner to prevent labor agitators and other safety risks. The only big complainers, beside the Prescott and Yuma businessmen, were the traveling preachers, who waved Bibles over their heads and condemned him to hell because he refused them access to the construction zone too. The wagon town suited the prostitutes, but the preachers wanted to reach the workers before they squandered their pay on beer and dice, or went to the women in the wagons.

Wylie barred the preachers on the grounds they might be labor agitators. Look at the uproar the preachers caused as soon as they arrived and went after the businessmen with the wagons of women. Wylie figured as long as the preachers and Prescott merchants quarreled with each other, he and Big Candy had nothing to worry about. Time and again, Wylie had watched the two forces squabble at the federal job sites he'd superintended. One of these days, Congress might get around to changing the law that gave the site superintendent such authority at government project sites. Wiley wasn't concerned; he and Big Candy would be long gone by then.

Wylie wanted to retire by the sea in southern California, where it was warm; Long Beach suited him just fine. They'd done so well as business partners over the years, Wylie was reluctant to part with Big Candy. He tried to persuade Big Candy the weather in Denver was too cold and Negroes weren't welcome, even if they had money. Now, in southern California they welcomed a man with money, whatever his skin color. Candy wanted a hotel and restaurant, but why not in Los Angeles? Big Candy was a Louisiana man; he'd hate the Denver winters. But Candy wanted to live near big mountains; Louisiana didn't have big mountains, and neither did Los Angeles.

Despite the impressive receipts, Big Candy seemed subdued; Wylie asked if there had been trouble with a drunk in the casino the night before. Just from the way Candy shook his head, Wylie knew it was woman trouble. He poured them both another glass of brandy; how could that girl of a squaw make trouble for an ex–army Indian fighter like Candy? he wanted to know. Candy sipped the brandy and shook his head. The girl had a little baby—his baby—but it was born too soon and sure to die.

Wylie shook his head, then downed the brandy and poured more. The constant moving from job site to job site barred a man from a family; Wylie was glad of it—but he could see sometimes Big Candy was lonely.

Wylie patted Candy on the back and poured him another brandy; he'd never known a man, white or colored, as honest as Big Candy. They never discussed how or why they got along—they had an understanding that developed effortlessly, at least Wylie thought so. He didn't presume to know what effort it took for a colored man to get along with a white man. Maybe Candy put in more effort than he let on; maybe that's why he kept talking about Denver. Wylie still hoped to talk Candy into southern California; that way he could eat Candy's cooking anytime he wanted. It was a shame about the infant, and he had nothing against the Indian girl, but Wylie was confident his friend could do much better for a wife in California.

Wylie knew how to cheer up Big Candy. He complimented him on the pork ribs that evening. Then he talked about steamed Pacific blue mussels in white wine and mushroom sauce he once ate in San Francisco. Candy's expression relaxed a bit and his eyes brightened.

"Scallops," Candy said. "I've been thinking about sea scallops poached in white wine." Candy knew this was Wylie's way to try to persuade him to go to Long Beach instead of Denver. Wylie remembered all of Candy's best dishes, and could describe each one in detail months, even years, later. Wylie's appreciation of fine cooking kept Candy inspired.

The rain brought the first relief from the heat in months, and the sticky, slippery red clay mud gave workers the vacation their bosses had refused. The soil was too wet to work and the workers celebrated their holiday with pails of beer and loud whoops and yells at the dice and cards. A little later there were gunshots followed by cheers. The little black grandfather stiffened and twisted around in his cocoon at the first loud sounds and refused to nurse. He was angry too because his own father believed he would die. Each day the baby lived would persuade Big Candy that he was wrong. You have to be patient with your father, she whispered to the little fists jabbing angrily from the bundle.

Big Candy was wet and muddy from reburying the safe when he came to look in on her and the baby. He brought her a plate heaped high with pork ribs, corn, beans, and potatoes and gravy. Maytha and Vedna still had not returned from Needles, which left him without enough help now that the workers had a holiday. He looked at her and then at the bundle in her arms and she knew he was thinking about asking her to take the baby and help Juanito sell beer. But he knew better; instead he asked when she thought the Chemehuevi sisters would come back. She shrugged her shoulders; the noise of the workers on holiday increased around them, and the little one began to cry angrily because his father did not speak to him. Just then one of the white men who dealt blackjack called out for Big Candy to come—a fight had broken out and they needed him!

She rocked him in her arms until he took her nipple again, and then she ate; she left the ribs for last, hoping that he'd fall asleep and not scold her for eating greasy food. The ribs were well roasted and lean—not much grease—and she was so hungry; as soon as his eyes closed she took a bite of the crisp meat along the edge of the rib. I have to eat meat of some kind, she whispered to him as his eyes opened; all the grease is cooked out of this. The little grandfather's shining black eyes watched each mouthful she took, but he kept quiet, distracted by the voices and shouts outside. The noise seemed to interest him now. She ate until she was full and still there were ribs left over on the big plate.

Now that the sun was up, the tent was getting warm inside. The coolness of the storm was giving way to the heat, though it wasn't as fierce as before. She unbundled him to give him a dry diaper; at first he gasped at being uncovered. His legs and arms kicked and waved, but he didn't cry. His little bottom was still skinny as an old man's, but she thought his legs and arms looked a little more plump. "Little black spider baby," she whispered to him, "let's go for a walk." She filled her gourd canteen and wrapped up the bones and the leftover ribs in old newspaper, tied with a string she wore over her shoulder, then gathered him up for a visit to the dog woman's camp.

The rain left the air humid and warm even in the deep shade of the tamarisk and willows along the riverbank. She didn't care; she was glad to get away. The little black grandfather fell asleep as soon as they got away from the commotion around the tents. Before long she could hear yips and barks in the distance—the dogs sounded excited. When she reached the sandy clearing under the big cottonwood trees, an amazing sight greeted her.

The black dogs were racing in a circle around the crippled dog, who stood with her tail wagging, giving them barks of encouragement. From time to time one of the racing dogs broke out of the circle to leap over the crippled dog's back without interrupting the rhythm of the speeding circle. Suddenly the circling dogs began to leapfrog over one another and there were collisions—dogs sprawled and piled up on one another, and instantly all the dogs, even the lame dog, began growling and fighting fiercely with one another. Though these were not large dogs, Sister Salt saw immediately how dangerous they were together; when they suddenly stopped and turned in her direction, sniffing the air, she felt her heart pound. The pork ribs! If they started to attack, she'd throw them the ribs.

Just then Delena called out in Spanish from the deep shade where she was sitting and the dogs ran to her. After they gathered around her, she stood up and called out to Sister it was safe to come. The little grandfather's eyes were open wide but he didn't make a sound. Delena ordered the dogs to lie down; they obeyed but their noses moved constantly, savoring the odor of the ribs.

Delena plumped up a burlap dog pack for Sister to sit on; spread all around on the smooth sand were the other burlap packs and on top of them, the dog costumes made of brightly colored scraps of shiny cloth, decorated with buttons of all sizes and acorn-size tin bells. What a delightful morning they had! While Delena finished the pork ribs, Sister nursed the baby until he was asleep; afterward Delena divided the bones and fed the dogs, keeping a distance between each bone pile to prevent dogfights. Then they settled back in the shade to talk. Delena was full of questions. She wanted to know about the construction site, about Sister Salt's tent, and about Big Candy.

It was good to be free of the school and the reservation at Parker; they earned good money doing the laundry and going with the workers. Delena's eyes widened at the mention of money. Sister Salt shrugged; so the dog woman was just like others: money, money was all she thought about. So Sister bragged about all the money she and the twins had made in little more than a year. They made enough money to buy a little piece of land from their old Chemehuevi auntie upriver. They made enough money they didn't have to come back to work ever unless they just felt like it. The longer Sister talked, the happier Delena became.

If money was what interested Delena, then she came to the right place because money was all anyone here ever thought of except for her. In the beginning even she was excited by the stacks of silver she earned; but she was tired of money, tired of the noise the boredom and the dust required to make money; tired of the worry money caused over thieves and floor safes buried in the sand. She had promised Big Candy never to mention the safe to anyone but somehow it just slipped out; the dog woman didn't seem to notice anyway. Candy would never find out—he was too busy making money; even if he did, she didn't care—he couldn't stop her! She enjoyed telling Delena everything she wanted to know.

Sister described the tents in the shade of the cottonwoods where the workers and now the off-duty soldiers lined up to play at one of the eight tables in two tents. Her husband, Big Candy, was partners with the site boss and all the money they made off the laundry, gambling, beer, and meat, Wylie and Big Candy split fifty-fifty.

Delena's dark eyes lit up when Sister Salt described the canvas money-bags Big Candy delivered to the boss every day before dawn. Yes, this was the right place! Her dog circus would do well here, she was sure of that. Sister noticed the long thin scar down her face seemed to redden while she spoke.

Sister was enjoying the conversation and she didn't want it to end.

"Now the safe's buried somewhere only Big Candy knows." She had the compulsion to mention the safe again, she didn't know why. The safe had all their money—Wylie's, Candy's, and hers too; only Maytha and Vedna took their money out to buy land.

Delena watched her adjust the baby's wrappings and casually asked what Big Candy thought of his baby. A lump made of anger and sadness pushed into Sister Salt's throat. She shook her head and did not look at Delena.

"He thinks the baby is too small and will die." She spoke in a loud whisper so the little grandfather couldn't hear. Delena leaned over her sewing and gently patted Sister Salt's hand.

The humid heat and all the answers to Delena's questions left Sister Salt feeling drowsy, so she stretched out on the sand alongside the sleeping baby while Delena sewed satin ruffles. She did the talking now as she patiently threaded the needle; the dogs liked to tear off one another's costumes during their performance, she said, and at this Sister laughed with her eyes closed. Audiences were excited by the spectacle of torn satin ruffles and little bells ripped off; they roared with laughter as the dogs pulled off their lions' manes and tails of unraveled burlap, so she did not stop them but made it part of every show. Now that the pups had learned their routines, it was the repair of the costumes that required the most work.

Sister Salt had as many questions to ask as Delena had, but she was too sleepy. She wanted to know where Delena came from and what made that scar down the middle of her face. She wanted to know if Delena had children or any family or a husband somewhere. As she fell asleep she wondered where Indigo was, what she was doing at that moment, and Sister dreamed she was back at the old gardens; the apricot seedlings by Grandma Fleet's grave had grown taller than she was and their branches were heavy with ripe fruit. The little black grandfather was no larger than he was now, but toddling, then crawling in the sand under the tree. From the direction of the sandstone cave and the spring, she heard voices,

Grandma Fleet laughing and Mama and Indigo joining in. Oh how happy she was in that dream! They were so happy to see her they hugged her close, and they were delighted with the baby, who hid his face in her skirts and giggled each time Grandma Fleet tried to pick him up.

When she woke, the dog costumes and the needle and thread were put away; in their place, Delena had spread a square of red silk. In the center of the silk she was carefully arranging cards—not poker cards but cards with parts of pictures that made no sense. She checked on the baby, who slept peacefully, then watched Delena turn over the cards one by one. Now it was Sister Salt's turn to ask questions about where Delena came from.

She glanced toward the south before she replied she came from a war in the south. Yes, Sister Salt knew about war. War was the morning the soldiers and Indian police descended on them and the other dancers to arrest the Messiah and his family. Delena looked up from the cards. In Mexico the soldiers killed everyone—even women and children; that's why the people had to defend themselves.

Sister nodded. War explained the scar down her face; war answered the question of whether she had any family. What confused Sister Salt was why the Messiah didn't stop the killers. The Messiah told the people here not to take up weapons but to dance until the great storm winds of heaven scoured the earth of killers. She did not like to admit she was beginning to have some doubts about the Messiah's promises. Delena said they were lucky to have the storm winds do the work for them; in the south they had to do the fighting themselves.

Delena kept turning the cards. In the south everyone would be dead unless they defended themselves—Nuestra Señora de Guadalupe appeared not long ago and told them to go buy good rifles across the border in the United States.

Sister Salt's eyes widened. This was the first news she had of the Messiah's Mother. How long ago? This past January. Of course, Sister thought, during the cold weather. But where were the Messiah and the others? Sister Salt was disappointed she still didn't know where Mama was, and now this stranger told her they were seen in the mountains of Mexico. She wanted to like Delena, but some of the things she said were a little difficult to believe.

They sat awhile in silence, though off in the distance the sounds of laughter and gunshots drifted downriver. Sister asked what she was doing with the cards.

Delena shook her head as if she could not talk right then; she kept her eyes on the cards, shifting them around in their places until some of them formed complete pictures. Sister Salt watched quietly for a while, but finally she asked how did the cards know anything—they were just pieces of paper.

These are Gypsy cards, Delena explained; the pieces of cardboard were specially blessed before they were painted, and the figures and colors and marks on them attracted certain powers or beings. These cards belonged to the kind woman who raised her. Sister Salt looked hard at the deck after she said this, but could see no sign of any spirit presence.

"They'll answer questions and give warnings if you know how to read them."

Gypsy cards! Gypsies! Sister Salt remembered when they lived in Needles how the news of Gypsy wagons approaching excited the town. Storekeepers locked their doors in the middle of the day because the Gypsies came in groups, always friendly and smiling, and tried to sell charms and trinkets to the storekeepers while their companions picked up merchandise, admired it, and asked questions all at once to confuse the store clerks while they walked out with items and food hidden in their shirts and under their skirts. Grandma Fleet said they didn't hurt anyone—they only went after storekeepers who had plenty anyway—but some of the Mojaves feared Gypsy witchcraft.

"You don't look like a Gypsy," Sister Salt said, and Delena smiled. "I'm Yaqui," she said, "but the Gypsies found me and took me in after my family was killed; that's how I learned about cards." She ran a finger down the thin scar on her face. "The soldiers left me for dead with the others." Sister Salt nodded slowly and leaned over to shoo a fly away from the sleeping baby's head. Now they were even; her questions had raised as many sad memories for Delena as Delena's had raised for her; so to change the subject, she asked about the cards. What did they say?

"I asked the cards about you," she said, and looked up at Sister Salt.

"See, this four-leaf clover is upside. It tells me things were green and growing, then suddenly uprooted—grief and disappointment." Me and Candy, Sister thought to herself.

Under the cards was a bright patchwork of satin scraps and remnants; the colors of the patches made the cards more difficult to see. Sister managed to recognize half of an image of a Horse here; and half of a Bear, half of a Rooster over there.

Delena pointed to the first row of cards; up here means this happened in the past. Sister nodded; it was true that once the old gardens were green and growing before the starving people came. When they returned with Grandma Fleet once more green shoots appeared but Grandma Fleet died and again grief and disappointment.

In the same row of the past sat the cards that formed a blue moon's upright image amid a golden shower of stars; she picked up the Moon card as her favorite even before Delena told her its message was a peaceful life of happiness. Yes, she and her sister and mother had so much happiness as long as they all were together—no matter if they were at the old gardens or along the river in Needles. The people one loved mattered most, but now Sister Salt saw how places forced loved ones apart.

Bright datura Moon, silver shower of falling stars, of course this card was good luck, but it was in the row called the Past.

In the next row Sister Salt saw the Owl's feet first, upside down, and knew this picture spelled trouble too. Delena pronounced its meaning as failed plans, things that never worked out, though one waited hopefully. Right next to the Owl was the hindquarters of the Pig on its snout, a bad omen—Sister guessed this before Delena said it meant greed will be punished. Next to the Pig and immediately below the Owl was the Fish, belly-up—just like the poor fish stranded in holes when the river was diverted. Here was the worst message yet! Sister Salt felt certain. Would something bad happen on the river to leave more fish belly-up? More heavy rain and the embankments would weaken and break, and the entire campsite would be washed away in a flood. She heard a snuffling sound from the bundle and turned to see little dark fists punching into the air. She leaned down and put her face close to his to smell his sweet baby's breath and to let him feel hers as a blessing. "Yes, you were right," she whispered to him in Sand Lizard language, "this place isn't safe much longer." The upside-down Pig and even the Owl might be signs of the flood that would drown all in its wake.

Delena listened to her, then shook her head. The healthy Fish swam upside down, and even used this ability to escape trouble. This card, said Sister, would come out on top, after greed was punished. The fourth picture was a Scale on its side, which Sister did not recognize; Delena explained the Scale's connection with justice; on its side, the image of the Scale meant you must keep your balance to survive. These pictures formed by the cards touched one another, which meant all these things were to happen about the same time, not far in the future.

Sister Salt did not pay much attention to the images after the belly-up

Fish; neither the Scales nor the silver white Lilies on their sides mattered after she saw the position of the Fish. Delena tried to reassure her: The message of the silver Lilies was exceedingly good—heavenly happiness hardly imaginable now, she said, smiling. Everything will turn out all right! But Sister didn't care if the dog circus woman said it was a good omen or not. The little black grandfather knew better; he wanted them to go away from there, partly because something was going to happen and partly because his father didn't believe he would live.

Sister Salt gathered up the baby and gently brushed the sand from his wrapping; then she stood up and shook the sand from her skirt. She had to get back; maybe Maytha and Vedna would be there and they could discuss the meaning of the belly-up Fish. At least the Gypsy cards had more confidence in the baby than Big Candy did—they made no mention of death.

Delena and her dogs walked with her partway; next time they'd ask the other deck of cards—the Mexican cards, which Delena used only for herself. Sister Salt nodded; she wanted to ask the cards about Indigo and Mama. Before Delena turned back, she asked Sister to tell Big Candy about her dog circus. She wanted permission to put on a performance there.

As the sounds of the camp became louder, the little grandfather woke and began to squirm. "I know, I know," she whispered to him, "but there's nothing we can do now except move, and everyone is too busy to help us with the tent." If Big Candy would only welcome his son, the baby might learn to tolerate the noise from his father's casino and brewery.

Sister Salt was delighted to see the twins were back, but what were they doing? Maytha and Vedna were outside their tent, both of them bent over, tying bundles. As soon as they saw her, they came running; before they even spoke they pressed close to see the baby.

"He's cute! He's not that tiny!"

"No! He looks strong!"

Sister Salt felt so much love for her friends at that moment as they put their faith in her baby's strength and health. That's what Big Candy didn't seem to understand—doubts weaken tiny babies. Think happily of the baby or stay away!

That Mojave woman was the one spreading the rumors the baby was too small to live; that woman was full of hate toward Sister Salt. The woman wanted to be rid of her and the twins to run the laundry as well as the brewery for Big Candy. She probably wanted Big Candy all to herself.

"She's a witch," Vedna whispered. The twins didn't want to take any chances with that woman, so they were packing up. Big Candy offered them more money if they'd stay, but their minds were made up. They were going to live on the little piece of land their old auntie sold them down-river from Needles; Sister Salt was welcome to come with them.

Maytha went around the back of the brewery tent and brought them a lard pail of beer to drink for their going-away party. It was just the three of them sitting outside the tent as the night began to cool off. All the beer they drank dimmed the noise of the shouting dice players and drunks at the tents nearby. Maytha got so drunk she started to dance around and she stumbled into Vedna and they both sprawled laughing on the ground near Sister Salt. She laughed with them and drank more beer, but she was both-ered to learn about that Mojave woman's harmful intentions. She couldn't stop thinking about the Gypsy cards of the overturned Pig and the belly-up Fish. Although the baby in his bundle was safely in the corner of the tent, barricaded with old blankets, Sister Salt checked on him often in case their laughter woke him. He slept soundly with his little fists up beside ei-ther cheek, as if ready to defend himself.

They finished off the first pail of beer, and this time Vedna went for more because Maytha was so tipsy she'd spill it all before she got back. The twins passed the pail back and forth to Sister Salt and talked about their new life. They'd sure miss all the men who paid them for sex—they joked the Chemehuevi men were all married and the wives bitterly opposed their re-turn.

"It's because our father wasn't Chemehuevi," Vedna said, and Maytha nodded. But their old auntie sold them the land, so the others were stuck with them.

Sister Salt told them about the dog woman, Delena, and the Gypsy cards.

"See! I told you! The Gypsy cards know about that Mojave woman!" Maytha said, and Vedna nodded in agreement. Fish could swim upside down, then right themselves; maybe Sister Salt was the Fish. That's what Delena said too. Sister was beginning to see the good in the upside-down Fish, and she found herself feeling more lighthearted now, and reached for the pail of beer again.

The twins were more interested in the dog circus than the Gypsy cards. Damn! Maybe they should accept Big Candy's offer to work another week just so they could see the dog circus perform. Vedna drank more than Maytha but she didn't stagger and she never seemed drunk until she brought out the Bible with all the pictures. All three of them avoided the traveling preachers and missionaries who shouted and scolded, but they liked to look at the strange pictures in the Bible. Vedna read the words sometimes, but Bible language was different from the English they spoke, and pretty soon she'd give up.

Vedna closed her eyes and turned the Bible around and around in her hands, then let the Bible fall open on her lap and let her finger drop on a page—that was how good Christians told fortunes.

"Oh!" she exclaimed as she opened her eyes, and Sister Salt thought she must have got one of their favorites—the children in the fiery furnace or Daniel surrounded by lions. Maytha's favorite was Jonah as he was swallowed by the whale. The picture was crowded with human skeletons and corpses, a few in shrouds, by the light of a full moon peeping out of the clouds, as the prophet looked down on them. The dead looked anguished and tormented, especially the skeleton at the lower right corner of the page who groped for his lost skull. They burst into laughter, and Maytha said, "Oh-oh! It looks like that Mojave woman and her friends!" So they laughed even harder as Vedna began to read: "The hand of God was upon me and carried me out and set me down in a valley full of bones—"

"That's right!" Maytha interrupted. "We live in that valley!" Vedna frowned.

"Do you want me to read, or not?" Her tone was impatient and her eyes red from all the beer. She cleared her throat loudly and continued: "He caused me to walk all around them, and the bones were very dry. He asked me, 'Can these bones live?' I answered, 'God, you know.' And he said to me, 'Prophesy concerning these bones and say to them, "Oh dry bones, hear the word of God!" ' Thus said God to these bones: 'I will cause breath to enter into you and you shall live. I will lay sinews and bring flesh upon you and over you with skin.' "

"Ugh!" Maytha pretended to be squeamish.

"Shut up!" Vedna commanded.

"She thinks she's preacher!" Maytha said just before Vedna tried to kick her.

"So I prophesied as God commanded me and there was a noise, then an earthquake, and the bones came together, each bone to its joint. I looked and the flesh and skin covered them, but there was no breath in them. Then God said to me, 'prophesy concerning the breath, say to the breath:

"Come from the four winds, O breath, and breathe into these slain that they may live." '

"So I prophesied as God commanded and the breath came into them, and they lived and stood up on their feet, an exceeding great army." Vedna was about to close the book when Sister Salt asked to look; she plopped the open Bible in Sister's lap and took the beer pail from Maytha.

Here it was even in the Bible—everything Wovoka said was true. With winds from the four directions scouring the earth, their slain ancestors would rise up into armies. The twins shared the last of the beer and argued over whose turn it was to go for another pail. Sister Salt felt the headache beer always gave her; she gathered up the sleeping baby to go to her tent. What the dog woman said must be true—the Blessed Mother of the Indians said to defend themselves, and don't fear death.

Toward morning she heard Big Candy come into her tent and smelled the warm food he brought her, but he did not come kneel beside her to kiss her forehead until she woke, as he used to before the baby. This morning he set down the food and left. She listened to his footsteps recede and thought about going after him; but if he didn't want to be with them, then she didn't want to ask.

Sometimes those tiny babies lived for days, even weeks before they gave up the ghost; Big Candy's mother used to say that was the cruelest thing those little babies did—stay alive long enough to give you false hope, and then break your heart. Poor mothers! Sometimes they held on to those babies for days after they died—one young mother even forced her nipple into the cold little mouth. The prospect of all that sadness and loss for a young girl who had already lost all her family made him feel exhausted and discouraged. It didn't help that Wylie had a telegram from Washington that gave the military jurisdiction over access to the construction site in thirty days.

Big Candy tossed and turned without sleep; he knew he should be with Sister to comfort her, but she resented what he knew as inevitable. Better to let her have this time with her baby undisturbed. He lay thinking about the future and what they would do. Once the campsite was opened up to competitors, Wylie and he knew they'd see a big drop in their receipts; luckily they'd made hay while the sun shined, and he and Wylie were set. From here they each had enough to go anywhere and retire. He drifted in and out of sleep, aware of the shouts and occasional gunshots and laughter. He dreamed an elegant dining room in a fine hotel—out the windows all around were high mountains covered with snow. Wylie sat at the head of the table with men in military uniforms. They drank red wine from crystal goblets but no food had been served. In the kitchen Candy found a tiny black child wearing only a diaper by the stove, where it played with a black dog. The child was no larger than a baby but it could walk, and it smiled at him with a full set of teeth as it climbed on and over the dog's back with strange agility. When he lifted the lids on the pots and on the roasting pans in the oven, all the food was gone, and only scraps, skin and bones, remained in the grease.

Even after he woke and struck a match to see the face of his pocket watch, Candy still felt agitated by the dream. He had to get more sleep or he'd feel weak and sick all day. He reached for the bottle of good bourbon he kept for medicinal purposes and took three big mouthfuls. The warmth of the spirits radiated out from his stomach over his entire body and one by one he felt his muscles relax until he felt himself drift weightlessly. He dreamed a small coffin partially uncovered, pushing up through the earth in a big military cemetery of identical white crosses. What was a baby's coffin doing there? As he got closer he saw that the small coffin oddly resembled a floor safe. He woke with a start, his heart pounding. Had he reburied the floor safe deeply enough? Had he brushed over the disturbed sand and disguised the area under the tree well enough? He had been in a hurry and it was difficult to see by lantern in the dark. He'd have to check it later. The dream must refer to the baby's death, though it had already survived longer than he thought it would. Sister's baby was too small to live—even the Mojave women who tended the beer agreed about that.

Wylie complained he hadn't slept well either. It was no wonder, with the soldiers bivouacked above the workers' camp and more wagons arriving from Yuma and Prescott, even from Phoenix, in anticipation of the shift in authority over the construction site. Candy put the coffee on to boil first, then stirred the eggs into the batter and cut the bacon while Wylie sat in his long underwear at the table. Cigarette butts and spent matches filled a saucer next to an empty brandy bottle.

They'd made their stakes in the nick of time; these next few weeks they could coast along and still make plenty of money until all the others set up gambling tents and started to sell beer and barbecue. This was a good time to retire from federal projects anyway; Wylie's political connections in Washington had been weakened by the scandal that followed the Panic of 1893.

Next year at this time they'd be retired and settled into their new lives—Wylie avoided mention of California or Denver because he still hoped to persuade Big Candy to settle on the West Coast with him. Wylie smiled to himself. He knew how to win over his friend—it was with the abundance of fresh seafoods not available before for Big Candy to prepare and serve. Wylie knew the fresh abalone steaks and butter clams were the way to Candy's heart.

◆　◆　◆

At dawn Delena lit a fire to boil the water for coffee, then settled back to watch the pups. They woke up one after the other, and they yawned in unison. When they crowded around her, they leaped up at the same instant. They easily learned to run one after the other over barriers and kept their balance on narrow planks. When excited, they easily stood on their hind legs, so it didn't take long to teach them to dance. She watched them tug and pull one another with a piece of old rope one of the dogs found; three pups tugged on each end and they whirled and spun around one another effortlessly.

The crippled mother dog stayed by her side, out of their way, because from time to time the pups fought over the rope. Their snarls and growls sounded terrifying; clouds of dust flew all around the knot of biting dogs as they tumbled over and over.

The first few times they fought one another like that, she feared a dog or two might be injured or killed. But when they finally stopped, the two dogs on the bottom of the heap emerged with nothing worse than bloody torn ears and dog saliva and dirt caked on their fur.

Later, with a tin cup of black coffee in one hand, she brought out the deck of Mexican cards. On the scraps of satin remnants she laid out the cards in the formation of the cross and the lance, then studied the figures and the *dichos,* or sayings, that belonged to each card.

The first card, La Rosa, the Rose, turned up to represent her! What good card this was! The Rose was the influence affecting her and its saying was *"Rosa, Rosita, Rosaura"*—"Rose, Little Rose, Rosiness"! The rose was a sign of the Señora of Guadalupe as well; roses were her blessing and sign to the poor Indians at Tepeyac.

The second card, which crossed the Rose, was the Barrel, but on its side, as if empty or dumped. The saying of the barrel was *"Tanto bebió el albañal que quedó como barril,"* or "The bricklayer drank so much he became the shape of a wine barrel." As a card that crossed her card, the Barrel wasn't much opposition at all! Any obstacles she might encounter would be overturned as easily as an empty barrel.

The crowning card was the Rooster card, reversed—a good card to reverse because it had an ominous *dicho*—"*El que le cantó a San Pedro no le volverá a cantar*" ("The one who sang for St. Peter will not return to sing"). Probably because he got made into soup. The fourth card stood for her foundation, her origin; El Pino, the great Pine, stands proudly. "Always cool, fragrant, and always beautiful," was the saying that went along with this card. A solid foundation in the pine forests of the highest mountains was where the people fled from the army before Delena was born.

Behind her, representing the past, was the fifth card, the card with the red, white, and green Flag of Mexico, upside down, draped around its pole. A Flag reversed was a distress call; someday the poor would prevail over the government, and not one but many Mexicos would spring up overnight.

The handsome Guitar Player upside down stood for her immediate future; here was another card that was better reversed than upright because its saying was oddly phrased: "The musician's rubber trumpet doesn't want to play," a silly saying about a limp penis. Reversed, this card might not be so bad—maybe the trumpet would play and success would be hers.

The seventh card indicated Delena's position in the present instance, and here the accuracy of the cards gave her a chill because it was La Mano. The *dicho* called it "the hand of the criminal," though luckily it was reversed, which meant the criminal hand was hers!

El Nopal, the Cactus plant covered with red fruit, the eighth card, represented her present home, but the card was upside down, to reflect the truth—she was uprooted like the Nopal, her homeland torn open by war. Its *dicho* was bitter: "All anyone sees is something to eat." Plundered lands, the animals, even the people plundered. Even reversed the Nopal card was a good one, because although uprooted, neither the Cactus nor its fruit was destroyed; in fact the Cactus was able to take root again upside down, even broken apart, almost anywhere.

Her hopes and fears were represented by the ninth card, El Corazón, the Heart, with a bloodied arrow through its center. "Don't banish me, sweetheart," the saying went; "I'm returning by wagon." Perfect. The Heart might mean romance but the bloody arrow was shot by a warrior. An arrow through the center of the Heart meant success at the heart of the matter— her sweetheart was the uprising in the south, and they would prevail. Yes, she would return with a wagon, loaded with supplies.

The tenth and last card represented the future, the outcome of the present enterprise, and here was La Sandia, the fat ripe Watermelon; its sliced, succulent red flesh meant success, success! The dicho said, "*La barriga que Juan tenía, era empacho de sandia*"—"Juan's belly is glutted with watermelon." Only the best conditions produced big ripe melons or permitted Juan to gorge himself—this card told her the conditions were perfect. Clearly it was time to take the dog circus to perform at the construction camp.

Despite the noise of the camp, and his father's fear, the little black grandfather was growing. Now Sister teased him and called him Little Black Spider because his legs and arms seemed longer as he grew. He still fretted over the noise unless she held him and sang louder than the outside noise. Hour after hour she sang, and when she ran out of songs she sang sounds that were parts of words—Sand Lizard, Spanish, and English nonsense words seemed to calm him and drown out the noise best.

She bundled him onto her back, secured with her white cotton shawl, and took him for a walk away from the tents. As the earth was heaped higher across the riverbed, the dam resembled more and more one of the monster stories Maytha and Vedna learned from their father. This monster ate up all living things up and down the poor river. Upriver, the backwaters flooded the cottonwoods and willows; now they were beginning to die. The watercress and delicate mosses that used to fringe the river's edge were submerged, and the silver green minnows disappeared. She sat at the river's edge for hours and watched the slow currents move through the tall reeds and mosses while the little one enjoyed a deep sleep. She thought about Indigo and Mama then, and about the Messiah and the dancers. She was beginning to think they would not see one another again.

Later, Sister Salt offered to take Maytha and Vedna to meet the woman with the dog circus so they could ask the Gypsy cards about their future. Sister Salt wanted to ask the Mexican cards about Mama and Indigo. But the twins seemed reluctant; it was true the woman gave water to Sister right after the baby was born; still, one had to be careful of traveling strangers. Vedna had to laugh because soon they were going to be traveling strangers themselves. Still, they wanted to see the dog circus perform, and the decks of cards that foretold the future; so they decided to stay for a few more days.

Sister Salt intended to tell Big Candy about the Mexican woman and the dog circus, but she didn't have a chance because he was so busy. The next afternoon as Sister and the twins relaxed in the shade with the sleeping baby, two black dogs suddenly appeared, dressed in patchwork capes of bright satins with little horned caps decorated with bells tied behind their ears—jokers' caps copied from a deck of cards. The dogs were quite friendly and bells rang as they wagged their tails.

Juanito called Big Candy out of the brewery tent to watch the dog circus arrive. He was astonished to see a dark woman who wore a white cape sewed with bright red satin figure of the queen of diamonds over her dress; she was flanked by more black dogs that wore satin capes sewn with scraps of satin to form the figures of the king, the jack, the ten, and nine of diamonds. She didn't notice Sister or the twins under the tree until Sister called out a greeting. Delena acknowledged them with a wave, but remained where she was, talking in a low voice to the dogs.

Slowly the dogs began to canter around the sandy clearing behind the tents, and as they gradually increased their speed, a small crowd began to gather. The dogs began to leapfrog over one another in a dead run; playfully the dogs began to tear at one another's costumes, and bells and bits of the costumes began to litter the sand. Even the gamblers stopped to come take a look, and they laughed and laughed and cheered on the dogs while the woman in her odd costume watched.

When the dogs finally stopped their tug-of-war with the costumes and gathered around their mistress, Sister and the twins joined other spectators, who cheered to see more of the dog circus, but Delena ignored them. The exhibition was over. Gradually the crowd drifted away to the gambling tents as she praised the dogs in a high soft voice. She patted and spoke to each dog separately as she retied the bells and adjusted the capes, examining the damage to the costumes. When Big Candy approached from the gambling tent, she turned away from the dogs to straighten her queen of diamonds cape before she greeted him.

Sister Salt picked up the sleeping baby and the twins followed. They stood nearby to listen as Big Candy and Delena negotiated a price for the dogs' performance. Candy said he had to consult Wylie before they had a deal, but he was sure the boss would go for it. Candy hadn't smiled like that in days. He really enjoyed the spectacle of the playing card costumes—together they formed a royal straight flush, a winning poker hand that would be inspiration for his customers! Sister felt a pang of sadness as she realized the birth of the little grandfather brought Candy worry, not happiness; Candy seemed far happier to see a dog circus than his own son.

Candy offered the dog circus woman empty crates, and kegs, even planks if she wanted them, for the dogs to leap over. A bit embarrassed by Candy's enthusiasm, Delena nodded, and he immediately called Juanito to bring the items he requested.

"Ooh ooh!" Maytha said after Delena and her dog circus accompanied Big Candy to Wylie's tent. Vedna squeezed her mouth and eyes shut tight in mock disapproval that made all three break into laughter. Sister announced she didn't care if Big Candy went off with her—Delena was nice. Anyway, the little black grandfather still refused to forgive Candy for believing he would die. They were better off apart, especially the baby.

Before long, Delena and her dogs came back alone. Big Candy stayed at Wylie's tent to start cooking for Wylie's big dinner. His important business connections from Prescott and Yuma were coming day after tomorrow. Sister and the twins helped Delena pick up the pieces torn from the costumes. Delena wasn't worried; she kept the bear and lion costumes for the dogs to wear until the diamond suits could be repaired. Now that they'd met her, Maytha and Vedna agreed with Sister; the dog circus woman was really interesting and she seemed nice.

Delena mentioned Big Candy had invited her and the dog circus to camp there next to the tents, then made them laugh as she repeated her reply: "Thanks but no thanks!" Her dogs would bark all night at the drunks stumbling around. She made it clear she wasn't going after Big Candy even though he was interested in her—they all could see that. Sister had almost given up on Candy; still, she felt relieved Delena wasn't after him; she and the twins liked her even more now. They told Delena she was right—the place was getting noisier at night now that the soldiers were camped nearby. That's why Maytha and Vedna were leaving, and Sister might go too.

They all walked her and the dogs back downriver to her camp hidden in the tamarisk and willows. The dogs fanned out ahead of them, bounding along then stopping to sniff a rock or to urinate on a dry log. They hadn't gone far when Delena stopped because there were only six dogs; the crippled dog was missing. They were about to go back to look for the dog when she limped out of a tamarisk thicket, her tail wagging.

"Ooh look! What's that in her mouth?" Maytha exclaimed. The others bent down for a closer look; they were amazed to see a $1 bill in her mouth.

"Some drunk dropped his money!" Sister Salt laughed, and the baby let go of her nipple with a soft pop to stare at her merriment.

"We need that kind of dog!" Vedna remarked.

Delena smiled but said nothing as she folded the banknote into a tiny square and reached under the satin cape to tuck it down her blouse between her breasts. The seven black dogs were her army.

In her shady camp, they shared two bottles of beer the twins swiped from the brewery tent while the Mojave ladies were gone. No more green beer by the pail like the other night, they laughed; the hangovers were too brutal. The beer got Maytha and Vedna excited again about how amazing and funny the dogs' performance had been. Just wait, Delena told them; that was just a little rehearsal. Wait until they saw the big show!

They sat awhile without talking, and the sudden quiet woke the little grandfather, who peered sternly at the young women until Sister offered him a breast. After he was nursing contentedly, Sister asked Delena to bring out the Mexican cards to see what they knew about Mama and Indigo.

OK, but first she had to understand the cards might bring bad news, Delena explained. The Gypsy woman—she called her Auntie—who took her in and began to teach her about the cards was strong, never sick. That winter in Chihuahua she came down with a cold; she wasn't very sick—she still was up around the camp. Delena was still learning the cards then, and just for practice she asked the cards when her auntie would get over her cold. She shuffled the deck four times as she had been taught, then took the first card off the top for the answer. It was La Campana, the Bell, upside down. She had not seen that card reversed before, and was not sure of its meaning after she recited the card's *dicho:* "The bell and you beneath it."

As she was talking, Delena took the Mexican cards out of their woven bag and unwrapped them. She paused to look up at them before she continued.

"I took the card to Auntie to ask her how the reversed Bell should be read." Here Delena paused and swallowed.

"Auntie said, 'That's my card, isn't it?' " Now tears streamed down Delena's cheeks, and the twins looked at each other and Sister.

"The Bell means good fortune when it is upright—the church bell rings and everyone dances under the bell at weddings and baptisms and other happy occasions. But reversed, the Bell lies upside down on the fallen beam that supported it; to be under the Bell, then, can only mean disaster."

Sister glanced down uneasily at the baby in her arms, and Maytha and Vedna shifted their legs under them to restore circulation. Delena smoothed out the patchwork cloth of colored satin and shuffled the Mexican cards over it. Vedna tipped the empty beer bottles to her mouth one after the other for any remaining drops.

"She died?" Maytha asked in a soft voice. Delena nodded as Vedna elbowed her and whispered loudly, "What do you think, stupid!"

Sister shook her head at them both. Delena was laying out the cards, and Sister didn't want the message of the cards affected by the twins' quarrel. Now as Delena began to lay down the cards they didn't take their eyes off them. All three inhaled sharply at the first card, La Muerte, the skeleton with the big scythe. Delena frowned and shook her head at them; their reactions might influence the cards.

"Yeah, be quiet!" Sister Salt warned them. "Don't spoil the cards for me!"

So in silence they leaned close to watch Delena lay down the cards; each time the Bell upside down did not appear, Sister whispered thanks to the old ancestor spirits. When the last card went down and no overturned Bell appeared, she exhaled deeply, her heart pounding.

Delena studied the ten cards for a long time before she began to read them. The skeleton, Death, the first card, was gracefully covered by the Flowerpot of red blossoms, and both were crossed by the Sun. This looked very promising, indeed, she said, and both twins patted Sister on the back enthusiastically. La Muerte has a good *dicho,* she told them: " 'Death's here, death's there'—that's nothing unusual. That's the way life is; it means some sort of change."

The *dicho* of the Flowerpot said, "One born in a flowerpot does not leave the room"; this was a reminder each being had its limits. "Cover for the poor" was the *dicho* of El Sol, the Sun card; all the poor have over their heads is the Sun, but that is enough because the Sun is a mighty presence. The Sun card might also be read as the Son of the God who shelters the poor in the world. This was among the best cards in the deck.

Sister was so happy to hear this, she leaned down to kiss the little sleeping grandfather on both cheeks.

Following those three cards was the Spider's Web, which indicated a struggle but also one who refused to give up. The Web might look delicate but it wasn't weak and didn't give back anything entangled in it. The Cooking Pot card overturned meant some upset or trouble, but the *dicho* said it was "little"—the Spider's Web more than balanced the Pot upside down. Sister wondered if this Cooking Pot card had anything to do with the big dinner Candy was preparing for the boss and his friends.

Above all these cards was the lovely card La Estrella, the Star. "The shining guide of the sailors" was its *dicho,* and it was the most important—it meant Sister would find her way back to her sister.

The Watermelon card—a fat slice cut from the ripe red fruit—came up again for Sister, with its tidings of abundance and success. Sister recalled the delicious melons they shared from the old gardens, and the wild melons she ate the day the little grandfather was born.

The Apache card above the Flag card and the overturned Rooster card meant the people hiding in the mountains from the soldiers would escape destruction. This was the only time Delena looked up from the cards to smile and nod at them. Sister knew she was thinking of the people in the south where she had come from, as well as the Messiah and the dancers here.

"The last card is the most important of all," Delena said, tracing her finger over the ocean blue of La Sirena, the Mermaid. As Delena recited the *dicho*—"Don't get shipwrecked by siren songs"—Sister realized it was some kind of warning; but when she asked her, Delena only shrugged. Maybe the card wasn't hers; maybe it was Big Candy's.

Edward was shocked, but he did not protest after she booked separate cabins and shared hers with Indigo. He wanted to explain, but each time he started, Hattie shook her head and turned away from him. There was nothing to explain. It did not seem to occur to him she wanted apologies, not explanations.

She occupied herself with Indigo; they were reading about gladiolus and they'd nearly finished the book of Chinese monkey adventures. There were moments when she forgot about the arrest, but then the awareness swept back over her, and she scarcely noticed the sun's warmth against her face or even the refreshing ocean breeze. Sometimes she experienced an odd breathlessness while resting and could think of nothing else but the poor giant beetles suffocated under their bell jars at the Natural History Museum. Behind the glass she felt nothing, yet all was visible.

She experienced strange dreams that took her back to Laura's garden of aloes and sand, where she was alone but did not miss the others or wonder where they were. Variations of the dream took her to Laura's wild forest, where she always felt fearful alone and turned and ran back, to awaken bathed in sweat and shivering. She slept a great deal on the return voyage—often twelve hours each night. Awakening was the most difficult because she forgot and was happy for a moment before she remembered Edward's treachery; then her heart raced and she felt her spirits sink into her stomach, where the flutter stirred a vague nausea. Fortunately she had

Indigo along to remind her here was an opportunity to rearrange her life's priorities. She scarcely thought of her thesis now; it was already part of another life, and another person, not herself.

After she refused to hear his explanations, Edward assumed Hattie simply wanted to put the incident behind them, and made no further mention of it. Though he was initially stunned by his arrest, his shock gave way to an odd sense of relief as if some dreaded task were now over. He was confident his contacts in the Plant Industry Bureau would persuade the customs authorities in Livorno to drop all charges. He was weary of plant collecting for others when the large profits lay in the propagation and sale of hybrids. Already he was developing a new plan.

The customs authorities seized all the twig cuttings, but Indigo was delighted to discover all the cloth sacks of gladiolus corms were intact; she'd counted them before and not one was missing. Likewise, all the little envelopes of seeds from Aunt Bronwyn and those from Laura were safe; and even she found the cloth bag of green and yellow feathers she saved whenever Rainbow dropped them. Now they were moving west with the sun, and Indigo began to feel a stir of excitement each morning when she woke: going home! Rainbow seem to sense it too, because he began to call her as soon as the sun rose. While Hattie sat motionless in the deck chair or slept in the cabin, Indigo talked to Rainbow about where they were going, and about their real home. First they had to return to Riverside to get Linnaeus and for Hattie to contact the boarding school superintendent. Then they'd all go on the train to Needles together; Hattie promised to hire a driver and buggy for the two of them to search for Sister Salt and Mama until they both were found. Rainbow would have to be patient and get used to Linnaeus little by little. When they got to Needles, both of them must stay close to Indigo at all times or someone might steal them or a golden eagle or big hawk might carry them away and eat them.

They enjoyed lovely weather over the Atlantic crossing; the days were sunny and clear, and they encountered no storms, only light rain showers. The fair weather had a tonic effect for Edward, though it did not seem to cheer Hattie much.

When they stopped to refuel in St. Augustine, Edward wired Susan and Colin to propose a final settlement of the estate, and a cancellation of all his indebtness to them. The citrus groves around the Riverside house would be sold at once, but he proposed to lease the house from Susan and Colin until his new propects began to pay dividends.

In New Orleans, Hattie and the child rested at the hotel before their departure on the train the next morning. Thoughts about the details of his new plan left him restless; were it not for this restlessness they might have stayed a few days in New Orleans, time enough for his sister and her husband to wire him their response to his offer. He sent a telegram to his new business associate, Dr. Gates, at the Albuquerque address he gave. Then, out of habit, he walked to the waterfront to search out curios and oddities and, of course, unusual plants.

Among pallets of green bananas on the dock, Edward saw pallets of burlap bags of vanilla beans, then noticed a pallet of bundles with delicate green stems pushing heroically through the burlap. On impulse he lifted a bundle from its pallet for a closer look. Here were dozens of Guatemalan orchids—robust specimens of *Brassavola nodosa* with huge white birdlike blossoms of a heavenly fragrance. They'd be just the orchid to win over the public. Sun priests of the Maya reputedly held the orchid sacred because it invariably bloomed on the autumnal equinox. Flowers of the gods! He could imagine the ads in magazines now. He was in such high spirits he bought bunch of bananas for Indigo to take to her monkey. He had to hire a cab to bring him and his purchases back to the hotel.

Hattie took one look at the orchids and bananas and thought perhaps he was suffering a breakdown of some sort, as Edward excitedly described the palletload of fifty *Brassavola* plants he'd managed to buy. She did not ask what he planned to do with the orchids because with Edward all comments led back to explanations, and she did not have the energy to listen to him then.

After he left to supervise the packing of the orchids for tomorrow's departure, Hattie ordered a simple dinner—split-pea-and-ham soup and bread, brought to the room for her and the child. When Edward returned later, he asked if they would like to dine with him, but Hattie merely shook her head and turned back to the child's sketchbook; Indigo's drawings of the parrot and her sketches of gladiolus blossoms in color pencil were quite wonderful. Together they'd begun to read an English book about gladiolus culture that Laura sent along. There was a wonderful description of the first time a European saw the thousands and thousands of violet-and-white flower spikes of the wild gladiolus flourishing in the coastal desert of North Africa. Indigo began a sketch of the scene as she imagined it, but fell asleep with the sketchbook and white and purple pencils in her bed. Hattie carefully retrieved the sketchbook and the pencils, then pulled the bedcovers over the sleeping child. She was ashamed to admit that some part of herself hoped that Indigo was an orphan, that her mother and sister would not be found.

After a meal alone in the hotel dining room, Edward returned to his room, which adjoined the room Hattie shared with the child. He saw light from under the door but it was extinguished almost at once, as if Hattie heard him. She was exhausted from travel now, but after they got home and she had a chance to rest, he was confident she would understand.

Hattie and Indigo shared one sleeping compartment while Edward shared his compartment with the orchids he dared not trust to the baggage car. As the train left the coastal plain outside Houston, he sprinkled each plant once lightly with water, though rot was more of a threat to these plants than drought. He wanted to optimize their survival rate so he would have plenty of breeding stock. Though he still could not bear the heavy scent of gardenia or honeysuckle since his father's funeral, the night scent of the *Brassavola* was so subtle and refined he could inhale it with pleasure. The orchid's flowers resembled exotic white birds, wings spread in flight. He would create his own fragrant orchid hybrids to sell to florists from Los Angeles to San Francisco. The *Brassavola nodosa* with its dark green stick-like leaves was used to heat and occasional dry spells; it would tolerate the heat and dry air during shipping more easily than the hybrid *Cattleya* found now in florist shops.

His plan was to ship florists the *Brassavola* blossoms, plant and all; later, when the blossoms ended, the customer returned the plant to him. As Hattie listened to his new plan she realized a quality of tone in Edward's voice had changed or perhaps her hearing changed. She no longer recognized the connection she'd once felt with him, perhaps because she no longer trusted her own judgment. The glowing light in Aunt Bronwyn's garden and the disembodied mask she dreamed seemed more real now than her manuscript or her marriage.

Indigo was delighted with Edward's gift for Linnaeus, and while she let Rainbow get a closer look, she was careful the parrot did not take a bite. The fruit was so fragrant and each day she watched the color of the smooth green skin change ever so slightly. She could hardly wait to see her dear little friend again and to give him the wonderful gift.

The days were still hot as the train left El Paso, but already the nights were cool; the days were growing shorter now. She and Hattie continued their geography lessons with the map, and Indigo counted the days, then the hours, before they reached Yuma. She missed her best chance months ago in Needles; this train they were on followed a southern route through Yuma; Indigo didn't know her way around Yuma.

The moon was low in the sky; its first quarter shone brightly through the window of the compartment onto the bananas on the seat; in the strange light they reminded her of a giant severed hand. She could hardly wait to see Linnaeus to give him his gift. Just as she was going to sleep, she felt the train slow and heard the conductor call out, "Yuma." Hattie did not stir despite the jerks and creaks of the train. Rainbow slept with his head tucked under one wing; she thought she saw one eye open at her from under the wing, then he went on sleeping. If she wanted to get away, here was her chance. She pressed her face against the coolness of the window glass: the sandy hills approaching the river were a dark blue silver from the moon. She tried to see if she could locate the place where the Indian police held her and the other children—the last place she had seen Sister Salt—but all that seemed so long ago; she recognized nothing. She looked at the bananas again—she promised Linnaeus she'd come back. How could she leave Rainbow behind? Yet she couldn't jump off the train with him; he might be killed. Tears filled her eyes, and she felt swallowed by loss— Mama, Grandma, and Sister—all over again. Hopelessness paralyzed her and despite the voice in her head that told her to go now, hurry, before the train picked up speed, she did not move.

With her cheek cold and slippery against the train window, she cried herself to sleep. She dreamed Rainbow was perched in one of Grandma Fleet's apricot trees and she sat in its shade while Linnaeus played in the sand nearby. But in the terraces between the dunes, planted among the corn, beans, and sunflowers, were bright swaths of red, pink, yellow, orange, purple, and black gladiolus flowers as tall as the tasseled corn.

The train arrived in Los Angeles a little past four that afternoon. Edward insisted the cab take them directly from the train station to the lawyer's office, where they left him, but not before he instructed the cabdriver how to gently unload the orchids at the hotel.

Hattie removed her shoes and rested on the bed while Indigo played with the parrot on the floor. Tomorrow the train would return them to Riverside, and a house that was no longer theirs, if it ever had been. Fortunately she hadn't had time to settle into the house, so she would not feel much loss. But she'd grown so fond of Indigo she wasn't sure if she could bear to let the child go, especially now. She was determined to take the child out of the Indian boarding school and help her find her mother and sister. If Indigo was orphaned, then Hattie would spare no expense until she adopted the child.

Edward returned from the lawyer's office with letters and telegrams and good news: All was well in Riverside. The monkey was healthy and played happily with the kitten; the two curled up with each other at night. Edward smiled at Indigo as he said this, and she returned his smile. Poor man, he wasn't so bad—there were worse.

Indigo turned to Rainbow in his cage and told him not to worry—she loved him as much as she loved the little monkey. Now they could all be together. She showed the parrot the bunch of bananas, the gift for Linnaeus. At first the two of them would have to become acquainted—Rainbow had to watch out the monkey didn't accidentally hurt him; they had to be especially careful of the kitten Linnaeus adopted.

Edward gave Hattie the telegram to read for herself; Susan and Colin agreed to lease the house and gardens to them, but the citrus groves must be sold. Fortunately, orchid culture did not require extensive acreage. The sale of the citrus groves meant all the debts could be paid, with money left to build glass houses for the orchids.

He waved another letter at her; more good news! In a letter sent from Albuquerque, his Australian doctor friend reported specimens of meteor iron were obtained from a sheep herder who sold them to a prospector. When the assay laboratory in Albuquerque attempted to saw open the specimens, the hardest steel blades were quickly dulled, and finally a pneumatic spring-loaded chisel had to be used. Inside the nearly pure cadmium were threads of pure silver and gold; but more astonishing yet, the specimens were shot through with black diamonds that penetrated with great velocity! Dr. Gates urged Edward to come out to the Arizona crater site as soon as possible. Hattie could only nod her head; she would never forget the doctor's long hands and that slow predatory examination during her illness. She swore never to be in the same room with that vile man again. She might have been able finally to rationalize Edward's zeal to acquire the citron cuttings for the government, but his association with Dr. Gates was beyond the limit.

The journey by train to Riverside was not long, but the time seemed interminable to Hattie, and she was reminded of descriptions of purgatory and hell. She realized she no longer believed; if they existed at all, purgatory and hell were here on earth. She was exhausted but could not sleep as the train lurched along; her clothing felt untidy and she felt a sick headache coming on. Only when she looked at the child whispering excitedly to the parrot was her heart eased. The child was thriving; her dresses were a bit short and snug around the waist and she outgrew her shoes. Hattie found comfort in making plans for Indigo's return. She would need proper clothes herself to travel in the sun and heat of Arizona.

Edward reread the letters and the telegrams; he was more confident than ever of success with the mining venture. Of course their new company would require funds immediately, and the settlement of the estate with Susan and Colin might take months. He felt confident he could persuade Hattie to lend the money, only until the estate was settled.

The sun had set but the twilight was still bright as they drove through downtown Riverside, past the businesses and the stately Mission Hotel, where the oil lamps were already lit along the entry promenade; from inside, music from a piano could be heard faintly as the coach passed. Once they'd left behind the downtown businesses and streets lined with houses for the farmland and orchards on the outskirts, Indigo pulled herself closer to the window and she began to watch for the Indian school buildings. Dim light shone from the windows of the dining hall, and her heart beat faster when she sighted two long lines—girls in one, boys in the other—marching toward the dormitories. She felt light-headed with relief once they'd passed. Last year at this time she had been one of those girls in line—pushed from behind and pinched by the others.

The coach had hardly stopped in the driveway when Indigo scrambled out; the instant her feet touched the flagstone driveway, she was off to see Linnaeus, the handle of the parrot cage in one hand, the bunch of bananas clutched in the other. The twilight was bright in the glass house as she entered; Linnaeus was angry and pretended he didn't remember her. He ignored the fragrant gift of bananas she offered, and sat on his rope swing near the top of his cage and watched the cat climb to the top of the wisteria. Indigo didn't blame him—locked in the cage the whole time they were gone. The cage door was padlocked so she left the bananas on the floor, pushed against the cage bars, where he could reach them while she went for the key. On the steps outside the glass house, in his travel cage, Rainbow heard her voice and began to squawk. As soon as she unlocked the cage Linnaeus would forgive her!

Edward greeted the household staff and the gardener; the cook had their dinner prepared, and though the table was set, he went immediately to unpack the orchids the coachman carried upstairs to his study. Later he would examine each plant and make note cards with numbers corresponding to numbers on small brass tags tied to each plant. In the morning the glass house must be swept and wood chips and light soil prepared for potting the orchids.

After dinner, Hattie went from room to room to open windows to rid the house of the odor of furniture polish and wax. The dark oak floors and oak paneling all around felt too close after the pale plaster walls and tile of Italy; even the stone walls of Aunt Bronwyn's old cloister were more welcoming. Dark oak made her think of coffins. The lamps and cabinets were spotless, each in its place just as they had been when Mrs. Palmer was alive. She opened her valise on the bed to unpack the books and papers but could not bring herself to touch her manuscript notes.

Why bother to unpack at all? As soon as she'd obtained the information and the permission to return with Indigo to Arizona, they would be off again. In any case she did not wish to remain in the Palmer house any longer than necessary. She was relieved Edward's attention was fixed upon the orchids; he slept in the small guest bedroom on the third floor to be closer to his laboratory and the orchids.

Indigo was delighted the next morning when Edward brought her Linnaeus to watch while the gardener and helpers dismantled the monkey cage and moved it out of the glass house to a shady corner at the end of the long arcade. Edward did not want to risk damage to the orchids in the event the clever monkey managed an escape. It took all day for the cage to be moved and reassembled, so Linnaeus ran freely from garden to garden, chased by the kitten.

That night Hattie told Indigo Edward was not inclined to let them take Linnaeus along. Arizona would be difficult enough for a woman with a child and a parrot in tow. Indigo could tell just by the way she said it, Hattie wanted her to have Linnaeus. Indigo wiped a fist across her eyes and swallowed back the hurt; she pretended to accept the decision even as she was making a plan. She brought Linnaeus upstairs to her room and let him crawl under the bedcovers and play with his cat in the trunk and valises that she'd begun to pack.

Those last weeks in Riverside, Indigo kept Linnaeus with her constantly; Hattie even allowed her to keep him in the bedroom, where he slept curled next to her under the covers all night. If Edward noticed, he said nothing despite complaints from the cook about fleas and disease. Linnaeus rode on her right hip, his arms around her waist while Rainbow perched high on her left shoulder out of the little monkey's reach. As their departure day neared, she told herself, Don't be afraid, you know what you can do. All day she held Linnaeus and let him play with her fingers and nibble the edges and lobes of her ears. Rainbow was terribly jealous and in-flicted the first attack, driven by jealousy, after the monkey's long tail snaked around behind the bird and startled him. Indigo cried when she saw the blood, and held Linnaeus close the rest of the afternoon while Rain-bow sulked in his cage.

The last few weeks before their departure were filled with tension. Ed-ward did not understand why they could not travel to Arizona together; the meteor crater was only three days' travel by coach from the Colorado River Indian reservation. He saw no reason for the haste, and could easily accompany them if only they'd delay the departure until he had the new orchids securely established. They'd scarcely been home a week, and now Hattie wanted to be off again.

Hattie refused to discuss her plans—why should she, when Edward never bothered to consult her? What was she to say to him anyway—their marriage was a mistake. If it was money Edward wanted for the mine ven-ture, then she would arrange a letter of credit for him. In any case, she vowed never to set eyes on the Australian doctor again. But Edward con-tinued to press her—he wanted to show her the mine site at the meteor crater. Finally she had to confront Edward again about the doctor's lewd conduct during her illness.

Edward listened and nodded his head, but Hattie could tell by the ex-pression in his eyes, he thought Hattie must have dreamed or hallucinated. He refused to believe the doctor behaved improperly; again he tried to sug-gest it was the nature of her illness that caused her to mistake the doctor's medical examination for an assault. This time she slammed the bedroom door in his face as he followed behind her attempting to explain.

The longer she cried, the better she felt—the numb misery washed away in the tears; it was as if her old self molted away as she cried, and with it went the disappointment. She slept soundly until dawn, when a shaft of light came between the curtain and the window and illuminated the wall above the bed. She lay back on the pillow to watch the dust specks glitter, rising and falling in the light. How beautiful and perfect it was—there was no need for anything more, certainly not her attachments to the past. She was up and dressed in no time; she didn't bother about her hair. She shut the valise without giving the manuscript another look. She wanted to get outside before the others were up. The air was fragrant and cool; the wrens and sparrows chirped, still roosting in the tree. She took a spade from the gardener's shed and walked toward the sun, past the last rows of lemon trees at the edge of tall weeds and the sand of the desert. A few inches down, the sand was dark and sweet with moisture and she was able to easily dig a resting place for the valise.

As the day of their departure approached, Edward went out of his way to be kind to her and the child; he gave Indigo four hearty specimens of *Brassalova nodosa* with signs of developing buds despite their long journey. Edward did not press her to wait and travel with him, but he talked about where they should meet: Flagstaff, he thought, because it was halfway between the meteor crater and the Indian reservation on the river. Then one evening over dinner, Edward surprised them with the announcement that he had reconsidered his earlier decision: Indigo should have Linnaeus after all. Further he decided the gardner could tend the orchids without him; his bags were packed. He asked if he might go with them. His change of heart moved Hattie to relent: yes, he might travel with her and the child but only as far as Needles.

As the packing and last-minute arrangements fell into place, Hattie felt a flicker of anticipation and excitement at setting out for Indigo's homeland in parts unknown. It was just the change she needed.

Part Nine

THE PERFORMANCE of the dog circus drew a big crowd—not only the construction workers and off-duty soldiers, but miners and cowboys from outlying areas heard about it and came. The early arrivals bought beer and tried their luck in the gambling tents just as Big Candy hoped they would. A quick survey of the cash receipts proved this day to be their best by far. Even the women who worked in the wagons and the Prescott businessmen they worked for came to see. Candy estimated their number at close to two hundred, and both Wylie and Big Candy were enthusiastic about hiring the dog circus to travel with them when the construction camp moved to Twentynine Palms.

It took a good while to dress the seven dogs and to keep them from tugging at their lions' manes of horsehair and the long striped tiger tails of painted burlap. For the mother dog, who led the troop despite her lameness, Delena had fashioned a strange cape of long black horsehair, which was quite unsettling as the dog approached, so Sister Salt and the twins dubbed her the Bear.

Delena covered her dress with a long cape of burlap covered almost entirely with bits of red, yellow, green, blue, and white ribbon that flickered in the breeze, trimmed with dozens of little dangling baubles made of tin cans, which jingled as she moved. By the time Sister Salt and the twins helped Delena arrange a circle of smooth river stones for the ring and piled kindling on two sides of the circle, the sun was down. The girls took turns beating an old tin bucket with a stick to announce the performance. More and more onlookers gathered and the buzz of voices and barks of the dogs added to the excitement.

Delena called to the crippled dog, and the others followed her inside the circle of stones. She talked to the dogs constantly in a low voice Sister Salt could barely hear, but it soothed them and kept their attention on her. In pairs, the black dogs danced together on their hind legs around and around as Delena waved her wand—a willow stick tied with strings of sparrow feathers; the crippled dog sat motionless on a keg in the center of the ring.

Delena left them dancing while she lit the oil-soaked rags wreathed around two hoops she fashioned from scraps of wire. As the crowd cheered her on, a fiery hoop in each hand, she called first to the crippled dog, who leaped off the keg and through one hoop after the other to wild applause from the audience that had consumed a large amount of beer. The other dogs followed their mother through the hoops eagerly, and barked excitedly as they raced around the ring.

Next Delena rolled in other empty nail kegs and arranged scraps of corrugated tin roofing for an elevated track around the ring, which made resounding thunder as the dogs raced over it. While the "lions" and "tigers" pounded the tin, now gaily chasing one another's cloth and horsehair tails, Delena stepped out of the ring, and the crippled black dog in the bear costume followed her into the shadows, where a moment later she returned with an old ladder, which she held upright in both hands while one after the other the dogs climbed on, until she had six dogs at once balanced on the rungs of the ladder. Later the twins and Sister Salt did recall the absence of the crippled dog in her bear costume; at the time they did not make much of it—they assumed the dog was too disabled for the ladder trick.

The last trick consisted of the dogs each sitting up on their hind legs on a keg while Delena rapidly tossed them wild gourds, which they caught and held in their mouths before dropping to catch another. When each dog had six gourds by its keg, Delena bowed to the crowd with a flourish, spreading both arms to direct their applause to the dogs on the kegs behind her. Then, while the crowd continued to whistle and cheer, Delena reached down into her gunnysack of costumes and props and brought out a strange doll almost two feet tall, made of white canvas, with a long beard of white horsehair and a matching wig topped by a paper top hat painted with stripes of red, white, and blue. The doll wore no clothing, but around his neck was a string of little round tin bells.

At the sight of the doll, the dogs became alert and some of them began to wag their tails in anticipation; Delena sternly commanded them to stay put before she took the doll's hands in her hands and began slowly to dance around and around the ring. The light from the lanterns and from the two small fires at either end of the ring trees threw giant shadows of the doll and the woman across the audience, which was drunk and disorderly now; those in back attempted to push forward to get a better view. A drunk miner bumped a drunk soldier, who stumbled against a drunk cowboy, and a fight broke out in front of the gambling tents. Big Candy ordered the dealers to shut down until the crowd was more orderly, and halted the sale of beer for the time being to avoid more trouble.

Now as Delena whirled faster and faster with the strange doll, and her dogs danced around with her on their hind legs, barking excitedly, a drunk soldier staggered into the ring and pulled the white doll out of her hands to dance with it himself. The dogs took this as their cue to grab the white doll for their finale, and grabbed hold of its legs and arms and head. The drunk clung to the doll's torso with both hands even after the dogs pulled him facedown hard and began to tug and pull the doll and him around the circle. Once the dogs tore off the doll's hat and wig, they pulled off the beard and tugged at it between them before one of dogs grabbed hold of the drunk's shirt, and then all of the dogs were on the man, pulling and tearing at his clothing while the crowd laughed and urged them on.

Soldier friends of the drunk who tried to push their way through the crowd to stop the dogs met with resistance; the resentment many felt toward the presence of the army surfaced, and fistfights broke out. Oblivious to the disorder that spread through the crowd, the dogs gaily tore to pieces the drunk's uniform but ignored the naked man on the ground. Once the uniform was shredded, the dogs began wild tugs-of-war with their own costumes. In their excitement they tore off the horsehair lions' manes and tigers' tails and the burlap capes trimmed with tin jingles. Their mistress made no effort to stop them; in fact, Delena was nowhere in sight.

The crowd surged, then swelled like floodwater over one another to the protests and yells of those pushed and trampled. Sister Salt held the baby close to her in both arms as she ran to escape the fighting mob. Out of the corner of her eye she saw Big Candy with a shotgun cradled in his arms in front of the gambling tents. She ran a short distance downriver until she saw a dense stand of willows; with the little black grandfather safely cocooned she crawled as far back into the willows as she could. She could hear the voices—the curses and shouts, and then the shotgun blasted twice, followed by three or four pistol shots and more shouts. The little black grandfather's eyes widened at the gunfire and he waved his arms furiously but did not cry. "Yes, you were right all along," she whispered to him, and the cards were right too—a big flood came all right, but it wasn't the river that wiped out everything.

Wylie was on his horse behind the crowd when the riot broke out; he pulled the six-shot thirty-two special out of his right boot and took the two-shot thirty-eight derringer from the left boot. He regretted leaving his sawed-off shotguns in his tent. He could not see Big Candy for the mob that boiled around the tents, but he heard Candy's shotgun fire and then more shots. Wylie knew there were bound to be off-duty soldiers involved, so he turned his horse away and raced off to alert their commanding officer to send military police.

Suddenly Sister Salt saw fire—flames engulfed all the tents. Not only were the gambling tents and laundry and brewery destroyed; the tents the twins and Sister Salt lived in went up in oily black smoke. Fortunately Maytha and Vedna had already moved out of the tent and kept their bundles of belongings with them that terrible night.

Was the fire an accident, or deliberate? The crowd had been drinking beer since early afternoon, and the workers were unhappy about overtime work without pay. By the time the military police were summoned, the rioters ran up the ridge to the wagon town and robbed and looted until the military police fired warning shots to disperse the crowd.

The fires consumed the tent canvas and left only the smoldering skeleton of chairs, oak kegs, and planks that served for poker and dice tables. Up on the ridge a number of wagons burned and a Prescott businessman was accidentally shot, but no one was killed, and the commotion didn't end until sunup.

At daybreak, the first question from Wylie was, where in the tents was the money kept? He passed Big Candy his silver brandy flask from the saddle. The cash boxes were fireproof, but they emptied the flask waiting for the fires to burn out and the ashes to cool off enough to search the smoldering debris.

Big Candy used the smoking remains of the gaming tables to orient himself in the ashes. With a shovel he cleared away the hot coals to the scorched sand and struck metal; the box itself was still chained to the smoking wood stub of a table leg, but the lid of seared metal was wide open; a piece of baling wire used to pick the lock was still stuck in the keyhole. Candy felt light-headed and nauseous when he saw the wire in the lock; he ran with a shovel to dig up the cash boxes from the other tents.

Wylie found him exhausted and brooding in the shattered bottle glass and smoldering remains of beer barrels, the melted remains of an open cash box at his feet. Neither man spoke at first. Wylie commented whoever robbed them knew the layout. Then Candy inhaled sharply—the dream about the exposed open coffin shaped like a safe! That had been a warning; instantly the sweat on his brow felt icy; Candy left Wylie standing there without a word and took off. He ran fast for a man his size; the white sand of the path reflected the dawn light but the willows remained in deep shadows. Candy prayed as he ran: Let the floor safe be buried deep enough!

The deep shade of the big cottonwood hid the truth until he stood on the pile of damp sand above the hole where the floor safe lay, its thick lead door wide open, empty. Candy tried to swallow but his throat was dry; he coughed until tears filled his eyes. He cried out in fury at the top of his voice; off in the hills above the river, coyotes howled in reply. Dog paw prints were everywhere in the sand around the base of the cottonwood tree, and he found one set of small wide shoe prints but no others. So the thief was that Mexican dog circus Gypsy! He knew he could catch her.

Wylie let him take his good walking horse. He took a canteen but no food—he was too upset to eat anyway. He rode south for hours searching for tracks in the sand along the river until he began to feel the horse tire. They'd lost all their savings—he didn't want to kill Wylie's favorite horse too. There were no traces of the dog circus woman; she might have gone any direction. He leaned away from the horse to vomit until he had dry heaves. He got off and walked to spare the horse; it was late afternoon before he got back to the ruined camp.

Big Candy was half crazy, frantic to recover the money. Sister Salt could tell by the expression in his eyes he blamed her and the twins because they were friendly with the woman. She pointed out she had lost everything too, but Big Candy's face was rigid with anger. He didn't look at her directly and he didn't glance down at the baby, whose face was getting fat and cute now. At that moment he wasn't the man she knew; he was someone different. He wanted to know what she knew about the dog circus woman and where she might have gone from here. When she shrugged, he looked as if he wanted to strike her but managed to hold his temper.

Sister told him what she knew about the uprising in Mexico, and about the crippled dog trained to sniff out cash. But she didn't tell him Delena bragged about how much the dog circus would make for her that night. Sister remembered vividly the amused expression on Delena's face as she said, "A dog circus like this can make more money than you might think."

"How's that?" Maytha had asked, and Delena only smiled and nodded slowly; just wait and see, she told them. Now they all saw but it was too late.

◆   ◆   ◆

That floor safe was so full of cash and coins, the money-sniffer dog easily located the safe's burial spot days before the finale. The most difficult part of the operation had been to learn the safe's combination. Though she disliked high places, she climbed the cottonwood tree above the buried floor safe to wait in the dark for the bobbing light of Candy's lantern. Candy had been full of the boss man's brandy by the time he brought the sacks of the day's receipts to the safe; often he was singing and talked to himself. But the hours watching from the treetop paid off because each night she listened intently and counted the clicks of the safe's dial. The sand stuck in the dial and some nights he had difficulty getting the safe open, and he'd get impatient and repeat some of the numbers out loud as he turned the dial again. Once she knew how to open the safe, she might have emptied it any night and fled; but she wanted to make a clean sweep.

What a night it had been! The dogs were amazing and did everything she taught them. That audience got their money's worth all right! The banknotes, silver, and gold locked up in the airless darkness deserved to be set free, to go south where it was needed, where it would be circulated—where the little gold pieces and $5 bills would get free air and sunshine!

She dared not follow the river because searchers would go that way; so she and the dogs headed for the hills toward the southwest, in the direction of the old gardens Sister Salt used to talk about. She packed each dog with a portion of the cash and coins, but the dogs' packs carried only water and no food, to reduce the weight of the load. She went south, along game trails in the foothills far from the river, to create a hardship for her pursuers' thirsty horses.

She memorized the creeks and rivers from confiscated army maps before she left on her mission. In a sandy floodplain she used yucca to wipe away their tracks before she and the dogs abruptly doubled back a distance north again to reach a creek that later joined the Havasupai River, then south to the Gila River junction with the Santa Cruz. From there it would be a straight shot south to Tucson, where their group had dedicated supporters and the local merchants loved money far more than they feared the law. They would sell as many boxes of rifles and cartridges as she wanted to buy for cash—no questions asked.

◆　◆　◆

The disturbance and fire so near the construction site spoiled the dinner plans with Wylie's associates; strangely this cancellation of the dinner seemed to accelerate Wylie's replacement as site supervisor by the army officer with the troop detachment. Although the water dispute between California and Arizona farmers that initially brought the troops had subsided, the camp rampage was evidence of worker unrest and the possibility of sabotage to the new dam.

Wylie was placed on leave with full pay and benefits for the duration of his contract; an assistant to the secretary of the Interior Department wrote Wylie a letter commending his years of service on federal construction sites. Wylie looked at his dismissal as a paid vacation; besides, he'd lost much more money in the bank crash of '93.

Wylie tried to put their loss into perspective: Candy had escaped losses in '93 because he never used banks. One time it paid Candy not to use a bank; but now Candy suffered a loss that a bank prevents. Even so, Wylie still preferred to take his chances with his money in a hole before he'd watch the bankers rob him again. Bankers were untouchable, but the Mexican woman and her dogs might be tracked down and caught, though it wouldn't be easy. She might be dangerous, she might ambush Big Candy along the river, and one man could never fight her and shoot all those dogs at the same time. She might have accomplices hiding out in the hills who would pick off any pursuers one by one. If they got the army or law enforcement involved, they'd never see the money again even if the woman was caught.

"No, forget it," Wylie told him. They would make back that money in a year or less if they opened a hotel and restaurant together in Los Angeles. Wylie had money buried in the backyard of his mother's house in Ohio. Enough to get them started. Think of the abalone flesh white as the breakers, their taste as delicate as the scent of the sea breeze; only Big Candy knew how to make the delicate breading of sherry, egg white and walnut flour before he braised the abalone in sweet butter. Los Angeles was waiting for a chef like Candy to show them how to cook.

Candy felt anger sweep over him as Wylie spoke. Easy for Wylie to talk—he still had money. Hell, he started with money! Candy lost everything—years of working day and night. A man could do nothing for himself without money; here a man, white or colored, was nothing without money.

He saw Wylie truly wanted him to accompany him, Wylie really was his friend—he didn't blame Candy or criticize his judgment. But somehow that only made the loss worse because his friend Wylie trusted him to take care of the floor safe and he failed. Now everything was meaningless except recovering the stolen money as soon as possible.

Wylie even invited Sister Salt and the baby to come along too, but

Candy shook his head. He told Wylie to go on ahead to Long Beach without him. He couldn't explain to Wylie but he was consumed by the feeling he had failed to measure up, and only by finding that dog circus woman and their money could he be restored.

Wylie was amazed at the effect of the theft on Big Candy; he was inconsolable, transformed so Wylie barely knew him. Nothing else mattered—Wylie even offered to loan Candy money to go ahead with his plans in Denver, but Candy refused.

Before he left, Wylie gave Candy the address in Long Beach where he'd be staying. He finally persuaded Candy to take his old shotgun, $50 for food, and one of the big mules to ride. All Candy needed was a little time and he'd get over it and start thinking clearly again. Wylie just hoped, in the meantime, Candy didn't go off and get himself killed.

Delena and the dogs trotted slowly but steadily away from the river over the sandy ridges to the dry gravel flats that stretched east and south. From time to time they stopped to rest, and she checked each dog's pack to make sure it was secure, and not rubbing off any hide. Though the days were still hot, now as the morning star rose a light wind stirred and chilled her until she started moving again. Finally, just before dawn they reached the precipitous edge of the big arroyo that would take them to Havasupai Creek.

She waited while the dogs scouted the steep clay bank until they located a game trail down. Even so she found herself sliding down on her seat, the slope was so steep. It was much cooler down there; as she hoped, there were still muddy water holes along the creek bottom from the rain the month before. After she drank and refilled her canteen, she walked until she found a pocket of deep fine sand at the foot of the clay bank. Oh the soft sand felt so good as she dropped to her knees and hands; she removed her backpack to scoop out a bed for herself. She used the pack for a pillow; it was heavy and hard, not with cash but with the big canteen and the chunk of roasted beef she grabbed off the grill. That and any rats they might catch was all they had to get them to the Havasupai River. The money sniffer curled up with her and one by one the other six dogs took their place until Delena was covered with dogs. She patted and scratched each dog—not too long or the others would get jealous and want to fight. Yes, I know you love me, she said; you love me for that big piece of roast beef in my pillow.

The last few days and nights she got very little sleep as she feverishly prepared the dog circus performance and spied on the buried safe. Now she was exhausted. Almost as soon as the last dog pressed itself across her shoulders, she was asleep so deeply the dogs' barks at coyotes scarcely roused her.

When the sun was midway overhead, the dogs began to get up, stretch, and go off to relieve themselves and drink. When only the crippled money-sniffer dog remained, Delena sat up; the warmth of the sun felt so good she wanted to lie down again and sleep more, but she knew they had to get going again.

She was curious about her pursuers so she brought out the Gypsy deck from the bag she wore inside her dress, around her waist, and spread the satin cloth over the sand to see what the cards had to tell her.

The Gypsy cards were oddly unmatched and had little to say about her pursuers; she realized then there must be only a few pursuers, maybe only one, and that was the reason for the cards' meager information. The unusual disarray of the cards gave her suspicions of invisible intervention to protect her lone pursuer. He must be a fool to come after me and my dogs by himself. No wonder his ancestors took pity on him and tried to block the cards. Still, she could feel the golden threads of the radiance from across time that turned the cards and spoke the truth about her pursuer, like it or not.

The figure of the Owl was lying on its side against a blood red background; the Owl wore a gold crown and was tied to a branch with a golden chain. Too bad for her pursuer! The Owl's position meant his plans will fail! She let out a shout of joy that brought all the dogs to stare at her. She remembered the message of the cards to the Sand Lizard woman, that greed would be punished—this Owl bound by a gold chain must be the Sand Lizard's husband.

The figure of the Four-leaf Clover on dark purple lay on its side, the same as the Owl, and meant a misunderstanding, something her pursuer didn't know, maybe about her or maybe about himself. Good, good, she whispered to the cards, and the dogs nearby wagged their tails.

The last figure was of the white Lilies upside. "Oh poor Sand Lizard girl, your husband is very confused." The poor man was beset by useless doubts for no reason. Now that she knew who her pursuer was and his state of mind, she wasn't in such a hurry. Even a good tracker would find it difficult to tell the difference between coyote tracks and her dogs' tracks; their paws were callused like the coyotes'. She was careful to walk on hard-packed ground and in the sand to step from rock to rock when she could; on long stretches of sand she stopped from time to time to wipe away her tracks.

391

Her pursuer had to decide which way she went, and the fastest, easiest route to Mexico was straight south along the river to Yuma. Even if he guessed right and rode east, he still had to catch her; the most stout horse or mule would soon tire from toting a man that heavy; the mount would need water and food—a great deal more water than he'd find on the route she was on.

She and the dogs slept in the shade all afternoon, moving from one side of the wash to the other as the sun shifted. As the air cooled off before sundown, the dogs got up, stretching and sniffing the air. They managed to locate a nest of baby cottontails in the clay bank, but gobbled them all before Delena could get any for herself. "OK," she said, "if you won't share, then I won't either"; she cut herself big pieces off the roast in her pack but gave none to the dogs.

She drank and washed her hands and face a last time in a rainwater hole the dogs hadn't muddied. Before she set out again, she peeked at the Mexican cards in their pouch: she was happy and relieved to find La Estrella, the Star, on top of the deck. The stars were celestial beings, all related to the most beautiful and beloved star, the morning star. She never forgot the devotion in her homeland to the Shining One the Christians call Messiah.

Indigo was too excited to sit still. She opened the hatbox to give the orchid plants sunshine after the first night on the train, just as Edward suggested. Hattie said they were among the nicest plants he had. She must remember to give them morning sun but not too much water or they would rot. She checked to make sure the paper envelopes of seeds were still neatly tied so none spilled, and felt each little cotton sack of gladiolus corms to make sure they were still dry in the bottom of the valise.

Hours before the train approached Needles, she cleaned the monkey's cage as she promised she would if Edward allowed her to bring Linnaeus along. She put down clean newspaper she saved after Edward finished reading it.

Out the window she saw the jagged dry peaks of the Paiute mountains hazy blue in the distance across the gravel and sand of the plain. As the sun got lower in the sky and they got closer, the mountains changed colors— light blue to violet to fiery red-orange as lovely as any flowers. Then as twilight settled over them, the fiery reds shifted to bright pinks that settled into lavender and finally dark purple. The window in the compartment was open only a bit but Indigo put her face to the rushing air and was delighted to smell the greasewood and the rocks.

It was not dark yet when the conductor called out, "Needles." Indigo felt her stomach flutter and her heart beat faster. As the train pulled into the station, she saw the station lanterns were lit along the platform, where eastbound passengers and people meeting the train were gathered. She dreamed and imagined many times Mama and Sister Salt would be there in their place on the platform beside the Walapai and Mojave women.

She was so excited she could hardly wait. Even before the train jerked to a stop, Indigo was ready; the cover of the parrot cage was on and Linnaeus was in her arms, his cage left with the other luggage. She walked ahead of Hattie and Edward, but the other passengers swept around her and she had to hold the covered parrot cage tightly in both arms to keep hold of it. Hidden inside, Rainbow endured the bumps and noise in silence while Linnaeus clung to her piggyback with his eyes hidden against her shoulder. Here she was at last! The smells of the burnt coal, tar, and hot axle grease of the platform were just as she remembered from years ago. As the crowd of passengers and others began to clear the platform, her heart pounded with anticipation. She had dreamed about this moment so many times— how Mama and Sister Salt would be shocked, and then come running to greet her.

She stopped until the surge of people passed around her, and lifted the cage cover a bit to give Rainbow fresh air. She heard Hattie call out to ask if she was all right, but she was intent on the end of the platform blocked by the crowd. But as the platform cleared, she saw that the place near the station door where Mama and Sister Salt used to sit was empty.

As she looked up and down the long empty platform, the burning ache in her throat hurt so much when Hattie reached her, she was in tears. Her sobs frightened the monkey, who gripped her neck tighter until she had to set the parrot cage down on the platform and take him in her arms. They were gone, they were all gone, and now she'd never find Sister or Mama.

At the hotel, Hattie tried to reassure Indigo as she helped her pull the bedding onto the floor the way the child liked it. At dinner Indigo refused to eat or drink anything; then as the meal was over, she insisted that the food on her plate be wrapped to take back to Linnaeus and the parrot. Edward, annoyed at her insolence, attempted to correct her but the child shocked them by telling him to go to hell, then refused to speak at all.

Hattie had anticipated a joyous arrival and expected Indigo to be in good spirits now she was in her homeland. The return of the child to her family had become the primary focus of Hattie's attention, especially now that she and Edward agreed to separate. She realized she loved Indigo dearly—Edward's deception and all the rest did not matter so long as she secured Indigo's happiness.

Hattie again promised they would not leave the Colorado River until her sister and her mother both were found. But the child was inconsolable; tears rolled down her cheeks even as she arranged the parrot cage and monkey cage on either side of the bedding on the floor so she could touch them during the night.

In the adjoining room, Edward was at the table by the lamp, reading. He marked his place with a slip of paper before he closed the book and looked up with a smile. Now that they had agreed to live separately, the tension between them was gone. Tomorrow Edward would take the train to Winslow for the buggy ride to the meteor crater while she and Indigo would begin the search for her sister and mother.

In Riverside they agreed neither of them was suited to the married state, and left it at that. No further mention was made of his reckless deception or his unforgivable defense of the Australian doctor. The child seemed to be calmed now, no need for concern. They said good night and Edward turned back to his reading as she closed the door.

She was still saddened Edward seemed so relieved by their decision; she must have only imagined Edward's devotion to her just as she misread Mr. Hyslop's attentions. In any case, she would not make that mistake again. Before they left Riverside, she wrote to her parents to announce the mutual decision to obtain a legal separation as soon as possible, but gave no explanation. They were bound to hear all the details from Susan and Colin.

She agreed to a generous separation settlement and made arrangements with her bankers in New York to arrange a line of credit for Edward until his mother's estate and his debts were settled. She had no plans beyond the immediate goal of finding Indigo's sister and mother, but she did not want to return to New York. Oyster Bay belonged to a previous life, dead and buried with her manuscript.

Perhaps she would return to England or Italy—she dreamed about the gardens often. Aunt Bronwyn's old stones danced in one of her dreams, and in another dream, Laura's figures of the snake and bird women sang a song so lovely she woke in tears.

◆ ◆ ◆

The wagon road above the riverbank was dusty and hot. The footpaths through the willows along the river were shady and cool, Indigo told Linnaeus and Rainbow. The buggy had a cloth top but it was black and held the heat. She amused herself by pointing out places along the river and telling Linnaeus and Rainbow about the escape she and Sister made downriver the morning the dancers were attacked.

She felt more hopeful today because, the night before, she dreamed she was with Sister Salt at the old gardens, which were filled with great tall spikes of gladiolus flowers in all colors of the rainbow. Sister Salt cradled Linnaeus like a baby and Mama let the parrot sit on her shoulder; even Hattie was in the dream—she carried water from the spring in a big gourd balanced on her head.

As they drove out of town, Indigo watched people on the street point and stare at the empty monkey cage on top of the pile of luggage, and Linnaeus in her arms. The sandy hills were green with grass and weeds—a sign of good rain weeks before, and good news for the terrace gardens in the dunes. The corn plants would be tall, the amaranth thick, and the bean plants and sunflowers fat with seeds enough to see them through the winter. She had forgotten how big the sky was and how blue it could be when there were no clouds. Sand Lizard girl, you are almost home now, she whispered to herself.

Just south of the Chemehuevi reservation, they stopped for the night at a small trading post called Road's End, where the storekeeper's wife accommodated overnight guests in a small back room. At first the wife was reluctant to allow the monkey and parrot cages indoors, but Hattie gave her an extra half-dollar and promised to keep them caged, a promise Indigo did not keep. There was scarcely room for the cages and luggage around the small bed they shared. All night Hattie tossed and turned, and each time she felt another horsehair poke through the bedding from the mattress. In the morning, Indigo kept scratching at her legs and when they looked they saw little red welts of insect bites.

The following morning, the table in the kitchen was set with only two places; their driver seated himself at one but when Hattie asked, the wife told her the Indian girl could sit in a chair out on the front porch. Hattie said nothing, but removed her plate and cup from the table and joined Indigo, who was already out on the porch playing with the parrot and monkey, the four pots of orchids out of the hatbox in the sun.

All morning Hattie felt out of sorts from the wife's rude behavior, and exhausted from lack of sleep. The reflected glare of the sun off the metal of the horse's bit temporarily blinded her but when she closed her eyes, the burning white flash remained and quickly developed into a headache. She managed to sip a little paregoric from the bottle in her purse and then leaned back and closed her eyes to try to sleep. Instead her thoughts swarmed around and around—her mother's disapproval, her father's disappointment, her foolishness in believing Edward truly cared about her. She tried to control her thoughts by visualizing the lovely carved gemstones from the spring at Bath, the bright orange carnelian carving of Minerva seated with her serpent at her side, a pale yellow carnelian of a long-neck waterbird standing on its nest with its chick, and the cloudy chalcedony of the three cattle under the oak tree.

Edward was reluctant to part with any of them, but felt obliged after she agreed to make the loan. He sorted through the gem carving and gave her the three he didn't want. Perfect, she thought; I don't want anything he wants!

Indigo called out and Hattie roused herself to see what it was; up ahead on the river was a large earthwork—the dam to feed water to Los Angeles. Indigo was amazed at the changes all around; the river was trapped, and only a narrow stream, muddy red, flowed south. The river was stripped naked; all its willows and tamarisks were gone, its red clay banks scraped; and exposed piles of white skeletons of cottonwood trees dotted the swaths of scraped red earth. The deep gouges made to build the dam had trapped rainwater and now were filled with weeds and sunflowers. Rows of army tents lined the ridge above the river, and nearby were clusters of wagons, their canvas covers painted with prices for lamp oil and tobacco.

As they continued south, Indigo noticed the cottonwoods and willows were dying of thirst because the flow of the river was so meager. Parker wasn't actually a town; it was more like a stagecoach station at the edge of the reservation. A barbed-wire fence marked the entrance to the reservation. As they arrived, the children ran out to meet the buggy and they pointed at her and at the monkey and parrot and they shouted and laughed.

As they neared the superintendent's office, someone—probably the older boys—threw rocks at the buggy until the driver turned on the seat and swore at them, with no apology to Hattie. Dirty animals, he called them. He was the son of the livery stable owner who kept a toothpick in the corner of his mouth, and he made it clear he thought Hattie a fool or worse. The driver let them off outside the office of the reservation superintendent and drove away without a word, in the direction of the trading post.

Indigo waited outside the superintendent's office with the parrot on one shoulder and the monkey on her hip. She was careful to stand close to the wall around a corner where no one passing by the office could see her because she was afraid the children might hit Linnaeus or Rainbow with a rock.

Hattie was heartened by the reservation superintendent, who was new to the job but nonetheless located a file of correspondence written on behalf of Indigo's older sister, named Salt. Hattie noticed on the file Indigo's surname was listed as Sand. The last known address for the sister was in care of the construction site at the Parker Canyon dam. However, there were no records of their mother, but the superintendent admitted there were many more Indians along the Colorado River than were listed on the Indian Affairs census. The Indians moved a good deal. Apparently some of the tribes did not get along with one another and others complained the river bottom land wasn't healthy.

The superintendent shook his head. He had just transferred here from Oklahoma two months ago. The Indian Bureau lacked the resources to hire more officers to keep them on the reservations and to track down those who drifted back into the canyons and hills. He hastened to add they posed no threat to white people.

He picked up the file on Indigo for a moment before he glanced up to ask if she intended to adopt the child. Hattie was so surprised at his question she felt her cheeks flush, and for a moment she lost her composure.

There was no reason to adopt the child if she had an elder sister nearby, was there? The superintendent shook his head and moved another file on top of Indigo's file. The child's elder sister had been jailed for theft by the previous agency superintendent. She might still be there if her fines had not been paid by a contractor hiring workers for the site of the dam construction. The superintendent's face colored a bit as he added young squaws the sister's age often resorted to prostitution.

Hattie gathered her purse in her lap and thanked him for all his help. He reminded her the child was under his jurisdiction; if she was not returned to the boarding school in Riverside, she must be turned over to him, under penalty of federal law. Hattie assured him that she understood the conditions and promised to stay in touch.

The driver had bloodshot eyes when he finally returned for them; Hattie was furious because he kept them waiting on the porch of the superintendent's office for more than an hour, but the odor of liquor on his breath persuaded her to say nothing. Indigo's excitement and happiness at the good news far outweighed the irritation of the rude driver. Indigo could hardly wait to get there to see her big sister; if they got going now there was still time to get to the dam before dark, so Hattie directed the driver to go back upriver.

Hattie could not get the superintendent's words off her mind. What would happen to a child like Indigo, accustomed now to decent shelter and clothing and nutritious food? All the education she'd managed to get would be for naught if she came back to live here. Except for the vicious rock throwers, the reservation at Parker seemed lifeless; the few Indian women and men she saw had eyes full of misery. Indigo's beloved little monkey and the parrot would likely be stolen or killed almost at once. Perhaps adoption would be best for Indigo; the superintendent implied he could authorize the adoption himself.

Sister Salt recognized the old Walapai woman at the street corner in Needles and called to her. The old woman looked a long time as if trying to identify her, then suddenly a big toothless grin spread over her face and she called out and motioned for Sister to come over. First she wanted to see Sister's baby, and pronounced the little black grandfather healthy and fortunate, then she asked if Grandma Fleet was still weaving those little baskets shaped like turkeys and frogs. Sister Salt's face fell and she shook her head slowly; the Walapai woman knew immediately, and tears filled into her eyes. "And your mother?" she asked. "Is she still traveling with the dancers?" Sister Salt nodded, then asked if anyone had heard news of their whereabouts.

How long had it been—two winters almost, wasn't it? Sister Salt nodded. People here were afraid to dance because of the soldiers and Indian police. But if the people would just dance like before, then the Messiah and the dancers would return.

Maytha and Vedna were waiting for her across the street. They'd come into Needles to buy nails and check the town dump for pieces of scrap wood or tin they might use for their new house. They paid to ride on the back of the freight wagon that carried the mail between Parker and Needles twice a week; it was a two-day ride from Road's End to Needles, so they had to bring along their own water and food. The little black grandfather began to twist around in his bundle impatiently, and Sister Salt was about to excuse herself to go when the old Walapai woman put a hand on her arm.

"Wait! I've got important news for you," she said, "about your little sister." Sister Salt's heart pounded as she listened. Two days before, the Walapai woman saw Indigo get off the eastbound train; at first she didn't recognize her because she'd grown so much, and she wore fine new clothes and shoes. But it was her! She carried a colorful caged bird, and a funny furry creature clung to one arm; she was accompanied by a rich white man and woman with a great deal of luggage. They left the station in a rented buggy.

The woman's Walapai sisters agreed; they'd seen them too. But other Indian women, mostly Havasupai and Mojave, came over to disagree with the Walapai women. They said not to listen to her; the old Walapai woman had been crazy since she was kicked in the head by a cavalry horse, and her Walapai sisters drank too much beer.

Sister Salt politely thanked the old woman and her sisters; were they mistaken as the others said? Indigo was at boarding school in California, not with a white couple; she must have seen another girl. Deep down though, she felt hope and excitement; what if the Walapai women were right?

Later Sister showed the twins the place along the river just south of town where their lean-to had been; the ring of blackened stones that marked their hearth was still there, but nothing else. On trips to Needles with Big Candy, Sister used to avoid the place; for a long time she couldn't even bring herself to look directly at the high sandy hill above the riverbank where the Messiah and his family fled that morning. Instead she glanced at the hill from the corner of her eye, afraid that if she looked directly at it, she might cry.

After the dancers were arrested, all the shelters were torn down and burned. The Walapai women and the others relocated to the dry wash behind the train yard, so they had the riverbank by the town dump to themselves. But now, with the little bright-eyed grandfather in her arms, she felt heartened to be at the place they last were all together and happy, even if it was Needles. In the midday glare of the sun, the sandy slope of the hill looked different than it had that morning after dawn when the raiders came.

The days were shorter now, and the nights were cool. In a few more months the snowstorm clouds would return to the mountain peaks, and with them the Messiah and his family and the dancers. If the people gathered here and danced again, the Christ and the others would return, and Mama with them.

The twins suggested they camp there until they caught the mail wagon back to Road's End. As she lit the fire on the same hearth Mama and Grandma had used, she felt happy. But as the night wore on, she was saddened only the circle of burnt stones remained. Big Candy was gone, and with him went the help she needed to find Indigo. All the money she saved for the search and their return to the old gardens was gone. Damn money! She hated it but needed it too.

God damn that Mexican woman and all her dogs! God damn the war that sent her their direction! Sister knew better than to talk to strangers, but Delena seemed so nice. Although Big Candy didn't accuse her or the twins of aiding the thief, still in his mind they were connected, and that was enough. Even if Big Candy caught up with the woman and got back the money, Sister doubted she would ever see him again.

So much for the Sand Lizard notion that sex makes allies of strangers. She had months of sex with Candy but lost him as her ally anyway; he went off crazy after that Mexican woman and the money. Money! You couldn't drink it or eat it, but people went crazy over it.

That night the little grandfather snuggled against her breasts and talked to her as she slept. When she woke herself answering him, she found his black shining eyes gazing at her; the approach of dawn was milky gray across the east horizon. He wanted to return to the old gardens. Money wasn't necessary there—all the food the two of them needed could be gathered there. His little auntie, Indigo, would return there—she wouldn't forget the way home.

She pulled her shawl snuggly around them both, and adjusted the old blanket across her legs, careful not to wake Maytha and Vedna, both snoring softly nearby. As sunrise approached, she watched the light touch the slope of the high sandy hill, and imagined the Messiah and the others slowly descending the slope, ankle deep in the sand. But the angle of the sun was wrong—still too steep this time of the year—and she knew she could not see the Messiah and the others yet.

The twins stocked up on the things they'd need to live at Road's End—everything cost so much. The twins were good to her and shared their food without reproach or meanness, so Sister made herself useful by staying at their campsite with the little grandfather to guard the supplies the twins already bought. She bundled him onto her back and searched along the river for wild onions and watercress; she dug up cattail roots to boil for soup.

She was grateful now for all the meat and grease Big Candy fed her because her fat made milk for the baby even if she didn't have much to eat. He was getting so big and plump now and he could lift himself up and roll over; but the expression in his gleaming black eyes was still piercing and cranky, like that of an old man. He wanted to return to Sand Lizard country, away from the river dampness that caused fevers.

Bright Eyes she called him one day when he was gurgling and smiling on his blanket—he loved to feel the air on his bare bottom. She wanted to buy cotton cloth and a wool blanket to keep him cozy the coming winter, but she had no money. When they got back to Road's End, she would cut and soak yucca leaves and try to make little yucca baskets the way Grandma Fleet had—in shapes of turkeys or dogs; then she could bring the baskets to sell at the depot every two or three months. She practiced braiding and tying willow bark while Bright Eyes slept.

The day before the mail wagon left for the south, while the twins were busy tying bundles and packing, Sister went to visit the old Walapai woman a last time. Road's End was so far from any place—she didn't expect to get back to Needles again for months, and she wanted to see if the head injury really had affected the old Walapai woman, the way the others alleged. What if Indigo had returned with the rich white people?

Earlier she heard a westbound train arrive, so Sister looked for the women on the outdoor platform of the station. But when she saw the tourists flock around the women to buy their strings of cedar berry seeds, three for a penny, Sister stopped.

She was about to turn to leave when two tourists surprised her from behind and asked her and "the papoose" to pose for their camera. Sister started to turned away from them but out of the corner of her eye she saw a silver dollar between the white man's fingers. She'd seen only lucky gamblers with silver dollars; the workers used to pay her for walks along the river with nickles and dimes. Sometimes it might take her two days to earn a dollar, but she had fun naked and laughing along the river with the men.

She turned back to the tourist and nodded at the silver dollar in his hand. She gripped the silver dollar in her hand, her face hot with shame, and refused to look at the camera; instead she stared down at her feet. Hastily she pulled the baby's wrap up around his ears and chin so the glass eyes of the camera could not see his face and steal his energy. When the tourist finished she felt so ashamed she hurried away without telling the old Walapai woman good-bye.

She vowed never to let that happen again, no matter how much money she was offered. Fortunately the baby was not affected, but she felt weak and slightly nauseous after the encounter with the camera. The eye of the camera was the worst! Preachers condemned the sale of sex, but Sister always felt happy after her walks with the men; they always told her she was the prettiest—way prettier than the mattress women, who cost more. Naked on the river sand she always felt as free and joyous as that River Girl character in the old stories the twins heard at Laguna. The River Girl walks with Whirlwind Man and the poor receive venison and deer hides; when she goes off with Buffalo Man during a famine, the buffalo agree to give the starving humans their meat.

On the wagon ride back to Road's End, she surprised the twins with the silver dollar, for her share of the expenses. Maytha asked how she got it, but Sister shook her head and avoided her eyes. Vedna pestered her to tell until she confessed. They were concerned about the weakness she experienced immediately after the photograph; they'd heard stories at Laguna about old people who died within days of being photographed.

The people at Road's End were Chemehuevi Christian converts who kept to themselves. The twins found sheep and goat droppings on one end of the land—evidence their neighbors had been using their auntie's land in her absence; probably they hoped no one would claim it after the old woman died.

The day after they got back with their supplies from Needles the three of them were struggling to get the hole in the roof patched. Maytha stood precariously on the roof to pull the rope while Vedna, on a ladder, and Sister Salt, on the ground, lifted and guided the sheet of corrugated tin up. Just then a kind Chemehuevi man passing by on the road saw their struggle and stopped to help them. He was not young, but he was able and strong as he climbed the old ladder and took hold of the end of the tin and guided it into place. He was on an errand somewhere, because he carried a rope halter, but he stayed and helped them lift the other piece of tin roofing into place and even showed them how to nail it down to prevent leaks.

Late that afternoon, before sundown, the work was finished and they invited him for rabbit in amaranth soup, and he quietly accepted. He said nothing while they talked excitedly about how fast the old roof was becoming snug again. Now that the roof was on, they could welcome the winter rains, and not shiver.

They each thanked the man for his help before he continued down the road, the rope halter over one shoulder. But the following morning they were shocked to see an angry wife and her two sisters walk into the yard, their walking sticks firmly in their hands, ready to thrash someone. They called the twins and Sister prostitutes and told them to keep their hands off other women's husbands or else they'd call the Indian police to arrest them. They'd heard about the twins and their Sand Lizard pal going to jail in Yuma for stealing soap, so they better not steal anything else either.

Edward was saddened to see Hattie and the child on the station platform waving good-bye to him; the sight of the little monkey frolicking on the child's back brought tears to his eyes. He never imagined the marriage would end like this. Perhaps they were better suited to each other than to marriage itself. He had no regrets—he was accustomed to the single state. But he felt sorry for Hattie, who apparently suffered from the sort of nervous disorder recently reported in German scientific journals, an affliction found almost exclusively among highly educated women. In any case, they would remain cordial with each other; if Hattie later wished to petition for annulment, he intended to cooperate fully. She generously arranged a line of credit for him at her bank since time was of the essence in the purchase of the mining claim. Dr. Gates was negotiating with the prospector who owned the mining claim on the meteor crater site.

As the train traveled farther east, the bleak plain of gravel and sand scattered with sagebrush gave way to the juniper and piñon of the higher elevation. Now the great majestic peaks of the San Francisco Mountains could be seen, pale blue in the distance; though it was only September, caps of snow gleamed on the peaks. He was glad he packed along his camera despite its bulk.

Dr. Gates met the train and accompanied him to check into the hotel next to the train station. The following morning, after breakfast in the hotel restaurant, they set out in the buggy for the crater, some twenty miles to the southwest. The dry grassy plain was scattered with pale yellow sandstone ridges and occasional dark outcroppings of volcanic rock and crossed by a number of ravines that, though sandy and dry now, carried enormous floods of runoff during the wet season. The air was so clear the San Francisco peaks, snow-tipped and blue, stood out vividly on the horizon to the west.

The low silhouette of the ridge formed by the debris from the meteor impact was visible in the distance when the doctor directed the driver to turn the buggy into a sandy wash. They followed the wash some distance to the foot of a pale yellow-orange sandstone mesa forty feet high.

The prospector made the discovery the previous week while digging for Indian pots. They walked forty or fifty yards from the buggy up a sandy slope to the foot of the sandstone formation, where a large crevice provided hand- and footholds to reach the mesa top. The doctor halted on a ledge below the final ten feet to caution Edward: here the Indians must have used a ladder of some sort because the sandstone was steep and offered few hand- or toeholds to a climber. Edward looked up and then he looked back; he had come this far and he did not want to stop. He nodded for Gates to proceed and watched his companion scramble skillfully up the sandstone, his fingers and toes barely braced in shallow indentations of the rock.

Once on the top, Gates knelt and offered a hand to Edward, who took a deep breath and sprang upward, arms and feet seeking any means to hold long enough to propel him higher to the doctor's outstretched hand. For a moment he feared he would not have the momentum to make it, but he threw himself with all his might upward and the doctor pulled him to safety.

He was out of breath but exhilarated to reach the top of the mesa safely, and it wasn't until he followed the doctor over the low mounds of grass and fallen stones that he realized he might have strained the muscles in the weak leg. He stopped then briefly to gently stretch the leg to prevent its stiffening.

Gates led him to a mound next to a large boulder where the outline of a dwelling was visible. Next to the boulder Edward saw piles of freshly disturbed sand at the corner of a room. A large piece of canvas covered the excavation, which reached into the wall and under the boulder. Gates pulled back the cover with a flourish, and there in the stone cavity, Edward saw a most remarkable object: wrapped in the remains of a garment of feathers and cotton string was an iron meteorite. On one end of the iron were tiny stone beads once strung as a necklace, and nearby were two small pottery bowls. The doctor reached into one of the bowls and handed Edward a tiny pottery whistle in the shape of a bird.

"Amazing, isn't it?"

"Oh quite wonderful," Edward replied as he turned the little clay artifact over in his palm. The burial objects with the meteorite—the tiny stone bead necklace and the toy whistle—were intended for a child.

"Well you haven't seen anything yet!" his companion exclaimed as he carefully pulled back the remains of the feather blanket from the "head" of the meteorite to reveal a glittering "eye" in the lustrous black iron.

"White diamond!" he said triumphantly.

Edward spent a good deal of time on his hands and knees examining the object and its site. He regretted his camera was down below in the wagon and the ascent so difficult; otherwise he might have recorded the Indian burial of the meteorite. In the catalogue of North American meteorites he had been amazed to read about a three-thousand-pound meteor iron discovered in Indian ruins in northern Chihuahua in a room with human burials, wrapped in native cotton just like the others. The prospector wanted to removed it at once, but the doctor managed to persuade him to wait until Edward could see the wonderful object just as it was found. Edward hoped the prospector would agree to sell it at a reasonable price.

From the mesa top the doctor pointed southeast, where the circular lip of the crater easily could be seen; tons and tons more of diamond-bearing iron waited for them there.

The descent was made easier thanks to the rope their driver tossed up and the doctor secured around a sturdy boulder, but effects of the strain on his leg were evident. The pain subsided as long as he managed to keep the leg propped up straight in the back of the buggy during the remainder of the ride. Later that evening in the camp on the rim of the crater, the doctor examined the leg and the redness and swelling around the scar. He gave Edward a handful of morphine tablets to take as needed for the discomfort but saw no need for concern. The buggy driver was a retired railroad engineer who hired on to drive and to serve as the camp cook. That evening he prepared a brace of quail he shot the day before, and Gates brought out a bottle of fine brandy to celebrate Edward's arrival. The brandy enhanced the effect of the pills, and the pain subsided.

The prospector arrived after dark on a mule, towing a donkey loaded with his gear. He was a tall wiry man with a trimmed beard; he wore dusty overalls and a faded shirt, but his boots were new. His skin was sun darkened black as a Negro's but his bright blue eyes and long, pinched nose allowed no mistake, nor did his hair, sun bleached white-blond even under his wide-brim hat. The prospector was content to let others do the talking, but behind the wire-rimmed glasses, his blue eyes took in everything.

The following morning, despite the stiffness and swelling, the doctor pronounced the leg safe to proceed. Edward swallowed more pills for the pain and eased himself up into the buggy for the half-mile ride to the bottom of the crater. The test drilling rig was in place to begin a first series of test holes and there were high hopes all around. The plan was to put down test holes to determine the locations of the largest deposits of the meteor irons.

The bottom of the crater was covered with strange white and gray silica flour—melted sand particles pulverized in the meteor's collision. The drilling rig was sidelined by water seepage into the drilling hole; the crater was a natural rain-catchment device. Heavy rains some months before had flooded the ponds they used to dispose of water pumped from the drill hole. Now long canvas fire hoses snaked out of the pond of standing water around the drilling rig. The mule team was hitched to a large cylinder that operated bilge pumps to clear the exploration hole of water seepage, but an equipment breakdown halted all activity.

Dr. Gates and the drilling foreman spread open the map to show Edward the distribution of meteorite debris, which suggested the main mass of metals would be found here in this northeastern quadrant. The prospector stood by patiently with the assay lab reports in his hand. They estimated the mass was buried under the southern wall some two thousand feet deep, and the meteorite itself weighed ten million tons.

Edward could hardly control his excitement as he read the assay reports. The most recent samples taken from the test hole proved to be almost pure cadmium with platinum, and traces of iridium, and palladium studded with white and black diamonds of industrial quality.

The following morning on their way back to the hotel in Winslow for baths and clean clothing, Gates confided the prospector was bored with the test drilling, accustomed as he was to roaming in search of mineral samples or Indian ruins to dig. The prospector decided to sell his mining claim, and offered it to the doctor first.

Naturally Edward understood the urgency of buying the claim lest a stranger buy it and gain control of the site. As soon as they reached the hotel and washed up, Edward sent a telegram to the bank in New York City for funds to be wired to the bank in Albuquerque.

♦ ♦ ♦

At the construction site Hattie spoke with the army officer in charge, who could only tell her some weeks before a number of workers and others had left after a violent disturbance broke out. Indigo stayed in the buggy to make sure Linnaeus and Rainbow had plenty of shade. She was teaching the two of them to get along with each other—Linnaeus learned to hold a sunflower seed in two fingers between the cage bars for Rainbow. As long she watched him, the parrot politely took the seed, but if she turned away, Rainbow tried to pinch the monkey's fingers with his beak.

The officer in charge consulted with his aide-de-camp, who left the tent to find the young Mexican, Juanito, who might know. The young officer insisted Hattie take his field chair and have a cup of water while they waited. He was from Pennsylvania and this was his first assignment out west. His face lit up when Hattie mentioned New York and Boston; the dust and the heat here were almost unbearable.

The aide returned with a young Mexican man, who listened to Hattie's description of the young Indian women she sought; yes, of course he remembered them, he said with a smile; they were a lot of fun. Hattie's cheeks colored and she looked away; the captain cleared his throat. Did he know where they went? Juanito nodded. The Chemehuevi girls bought land at Road's End and the other girl went with them.

Hattie asked if there were accommodations for travelers nearby; it was half past four, much too late to start out for Road's End. The captain consulted with his aide briefly, then offered her and the child his tent for the night, and invited them to dine with him. Gallant Captain Higgens even found space in a tent with enlisted men for the buggy driver, who declined the offer with a sullen shake of his head. Hattie was determined to replace the man as soon as they returned to Needles.

Indigo took the monkey cage down to the river to clean out and wash; the buggy driver muttered under his breath about "the stink of monkey shit and Indians." She found a shallow puddle and washed out both cages even though Rainbow's wasn't dirty.

Later that evening, over supper, the captain alluded to the driver's rudeness and local resentment at the presence of federal troops. Of course, Arizona had been Confederate territory, and the captain suspected the locals resented the army's protection of the Indian reservation boundaries. He smiled at Indigo. She certainly was intelligent and well mannered, thanks, no doubt, to Hattie's efforts.

Hattie smiled and nodded, but she was beginning to feel a bit uncomfortable with the captain's enthusiasm. Her wedding ring was in plain view but he may have assumed she was widowed. She told Indigo to get ready for bed, and the captain excused himself and said good night.

The army cot was terribly uncomfortable, and in the middle of the night, Hattie pulled the bedding to the tent floor next to Indigo. She fell into a deep sleep then, and dreamed she was back in the hidden grotto in Lucca alone with a cleft oval stone, which began to softly shimmer and glow until it was lustrous and shining, too bright to look at directly. The light itself, not the stone, spoke to her, though not with words but feelings.

She woke still embraced by a sense of well-being and love; she wept from a happiness she did not understand. Later she decided the young captain's attentions, not surprisingly, had affected her sleep. In any case, the captain and his men were gone by the time she and Indigo got dressed and repacked. The captain's cook had set a table in the officers' mess tent for the two of them. Eat hearty, he warned them; Road's End was a long way from anything like real food. At the end of the meal Hattie asked if they might wrap up some biscuits to take along. Later the cook not only gave them biscuits; he rinsed out a whiskey jug and filled it with fresh water.

In the early afternoon the driver stopped to rest the horses under a lone cottonwood tree at the mouth of a gulley near the road. Hattie and Indigo walked a distance away into the greasewood brush to relieve themselves; they took turns keeping watch for each other in case the driver followed.

They ate biscuits in the buggy in silence and did not try to offer the driver any. The young man fairly seethed with anger if Hattie even asked the distance they'd gone. Whenever he stopped to rest the horses, out came the knife to carve more toothpicks from green twigs off the nearest tree. The first few times she saw the knife, Hattie felt sick with apprehension, but gradually she became accustomed to his hostile behavior.

They reached the trading post at Road's End in the afternoon before sundown. An Indian woman and her little boy were browsing in the aisles of the store, but Hattie saw very little to buy on the dusty shelves; some dented canned goods, peaches and tomatoes, matches, lamp chimneys, nails. The trader and his wife seemed barely to recognize Hattie from their stop there night before last until Indigo peeked in the door with the parrot on her shoulder and the monkey in her arms. The couple scowled in recognition, and the trader's wife announced no animals in the store.

Hattie inquired about the three girls who recently moved there—twin sisters and their friend—but the trader shook his head while the wife turned away her face full of contempt. Don't ask them; ask the Indian agent.

Hattie pretended to shop but she wasn't sure she wanted to touch anything in the store; the thick gray dust on the shelves was peppered with rodent droppings. Finally she picked up a can of coffee, a can of peaches, and a can of cream corn, and asked where the sugar and flour were kept. The trader indicated two wooden bins behind the counter where he stood and she asked for five pounds of each. As he poured the flour from the scoop into the paper sack on the scale, Hattie could see the tiny weevils wiggle. The last item she bought was a half-gallon tin of lamp oil, which she regretted almost immediately because its odor seeped out no matter how tight its lid. Hattie was surprised at how much these few items cost, then remembered this was the only store for miles. The bright-colored candy balls in the glass jar next to the cash register were the most appealing items in the store, so she bought a sack of them for a quarter.

The woman and her little boy stopped their browsing to watch Hattie, and the boy's eyes widened when he saw the big sack of candy balls. As Hattie passed them on her way out, she reached into the sack and gave the boy a handful of candy. The boy smiled and his mother nodded, and they followed Hattie.

Outside the boy and his mother watched with amazement as Indigo showed them the parrot and the monkey; they wanted to touch the monkey, so Indigo showed them how Linnaeus would shake hands. The little boy shook hands with the monkey, then looked at Indigo closely and asked if she was an Indian. His mother nudged him and whispered in his ear. "Oh," he said and looked down.

Hattie explained Indigo was sent away to school, but now they were looking for her sister, who was living with two other girls, twin sisters.

The driver was annoyed at the delay and moved the buggy out from under the cottonwood tree to signal his impatience. Just as Hattie and Indigo were about to go, the Indian woman pointed east to the ridge above the river.

"See?" she asked, still pointing. Hattie squinted and looked in the direction she pointed, but could see nothing that resembled a house. She thanked the woman and got into the buggy after Indigo. She pointed in the same direction the woman had for the driver, who shook his head and exhaled impatiently as he picked up the reins and released the brake.

All along the river there were large fields with plows and cultivators parked nearby; melons, beans, and corn grew by the acre. There was another crop, which Indigo did not recognize at first glance—dark green bushes covered with small white flowers. Hattie pointed out the bolls of cotton Indigo mistook for blossoms. Here and there at the edge of the fields they saw little lean-tos for shade, but no people.

Above the river on an ancient floodplain, they passed a small wooden church neatly painted white amid a cluster of small wooden houses also painted white. Each house had a little garden of corn and sunflowers; some had pens with chickens or goats.

Was the buggy high off the ground, or what? Indigo wondered, because everything seemed so small. So this is what happened to your eyes if you looked at white people's things too long. Hattie wanted to ask someone to be sure they had the right directions but no one seemed to be home. Indigo kept quiet; she knew no one would come out while the white man was there. They continued up the sandy road to the low ridge above the river bottom where the woman pointed.

Now that they were close, Indigo put both the monkey and the parrot back into their cages; her heart beat faster as they started up the last incline of river stones and sand to a little house of mud and stone with patches of new tin on its roof.

The clatter of the buggy wheels over the river cobblestones at the top of the ridge brought two heads cautiously out the doorway; they looked just alike—twins! This was the right place! She grabbed the sideboard and swung herself down to ground before the buggy was fully stopped, landing so hard her feet stung.

The sight of the loaded buggy, and a dark girl in a fancy blue dress who jumped before it even stopped, left the twins speechless for a moment. Inside Sister Salt was nursing the little grandfather but he let go of her nipple to listen, and ignored the drop of milk on his cheek. For an instant Sister was worried and gathered him up, ready to run; but Vedna turned back from the door, eyes wide, and nearly breathless. She said, "I think it's your sister!" then followed Maytha outside.

Sister stood up with the baby just as Indigo appeared in the doorway. For an instant she almost didn't recognize Indigo because she had grown so tall; now her features resembled their mother's a great deal. Indigo threw her arms around Sister and she put her free arm around Indigo and they embraced each other, while the little grandfather squirmed between them. They held each other and cried until the baby got angry at being squeezed and let out a howl that made Indigo step back.

"Oh Sister! A baby!" she said, tears still running down her cheeks. "Look at him! He's cute!" The twins stood in the doorway and watched them, but they kept glancing outside too. Finally Sister got curious and turned to look outside too; then Indigo remembered Hattie in the buggy and her pets.

"Come meet my friends," she said.

They ignored the driver, who sat in the buggy and glowered at them as

410

they invited Hattie inside. They gave Hattie the crate they used as a table to sit on while they sat on their bedrolls on the floor. Sister and Indigo talked nonstop in a mixture of English and the Sand Lizard language.

At first Hattie and the twins listened while the sisters talked, but after a while Maytha got bored and asked Hattie questions about where they'd been and how they tracked down Sister. Hattie described the visit to the superintendent at Parker and the stop at the site of the dam. When she mentioned the kind woman with the little boy who directed them here, the twins exchanged glances, and Vedna remarked, "Oh I guess someone here doesn't hate us!" Then she laughed.

Outside in the wagon, the parrot began to call Indigo with loud screeches, which silenced Sister and the twins. Oh! Indigo jumped to her feet and looked at Hattie. They all went outside and Indigo handed the parrot cage down to Hattie and opened the monkey cage for Linnaeus, who climbed on her back; the empty cages were easier to lift. Indigo pulled out her luggage and the hatbox with the orchid plants from Hattie's luggage piled in the back of the buggy and handed them to the girls. The driver looked straight ahead, chewing hard on a toothpick, and made no move to help. Maytha nudged Vedna and they both made faces at the driver behind his back, then laughed.

Hattie saw the driver look around at the lengthening shadows, then glare at her impatiently as the sun settled toward the horizon. Finally as the girls took Indigo's luggage inside, the driver cleared his throat loudly, spat on the ground, and asked her if she was staying or going. She better decide—because *he* wasn't staying here tonight.

Hattie felt her face flush, and the palms of her hands were damp; her heart pounded and she began to feel light-headed. She told the driver to wait for her in a sharp tone of voice she hadn't used before, and scarcely noticed his scowl. She realized she hadn't prepared herself for parting with Indigo; she hadn't really believed they'd locate her sister so easily or so soon. She parted with Edward because it was the right thing; neither of them wanted the marriage to continue. But she loved Indigo with all of her heart; without the girl she didn't know what she would do.

Hattie watched from the doorway as the girls chattered happily inside, laughing all together. It was clear how much Indigo's homeland meant to her, and how she loved her Sister Salt. The two girls delighted in each other. She'd never seen Indigo's face glow with such joy. She scarcely would have recognized the laughing, chattering child as Indigo.

Hattie felt relief and pride too that she'd reunited the sisters, but another sensation began to emerge—a dreadful sense of how alone she was. But that was silly, she scolded herself; both her parents were in good health, and Edward and she were not estranged; they would still correspond.

She had to get hold of herself for Indigo's sake. The two sisters were reunited, but what about their mother? If the mother could not be found, would the authorities allow Sister Salt to care for Indigo? The reservation superintendent said the law required Hattie to give him a full update on Indigo's whereabouts, the sort of family her sister had, and what school she would attend.

Out of the corner of her eye, Sister saw the white woman watch them from the doorway, and she wondered what the woman wanted. Why did this woman take Indigo away from the boarding school?

"Good-bye," Indigo heard Hattie call and looked up from her unpacking.

"Oh! I thought you would stay longer," Indigo said as she walked Hattie to the buggy. The other girls followed; Sister held up the little grandfather so he could get a good look at Indigo's white friend. Maybe tonight after they were asleep, the little grandfather would give her information on that woman. He watched his auntie and the white woman intently.

Hattie hugged Indigo once and then again; she'd be back to check on her next week, and maybe have some news for the girls on the whereabouts of their mother.

"You could stay here if you wanted," Indigo said, glancing at the driver, then looking Hattie in the eyes. They both knew what she meant.

"I'll be fine, don't worry," Hattie said, but she was too upset by their parting to worry about the driver. She doubted there would be any trouble because he was in such a hurry to get to Needles. He started the horses almost before she was seated, but Hattie had to smile because the girls all made faces at him for her benefit. Hattie was beginning to have a plan for the weeks to come; it all revolved around Indigo and her sister.

Indigo gave the twins the smelly can of lamp oil and the bundle of canned goods, sugar, and flour Hattie bought at the trading post. She opened the valise of seeds and gladiolus corms only long enough to remove the tin of seeds and grain to fill the cup in Rainbow's cage, and filled the other cup from their water bucket with the flat sandstone lid.

"Oh candy balls!" Maytha called out as she held up the paper sack.

"Too bad she didn't buy us some lard or coffee—we could have had tortillas and coffee for supper!" Vedna said as she stuffed two candy balls into her mouth. They all helped themselves to the candy.

Indigo took out her color pencils and her notebook to show off her drawings of flowers to Sister while the twins lifted the fine linen underwear and petticoats from the trunk. They oohed and aahed over the chambray dresses trimmed in satin ribbon, and joked with one another about how much money they could sell them for—enough to eat for months, they laughed.

Indigo unpacked her two other pairs of new kidskin slippers and held them next to Maytha's bare feet; the shoes were too small, but Maytha and Vedna didn't care. They stretched the kidskin and forced the slippers on their feet, and wore them proudly.

The little grandfather was in his bundle proppped up in the corner of the room so he could watch. Sister opened the big hatbox and lifted up a pot of orchids for a better look. Indigo cautioned her sister to be careful with the plants, which irritated Sister.

"You think I don't know what a flowerpot is?" She put it back in the hatbox just as she found it. Indigo saw Sister's hurt expression and felt terrible; she apologized over and over until Sister told her it was all right. Indigo tried to hand her the hatbox of orchids—she insisted she take them, but Sister shook her head; she knew nothing about these plants; she'd only kill them.

Indigo hated herself for hurting Sister's feelings—she loved her more than anyone, as much as she loved Mama and Grandma Fleet. If Sister didn't want the orchids, then Indigo didn't want them either. She tossed the hatbox out the door; it landed with a thud on the sand, and all the pots overturned, dumping bark, orchids, and all. Later Sister took pity on the poor orchids and scooped them back into their pots and gave them a place on the windowsill.

It was getting dark now and Maytha filled their lamp with oil; they hadn't bought lamp oil in so long they didn't bother to replace the lamp chimney after it shattered. They used a piece of rag for the wick, and Vedna lit one of their precious matches; a lovely orange-yellow flame glowed in the dark room. Without the proper wick or chimney it gave off puffs of sooty smoke, but they didn't care.

They finished off the candy balls but had no way to open the tins of peaches and corn. Sister laid down the sleeping baby and took the cans and the axe outside. Whack-whack-whack, they heard, and a moment later Sister returned, both hands cupped around the can dripping sugary peach juice. Indigo shared her portions of the peaches and the corn with Linnaeus, then put him to bed in his cage next to Rainbow. After they finished off the can of corn, the twins and Sister took the tin of tobacco and rolling papers outside for a smoke before bed.

Indigo realized then she had no bedding, no blanket, so she arranged her wool coat and raincoat on the sandy floor near Sister's bedding. For covers she used her nightgowns one on top of the other, and slept in her clothes as the other girls did.

◆ ◆ ◆

Hattie noticed the buggy driver was acquainted with the trader and his wife; all the white people here seemed to know one another. "Strength in numbers," she supposed, since whites were outnumbered by Indians here. The driver probably stopped there overnight each time he drove to Parker or Yuma. Hattie smelled fried chicken and biscuits, but the woman said nothing about food. She wasn't really hungry anyway; she was worried about Indigo. Maybe she was wrong to leave the child at Road's End. Indigo's sister and her friends seemed nice enough, but they'd created a good bit of notoriety for themselves along the river.

The trader's wife put her in the same room as she and Indigo had shared the night before last; the sheets on the bed had not been changed. She brought out the bottle of paregoric syrup Edward gave her for emergencies, to help her sleep. She pulled the bedding to the floor off the horsehair mattress, and wept because this was Indigo's custom, to sleep on the floor. Blankets! Indigo had no blankets, nothing!

Hattie rolled over and sobbed facedown in the pillow, so the others did not hear. She took two good swallows of the paregoric and lay back with her eyes closed, listening to her own heartbeat. Gradually her heart and her breathing slowed and the anxiety over Indigo without blankets gradually passed. Her sister and the other girls would take care of Indigo; it was plain how much her sister loved her, and the other girls seemed very kind. Hattie would simply buy Indigo blankets and other necessities the girls might need and return to Road's End next week, but this time with a new driver. She drifted away to sleep as she imagined warm white wool blankets piled next to the parrot cage in the little mud house.

She dreamed the bright orange carnelian carving of Minerva seated with her snake was a life-size sculpture in a fantastic garden of green shady groves and leafy arcades. Next to the path stood a life-size waterbird and her chick carved from pale lemon yellow carnelian. In a thicket of holly she heard rustling and twigs cracking as if something large were approaching. Oddly, she wasn't afraid when she saw the old tin mask rolling down the grassy path as if it were alive.

She woke and struck a match to see the clock: half past twelve. She lit the lamp on the table and opened the trunk and brought out the little carvings. She arranged them on the nightstand so they were at eye's level from her pillow, and thrilled at their lustrous surface and transparent glow. Where were you in my dream? she asked the milky chalcedony carving of the three cattle. She took a sip of water and put out the light; oddly, the tin mask no longer seemed threatening.

Hattie ate the breakfast the woman served them, and was surprised at how good the eggs with biscuits and slices of smoked ham tasted. She was relieved the others at the table ignored her; nothing she could say or do would change their opinion of her: white squaw. Fortunately, her year of graduate classes prepared her for obnoxious conduct.

Now that she had decided her course of action, even the ride back to Needles seemed shorter. As the buggy passed through the business district of Needles she noticed a large mercantile and dry goods store on the corner; tomorrow she would shop there for Indigo's blankets and the others things the girls should have. She needed to visit the local bank to arrange for a transfer of funds from her account in New York.

The hotel desk clerk studied her signature after she signed the guest book and handed her a letter from Edward, postmarked Winslow. Edward described the campsite at the bottom of the meteor crater and the sorry condition of the equipment, especially the drilling rig, which broke down more days than it worked. But all that would be corrected very soon. He and the doctor were about to board the train to Albuquerque with the latest discovery—a wonderful meteor iron studded with white diamonds—to have it assayed. New mining equipment would also be purchased on this trip, and he hoped he did not have to exceed the credit line she arranged for him.

He described in colorful detail the mesa climb and mentioned "a slight stiffness" in his leg, but devoted the remainder of the letter to a description of the Indian burial—the "baby," or meteor iron, wrapped in layers of feather blanket, wore a tiny necklace and matching bracelet of tiny beads. Funeral offerings of food and a toy whistle were carefully arranged in the stone cavity with the meteor iron.

That night Hattie dreamed Sister Salt's live baby was in the stone cavity, but Edward and the Australian doctor insisted on using a large steel pick and heavy shovel to excavate the baby. She woke soaked with sweat and shaking; in her dream one of them struck something and Edward yelled. She saw blood spurting everywhere and a tiny severed leg; but the infant in the stone cavity was unharmed, even smiling.

She just finished dressing when there was a knock, and a telegram envelope was slipped under the door. Her heart beat furiously in those moments before she opened the telegram. It was sent from Albuquerque and all it said was: "Urgent. Come at once. Your husband hospitalized." It was signed by the chaplain of St. Joseph's Hospital.

If she packed only one bag and hurried, there was still time to make the eastbound train to Albuquerque. She felt light-headed and had to sit down on the edge of the bed.

◆ ◆ ◆

Indigo woke up before the others and took Rainbow and Linnaeus for a walk along the river; the sun had just come up and she thought the early start might get them more food. The first day she walked the river, Indigo realized others from the settlement of houses by the church walked along here to search for greens or other plants to boil and eat. Before the government drew reservation lines, there was plenty for everyone to eat because the people used to roam up and down the river for hundreds of miles to give the plants and animals a chance to recover. But now the people were restricted to the reservations, so everyone foraged those same few miles of river.

Up in the sandhills and high foothills, Indigo's luck was better; she knew the higher ground and what grew there better than she knew the riverbank. Anyway, long ago when they asked why Sand Lizards refused to live along the river, Grandma Fleet told them that too much time along the river put one at risk for fevers.

Indigo found a stand of sunflowers gone to seed near the mouth of an arroyo; ordinarily she would have only taken some and left the rest for the next hungry being who came along, but she was afraid her parrot would suffer if she did not take all the seeds, so she filled the pockets of her skirt. Linnaeus loved the seeds too, and Indigo began to plan a small winter garden for peas and greens and beans. Too bad the sunflowers had to be sowed in June, but next season she would sow rows and rows of the giant sunflowers. Next year she would harvest the big flat faces full of seeds for them all; but this year they were going to have to sell some of her clothes and things to buy food.

When she returned with her cache of sunflower seeds, the twins were snoring in unison, but Sister was sitting up on her bedding with the little grandfather at her breast. She proudly showed Sister all the greens and seeds she'd collected for the monkey and parrot. "What about me?" Sister asked. "Won't you offer me any?" She made the words sound like they were a joke, but Indigo knew there was truth in the joke too—if they barely had food for themselves, how could they spare food for pets?

Indigo opened the trunk to the compartment with the dresses and her light wool coat; she took them off the hangers and folded them carefully in stacks on top of the open wool coat. She tied the arms of the coat around the bundle and turned to Sister.

"Maybe we can trade someone this stuff for some beans and corn, and maybe some meat." Sister gave a short laugh at the mention of meat. The people here were Christians but they were still poor. Who could afford to trade food for a dress? Only the trader and his wife might have the money. It would be better to sell them in Needles, if only Needles were not so far and rides on the mail wagon didn't cost so much.

That afternoon Indigo put Linneaus and Rainbow in their cages, and Vedna snapped the huge padlock on the door of the little house; they were off to the trading post with the dresses bundled in the wool coat. They were disappointed to learn the trader was gone to Yuma, and they almost left the store before the trader's wife asked if they had something they wanted to sell.

First she reached for the wool coat, but Indigo held on to it, and told her it wasn't for sale. The wool coat was part of her bedding. The woman held up the dresses at arm's length and examined them carefully, although a number of them had not been worn even once. She bought all the dresses, then called her Chemehuevi laundress from the back room to boil the dresses. Indigo protested that the dresses were clean, but the other girls shook their heads to quiet her. As it was, the trader's wife allowed them only $7 in trade for all the dresses.

The twins motioned for Sister to come to the rear of the store, where the three of them huddled and discussed something—Indigo wasn't sure what it was about. They left the trading post with big sacks of beans and cracked barley, a little coffee, a small can of lard, and a big sack of colored candy balls; they still had the sugar and the wormy flour Hattie gave them.

It wasn't much for the lovely dresses trimmed in blue satin ribbon, made especially for Indigo, but it was better than starving. They walked back to the house with their mouths full of candy balls and smiled. The cracked barley was to brew beer or something similar to it; they didn't have all the other ingredients but they'd watched Big Candy and they figured they could get the recipe close enough to brew beer or ale or something to get people drunk. Maybe the Christian Chemehuevis at Road's End would not buy it, but the twins said drinkers would come from miles around. At least they could make enough money from the brew to feed themselves until the garden fed them.

They put on a big pot of beans to simmer on the coals all day while they all pitched in to prepare the garden to plant the winter seeds. The land the twins bought from their old auntie was across the road from the best farmland, irrigated by a system of ditches from the river. At one time the ditches brought water to their land too, but they were buried under the sand now.

In the rich moist fields close to the river, tiny green sprouts could already be seen; seeds planted too early sprouted, but quickly got scorched to death in the fierce autumn sun. If they didn't get their seeds planted now, later the ground would be too cold to germinate the seeds.

Among the old and broken hoes and rakes the twins found when they moved in were tobacco cans of seeds saved by their auntie. Maytha and Vedna argued over the worth of old seeds, but Maytha was right; these seeds were all they had except for the seeds Indigo brought; those seeds might not know how to survive here. At least a few of the seeds in the cans were bound to germinate, so they all worked away with rakes and hoes; none of them had gloves, so their hands got blisters and calluses. The twins and Sister joked farming wasn't any better than laundry for a lady's hands.

For their winter garden, they planted amaranth and all kinds of beans and black-eyed pea seeds they found in the cans. Indigo planted only a few of the seeds from her collection; all the others she intended to plant in the old gardens when they got home.

Linnaeus learned to follow along behind Indigo without disturbing the seeds she just planted, but Rainbow was naughty and hopped off her shoulder to rake his beak through the sand to expose the seeds and eat them. His parrot waddle was so cute she couldn't bear to scold him or lock him in his cage. She picked him up and kissed him and told him to stay put on her shoulder, then replanted any seeds he ate. But Linnaeus was a good worker; with his sharp eyes and quick fingers he caught sucking beetles and cutworms and ate them head first.

When they took a break for lunch back at the house, Indigo opened the trunk to the compartment with her seed collection; she untied the drawstrings on the cotton sacks of gladiolus corms Laura gave her and felt each one to make sure they remained healthy. At the time Laura gave her the seeds, Indigo used her color pencils to write the color names on the envelopes of gladiolus seed. Now she couldn't resist the temptation to plant just a few gladiolus corms among the pea seeds Aunt Bronwyn gave her. Since she and Sister probably would be moved back home by the time the corms grew blossoms, Indigo decided to plant just a few gladiolus.

Then Indigo found she had a great many black gladiolus corms, so she planted them for a border around the peas; between the beans and the spinach she planted two each of the scarlet, purple, and pink gladiolus. As she planted them, she imagined how this corner of the field would look, and she added white and yellow corms too. What a surprise the twins would have in a few months!

Later that day, when the planting was finished, Sister sent Indigo and her pets down the road to the neighbors' corral to look for long strands of tail hair the horses might have snagged. Sister and Indigo wove horsehair snares the way Grandma taught them and carefully strung them in the weeds around their garden; later that evening they had fresh rabbit meat to go along with the beans.

After dinner they sat outside to smoke and watch the stars before bed; there was no moon and the stars seemed to shine closer and brighter than Sister ever saw; Grandma Fleet said the stars were related to us humans. The twins agreed; at Laguna they'd heard stories about the North Star, who acted as a spy for Estoyehmuut, Arrow Boy, the time his wife, Kochininako, Yellow Woman, ran off with Buffalo Man. The North Star tipped off Arrow Boy, otherwise he never would have found her.

At first he was uncomfortable outdoors at night, but quickly Big Candy got reaccustomed to the soldier's life out on the trail. He didn't build fires and slept with his shotgun in his hand. The mule was young and stout; but on the morning of the fourth day of the chase, the mule pulled up its left hind leg and refused to leave Tonopah. Big Candy traded the mule for dried apricots and mutton jerky, and an old handcart he towed with a strap around his chest. That first day the miles blistered his feet, but he shot a covey of quail before dark and cooked himself a feast. His feet healed after he took a knife to the boots and cut them open at the heels and the toes.

This wasn't a race. He would keep on her trail steadily, and he would find her. He didn't care if he had to follow her all the way to Mexico City and back; she wasn't getting away with his money. The days were still hot but nothing like the summer, and the nights were almost cold enough to want a fire.

The next day the going got harder, as the trail left the Aguila valley and ascended the stony brush mountains of Gila Bend. Here the wheels of the cart hung up on lava rock outcrops in odd shapes that reminded Candy of the mushrooms he once stuffed and cooked for Wylie.

He camped outside town at Gila Bend so he could scout the trails to the west and south to make sure she did not double back on him and head for Yuma after all. The extra miles to sweep the trails left Candy too exhausted to eat that night. After the first week, the waist of his dungarees was too loose to button; he tightened his belt two notches and recalled the old stories Dahlia told about their Red Stick ancestors who trailed enemies for months through the swamps and bayous as silent and swift as water snakes. Those first days he dreamed about the trail and the tracks he followed by day, over and over; if he thought about Wylie or Sister and the baby, he quickly refocused his thoughts on the pursuit.

When he did not turn back at the Sand Tank Mountains, Delena realized how bitterly determined her pursuer was; so she took the long hard way across the mountains to give the fat man a good workout. After the first day, she doubled back to see if he gave up and turned back yet; but no, there he was, trudging along with his food and supplies in a pack strapped to his back. He abandoned the handcart, which wasn't suited to the narrow trails. He was thinner now but still looked strong.

Seven dogs drank a good deal of water, so he tried to anticipate her trail according to her dogs' requirements for water; he didn't know about the big canvas water bags each dog carried in its pack. At Quilitosa, the tracks of the woman and her dogs abruptly changed course and followed a dim old path into the mountains to the west. This could be a trick, or she could be headed for Yuma after all. She must know some spring or rainwater pool not shown on the map. The water he carried should last him three days if necessary, and according to the map, he'd be out of the Sand Tank Mountains in two days. He was wrong, but by the time he realized his error, he was too far to turn back.

In the mountains she and the dogs were concealed and it was cooler, so they traveled by day. Every morning she rationed out the water to the dogs as they sat in a row to wait their turn for water. From each dog's pack she took its water bag and filled the tin pie pan. They lapped up the water eagerly, then looked up into her eyes to beg for more; they were hungry too—even the pack rats were scarce in these mountains; the dogs had only found grubs and roots since the day before. She smashed pine cones for the green nuts and built a small fire just to roast the agave hearts and roots she gathered. She didn't care if the fat man saw the smoke—he'd never catch her.

Later that day, a breeze came up from the southwest, followed by big fluffy clouds moving rapidly overhead. "Stop awhile over these dry hills," she said to them, though one look around told her something was wrong here. Too much taken away and not enough given back—the clouds avoided places where people showed no respect or love.

Distances were deceptive in the dry clear air but she had not counted on the broken rock or the steep incline of the trail. When they finally came down out of the mountains, she had finished off her water and the dogs' water, and they were still a day and half or two days from water. The risk to herself and the dogs was worth it; these mountains would stop the fat man. To save her strength, she no longer bothered to double back to spy on the fat man's progress after he followed her into the mountains; if he turned back now it was still too late for him.

The following day she figured the fat man was just about finished, but now she would be lucky to get herself and the dogs to water before they died. She and the dogs traveled much more slowly now, and they stopped to rest more often. The clouds still passed overhead in great woolly herds, though not as fast as before; in the shade with the dogs lying around her, Delena began to think about her comrades in the south; they fought the federal troops from ambush with sticks and rocks. What a difference repeating rifles would make!

She asked the ancestors for help to get her and the dogs safely to water now that they were back on the hot gravel plain. What a pity it would be to die here with so much money the people needed so desperately.

Big Candy made two days' water last until the morning of the fourth day, when the trail descended out of the mountains onto the dry plain. He stood and gazed into the distance on the plain for a long time but saw no sign of water or even a mud hole left over from past rain. No water behind and no water ahead—the words repeated themselves to the rhythm of his feet on the trail. In the army he heard plenty of stories about those who choked on their tongues swollen out, blistered, and black; some thought the hallucinations of the dying gave them comfort in their last moments—

they often raved as if they were bathing in cool water as they rolled on the ground and tried to swallow the sand. He intended to use the shotgun before that happened.

At night Big Candy woke himself again and again with dreams of water—icy glass pitchers of pure water, cascades of springs over rocks, topaz blue pools shaded by tall trees, even the muddy red Colorado water swirled around him so invitingly. Sometimes in the dreams he saw the tiny black baby near the water—it walked and moved as if it were grown up and it laughed at him but never spoke. Candy knew his meaning—the baby was alive and would live; he was the one who was going to die.

Before dawn he woke to the sound of a drum; it wasn't his heartbeat, he was sure; he sat up and listened but heard nothing but the breeze over the rocks. When he laid his head down again he heard it distinctly—the drumming was underground. So this was how it begins, he thought, not at all as he imagined dying would be. Who were the drummers who came to accompany him? He drifted off to sleep again, where the little black baby stood at the edge of a clear fast-moving stream to gesture and jeer at him. You're the one who's almost dead, not me!

He woke crying but he had no tears; he failed the Sand Lizard girl when the baby was born—in Dahlia's kitchen they always praised the tiny newborns, and spoke cheerfully to encourage them. Poor Sister! He let her down when the baby was born and now all the money she'd saved was gone too. He felt the need to urinate but was too weak and dizzy to stand up; he rolled over to one side, unbuttoned himself, but was able to make only a few drops of urine. His eyes would quit first, so he kept the shotgun right by his side.

Delena looked back at the mountains of grayish purple stone and wondered if the fat man turned back in time. As the sun moved overhead, she and the dogs crawled under the greasewoods for shade. She shook her canteen and listened to the last mouthful of water slosh inside; the big clouds moved slower today, their silver backs and bellies streaked blue-violet. Ancestors, she said, never mind about me; what about the others who are depending on me—hear their prayers!

That day months ago as she set out with her dogs on her mission, the old women and old men cried as they embraced her one by one; their task was to pray for her every day she was gone until she returned. Others prayed for their people fighting the federal troops, but her mission was so important, those assigned to pray for her had no other task but to bring her back safely with the rifles.

Now that the water was almost gone, the best strategy was to keep still in the shade; this trail across the dry plain wasn't much traveled but someone—maybe prospectors—might happen along before death came. She always wondered how the cards would tell her about her own death; she shuffled them and began to lay them down: First the card that stood for her, the Guitar upside down. Useless for play—yes, that was her! Next the Flowerpot upside down on its flowers—yes, this was her situation all right! Even the saying that went with the Flowerpot was true: "The one born in a flowerpot doesn't leave the hall"—beings that depend on water should not cross the dry plain. There it was! The Bell overturned, the third card, which represented the obstacle—death—that must be overcome. She had to smile; even at the end, the cards spoke truthfully.

She lay down the others. The Songbird upside down couldn't make anyone's heart sing, but the Rose upside down still was lovely; Mother of the Indians, Guadalupe, was still there. But then she turned up the Frog by a pool of water, followed by the Umbrella upside down to catch the rain, not shed it. Good to see the Frog, child of the rain, with the Umbrella, also a companion of the rain. The Drunkard card was upside down, so the liquor in the bottle poured into his mouth; the Heart was upright and its saying promised, "I will return." The Apache card stood upright under the Sun card—the warrior strong and ready under the Sun, who is the protector of the poor. The overturned Bell was the truth—she faced death, but the other cards were her hope.

She glanced up at the sky at the clouds; they were no longer in such a hurry as they swelled and ascended into great pyramids and towers thousands of feet high.

"Oh you are beautiful!" Her throat was so dry her words made a croaking sound; all seven dogs feebly wagged their tails, mistaking the compliment for themselves. Poor dogs! Dumb to the end!

"My good soldiers!" she said and patted each one's head before she removed their packs with the empty canteens and the cash bundled up in old rags. Let the poor dogs at least die in peace without burdens. She piled the bundles together. Far, far in the distance a coyote howled for rain, and one by one the dogs began to howl mournfully in reply. She knew it was their death song and hers too—no one would pass by on this trail in time to save them.

She opened each bundle to expose the stacks of currency and the silver and gold coins; as she did, the money-sniffer dog wagged her tail and laboriously got to her feet to press her nose against the stacks of bills. Besides her dogs, her most prized possessions were the decks of Mexican and Gypsy cards. She removed them from the cloth bag around her waist and laid both decks on top of the money.

She glanced up at the clouds again. She found it difficult to swallow now, and took the canteen with the last mouthful of water and sprinkled it over the dogs. She removed her dress and her shoes and placed them on the money pile, next to the decks of cards. This was all she possessed except her last breath and her body. Take it all, she told the sky.

She lay down in the greasewood's thin shade and looked up at the clouds pushing and bumping one another as they climbed the pyramids and towers that darkened under their weight. Now her eyes felt dry and it was more comfortable to keep them closed; the dogs were all lying close to her now. "Good dog army," she said as she drifted off.

Hattie took a cab directly to the hospital from the station. She carried her small bag with her; it was heavy and made her regret she had not checked into the hotel first. The nun at the reception desk showed her upstairs to the third floor, for the most critical cases. Three doctors were consulting in the corner of the room; Hattie felt her heart lurch when she heard that awful Australian accent chime in with the others—of course Dr. Gates would be here. Edward seemed feverish but he recognized her at once and called out her name. She felt her cheeks redden as the Australian turned to look at her.

Edward looked grayish and weak, but she forced herself to smile and asked how he was feeling. He sat up and leaned forward.

"How dear of you to come," he said as he took her hand between his hot dry palms. The diagnosis was pneumonia, he told her, but he felt better now. Dr. Gates was concerned about the possibility tuberculosis would follow the pneumonia, although the other doctors disagreed. Today the fever seemed on the wane, after Dr. Gates's experimental doses of manganese and raw gland tissue extracts to fortify his blood.

Though obviously quite ill, still he seemed alert and did not appear to be dying. Now Hattie regretted her haste—she might have taken Indigo the blankets and other things she would need for the winter, then come to check on Edward. He was in good hands here with ample medical resources, not to mention the moral support of his business partner, who oversaw his treatment.

As the doctors left the room, the Australian with them, Hattie exhaled slowly. To be in the same room with Dr. Gates was almost intolerable; she was determined not to speak to him. She would enlist the hospital chaplain to speak for her if necessary. Though somewhat feverish, Edward seemed anxious to visit with her. He caught cold one afternoon as he hiked the rim of the crater. A sudden thunderstorm came up; as he hurried to rejoin his companions at the drilling site, the stiffness of the old leg injury slowed him, and in the confusion of the lightning bolts, the others drove off without him. He was drenched and shivering by the time his companions realized their error and returned for him. The cold lingered no matter what he tried, and then last week, when they brought new assay specimens to Albuquerque, a high fever developed.

He began to cough and fumbled for the basin; Hattie gave it to him then turned away as he spat. It was a mistake to come—the legal separation was almost final, she thought irritably. Why had Edward asked the chaplain to send her the telegram?

Hattie felt exhausted, almost ill herself. What could she do? What did he expect? Nurses in white habits appeared pushing a cartload of medical instruments and an odd apparatus that looked like a bellows connected to a piece of rubber tubing. It was time for his breathing treatment and the nurses asked her to wait downstairs.

Back at the hotel she soaked in the bath until the water cooled off, trying to sort out her feelings. She missed her parents, especially her father. She deeply regretted the disappointment they must feel over the separation, but she saw it in a positive light—she wasn't suited to marriage. After her bath she sent Susan a telegram to come at once, Edward was seriously ill. She would stay to look in on Edward until Susan arrived.

Her letter to her parents began with a description of Aunt Bronwyn's white cattle grazing under the old apple trees in the ruins of the cloister orchard. She wrote of her amazement at the cloudy chalcedony portraying three white cattle under a tree, excavated from the sacred spring at Bath. Aunt Bronwyn with her old gardens and old stones changed her outlook entirely. She did not tell them Edward's betrayal influenced the change as well.

She knew her father would be interested in her bout of sleepwalking and the luminous glow she'd seen; she wasn't the first to see such a light in Bath. She recounted the story of the queen terrified by the luminous glow in the King's Bath. She experienced a gravity of well-being and peace as she gazed at the glow; later she felt traces of that odd gravity from the old stones Aunt Bronwyn protects; it was the same gravity exuded by the carvings in her possession.

"I wish you had been with me to see the *professoressa's* black gladiolus garden with the 'madonnas' in their niches," she wrote. "The rain garden serpent goddesses were quite wonderful. They won me over entirely.

"I know Mother will be relieved to hear I've abandoned the thesis." She gave no further explanation, except she wished she had studied old European archaeology instead.

"The child was a good traveling companion, and the parrot was lost and found again only once," Hattie wrote, but could not bring herself to write anymore about Indigo, so she wrote about Edward's illness, and how anxious she was to return to Arizona to look in on Indigo and her sister. She made no mention of their detainment by authorities in Livorno.

Susan did not reply to the telegram; another week passed as Hattie made brief visits to the hospital twice each day, and learned her way around Albuquerque to shop for Indigo. Although Edward seemed better, Dr. Gates ordered the treatments increased so there was scarcely a time she found poor Edward in his bed.

Edward tasted camphor and felt its vapors in his lungs for hours after the treatments. He did not remember much about the procedures beyond the face mask and the pump for the camphor because Dr. Gates gave him injections before and after the treatments. He did not ask what the injections contained, but recognized the morphine from the sense of well-being and euphoria it gave him. Dr. Gates discussed his theory behind the experimental therapy with Edward, one scientist to another: Gates believed there was a great risk of tuberculosis following pneumonia unless special treatments were given.

The hotel next door to the train station had a small courtyard garden with a quaint Spanish-style fountain; the sound of the splashing water soothed her. She calmed her anxiety with long walks through downtown Albuquerque. Here the cleaning and menial tasks seemed to be performed by Mexicans. She saw very few Indians on her walks except at the train station, where Indian women sold small pottery and beaded pins to the tourists. On the whole the Indians here looked much more prosperous than the poor women she'd seen in Needles. She added items to her list and began shopping for Indigo and her sister.

What was wrong with Susan and Colin? Were they away on vacation? Or was their silence an expression of their disapproval of Edward, or of her? Still she could not simply abandon him; he was quite ill, and asked her to stay until Susan arrived. She didn't tell him Susan hadn't responded. The weeks of illness changed Edward's appearance dramatically; the hair at his temples had grayed noticeably. His hands suffered tremors now, and he was terribly thin with no appetite; yet he seemed to be in high spirits.

In downtown courtyards and along the Rio Grande, the leaves of the cottonwood trees went from greenish yellow to pale yellow and finally to a golden yellow in the weeks Hattie was there. One morning she woke to see snow on the tops of the mountains but the weather in Albuquerque remained sunny and warm. She was anxious to get blankets and supplies to Indigo before the nights were freezing cold; if she did not hear from Susan by the end of the week, she was determined to return to Needles.

The nights were chilly, but the days were lovely; she took long walks from the hotel down Central Avenue to the old town square in front of the church. The spice of burning piñon wood filled the air. From a bench in the shade by the bandstand she watched the old Hispanic women dressed in black file inside for mass. Sometimes she heard snatches of the chants or caught a whiff of the incense as the church doors opened and closed, but it seemed quite remote and strange to her now.

The repeated bouts of therapy with the bellows and rubber tubing wore Edward down, and the raw extracts of glands upset his digestion. On Sunday Hattie found Edward dozing in his bed; he looked much weaker, and his color was not good although the fever subsided. The local doctors disagreed with Dr. Gates over the treatments and withdrew from the case, but Edward insisted the experimental treatments be continued. He said the local doctors couldn't be blamed for their lack of sophistication in regard to the latest scientific developments.

Hattie feared the local doctors were right, but if he refused to listen to the medical doctors, he would not listen to her—better to agree and reassure him. Hattie was grateful not to encounter Dr. Gates at the hospital, but gradually she realized he must be trying to avoid her as well. At last a telegram announced Susan's arrival the next week, but on the appointed day, another telegram came with a new arrival time three weeks away.

The injections left him in a dreamy state for hours; he drifted in and out of consciousness, deliciously numb. The injections slowed his breathing but relaxed the bronchial spasms as well. Later as the injection's effects waned, he felt quite lucid and energized. He kept a pencil and paper on the table at his bedside and made notes of ideas for the locations of the other mine shafts or questions to ask his friend Dr. Gates.

By then his thoughts were as vivid and detailed as dreams and he was content to sit back and think for hours on end. If he thought about the mine, immediately he envisioned a long glittering tunnel into the center of the crater, its walls embedded with black and white diamonds. At the end of the tunnel was the ore body of the meteorite itself, lustrous soft alloy of pure silver streaked with gold.

He and their company would be able to repay Hattie's loans, and he could settle all he owed Susan and Colin. He recalled Susan the night of her ball in the rich sapphire blue silk brocade that cost hundreds. The mother lode of the meteor crater would put him back in good standing with them. Livorno, even Hattie and the separation, would scarcely matter beside the wall of silver and gold.

Now when he dreamed, not only was the Riverside property all his, but his father was alive in the dream, standing with him between rows of mature citron trees directly west of the house. But when he looked back, he saw only the terrace fountain and lily pond and the terrace garden walls, but the house and all other outbuildings were gone without a trace, as if they had been removed long ago.

He intended to discuss with Hattie the equipment purchases and the overdrafts in one of his lucid periods between the injections. He wanted her to know her loan to him was secured by the machinery and the leasehold. But when she came that afternoon, she was upset over Susan's silence, and he had to reassure her.

Hattie was furious with the woman; what was wrong with her? She refused to be delayed with her plans any longer, and began packing the blankets and other supplies for the girls in sturdy tin trunks. Prices and quality were much better in Albuquerque, a much larger town than Needles. She bought a great many canned goods, and found dried apples and dried apricots, dried beans, and corn sold by the local farmers. When she had everything packed, she realized her luggage would completely fill a buggy. That night she slept more soundly than she had in weeks, and woke early for breakfast and a visit to the hospital before the afternoon train west.

Edward was confident he wasn't dying, but he felt strange and not entirely in his body since the last treatment. Now as the effects of the injections began to wane, he experienced agitation from disquieting thoughts laced with regrets. He should have bribed the customs officers in Livorno before they embarked to Corsica. He should have concealed the citron slips more ingeniously.

What bothered him most was his memory of the piles of meteor irons he left behind in Tampico; he always intended to return to the town market to acquire those meteor irons from the hostile blue-faced woman. Oh the burn of regret lest someone knowledgeable see the neat pyramid stacks of the irons and buy them before he did! He drifted off on the Pará River once more, his head rested on gardenia blossoms in the big Negress's lap in the canoe; when he looked up at her face it was sky blue.

Hattie saw the Australian doctor and the nurses outside Edward's room and her heart sank. She did not make eye contact with the doctor and was about to enter the room when one of the nuns told her the priest was with him now to administer the Last Rites; Edward slipped into a coma during the night.

Hattie burst into tears and surprised herself with the grief she felt; she knew she was mourning the absence of Indigo as well as the loss of Edward, who was still a friend, after all. Dr. Gates hurried away down the hall as if he sensed her anger. That wretched Australian criminal! His quack treatments destroyed Edward's health!

When the priest left, they allowed her to stay alone with him; his breathing was in slow labored gasps and she reached down to take his hand in hers and whispered, "Rest in peace." Poor thing! Moments later his breath left him in three loud snores.

The nuns offered condolences and the priest offered to accompany her to the chapel, but Hattie firmly declined. She shocked them further when she announced Edward's sister would make the funeral arrangements. She paid the hospital bill and left a bank draft with the hospital accountant to pay the undertaker to keep Edward's coffin in the icehouse until Susan arrived.

Part Ten

THE LEVEL of the river rose a little higher each morning Indigo took the monkey and the parrot to forage for seeds and roots. The little black grandfather was teething and cried irritably at the least sound, so Indigo kept her pets away for a good part of the morning. At first the tamarisks and willows perked up from the extra water, but as the water began to cover the base of the trees, the leaves yellowed and died.

Once the watercress and other tender plants were submerged, they stayed higher on the sandy bank, where she let Rainbow down to walk with Linnaeus to browse among the sunflowers. She kept a close watch for hungry foxes, who looked for rabbits and water rats displaced by the rising water; a great many tortoises and water snakes hid in the tall grass above the water.

At first the girls all made fun of Indigo for speculating on how high the water would rise; they didn't see the river every day. But the morning they all took buckets to bring water from the hydrant by the church, the twins and Sister stopped in their tracks when they saw how high the water had risen in such a short time. Even the little grandfather, tied piggyback on Sister's back, gazed at the high water.

"It's all going to be flooded," Vedna said. "I didn't believe it before." They stood in silence a moment before Maytha whistled slowly and shook her head. The irrigated river bottom land was the best land, where the winter crops of beans and peas, already knee high, were about to be drowned.

At this rate, all the houses and the little church with the hydrant would be underwater too; then where would they get their drinking water? Maytha joked their land would become prime irrigated farmland soon. The sprouts in their dry garden were tiny compared to those in the river bottom fields. Vedna said this must be what the Bible meant about the least shall be first. Sister Salt looked at the houses, where people watched them but never came outdoors or spoke to them. She shook her head. When the land here was flooded, the people would hate them even more.

They hauled water all morning to fill the iron kettle and the two tin washtubs to boil for beer. After the water cooled to lukewarm, they added the yeast cakes just as Big Candy did. Vedna wondered aloud what became of him, chasing after that Gypsy. Sister Salt shrugged as if she couldn't care less, but she wondered sometime too; the one she loved to dream about was Charlie, even if he was married in Tucson. Sometimes she caught herself daydreaming his wife got ill or had an accident and died; no, she didn't want to get him that way. Probably he didn't even remember her now.

Their house reeked of green beer; every available pot and pan was full of it; Sister and Indigo gathered dried gourds and cleaned them out for beer containers. Candy used glass bottles to get the fizz in the beer, but the glass sometimes exploded. At worst, the gourds only fizzed and foamed.

The twins went to visit their old aunt upriver and took some beer samples with them to give away. They were gone overnight; it was the first time the sisters were alone since Indigo returned. Indigo put the parrot and monkey to bed and joined Sister, who was outside nursing the baby and watching the stars. They shared Sister's shawl over their legs; later there was a chill in the breeze that made them scoot closer together. Sister couldn't resist tickling Indigo's ribs, and she squealed and they both laughed. The little grandfather let go of Sister's nipple and studied both their faces; he and Indigo were jealous of each other, which made Sister laugh. He was rounder now, with fat little wrists and ankles that would have pleased Big Candy. She still felt sad he didn't give the little grandfather a chance. The baby was crawling now, and beginning to try to pull himself upright. He was a serious baby who didn't smile often but who cried only when he was angry; wet or hungry, he remained silent because he was a grandfather and not someone new.

Indigo wanted to make friends with him, and started to help Sister care for him. At first she only watched; each time Sister gently scooped the warm water over his legs and bottom in the shallow basin, he took deep breaths and held them. He screamed if Sister tried to put him in Indigo's arms, so that day Indigo picked up Linnaeus, then cradled the monkey close to her face. The little grandfather watched, then screwed his face up in fury.

"Did you see that?" He knew Indigo was mocking him. Sister nodded. That was why she called him grandfather; they must not tease or mock him.

The twins returned the following evening with a dozen or more guests, mostly Chemehuevi relations but also Walapai and Havasupai friends. Sister and Indigo heard their laughter a half mile away the evening they showed up. They all sat on their blankets on the smooth-packed ground in front of the house; when it began to get chilly, the twins built a fire. They celebrated the new beer and their new friends. They told stories about the old days when the people drank cactus fruit wine in late July to contact the ancestors to rain down their love on them. They made jokes about the rising river, the government's plan to drown all the Indians, and they all laughed and laughed until tears filled their eyes. The only good land left to them now was about to be taken away by the backwater of the dam.

The next morning their guests woke up in the front yard with ailments from drinking so much green beer. The girls cooked up the rabbits they'd snared with the last of the beans and used the last of the flour for tortillas to feed the guests breakfast. As they departed, their new friends promised to say good things about the beer to people with money or things to trade.

Later that day as they rinsed clean the beer gourds, Sister asked Indigo if they could sell her big trunk for money to get food and supplies to make more beer. That evening Indigo began to remove the few remaining clothes from the trunk, and her color pencils, notebooks, and gladiolus book. She had room in the two valises to keep what remained. She didn't need the trunk any longer. It was a fine leather-and-wood brass-bound trunk with compartments and many small drawers, which Indigo loved to open and close. She gave it a pat and hoped they could get a lot of food in trade for it.

In a few more weeks they'd have baby peas to eat; Indigo checked their garden every morning to see how many rabbits they'd snared. At the old gardens they used to sleep out with the plants to keep the rabbits away, but here snares seemed to be enough. That morning, though, as Indigo approached she saw at once something had eaten rows and rows of baby pea plants.

Maytha and Vedna shook their heads in unison when Indigo proposed she and her pets sleep down in the garden. This wasn't the old Sand Lizard gardens, this was Road's End, where wicked men prowled at night and jumped on sleeping women.

After their morning excursion along the river to look for tidbits, Indigo took the parrot and monkey to the garden. First they checked the rabbit snares; in the beginning they caught two and three rabbits a night, but as the river rose, rabbits were scarce. Birds became the main threat, so Indigo would bundle up her color pencils and notebook, some stale tortillas, and a gourd canteen of water, to guard the plants all day. Old Man Stick, the scarecrow they made out of twigs and horsetail hair, scared the newcomers for a while, but the resident birds perched on Old Man Stick.

Patiently she taught the monkey and parrot to leave alone the garden plants but to pull the weeds. She always stayed with them to be sure they didn't get confused. Later when they got tired of weeding, they went to the little lean-to for shade and rest. She drew gladiolus flowers of all colors, and sunflowers, even datura flowers.

The gladiolus corms sent up bright green blades that grew far more quickly than the bean sprouts and peas. When Sister and the twins asked what those rows were, Indigo told them it was a surprise.

The water kept rising, creeping closer and closer to the best fields of tall beans and peas; the people banked the soil higher and higher to protect them. One morning when Indigo started down the trail toward the river, Rainbow began to squawk as if he spotted a hawk or eagle. She looked up at the sky first but saw nothing; but as she gazed all around she was shocked to see a bright sheet of water had flooded the riverside fields during the night. She ran back at once to tell the girls the news.

They left off the beer making to come look from the ridge; down below they watched as a group led by the Chemehuevi preacher approached the flooded fields to pray. "How high would the water rise?" Sister wondered out loud. The twins shook their heads. By the following week, more fields were flooded; all the people could do was pull up the wilted plants and boil them for lunch.

Steadily the water advanced, and began to threaten the church and the small, neat houses and gardens. The twins no longer made jokes about their cheap dry land becoming irrigated bottomland. Now Sister came along with the baby on her back when Indigo went to check on the water's level. Off in the distance they watched the people help one another move their belongings to higher ground. Wagonloads of church pews and Bibles were unloaded on the old floodplain not far from the twins' house.

The girls went down and pitched in to help unload the wagons. The people did not smile, but they did not object to the girls' help. Sister leaned the little grandfather's bundle against a big rock a safe distance away so he could watch her and the others. His black shining eyes took in everything and one look at him made Sister feel so happy—buoyant with overwhelming love she felt for him and so proud of his special qualities. She had never loved anyone so much before; she always wanted to know her ancestors, and now the little grandfather had come to be with her and to love her.

When the wagons were unloaded, the girls politely excused themselves, but their neighbors ignored them. The twins walked in front and Sister and Indigo with the baby on her back followed. No one spoke. Just then they heard a man's voice call out behind them: the wantonness and drunkenness of them and others had angered God so much he sent this flood!

They turned and suddenly were face-to-face with a short fat Chemehuevi gentleman in a black preacher's suit and white shirt. The exertion of hurrying after them left him breathless and sweaty across his brow. While he mopped at his forehead and caught his breath he glared at them; they were not really Chemehuevis but Lagunas and didn't belong there. They were damned, contaminated—a risk to all others.

The twins took off running and the girls followed; even with the baby on her back Sister was a strong runner; Indigo ran beside her. The preacher got winded and when he stopped, so did his congregation.

When they got back to the house, they were cheered to find the yard full of visitors camped for the night. The guests kept their word and spread news of the beer makers up and down the river. The new batch of beer was barely old enough to drink but they filled the gourds for the guests to sample. The guests shared the venison jerky and parched corn they'd brought along.

After the baby and the pets were put to bed, Indigo sat outside with the girls to listen around the campfire to the news the visitors brought. The backwaters from the dam were going to make a giant lake and everything, even this land here, would be flooded. No! other guests disagreed; the water would not come this far, but the Chemehuevi reservation superintendent was going to send the flooded-out families to live on the reservation at Parker. The night was clear and still but cool enough that everyone wrapped themselves in blankets and shawls around the fire.

Indigo didn't like the smell or taste of the new beer, but Sister and the twins drank along with their guests wholeheartedly; Indigo liked to listen. As the midnight stars rose and fell, they talked and laughed about the old days before the aliens came with the fevers and killed so many. Some who drank too much beer started to cry for loved ones lost.

Indigo didn't like to hear the crying and arguing that seemed to follow the beer; she was tired and about to excuse herself to go to bed because she knew the monkey and parrot woke early and wanted to go browsing for breakfast. But Vedna brought out her Bible, so Indigo stayed up.

Vedna closed her eyes and turned the Bible around and around in her hands, then opened it with one finger and looked to see what passage her finger touched.

"And this house which Solomon built for the Lord was in length sixty cubits and in width twenty cubits and in height thirty cubits," she read, then laughed out loud, and Maytha joined her. Soon the visitors joined, and they laughed because the twins barely kept a roof over their own heads, and the Bible asked them to build the Lord a big house. One of the visitors pointed out the last house built for the Lord there was up to its steeple in water, and they laughed some more.

Sister Salt waited for the laughter to pass, then she told them "a house" means a circle of stones, because spirits don't need solid walls or roofs; but it must have two hearths, not one, to be the Lord's house. The visitors all looked at her, but no one joked because Sister was serious. The circle of stones must be made at the same place as before on the riverbank below the big sandhill near Needles.

"Too bad for the Lord," Maytha said. "We can't go to Needles now. If we leave for even one night, the flooded people will call our place abandoned and move in."

The conductor commented it was early for so much snow in Flagstaff. The tall pines were blanketed and Hattie shivered though the train compartment was warm. How pure and quiet the snow was, how inviting the forests and the great mountain peaks above the town. The conductor asked if Flagstaff was her stop, and seemed surprised to learn her stop was Needles.

Outside the station at Needles, Hattie saw the buggy and sullen young driver but ignored him and hired a porter with a handcart. The townspeople of Needles took notice of her return; though she'd been in Albuquerque more than six weeks, the stationmaster remembered her, and the hotel desk clerk recognized her and even asked if Mr. Palmer was going to join her later. She sensed at once the clerk was prying, and imagined them all—the stationmaster, the clerk, their wives—exchanging rumors and observations of a white woman traveling alone.

How odd it was to think, only weeks before, Edward signed that hotel register, alive and excited by the prospect of seeing the meteor crater. She felt a melancholy creep from her heart over her body. Human life was woefully short and ended so suddenly; she fought back the tears, aware she was the center of attention.

The porter had to make three trips with his handcart from the station to the hotel. The trunks and boxes of supplies with her own luggage filled every corner of the hotel room. As soon as she was alone, she unpacked the carved gemstones Edward gave her from Bath; if she acted at once the gloom might not overtake her. She unwrapped the lemon carnelian carving of the long-neck waterbird with her chick bright with yellow translucence; the birds appeared almost alive. Carefully she set the bright orange carnelian of Minerva and her snake next to the cloudy chalcedony of the three cattle under the tree. One look at the carvings and Hattie felt the immediate joy their beauty and perfection gave off.

Despite the snow on the tips of the distant mountain peaks, the weather in Needles was mild and dry. After dinner in the hotel dining room she slipped on a light coat for a walk around the small commercial district next to the train station and hotel. She hoped to find a different livery service to take her to Road's End the next day, but she soon realized in a town that small, she would not find another. She resolved to ask the owner to drive her himself even if she had to pay extra.

She had just crossed the street before the train station when she heard loud laughter and voices; at the end of the dark alley she saw a small fire with four or five figures warming themselves. The instant she heard the voices clearly she knew they were Indians, all women, she thought, by the tones of voice. One started singing and the others joined, and Hattie realized the women were drunk. The twilight was fading to darkness, but she lingered to watch them from a safe distance; how terrible it was to see— had Indigo and her sister lived like this with their mother?

The owner of the livery service charged her extra and sent his hired man to drive her; she recalled then the sullen driver was his son. The hired man stole glances at her and she wondered if the sullen driver had talked about her and the visit to the girls. But she was so happy to be on her way to see Indigo, she scarcely noticed the man.

They reached Road's End well before dark. Hattie did not want to spend another night on the horsehair mattress or see the expression in the trader and his wife's eyes, so she directed the driver along the river, then up the old floodplain to the twins' house. As they drew closer, Hattie felt excited but anxious too—what if her nightmare of the empty house came true?

She was never so happy to hear the parrot's screech as she was at that instant; a moment later out came Indigo with Linnaeus on her hip and the parrot on her shoulder. Hattie began to wave wildly, but the child paused before she waved back. That hesitation made Hattie anxious. She knew she was an intruder here, but she only planned to drop off the blankets and supplies, perhaps spend a night or two, then return to Needles on the mail wagon.

She wasn't able to give Indigo a proper hug because of the monkey and parrot but she kissed her forehead and smoothed her hair. She was aware she was being watched and looked up to see the sister with the baby. Indigo's sister didn't trust her; that was apparent from the expression on her face.

Once they carried indoors all the parcels and bundles from the wagon, the one-room house was crowded; the tubs of new beer needed the warmth of the house now that the nights were cold. Hattie felt a bit more relaxed as the twins joked about having their own trading post now as they stacked the canned goods and sacks of sugar and flour, onions and potatoes along the walls.

Vedna teased Hattie about forgetting the sack of barley they needed for beer, and they all laughed except Sister. Indigo was delighted to find sacks of millet and sunflower seeds for the parrot, and a big bag of special biscuits for Linnaeus. Indigo unpacked the two new lamps, filled them with oil, and lit them before it was even dark.

Sister sat on her bedroll and nursed the baby while Maytha and Vedna fried up the onions and potatoes Hattie brought with the jackrabbit they found snared that morning.

Hattie waited to tell Indigo about Edward until they'd finished eating and the older girls went outside to smoke. Indigo was bedding Linnaeus and didn't react to the news but continued to arrange the parrot's cage. Hattie was embarrassed by the sound of her voice in the little room as she repeated the news of Edward's death. Indigo looked down and shrugged her shoulders before she looked at Hattie.

"Are you sorry?" Indigo asked.

The question took Hattie by surprise, but she recovered quickly. Yes, she was sorry because Edward once meant a great deal to her. Indigo looked into her eyes as she spoke, and did not blink; she had not thought about

Edward since they said good-bye at the train station. The world Edward lived in seemed distant from the world of Road's End. Indigo recalled the day he gave her Linnaeus and how he showed pictures of parrot jungles and orchid flowers. Except for the big glassy eye of his camera, Indigo thought he wasn't a bad man.

"Poor thing. I guess he was old," Indigo said.

Hattie nodded and fought back tears. She was shocked at the awkwardness between them in a matter of only six weeks. What a fool she was! Indigo returned to the life and sister she had before she was taken away to boarding school. Hattie realized, oddly enough, she was the one who no longer had a life to return to. Although they would welcome her, she could not return to her parents' house.

Hattie looked very tired so Indigo showed her how to make her bed with three of the new blankets—two on the bottom, roll yourself up in the top blanket. When Hattie took her nightgown from the train case, the book of Chinese monkey stories was under it. She held up the book for Indigo to see, and her face lit up with anticipation. She scooted close to Hattie on the blankets and looked down at the page. Now at last she and the child resumed their former ease with each other as she began to read aloud.

Awhile later, Hattie looked over and saw that Indigo was asleep; the girls were sitting near the doorway listening. The twins were curious to know more about the adventures of Monkey and his companions, but Sister Salt said nothing.

The next day Indigo took Hattie along on her morning excursion with the monkey and parrot along the water's edge. Hattie was saddened at the sight of church steeple rising out of the water. Didn't anyone ever tell the people here about the lake made by the dam? Indigo shrugged; they told the people the water wouldn't come that high.

Indigo showed Hattie the sprouts from gladiolus corms; the corms sent up long green blades, but they wouldn't bloom until after Christmas, when the days got longer.

The beans and black-eyed peas in the girls' garden looked promising, but even with the amaranth and greens the garden seemed meager. Hattie thought some chickens and goats might be good for the girls, too, or one of those pigs her father raised. She did not want to antagonize Indigo's sister on her first visit, so she made it short. The following morning Indigo and the twins walked with Hattie to the trading post, where the mail wagon took on passengers or freight for Needles. The mail wagon driver recognized the twins and was friendly enough as he took Hattie's valise and helped her up into the wagon. The store man and his wife brought out the sacks of mail. They stared past Hattie as if she were invisible, even after she murmured hello to them. The twins whispered to each other and laughed out loud; the storekeeper and his wife stiffened their backs and glared as Indigo started laughing too. The driver clucked to the horses and the wagon creaked, and the harness jingled as they pulled away from Road's End. Hattie turned on the seat and waved at the girls, who waved back until the wagon went over the hill.

The mail wagon driver was a talkative man who didn't seem to mind Hattie's reluctant replies. He asked if she was a missionary of some sort and if she planned to settle around there. He added non-Indians weren't allowed to reside on the reservations without government permits, and only merchants, missionaries, and schoolteachers could obtain them.

To change the subject Hattie asked about farmland for sale in the area; the driver launched into a long account of locations and prices and availability of irrigation water or wells. If she didn't mind being around Indians, the cheapest way to go was to lease Indian land from the Indian Bureau. Forty-year leases were cheaper than the ninety-nine-year leases and just as good, with options to renew for another term.

By the next day, the hotel clerk knew about her interest in land, and so did the bank manager when Hattie went to arrange another transfer of funds. The banker had a list of real estate, mostly farmland for sale and for lease, which he would be delighted to show at her convenience. By the end of the week Hattie had received two dinner invitations—from the banker's wife and the minister's wife. But before she could respond to the invitations, unsettling news came in a note from the bank. Her bank in New York indicated the amount of the cash transfer she'd requested exceeded the balance in the account.

"But that can't be!" she said aloud, and began to fumble with the valise that held the account book.

Delena thought she must have reached the edge of the land of the dead or some kind of hell because a terrible howling wind stung her face with grit and dust. When she choked and coughed it hurt so much she knew she wasn't dead. A moment later big cold raindrops began to slap her face and arms. She heard the dogs stir; they'd been without water longer than she had, and she feared she might lose some of them. Her arms and legs were so stiff they hurt to move, but she managed to roll over on her back. Her lips and tongue were swollen and cracked; at first the raindrops stung. She leaned her head back so the rainwater bathed her dried-up eyes; if eyes dried out too long they were blind forever.

The wind increased with the rain and carried with it grit the size of seed beads, then the size of peas; as the wind's scream increased even pebbles the size of small acorns were blasted against her, and she felt her clothing about to be torn from her body. Then the deluge came as if someone was dumping water from canteens, then from barrels, and suddenly it was as if a river in the sky cascaded down; even the wind got washed away.

The rainwater ran down her face into her mouth; at first her tongue and throat were so dry she almost choked on the water. Before long she felt rain seep along the ground beneath her, and rolled over to put her lips to the ground to suck the glorious cool water until her thirst was satisfied.

After a while she felt the water rise, up to her ribs, then to her ears. She rolled over again on her side with her legs drawn up, shivering in the cold stream of water. Once moistened, her eyes began to burn; they felt swollen so she did not try to open them; she could wait to find out if she was blind.

When she woke again, a light rain was falling and the dogs were standing over her licking her face; one dog licked her eyes with special vigor, gently using its teeth to remove the matter that caked them. She reached out and felt the crooked legs of the mother dog, the money sniffer. She let the dog saliva work its healing power for a while and then she had to find out.

It was so dark at first she feared she was blind; then she realized it was only dawn, and the storm clouds covered the rising sun. Gradually she could make out light and darkness in the sky, but the light hurt and caused tears to stream down her cheeks. Still she could make out forms—all seven dogs were there and she could see the motion of their tails as they wagged to greet her. "Well we made it, after all, didn't we?" she said, but was shocked at the croaking sound she made when she spoke.

All morning she and the dogs rested, getting up only to drink water from the standing pools; she tried not to open her eyes unless it was to see what little rodent the dogs caught. After the rain, the desert creatures all came out and the dogs made short work of any cottontails or rats they saw.

She let them have the first three or four before she took a rabbit for herself; by that time the sun dried the grass and twigs enough she was able to kindle a fire; she was so hungry; she didn't care who saw the smoke. A big man needed more water so her pursuer was probably dead before the rain came.

Delena and the dogs stayed as long as there were puddles of water, and she filled all the water bags while the water was fresh and plentiful and saved it for the journey. The dogs and she alternately rested and hunted rabbits and birds for the first few days, but as she and the money-sniffer dog regained their strength, she took the dog to the soggy pile of dog packs and the wet cloth of the bundles she'd opened as gifts to welcome the storm clouds. The fierce winds took away all the cards of both decks and all the currency; bless the silver and the gold coins, they sank in the wet dirt but stayed put even in the driving rain and runoff.

A short distance away, wedged tightly between two rocks, was one of the Mexican tarot cards, terribly curled as it dried out. This will be the last reading of my poor cards, she thought as she leaned down to pick it up. She was encouraged to see it was La Estrella, the Star, companion and guide, the one who brought the rain. She found another card stuck in prickly pear needles—El Tambor, the Drum; its *dicho,* "Don't crinkle the old leather, I want it for my drum," made her think of the father of the Sand Lizard girl's baby; now he was wrinkled up and dead for lack of water. The Sand Lizard girl didn't want to be married to him anyway.

A short distance from the card the dog sniffed out a $20 bill blown around the spiny base of the ocotillo, which wore small holes in the paper. Nearby the dog sniffed out two $5 bills. The storm winds swept the money and cards ahead of the storm in the direction of the mountains they'd come from. She and the dog searched every day, and by the time the pools of rainwater began to dry up, the dog had found all but $40 of the cash. She was not so lucky herself finding the cards, which were too stiff to snag on branches and rocks the way the currency did. She found the Deer, the Mandolin, and the Soldier, but not even one of the Gypsy cards. When she studied the cards, the appearance of the Soldier card with the Deer persuaded her the fat man was still alive. Oh well, he wouldn't be in any condition to trouble her for a while.

The rainstorm left large pools of standing water all the way to Tucson. They kept to the dry washes and game trails to avoid soldiers and other criminals who might endanger the cash the dogs carried. Delena had not seen the desert so green in early autumn. Wild amaranth sprouted in stands as tall as she was in some places in the washes. The rains brought newborn rabbits and rats, so she and the dogs ate well too. Still, she was re-lieved to reach the safe house in Tucson to eat beans, red chile, and tortillas after so many little roasted rodents.

◆ ◆ ◆

The big baked ham had a thick shell of honey sugar glaze garnished with small garnet cranberries and fat brown raisins. All around the ham, side dishes brimmed with baby peas in butter cream sauce, candied yams in ap-ple butter, baked pears in lemongrass pudding, and black-eyed peas in ham gravy, and a platter of biscuits puffy and light as clouds flanked with little dishes of strawberry, blueberry, and raspberry preserves.

There was no one in the room to serve him, but the ham was sliced and he was about to fill his plate when he realized what he really wanted was a drink of water; but the fine crystal goblets above his plate were empty. He circled the table but found no water or wine, which annoyed him enough that he opened the door.

Before him was a much larger room, a wonderful dining hall with high ceilings and big bay windows with snowy mountain peaks in the distance. The great long table was laden with racks of lamb and veal, a pheasant and a suckling pig, platters of crab legs and lobsters still hot, casseroles of wild rice, baby onions in walnuts, green beans with corn, and squash with pine nuts. Loaves and braids of bread—sweet fig bread, apple bread, zucchini bread, and spicy rolls—surrounded fruit pies and cream pies, and towering cakes iced in whipped cream and chocolate fudge.

The odors of the food were sublime but he could find no wine or water or coffee anywhere on the great table; now his hunger was exceeded only by his thirst. The snow out the windows looked so inviting! He would gladly forgo the tables of luscious food for a handful of snow, and looked for an-other door out of the room; but the only door led back to the smaller din-ing room. He would have to smash the bay window and find a rope or way to let himself down to the ground some twenty feet below.

He kicked the glass and was shocked to see the fragments splash and rain down like water; he tore loose a thick green velvet panel of drapery and tied it to the window frame before he let himself down to the ground. It was freezing cold outside but the stony ground was dry; he could find no snow, and he could not control the shivering.

The last he remembered was the animated voices in a heated discussion louder than the drumming he heard; they talked about him. The Africans and the Indians—all his ancestors argued whether they should bring him home or let him stay longer. He didn't remember his ancestors or care about their feelings; yes, he was a good boy and loved his mama, but once a grown man he wasn't worth a damn except for moneymaking. He didn't remember the ancestors with even one drop of liquor or even corn pollen or a plug of tobacco. He abandoned the little grandfather, his son, to chase after money. That's how he got himself in this predicament in the first place—so crazy over the money he didn't carry enough water. Any human that weak might as well be dead.

Candy was saddened at the unfairness of the spirits, who seemed not to know that these days money was necessary to buy one's freedom day after day. Part of the stolen money belonged to Sister Salt; he always intended to return it to her. He was the one who assured her the safe was better than a hole in the ground. His eyes would not open anymore, and he could hardly swallow; but he spoke to them silently: If it was too late to save him, what were they arguing over? He had almost crossed over and was relieved to be finished—life was certainly more difficult than death. The voices ignored him; maybe he wasn't as far gone as he hoped.

No one was going to come along with water in time to save him—with the last of his strength he pulled the shotgun up beside his face. Now the drumming was so loud it deafened him and he no longer heard the voices; he felt the gusts of wind grow stronger until tiny pebbles stung his face and hands.

At first he feared the odor of rain in the wind was another hallucination, but a crash of lightning and thunder shook the ground beneath him.

He drank and drank, then tore a rag from his shirt for a wet compress on his eyes; it seemed like he slept for days before he drank enough water to need to urinate. After the storm passed, the sun came out and warmed him. He drank but oddly he wasn't hungry; he recalled the strange mountain dining hall tables of food without any desire for it. Instead he lay on his belly, his back to the sun for hours as he looked into the clear shallow pool of rainwater that collected on the flat stones. How magical water was— shifting its form endlessly, embracing the sunlight with little rainbows above its surface.

He was grateful his kidneys weren't damaged by the long thirst. During his army years he heard stories of agonizing death—burns, impalement, and poisons—but dying of thirst in the desert haunted all the troops. Now he had to agree; he got so weak toward the end he couldn't even lift the shotgun or pull its trigger. Gradually he regained his strength; when he pulled himself up to lean against a boulder, his denim pants slipped down around his knees. He looked down at himself and realized the past weeks and then these last days had whittled him away; he felt himself and found only skin and bones.

He was dozing when the odor of horseshit woke him; when he pulled the damp rag from his eyes he saw blurred blue outlines but there was no mistaking the rifles; he was surrounded by soldiers. They had orders to find a black soldier AWOL from Fort Huachuca. Candy told them his name and where he came from; the sergeant listened but was not convinced. They'd tracked him from Tonopah after reports a black man stopped there. Candy pointed out he was too old to be the man they sought, but they handcuffed and loaded him onto a mule anyway.

He asked for food and they gave him hardtack—as much as he wanted; the flat hard biscuits tasted far better than he remembered from his army days. Later when they camped for the night, they brought fried salt pork, but after a few mouthfuls he felt his stomach turn, and he was able to finish only the hardtack and boiled coffee. They took the long way around; all the way to Tucson he tried to eat the fried salt pork they offered him, but the mountain ordeal weakened his stomach, and all he could tolerate was hardtack and flapjacks.

◆　◆　◆

Indigo marked a dot in her notebook for each day that passed after Hattie left, but even when there were forty-six dots, there was no sign of Hattie. Sister Salt stole a peek over her shoulder and realized she was counting days until the white woman returned. Didn't Indigo remember how white people came, claimed they'd stay, but then later they were gone?

Sister hoped the woman never came back; yes, she was kind to Indigo and generous to all of them. But Sister felt uneasy whenever the woman came around; she knew the woman thought about taking Indigo away for good—she could tell by the expression in Hattie's eyes whenever she looked at Indigo.

Before she left on the mail wagon, Hattie promised Indigo to write in care of the trading post if she was delayed. Indigo wanted to see if there was a letter. The weather was changing; it was overcast and windy that morning, and Sister didn't want to take the baby out in the dust. But Maytha and Vedna came along with Indigo to buy more sugar to make beer.

The trader's wife barely skimmed the surface of the bushel basket where mail for the Indians was kept, but said Indigo had no mail. Indigo knew Hattie preferred small fancy sheets of paper with small matching envelopes, which might easily slip to the bottom of the basket. Indigo stayed put in front of the counter, and after a while the trader himself asked if there was something else she wanted.

"I know she was going to write," Indigo said.

"Oh. Her," the trader said and shook his head. He looked at Maytha and Vedna, who held sacks of sugar, waiting patiently for Indigo.

"Someone better tell the girl. Those society women come out from back east, interfere, and then they leave and never write." He turned his back to them and shoved the basket of mail back in its corner. Indigo's heart pounded so loudly she hardly noticed Maytha's hand around hers; she didn't cry until they stepped out into the dust and grit driven by the cold gusts of wind.

When the girls returned from the trading post, Sister saw streaks down Indigo's cheeks, where fine dust stuck to the tears. Despite the monkey's somersaults and the parrot's screeches to be let out, Indigo went straight to her bed. Sister was so angry at that white woman tears filled her eyes, and she could not stop herself.

"She's not coming back!" Sister used a loud whisper not to disturb the little grandfather's nap. Both twins nodded solemnly at Indigo.

"She's really nice—"

"She's really generous, too," Vedna interrupted.

"But the thing is, Indigo—"

"She wasn't *lying*—"

"No! She means well, poor thing."

Sister Salt angrily shook her head. Maytha and Vedna hurriedly wrapped themselves in their shawls and took the axes to go cut kindling above the riverbank while the sisters worked things out. They were expecting guests later that evening and the twins didn't want the party spoiled with arguments or tears from Sand Lizard girls.

Indigo sat up on her blankets; the little grandfather was wide awake, propped up in his bundle, listening and watching everything. Good, Indigo thought, let him see how his mother-granddaughter repays the kindness and generosity of a stranger.

"I notice you eat the food she brought; you see by the light of the lamps and oil she brought," Indigo said.

"You sound like a white girl! Listen to yourself!"

"Listen yourself! You're the one! You hurt feelings without a second thought just like white people!"

Indigo watched the little grandfather's eyes move from one to the other as they argued, but could not tell whose side he was on. Sister said even if Hattie came back this time, and the next time, someday she wouldn't come back.

How do you know?

Stories Grandma told, about a long time ago. People worked for the Mexicans for money, and bought their food and clothing. For years these people were wealthy, but one day the Apaches came and killed all the Mexicans and took all the sheep and the goods. The people who got rich working for the Mexicans began to get hungry. Crops were meager that year so the people with corn traded a handful of corn for a handful of silver coins; before long the rich were poor like everyone else.

As Indigo listened she realized her sister was right; Hattie couldn't live there and she couldn't come month after month or year after year. Grandma Fleet did use to warn them to remember other locations of water and places of shelter, just in case something happens—as it happened to Mama, or to Grandma Fleet, who didn't wake up.

The baby did not seem to mind but the argument upset the monkey and parrot; it was too windy to take them outside, so she let them out of their cages to quiet their noise. Sister Salt frowned but said nothing as long as Indigo stayed right there with them to stop any mischief. Sister was afraid the pets might bite or scratch the baby, but Indigo was confident they wouldn't harm him. She could not be so sure about the tubs of new beer—both the parrot and monkey liked to perch on the rims of the tubs, and she caught the parrot nibbling at the orchids on the window ledge.

Fortunately she stopped Rainbow before much damage was done—he peeled some green skin from two or three leaf tips. The orchids became everyone's favorites because they put out fragrant white-winged blossoms for weeks since the fall equinox, just like Edward promised. They had survived Indigo's anger—tossed and dumped from their pots—and even neglect; their stick-shaped leaves stored water like a cactus, and the flowers lasted weeks.

How strange to think these small plants traveled so far with so many hazards, yet still thrived while Edward died. Grandma Fleet was right—compared to plants and trees, humans were weak creatures. Indigo wondered how Grandma's apricot trees were. The shallow sandstone cave at the spring above the old gardens was a perfect place to keep the orchids when the hot weather came next year.

She had been thinking of the old gardens more and more. She didn't tell Sister or the twins, but the other day, while she and her pets were weeding the garden and keeping the birds off, two or three of their flooded-out neighbors came and began to pace off the perimeters of the garden and set marker stones at each corner. A few days later the Indian preacher from the flooded church came with some others to look at the new fields planted next to theirs. The Indian preacher looked right at Indigo and even from a distance she saw his anger. Of course their beans and peas were already blossoming, and their amaranth was tall, while the crops in the new fields had barely sprouted. The twins said it didn't matter that the flooded people planted late because white churchpeople sent them a wagonload of food once a month.

Maytha and Vedna returned around sundown after the wind died down; not long after, the guests began to arrive with their bedrolls and bundles of firewood. The little grandfather was awake and Sister asked Indigo to watch him on his blanket while she helped the twins serve gourds of beer outside. As it got dark, Linnaeus curled up next to Indigo on her blankets and Rainbow climbed on top of his cage and tucked his head under his wing to sleep.

The argument with Sister left Indigo exhausted. She did not remember falling asleep, but when she woke the sun had been up for a while but so had Linnaeus and Rainbow. She forgot to shut them in their cages before she fell asleep and now both of them were gone. Indigo could see where the monkey played with the empty beer gourds and the parrot chewed off the gourd rims soaked with beer. They found her notebook and scattered her color pencils, but none were chewed. The orchids on the window ledge were untouched.

Sister was asleep with the little grandfather in her arms, and the twins slept outside with the guests, but Indigo woke them. Had they seen the monkey and the parrot? No. They rolled over again—even Sister didn't care.

She walked among the sleeping guests and the campfire burned down to white ash but saw no trace of them. If only the weather had been colder, they would not have wandered out of the house. She felt the panic rise up her spine. Linnaeus would be killed by the neighbors' dogs, and poor Rainbow torn apart by an eagle or a hawk. She had to find them fast.

Indigo ran to the garden. Around the pea plants she found parrot-shredded remains of pea pods, and neatly opened bean pods—the work of the monkey fingers—all freshly picked; good thing the girls didn't come down to the garden very often. They left the garden to Indigo now that they had guests nearly every night.

The parrot and the monkey were probably in the amaranth now because it was tall and thick enough to hide them; she called their names as she waded into the thick stands, shoulder high in some places. The amaranth grew all the way to the back boundary of the field where they set their horsehair snares for rabbits; maybe she'd find them trapped. But the web-like snares were empty, and her heart began to pound in her chest as she realized the two had gone into their neighbors' gardens, where the plants were smaller and more tender.

As she stepped over the low sandy ridge that formed the boundary, she saw the damage at once. Limp, wilted pea and bean plants were strewn all around; in the rows of beans closest to the road she spotted them side by side; the monkey had both fists full of baby plants; the parrot worked rapidly, tasted only the tendrils, then dropped the rest. The monkey picked the seedlings more carefully and ate all but the roots.

"No!" she called out. "Stop that!" They both looked at her calmly and went on with their feast until she reached them. Linnaeus looked up at her with big eyes and extended a fist full of bean seedlings to her, and Rainbow waddled over and grabbed hold of the hem of her dress with his beak to climb onto her until she lifted him to her shoulder. They were so dear; she loved them so much, she couldn't bear to scold them; how could they know these plants belonged to the neighbors?

Quickly she removed all the evidence she found—torn plant remains and any parrot and monkey tracks she saw. She looked around but saw no one and hurried back to the house; she hoped the neighbors would blame ground squirrels or sparrows for the missing seedlings.

◆ ◆ ◆

Hattie did not intend to stay in Albuquerque so long, but there was little the bank officers there could do, except advise her to contact her New York bank directly. Though she was low on funds she hired a lawyer, Mr. Maxwell, to make sense of what the bank had done when Edward over-drafted the line of credit. Mr. Maxwell was an older man, whose announcement that he was a widower left Hattie feeling uncomfortable, especially after he sent a dinner invitation to the hotel.

The wait for a reply from the bank in New York left her sleepless with anxiety; she never bothered to ask about liability if the line of credit were somehow exceeded. At the time of the wedding her parents quarreled over the sum released from the family trust; her mother wanted to retain half the sum until the birth of a child, but her father's generosity prevailed. The remainder of the trust was just enough to see her parents through. How clearly she recalled her father's pride as he persuaded her mother Hattie was a bright educated young woman who deserved to dispose of her legacy as she saw fit. Oh misplaced trust! Her father's and hers!

As the weeks passed, she regretted her promise to Indigo. She could not get back to Road's End in thirty days as she thought; a dozen letters and telegrams were sent and received over the bank account.

It was much colder now in Albuquerque and she wished for the warm boots and clothing she'd left behind when she moved from New York. She waited until the sun warmed the air around midday for her walks down Central Avenue; fragrant piñon fires scented the crisp air; she hoped Indigo and the girls had enough firewood. Road's End was much farther south and at a lower elevation, so the winter was milder. The hotel clerk commented it usually wasn't that cold in early December.

Most days it was too cold to walk all the way to the old town square and the church, but now she slipped in the back of the church behind the pews to warm herself. She passed the holy water font by the door, and ignored the crucified Jesus in the center of the altar; instead she stood in the alcove with the statue of Mary with the baby Jesus in her arms. How false they seemed after the terra-cotta madonnas in Laura's black garden. *My Mother, my Spirit*—words from the old Gnostic gospels sprang into her mind. *She who is before all things, Grace, Mother of Mythic Eternal Silence*—after months in the oblivion of its shallow grave, her thesis spoke to her. *Incorruptible Wisdom, Sophia, the material world and the flesh are only temporary—there are no sins of the flesh, spirit is everything!*

Though she declined his invitation to dinner, the lawyer worked diligently on her behalf. Since her loan was secured by Edward's interest in the meteor ore venture, Mr. Maxwell, the lawyer, suggested they go to the crater to see for themselves what the mine might be worth. Hattie was adamant about avoiding any contact with the Australian doctor, and the lawyer assured her he would take care of everything.

The train arrived in Winslow in a snowstorm the morning before Christmas. While Hattie got settled in her room, Mr. Maxwell made inquiries around town and learned the Australian doctor had not been seen for weeks. He left behind two small crates of rocks, which the hotel manager seized for the unpaid balance the doctor owed.

It became her practice to first unpack the box of carved gemstones to arrange them on a bureau or bedside table where she could see them. Given the least backlight, the gems had an almost magical translucence. How she envied the timeless space they occupied while mortals stumbled along in disgrace. She was weeks late to see poor Indigo! If the lawyer was encouraged by what they saw at the meteor mine site, Hattie planned to try to sell her entire interest to him for a modest sum—enough to provide for Indigo and to take her to England to Aunt Bronwyn.

Christmas morning was sunny, but as the snow melted, the roads in and around Winslow became nearly impassable. They were the only guests in the hotel dining room for Christmas dinner, but the hotel manager and staff were quite hospitable; perhaps they hoped Hattie or the lawyer might want the crates of rocks and pay the bill.

The following morning Mr. Maxwell hired a buggy complete with a heavy wool rug to cover them during the drive to the meteor crater. The snow was not deep but transformed the plain and the low hills and mesas beyond. The view from the crater rim dizzied Hattie, and the sharp winding trail into its depths unsettled Hattie's stomach and gave her a headache. What had Edward's last letter said about a meteorite fragment buried as if it were a baby? She wished she had stayed at the hotel—too much of Edward and the Australian were still here.

No one seemed to be at the mine site at the bottom of the crater. After a brief inspection of the machinery, Mr. Maxwell doubted much of the money went toward the purchase of new mining equipment. The only new piece of equipment was a giant spring-loaded cutter used to slice open the meteor irons; beneath the heavy sharp blade Hattie saw piles of fragments left over from poor meteor irons guillotined to reveal any diamonds or precious metals. Nearby, other crates of meteor irons awaited the blade.

The mud and standing water at the bottom of the crater lapped at the edge of the wagon road. The drilling rig and other equipment looked old and poorly maintained; Mr. Maxwell pointed out the hoses and pumps and speculated the shaft constantly flooded. While he walked around the ramshackle tents and shed, Hattie directed the driver to load the two crates of meteor irons into the buggy.

Mr. Maxwell gave her his assessment on the drive back to Winslow: except for the cutter, the equipment was nearly worthless, and the mining lease devalued by the seepage, which must be pumped constantly to keep the shaft dry. He thought he would be able to sell the cutter and the other equipment to cover his fees and her expenses thus far, with some money to get her on her way—but that was all.

Mr. Maxwell expressed concern about her plan to go to Needles; it wasn't safe for a woman to travel alone out here. He wanted her to return to Albuquerque.

Nonsense! She'd been traveling alone for months quite safely.

After Mr. Maxwell departed, Hattie asked to see the rocks left behind by the Australian doctor. As she suspected, they were meteor irons, and despite her limited funds, she paid the hotel bill to get them.

At the depot in Needles the crates of meteor irons proved too heavy for the luggage cart even for the short trip around the corner to the hotel. The station attendant went for help, and to Hattie's discomfort, returned with the sullen young man and his buggy. She gave the station man a dollar to send the crates and her valises ahead—she preferred to walk.

The hotel desk clerk appeared surprised to see her again; he handed her a letter that arrived weeks before from her father. The desk clerk asked she pay for the week in advance, which seemed odd until she realized the banker or the telegraph clerk alerted the others to her financial difficulties. After he struggled to bring the crates, her valises, and the trunks of supplies, she tipped the bellman a half-dollar to dampen the rumors about her insolvency.

Her father's letter brought her to tears. He begged her to come home to them; they loved her so much and they were so proud of her no matter what anyone might say. They both were getting on in years and one day the house and land would be hers—she might as well come live there now. He knew about Edward's overdrafts on her bank account from Colin, who was executor of Edward's estate. She mustn't worry—it was only money. Please come home.

She put the letter on the bed, and unpacked the little box with the carved gemstones. She held up each one to enjoy the play of light through the chalcedony and carnelian. She arranged them on the night table with Minerva and her snake flanked by the three white cattle and the waterbird and her chick.

No, she'd rather wander naked as Isaiah for years in the wilderness than go back to Oyster Bay to endure the stares and the expressions of sympathy. She refused to serve as the living example to frighten young girls judged too fond of studies or books.

◆ ◆ ◆

The Sand Lizard sisters packed up and left Road's End after a guest revealed the flooded minister had contacted the Chemehuevi reservation superintendent about unauthorized Indians living at Road's End.

The twins didn't want them to go, but Sister and Indigo knew if they stayed there'd be trouble; they didn't belong there. The twins lied for them, and told everyone the Sand Lizard sisters returned to the reservation at Parker. The day they took the mail wagon to Needles, they covered the cages with a tarp and hid themselves, crouched down in the deep bed of the freight wagon. Linnaeus and Rainbow both sat solemnly in their cages as if they understood their garden crimes had contributed to the trouble.

The twins stayed to care for the garden and assert their rightful ownership of the land their old auntie sold them. Their flooded neighbors wanted that land for gardens to feed themselves. The twins didn't blame the neighbors; good farmland was in short supply. But Maytha and Vedna had to eat too. They paid old auntie two hundred silver dollars, and they had proof.

No one lived on the riverbank south of Needles after that winter the soldiers and Indian police broke up the dance for the Messiah. The driver of the mail wagon was kind enough to stop south of town to let them off and even helped unload the cages and some of the bundles. Sister showed Indigo the very same hearthstones they'd used before with Mama and Grandma.

While the weather was still dry, they got busy building. They used sturdy pieces of crates and other scrap lumber they found in the town dump, which was full of useful materials. Of course the Mojaves and Walapais and others who lived around Needles searched the dump every day too. The girls didn't find any large pieces of tin, but they patiently pounded tin cans flat, and with nails they pulled out of the old lumber, they were able to cover the scrap lumber entirely with tin.

On the shortest day of the year a big storm came with much rain and even sleet and hail to test the lean-to they built on the riverbank. The wind whined and the wood creaked and groaned and the rain and sleet whipped against the walls; it wasn't snug like the little stone house at Road's End, but it kept them dry.

They stuffed the cracks with Indigo's stockings and arranged their bundles and Indigo's remaining valises against the thin walls for added warmth and protection. They all huddled together—the girls and baby with the monkey and parrot—wrapped in the good blankets Hattie gave them.

Sister felt a little regretful for the mean feeling and thoughts she'd had about the white woman who was so generous to her sister and her. They'd been so busy packing their last week at Road's End, Indigo didn't have time to check at the trading post for letters.

The morning after the storm, the girls woke to the sound of dozens of crows calling from the bare white branches of the cottonwood trees along the river. The girls were overjoyed; the Messiah and his family must be on their way! They drank the last of the coffee as they discussed the preparations that must be made.

Later they took turns carrying the little grandfather, who watched intently as the sand over the stones was brushed away and missing stones replaced in the big circle that formed the spirit house of the Lord.

More crows still had to come, and of course the girls had to get people to come dance or the Messiah and his family could not appear. Once the stones of the circle were in place, the girls began to gather firewood. On days the mail wagon went south, they watched for Chemehuevi people going as far as Road's End; a girl about their age agreed to get this message to the twins: The first crows have arrived.

While the girls scoured the riverbank for snags of driftwood under the tamarisks and willows closest to the river, the racket of the crows accompanied them. Linnaeus clung to Indigo's side until he saw some plant delicacy and slid to the ground; now that Rainbow's wing feathers had grown out, he flew ahead to reach plant sprouts ahead of the monkey. Indigo recalled how the crows in Aunt Bronwyn's garden welcomed her and Rainbow, and again in Italy the crows reminded her the Messiah and his family were not far away. Sister didn't say anything; from her expression Indigo saw she didn't believe her.

"Maybe those were a different kind of crow," Sister said. They stopped to rest on the sandy bank in the sunshine. Sister unbundled the little grandfather from the shawl on her back and spread it over the ground so he could crawl. Indigo shook her head slowly; no, it was true; she'd seen for herself. In a little town the people gathered to pray and the Messiah's Mother showed herself on a stone wall.

Sister made no comment as she offered her arm so the little grandfather could steady himself as he tried to pull himself up. Now the monkey and parrot rejoined them; Linnaeus was fascinated by the baby, but Rainbow only wanted to chew the edge of the blanket they were sitting on.

Indigo described the old stones Aunt Bronwyn cared for in her gardens; these stones used to move and to talk until the churchgoers smashed them. Sister nodded; she believed that. One night the stones even called Hattie out of her bed and she woke up in the garden! Sister laughed and Indigo joined her. Grandma Fleet knew stones that played tricks! Remember the stone that sweats and the other that urinates? They laughed again.

Indigo said in England there were a great many Christ Churches but the Messiah and his family seemed to travel most of the time. Sister nodded.

That was because so many greedy and cruel people did damage only the Messiah could repair. Trouble was in so many places, he had to travel constantly, and so did the Mother of God, who often went to help alone.

The warm sunshine felt so good after the cold weather that followed the big storm; Sister stretched out on the blanket and the baby crawled up on her chest and pulled at her dress for a breast until she unbuttoned and gave him one, then lay back to stare up at the sky. Indigo described the stone figures, half man and half horse or bull, hidden in shady green woods, and how they startled her and Hattie. There was even a giant head of a woman who kept baby snakes in her hair. Sister was interested but not shocked: Grandma Fleet always said humans were capable of sex with anything and on rare occasions these strange creatures were born. The stone figures were proof of the strange offspring.

The wind came up and small puffy clouds began to move across the sky; the baby was asleep with her nipple half out of his mouth, so Sister gently laid him on the blanket beside her and buttoned up.

Indigo told Sister about the gardens. All flowers? Nothing to eat? Yes, like the little flower gardens in front of houses in Needles. Only their friend Laura had big, big gardens—one was all black flowers, black gladiolus Laura raised herself. The black flowers honored the first mothers—half human, half bird, half bear, half snake, their clay figures carefully placed in little spirit houses in the black garden. Best of all was the rain garden of sand and tall succulents; their spikes of yellow, orange, and red flowers towered above the snake girls with basins on their laps to call the rain.

The sun moved around and left them in the shade and it got chilly. Sister sat up, her face bright with enthusiasm; Grandma Fleet always said snake girls and bird mothers were everywhere in the world, not just here!

News traveled up and down the river about the return of the crows and the encampment near Needles. People came from up and down the river; some Paiutes claimed no one told them about the camp but a big flock of crows led them south as they had before, when the soldiers attacked the holy family and the dancers. Soon small campsites with lean-tos of willows and cottonwood branches appeared on the riverbank not far from the sisters' tin shack.

Flocks of crows continued to arrive; the leafless cottonwoods were black with them roosting. They scavenged for oats and milo in the freshly harvested fields the white farmers had along the river.

Sister Salt brought out the practice baskets she made at Road's End, and pronounced them good enough to sell to tourists off the trains. She didn't want the baby around the strangers and left Indigo and her pets to watch the little grandfather while she went to the station. As long as the weather stayed dry, the tourists got off the trains during the stop, and each day Sister sold all the baskets she brought.

With her turkey, dog, and turtle baskets set out on the ground in front of her, Sister waited with the other Indian women on the driveway next to the station platform. Now the stationmaster barred the Indians from the passenger platform, but allowed them on the driveway for the amusement of the passengers who liked to photograph the Indians and their crafts. While she waited, Sister worked the damp yucca strips into turkey figures because those baskets always sold out first.

All morning, though, even before the train from the east arrived, Sister had an odd feeling of worry and sadness despite everything going along so well since their move from Road's End. The train from the west was due, but its passengers usually bought less than the easterners, so Sister packed up her remaining baskets and went home early.

Even before she reached their shack, she could see a pile of bundles outside so she was not surprised to find Maytha and Vedna inside; but she was surprised to find Indigo with tears streaming down her face even as she gently bounced the little grandfather on her lap. Sister greeted the twins, then asked Indigo what was wrong.

Tears welled up in Indigo's eyes and she looked at Maytha and Vedna.

"They took away your land?"

"Not yet!"

"Well why's she crying?"

The twins seemed hesitant. It was something about the white woman, wasn't it? They nodded. She'd been found wandering naked and dazed beside the road near Topock, at the northern edge of the Chemehuevi reservation. The twins heard about it from a guest at the beer-sampling party. The guest, an off-duty Indian policeman, said someone had beaten her head with a rock, then left her for dead beside the road. They later found the place it happened—her luggage was dumped and rifled and scattered in the ditch. Blond hairs and crusted blood were found on the heavy iron rock her attacker used; they found other, similar iron rocks nearby, dumped and scattered from small wooden crates.

"She must have been coming to Road's End," Maytha said, "because they found sacks of flour and sugar torn open—"

"Even fresh things like bacon and apples—"

"Wasted! Dumped out on the ground!"

Sister knelt next to Indigo and put her arms around her while the little grandfather grabbed hold of her and crawled into her lap to nuzzle her breasts.

"There, there, little sister, don't cry. We'll pray for your friend."

◆ ◆ ◆

She was frozen in the gray ice swirling around her head; it drilled into her skull until she screamed, but hands pinned her arms and a sharp weight pressed her flat until she lost consciousness. Later she woke to the taste of blood; her tongue and lips were bitten and bleeding. How did this happen? What sort of dream was this where the pain only increased as she woke? She slipped back from the pain into the comfort of the dim gray light and did not try to surface again for a long time.

Later she woke in the sand beside a road with a crushing pain in her skull so terrible she could not see clearly at first. She attempted to stand but the pain and dizziness brought her to her knees. The sun overhead warmed her, and after a while she was able to stand but the pain made her vomit, and she went only a few steps before she sat down by the road to wait for help.

Indians found her. She remembered that. Had she managed to walk a bit farther down the road? Men and women approached, then dropped their rakes and hoes to run to help her. From the shocked expressions on their faces, she realized she must look terrible. It wasn't until one of the Indian women wrapped a piece of cloth around her shoulders that she realized she was naked. She felt something warm running down the back of her head, and when she reached back to touch it, fresh blood smeared her hand. She felt hard crusts matted in her hair. One of the women spoke English and told her not to be afraid, they would take her to their house and send for help. They steadied her between them as they slowly walked; even then the pain and dizziness caused her to stumble and she had to vomit again. They helped her down to a soft pile of blankets and quilts, where she sank into the gray light again.

Later the women helped her into a blue gingham dress much too large for her before the men lifted her into the back of an old wagon they filled with blankets and quilts. The wagon went slowly enough, but even the least bump sent fiery pain through her skull, so she had to hold it tight in both hands.

When the wagon finally stopped and she opened her eyes, she saw the familiar downtown storefronts of Needles. As soon as the deputy sheriff came out, the store clerk, bank teller, and others gathered around the wagon to stare. Another deputy helped carry her from the wagon to the barber's chair.

As he gently snipped the hair from around the wound, the barber explained he'd studied medicine for two years in Philadelphia; the nearest doctor was in Kingman. She was lucky to be alive because her skull was cracked. The alcohol stung and ran into both her ears as he flushed the wound of dirt. The barber and his wife kindly offered a cot in their pantry until she got back on her feet. The barber offered to send a telegram to her family but she felt too dizzy and weak to reply.

For three days Hattie slept, waking only to drink water or use the chamber pot. On the fifth day her appetite returned and she ate a bowl of potato soup. Later the barber's wife heated water for a bath; as soon as she sat in the warm water she felt the other wounds her attacker inflicted, and tears of anger filled her eyes. She found so much sand with weeds in her clothes she put on the blue gingham dress again.

Her rescuers had gathered up what they could of the scattered clothing and belongings, but the little wooden box with the carved gemstones were gone. In a way, the loss of the carvings was worse than the outrage done to her body; she had no recollection of that, but her anguish over the carvings grew by the hour. The gemstones were perfect and beautiful, yes, but in their presence Hattie felt cherished in the way her father loved her. Now they were gone.

She cried so bitterly the piercing pain returned to her head and made her vomit; the barber gave her laudanum, which dulled the pain. The low ceiling of the pantry resembled a tomb. She was sorry she survived the attack—how much easier death would be than this.

The deputy came to make the report the next day. She was careful to move her head slowly and to answer his questions slowly or the pounding pain in her skull came back. The last thing she could remember was checking into the hotel from the train station the day she arrived; she lost all memory of the day of the attack. The deputy asked if there were other injuries beside the blow to the head, and Hattie could tell by the deputy's averted eyes he wanted to know if she'd been raped. She hesitated, then nodded, but she didn't cry; she didn't feel anything.

The deputy did not look up from his report.

"All your money and other valuables were taken?"

She nodded, then as she described the little box of carved gemstones, tears filled her eyes.

Though she could not remember, it seemed obvious she was on her way to Road's End the day of her attack. Surely the desk clerk at the hotel remembered who drove her—after all, she checked out that morning with a good many bundles and all her luggage. The deputy kept writing. At last he looked up, and promised to get back to her after his investigation.

The deputy completed his inquiry in one afternoon. The desk clerk recalled her checking out but neither he nor the bell captain saw her leave the lobby. Hattie was incredulous—the hotel staff would have had to help load all her luggage and the crates of meteor irons. The deputy looked her in the eyes: the livery stable had no record of a fare from the hotel on the day of her attack.

"But that can't be!" she cried as she realized the townspeople protected one another. The deputy said the case would be left open for one year from the date of her attack; any new information she might have as her memory returned should be submitted to his office.

So this was how it was done in Needles, California—it wasn't terribly different from the way it was done in Boston. Now it was clear to her, she could never return to her former life among the lies. She had to leave at once.

The barber's wife was kind enough to wash and iron her clothes, but Hattie insisted on wearing the blue gingham dress even when she slept. The woman tried to persuade Hattie people would think her strange if she continued to wear the dress—a squaw dress—much too large for her. When Hattie made no reply, the woman warned if she wore that dress around town, it wouldn't help matters.

"What matters?"

"You and the Indians," she replied. "People here don't welcome outsiders who meddle." She looked away from Hattie. A new Indian encampment started down along the river about a week ago; her attacker was probably one of them, full of green beer.

Hattie was so happy to learn of the encampment, she ignored the woman's last remark. She knew she would find Indigo there. Hadn't the girls talked about a winter gathering near Needles? She felt so much better just to know Indigo and the girls were nearby.

Hattie wired her father collect to ask him to please send the barber the money she owed for her treatment and room and board. She took her winter coat and all the warm clothes she could layer under the blue dress but left her luggage and all the rest with the barber as collateral until the money arrived. Her telegram told her parents how much she loved them, and please, not to worry. She was in the hands of God and no harm would come to her.

The sun was bright and the air mild and dry the morning she set out on foot from the barbershop for the encampment down along the river. As weak as she still was, she was glad to have nothing more to carry than a thick wool blanket and a sack of hard candy balls.

What idiots these military police were! The U.S. magistrate saw at once they brought in the wrong Negro. This man was twice the age of the deserter. He asked Big Candy if there was anyone in Tucson who might verify his identity.

In Tucson? He couldn't think of anyone. He would have to send a telegram to the address Wylie gave him, though it might be weeks before he got a reply. Then he remembered that construction worker from Tucson—Charlie—what was his name?—Sister Salt adored him—he might even be the baby's father—Charlie Luna! If they could find him, he would confirm Big Candy's identity.

Big Candy expected he might have to wait a day or two before Charlie Luna could be located, but later the same day, he was brought before the magistrate again. There stood Charlie Luna. For an instant Charlie almost didn't recognize Candy because of all the weight he'd lost. Charlie broke into a big smile.

"Yes sir!" He knew this man!

The magistrate ruled Big Candy was free to go. He was flat broke and he still didn't feel fully recovered from the ordeal. He walked out of the courthouse with Charlie to thank him.

"I almost didn't recognize you," Charlie said. Candy nodded and smiled. He didn't recognize himself the first time he stood in front of a mirror.

"You took a wrong turn?"

"You could say that. Ever hear of the Sand Tank Mountains?"

Charlie nodded; he used to worry Candy hated him over Sister Salt, so he was relieved to be able to help him. Now it was clear there were no hard feelings; Charlie felt so happy he invited Candy to dinner.

Both men avoided any mention of Sister Salt. Charlie's house was full of children and in-laws and relatives from three or four generations. Candy was reminded of his cousins' houses in Louisiana.

On a long bench flanked with old women and children, Candy ate three bowls of posole and a small stack of tortillas, which pleased Charlie's wife immensely. Charlie rattled on in Spanish, using his arms to show her how big around Candy's belly used to be. He told them how Candy cooked all sorts of roast poultry and rich meats—the odors used to waft through the workers' tents at night and made their mouths water because all they got was tortillas and beans.

Candy explained since his ordeal without water his stomach somehow was affected and he no longer was able to digest any meat or poultry. From time to time he tried a bite of lean pork or venison, but a second bite brought nausea. Even the odor of cooking meat and grease made him feel weak and ill; his passions for new recipes and unusual game or seafood were gone. Wylie wanted him to go to Los Angeles to open a restaurant, but that wasn't possible now.

Charlie Luna shook his head slowly; yes, he'd heard similar stories about people who suffered a terrible event and overnight their hair turned completely white or they no longer went outdoors or never left their beds. Everyone agreed: a person really could be changed overnight if an incident was drastic.

In the big yard next door, Candy noticed freight wagons and corrals of mule teams outside a big warehouse. Charlie's aunt owned a freight line between Tucson and Caborca, Sonora. He needed a relief driver to go with him to Hermosillo in the morning. The cargo was something special—Charlie raised his eyebrows expressively—and the pay was very generous.

Candy figured it was some kind of contraband but he didn't care as long as the job paid good money.

◆ ◆ ◆

Delena's mission was finished as soon as the Tucson contacts finished the purchases and made the arrangements to ship the rifles to Hermosillo. Her orders were to return to Caborca. The dogs had regained all the strength they'd used up in their travels and were becoming restless, unaccustomed to the inactivity. They smelled a rat under the floor of the barn and chewed away one edge of a warped plank while she was in the house at dinner. She slept in the barn with them to keep them from barking and howling at night; they piled around her and wrestled one another for

463

the honor of sleeping across her legs; twice their wrestling with one another resulted in loud dogfights that brought the neighbors out to the alley. It was time to go.

The last evening at the safe house an old man leading a mule loaded with firewood stopped outside. The man of the house went out immediately to pretend to buy the wood so the neighbors didn't get suspicious. Delena did not recognize him, but he was sent by their people in the south to find out if she was alive and if they could expect any supplies soon.

They sat up late into the night in the kitchen to hear the old man's accounts of recent skirmishes with the federal troops in the mountains. While they talked, Delena threaded her bone awl to mend the burlap dog packs as the woman of the house busied herself cooking and packing food for Delena's long walk south.

The last thing she did was fill the canvas water bags from the well in the yard; free of the cargo of money, the dogs could carry all the water they might need and bones to eat. A light wind out of the southwest carried a faint scent of rain—a good companion for the desert crossing. After midnight, the woman finished packing the food, and Delena went out to the toilet and was amazed the sky was so bright with stars. She didn't need any Gypsy cards to know this was the best time to set out.

The old man was already asleep in the barn as she checked the ties on the dogs' packs a last time to make sure they were firm. Delena thanked the Tucson couple for the food and the safe haven but also for their tolerance of her dogs. The man of the house shook her hand and the woman embraced her. They prayed for the people and the struggle every day, and they would not forget her.

In the brightness of the stars at that hour, the silhouettes of the black dogs with their backpacks were plainly visible in the gateway; she heard the dogs pant eagerly for the signal to go. As she turned to go she said, "We will outlast them. We always have."

◆ ◆ ◆

Just ahead of the storm clouds came more flocks of crows, followed by people in groups of three and four. The encampment was not nearly as large as the one before, but Sister said that didn't matter; maybe with a smaller gathering, the authorities would leave them in peace to dance for the Messiah. So far no old-time Mormons showed up like they had last time; but who could blame them after their punishment?

Off in the distance on the road from town, the twins noticed a figure coming slowly their way. They thought at first it might be some old Mormon woman brave enough to join them, but as she came closer, Maytha recognized Hattie; so their prayers for her had done some good!

Vedna ran to tell Indigo, who instantly looked at Sister Salt for her reaction to the news. No one may be turned away from the gathering, Sister said; otherwise, the Messiah will not come. Indigo shut Linnaeus and Rainbow in their cages for safekeeping, while Sister bundled the little grandfather onto her back, and they went to greet Hattie.

Even from a distance they could see her face was bruised and swollen, and she moved unsteadily on her feet. Indigo was shocked at the swelling of her face—she hardly looked like the Hattie Indigo knew. She seemed to have trouble with her eyes and did not seem to recognize Indigo at first, but then she gave a shout and dropped the blanket and sack of candy to hug Indigo. The twins dropped to their knees at once to pick up the spilled candy balls and wipe the sand off before returning them to the sack.

Hattie started to cry and hugged Indigo so hard and long Indigo finally had to pull loose from her embrace, and left Hattie wobbling on her feet until Maytha and Vedna steadied her between. Sister Salt watched Hattie's shaking hands and the difficulty she had focusing her eyes.

They nearly killed her, Sister Salt said bitterly after they helped Hattie lie down on Indigo's blankets. Poor woman! She was in bad shape; she might not recover. She told Indigo to sit awhile with her until she got settled. Don't talk about what happened—talk about good things.

Linnaeus sat on Indigo's lap and watched Hattie solemnly; he didn't even try to tease Rainbow by pulling his tail feathers. She held Indigo's hand in hers and lay back with her eyes closed and moaned softly. Indigo began to talk about the crows and the snow clouds and the people who came to dance for the return of the Messiah.

Gradually Hattie's grip on her hand relaxed, and Indigo saw her body relax as if the intensity of the pain was beginning to subside. Sister said Hattie should not have walked even a short distance, as badly hurt as she was. After Hattie fell asleep, Indigo gently slipped her hand loose from Hattie's. "We will pray for you every night of the dance," she said softly, then took the monkey and parrot outside to stretch her legs.

Outside the shack around the fire, they passed around the sack of candy balls Hattie brought them; big snowflakes began to fall and hissed in the fire. Hurt as she was, still she brought them a gift. Big tears welled up in Indigo's eyes. Vedna offered to consult the spirits about Hattie; she took her Bible and closed her eyes and turned it round and round, then stuck her finger on a page, then read aloud: "Do you see this, O Son of Man? Turn around again, and you shall see greater abominations than these.

"Ezekiel," Vedna said. "I don't know—it doesn't sound so good if it's about Hattie. Maybe it's about us—Ezekiel's trying to warn us."

"I think it means if we camp here too long they'll come after us," Sister said.

The girls shared a cigarette Maytha rolled, and watched the snow clouds push in above the river. In only a few more hours the two fires would be lit, and the dance would begin. Already they were applying the white clay paint to faces and hands, and a Walapai man shared the sacred clay Wovoka gave him and blessed each camp and lean-to with a pinch of the red dust. Sister watched the tall sandy hill above the river where last time the Messiah and his family walked out of the falling snow.

Sister went to nurse the little grandfather inside the lean-to before the dance started; he was bright eyed and nursed heartily but refused to fall asleep, as if he wanted to see the dance. You're too little, she told him; I might see Grandma Fleet or someone and fall to the ground or drop you. She rocked him in her arms as she stepped over to check on Hattie. The skin was terribly pale around the swollen purple bruises on her forehead; Sister had to watch carefully a long time before she was even sure Hattie was still breathing. The swellings around her lips and cheeks were going down, but all she did was sleep. Wasn't there anyone who cared about Hattie but them?

As the fires were lit, the snow seemed to fall faster—a sign the Messiah and his family were on their way. They did not all have white shawls—some shawls were burlap or old army blankets, but the Messiah would understand. They had to make do with what they had. Wovoka the Prophet could not be there because the soldiers wanted to arrest him.

As everyone prepared for the first dance of the night, Sister nursed the little grandfather and Indigo offered Hattie water mixed with a little blue cornmeal, which was all she could eat because her mouth was injured. She seemed more alert as she sat up; she watched Sister change the baby's wrapping and noticed Linnaeus and Rainbow in their cages by the bed. When Indigo told her the first dance was about to begin, Hattie managed a bit of a smile despite her swollen lips.

Maytha and Vedna promised to look after the little grandfather, and to watch Hattie and the parrot and monkey if Sister or Indigo were visited by the spirits. What if they all were visited at the same time? That was not likely, Sister said, but if that happened, then the baby, Hattie, the pets—all would be blessed and protected by that presence.

The snow covered the ground and continued to fall lightly as the drum called them to the spirit house, where they sang the new songs, each in a different language—Sand Lizard, Paiute, Chemehuevi, Mojave, and Walapai—because in the presence of the Messiah, all languages were understood by everyone.

They all joined hands and moved in the direction of the sun around the circle of stones.

"Across the snowy stars," they sang. More voices joined as they repeated the words, "Over the Milky Way bridge—oh the beloved return!"

They danced slowly, careful to trail their feet gently to caress Mother Earth. The wind was still but now the snow fell faster, and it was difficult to see the lean-to and the camps on the far side of the circle.

> Bare cottonwood
> Black with crows.
> They call
> Snow clouds on the wind.
> Snow clouds on the wind.

As the snow clouds closed around them and reflected the light of the fires, Indigo noticed how the white paint transformed their hands and faces, and the white shawls wrapped around them made the dancers almost invisible in the snow.

> We danced four nights.
> We danced four nights.
> The fourth dawn Messiah came.
> The fourth dawn Messiah came.

They stopped dancing around midnight, and stood around the big kettle to share cups of hot tea made with sweet grass and little mountaintop herbs. Although they danced for hours, no one seemed tired, especially not the older women and men, who talked excitedly about their dear ones they hoped to visit on the fourth night. A Mojave man passed around a big basket of goat jerky and a Walapai woman passed a basket of roasted blue cornmeal; then they returned to their lean-tos and tents to sleep.

The girls all piled together under the old quilts and all the blankets, which they moved toward Indigo's corner so they could keep Hattie and the parrot and monkey warm.

Midmorning the sun pushed through the clouds briefly and fog clung to the riverbed and drifted near their camp. Later, most of the snow melted, but by early afternoon the wind brought low gray clouds, and before sundown, sleet mixed with snow whipped against the shacks and tents.

Hattie slept like the dead for hours on end; after the wind came up, she woke. She was weak but the pain in her head was not so sharp as before. She drank roasted blue corn flour in water and went to sleep again.

◆ ◆ ◆

The storm clouds moved on; the afternoon was sunny and mild, so Indigo took Linnaeus and Rainbow for a walk along the riverbank to browse on the fat seed heads of rice grass and to dig cattail roots. The crows in the cottonwoods scolded as they passed by, so Rainbow fluffed his feathers and flexed his wings to appear larger to discourage attacks. He gripped her shoulder firmly and pressed close to Indigo's head, and did not reach for the monkey's tail as he often did.

Indigo stopped to look up at the crows. Their glittering black eyes were merry as they tussled and hopped along the branches. What did they know about the Messiah and the others? Would Mama return with them tonight?

The sound of her voice silenced the frolicking crows; the silence lasted for as long as she looked up at the crows until finally Linnaeus tugged at her dress, impatient to dig roots in the shallows of the river.

The crows' silence left Indigo discouraged even after they gathered a fine load of seeds and roots for Rainbow and Linnaeus on their journey downriver tomorrow. As she neared the lean-to, she was heartened to see Hattie, a blanket around her shoulders, outside in the sun with Maytha and Vedna. Sister Salt was on a blanket, helping the little grandfather stand up in the little moccasins their Paiute friend gave him.

They watched the baby as he cautiously took a step and then another around his mother while he gripped her hands for support. Sister confided to Indigo his desire to walk so young was another sign he was the old grandfather's soul returned.

The girls took turns walking the perimeter of the campsite every morning to check for signs the townspeople were spying on the gathering. Sister Salt worried someone would come looking for Hattie and make trouble, but no one came. After the first night, they found four sets of boot prints at the edge of a willow grove; but after the second night they found no trace of spies. Their gathering was too small to concern the white people of Needles.

◆ ◆ ◆

The sky was clear and the stars' light reflected off the sandhills with patches of snow on the third night. The waning moon did not rise until after midnight, but suddenly the night became so bright the willows along the riverbank and the sandy hillside were clearly visible in a pale blue silver light. Freezing air descended from the mountains, and ribbons of steam rose around the dancers' heads as they sang.

> I saw my slain sister, Buffalo.
> I saw my slain brother, Condor.
> Don't cry, they told me.
> Don't cry.

A dancer sank to her knees moaning, then lay flat to embrace the ground; her companions pulled her shawl up to keep her warm while she visited with her dear ones. They stepped over her and the others who fell to the ground twitching and babbling, and kept dancing as the starry bridge of the Milky Way arched over them.

The dancers stood near the fires to keep warm as they rested before the last song; Indigo went with Sister to the lean-to to check on the baby and to see if Hattie and the pets were keeping warm. They all were asleep and snugly covered; Sister put a small piece of wood on the fire outside and they returned to join in the final round of songs.

As they sang and danced the circle, Indigo lifted her eyes to the high sandy hill above the river to the northwest, and sang with all her heart for Mama to come. Just as the morning star rose above the mountain horizon, Indigo felt her sister's grip on her hand tighten before Sister Salt sank to the sand and lay crying softly and moaning. Indigo felt her heart pound with the drum until she was enclosed by the sound that shook the ground under her feet. Now the Messiah and his followers were near, prepared to come bless the dancers on the last night. She held on to the twins' hands even tighter to keep her balance on the pulsating earth.

> Winds dance
> In the green grass.
> Winds dance
> In the yellow flowers.

They covered Sister Salt with a blanket while she lay motionless on the ground, and later helped her back to the lean-to to sleep. Visits left the dancers exhausted.

Indigo had difficulty getting to sleep and wanted to be up early when Sister woke to feed the little grandfather. If it was Grandma Fleet who visited Sister last night, did she have any news about Mama? It was still dark when she woke and heard the others snoring; outside a crack between the wood and tin, dawn was approaching behind low foggy clouds. Faintly, in the distance, she heard beautiful singing and realized the singing she heard was not from the encampment—all the dancers were asleep. The sound was in the distance but closer now. Careful not to wake anyone, Indigo took her shawl and stepped outside before she wrapped herself against the freezing air. On the high sandy hill she thought she saw some movement in the mist and fog.

As she began to climb up the deep sand of the slope, the fog and mist swirled down to meet her; now the singing was near and very beautiful—a song in the Sand Lizard language she'd never heard before.

> Dance, little clouds, your sisters are fog!
> Dance, little clouds, your brothers are mist!
> Play in the wind! Play in the wind!

Mama was rocking her—she was so snug and warm. What a happy, beautiful song! Mama kissed her and held her so close.

Indigo woke in her bed and saw it was still dark. She felt so much love she wept; she knew then where Mama was and always would be. Dance, little clouds, dance! Play in the wind!

For an instant Hattie did not know where she was, then she heard the drum and the voices. Outside the soft yellow glow must be the approach of dawn; the lemon yellow light was the same color as the lost carnelian carved with the waterbirds. The crushing pain was gone and her head felt clear; all her senses were alert for the first time since the assault. Dawn was the time the Messiah and his family were expected to come. She wanted to see for herself.

In the soft light she could make out the sleeping baby, the quilt carefully tucked around him; the parrot and monkey both were awake in their cages and watched her put on her shoes. As she approached the blanket over the lean-to entrance, the light outside became brighter and more luminous—she recognized it at once and felt a thrill sweep over her. How soothing the light was, how joyously serene she felt.

She lost all sense of time and of how long she stood at the entrance, the luminous glow streaming in all around the edges of the blanket. She was too awed to step outside to face it.

The girls were surprised to find Hattie up when they returned to the lean-to after midnight. She told them how she woke feeling so much better and then noticed the beautiful glow outside the lean-to, so much like the strange light she saw before.

The light she saw was the morning star, who came to comfort her, Sister explained. How could she have seen the same light in the garden in England and in a dream on board the ship? Oh the Messiah and his family traveled the earth—they might be seen anywhere. Tomorrow he would come as the Messiah with the others and speak to them.

But on the morning of the fourth day, three white soldiers and two Apache policemen rode up; while the soldiers watched from their horses, the Apaches went around to question all the people about their assigned reservations. The policemen were polite, even friendly when they spoke to the dancers, but they let them know they must break up the gathering at once or be arrested.

Many wept at the news, and Sister and others pleaded with the police to let them dance just one more night—the Messiah and the others were so close now. But no, the Apache cops pretended they didn't know what the people were talking about.

People started to cry as they realized they would not be permitted to dance home their ancestors and the Messiah that night. Sister Salt was furious and cursed the policemen and soldiers in English: Masturbators! Donkey fuckers! Maytha spat at them but Vedna brought out her Bible and waved it in the cops' faces. The soldiers moved in on their horses to protect the cops but Vedna stood her ground and let the Bible fall open, then began to shout the words on the page: "Even though you make many prayers I will not hear you. Your hands are full of blood!"

The Apaches retreated quickly to their horses to confer with the soldiers; they were afraid the girl shaking the Bible might put witchcraft on them. Many people were crying and all appeared stunned; only the girl with the Bible appeared to resist.

Indigo cried and cried; now they'd never find Mama or get to see Grandma Fleet except in dreams. The Messiah and the others were so close, but now they could not come. Her tears were hot and bitter and burned her eyes, so she had difficulty seeing what it was Maytha was pointing at in the distance. A wagon! Was it more police coming to haul them away?

Hattie was shocked to see her father beside the Indian policeman in the doorway. His expression of joy at finding her quickly faded to concern over the bruises on her face. He hesitated before he stepped inside to kneel on the quilt beside her to get a better look. The parrot squawked loudly and the monkey screamed; the baby woke and began to cry. Hattie burst into tears—her father knelt and gently put his arms around her but she pulled away.

At the baby's first cries, Sister Salt burst into the lean-to past the Apache cop and white man, to pick up the little grandfather. Indigo followed, and recognized Mr. Abbott at once and greeted him politely. The monkey and parrot calmed when they saw the girls.

Mr. Abbott said Indigo grew so much he almost didn't know her. Sister held the baby close to her chest and stood ready to flee even after Indigo reassured her Hattie's father was kind.

Now one of the white soldiers joined the Apache cop in the doorway; Sister spat in their direction and turned her back to them. Outside she could hear people pray, and some wept softly for the losses—their hopes to be blessed by the Messiah were dashed. How they dreamed and yearned to see beloved ancestors and dear ones passed on, and that was not to be.

Hattie realized the police and soldiers came to break up the Indian gathering because of her—because they came looking for her there. She already knew the townspeople blamed Indians for her assault. Hattie stopped weeping to beg her father to intercede for the dancers. She did not hide the anger she felt as she told him the authorities might have ignored the gathering one more night if he had not come looking for her there. Her father seemed shaken by the fury of her accusation, and the others were motionless as she went on; this fourth night of the dance she hoped to see the Messiah. Don't let the authorities interfere!

Her father seemed overwhelmed, even a bit dazed, to find himself in the middle of such a conflict. He gestured out the door; her mother and the Albuquerque lawyer, Mr. Maxwell, were waiting in the buggy. "Get the lawyer to do something!" She got to her feet with her father's aid; she told the girls she'd be right back; she held her father's arm as she slowly made her way out the door.

Hattie looked the driver of the buggy in the eyes; no, he wasn't the one;

she knew it was either the son or the owner of the stable. She felt furious and strong; her attacker walked free in that wretched town!

The lawyer removed his overcoat and Hattie's father put it over her shoulders and rolled up the sleeves that were too long. It smelled vile—stale tobacco smoke and man sweat—but a chill wind had come up and she had to keep warm in order to keep going.

She barely greeted her mother before she began to argue: This fourth night of the dance was to bring the Messiah! Didn't they understand? The urgency in her voice unsettled her mother and the lawyer, but her father patted her hand.

The dancers' prayers saved her life—each night of the dance she recovered a bit more as the Messiah drew nearer. She wept with fury when she saw her mother and the lawyer whisper to each other—they believed she was ill, out of her head.

"Oh Hattie! Just look at you! You've suffered a terrible shock!" her mother exclaimed. Hattie knew she meant the Indian dress and her unkempt hair. That was enough for Hattie. She let go of her father's arm and turned to go back to the camp. But her mother cried out for them to stop her—her daughter was ill and needed help! They must get her on the next train to Albuquerque to the hospital. Her head injuries required treatment at once.

Hattie managed to break free of her father and left the lawyer holding the empty coat; but the soldiers dismounted and helped them subdue her. She saw the people who were packing up stop to watch, then hurry on their way, as if they feared they'd be seized next. Sister Salt and Indigo watched outside the lean-to as Hattie struggled with her captors. After they lifted her into the buggy and Mr. Maxwell and mother held her arms, Mr. Abbott, his face pale with distress, hurried over to say good-bye to Indigo, who wept for Hattie. Inside the tent, the parrot shrieked, furious his beloved was crying, and the monkey called Indigo frantically.

Just as Mr. Abbott spoke, Sister Salt stepped forward and spat in his face. For an instant he seemed shocked, but then he closed his eyes and stared down at the ground; he made no effort to wipe his face before he got back into the buggy.

In the train station lobby Hattie pretended to collapse long enough for her father and the lawyer to leave her alone with her mother while they saw to the tickets and luggage. She waited until they were out of sight and her mother rummaged in her purse to make a run for it.

Her fury gave her strength and will to run down the alley and cross another street; but instead of returning to the river where the girls were, she headed down another alley; she didn't want to bring any more trouble for the dancers.

She stopped behind a stack of oak kegs in the alley to catch her breath and to listen for her pursuers. Piles of dirty snow lined the north side of the alley and made the footing there treacherous. The fresh air did her good; her head felt clear, and the excitement of the escape gave her strength.

Now the breeze down the alley chilled her and she shoved her hands deep into the coat pockets and felt objects in both pockets. In the right pocket she found a fresh starched handkerchief and a small box of matches; in the left pocket she found a key that she tossed into a dirty snowbank and a small pouch of tobacco she threw down. But she kept the little pack of cigarette papers, and pulled one out and struck one of the little matches to it. For a moment the warmth of the flame around the paper was delicious before she had to let go of the bright ash.

She looked both ways before she continued down the alley, which was cluttered with trash and debris—rotting garbage and overturned barrels— filthy just like the town and its people. She caught the odor of horses and saw corrals up ahead; manure and old straw were piled outside: it was the back of the livery stable. Her heart began to pound wildly; she could turn back and go down a side alley, but she crept closer, careful to remain in the deep shadows as she listened and watched. The horses were calmly chewing their hay and paid no attention as she crept up.

What a disgusting stinking mess outside the back door—she stepped over dirty rags and manure. Straw and hay were strewn everywhere. The smell of rotting urine and manure was terrible as she peeked around the corner of the wide barn door. She listened and watched, but no one was there. Inside it was almost dark, but she could see the buggies and wagons parked along the far wall; above them big metal hooks held the harnesses. Everywhere the floor was littered with hay and straw; along the near wall by the door were the haystack and burlap sacks of feed, and a workbench. Something familiar caught her eye and sent the hair on her neck straight out: among the scattered tools was a big steel vise, and clamped in it was a meteor iron partially sawed in half. She saw other fragments of meteor iron among the chisels and saw blades on the bench. She shivered—from the cold or from the sight of meteor irons, she didn't know.

She knew exactly what must be done; the crumpled cigarette papers flashed under the match; all the starch in the handkerchief caused it to flare up nicely in the loose hay on the floor. Little wings of flame gave off a lemon yellow glow that recalled the lost carving of the waterbirds. What a lovely light the fire gave off as she warmed her hands over it; but as the rivulets of fire spread to the haystack, the heat drove her outside.

At the corrals, she let the terrified horses run free, and followed them to a hill east of town, where she watched—amazed and elated by the beauty of the colors of the fire against the twilight sky. As the flames snaked over to catch the roofs of buildings on either side of the stable, the fire's colors were brilliant—the reds as rich as blood, the blues and whites luminous, and the orange flame as bright as Minerva's gemstone.

◆ ◆ ◆

By the time they got everything packed and took down the lean-to, it was too late to get very far downriver. Even with the help of the twins it was a struggle to get all their belongings, the pets, and supplies to the road where they could catch the mail wagon the next morning.

Indigo still cried when she thought of Hattie lifted bodily into the buggy, though the twins reassured her Hattie was strong; she'd been blessed by the light of the morning star. Sister Salt was still too angry to speak; only the little grandfather's laughter at the antics of the monkey softened her fierce expression.

They made a little campfire just as the sun went down and shared cold tortillas and bits of mutton jerky in silence. The turmoil left them exhausted. Rainbow noticed the flames to the north first and flapped his wings and squawked excitedly as he clutched Indigo's shoulder.

All night the flames lit the sky, and they sat bundled in blankets and quilts to watch. At first they didn't know what was burning, and Maytha joked the town dump must have caught fire, but later the flames went so high, Vedna said it had to be the town that was burning. At first they didn't mention what night this was to have been or that somewhere in the mountains the Messiah and the ancestors still waited and loved them.

The next morning a line of blue-gray smoke still rose above the town, and Vedna joked whatever else happened, at least they got to watch the white town burn to the ground. Or maybe it was only the town dump— they didn't know until they flagged down the mail wagon and loaded their belongings. The driver said it was no joke—half the town of Needles burned that night, though no one was injured.

Maytha and Vedna came to visit in the early spring before it got too hot. They found their way back without any trouble, although they'd been there only once before to help the girls move to the old gardens.

The twins arrived around midday. Even from a distance the bright ribbons of purple, red, yellow, and black gladiolus flowers were impossible to miss, woven crisscross over the terrace gardens, through the amaranth, pole beans, and sunflowers.

Sister warmed rabbit stew for them while the twins teased them about the waste of precious garden space and rain on flowers. Remember how outraged their neighbors were when they found out Indigo's plants produced only flowers?

They brought Indigo the two orchid plants she had to leave behind. They teased Indigo they'd kept the two biggest plants for themselves. They had grown and filled their pots nicely despite being thrown out the door last year and nibbled by Rainbow.

The little grandfather was shy and hid his eyes from them at first, but then he began to play peek with Vedna, and Maytha finally persuaded him to toddle over to her so she could pick him up. What a big boy he was now!

With the gourd bowls of stew, Sister unwrapped red amaranth tortillas, cold but freshly made earlier that day. The little grandfather took a bite from his tortilla, then offered some to Maytha; he was more shy with Vedna; then he handed Linnaeus a piece of tortilla and gave Rainbow the rest. He was too excited by the visitors to eat; he began to bring out his toys—his corncob doll and a small gourd dish of round pebbles.

The twins remarked what good stew it was. Sister motioned with her chin at Indigo, who smiled proudly. They asked the ingredients beside rabbit, but she would only tell them, "A little of everything."

The twins brought all kinds of news from Road's End, and a letter for Indigo from Hattie. The envelope was covered with strange stamps and a smeared postmark from England. Inside Indigo found a lovely tinted postcard of Bath and a folded blank sheet of paper that held a folded $50 bill and a glassine envelope of postage stamps.

The postcard showed the big pool at the King's Bath dotted with the tiny figures of white men wading and swimming. They took turns looking and laughing at the picture before Indigo read the message.

Hattie sent her love to Indigo and the girls and, of course, the little grandfather. The weather was too cloudy and cool for anything more than pussy willows, snowdrops, and pink ladies.

Next week they would take the train to Scotland to visit the old stones. In September they'd cross the channel and go by train to spend the autumn with Laura in Lucca.

Indigo broke into a big smile. What a relief it was to know Hattie was all right. She unfolded the money and the girls passed it around. They'd never touched a $50 bill before. The stamps Indigo would use right away. She would write Hattie and send the reply back with the twins.

Now for the news from Road's End, Sister teased the twins. Were they at least pregnant or engaged yet? They all laughed and shook their heads. It sure was good to see one another again. Yes, the news was they'd managed to save up enough money so they didn't have to live in a wallow of green beer anymore. Rumors had it they were about to be arrested for bootlegging anyway.

They used the money to buy two milk goats, six turkeys, and two dozen chickens. With egg and milk money they bought peach and apricot seedlings out of a California mail-order catalogue. Only thing was, now when they wanted to be gone more than a day, they had to hire a neighbor to sleep at their house to care for all their livestock.

Remember all those gladiolus spuds Indigo planted in their garden and everyone scolded her for planting useless flowers? Guess what? Big spikes of buds appeared in the first warm days after Christmas, and in no time white, lavender, red, and yellow flowers opened. People passing by on the road stopped to stare—the flowers were quite a sight.

When no one was around, the twins took an old bucket full of freshly cut flowers to the brush-covered shelter the flooded Christians used as a church. At first the twins weren't sure if their peace offering would be accepted by their neighbors. But the next week, they found the old bucket at their gate, so they refilled it with flowers. Their neighbors received all sorts of food donations from other churches each month; but no one up or down the river had such tall amazing flowers for their church. So those flowers turned out to be quite valuable after all.

Indigo scooped up some stew with a piece of tortilla.

"Look," she said to the twins. "Do you recognize this?"

"Some kind of potato, isn't it?" Vedna fished one out of her stew and popped it into her mouth.

"Ummmm!"

Maytha stirred her stew with a piece of tortilla and examined the vegetable—it was a gladiolus spud! She laughed out loud.

"You can eat them!" she exclaimed. Those gladiolus weren't only beautiful; they were tasty!

After the twins finished lunch, they all walked up the path to see the gardens and the spring. Now Rainbow flew along above them until he saw a hawk and returned to Indigo's shoulder. Linnaeus walked ahead of the little grandfather to scout for any danger, Sister liked to say. Their parrot and monkey warned them if strangers approached even a mile away.

The twins especially like the "speckled corn" effect of the color combinations Indigo made with the gladiolus she planted in rows to resemble corn kernels. Maytha agreed with Indigo; their favorite was the lavender, purple, white, and black planting, but Sister and Vedna preferred the dark red, black, purple, pink, and white planting. They were closed now, but in the morning sky blue morning glories wreathed the edges of the terraces like necklaces.

Down the shoulder of the dune to the hollow between the dunes, silver white gladiolus with pale blues and pale lavenders glowed among the great dark jade datura leaves. Just wait until sundown—the fragrance of the big datura blossoms with the gladiolus flowers would make them swoon, Indigo promised.

When the girls first returned to the old gardens the winter before, Grandma Fleet's dugout house was in good condition but terrible things had been done at the spring. Fortunately Grandma Fleet had warned Sister Salt during her visit the third night of the dance, so the girls were prepared for the shock. Strangers had come to the old gardens; at the spring, for no reason, they slaughtered the big old rattlesnake who lived there; then they chopped down the small apricot trees above Grandma Fleet's grave.

That day they returned, the twins helped Sister Salt and Indigo gather up hundreds of delicate rib bones to give old Grandfather Snake a proper burial next to Grandma Fleet. They all wept as they picked up his bones, but Indigo wept harder when she looked at the dried remains of the little apricots trees hacked to death with the snake.

Today Indigo and Linnaeus ran ahead of the others with the parrot flying ahead of her. At the top of the sandy slope she stopped and knelt in the sand by the stumps of the apricot trees, and growing out of the base of one stump were green leafy shoots. Who knew such a thing was possible last winter when they cried their eyes sore over the trees?

They took turns drinking the cold water from the crevice in the cave wall and sat on the cool sand on the cave's floor to listen to the splashing water for a while.

They sat so quietly the twins and the little grandfather dozed off; something terrible struck there, but whatever or whoever, it was gone now; Sister Salt could feel the change. Early the other morning when she came alone to wash at the spring, a big rattlesnake was drinking at the pool. The snake dipped her mouth daintily into the water, and her throat moved with such delicacy as she swallowed. She stopped drinking briefly to look at Sister, then turned back to the water; then she gracefully turned from the pool across the white sand to a nook of bright shade. Old Snake's beautiful daughter moved back home.